KU-020-060

RING OF LIGHTNING

Dance of The Rings: Book One

Jane S. Fancher

DAW BOOKS, INC.

DONALD A. WOLLHEIM, FOUNDER

375 Hudson Street, New York, NY 10014

ELIZABETH R. WOLLHEIM
SHEILA E. GILBERT
PUBLISHERS

First Printing, July 1995

3 4 5 6 7 8 9

DAW TRADEMARK REGISTERED
U.S. PAT. OFF. AND FOREIGN COUNTRIES
—MARCA REGISTRADA
HECHO EN U.S.A.

PRINTED IN THE U.S.A.

To the Writers Group From Hell.

It's possible I could have done it without you,
but it would have been a lot harder
and a lot less fun.
Thanks for not letting me off easy.

And to Betsy,
for renewing my faith
and for three good-looking guys on the cover.

Excerpt from Darius' *History of Rhomatum*
Reconsidered, **by Berul dunSegri, written and published in
the year 284 after the Founding and found in the private
library of Nikaenor Rhomandi dunMheric, 18th
Princeps of Rhomatum.**

*. . . It is frankly naive to accept any written history as abso-
lute fact, as all events are filtered at least once through the
eyes of the participants and again through the eyes of the
recorder. Even if the recorder and participant are one and
the same, written history remains a record twice removed
from fact, as one must always interpret one's experiences in
retrospect, and one is never quite the same before or after
the interpretation, much less the events themselves.*

*With regard to the history of Rhomatum, this limitation is
particularly evident in the decades surrounding the Foundation. We have a paucity of documentary evidence regarding
the—presumably—decades of events and thoughts that led
to the Darian Exodus from the ancient city of Mauritum
and the founding of our own fair city. This dearth of knowledge may be partly attributed to the inevitable attrition of
sources over three centuries and the likelihood that the most
interesting sources remain in Mauritum, inaccessible to this
conscientious scholar. Yet these are not the only reasons for
our ignorance, nor are they the greatest. Darius Rhomandi
himself, our city's founder, must be judged the architect of
our ignorance.*

*By his own decrees, in the thirty-third year after the
Founding, Darius severed his creation from the city which
had created him. With a single stroke of his pen, our
Founder proclaimed his own recounting of the Founding
and his own memories of Mauritum, which he'd set forth in
his three-volume* History of Rhomatum *were all the past*

Rhomatum needed for the future. All other substantial evidence of Mauritum was henceforth banned in Rhomatum.

Books were burnt—not just the tomes of interpretive history Rhomatum's first settlers transported into Rhomatum along with their other baggage, but letters, private diaries, and all the other intimate documents of people in their own time, without which the conscientious historian is reduced to evidence scarce removed from rumormongering, hearsay, and gossip.

Having excised their Mauritumin past from Rhomatum's collective consciousness, our Founder then signed the second decree of the Reformation, thereby sealing his city's fate of isolationist ignorance.

I speak, of course, of the establishment of the Darian calendar which, within the limits of nature (since not even Darius could adjust the speed with which we circle the sun), divided the year into nine equal months of four equal weeks of nine days. To those seven (and sometimes eight) embarrassingly inescapable intercalary days, he assigned the sole state-sanctioned holiday, the now notorious Transition Day Festival.

In his ongoing attempts to salvage our collective consciousness from the "insidious effects of unconscious aggrandizement," Darius declared those months and days be named not for forgotten kings, like Mauritum's fourteen unequal months; nor ancient gods like the eight days of Mauritum's week; but numbered, simply and rationally, beginning with the day Darius himself set the rings of Rhomatum into motion.

Today is the third day of the second week of the seventh month of the 283rd year after the Founding. But what day is it in Mauritum? I do not know. No one in Rhomatum does—lest he admit illegal commerce with our ancestral city.

Oh, Darius! The good you did for your children and your children's children when you set the clocks and calendars of Rhomatum running on their own time was a curse upon historians—as well you knew it would be! From the lands beyond our own ley-determined borders we have a plenitude of tales, nothing more. No kernels of dates or documents which a conscientious historian might plant and nurture into a hedge linking the here and now of Rhomatum to the there and then of Mauritum.

Yet I, Berul dunSegri, shall try to piece together some

understanding of Mauritum's ancient past—and by painstaking extraction, some notion of how the Rhomatum I know and love came to be.

... [We] know Mauritum's ring legacy goes back a thousand years and more, and Rhomatum's a mere three hundred. This simple fact would indicate that we did indeed originate, physically, culturally, and technologically, from Mauritum. While this might seem obvious, one must remember that Darius controls our knowledge, and so our ability to logically extrapolate from a given set of information. Realizing where our beliefs originate helps us to examine their inherent reliability.

... [The island of] Maurislan in general, and the city of Mauritum in particular, was, by all available evidence, the birthplace of the leythium ring disciplines around which Rhomatum society is structured. While we've no reason to presume the leylines and nodes which provide the basis for those disciplines are unique to our small corner of the continent, elsewhere in the civilized world, people appear to have either ignored, rejected, or never discovered the advantages of ley energy.

Elsewhere, people live much as the hill-folk and the between-ley farmers, in towns and villages and individual homesteads, dependent upon candles for light and fire for heat. Even where great and powerful leadership results in cities to rival Rhomatum in both size and population, those citizens still conduct their lives under the most primitive of conditions, where the very necessities of life create filth and stench unimaginable to a citizen of Rhomatum.

These have a long and complex history of petty kingdoms and empires with which Darius, in his Histories, *was notably unconcerned.*

The conscientious scholar can't but wonder whether this lack of interest on the part of Rhomatum's founder in the World Beyond the Web (a tendency which to this day, Rhomatum herself displays in her extra-web dealings) indicates (1) an idiosyncrasy endemic to any node city, (2) an isolationist tendency inherited from Rhomatum's sociotechnologic progenitor, or (3) a simple echo of Rhomatum's founder's own limited interests and biases. . . .

... insofar as history can be described as 'fact,' insofar as we have a multiplicity of accounts to substantiate those

'facts,' we have ample reason to believe the following to be 'true':

1) In the spring of the thirty-ninth year of Matrindi's reign in Mauritum, Darius Rhomandi, of no proven patronage, led 257 adult males, 199 adult females and an unrecorded number of minor children out of the city of Mauritum and across the Amaidi Channel to the mainland valley where they founded the city of Rhomatum.

2) That Darius was ultimately responsible for capping and controlling the Rhomatum leynode also appears undisputed, as is the case with Darius' claim to Maurii priesthood, though he was apparently a very minor priest, most likely of the metal-working order, considering the endless detail with which he describes the casting of the Rhomatum rings.

3) According to hill-folk tradition, a tradition substantiated by the ruins scattered throughout the valley and foothills, the Darian refugees were by no means the first inhabitants of the valley. However, none of the physical evidence supports the current, highly popularized theory that Darius led an army into the valley and destroyed the Tamshirin of local folklore: the patterns of destruction still extant on the ruined castles and altars, while not indicative of natural weathering and decay, have more in common with ley-invoked lightning storms than with any human engine of war. Nor is there evidence in the remaining architecture to suggest other than human origin.

Indeed, in this, considering the deserted sites, rubbled victims of Rhomatum's shunted lighting storms, now extant on the Rhomatum Web's own borders, we can trust Darius' account that the valley beyond Persitum Node had become a maelstrom following Mauritum's capping of Persitum. A constant pounding of lightning would seem, at least to this humble scholar, sufficient inducement for Rhomatum Valley's former inhabitants to have taken their leave. . . .

. . . Of Mauritum itself, we have little solid evidence to support or defy Darius' unquestionably biased account; the reports of mutual trade interests, however, substantiate his contentions of massive overpopulation within the island cities, as well as the enormous sociopolitical power he attributes to the Maurii priesthood.

Granted these two 'facts,' Darius' demand that the mainland satellite nodes swear fealty to Rhomatum alone or be *cut out of the web was destined to create antipathy between Darius' Rhomatum and ancient Mauritum.*

According to Darius, there were actual armed assaults on Rhomatum in those early days; however, considering Mauritum's limited martial resources—by that time the world beyond considered them invincible, and they hadn't mounted an army in generations—and considering also the fact that by the time such assaults could have taken place Darius' original small band had grown to thousands, Darius' colorful depiction of Maurii soldiers breaching the outer walls of Rhomatum and threatening the Tower itself might well be all color and little substance.

A created cultural paranoia, if you will.

Then again, the accounts might be word for word, event by event, accurate. One simply cannot know. . . .

. . . and lacking a contemporary outside perspective, reconciliation of [Darius'] acts with his espoused goals and beliefs is virtually impossible.

What appears indisputable to this scholar is that two great powers have been poised in equilibrium for three centuries: one structured ostensibly around the will of great and powerful gods, the other (also ostensibly) around human free will.

That the god Maurii lusts after additional followers is a virtual given—such is the way of gods. What Darius intended, what goals Darius has passed on to his descendants, is far less certain to those of us who live outside the Tower.

For three hundred years, these two powerful, isolate entities have stood side by side, looking carefully past one another, their peaceful coexistence based upon their own invincibility upon their own soil. If, however, each of these aloof giants in fact desires the other's power, when that balance shifts, as some day it must, they will be forced to look upon one another in truth, without a god's—any god's, Maurii's or Darius'—intervention. . . .

Prelude

High in the atmosphere above Mount Khoratum, moisture-laden froth boils higher, deeper. Denied escape, caught between the freezing air above and the shifting energies below, particles roil in ever-increasing ferocity, swirling on fierce, invisible currents, twisting, rubbing, chafing . . .

Deep within the heart of Mount Khoratum, in a leythium-draped chamber deeper than the deepest human mines, Mother laughed, revelling in the flow of pure energy that slithered tingling tendrils across her skin, and for a time, it was sensuality alone that dictated her moves, that drove her to keep that brewing storm contained.

It is an ancient, elemental ritual, this periodic convergence of power, frustration, and obstinacy; a ritual compelled by laws as primordial as the earth herself toward its inevitable resolution:

Lightning arced between clouds.

"Oo-oo-oo . . ." Mother shivered in victorious ecstasy. *"Yes!"*

On the mountain's surface, midway between leythium cave and lightning cloud, in the Tower overlooking the human-built city called Khoratum, in a chamber where the seven leythium-coated rings of Khoratum spun solemnly about their common center—the Khoratum free radical echoed that sky-born bolt with a quivering deflection of its own sinuous path.

It was a tiny shift, a disturbance only the most observant would note: the radical (an amorphous streamer of pure leythium that skipped and danced freely among its more rigid cousins) was prone to random motion. A tiny disturbance, but significant. A power flux—tiny, but significant—that only a most Talented human ringmaster could correct . . . without consumer awareness.

Visible to no one within that notably empty room, baneful energy sizzled along the radical, arced from radical streamer to the outermost Cardinal Ring. The Cardinal shuddered, its heartbeat-regular rhythm faltered, and the energy mote leapt inward, disrupting the painstakingly aligned orbits of Khoratum Tower's rings one by one.

On the innermost, it paused as if savoring its triumph, then penetrated the central sphere itself. The scintillating orb flared, a momentary localized nova extending well beyond the Cardinal's radius, then faded to lightless black.

The rings faltered and tumbled to the tiled floor.

Lights within the embryonic city blossoming ripplewise from the Tower's base—flickered and died.

Sirens sounded. Briefly.

Unchecked, the mote fled the Tower and skipped triumphantly along city streets vacant on this fearsome afternoon and midnight-dark between stormy skies and mountain shadows. It slithered sullenly past wattle and daub huts aglow with light, oil lamps impervious to the mote's presence, then flowed like spring rain runoff along the leyline, down the mountain pass toward the fertile Rhomatum Valley.

It was a route marked with dead and dying trees, the unnatural byproduct of Khoratum's recent capping. Before the humans, the ley had created but small disruptions to the natural surface growth; the narrow lines of sterility marking its underground structure had been part of the natural scheme, rivers and streams.

But the humans capped the nodes, concentrated the energy flows, and spread the pathway, making of the natural ley a wound, a perversion. And to that perversion, the humans added gravel and paving stone: a road for their traveling convenience.

On that leyroad came a cargo hauler bound for Khoratum, foolish and greedy driver to be out on a leyroad on such a day, daring the elements to interfere with his schedule.

Like some giggling, formless gremlin, the spark infiltrated the hauler's heater-core and brushed the tiny leythium web contained there with an ephemeral kiss. The web shriveled; the heater died. Deprived of buoyancy, the hauler's towering balloon wilted, throwing the cargo bed's full weight onto woefully inadequate wagon axles. The draft horses stopped dead in their tracks, and the lead gelding cast an accusatory glance over his broad shoulder toward the silk-draped, disgruntled driver.

The sparking mote, heedless now of the havoc in its wake, scampered through the Khoramali foothills, ignoring equally the thriving watchtowers of the current human populace and the ruined altars of the previous inhabitants. It bounded relentlessly toward the valley's southernmost reach, toward another ley-rich node, another ringchamber, another tower-dominated city.

Mount Rhomatum: eroded with time—as Mount Khoratum was not.

Rhomatum Node: where nine major leylines converged—to Khoratum's six.

Rhomatum City: a web of carefully plotted ringroads and radial spokes: leyroad connections to other nodes, other cities—of which Khoratum was youngest.

But far from least.

Rhomatum: home of Ringmaster Anheliaa dunMoren, architect and instigator of the profane Khoratum Tower.

Gaining momentum and gleeful purpose with each passing instant, the spark traversed its barren path, a gravelled slash between lush, cultivated fields, and streaked through the outer-city livestock market, unnoticed by any save cattle and chickens.

Almost sentient in its excitement, the lightning-born calamity reached for the City's outermost wall, the human-made buffer against human flotsam seeking Rhomatum's energy-rich harbor.

It gained the innermost stone . . .

And died.

Unnoticed.

Unappreciated.

(Sigh.)

Ignored.

And, as yet another leythium strand quivered in sympathetic resonance to the firestorm raging above, Mother kindled another . . . event.

SECTION ONE

Chapter One

The impending deluge erupted just as Deymorin Rhomandi dunMheric raced beneath the palisade gate that marked the Rhomatum umbrella's outermost perimeter. A single stride within, Deymorin's horse, wise to the idiosyncrasies of the City and disdaining anything so plebeian as a signal from his rider, slid to a plunging, bucking halt, spraying sand and gravel over the gate attendants scattering from his path.

Deymorin himself, wise to the idiosyncrasies of his horse (having raised him from a fractious colt), lifted a careless hand to stop the single, brave (but ill-advised) soul who rushed forward to help control Ringer's extravagant display. Having failed to unseat his rider, the horse froze, four feet square, then shook from toe to tail, as if the handful of drops that had pelted them at the last had drenched him to the skin.

"Silly creature," Deymorin murmured fondly, and leaned forward to slap the sweat-darkened neck. When he straightened, it was as if every vertebra snapped and grated before settling into place. He gave his aching shoulders a backward stretch, signalled his thanks to the alert gatekeep, who'd had the gate open and waiting by the time he reached it, and sent Ringer on toward the stables with a gentle pressure of leg and rein.

Outside the palisade the air was roiling grey and deluge; here, at the power umbrella's outermost edge, where only the smallest, simplest and purest leythium crystal would glow, the glimmer of sun through broken clouds cast the occasional shadow; shadows whose midafternoon length reminded him of his woefully belated arrival.

Easy enough to find excuses, if excuses he desired. Excuses Nikki would understand: the weanling cull running a month late, the overall high quality of the foals making the choice of which to keep and which to sell nearly impossible:

a fact that would please him, once he'd had time to consider; and there was desperately needed hay that lay curing in the fields about to be storm-flooded, and a prize brood-mare in danger of aborting what might well be her last foal . . .

Time-critical problems, all of them. Small wonder Tonio's gentle reminder early this morning had caught him un-awares and at his stud farm, Darhaven, rather than in Rhomatum.

Small wonder, but unforgivable: older brothers had . . . obligations.

And the morning of the eighteenth day of the first month of the year 317 should have found Deymorin Rhomandi dunMheric, brother of Nikaenor Rhomandi dunMheric, if not in Rhomatum itself, at least at the valley estate, Ar-mayel. When a man's family owned multiple seats, a man really ought to make use of them.

Darhaven was in the foothills, two *sensible* days' ride from Rhomatum; Armayel, an easy morning's jaunt. Nikki would have understood his sleeping over at Armayel to minimize his time in the City; Nikki would *never* have for-given him missing tonight's festivities altogether.

Well, he hadn't spent the night at Armayel, but he wasn't going to miss the party either, though he might well fall asleep in the middle of dinner. It had required his best and bravest—he ran a grateful hand down the sweating arch of mane and muscle—to get him here at even this truant hour.

He tightened his legs and Ringer surged willingly into a jogtrot, the fastest pace the law allowed within the palisade. The horse was tired, as Deymorin himself was, but eager for the warmth and comfort awaiting him in the stables.

If only, Deymorin thought as he ducked to miss the low beam at the barn's back entrance, Ringer's rider felt a simi-lar anticipation toward his *own* . . . stable.

A nickering duet greeted him as he eased numb feet to the packed and raked ground outside the tackroom, and fluttering nostrils on two near-identical black-nosed heads with identical white stars appeared over neighboring stall doors. He dropped Ringer's reins and palmed a handful of dried apple treats from the pouch hanging just within the tackroom door, a move that raised an expectant rustle be-hind him.

"Don't even think it," he said, without turning.

With a dejected *whoof*, that sense of *horse* at his shoulder disappeared. Ignoring the big bay gelding, he limped across the aisle to the greys' stalls, speaking softly to them, scratching the snip on Storm's nose, the tiny scar on Ashley's—the only notable difference between them—his eyes reflexively noting their condition.

They were undoubtedly the best matched team ever bred at Darhaven, by himself or any of his ancestors.

Theoretically, the greys belonged at Armayel, but somehow they rarely stayed there for long. Not that he minded: better here where they'd be exercised and loved than waiting around for his infrequent needs. Personally, he preferred to ride—as had Nikki. Once. Before the boy found it impossible to ride two horses at the same time.

He scratched an expectant chin with one hand, with the other patted a neck solid beneath a silken black mane . . . and recalled a scrawny, blond-headed kid and two scrawnier foals, and himself and Gerhard bastardizing their better sense for a pair of pleading blue eyes.

And Nikki had been right, in his blind-child-luck way. The twins had lived, and flourished, to become a matched team any horseman would cherish—as the scrawny, blond-headed kid had grown into a man anyone would be proud to call brother.

Well, most of the time.

He did look forward to seeing Nikki. His youngest brother's visits to Darhaven occurred far too infrequently these days, and when Nikki *was* there, he seemed distracted, more interested in the library than the horses. Deymorin suspected their mutual brother Mikhyel's hand in both that dereliction and that distraction, as in much else that transpired—or didn't—in the boy's life.

Dear, pious, priggish Mikhyel. Sometimes he thought he'd be perfectly content if he never saw his other brother again, but if enduring the middle Rhomandi brother's presence was the price he must pay for time with the youngest, he'd pay that and willingly to be with the boy tonight.

Boy. Not any longer. Nikki was seventeen now, and legally a man—or would be, soon enough, after the announcements had been posted, the oaths taken and the Citizen contract signed.

Gods will Nikki's would be a less . . . eventful . . . passage into adulthood than Mikhyel's had been. He'd lost a

brother that night—ten years ago next spring—though not
to death. Death would have been easier, cleaner. Instead,
he'd been left with a hard-faced, ambulatory shell that bore
only a superficial resemblance to the brother he'd grown
up with.

He'd lost one brother that night; he wasn't about to lose
a second tonight.

He ran a final, loving hand down each dark grey jowl,
gave Storm's overactive black lip a gentle tug, and returned
to Ringer, hands harboring one final treat behind his back.
They were gathering an audience, he and the big horse:
grooms versed enough in his ways not to interfere before
his signal, and familiar enough with those ways to stand
where they could enjoy the show.

"Well?" he asked.

A black-rimmed ear twitched. The bloodred head with
its narrow blaze drooped low, the long forelock falling
across half-lidded eyes: a picture of equine exhaustion requiring only shuddering sides and quivering knees to complete. Unfortunately for Ringer, his sides moved in long,
even breaths, and his legs were as sound as they'd been
that morning.

"I'm not impressed, you know."

The large head raised to rest its chin heavily ... pitifully
... on his shoulder.

Laughter escaped despite tight-clamped lips, and Ringer,
with a smug toss of his head, shoved Deymorin's chest with
his nose, demanding his reward, which Deymorin willingly
provided.

Handing the intrepid gelding over at last to the team of
chuckling grooms, he freed his silver-handled cane and pistol from the saddle and headed through the stable toward
the market and the inner wall, pausing only to check the
pistol at the armory.

A man never forgot that twice. If he somehow got past
the guard with it, chances were it would shoot off something important, without warning and before nightfall.

Ley and gunpowder, like ley and lightning, did not mix.

The Oreno market closed around him, banners and
booths combining to obscure the stable. Once one of several private facilities situated well outside the city wall
among productive farmlands, where there had been space

in plenty for paddocks and arenas, the Rhomandi stable was the final vestige of that original agrarian use of this land.

Nearly ten years ago, his own dear aunt Anheliaa had realized her greatest ambition and capped Khoratum Node, making her the first Rhomatumin ringmaster ever to have the full power of the Rhomatum Web available to her. The most immediate and inescapable effect of controlling that last of Rhomatum's satellite nodes was the extension of the Rhomatum City power umbrella—by as much as five miles in some directions.

The City had immediately constructed a new perimeter wall, a physical demarcation of that new municipal boundary, and the property values—thanks to overzealous speculators—between the old wall and the new had flared out of control, taking property taxes with them. Ten years after the fact, prices had settled, the taxes had, but much of the land between the old wall and the new still lay fallow, no longer fit to grow anything but roses, the previous owners, mostly farmers and horse breeders, driven out, those overzealous speculators considering themselves fortunate when they managed to break even.

Deymorin himself had eventually given in to Mikhyel's pressure and sold his own training facilities (twenty paddocks, two outdoor arenas, and one mirrored, indoor arena, as well as two of his three barns) to some faceless Oreno Syndic, whose favor Mikhyel had been courting for some internode economic alliance. His only consolation when he passed the vacant paddocks was that the new owner, who had purchased the facility when the market was at its peak, had yet to resell the land and lacked the capital to develop it himself.

And Mikhyel's deal had fallen through.

None of which mattered significantly to Deymorin these days. He had moved his in-training stock (and himself) permanently to Darhaven, and overall, he preferred the change. But he'd keep this small barn (if only to spite his miserly sibling at each tax assessment of the Family estate) until that miserly sibling managed to push through some law that made the barn illegal—and even then, he might choose to challenge that yet to be written law, just to see whether that miserly sibling—who was also the family barrister—would dare prosecute his own brother, who also happened to be the Princeps of Rhomatum.

That would keep the gossips busy for at least a month. . . . And Mikhyel hated scandal.

Outside the palisade, in the new country edge, no civilian stables had grown up to replace the old. Professionals, such as the long-haulers or the internode passenger coaches, had already built their own private stables, convenient to the leylines between node cities, but well beyond the reach of city taxation. Around those stables, communities had grown: inns, farriers, everything needed for the stock, the drivers and those who cared for them. Most Outsiders forced to visit the city now put themselves and their horses up at these small villages, then took the commercial floatercoaches into the city itself.

The casualty of the Khoratum expansion that was likely to prove the most costly of all had been the dissolution of the military training grounds, facilities that had once drawn recruits from all over the web. Stables full of well-bred horses, gymnasiums and practice fields, shooting ranges—everything needed to train young men to defend their families and homes—had been reduced over the years to a single gymnasium, a fencing salle, and a handful of ill-trained equine slugs Mikhyel and his City Council cronies allotted the city to keep the Guard in practice.

'In practice.' Only Mikhyel could conceive so inane a concept. Men didn't stay in practice for war, they kept prepared—which meant more than a twice yearly jog about a covered arena and crossing epees in a salle.

But Rhomatum didn't require such readiness any longer—just ask his dear brother. The Rhomatum Web was civilized, her satellites content with the status quo, her traditional adversary, Mauritum, was ready to sign trade agreements . . . any day now . . . for the last twenty-five years and more.

Anheliaa had capped Khoratum, and suddenly Rhomatum was invincible . . . at least, that was how the city-bound members of the 36th Council of the City of Rhomatum apparently viewed the situation.

As those sagacious leaders viewed the situation, no conquering warrior could take Rhomatum without destroying that which made her the most valuable: her precious leythium-harnessing rings. Ringmasters weren't interchangeable.

Common knowledge held that training a master required years of orientation and personal supervision by the sitting master. Without a ringmaster, the rings themselves would falter in their paths and the power that ran the city would cease to flow; and since only Anheliaa dunMoren could train the next Rhomatum ringmaster, Rhomatum was, so Council believed, completely safe.

Which reasoning presupposed that that faceless conquering warrior *wanted* the rings. At the moment, the Kirish'lan Empire that controlled the majority of the lands along the Rhomatum Web perimeter was apparently quite content without ringpower. Content or uninterested. Fortunately for Rhomatum, they seemed equally uninterested in the Rhomatum Valley.

That hadn't always been the case, and likely would not be again at some unknowable future date.

What those Rhomatum leaders failed to realize (or refused to acknowledge) was that the land surrounding Rhomatum was immensely vulnerable, not only to some theoretical invasion, but to the very real and increasingly unpredictable whims of nature. Without her associated farmland, Rhomatum would starve within a year, despite her much-vaunted reserves.

But Rhomatum councillors didn't think of that. Rhomatum citizens as a whole had forgotten where bread and milk and cheese came from, thanks to ancestors who had moved into an extremely fertile valley that had been blessed, with the capping of Rhomatum, with unnaturally reliable weather patterns, where those who would be farmers could ply their trade with maximum output for minimum effort.

A society grown content, that was Rhomatum.

Deymorin had personally replaced those neglected martial facilities, basing the new facility at Parawin, yet another of that multiplicity of Rhomandi estates. He'd made them available to any who requested. Sometimes those who came paid for the privilege; frequently they could not. For the sake of the future of the valley, he and other like-minded landowners throughout the entire web absorbed the expense, never bothering to ask Rhomatum for subsidy.

He'd tried that once, five years ago, and discovered the hard way just how blind stupid a majority rule could be when the majority was ignorant and refused education.

After that eye-opening debacle, when something had needed doing, he'd done it himself.

And Mikhyel wondered why his elder brother's pockets were always empty. When it came to Outside matters, Mikhyel was as blind-stupid as the rest of the Council.

Outside, Inside, the Darkness Between the Lines ... as if any of those parts existed apart from the whole. The Web was the Web: Rhomatum, her eighteen satellite nodes—from the oldest, Persitum, to the youngest, Khoratum—and all the lands between. The perimeter of the web was a well-defined zone of frequent storms and generally unpleasant living conditions.

Insiders lived under a node city's power umbrella, Outsiders did not. Pockets of Outsiders had settled along the leylines themselves that ran between those nodes, narrow strips where the ley energy dimly manifested—enough for running a limited number of floater balloon heaters and making lights glow dimly—but the encroaching Darkness had proven too unnerving for the average Insider citizen's delicate sensibilities to endure for more than the night or two needed to travel between nodes.

Encroaching Darkness. In the average Insider's mind—and more ominously, in the minds of the Rhomatum Council and the House of Syndics—no sane person would willingly dwell in those uncivilized segments of the web. But people did. Outsiders, who produced useful things ... like food ... and who required governing.

So were boundaries established, jurisdictions surrounding each node over which the included node city held authority. Some cities treated that responsibility with great respect. Others took their cue from the node of nodes, Rhomatum, and left the Outside to fend for itself, interfering only when taxes weren't paid or produce didn't appear in the marketplace.

An attitude which, at least in Rhomatum, was proving dangerously shortsighted.

In recent years, according to the oldest farmers, the once reliable weather patterns that had for three hundred years blessed the Rhomatum Valley with outstandingly predictable growing seasons had undergone dramatic changes, creating drought in some areas, flooding in others. He hadn't the personal perspective to know how rapidly those conditions were changing, or in exactly what fashion, but after five years of tracking gross groundwater and water-flow conditions throughout the valley, he knew they could no longer rely totally upon nature for watering crops and drainage.

The Outside landowners knew what needed doing, and were ready to commit men and equipment to dig the drainage ditches and build up the low spots, but to accomplish the overall plan they' needed dispensation to build the ditches across seven leylines. And they needed funding—or at least, tax relief—until they had recovered from the effects of lost crops, reduction of available useful land, and the problems of housing flood-displaced sharecroppers.

They'd left that up to him. After all, he *was* the Princeps. Council *couldn't* deny him anything, could they?

Nice to have the confidence of one's peers. . . . Outside.

If he and Mikhyel had any sense, he supposed they'd follow the example of other founding Families and split the household amicably into City and Outside septs, with separate caucus representatives for each sept. It wouldn't affect the overall city-biased power balance within the Council, but it might ease tensions within their own household.

Unfortunately, while those other Families had, over the eight generations since the Founding, grown sufficiently numerous to fill every available nook under the power umbrella and beyond, Darius Rhomandi's get had proven woefully unfertile; the Rhomandi rarely had more than a handful of adult carriers of the name alive at any point in time.

House Rhomandi: the largest estate in the Rhomatum Syndicate, heir to the singular honor Princeps of Rhomatum, traditional controller of the Rhomatum rings, and there were just the four of them left: Mikhyel, Nikki, himself . . . and Aunt Anheliaa, of course. One couldn't forget their paternal grandsire's sister . . . however much one might care to.

He supposed some would say Mheric Rhomandi dunFaren's three sons all living to adulthood should, in itself, be cause for some sort of celebration.

Of course, one must also suppose, others might just as soon the entire name simply die out altogether and let the syndicate—and the rings—revert to the people, as Darius had intended.

There was, as in most such dichotomous situations, a relatively simple answer: the Syndicate could vote to eliminate the Princeps as quickly and easily as they'd instituted the position. But they wouldn't—not as long as the Rhomandi Family controlled the Rhomatum rings.

The Oreno marketplace crowded in around him, merchant and casual acquaintance alike vying for his attention, all wanting to know where he'd been, how he'd been and with whom, the usual friendly distractions one encountered in the market, but today he settled for a wave or a shouted, good-natured jibe, and hurried on, though his riding boots slipped and slid over the cobblestones, jarring already aching joints, and the uneven surface caught and held the cane's tip when, leaning too heavily, he depended too much on its support for balance.

An open-faced hand-cab stopped directly in front of him. "Give 'ee a lift, zur?"

A man would laugh, who wasn't exhausted, whose leg wasn't throbbing like a broken tooth. The cabby hadn't given him much of a choice, pulling up where he had. It was accept his offer, or push through a smithy's display.

"Oreno Gate," he said, and eased back into the two-wheeled cart, disgusted when he had to set the cane on the floorboard and use both hands to draw his off-leg in after him. But the bad right leg was a reality of his life, an old injury, and he had to admit, as the cabby set off at a goodly pace for the gate, it was a relief to let his back and hips sink into the soft leather cushions and let other legs do the work.

At the inner gate, a backup at the turnstile threatened further delay. Registration. Declaration of legitimate city business, projected length of stay.

Visas: one of those City-biased legal decisions.

He could, if he so chose, force his way to the front of the line: he wore a ring on his left hand that would clear his path in a quasimagical instant, should he choose to invoke its authority, but he resented using *that* ring in such a fashion almost as fiercely as he resented the quasiroyal power of the silver-filigree crest it bore. That he wore it at all was solely a matter of family pride. Whatever else he was or was not, he was the Rhomandi, eldest living male of the Rhomandi Family.

On the other hand, who was to say the Rhomandi's business was any more important than that of these other folk mumbling and complaining amongst themselves?

A philosophical opinion which forced him to flatten his already lean pouch by another few coppers to the cabby for standing time. Princeps of Rhomatum, theoretically the most powerful citizen in the Rhomatum Syndicate, and he rarely had a silver-piece to his name.

Mikhyel would claim it was his profligate ways, that he tipped too much, that he gambled too wildly and lent money too easily and on uncertain collateral.

He considered it . . . spreading the wealth, in a way honorable for both parties.

Besides, it made him feel good to send a hard worker away with a smile on his face rather than disappointment— like the cabby when at last his turn at the stile arrived.

"Papers, please." The registrar's voice was as bored as the eyes that looked right through him.

"Papers?" Deymorin kept his voice low, controlled, fighting the fatalistic disgust rising in him. "What *papers*?"

Possibly his face did not match his tone. Certainly the drab assistant wielding the pen blanched quite markedly. The registrar held out his hand and repeated, blindly oblivious:

"Identity papers, please. All Rhomatum citizens have been issued them, all visitors are instructed to pick them up at the outer palisade. If you haven't filled them out, I must ask you to step to the back of the line and do so. —Next!" The registrar's head dropped in total disinterest. "State your name, your business, length of stay . . ."

"My name is Deymorin Rhomandi dunMheric," Deymorin said tightly, without moving a step.

The assistant's pen dropped.

"I'm a free man, a citizen with no arrest record of significance." Deymorin began jerking his left glove free, one finger at a deliberate time.

The registrar's eyes suddenly blinked into awareness, his litany slowed to a stuttering halt as Deymorin's hand—and the unique silver-webbing over gold of the Rhomandi crest—cleared the pale kidskin.

"I'm bound for House Rhomandi. My business there is damnwell my own. And my brother can take his bloody papers and use them to light his way to the eighteen hells above Rhomatum."

The assistant backed away, a slow step at a time, and, with a mumbled excuse regarding *nature* and *necessity,* disappeared into the garderobe within the wall itself.

The registrar, evidently made of sterner stuff—or perhaps, with his line of escape already occupied—cleared his throat and said haltingly, "You understand, y'r grace—"

"Rhomandi." Deymorin corrected firmly. "The name's *Rhomandi.*"

"Yes, y'r grace Rhomandi."

My grace, your grace, lords and ladies: it was ridiculous. Rhomatum had been founded by men and women defying such class distinctions, yet three hundred years after the fact, with no rules of usage, no legal or philosophical justification for such nonsense, the words and attitudes persisted.

"You understand, y'r grace, I *had* to ask, y'r grace."

And it was senseless trying to fight the ancient tradition—particularly in so obsequious an individual.

"I understand nothing about *papers.*"

"Identification, y'r grace. Standard procedure as of two months ago, y'r grace."

"And if I'd had no ... identification?"

"You'd have had the choice, y'r grace, to leave or fill out the papers and wait in the confining area until—"

"Until my sick uncle died, or the critical business meeting was over. How ... hospitable of us."

"It's the law, y'r grace."

"You mean, it's my *brother's* ..." He bit his tongue. "Oh, never mind. May I pass, *m'lord* Registrar? Before these good people storm the gate and trample us both?"

A titter from behind assured him the little exchange had not gone unnoticed, and the registrar's frustrated glare assured him it would not soon be forgotten. But the registrar released the turnstile and waved him through. Deymorin smiled sweetly and sauntered into the City, beyond the titters, beyond the cobblestones—and completely beyond the sun-dimming clouds.

Storm without the umbrella, clear skies within. He'd experienced such sudden weather changes throughout his life, but his gut had never reconciled to them. It wasn't natural. Nature was storms the day before harvest, drought when the seedlings were most vulnerable. Nature was a twenty-year-old mare aborting and twin foals dying. . . .

Half the joy of living was racing to beat nature's odds.

But in Rhomatum, the odds never changed. In Rhomatum, rain would happen in the evening, every evening, just before dusk and end before the street-lighting. Just enough rain to flush the streets and water the roses. Predictable time. Predictable amount. Predictable results. . . .

And the roses never mildewed. Gods, it must be boring.

The floatercab dock nearest the Oreno gate was empty save for a waiting line of chattering, package-laden market-grazers, all the cabs evidently engaged, enroute to one end of the City or the other. By the time he made it through that line and negotiated a floatercab, he could be halfway home.

Besides, his heartrate was up, thanks to the registrar, he was rested, thanks to the impudent cabby in the market, and, deciding his legs could use a bit of a shake-out after the long ride, he bypassed the dock without slowing his stride and headed up the boardwalk toward Tower Hill.

Unlike the gregarious market, on walks inside the City, and particularly along the leys, delays for the sake of gossip were unlikely. But then, within the City, everyone always seemed to be hurrying in one direction or another, too busy, and too self-important to involve themselves in anything or anyone outside their tiny sphere of pseudo-civilization.

He feared even Nikki was catching the malady, if his decreasing visits to Darhaven were any indication. At least the lad still made regular treks Outside—the greys' condition was evidence enough of that; when the day arrived that he had to come and drag Nikki away from the City for the foaling season, he'd drag him away, all right, and never let him return.

Rhomatum was an unhealthy environment for a growing mind and body. Besides holding nature at bay, it was a fantasyland of consumer improbabilities—more so than any of her eighteen satellite cities. They at least had some quantifiable output: fabric mills and sericulture, glasswork, mining . . . two were primarily hospital nodes, noted for their healing waters.

Rhomatum produced politicians and the industry of diversions necessary to entertain visiting dignitaries. In

addition to her own Councils and debating Assembly, she
played year-round hostess to the web syndics, elected offi-
cials of the satellite nodes who gathered here to pontificate
ad nauseam on the needs of the web itself and their little
corners in particular, juggling their carefully narrow-fo-
cussed statistics and surveys to prove whatever legal or
moral point they currently espoused. Lawyers, all of them,
regardless what they claimed. Tweaking rules to finagle one
more iota of perceived advantage.

A city full of politicians and lawyers—and Mikhyel was
worried about unregistered visitors?

Registration papers. Darius save them, where had Mikhyel dreamed that one up? It was of a piece with Mikhyel's obsession over street safety and his fascination with
statistics: assassins or cutpurses or unaffiliated prostitutes,
Mikhyel didn't care, provided the reported instances of
crime were within 'allowable parameters.'

He'd love to get Mikhyel at the business end of a
parameter.

Tower Hill loomed above him sooner than he expected. Literally above: his feet had taken him down the
tunnel to the northside service access, where servants
welcomed him with grins and handshakes and made room
for him atop a load of laundry bound for the House Rhomandi kitchens.

He settled comfortably, balancing his cane across his lap
as the grille slid into place, then waved at the head disappearing between his feet.

He could have taken a more civilized route up Tower
Hill: floaters made the circuit of the whole damned government complex on a regular schedule, weaving among the
governmental buildings and public libraries and museums,
arriving ultimately at House Rhomandi's marbled entrance,
but he never used them, willingly, and saw no reason to
break his personal tradition today when the service elevator
could lift him quite comfortably and quietly through the
heart of the small mountain, avoiding barristers and councillors and lobbyists alike.

His arrival in the kitchens caused no more stir than it
had when he was ten. Cook hugged him, scolded him, and
slapped his hand when he kyped a crumpet; he kissed her
forehead, laughed, and, cane on his shoulder, skipped out

the door and up the stairs toward Nikki's apartment, exhaustion and aches vanishing at the suddenly near prospect.

*   *   *

Lights within the Rhomatum City Library flickered, an extraordinary event that caught the assistant to the curator with one foot in the air above the slick marble downstep and tilted precariously beneath an enormous codex. The young man staggered, a single shift of balance, as thunder muttered in the distance.

"Be careful! *Careful,* I said!" sputtered the curator himself, his fluttering presence posing a far greater hazard to the timeworn tome than anything the harried attendant had done trying to transport the book into the private study.

Nikki bit his lip on a grin and surreptitiously shifted notes and scrolled maps to clear a spot on the cluttered table, then turned to take the book's weight into his own hands.

An instant of sharply contrasting textures: ancient, travel-weary leather, the velvety, unscarred freshness of the table-top ... it was as if his fingertips were caught between two ages. It was a feeling not exclusive to his fingers: every time he accessed this, or any of the archive manuscripts, he felt this ... oneness ... with his ancestors.

Exerting immense control, he freed his hands from the source of that deliciously eerie sensation and forced a warm smile to his lips.

"I promise I'll be very careful with it, Gomarrin," he assured the curator, though he was by no means obligated, the book being his own family's property, on permanent loan to the city archives.

"I know *you* will, m'lord," the curator said, then glared at his attendant, who just dipped his head respectfully and faded into the shadows between book cases. "It's that ham-handed oaf I don't trust."

The lights flickered a second time and the curator shot a worried glance at the overhead chandelier.

"Don't worry," Nikki reassured him absently, thrilling to that leathery touch, "my aunt was on duty when I left. It's a big storm brewing over Khoratum, that's all."

"If you say so, sir." Gomarrin edged away as if reluctant

still to leave his prize in the hands of an amateur. "If there's anything else I can do?"

One did try to think of the book as a State Treasure, not personal property, and one did try to remember that the library was Gomarrin's life, not his hobby. . . .

And one did try to remember that one's merest expression of displeasure could threaten that livelihood, even while one tried, as Deymorin said, not to build too highly on that privilege of rank. . . .

"Nothing, thank you," Nikki said, quietly but firmly, ignoring, with near intolerable fortitude, the allure of the leather cover lying just below his knuckles.

And in a moment of exquisite self-torture, telling himself it was simple courtesy, he waited until the curator had gone before taking his seat in front of The Book . . . to discover he'd resisted a single moment too long: the sensation was gone, thoughts of Gomarrin and the rights of those like him intruding upon the romance of a past filled with kings and priests, wizards and magic.

One tried, one sincerely tried to remember that all citizens were equal under the laws of nature and Rhomatum, but it was very hard when tradition refused to relinquish the honorifics and manners of an earlier era, and when daily reality was just . . . different . . . for himself than for his friends in the stables, or Gomarrin, or the Rhomandi House servants.

Mikhyel said the patrician traditions were just a courtesy, the self-biased citizen's way of acknowledging the efforts of those dedicated to making the machinery of justice and economy run smoothly; that it wasn't words, but how you treated people in the courts and on payday that was the ultimate arbiter of social justice.

Deymorin said that Mikhyel had his head buried somewhere less than sanitary and that people who got called lords eventually thought of themselves that way, so *he* was just Deymorin, Deymio, or Rhomandi to everyone—servant, citizen, and brother alike.

Which was theoretically very nice, but functional reality placed Gomarrin's neck on the line should anything happen to this book, or any one of the treasures housed here, and functional reality allowed Nikaenor Rhomandi dunMheric to sit here day after day taking what might well prove to be useless notes regarding information Gomarrin spent his life protecting and never had the time to read. Functional reality gave common-born Gomarrin a purpose in life, and left the third son of Mheric Rhomandi dunFaren with more money and time than he knew what to do with, and no purpose or function whatsoever.

Though not for lack of trying. Someday, somehow, perhaps within these venerable records, Nikaenor Rhomandi dunMheric would *find* that purpose. . . . He just wasn't sure *exactly* what that purpose might be—yet.

Granting the scarred leather a final lingering caress, he lifted the cover with a disposition approaching reverence. Delicate, time-yellowed pages crackled beneath his fingertips; ruffled, uncut edges of an earlier era crumbled to fine powder at his touch. And on the pages themselves, ridges of ink, fading in places, gouges from an ill-considered scrape of a ragged crow-quill's tip . . . Darius' own notes. Written by Darius' own hand over three hundred years ago:

Today I looked into the rings and saw a new and better world . . .

Those heretical words—written in secret, by shaded candlelight (or so his inner self envisioned it)—had marked the beginning of a new era, not just for the man who wrote them, not just for those who followed where he led, but for the entire known civilized world.

Among the thousands of volumes in the Rhomandi House library were some seventeen different published editions of Darius' *Histories of Rhomatum,* not including the nine-volume, profusely illustrated, children's version, but somehow the words always *felt* different—*sounded* different in his head when he read them from this book and these pages, where Darius himself had written them. Somehow, following those faded words with eyes and fingers, he felt . . . part of those momentous events.

The pages separated, dust laden with mysterious scents caressed his nostrils, and suddenly, magically, he could smell and taste the past, could see, as if he'd been there, Darius' midnight invasion of the Mauritum Ring Tower where, in defiance of law and religious custom, he'd asked the god Maurii, directly and without sanction, for a vision, a hope for the future of Mauritum's hopeless, homeless masses—a vision of the sort the ancient node's god supposedly reserved for the city's high priests.

Out of that history-making illegal entry, Rhomatum had

been born. Modern scholars wrote monstrous treatises and held month-long debates over exactly what Darius did or did not see, what Darius did or did not do that night in the Mauritum Ring Chamber. Some argued whether or not the invasion of the Tower happened at all.

Darius claimed the rings had answered him, a junior priest, without dispensation or master intervention, thus proving his contention that the rings resonated to some inborn Talent, not godly sanction. Darius claimed a vision of a storm-wracked valley and a geas to go there.

Darius' modern detractors suggested Darius' stimulus wasn't a vision at all, but common knowledge, at least within the Maurii priesthood. That once Persitum had been capped, the ringmasters *must* have sensed the nodes beyond, certainly so powerful a node as Rhomatum itself. Each of those modern-day historians came up with his own theory as to *why* the Maurii priests hadn't pursued capping those obviously powerful nodes, theories as to *why* Darius had been able to pull off such a coup, but the fact was—they hadn't and Darius had.

It wasn't as if Darius had tried to use that so-called revelation to become a high priest, since he had abandoned the priesthood altogether and led his family and the other original Founders out of Mauritum in search of his valley.

Which they *had* found: Nikki's very existence, as well as the existence of those outspoken detractors, was proof absolute of that.

I find it small wonder now that my vision eluded me for so long. The veins are unbelievably rich. More leythium than anyone could have dreamed ... if not for the danger from the storms, one could strip the surface away and simply pump the essence out of the earth. ...

But the storms were there, and so every man, woman, and child who had come with Darius, regardless of their position in Mauritum, had participated in mining the silver and leythium from beneath the time-eroded leymound. That effort was the price, by Darian decree, that assured them a personal stake in the future city, a decree that, at one and the same time both assured their loyalty to Rhomatum, and destroyed forever the cultural taboos against any but sanctified priests handling the leythium.

When it came to the actual casting of the rings, Darius himself, using knowledge and skills gained as a Maurii priest, but passing those skills willingly on to any with the desire to learn them, had supervised the construction of the molds, and Darius himself had smelted and poured the silver, and coated the final product with liquid leythium.

And when he was done, atop those mines (whose shafts still existed beneath Nikki's very own bedroom, above the casting forms still on public display right where they'd been carved into the foundation stone) those Founding Families had constructed the first permanent building of the new hub-city: the Tower to house the precious rings.

And when that was done, one man and one man alone had aligned the rings and set them in motion, a feat that was, in itself, a minor miracle of the time.

... Today, the rings spun, for the first time ...

How little effort it took to imagine, sitting with one's hands resting on those age-dusted words, that ancient tower of rough-hewn granite, lightning raging all around, bands of blinding light reflecting off the concentric rings that lay lifeless on the stone floor, awaiting one touch to quicken them.

... All my life, terror has been a meaningless word, a weakness in other men to be scorned....

And a man alone, unwilling to risk a single innocent life, raising each ring, one at a time, by himself, eyes closing as he reached for some inner *sense* that would reveal the flow of the ley, aligning the ring with that flow and setting it spinning, the innermost ring first and working outward. And when the Cardinal Ring was in place, when its orbit matched the heartbeat of the ancient mountain's leythium core, the radical streamer, the band of pure leythium that was neither crystal, nor solid, nor liquid, would have uncoiled of its own accord, to weave and dance among the spinning rings....

... I scorn it no longer....

One mistake—one mismatch, energy flow to ring size, one misalignment, one ring confounding the orbit of another ... and Rhomatum would never have been born. Darius, his people, Rhomatum itself, would have been gone in a single, lightning-blasted instant.

Maurii would have won.

Instead, within moments of that radical's rising, the lightning stopped and the skies cleared above the Tower, and Rhomatum became the safe haven for all the refugees.

Thanks to Darius, the one adept among them.

Darius, one-time junior priest of Mauritum.

Darius, founder, architect, and philosophical sire of Rhomatum.

Darius, the original Rhomandi of Rhomatum. Nikki's own ancestor, seven—or was it eight?—generations removed.

—or was that remote?

Not that it mattered. Removed. Remote. Those were just words. Darius was . . . history . . . and the future. *His* future.

Nikki shivered, feeling that link to his famous forefather drawing at his very soul. It was . . . exquisite, this internal conviction that his very own, perhaps momentous, destiny lay somehow linked to this great man and history itself.

Because Darius, founder of Rhomatum and the Rhomandi line, *had* been great. Nothing the detractors could say could change the reality that the supposedly uncappable node had been capped—by Darius. Whatever speculations one might make about his character, Darius, alone of his peers, had had the courage—and the skill—to accomplish that great feat; and if such a man chose to employ a hint of . . . poetic license in recounting his story for future generations . . . well, it seemed to Nikki that the inheritors of that history—and of the comfortable lifestyle Darius had made possible—should applaud the evidence of yet another of Darius' talents rather than use that talent to devalue his undeniable accomplishments.

. . . on this 13th day of the 21st meeting of the House of Syndics, following the S7-node disaster, the Rhomatum ringmaster has been granted absolute veto-power over Syndic development. . . .

Which meant, of course, Darius.

But the decision had been inevitable. In the wake of Rhomatum's capping, with seventeen satellite nodes waiting to be capped and mastered, a flood of would-be ringmasters had arrived in Rhomatum Valley out of Mauritum monasteries. Having located the nodes through the Persitum Tower, they sought to cap them and claim them for Mauritum, disregarding their physical link to the rebel Tower of Rhomatum, possibly even in an organized attempt to force Darius into the Mauritum Web.

No one would ever know how many died in those wildcat attempts, since no one of those would-be ringmasters had dared announce he was making the attempt, and none had survived a failed attempt. But it soon became evident to even the most ambitious that no one capped a Rhomatum satellite without Darian sanction and Rhomatumin aid, and no one received that aid and sanction without adhering to Darian guidelines.

Which meant, quite simply, no more priests in the towers, no supernatural overtones to the leythium, and economic and political loyalty paid to Rhomatum, not Mauritum. Virtually anything else was, from the variety within the resulting Syndicate contracts, negotiable.

Variety which more than once had made Mikhyel express a wish that their illustrious ancestor had directed a fraction of the energy he spent worrying about the negative effects of a ring priesthood toward the production of truly viable alternatives.

But no one ever said Darius hadn't had his ... obsessions. All truly great people had obsessions. Obsessions were what drove otherwise normal people *to* greatness. And Darius had been obsessed with the corruption within the Maurii priesthood.

Darius had never written of his personal experiences within the Sacred Tower of Maurii, or of his life before the Tower, but the Darius who had entered that priesthood could not have been the embittered and angry Darius who led his family and a thousand others out of Mauritum and away from its gods forever. Nikki was as certain of that as if the decision had been his own.

Whether it was naive belief, a religious calling, or a rational faith in the value of the priests' work in Mauritum, *something* had once prompted an idealistic and intelligent young man to join what appeared to be a blatantly corrupt sect. That original True Believer was Nikki's elusive quarry in these crabbed and overwritten pages, a remnant of the young Darius that could ... cast the light of understanding upon the elder.

Perhaps, as popular scholarship maintained, Darius had planned the Exodus all along. As a *man* with no prospects, Darius might well have opted to become a *priest* with no prospects in order to create secular options for himself. Such scholars maintained it was unwise to make an icon of Darius, that the new social order he'd created was an artifact of Darius' own greed and therefore suspect.

But a single, obscure bibliographic reference to another ancient diary had sent Nikki on a search through all the family archives, a search that had culminated in the small, cozy library at Darhaven, a not altogether surprising end, as Darhaven had been Darius' sanctuary, his escape in the final years of his life.

Those diaries had suggested that perhaps Darius had hoped to change the priesthood from within, and that, as a true believer, he'd hoped to revitalize that which had been corrupted, and when he had discovered that righteous ambition to be impossible, he had founded the Exodus as a . . . as a creative option.

The Darius therein described, in such loving, intimate detail, had been a dreamer, a philosopher . . . the sort of visionary Nikki just knew, in his deepest soul, Darius *must* have been, and he sought today the subtle motivations and internal nuances that would make the autocratic engineer of Rhomatum society reconcile with the dreamer.

The author of the Darhaven diaries had been Darius' contemporary, Darius' third, least politically significant wife; her account of those years had gone unnoticed in serious circles . . . possibly because of the common belief that this youngest wife had been something of a butterfly-brain. A reputation which, one *had* to admit, from the overall tone and substance of the multitudinous volumes, might well have been justified.

But Nikki (who would, as Deymorin frequently pointed out, read the instructions on a bell-pull) had devoured the young woman's diaries and found, buried within the child-ishly round-lettered text, hints that Darius had confided in this wife as in no other. Hints between the lines of the songs the girl had written to delight her much older husband, that the true match for Darius' heart and soul had not been, as the Darius-endorsed histories would have them believe, the First Lady of his household, the woman who helped him organize the Exodus, and the coarchitect of Rhomatum . . . but rather this child of his dream city, among the firstborn of Rhomatum, whose very name was disputed among those who studied Darius' life.

Personally, Nikki believed Darius had carefully fostered that image of his child-wife to conceal the true intelligence of a woman without official power, but whose son had been the only one of Darius' nine recorded offspring to survive puberty.

Of course, it was also possible Darius had kept her cloistered to conceal the fact that his child-wife had also written songs to the mystical Tamshirin.

One was obliged to smile, in pragmatic company, at the mere mention of the 'people of the forest'—or 'spirits,' depending on the translation of the hill-folk's language one used. And one had to admit that unexplained disappearances in the forests, and visitations from old (and more often than not, dead) friends and lovers, did stretch the bounds of rational thought.

One tried to keep a properly receptive mind about such things, and a scholar such as Darius—or himself—given time and resources, was drawn to investigate the truth behind the tales. A poet, such as Darius' mysterious young wife—or, more modestly, himself—found such tales irresistible.

And as the real and spiritual descendant—one might even say the reincarnation—of that spiritual side of the Rhomandi Family, one felt compelled to investigate—and perhaps vindicate—one's ancestors.

A task which might prove easier if only the people to whom the Tamshirin actually appeared didn't always seem somewhat less than reliable. Drunks. Half-wits.

And, in particular, *ocarshi* smokers, of which Darius' child-wife, according to the less charitable biographies, had been one. . . .

*　　*　　*

The bitter stench of ocarshi lingered about the cloak Dancer flung into the far corner of the cell-like room. Disgusting stuff. Impossible to imagine what Rhyys saw in it.

Lightning skipped along the peaks outside the room's single window; thunder crackled a sudden staccato counterpoint to the low rumble that vibrated the very stones of this old and crumbling hall.

Close. *Very* close.

Dancer closed the door and shot the bolt, alone at last, and not likely to be interrupted, now that Rhyys had finally retired to the Ring Tower, which, as the Khoratum ringmaster, Rhyys *should* have done at the first sign of the storm.

But Rhyys had been at the Harvest Moon Festival, and, in Rhyys' casually voiced opinion, one had apprentices to see to such contingencies ... particularly when there was an important celebration in progress.

Never mind those apprentices were almost certainly *also* revelling, following, as apprentices were wont to do, their master's sterling example.

The formal robe of heavy brocade sailed after the cloak, and the beaded hair-clip bounced off the vanity to disappear beneath the rope-sprung cot. The wind's cleansing chill whistled through the battered window and whipped Dancer's hair free of its elaborate knot, twisting the fine strands around Dancer's body along with the supple linen undertunic.

With its cold and its inconvenient location in the outermost corner of the north wing, this room was undoubtedly Khoratum Ringmaster Rhyys dunTarec's notion of Rhomatum's hell on earth, considering it had been assigned to Dancer, and considering Rhyys had personally handled the room assignments.

Part of the original castle that had been deserted centuries ago, this room was far down Rhyys' list for renovations. The entire wing was battered and unreliable, half the staircases had rotted or burned long since, and rather than the delicate colored glass prevalent in the modern Tower, this room's window was a lightning-blasted hole.

Battered ... inconvenient ... icy-chill ...

And Dancer loved it.

In fact, had Rhyys allowed the novice ringdancers to select their own quarters, Dancer might well have chosen this very room, because, for all its inconvenience, for all the north winds channelled straight for its one, unshutterable window, this spot had the best view in all of Khoratum. From here, one could look out across wild mountain peaks and almost forget the city growing cancerlike below and to the southwest, buildings oozing down the ley-strand toward distant Rhomatum.

And from here, if one leaned just so, being careful not to dislodge what sill remained, one could see the stadium and the *other* rings of Khoratum, the only rings that mattered to Dancer.

Lightning flashed, so close the fine hairs on Dancer's arms tingled. If Rhyys didn't get at least the Cardinal reset soon, the Tower would take another direct hit before he had the rings reset from the last one. A wiser, more experienced, ringmaster could have prevented the storm in the first place, or at least directed it elsewhere. But Khoratum's ringdirector (one could hardly call Rhyys a *master* of anything) was neither particularly experienced, nor particularly wise.

Complacent best described Rhyys dunTarec.

{Rhyys is a certifiable dolt.}

Mother's sarcasm invaded Dancer's thoughts, and for a dizzying moment, Dancer allowed personal opinion to ebb and flow into agreement with her, that being the easiest option.

But only for a moment.

Dolt though Rhyys might well be, (Dancer maintained firmly) he must have at least some Talent, else why would Anheliaa of Rhomatum have endorsed Rhyys' application? Anheliaa was not a woman, to judge by all her near-legendary accomplishments, to make foolish judgments, and Anheliaa Rhomandi dunMoren, Ringmaster of Rhomatum Tower, had herself designed Khoratum Tower, commissioned its rings—after funding the expensive, and dangerous, mining operations—and Anheliaa herself had trained Rhyys in their—

{Dolt, I tell you. Like all his kind—including That Creature. Invading the sanctums, stealing the structure and substance of the lace . . .}

"Humans require the leythium for the rings—"

{Halt!}

Mother's rejection was a blow to the inside of a mere human's skull. Vision dimmed momentarily. When it cleared:

"Forgive," Dancer apologized, humbly, as one learned to do after seventeen years of salvaging Personal Opinion from Mother's insidious notions. "Humans are a lazy breed, requiring mental crutches for a process as natural as . . . passing wind."

{Better.} Smug satisfaction tinged the thought. *{—And?}*

"And I seek to transcend the limitations of my own humanity."

{Take that laughter from your mind, you irreligious squanderer of universal truth!}

"Yes, Mother."

{Oh, shut up.} Her 'voice' began to fade. *{Silly, undisciplined rascal. As if I had nothing better to do with my precious ti . . .}*

Her distinctive presence evanesced, leaving the question scintillating in her pupil's mind, leading Dancer to wonder, not for the first time, at Mother's interest in so imperfect a vessel—to wonder why, seventeen years ago, she'd transferred a human child from the surface into her cavern of miracles, why she had taught that child to come and go in her subterranean world at will, why she had provided a learning far different from that gleaned in any human school . . .

{Oh, shut your head up and hie your lazy butt down here.}

And to wonder, most of all, why she had never yet called in her debt, nor even so much as indicated what that debt might entail.

{And pick me up some drenal leaves on the way.}

Enough to make that flawed vessel just a bit nervous, even as that flawed vessel's fingers reached under the cot for the pot of oil hidden there.

{And don't forget the aphids!}

Chapter Two

On the far wall of this little-used library antechamber hung a painting nearly as old as Darius' journal. A depiction, Nikki personally believed, of the Mauritum of the age of the Exodus. He'd found the rendering hidden behind a false wall in a condemned building when he was only ten years old.

It had been his arguments alone that had convinced Mikhyel not to destroy the painting; his arguments that had persuaded Mikhyel that Darius' ancient ruling against all things Mauritumin couldn't possibly apply after all these years—particularly not with the long-sought trade agreement with Mauritum on the horizon.

Personally, he believed Khyel had been so amused at hearing his ten-year-old brother spout legalities at him, that he couldn't possibly have refused, but the important thing was, they'd negotiated a compromise so that seven years later and with that trade agreement *still* under negotiation, the painting remained intact, though hidden away in the Rhomandi Family Collection Wing of the public access library, where few but he, as he'd carefully pointed out to Mikhyel, visited anyway.

He often wondered who the long-dead artist might have been. Second generation, the experts had insisted, and stylistically one of three known names of that period. But for him, the detail, the loving sensuality of line and brush stroke, the fantastical glamour about the city itself suggested a more personal memory.

Perhaps, he imagined to himself, the artist had been some reluctant exile, leaving Mauritum in the wake of a disastrous love affair ... Or perhaps a failed spiritual reevaluation: a man—or woman—of unquestionable artistic ability, destined to scrub floors for the rest of their life because he—or she—hadn't garnered the money or political connections, to rise above the Maurii-declared situation. . . .

Or perhaps not an original follower at all. Perhaps the artist *was* second, or even third generation—recreating a memory for a beloved, dying grandparent, then forced, following the Darian Ruling of the twenty-second year After the Founding to hide a masterpiece behind a facade of mediocri—

Nikki sighed.

He had, according to Mikhyel, one besetting sin: he daydreamed. Mikhyel tried hard to cure him of it—for his own good, he never doubted it—a cure that sometimes left bruises he'd just as soon avoid, and if Mikhyel were here just now, his ears would ring for certain.

But he had to admit, his tendency to . . . examine multiplicities of possibilities . . . did absorb copious amounts of time, which he had little enough of today.

Of course, he wouldn't be here at all, would have had no time to waste if Deymorin had come as he'd promised faithfully he would at the Transition Day Festival.

But probably Deymorin had forgotten. Or, equally probable, Deymorin and Mikhyel were having another row about something or other no one had bothered to explain to him, and making a point with Mikhyel had taken precedence over any promise to him.

Which left him—having begged off (on the *slender* possibility Deymorin would arrive this morning) Bertran's and Phellrad's trek to see the Shanitum Node bell and candle dancers on-stage-for-one-day-only in Gartum market—with only his own company. The muse hadn't struck, his guitar strings were old and untunable, and if he'd gone to buy strings, which he'd kept putting off and then forgetting to do, he'd have had to go to Gartum market, where he'd naturally have run into Bertie and Phell and have had to explain that No, Deymorin *hadn't* shown . . .

Which had left the library, where Deymorin, if he bothered to make an appearance after all and cared to think on it, would know to look for him.

He could almost hear Deymio laughing: Which is it now, fry? Darius? the poetry of Belianus? the second century Ultra-romanticist school of frog painting? C'mon, brat, let's go for a ride.

Never mind it was storming Outside: Deymio was waterproof.

Mikhyel, at least, could have no objections to his being here today. Mikhyel would be proud of him for seeking a purpose ... a realistic goal for his future, unlike his past *obsessions,* as Deymorin called them.

Mikhyel would understand if he said his future lay in the Mauritum trade agreement. That was politics and law, things Mikhyel understood and *appreciated.*

As Mikhyel had understood the painting—or at least his ten-year-old brother's need to save his find from destruction.

What neither Mikhyel nor Deymorin knew was how that image had obsessed their youngest brother for years, or how it was meant, (he was just certain of it), to affect their younger brother's destiny. They didn't know, because their youngest brother hadn't quite figured *how* it was going to affect him. Their youngest brother only knew it drew him to it ... as Darius' journal or the child-bride's diaries drew him.

The painting depicted Mauritum Tower atop a rugged, sunset-lit knoll rising far above the flat plain of the city proper; and radiating out from that knoll, twelve save one irregularly-spaced roads sparkled with the familiar silver of leylight, the single darkened leyroad Mauritum's link to the untappable node lying beneath the ocean.

Those lighted streets were a disturbing familiarity in an otherwise exotic image.

The city in the painting was an interconnected webwork of curiously amorphous structures, as if the architects had intended the city to reflect the crystal structure upon which all Mauritum power, both real and political, was based. One had to wonder whether that depiction was mere artistic whimsy or based on the architectural reality.

... We'll have no dynastic webs here. And no lords, no kings, no graces. A man will be a man and of one family only, son to one man only ...

Family-webs. Multiple spouses.... Nikki had a difficult enough time imagining himself with one wife. But two ... or even more? And each of them with loyalties, and legal bed-mates, other than himself?

Not that such arrangements were unheard of in Rhomatum. A widow or widower often joined houses with a mar-

ried cousin or even sibling, for economic advantage or
simple convenience. And if joining households included
joining bedchambers ... well, it was only natural, wasn't it?

But with the lesson of Mauritum behind them, Rhomatum citizens knew better than to let such associations blossom into excessive offspring. There was finite space beneath
the node's power umbrella and all of that land was long
since privately owned, or if state-controlled, platted for
public gardens or other predetermined use. For the offspring of a family who had physically no more space within
the city, there was only the darkness between the lines,
those wide, untamed lands where the ley did not reach,
where the only source of light and heat was fire and where
other facilities were equally primitive.

(Personally, he rather liked fire. And horses. And chickens. And cats and dogs ... and all those other things you
couldn't have inside a city because they either weren't necessary or because they produced dirt or noise or static. But
one had to admit that leylight and leyheat and sewers that
ran into leylines and disappeared were pleasant conve-
niences.)

Early on, of course, population had not been an issue.
Early on, Darius' new city had flourished so well that, according to Darius, some of Mauritum's landed Families had
encouraged whole portions of their clans to relinquish their
landrights within Mauritum and follow the waves of immigrants to Rhomatum and its rapidly expanding web of satellite cities—until Darius, due to major philosophical
differences with those aristocratic immigrants, had ended
all contact with Mauritum, and ultimately, in the thirty-
third year of the Exodus, had ordered the destruction of
every image and book that referenced Mauritum—the ruling that had nearly demanded the destruction of his precious painting three hundred years later.

For a man who had proclaimed the Exodus as an escape
from the authoritarian rule of a handful of individuals,
Darius had certainly taken a dictatorial approach with his
own followers. But they must have agreed in principle,
since they had never, in Darius' fifty-three year tenure as
their absolute leader, attempted to depose him.

Not, at least, according to the histories Darius had per-
mitted to see publication.

Although, to be fair to his illustrious ancestor, neither

had any personal diaries or letters surfaced in the subsequent centuries to refute that record.

At least, not that any of Darius' descendants had allowed into the public eye.

It made for a suspicious—and dizzy—mind, considering history the way Berul insisted any serious scholar must.

Berul's contention that historical accounts were, of necessity and simple human nature, slanted by the writer's own political bias and personal history—was so obvious, and yet, at the same time, so very revolutionary a thought, such a simple insight, and yet no one prior to Berul had ever considered the possibility—or at least, not considered the possibility and made it into print. Certainly none of Nikki's private tutors had ever suggested that the Written Word might not contain all the truth necessary for understanding.

But he'd found Berul's privately published essays on his own, and on his own he sought now to apply them to his illustrious, but elusive, ancestor in general and to Darius' journal in particular.

Strikethroughs—some so violent the heavy paper itself was ripped, and sometimes the pages beneath, as well. *A man of temper,* Nikki's thought tasted of wry humor. Darius would have been right at home in the current Rhomandi generation.

Darius had been a fighter, as Deymio was—and as Mikhyel was, in his own way. Darius had fought Mauritum for independence of thought and personal freedom, and yet, considered in Berul's light, Darius' subsequent high-handed censorship made a sort of cold-blooded sense, an action, in that considered light, not entirely out of character.

Darius and his most ardent followers had wanted a clean break from the past. Perhaps they had seen such darian (a word coined by Berul himself) tactics as the only way to accomplish that separation from all Mauritum represented, and to prevent the newly arrived aristocrats from exerting their residual influence. . . .

Residual because in this new land, every citizen began equal.

Theoretically.

But then, everything they *knew* about that time, and particularly Mauritum, was theoretical.

On the other hand—a thrill of excitement shivered down

Nikki's spine—a breakthrough in that pending trade agreement with the ancient web suddenly bid fair to change that. The limited agreement signed two years ago was about to expand. Soon, trade would begin to flow freely. Three hundred years after Darius, trade relations between Rhomatum and Mauritum were regenerating, and it was going to take men with historical perspective on both sides to permanently heal the well-entrenched rift.

And, in one's most private thoughts, one did think one might be among those history-making peacemakers. One had, after all, had plenty of practice, having spent one's lifetime making peace between one's brothers.

And who better than the third son of the House of Rhomandi to fill one of those soon-to-be-named ambassadorial posts?

"M'lord?"

Who better to understand Darius, and by that understanding, perhaps understand Darius' passionate abhorrence of Mauritum and find the truth behind the fable?

"M'lord Nikaenor!"

The curator: standing on the far side of the table, flanked by two attendants.

"Yes, Gomarrin?"

Two quite large attendants.

"M'lord, the library closed some time ago."

Nikki tipped his head. "Closed? . . ."

For a moment, it was only a sound, not a word with meaning at all.

"M'lord, I must send my people home. You're the last one here. We must return the book to the vault."

"Oh . . . of course . . ."

Nikki was *not* in his suite—or in any of the other eighty-one private rooms in this damned monstrosity of a house.

Deymorin collapsed on the couch in the reading nook that was part of the small complex of rooms maintained year-round for his use, never mind that he only used them a handful of days out of that year and would as soon patronize Tirise's establishment on those nights he was forced to spend in the City.

But his staying at a brothel, regardless of its reputation, would horrify prudish Mikhyel's delicate sensibilities (which he didn't mind in the least) and hurt Nikki's feelings (which he did) so he said nothing and rattled about in unfamiliar surroundings, wearing unfamiliar clothing Mikhyel's tailor provided to keep Mikhyel's lamentably rustic elder brother presentable.

At least the wardrobe so provided wasn't solid black.

The wine he'd ordered arrived along with Jerrik, Nikki's so-called valet and erstwhile partner in juvenile chicanery.

"Where the hell have you been?" he demanded by way of greeting, and Jerrik, whom Deymorin had known since childhood, only grinned.

"Might ask you the same thing, *m'lord* Dee. Mighty upset, Nik was, when you didn't show last night."

"Oh, shut up and hand me a glass of whatever you've brought. Is it drinkable?"

Jerrik licked his lips and wiggled his brows, then handed a glass over, his expression turning woeful.

"Oh, pour one for yourself and park your rear. Lord, you remind me of Ringer."

"I'll take that as a compliment, m'lord Dee."

"So, where have you been?" Deymorin repeated, when Jerrik had settled in a chair opposite him. "And where's that pesky brother of mine?"

"Left early this afternoon, sir. Said he'd be back in plenty of time."

Deymorin snorted and Jerrik cast him an apologetic look.

"Sorry, sir, but I couldn't ride herd on him this time, could I? Had to get his party clothes ready, I did."

"No one blames you, Jerrik, but the lad's sense of time is deplorable."

"Family trait, m'lord Dee?"

"Oh, shut up. Where'd he go—the library?"

Jerrik's eyes dropped.

"Might have known. What is it this time? Tamshirin? The stratification of—no, it's Darius these days, isn't it? The boy's obsessed with the man and his little piece of fluff."

"He's *not* obsessed," Jerrik protested. "He just wants—" The young man broke off, obviously discomfited, obviously hoarding some knowledge he felt Deymorin should know. Deymorin, trying to hold back his growing alarm, said gently:

"Wants what, Jerrik? It's all right, son, you can trust me."

"I do, sir, you know that. I just don't want Nikki to *stop* trusting me. It's possible Nikki wants to tell you himself. It's not crazy—"

"I think maybe you should let me be the judge of that."

Jerrik took a long swallow. Then: "He wants to go to Mauritum."

"Of course he does: History incarnate. Probably dig the whole damn place up and get us sued for the damages."

"It's not like that, sir. He wants ... Rhomatum will need ambassadors to Mauritum, won't they? Rhomatum representatives within the city?"

"He's too young!" Surprise startled the truth out of him.

Jerrik bit his lip and frowned, refusing to meet his eyes, and Deymorin extrapolated carefully: "I mean, of course, that he'd be fighting an uphill battle getting Mauritum leaders to take him seriously. Perhaps someday ..." He let the thought trail off, not committing his support to the fluff-brained scheme, but not totally opposing it either, which never got anyone anywhere against seventeen-year-old dreams.

And Jerrik's shoulders dropped. "I know that, sir. I've tried to convince him, but you know Nikki."

"Too well. —Wait here." Deymorin rang for a footman and sent him off to the library to haul Nikki home. "And if the library has closed, have Gomarrin open it up. He could have gotten himself locked in ..."

"Again." Jerrik muttered, behind him, and he stifled a grin as he shut the door behind the messenger, and turned back to the young man.

"So, why did you really come down here?"

"Thought maybe you could use some help getting ready. I heard you arrived without Tonami."

"Appreciate it. Maybe you can make sense out of whatever Mikhyel's tailor has left in my closet this time. Find me something appropriate for tonight, will you? And if I'm not out of the bath by ..." He thought of long rides and weary bones. "Hell, by the time Nikki shows ... well, come and make sure the old man hasn't drowned, will you? *Before* seeing to that unappreciative wretch."

Jerrik grinned. "Aye, m'lord Dee."

As fate had it, he'd no more than settled into the steaming water, than the tinkling of the doorbell and Jerrik's quiet query stole the moment away. Jerrik entered, carrying a folded note.

A scented, folded note.

Addressed with Tirise romMarinni's distinctive, florid hand.

* * *

The storm raged on over Mount Khoratum. Deep within Khoratum's heart, Dancer watched the radiant leythium chandeliers respond to those atmospheric shivers, and wondered.

From above, the storm had seemed natural enough. Down here, where cause and effect remained manifest in the leythium strands, one suspected differently.

For seventeen years Dancer had watched weather systems flux the crystalline lace into semipredictable curves and twists, had learned through experience how those mutable shapes reflected surface-world mountains and valleys, as well as shifting clouds.

When storms built over distant oceans to the west or grassy plains to the south, the cavern's response would begin as the merest shiver of the outermost fringed edge; the shiver would grow to a billowing bulge as that seething energy crashed into land and mountain. Following familiar patterns, warps and wefts of living crystal formed from millennia of world resonances, the outworld storm should then weave in and around mountain and valley, leyline and tower: natural forces creating natural, logically predictable, effects in the ley.

Too often these days, something affected that pattern. Somewhere beyond three-node distant Mauritum—the limit of the cavern's awareness—something ... irritated ... the ley, not creating these storms, but certainly encouraging them, as sand in an oyster encouraged a pearl to grow. Sometimes, like today, that irritant would resonate with Khoratum, changing a simple rain cloud into something far more sinister.

The lightning blast that had blackened Khoratum had exploded the sparkling leythium cloud that represented/was Khoratum Tower. The cloud that was neither crystalline nor liquid nor gas, but something of all three, was rebuilding its integrity more rapidly than usual—and without help from Rhomatum. That was surprising. Rhyys' adrenaline must be pumping.

A shimmer in the veils: rain in the world above. A great deal of rain.

No surprise to someone newly transferred from the surface—water still dripped from Dancer's oil-slick skin and hip-length hair, to make rainbow pools in every nearby low spot.

Mother and her delicate taste buds. The drenal leaves *had* to be damp but *not* drenched, and the buds *must* have at least three aphids per petal. Never mind it was fall and aphids even harder to find than buds, Mother's human apprentice fetched whatever Mother might, on a whim, decide she required. Her flawed vessel of an apprentice . . .

Perhaps—Dancer grinned at the softly drifting lattice—one should say *vassal,* since one was expected to interrupt one's rare-enough within-time for those whims, to transport between cave and surface and back again, until one's skin began to glow with accumulated ley energy. A glow that, fortunately, faded quickly once one was back above.

The rain-shimmer intensified: the storm, defying all Rhyys' efforts, had stalled directly above Khoratum, and was releasing its bounty all at once, a deluge that must concern surface dwellers of mountain and valley alike.

The previous summer's storms had been all fire and thunder by the time they reached the Khoramali Range. That mysterious, faraway irritation had clashed too often with Rhyys' inexpert control of weather patterns, (and—one had to be honest—Mother's interference) causing the clouds to relieve themselves over the valley to the west. By the time the clouds had reached the Khoramali, they had lacked the moisture to placate the thirsty mountain soil.

The mountainside had turned hard and crusty, requiring a gentle soaking to open it again to life. Instead, it was to receive a deluge that would skim the surface and tax the limits of even the greatest river gullies.

The mountain-folk who built their stone and thatch cottages along the deep river cuts, would have been watching today's darkening skies in awareness and no small fear. And when the initial surge of water swirled, driving rock and tree before it, they would retreat to the altars cut deep into the rock beneath their homes to burn incense to the guardians of earth and ley, praying the flash floods would not pound their surface dwellings into rubble and wash the rubble downstream with the rocks and trees.

The strands nearest Dancer shivered, shimmering deepest violet.

Years ago, following a similar storm, when the earth itself had quaked in fear, Mother had found a human child huddled beside one such altar fire gone dead, the bloody seep from the tunnel's collapsed mouth—all that remained of the child's grandmother—thankfully invisible, gone with the fire's light.

But that memory was long ago and far (figuratively speaking) away. Dancer paid Grandmother's memory the loving respect it deserved and pressed it lovingly back into the past where it belonged. In moments, the leythium resumed its natural iridescence.

Flashes within the lace, a series of blinding crystalline novae: lightning, and a great deal of it.

Above and a bit to the (a mental pause to translate leythium-lace response to human surface association) southeast, the residents of Khoratum were looking to their precious Tower and sighing, resigned to another period of candlelight and smoky fireplaces.

Dancer had little sympathy for those valley-bred foreigners who, fifteen years ago, had invaded the once-tiny mountain village, polluting the fields and minds of the mountain folk, bastardizing the ancient wisdoms; had less sympathy for the city-dwelling natives, like Rhyys, who had welcomed those invaders, even to adopting their foreign naming practices. Those folk had known the risks when they pledged their lives to the new tower, and moved in, bringing industry and problems the mountain folk had never realized they needed—until they had them.

Another lightning string danced the lace.

The true disaster of the storm in the world-above would occur when that river swell reached the valley below: disaster by flood, against which not even the fabled Rhomatum rings had defense.

For those lowland farmers, Dancer did feel some sympathy, even though they were Rhomatumin. After previous rains had ruined two cuttings, a rich third lay curing on the ground, desperately needed hay to winter cattle and horses. Bumper crops of barley and corn—more than sufficient to offset last year's disastrous drought—stood a scant week short of harvest. Drenched one last time, and lacking summer's drying heat, the hay would mold, and the grains, already bending their heads under their own weight, would flatten to ground turned soft and unworkable.

As for those who lived in Rhomatum itself, on the far end of the Khoratum Line, those whose existence in the lace was a gentle breeze through loose filaments ... the Rhomatumin would feel no qualm, would probably not even have noticed the clouds gathering into ever-darkening piles on their northeastern horizon.

They were the lucky ones, they would acknowledge humbly (while privately assuring themselves that of course *luck* had nothing to do with their superior circumstance). They lived in the City (Rhomatum, to those Outside), the harbinger of the Modern Era, where the leylight and heat never wavered, and the floating cabs were never grounded; where crime was virtually nonexistent; where roses grew in the dead of winter, water ran cool and fresh year-round, and rain happened *predictably* an hour before sunset ...

Let the lightning dance about the distant clouds, Dancer could almost hear them say, *it will not affect Rhomatum.*

The Lady would never permit it.

{Lady?} Mother's disgust screeched between Dancer's ears, an instant before Mother herself appeared between two ceiling-to-floor crystalline veils. "That *creature* is no lady!"

The veils curled back on themselves, evading Mother's heated emotion, but relaxed and resumed their glimmering, glowing sway in an instant as she controlled that disrupting emission, and glided toward Dancer, hands outheld.

{Welcome, child.}

Never mind Dancer had long since delivered the drenal leaves to Mother's inner sanctum—Mother operated on a different time sense and Mother's flawed vassal had learned to accept acknowledgment when Mother deigned to make it and never take offense.

Not that offense would accomplish anything anyway.

Mother's embrace ended almost before it began, leaving behind a residual:

{Oil ... there's a good child. ...}

Dancer retrieved a translucent, leythium-traced bowl from a constantly metamorphosing shelf composed of living leythium crystal, dipped oil from a deep, narrow-mouthed pool, stood, and poured at her signal.

Mother spread the sacred oil over her hands and arms until the faint green scales glimmered with iridescent light, then turned to the Cauldron of Life to lift a bud from the Sacred Flame with her bare palms. Swaying and swirling to some internal melody, or perhaps in response to the earth itself, Mother showered the shimmering essence over the sanctuary floor in a seemingly (though Dancer knew better) random pattern. Where the drops fell, small flames flickered.

Sacred Flame. Sacred Oil. Cauldron of Life. Human religious terms for Tamshirin tools of the trade. Terms two thousand years old and more. Words the first human visitors to this cave had carried to the surface to describe the magical images and events they'd witnessed.

For Mother, the oil was simple precaution, insulation against energy surges, the Cauldron a reservoir of liquid leythium, unstable, volatile, the better to show the pattern she set.

Her preparations completed, Mother contemplated that pattern, flicked the final drops carelessly into the center of a glowing flower, then grinned, her glittering fangs reflecting the shifting, shimmering flames: rain would fall, lightning would strike when—and where—Mother decided.

Mother didn't create storms, but once they existed, she did tend to play with the results. And Mother, her resentment of Anheliaa tinting the ley with gleeful yellow, shifted the storm's course now, countering Rhyys' every defense, never sending the storm quite to Anheliaa's doorstep, but bouncing it instead right back toward Khoratum and Anheliaa's vulnerable prize apprentice.

Mother rarely took an interest in surface events; she didn't now, except to scratch the itch Anheliaa gave her. But Dancer was of the surface, and Dancer knew Rhomatumin history well, studied it with an eye to Khoratum's future, and Dancer cared about Khoratum's future because as that future went, so went the future of the Khoratumin ringdance—which meant Dancer's future.

Dancer knew, for instance, that Lady Anheliaa dun-Moren's uncanny knack for knowing which ring-related technologies to support, her own experimentation into uses of the rings themselves, would alone have guaranteed her

place in human history—a fact that would have left her as
minor an annoyance to Mother as Anheliaa's predecessors
had been.

However, Anheliaa had managed what her ancestors as
far distant as Darius himself had failed to accomplish: she'd
capped Khoratum, the last radical line out of Rhomatum,
its nature-given attraction leeching (or so human ring-
theory maintained) perfectly usable ley energy into useless groundflow.

Once Khoratum had been controlled, the sheer power
available to Rhomatum had, for the first time in history,
exceeded that required by the City itself, and Rhomatum
had begun to supply that surplus energy to lesser nodes—
for a price.

Mother didn't care about money. Mother had quite a
different view of how 'useless' that 'groundflow' had been.
Mother cared about—

{Hackers!}

Mother's thought was a darting thrust, penetrating, and
vanishing in an instant, but leaving a residual image of humans chopping and mutilating the delicate leythium fibers.

Mother didn't like careless exploitation of the ley energy.
Liked far less any unconsidered (in her opinion) experimentation with it. *Especially* where that experimentation
involved Khoratum Node.

Mother's node.

But according to rumor (a satisfied mental glimmer from
Mother), Anheliaa's experimentation had finally caught up
with her. According to rumor, taming Khoratum had cost
the Rhomatum ringmaster dearly.

{Of course it did!} Mother's capacity to manipulate the
ley and chatter at the same time never ceased to amaze.
{I'm not as easily cowed as my brothers and sisters. I'll never
comprehend why . . .} Her next reference—something about
drinking disgusting substances—was her personal image for
her counterpart beneath Rhomatum. {. . . allowed Darius
access in the first place. We could have handled the storms,
but no-o-o. Sucks-pond-water liked the taste of Darius'
mind, so Sucks-pond-water invited Darius into the valley,
and look what that got us. —Anheliaa.}

The sensory-rich image she incorporated into that last
'word' made 'Sucks-pond-water' quite palatable in contrast.

Dancer had only the most hazy images of the leythium

chambers prior to Anheliaa's capping of Khoratum, but the clearest memories were of sitting and watching the crystal patterns actively growing, overnight changes that now took months—even years—to achieve. Mother insisted the node had been growing, extending new lines, that she'd been able to sense the sun on the far side of the world when the full moon floated overhead.

The world-cavern Dancer knew could see only three nodes distant, and struggled to maintain its own integrity. New lines, which always grew in opposing clusters of three, would have made it a nine-line intersection, comparable in power to Rhomatum. If Mother was correct, another human generation and capping Khoratum would have been impossible, without Mother's aid.

It was possible Anheliaa had sensed that was true. Possible Anheliaa had risked her life to cap Khoratum precisely because it was her node's last chance for absolute dominance—and perhaps she'd sensed, even fifteen years ago, that the next generation would prove inadequate to the challenge.

Dancer had seen Anheliaa once only and then from a distance, when the Rhomatum ringmaster had travelled to Khoratum for the tutoring of Rhyys. Anheliaa had been frail and aging even at that time, and she'd had to have been aware that, even though she survived capping Khoratum, one day she'd be dead; all humans died.

One had to wonder if, on that day when Anheliaa had been carried through the streets of her conquered mountain village to the Tower she'd financed and designed, the Rhomatum ringmaster was feeling triumph over her gods, or betrayal by them.

Because in order to cap Khoratum, Anheliaa had had to draw on the power of all the other satellite nodes—for a venture that might, for all they knew at the time, have destroyed the entire web. In order to gain the cooperation of the satellites, Anheliaa had had to sign a variety of agreements. The terms of those agreements were unique to each node and secret, but rumor held little doubt those agreements held Rhomatum to severe standards of performance—both during Anheliaa's lifetime and after.

And in the perverse way of nature, following the most accomplished ringmaster of all time, House Rhomandi's uncontested control of the Rhomatum rings appeared in dan-

ger. Rumor held that none of Mheric's three sons possessed
even a modicum of skill with the rings, and they were all
(reportedly) without issue.

A derisive snort: a mental drowning.

*{Mheric's sons might have all the ability in the universe.
Won't do them any good whatsoever with that creature in
charge.}*

"But Anheliaa won't be in charge forever. And when
that day comes, Mother, you'll have someone totally unknown to contend with."

*{I contend with no one. And Mother knows everyone.
Now, go away. Mother's busy.}*

Never mind she'd instigated the conversation. Dancer
smiled, accustomed to her moods.

In all likelihood, Mother knew—if Mother cared to
know—who was destined to be Anheliaa's successor.
Dancer, who received only the vaguest of images from the
flickering, shimmering lights of the leythium web, had to
rely primarily on rumors overheard in Rhyys' court of social climbers.

Rumor held Deymorin, Mheric's eldest and heir to the
vast Rhomandi holdings, to be obsessed with Outside interests: hardly what one would expect of a ringmaster, certainly not of someone who could have near absolute power
within the City. But so far, Deymorin had abdicated that
power to his brother, Mikhyel.

Serious, dark-featured, and (so the ladies of the court
claimed) wickedly mysterious Mikhyel had for years held
his father's administrative offices—an important job in itself, leaving little time for Tower training, when one was,
as rumor held Mikhyel to be, meticulous and scrupulous in
his work.

Finally, there was Nikaenor . . . Nikki the Scholar, people
called him. Nine years the youngest . . . who apparently
emerged from his history books for only two things: wandering condemned buildings looking for what he called 'historical artifacts' . . . or riding brother Deymorin's horses.

Nikki the dreamer—the City's businessmen and religious
leaders agreed, and no one argued.

{Least of all me. Mother never argues. Now go away!}

Chapter Three

" '... and from the wind-swirled ashes, my love's spirit climbs—' " The voice from beyond the door paused, then: "I think, maybe, that should be 'soars,' don't you?"

"Nikki, Nikki, Nikki ..." Deymorin sighed and leaned his brow against the closed door, finding in its rough surface unexpected relief from an irritating itch. "What am I to do with you?"

"Don't worry, Dey-m'love." Long-nailed fingers brushed his temple, securing wayward hairs behind his ear. "Mayhap they're takin' a wee rest. Been up here a longish while, they have."

"I wish I could believe that," he told the door sourly. "How long did it take him to work up the nerve to come upstairs?"

Tirise laughed softly. "Oh, less than you, as I recall."

"I was a year younger."

"Two. *And* among a crowd of friends."

That surprised him. "Nikki's here on his own?"

"His birthday present to himself, as he was quick to point out when he arrived."

"Wanted to make clear right off he was legal, did he?"

Her nod brushed his shoulder. "Seemed right determined, just a smidge confused, if you take m' meanin'." Another soft laugh, a quick squeeze at his waist. "Bring th' laddie back, Deymio-luv. Mayhap I can straighten 'im out. I did think Beauvina—what with her innocent ways and all ..." Her cheek pressed lightly against his back, and he felt her sigh. "If only they hadn't looked so sweet together."

Sweet? Tirise was a closet romantic. He'd have had a different word for it, he'd wager. Still ... *Tirise* and Nikki?

He tipped his head, looking past his shoulder to the proprietress' full-bodied figure. Tempting. Sincerely tempting. Once—a very long once ago, so it seemed these days—

Tirise had introduced him to the finer things in life. Fifteen years later, she was still an extremely handsome woman, particularly in the soft backlighting of the hallway's silver leylights, but somehow ... legal age or not ... Deymorin shook his head reluctantly as he pulled her ample form to the fore ... "I don't think he's quite up to your weight yet, m'dear." ... and bending his head to hers, proceeded to erase any possible sting in his words.

Tirise was humming when she surfaced, and with a sultry smile, a sway of hip against hip, and a tug at his waist, she murmured, "Whaddaya say, lovie? Empty room, next. No charge for an old friend. Been far, far too long since you visited us."

With even greater reluctance, he resisted the pull and nodded toward the door. "Better rescue the fry before Beauvina guts him from sheer boredom."

Tirise chuckled, a low, warm sound, deep in her throat. "Little worry for that. 'Vina looked right impressed with his little verses down below. That's when I first reckoned they'd match."

"Ringfire," he exclaimed, in only partially feigned alarm, "she *encouraged* the brat? He'll be expecting *me* to read the damned things next. Now I *must* get in there. —Hold this for me, will you?" He handed her his cane, then reached for the latch. "Have you the key?"

The well-greased bolt moved easily, silently—and without *need* of a key.

"Never mind," he finished, disgusted.

Through the slightest crack in the doorway, he took the whole pitiful scene in at a glance:

Deep red draperies, gilt gold furnishings awash in the warm glow of candlelight, the soft, inviting texture of velvet, safe (and legal) this far removed from Tower Hill. Perched on the edge of her chair, clothing and hair still depressingly intact, was a girl—about Nikki's age, or a bit older—her kohl-darkened eyes wide, her reddened lips pursed in anticipation. On the bed, feet spread for balance, one hand to his breast (undoubtedly for dramatic emphasis), the other hanging at his side holding a thick sheaf of curling pages, was his scatterbrained brother.

Deymorin muttered a curse, then, with a, *Pardon me*— to Tirise, he took a deep breath and threw the door back.

It struck the wall with a gratifying crash.

For a single startled heartbeat, Nikki stared at the shadowed opening, mouth hanging open on a forgotten line.

In the second, Deymorin bellowed, *"Down!"*

In the third, his idiot brother dropped flat on the mattress, bounced once, and rolled to the floor on the far side of the bed, disappearing amidst a pouf of loose pages.

Deymorin waited a fourth and fifth heartbeat, allowing the dolt time to do something incredibly stupid, realized pleasant surprise when he didn't. Better, of course, if the fry had dropped without the cue, but overall . . . one took what one could get. Especially when one recalled one's own youth, when impressing the lady in question would have been infinitely more important than common sense.

Or perhaps not so common. Normal men didn't worry about assassination and abduction. Such concerns were limited to men whose family tended to irritate those with murderous tendencies.

Families like the Rhomandi. A fact of life Nikki had yet to realize.

Deymorin stepped into the candle-glow, and feigning nonchalance, leaned his shoulders against the doorframe and drawled: "Not bad, fry. You'd only have been dead twice over, this time."

Blue eyes blinked above the disrupted bedclothes. "D–Deymio?"

He raised an eyebrow. "You need to ask? You can come out now."

Smooth skin flushed bright red, then disappeared, and a muffled curse rose from beneath the rippling mass of golden, bane-of-his-young-life curls.

Deymorin waited patiently until, embarrassment evidently conquered, Nikki flung the golden mane back with a flourish, taming it with a practiced (undoubtedly before a mirror) two-handed sweep, and stood up with exaggerated dignity, ignoring the shirt hanging open at the throat, exposing him nearly to his cummerbund.

"Picturesque," Deymorin said, restraining a wicked urge to point out the childish roundness thus revealed, "but not highly efficient—for much of anything. Mind telling me what you're doing here?"

The slightly cleft chin raised another notch, hinting boyish stubbornness and little else. "I should think that obvious."

"Obvious." Deymorin swept a calculated and calculating gaze over the fully clothed young woman cowering behind her chair, past the boy's artistically loosened clothes, ending with a long look at Tirise's carefully neutral face—a look that ended in the merest hint of an off-side wink. "Just arrived, did he?" And Tirise, with the wisdom gleaned of several dozen young Nikkis, replied without missing a beat: "In the salon . . . oh, not half-an-hour ago, they were."

Deymorin schooled his face into determined sincerity and turned back to his brother. "Obviously, then, I've interrupted you at an awkward moment."

"Damn right, you did." Nikki's lower lip pouted ever so slightly.

"Not in front of the ladies, child," Deymorin chastised gently, and when Nikki looked daggers at him, perversely courted even greater youthful resentment with a firm: "Put on your clothes, we're going home."

"But—"

"*Now,* Nikaenor," he said, all tendency toward humor leaving him, and for a moment, he thought the silly boy was about to argue, but then Nikki's eyes widened, and:

"Damn. I *forgot.*"

"Forgot." Coming from anyone else, he'd have said that was impossible. Coming from Nikki, who had just been standing on a bed, reading his poetry to an enraptured audience of one . . . he could believe it.

"Deymio, I'm *sorry.*" The pout faded into heartfelt chagrin, a look the boy's angelic face did so well that in his less charitable moments, such as now, Deymorin suspected him of practicing it, too, in between those swipes at his hair.

"I know you are, brat. Just get dressed, will you?"

Nikki nodded, setting his curls to bouncing. "Miss Beauvillia—"

"B–Beauvina, Ni—m'lor'," the girl corrected in a charmingly lispy whisper.

"Oh. Ah. Yes, of course." Nikki ducked his head again, tucking his shirttail one-handed, shrugging awkwardly into his tailored coat with the other. "I—I'm sorry, but I'm afraid we'll have to—continue another time."

'Miss Beauvillia' expressed her regret—quite vocally—and amusement threatened anew, but Deymorin swallowed the chuckle and lent Nikki a hand with his coat. He brushed a cursory hand over the lightly padded shoulders and tugged the skirt-pleats straight with a snap of brocade (the boy was becoming quite the dasher), then pulled the blond mass back into a quick, barely respectable queue, securing it with a ribbon the redoubtable Tirise slipped him. Following a final evaluation of his brother's person to assure himself the truant wouldn't destroy whatever gentlemanly credibility he had remaining, he shoved Nikki unceremoniously into the hallway.

Beauvina darted past him and fluttered after Nikki like an oversized butterfly. Pretty little thing; one couldn't fault Tirise in that, but not to his taste.

Not even when he was seventeen.

Deymorin retrieved his cane and offered Tirise his arm; she accepted with a grace no simpering so-called lady of his acquaintance could claim, and they sauntered after the youngsters, down the silver-lit hallway toward the broad, sweeping staircase. "I can't thank you enough, Tess. I'd have been all over the City looking for him, and this—" He tapped his left leg with the cane. "—was already giving me fits."

She squeezed his arm sympathetically. "Wondered why you was favorin' it so. Sure you don't want to give it a rest?"

"No time. We're late as it is."

"Celebration tonight?"

He nodded. "If you hadn't sent that message ..." He cast his eyes heavenward. "I owe you."

She laughed and patted his elbow. "I'll remember that, lovie—" Her wink held nothing of girlish coquettishness; he laughed and finished for her: "—and remind me in your own good time, eh?"

She just smiled the smile of a cat with the key to the milk-barn.

"Ta, sweetling. . . ." A door shut behind them: another customer on his way out.

Deymorin glanced quickly down the hall: Nikki and his would-be paramour were safely out of sight, around the corner, and heading downstairs. With luck they would escape with the boy unrecognized—

"I say, there. Rhomandi, is that you?"

Unmistakable, that nasal voice. Deymorin's spine stiffened.

Not that Nikki hadn't every right to be here, but he *was*

cutting the age laws close, a law Mikhyel passionately supported, and Pwerenetti dunPatrin was ... less than discreet at best, and fully capable of running the tale straight to Mikhyel's ears, if he thought to curry favor by doing so.

And curry it, he could: Mikhyel had absolutely no sense of humor in such matters, and a damned *overblown* sense of Family dignity.

Damned prig.

Deymorin forced himself to turn and greet the ... prosperous ... individual hurrying down the hallway toward him.

"Long time, old man." The sweaty hand pumped his enthusiastically. "What brings you to the City?"

The things he did for his brothers. ... Gently disengaging himself, Deymorin curbed the temptation to wipe his hand on the nearest tapestry, and planted a smile on his face. "Business, Pwerenetti." And quellingly: "—*Family* business."

"Family?" Beady pig-eyes lit. So much for quelling; the old gossip's voice positively quivered with anticipated exclusivity, then: "Oh. Your brother's coming of age."

Deflated-sounding statement of fact: so much for Mikhyel's dignity. Deymorin nodded and turned to leave.

"I say, does this mean Anheliaa's to declare her heir at last?" The light of hope flared anew.

"I didn't say—"

"Of course not, old fellow. But she *is* getting old, isn't she? I mean, no one's seen her for *years*. And *someone's* got to replace her soon, isn't that so?"

The cane's carved ridges cut into his clenching fingers. "Having trouble with your power lately? Lights quit? Clocks stop spinning? Take it up with the Commissioner."

"No complaints—yet. Though we do get a flicker now and then, which never *used* to happen. We live in daily fear, now, don't we? Reassurance of a Talented successor would do *wonders* for market confidence...."

What had begun as a delaying tactic for Nikki's sake was rapidly developing into cold resentment. Whereas he and Anheliaa had had their (frequent) differences, she was Family, and as the eldest living Rhomandi deserved respect—particularly from leeches like Pwerenetti.

"Obviously, someone will replace her in the Tower eventually," he said carefully. "The last time I saw her, she was doing quite well, overall." Under the circumstances, one didn't admit how long that had been. "It's just that ever since Khoratum—"

Light, easy laughter interrupted him. "Come, Rhomandi. We're all friends here, now aren't we? We can be honest. Anheliaa's reclusiveness has nothing to do with Khoratum."

"I have no idea what you're talking about."

"Of course you do, old fellow. We all know these rumors about Khoratum crippling her are just to keep the un-washed masses content, now don't we? Rumor loves mar-tyrs, and rumors like the business at Khoratum—"

"Make our exalted state more ... palatable to lesser mortals?" Deymorin finished for him with deceptive gentleness.

"But of course."

While finding the revelation uncomfortably enlight-ening (Anheliaa should be relieved to know the daily tor-ment she suffered was nothing more than a political smokescreen), Deymorin found himself controlling an urge to smear the complaisant look on Pwerenetti's face into the floorboards.

"Comfortin' thought, that," Tirise said, nodding her head sagely. "One would hate to think the price of all this—" She swept an elegant hand through the air as they headed down the wide staircase. "Was somebody's *life*."

Deymorin aimed a slight smile in her direction.

Pwerenetti's eyes skated from one to the other of them, increasingly, almost pathetically, confused. Finally, he cleared his throat and said, "Yes, well, in any event, Rho-mandi, I wish you and your family well. And now, if you'll excuse me—"

"Now promise me, Nikki. You *must* come back and tell me the rest of the wonderful, sad story. . . ."

They'd reached the landing at the midpoint turning of the stairs. Deymorin glanced down—

"*Please*, Nikki, love ..."

—where, in the cross-fire of laughter and music from the mirror-image greeting salons, (Gents to the left, ladies to the right, thank you very much, darlings ...) poor, poetry-starved Mistress Bee had cast herself into Nikki's arms and was kissing him hard and on the mouth.

A salute the boy returned with apparent skill, and a

distressing oblivion to the impending approach of one of
the City's worst gossipmongers.

Deymorin tossed a panicked glance toward Tirise; she
returned a slight, knowing smile and, taking Pwerenetti's
arm, said:

"Y' can't leave me just yet, m'lord. Seems like months
since we last 'changed a word." And urging him gently
toward a side room, her private salon: "Come 'n set awhile.
Share a pint wi' me, eh? No charge, lovie." And with a
backward glance: "Not for an old friend."

Darius save him, another level of debt to Tirise dunMarinni.
With luck, she'd get the man so sloppy drunk, he'd be out
for days and not remember a thing about their meeting,
once he'd surfaced.

Downstairs, Nikki's rather energetic mouth had worked
its way down past Mistress Bee's white neck to her exqui-
sitely displayed bosom, and her red-painted fingers had disappeared under his coattails.

Trust Nikki to figure things out at the front door.

Before matters developed further, Deymorin grabbed his
brother's elbow and pulled him (protesting every step)
through the front door with its stained glass inset, past
dripping eaves, and down the stairs into the darkening
street.

The evening mist was rising rapidly. Silver leyglow
pushed that mist before it, marking the lightwatchman's
progress as he worked his way down Beliard Cross from
distant Gart Ley, one lamppost at a time, turning the bulbs
to the leylines, refining the alignments with a single deft
twist of his six foot long key.

Benotti dunTogan, like most lightwatchmen, was a retired Tower Guard. It was a lonely job, this wandering the
deserted streets with night coming on, one which, in the
past, had frequently required the lightmen to act as impromptu peace-keepers, there never, in the past, being
enough constables to man the streets effectively; consequently the Guard had long ago absorbed the necessary
task into its duties.

In recent years, thanks to Lady Anheliaa and the new,
tougher penalties for repeat offenders, crime had grown
rather less ordinary—some nights had become downright

boring, but the tradition still held, as much to reward old has-beens like himself as for the City's protection.

Oh, there were a few young recruits sandwiched among the veterans, those like dunRimble over on Westin Crossley, next street down-ley from Beliard; the Khoratum expansion of the city boundary had made it necessary. But those recruits were brought in from Outside (Citizens preferring their light to happen without personal effort) and like most Outsiders, those recruits were too easily lost in the maze of side streets and underpasses to be of much use in an emergency.

But emergencies on this misty evening were unlikely. Other than himself and a handful of early pub-jumpers weaving past, the street was deserted.

An outdated poster—a garish thing gone ragged on the edges, advertising the Transition Day Ringdance—was hanging by a single tacked corner. Ben worked the tack free of patterned stucco, located the fallen tacks in the cobbles, and shoved the lot into the trash bag he dragged behind him. Not all the lightmen worried about such things, there being a plethora of young ne'er-do-wells paying city penance to keep the streets clean, but Ben took pride in keeping his beat spif-spaf.

It had been a good dance that one advertised, better than the garish poster would suggest. The visiting troupe, from Beliard Node, had pulled some truly splendiferous moves on the whirling rings. Made a man wonder, who'd heard talk out of the hills, what the original dance must have been like. Dangerous, from the looks, but exciting, no doubt about it.

The next bulb turned, but failed to respond. He carried a spare in a bag slung from his waist, but bulbs rarely failed, their fine leythium-webs being near indestructible. Besides, Ben knew this particular post. Reaching with the key, he tapped the leythium-bearing end of the bulb itself. Once, twice ... on the fourth, it flickered and glowed as properly as you please. A final flick of the key, and that reluctant silver shimmer brightened to a cheerful gleam.

He grinned triumph at the post and moved to the next.

All about him, the buildings rose five stories and more, each sharing walls with its neighbors, their interconnecting walkways making lacework patterns in the overhead mist.

Within those vast complexes, thousands of individuals just like himself lived and loved and worked.

Old Darius would have been proud.

Another twist, another glow, a move to the next lamp-post.

His cousins from Outside the City marvelled at the ley-light and the floatercabs, at the smokeless heat and inexplicable coolth that circulated through the building vents. And they still refused to believe him about the sewers.

Sometimes, they even called it magic.

To him, the lights were—the lights. They did what they did, just as the floatercabs (for those too lazy to use their own two feet) provided effortless transportation along any ley—would likewise provide it along the cross-leys, but for the low overhead. Through her rings, the Lady of Rhomatum supplied the power that made the lights glow, and warmed the heaters for the floater-balloons and buildings. As for sewage, everything just went . . . down. Into the ley. That was just how things worked. Simple facts of life in the City.

But these buildings . . .

To a man who, once upon a time, had helped his Outside brother-in-law construct a simple lean-to, and had spent the ensuing years reinforcing that initial design and repairing the annual leak in its roof every time he paid sister-widow Lisa a visit, the City's engineers, carpenters, and masons were the true magicians.

Darius and his codesigners had set the initial codes and standards, all directed toward safety and maximum efficiency; the City Planning Commission had upheld those codes and upgraded them with each new architectural and engineering advance. Of course, partly that was because they *had* to, since all new construction and alterations within the City limits were required by law to pass the Commission before execution, but that august committee must have remained amazingly unpurchasable over the years, considering.

His course took him past Winemerchants' Row, where restaurants and taverns from within those engineering marvels rang with laughter, and where mouthwatering scents filled the air. Throughout most of the City, the roadside level was devoted primarily to shops and businesses, all

levels above to apartments. Even the street-spanning arch-
ways supported living space.

At Tinkers' Lane, the wide access tunnel marking the
halfway point of Beliard Cross, he paused, craning his neck
for sign of light from dunRimble's route.

Black as between. Teach the wet-behind-the-ears junior
a thing or two about 'old men'. He'd finish his row, then
swing down and finish up junior's for him.

Or maybe he'd just drop into Mully's for a . . .

"What in the name of all that's holy prompted you to
go *there*? And alone, for the gods' own sake."

It was a familiar voice that rang from the mist ahead.
Deymorin dunMheric, and none too happy, from the sound,
and coming this way.

"If you wanted to visit the ladies . . ." The young lord—
Deymorin, as he insisted on being called—took a lighter
note this time, as if he strove to soften the effect of that
previous facer. ". . . why didn't you say something? It's not
as if Tirise runs a cross-ley hovel; her girls are clean and
respectable, the business properly registered and overseen . . ."

Ben paused, squinted into the mist, striving to spot Lord
Deymorin through the leyglow. Unusual to find the Rhomandi in the City these days, but a pleasant surprise nonetheless. Or it would be, if m'lord weren't obviously involved
in reading the riot over someone's head. Had he been
alone, they might have gone to Mully's together.

Two shadow shapes strode free of the glow. Lord Deymorin, limping badly to keep pace with a strikingly handsome younger man, was saying: ". . . could have arranged
things first, taken you there, introduced you properly, explained protocol, made certain you had—"

The younger man's sulky mutter interrupted Lord Deymorin.

"Sorry, Nik," m'lord said, in a voice Ben had heard before. "What was that?"

Like when m'lord was trying to quiz, rather than bash,
sense into some young fool's head.

This particular young fool, unless this particular old
guard missed his bet, was the Rhomandi's youngest brother,
Nikaenor, which made it not altogether surprising when,
instead of relenting, the handsome lad's mouth set stubbornly. "I *said*, I don't *need* your help!" And the youngster
lengthened his stride for a few jogging steps, deliberately

opening a fair distance between himself and his limping disciplinarian.

Lord Deymorin paused, leaning heavily on his cane, and glared after the boy.

"Halloo, m'lord," Ben called softly, figuring a rescue from such dark thoughts might be considered welcome. "Evenin'."

The young lord started. His hand twitched as to an aborted salute: habit died hard, even in a lord, but only a twitch, these days; Deymorin dunMheric's cadet years were long since gone, and the dark scowl smoothed to a warm smile as Lord Deymorin approached him.

Still favoring the leg, though he chose his own pace. Damn shame about the accident; once upon, m'lord had been one of the best prospects the cadet corps had seen in years, regardless—or perhaps because of—his wildish ways.

But the accident *had* happened, and the corps' loss was the Outside's gain. Hard to imagine the young reprobate of the old days pulling garden weeds and training horses in rustic Darhaven, but there he was, most times.

"That young Nikaenor, m'—Deymorin?" Ben asked by way of opening, tipping his head after the lad.

Lord Deymorin nodded.

"Grown a bit since I saw him last. Ladies'll be after him soon."

"Already are," Lord Deymorin returned dryly.

"Thought that's what the skirmish was about, beggin' yer lordship's pardon."

His lordship lifted a casual shoulder, his attention fastened on his brother's retreating backside, until, with an obvious effort, he forced it back toward Ben. "Should have expected it, I suppose."

He lifted a brow toward the mist wall. "Tirise's?"

Lord Deymorin grimaced and he laughed.

"You boys always did have good taste." And as Lord Deymorin's distracted glance again sought his brother: "Don't let me keep ye, m'lord."

Made a man want to bite his tongue, who knew Deymorin dunMheric's feelings on the subject of titles. But if ever the honorific fit, if ever a man lived who took his responsibility for other lives seriously, it was this man. Fortunately his lordship didn't seem to be taking notice this night. His lordship only shrugged and said, "Hell, let him go. He's probably right in thinking he's safe enough in the city, and a bit of exertion is as good a cure for damaged pride as any."

"Interrupt something important, did ye?"

The sharp bark of laughter that answered him held little in the way of real humor. "He'd like to think so. I'd hoped to keep his escapade quiet, but the way he's acting, by tomorrow morning it'll be City-wide gossip."

"Gossip, m'lord? —Underage, perhaps?"

"Not any longer. That's not—" The young lord blinked and shrugged again, but there was something false about the nonchalance, something about this particular disappointment was cutting deeply indeed. In spite of that, a half-grin forced itself out, a sardonic brow lifted his way. "Hell, *let* the City talk. Not the first public squabble Mheric's sons have had." A breeze set a third-story wind-chime to singing. Deymorin looked up and shuddered. "This part of the City always feels ... claustrophobic."

"Prefer open fields now, do ye, m'lord?"

A very real grin answered this time, quite unforced. "Sacrilegious to a good City man, isn't it? But yes, give me open skies over catwalks and fireglow over leylight any day." He gave a breath of a laugh. "Or night, as the case might ..."

The grin faded, Lord Deymorin's glance falling again on the walkway-shadowed street and its single other occupant. The lad's pace had slowed as if he'd realized at last he'd left Lord Deymorin behind, but he didn't stop. Didn't turn back. Just kicked a stone or two ahead of him.

Stubborn, like all young lads, and if a bit more petulant than some, well, he'd reason to be a bit spoiled, coming from the family he did, and with his parents gone, and a brother like Lord Deymorin, openly affectionate, obviously inclined toward leniency, his other brother, by all accounts, too absorbed in the City to concern himself with mere Family affairs.

"I wish ..." M'lord's voice was little more than whisper.

"Wish what, m'lord?" he prompted, the wistful note in that whisper encouraging him to be bold.

"That I knew what to do with him. I'm fond of Nikki—I truly am—but ..."

"Meaning no disrespect, m'lord, do ye mind? Had a bit of experience with boys, you know."

A flash of even white teeth reassured him. "A bit, Ben? I doubt there was a cadet in my unit didn't spill his guts to you at some time or other; most of us on a regular basis.—It's simple, really. We've a family party tonight—reason enough for him to bolt, I suppose, but out of character for him. Nikki wasn't at home when I arrived—and I was late. Thinking to save us both from familial wrath, I went looking."

He glanced down with a puzzled shake of his head, and tapped his cane against his high boot-top. "The last place I'd have thought to look was Tirise's. If not for her message, I might never have found the boy in time. As it is . . ." He sent a speaking glance down the darkening street and shook his head. "Why tonight? Why Tirise's? Dammit, it's not like him to push the limit this way."

"On the other hand . . ." Ben ventured, "perhaps ye're still thinkin' o' him as yer little brother. He's a man now, what ye say, legally speaking, and men do tend to summat diff'rent goals than boys."

Dark brows knit in a worried frown. "You really believe it could be that simple?"

"Reason to think it could it be more?"

"It just seems so sudden, this—escape. I'm concerned about him . . ." And that worried look angled again toward the narrow cobbled street and the bend around which young Nikaenor had just disappeared, and the young lord began edging after his brother, drawing Ben with him. "He used to talk to me. Now—" A rueful smile pulled his lip. "I suppose I can't complain. I haven't been around much of late. Mikhyel's been so damned . . . but that's beside the point." M'lord's smile stiffened about the edges; m'lord's eyes took on a distant look. "Maybe Nikki just doesn't need me anymore. Makes a man feel a wee bit old."

"And mebbe," Ben ventured, "a wee bit sad?"

"Truth be told . . ." Dark eyes dropped to the cane he twisted between his fingers. ". . . more than a bit."

If ever a man needed a child of his own . . . But not the slightest hint of a rumor connected Lord Deymorin with an eligible wife. Pity.

The nervous twisting ceased and Lord Deymorin said, "You must think me maudlin, but more than the boy's manhood is at stake, Ben. He's careless, far too careless for his own good. He's an easy mark with his trusting ways—in constant danger from far more serious opponents than some female with a paternity contestment. By the time I was his age, I'd fended off three murder attempts."

"Assassins, m'lord?"

"I hesitate to give them the dignity, but it's possible they were that organized. These things happen. It's possible the danger is past, here in the City—though I'd argue against that complacency—but certainly outside its walls, and particularly with travel restrictions easing it's still a very real concern. Nikki's not like Mikhyel. He goes Outside with me. Has gone to Armayel on his own for years and will attempt further solo ventures soon enough—if he's not already. He *should* have had his stint in the Corps, but Mikhyel was so damned paranoid Nikki would be hurt, he wouldn't have it. Nikki hardly knows one end of a pistol from the other, is barely competent with a blade, and I don't—"

A muffled shout. The sounds of a scuffle from the misty residue leyward.

"Damn!" The next instant, Lord Deymorin, still quick despite his leg, was pounding the cobbles in his brother's wake, Ben hot on his heels.

Lightning above Khoratum generated a blinding display within the lace.

Mother's laughter rippled the folds, setting threads to humming musically.

A stabilizing impulse chased down the ley from Rhomatum: Anheliaa, coming to Rhyys' aid at last.

And as the Khoratum cloud reorganized, glowing a grateful yellow, an angry red pulse emanated from Rhomatum, thin tendrils, seeking answers.

Mother laughed again, and at the tip of each tendril, set a false trail, a maze of almosts and maybes ... simply to amuse Anheliaa.

So Mother said.

Lightning chained across the northern horizon, setting the mist aglow, casting the wet cobbles in sharp-edge relief, as Deymorin cleared the haze.

Heightened senses made a quick, on-the-fly assessment, and a sickening cause-and-effect filled him. As if his words had conjured them, three men surrounded Nikki, just outside the Winemerchant maze of ground level corridors.

But a second quick assessment, this time of his brother, set his immediate fears aside. The fry was a bit battered about the edges, but overall ... Deymorin skidded to a single-footed halt short of the struggle, lifted his weak leg to avoid a backward tumbling, would-be thug ... Overall, Nikki was doing just fine.

The would-be thug had landed in a shadowy tunnel between buildings. Only two adversaries left now, and as Nikki appeared to have them quite handily under control, Deymorin followed the grounded thug leisurely, pulling a protesting Ben after him.

"Maneuvering room," he murmured, and settled his shoulders comfortably against the stone wall. Still and all, he slipped the release on his cane ... just in case.

The thug lying at his feet stirred, and he planted a suggestive foot on the man's thick chest. The thug's unswollen eye swivelled in its socket, taking in his situation, sliding up past boot and cane, eventually reaching Deymorin's face.

Deymorin shook his head slowly; the chest beneath his foot heaved once, and the thug's head thumped back to the damp cobbles. Clever fellow—

An exclamation from Nikki; Ben's elbow jerked in his hand. But Nikki was still in control, the cry a frustrated curse, not dismay, so Deymorin tightened his grip, whispering, *"Hold...."*

... and slipped the fine-edged steel free of its deceptively innocent sheath.

A slow three-way circling; a glint of steel. At least one of Nikki's assailants was armed.

Deymorin tensed, but heeding his own advice, he waited. Let the boy test his own skill—which was proving, to an older brother's profound relief, cool-headed and—

Of a sudden, Ben sneezed.

The thug with the knife broke ranks and ran; the old guardsman jerked free and chased him down the street.

Nikki, momentarily distracted, caught the remaining thug's shoulder in his stomach, and fetched up hard against the rain-splattered wall. A shadowed hand struck upward, and Nikki doubled over; another shadow-hand brushed Nikki's waist; the clinch broke—

And the ruffian escaped toward Deymorin's shadow.

And Deymorin's grounded prisoner.

And Deymorin's extended foot.

Ruffian two sprawled over his partner, momentum carrying him beyond to the alley cobbles. He lay there, stunned, one hand clenching a knife, the other Nikki's purse, while thug one, on a suggestive nudge to the backside, darted unchecked into the darkness.

With a flick of his wrist Deymorin sent the cane-sheath spinning into the street, then tapped the prisoner's knife hand with the sword's tip, pressing further when the man glared up at him. The hand inched open; the knife, a wicked-looking stiletto with a simple, leather-wrapped hilt, dropped free.

"Here, brother." Deymorin hooked the knife hilt with a toe, and flipped it back toward the street, trusting Nikki to control it.

Holding the thug's gaze prisoner with a cautioning look, he lifted the sword and reached a solicitous hand to grasp the man's hairy wrist and pull him to his feet, shifting that hold to the elbow when imminent attack brewed in flexing tendons.

He tightened his grip, pressing his fingers into delicate nerves, a pressure that would numb the strongest man's arm, then tossed the sword-cane after the knife and extended his empty hand, palm up.

The man tried to jerk away; he exerted more pressure, and tapped fingertips to palm. With a gasp of pain and a heartfelt curse, the man hurled his prize at Deymorin's face.

Laughing in honest amusement, Deymorin released him to catch the purse, considering the trade—the man's freedom for Nikki's lesson in self-preservation—about equal.

The thug disappeared into the shadows; Deymorin turned, still chuckling.

"Well, well, well, Nik ..." Laughter died in his throat. Nikki was on the ground, hunched over his knees, and Ben was at Nikki's side, urging him to let him have a 'look-see,' Nikki all the while protesting and pushing Ben's hands away.

"Damn," he muttered, and joined the huddle on the rain-damp cobbles, growling at Nikki to shut his mouth and cooperate.

"Did you get him?" he asked Ben abruptly, no longer counting the score settled.

"Old legs couldn't keep pace, m'lord. Sorry."

"Did you recognize any of them?" He pulled at Nikki's tightly-clamped elbow, received a singularly fraternal curse for his efforts.

Ben shook his head. But:

"He yelled at me, m'lord, while he was runnin'—I think he mistook me for one of his—and his accent was strange. Not from Rhomatum. Not from any City I've heard."

Interesting. But then his hand came back damp and dark with Nikki's blood, and he forgot all about the cutpurse. Fingering Nikki's tight coat-sleeve with one hand, he waved his other vaguely toward the ground behind him: "Hand me the punk's knife, will you, Ben?"

"You're *not* ... cutting my coat!" Nikki gasped, and, apparently oblivious to the fact the coat was already ruined, staggered to his feet, taking a few wavering steps ... in the wrong direction.

"Dammit, boy—" Deymorin grabbed his recalcitrant sibling and held him while Ben worked the meticulously fitted garment off the boy's back, not much caring now if they hurt him. If he was so damned worried about a stupid coat, he couldn't be that badly off.

But he was. A deep stab wound that grazed along the high ribs under the armpit that would hurt like hell once the boy cooled off enough to notice ... which, at the rate he was leaking, wouldn't be long.

"Clear through, unless the scut got him twice," Ben muttered.

Deymorin bit back a curse. "Any chance the blade was poisoned?" he asked quietly, while they used Nikki's shirt to stanch the flow of blood.

"No," Nikki said on a gasp.

Ben extended a bloody sleeve into the leylight, sniffed, then shook his head.

"Color's good," he said to Deymorin. "Doubt it."

"Don't—don't talk 'bout me like I'm not here. —Think I wouldn't know?"

"Shut up, Nikki," Deymorin said absently, wondering how in hell to get the boy home and treated without creating a stir, knowing such a feat would be next to impossible tonight.

But the wound didn't appear, from what he could see in the leylight, to be that dangerous. The bleeding had already stopped, though there was no telling how long that would last if the fool youngster took it into his head to go lurch-about again, and it was just possible, if he could get it seen to, Nikki could muddle his way through the evening.

Possible, but not highly probable.

They tore the ruffled shirt into strips to effect a rough field bandage, then Deymorin got an arm under Nikki's uninjured side and, telling his protesting leg to be glad it was on the off side, muscled them both to their feet. He balanced against the stone wall, while Ben threw his warm cloak around Nikki's bare shoulders.

"Thanks," he muttered, and Ben said: "Just leave it in the Guard-room. I'll pick it up tomorrow."

Neither mentioned the bloodstained coat lying in a nearby, shadowed puddle.

Nikki was past noticing. The wrist he gripped, the arm over his shoulder, had grown limp and cold; Nikki's clasp on his hand where it rested at Nikki's waist, was weak and shaking.

"I can manage now, thanks," he said quietly to the light-watchman. And answering Ben's involuntary glance to his leg: "Don't worry, it's strong enough. Stronger than the other, when it's not complaining."

Ben's eyes dropped further, to the wet cobbles.

Deymorin laughed breathlessly, not the least offended. "Lord and rings, man, never mind. Just take care of the mess, will you? Then better finish with the lights. Folks will be out and about, soon, and wondering."

The old man nodded and bent to pick up the sword-cane, sheathed it, then stood holding it uncertainly.

"Nikki?" Deymorin asked casually. And more sharply into the silence that followed: "Nikki!"

The confused mumble confirmed his worst fears. He tightened his hold on Nikki's waist, with a little shake. "Listen to me, fry. Don't go out on me, hear? I have a job for you."

Awareness dawned on Ben's face; Nikki moaned and turned his face into Deymorin's neck, muttering something obscene. Deymorin laughed and shook him again. "It's easy enough." He nodded to Ben, who pressed the cane against Nikki's palm, whose cold fingers wrapped convulsively. "Drop it, brat, and I'll be forced to leave you in the street. Can't carry both it and you, now can I?"

Muted laughter—giggles, to a less discriminating observer—
added to Nikki's bodily tremors, but Nikki's hand tucked
the cane in against his chest, taking a fold of the cape with
it, and Nikki's arm grew less flaccid against his neck as the
boy took a bit more of his own balance.

"Take care, m'lord," Ben said. "Surgeon's in order, or I
miss my bet."

Deymorin nodded, then staggered as that new-found balance faltered and Nikki swayed against him. "Lord, boy,
what have you been eating? —Don't worry, Ben. Diorak
should be staying in-house—my aunt's not been well lately.
He can look after Nikki."

A blue eye glared at him from behind a silvery tendril,
the leylight turning all colors metallic: "Don't *need*—"

"Shut *up,* boy." And when Nikki's side heaved against
him, gathering wind for further protest: "Just tell the nice
man thank you, so we can go home."

The youngster's exhalation withered into a sullen *Thank
you,* and Ben pressed the boy's shoulder lightly. "Take
care, lad," he said, then watched helplessly as Lord Deymorin steered his brother toward Gartum Ley.

He plucked the boy's jacket from the puddle, folded it,
mud and blood carefully to the inside, and wrapped the
poster around it before placing it into his trash bag. The
boy seemed fond of it. He'd get the missus to clean it up,
see if she could mend it.

A brighter shine within the puddle's gleam: the thug's
stiletto. Not a distinctive style. Likely it would be no help
whatsoever in tracking the men down, but Ben slipped it
carefully into his belt anyway. He'd deliver it to the Tower
Guard in case the Lady could use it, perhaps even to locate
the bastards through the rings. Rumor claimed she could
do such things.

Laughter from a nearby tavern. Citizens. Lord and rings,
he was late. He hurried back the way he'd come, breaking
into a run at the last, and pulled up short of the halfway
point.

The wall of mist was gone. Light continued around the
street's bend, undoubtedly all the way to Berinor Ley.

And parked on the midway light, his skinny arse propped
on the decorative stand-off rail, a cocky grin splitting his

flat face, *his* key held upright like a lancer ready for battle
. . . was dunRimble.

Lightning raged about distant Khoratum, and with each
bass roll of thunder, Nikki shuddered beneath his arm.

"Almost there, boy," Deymorin gasped, risking a precious bit of his own breath on that reassurance, had his
reward when Nikki gave a little hiccup and managed the
final few steps to the floater dock mostly on his own.

Not much, but enough to give Deymorin's lungs a necessary respite, as the dockmaster walked into the streetlight,
suspicion in his every move. Warranted suspicion, Deymorin realized in sudden blind panic: he'd left his money
pouch, slim as it was, at home.

Deymorin pulled Nikki to a wavering halt, secured the
cloak to cover his bare shoulders and bandaged middle,
then jerked his glove free and extended his left hand, Family ring forward, for once not the least reluctant. The dockmaster's chin raised a notch, his narrowed eyes moving
from that ring to Deymorin's face and back.

"Rhomandi," Deymorin said flatly, his title, as head of
House Rhomandi. Time was, he wouldn't have needed to
make that identification—the price of changing venues: five
years since he'd moved permanently from the Tower house
to Darhaven, and it might have been a lifetime.

But the man's chin lowered. He squinted more closely at
him, at the ring, then at Nikki's shadowed face. His eyes
widened.

Nikki, he recognized.

Deymorin inhaled again, held it, then said: "Tower."
Which exhausted what breath he had left, but it was
enough. Without further question, the dockmaster rushed
them to his most elegantly appointed vehicle, half-carrying
Nikki in his eagerness to help, offering to send a runner—
at the cab company's expense, of course—to warn the
Tower of their imminent arrival.

Deymorin thanked him breathlessly, but, no, he didn't
want to cause a fuss, and the boy would be fine (A bit too
much, if you know what I mean), and accompanied it all
with a rather too-broad wink. The dockmaster, assured of
his conspiratorial status, returned the wink and patted
Nikki on the shoulder, and called him by name before low-
ering the floater door behind them. Surprising familiarity

that made an already anxious brother wonder just how often the brat had been carried home from this district.

Deymorin eyed the spacious interior somewhat guiltily. This had been a private car, once upon a time. Each brocade-upholstered bench seat had a matching gilt-fringed foot ledge, adjustable for personal comfort. Not to mention a dozen tasseled cushions.

Probably the best coach in the dockmaster's fleet.

"Don't you dare bleed, fry," he whispered to his brother, before easing them both down and propping Nikki between himself and a side window.

From his station outside the rear grill, the pedaller adjusted the heating unit until the coach drifted free of the docking cradle, then released the anchor and signalled the dockmaster to propel them into the stream. With a barely perceptible jar, the tether slipped from the parking track into Gart Leyside.

From there, it was a ley-straight shot to the Tower Hill spiral.

Settling back with a heavy sigh, Deymorin lifted his booted foot to the ledge to ease the throb in his leg. Poor old Ben, trying so hard not to notice. Stupid, but the stupidity had been his, and that one moment of idiocy had probably saved his neck in the long run.

It had certainly saved other necks.

A spasm rippled through his brother.

Just as well he hadn't had the breath to correct the dockmaster's instructions to deliver them to the front entrance of House Rhomandi. He'd have preferred the anonymity of the servants' entrance, but they were neither of them fit for a climb.

Another shiver.

He'd have to get Diorak up to Nikki's room without raising suspicions—somehow. Perhaps he could claim the boy had taken ill. Once there, he'd have to rely on the physician's discretion not to inform Anheliaa.

Or Mikhyel.

And perhaps a miracle would happen and Nikki would magically heal by the time they arrived at the Tower.

Rings. He wondered whether Diorak was taking bribes this week.

The shivers came in waves now, but he did his best to ignore them. The wound was far from life-threatening, and the way things were going tonight, Nikki would like as not take any further kindness as a personal affront.

Seventeen was such a hard year.

Still ... he reached past Nikki for the speaking tube protruding from the wall socket, pulled it to his mouth, and said quietly: "Bit chill in here, mate. Could you vent a bit more our way?"

And through the back speaker, the pedaller's cheerful: *"Pleasure, m'lor',"* preceded a welcome blast of warmth from the brass grill under the footrest. *"The young m'lor' looks a mite peckish, m'lor'. D'you want I should hurry it along?"*

A stolen glance toward Nikki. Closed eyes, white-edged lips pressed tightly together, a film of sweat forming beneath the curls ...

Deymorin swore softly, then answered in the same low tone: "Appreciate it."

"Right-o, m'lor'."

The vehicle's subtle vibration increased markedly as the pedaller picked up his pace. The fan blades behind the rear window blurred with his efforts. Probably hoping for a large tip, poor sod.

Evidently the stationmaster hadn't warned him it was a state job. And him without so much as a silver—

Nikki shivered: a single, bone rattling spasm.

Nikki. Nikki always had money.

Digging after the purse hanging heavy at his waist roused a muttered protest from Nikki. Deymorin ignored him and shook the purse's contents into his hand.

Seven gold darics, three silver rodari, a dozen coppers ... Damn, the kid was *shiny.*

"That's—*mine.*" Teeth chattered around that protest.

Deymorin raised an eyebrow. "Really? I lifted it off a cutpurse. I'd say that makes it mine."

A shaky scowl deepened the line between Nikki's brows, the girlishly full lower lip pouted ever so slightly. "Scum."

"Me? Or the cutpurse?"

"Both." Ridiculously long lashes fluttered down, masking pain-dulled eyes, before the curly head flopped back toward the window, finding a pillow in the heavy brocade drapes, pointedly ignoring the coins riding heavy in Deymorin's hand.

Shiny, indeed—unless Nikki had brought his entire savings: youthful optimism ... or ignorance of the going rate.

Deymorin dribbled the coins back into the purse—save for a silver and three coppers—and tucked the purse securely back into his cummerbund.

Another shiver; he pulled Ben's warm cloak tighter around the boy and murmured: "Soon, fry."

Nikki sighed again, an oddly contented sound, and shifted about, pulling his knees up onto the seat, curling against Deymorin's side the way he did at twelve, albeit a somewhat tighter fit these days.

Evidently his own transgressions were forgotten—at least for the moment. Probably forever: Nikki hated arguments, and tonight's little contretemps was the closest the two of them had ever come to one.

Deymorin chuckled softly and put an arm around the very unchildish shoulders: soon, very soon, now, the brat wouldn't need that stylish padding. "Don't worry, Nik, old man. You'll have it back. I just wanted a tip for the nice pedaller-man, is that all right with you?"

Golden curls brushed and bobbed against his chin. "Nice pedaller-man." Nikki's bare hand sought his gloved one and squeezed. "Nice brother-man."

Deymorin's throat closed. 'Nice brother.' Nice brother, who left his kid brother to explore life in the cross-leys on his own, never bothering to ask Did he want to; who stood aside and let that same mild-mannered kid brother take on three men with knives—alone—and consequently ushered him home with a hole in his side, late for dinner ...

And tonight, of all nights.

This dinner, of all dinners.

Nice brother? Not exactly how he'd put it.

Once, perhaps.

He recalled a time, not so very long ago, when Nikki *would* have come to him—a time when he'd been the recipient of all Nikki's boyish hopes and dreams, as he'd once shared his with Mikhyel and Mikhyel with him. Brotherly confessionals. A reward of siblinghood Mikhyel hadn't granted him in years—not since their mother had died—but which had been as natural from Nikki as breathing.

Tonight's escapade put a shadow over the past. Made a man think twice about trusts given and received. Made a man recall the new length and purpose of stride in the boy, and realize the breadth of shoulder beneath the stylishly tailored clothes, the grip which hinted at near-adult strength beneath that deceptive layer of baby-fat.

As Ben had pointed out, men did tend toward new goals, and most males—and females, at least of Deymorin's personal acquaintance—rarely waited for legal endorsement before exploring those not-all-that-adult goals. Certainly Deymorin had not: another fact Nikki well knew. *And* Nikki knew where he'd gone for that eye-opening experience.

While Nikki knew those worldly goals well ... from his endless consumption of theater and poetic nonsensicals, if not—he thought of that less-than-innocent farewell kiss— from real-life practice, *he* had never tempted Nikki, not with Tirise's, not with any Outside establishment. He'd learned years ago that another man's virginity was his own damn business, and a painful lesson it had been—for all parties involved.

Still, he sincerely doubted Nikki had ever taken it further, being Mikhyel dunMheric's younger brother, and so fully cognizant of the laws regarding premature procreation.

As if there were something magical about a seventeenth birthday that made a boy ready to be a father.

Nikki knew the legal consequences of breaking that law: Hell's Barrister Mikhyel had made certain of that years ago, damn Mikhyel's prudish soul, anyway. Mikhyel had swallowed the whole insane line of illogic right along with the rest of Rhomatum, and in the first of his patented birthday lectures had given a twelve-year-old Nikki nightmares for a week with his horror stories of what happened to such children with children exiled forever from the City.

Fabricated stories, all of them. Deymorin knew most of those exiles—the Outsiders took good care of them, and after the first year or so, it was the rare couple who expressed regret for that exile.

Perhaps the lesson had been necessary: Nikki *had* been of that age when experimentation *statistically* (rings, that *word* again) began, but a gentle warning would have sufficed for the socially underdeveloped and hypercooperative child Nikki had been at the time.

Regrettably, gentle wasn't in Mikhyel's barrister vocabulary.

However, Nikki had survived his nightmares, and Nikki certainly wasn't socially inept now ... tonight's performance notwithstanding. And while he was certain there had been other lectures, Nikki had never complained, had laughed and brushed the lessons off as justified when Deymorin found him unusually quiet and asked why.

Funny, though, how the need for Mikhyel's reprimands always seemed to arrive when elder-brother Deymorin was Outside and Nikki was in the City, alone with Mikhyel. Obviously, gentle, bookish Nikki had a dark side he kept buried when elder-brother was in town.

On the other hand, elder-brother would *never* have thought to look at Tirise's, so where did that place elder-brother Deymorin's cleverness?

Confused and worried, that was where.

It was possible this escapade was simply Nikki's way of expressing personal independence. Perhaps it truly marked the end of his childhood—and the little brother Deymorin had loved so well.

Depressing thought, that.

But if Nikki was claiming an adult's independence, he'd have to learn adult responsibility and adult caution as well, in a sense that had nothing to do with careless reproduction.

Over the years, he'd tried to make a game of self-defense with Nikki, trusting the boy's responses would, with time, become automatic, and that he'd never be forced to explain the reasons for such precautions in detail—remembering too vividly, perhaps, those childhood nightmares. Or perhaps just to avoid coming to blows with Mikhyel over the issue of safety in his precious city.

Mikhyel had limited Nikki's exposure to the Guard to head-sessions with theoretical tacticians of an army that hadn't taken the field in two generations.

Nikki's arms practice had been likewise theory without substance, save for time in the salle with a—Deymorin kicked the footrest impatiently—crippled sibling. Or so he'd believed: one had to admit, the lad hadn't done all *that* badly tonight, considering.

But how all those games he and Nikki played fit together ... that, he'd never quite gotten around to explaining to

Nikki, and if this independent, unannounced foray into unknown areas of the City, and that unlocked door in the brothel were any indication, he might have run out of time. He feared that tonight—tomorrow at the latest—he'd have to give his first, and hopefully final, surrogate-father lecture to the boy.

There had been attempts in the past, even within Mikhyel's precious law-abiding City, on the lives of the House of Rhomandi. Nothing Deymorin couldn't handle: a dispossessed, disgruntled farmer, a cutpurse with delusions of ransom, a zealot with dreams of reinstating the priesthood ... a Pwerenetti with delusions of blackmail; attempts about which the Barrister, cloistered safely in his Tower stronghold, knew nothing, even though two of them had been attempts on Mikhyel's life, not his—the would-be assassins having mistaken their brother.

Not that he hadn't tried to warn Mikhyel; Khyel just wasn't about to listen, and after a while, a man just lost interest in trying. If only Mikhyel didn't take it quite so *personally* when he suggested perhaps precious Rhomatum had a flaw or two and the Rhomandi brothers might do well to be prepared.

But if tonight's fiasco was any indication, these new and pending relationships with Mauritum could be adding a whole new element to the potential risk.

Not from any City I know ...

Part of the Tower Guard training was learning to recognize accents, to know city and district from a handful of words. That Ben had not recognized the accents, when Ben *did* recognize accents of every district of every city and province in Rhomatum's primary web, suggested that what might be sneaking into the City in these deceptively peaceful times did not bode well for the continued safety of Rhomatum streets *or* its treaty with Mauritum.

He should have settled this with both brothers years ago. Dammitall, he didn't *want* to lose either of them. Perhaps some good could come out of this evening, after all.

"Deymio?"

"Hmmm?"

"Thank you."

"For what, brat?"

"For not tr–treating me ... like ... kid. For letting me—" A pause for breath. "—handle it myself."

His throat spasmed again. He coughed it loose and said, "Sure, fry." And on a rueful afterthought, thinking of the dinner party they were both certain now to miss: "Happy birthday."

Interlude

A wave of yellow glee fluttered through the leythium chandeliers.

Mother liberated the storm, letting it snap like a released bowstring, right into Anheliaa's lap.

Another blinding flash sent a shivering ripple through the veil to break like an ocean wave upon the crystalline cloud that was Khoratum Node; Mother laughed and thrust a fist in the air, her long sleeve flying up, then drifting in an unexpected draft, a draft that set the veil's crystalline fibers to singing, a quivering musical hum within the cavern.

"Mother," Dancer asked, concerned for the veil's delicate structure, "isn't it enough? Can't we let Rhyys win now?"

"Win?" Her sibilant hiss seemed a part of those same currents. "Rhyys can neither win nor lose. Rhyys hasn't the ability. Anheliaa chose foolishly: Mother must remind Anheliaa of this fact." Her wide grin glittered even from Dancer's oblique vantage. "Constantly."

This was a new wrinkle in Mother's reality.

"Foolishly?" Dancer asked. "What do you mean?"

"You need ask? You, who should be ringmaster of Khoratum?"

"I? Never! I don't even wish for it."

"Never? How strange. I thought all humans wished to be ringmaster."

"Not this human."

{Then I've reared/raised/trained a fool.}

Mother's reversion to the internal voice made communication at once clearer and more confusing, stretching concepts beyond simple, singular human words.

Impossible, sometimes, for a mere human to comprehend Mother. Dancer had learned long ago to deflect rather than try. "Mother, much as I love you, you didn't raise me. You endured me."

{I'm crushed/distraught/disgusted/amused that you should think so.}

"You sound crushed."

Ears ringing from a well-deserved mental boxing, Dancer asked far more soberly:

"Mother, you've never expressed an interest in my life above. What's this all about?"

{You should have been ringmaster.}

Stubborn insistence: Mother at her most single-minded. All this time, Dancer had assumed it was the Khoratum rings in general to which Mother objected. This newest twist implied it was Khoratum's master, not the rings.

"But I was only seven when Anheliaa chose."

{Anheliaa should have waited.}

"She didn't know. Couldn't have. I was down here—with you."

{Anheliaa should have known. Anheliaa should have waited.}

Dancer, helpless in this battle of Motherly absolutes, shrugged and reminded her: "But I don't wish to be ringmaster. I *want* to be the radical dancer. I've *always* wanted to be the radical."

{Bat's poop.}

"Well, almost always." The Khoratum dance rings had only been constructed twelve years before. "At least, since I wanted to be anything."

And to this day, Dancer could remember lying on a cliff-edge hidey-hole, watching the foreign workmen raise the enormous structure, and the foreign dancers testing the equipment. Could remember watching the novices practice, preparing for years for the Khoratum Tower inauguration festivities.

Could remember praying to Grandmother's gods to be one of them.

Mother's slim shoulders lifted in a sinuous shrug, as if dismissing that artistic ambition as inconsequential.

"I'm a *good* dancer, Mother." Somehow, despite one's best efforts, one's insecurities always seemed to surface at the worst times.

{Good? Humanity's hell, human-spawn, you're the best/master/mistress/talent-elite.}

"How would you know?" And those insecurities found voice in unexpected bitterness. Mother was the only real family Dancer had had for years, and Dancer knew Mother didn't truly care, never had cared enough even to ask how practices went.

Now, in one of her quicksilver shifts, Mother swirled about and glided across the pulsating stone. Behind her, the veil fluttered and drifted, settling quietly as the storm began to follow its natural course toward Rhomatum. Stopping in front of Dancer, she stared down from her chosen lofty height.

Mother's clawed hand lifted, caressing. Face . . . chin . . . hair . . . and her wide, pupilless eyes grew soft and tender, losing the leythium-fire gleam.

And suddenly, her gown's semi-sentient folds floated around Dancer's shoulders, creating a safe, warm cocoon, unknown for years, but dear and alive in memory, and her sibilant whisper answered from close overhead:

"I named you, didn't I?"

Chapter Four

Lightning spasmed a continuous chain of fire that encircled the City as they stepped free of the floater and onto the Tower dock.

Above them, through the rose-covered trellis, there were stars.

Before them, leylight from the foyer chandelier traced rainbow patterns along bevelled-glass seams as the huge doors swung open with frustratingly massive deliberation.

Nikki swayed.

Deymorin dropped his cane to steady the boy with both hands; had to shift his hold to ease a stitch in his shoulder, and his stance to ease an ache in his leg.

Fine pair they were.

With luck, they could make their entrance undetected save by servants, who knew better than to ask unsolicited questions. He'd get Nikki to his room, clean them both up enough to escape particular notice, then sneak back downstairs to find Diorak and to make Nikki's excuses.

Without luck—

The door opened wide, a shadow fell across the threshold and their feet.

Words suggested themselves; Deymorin swallowed them and blinked sweat from his eyes.

Planted dead center of the foyer's patterned tiles, arms akimbo, Mikhyel appraised them like the king of Mauritum himself surveying a pair of recalcitrant hounds.

Nikki's breath caught, a quick, gasping inhalation, and he made a shuddering attempt to take his own weight, an effort that succeeded only in throwing them both off-balance.

"Easy on, Nik, old man, I've got you." Deymorin steadied his brother and drew him inside. The door closed behind them with a soft thump, and a light *shwip* announced his cane's entry into the stand by the door, before the doorman melted blank-faced into his shadowed nook.

Mikhyel stepped into their path. Curious how their rather undersized brother managed to look down his thin nose at two men taller than he.

"Drunk," Mikhyel pronounced, and Deymorin swallowed his resentment, seeing no reason to correct Mikhyel's supercilious misapprehension, drunk being easier to explain than the truth.

"Get out of our way, Khyel."

"The City's misfortune is your salvation," Mikhyel said, at his most abrupt and pompous. "Anheliaa's still in the Tower: the storm in the mountains, as I understand. Dinner has been delayed." Without ever really looking at Nikki, he dismissed them both with a nod toward the stairs. "Get him bathed and sober. If you hurry, she'll never know."

Deymorin snorted. "Not until it's to your personal advantage to inform her."

Mikhyel's brows tightened, his lower lip, so very like Nikki's despite his attempts to hide it under hair, pouted ever so slightly, the autocrat Mikhyel had become vanishing behind the defensive younger brother he used to be. "I won't tell—"

"No?" Deymorin asked dryly.

The hand clutching his arm squeezed a warning. "Th–thank you, Mikhyel," Nikki interjected softly. "I–I'll hurry."

Deymorin bit his tongue on a protest; if ever Nikki's ears needed boxing ... but he was much too weak at the moment. Mikhyel didn't have noble motives, as Nikki should have figured for himself by now. But Nikki didn't care about that. Nikki just hated arguments and came between them now to stop one developing, for which he was sure he should feel thankful and instead found himself resenting.

Peacemaking was Nikki's besetting weakness: a good dose of outrage might just get them up those cursed stairs.

"Don't delude yourself, boy," Mikhyel said, that damned sanctimonious stranger driving his vestigial brother out again. "It's for Anheliaa's sake, not yours. It would hurt her terribly, knowing what an ingrate she shelters beneath her roof."

Nikki's knees buckled; Deymorin swore softly and counterbalanced at some cost to his own knees.

"Mikhyel Rhomandi dunMheric," he said through clenched teeth, "either you move your pompous ass out of our way this instant, or I'll move it for you. Take your anger out on me, not the boy. —I'll even make it easy for you. I'll get Nikaenor settled, then meet you in the library, since I doubt you'd care to settle our differences in the fencing salle or the ring."

A muscle twitched in Mikhyel's jaw. Then he jerked his head toward the stairs and moved aside. "I'll wait for you in the Blue Salon."

Distrustful of so easy a victory, Deymorin dipped his head in wary acknowledgement, and said, "C'mon, Nik old man, almost there. Have to take the stairs, we will, but—"

"Is that *wool*?"

Deymorin swore again, not so softly. "The boy's not well, Khyel. One time—"

"Drunk or no," Mikhyel's claw-fingered hand grasped Nikki's shoulder and pulled him around, "he's not wearing *that* up those stairs. Especially—not—" Mikhyel jerked at the cloak-collar, seeking the clasp, his violence setting Nikki to coughing helplessly. "—tonight."

"I said," Deymorin hissed, "leave the boy alo—"

The cloak fell free, revealing Nikki in all his blood-stained, shirt-bandaged glory.

Mikhyel's lip curled. He stepped back, two-fingering the cloak to the footman who materialized beside him. "Get him to his room," he said coldly. "I'll send Diorak up. —And understand me, Nikaenor, you *will* be at dinner. Diorak will see to it. We'll say *nothing* of this to Anheliaa. You were at the library, lost track of time. Deymorin had to fetch you. Understand?"

Nikki blinked confusedly.

"Dammit, Khyel, the boy needs *rest*!"

Ignoring him, Mikhyel grabbed Nikki's chin, his fingers pressing the flesh white, demanding the boy's attention. "Do—you—hear—me?"

His own fingers itched to give Mikhyel the thrashing he deserved, but the Barrister's harsh grip was already squeezing tears from Nikki's eyes, and it took all Deymorin's fading strength to hold Nikki upright.

"I hear you just f–fine, Mikhyel." Nikki's whisper, though hoarse with exhaustion, and mumbled past Mikhyel's hand-clamp, came out utterly calm and collected.

"But unless you let me go, I'll have to dine as I am. Would you prefer that?"

Not exactly a peacekeeper's line, but it stopped the Barrister in his black-booted tracks.

Bravo, fry, Deymorin thought, and dropped his head to Nikki's shoulder, burying his triumphant grin in the golden curls, feeling quite magnanimous, now Nikki had won the round.

Deymorin had been right to insist they take the stairs—with Anheliaa still in the Tower, there was too much chance they'd intercept her at the lift door—but how he ever made it up a staircase that had acquired a disturbing tendency to bend and twist, turning in on itself while curling up overhead, Nikki would never know.

Khyel had been right to yell at him and force him to answer to stop his drifting. He knew that. It was Deymorin who took it wrong. Mikhyel knew he'd float off and forget all about what was important, like Anheliaa and the party and not making Anheliaa angry.

If only he weren't so cold, which he hadn't been before Mikhyel had stripped the cloak away, and he hurt—gods, how he hurt. But Mikhyel was right in that, too: one wore cotton or linen or smooth leather in the Tower, and the Tower included all the Family suites. Sparks threatened the rings. He'd known that rule since childhood.

So had Deymorin. It wasn't Deymorin's fault he didn't realize it just mattered more now than in past years—especially on a night like this when the lighting was flaring out of control. In-house reports of near disasters with the communication rings came with disturbing frequency these days, and Anheliaa warned of explosive consequences if they weren't careful. But Deymorin never heard those reports and warnings, coming to Rhomatum only for Occasions, the way he did.

No, one couldn't blame Mikhyel, certainly one couldn't blame Deymorin, which left ...

He sighed, and Deymorin paused to ask if he was all right, which of course he was; he was bloody wonderful, except he'd made a fool of himself in front of Madam Tirise and Mistress Beauvillia—and Deymorin.

Wonderful, except he had a hole in his side because he'd been an idiot and let that old lightwatchman's presence distract him for an instant.

In front of Deymorin.

None of which would have happened if only he'd behaved as he should and been at the Tower to greet Deymorin when he arrived, which he would have been had the ladies not gone on and on about his poetry, which he knew was short of perfect, but still it was nice to have someone say it wasn't.

But he didn't say any of that to Deymorin. He squeezed Deymorin's hand, and said *I'm fine, thanks,* and lifted a dead-feeling foot to the next step.

Deymorin had been right to wonder why he had gone to Madam Tirise's alone. And he'd have explained, willingly—if only he'd known the answer himself. That ignorance was the source of his anger, not Deymorin or anything Deymorin had said or done, which he'd tell Deymorin, if he could answer the other.

It wasn't a matter of manhood. Hadn't been at the time—not really. He hadn't consciously set out to prove anything to anyone. All he'd wanted . . .

His toe caught on a stair that surely must be higher than the others.

All he'd wanted, tossed from the library prematurely—on the verge of monumental personal discovery—*filled* . . . well, almost . . . for the first time with adult purpose and adult direction, was something . . . different.

He'd suddenly *really* realized it was his seventeenth birthday, supposedly the day a boy became a man, and doomed to be like every birthday before: dinner with his immediate family, a new perfectly hideous coat from Anheliaa to join the others mouldering in his closet because he didn't dare give them to the poor, sweets from Nurse he'd have to sneak out to the stable-boys so as not to hurt her feelings . . .

A lecture from Mikhyel on his newest responsibilities . . .

An I.O.U. from Deymorin who wouldn't have found just the right present, and who'd forget, after . . .

Always presupposing he'd *bothered* to show—which, obviously, he had after all, but he hadn't *known* that at the time.

He'd just wanted something . . . *more.*

This time, he managed to swallow the sigh that threatened.

And look where that *More* had gotten him: half-naked, with an endless climb up a swaying staircase, and his brothers arguing over him.

Arguing. Again.

Mikhyel's temper should fall on him, not Deymorin.

He *knew* Deymorin was going to take the blame; had *known* Deymorin would somehow instantaneously arrive—even from far-off Darhaven—to rescue him if anything had gone wrong.

As (he had to admit) it most certainly had, and (he also had to admit) Deymorin had.

He should have said something, should have made certain Mikhyel realized it was all *his* doing, not Deymorin's, would yell that downstairs now, if only Deymorin would turn his face downstairs instead of up. Which he tried to ask Deymorin to do. But Deymorin only shushed his protests, told him not to worry until the words and arguments he would have used with Mikhyel grew confused, twisting like the staircase.

He didn't deserve a brother like Deymorin. He wouldn't blame Deymorin in the least if he chose to drop him right here on the stairs and leave Rhomatum forever, brother or no, party or no, birthday or no.

But Deymorin didn't drop him. Deymorin was there, solid support on his left (though, from the way he took the steps one at a time, Nikki could tell his leg was bothering him), murmuring a steady stream of encouragement, and trying so hard to protect the wound from jarring, he would die before telling Deymorin that with each uneven step the skin pressed up under the hasty bandage, squeezing an ever-widening band of damp warmth around the wound and sending a tickling trickle toward his cummerbund.

A wound that wasn't Deymorin's fault any more than it was Mikhyel's fault when Mikhyel lost his temper the way he had downstairs. Mikhyel had pressures on him, pressures Deymorin couldn't—or wouldn't—comprehend. Pressures Deymorin didn't deal with, cloistering himself off in the country the way he did.

Like Anheliaa's increasingly ill temper. Downstairs, just now, Mikhyel had been like that because he was worried Anheliaa would find out. He wanted them both at dinner so she wouldn't. He knew that. Knew Mikhyel had run interference for him for years and years. Had seen Khyel come out of a session with Anheliaa white-faced and shaking, and taken the back of Mikhyel's hand and counted himself lucky.

But Deymorin didn't know that. Deymorin thought Mikhyel and Anheliaa agreed on everything, which he might not think, if Mikhyel wouldn't act like a stranger every time Deymorin came home.

Except (he sniffed: reaction to the change in humidity, he was sure) it wasn't Deymorin's home. Not anymore.

He'd come in late before—even staggered in drunk—and Mikhyel would just shake his head and cover for him, and tell him poetry was easier on a man's head the next morning; but now, possibly just *because* Deymorin had been with him, Mikhyel made an issue of it, evidently feeling the need to show himself the disciplinarian—as if he felt that otherwise Deymorin would blame *him* for their youngest brother's idiocy.

(Sniff.)

Deymorin couldn't know, as he did, that Mikhyel hadn't *dared* to look at him at first. He'd seen the laughter brewing behind the Barrister façade, knew it would shatter the instant their eyes met—which Mikhyel couldn't let happen in front of Deymorin; and if only Deymorin had kept his head up at the last, he'd have seen Mikhyel's fleeting grin—when Mikhyel finally did look at him—the look that assured him Mikhyel was sorry he'd yelled and sorrier if he'd hurt him and relieved he was all right and confident Nikki would be *able* to come to dinner, if only he'd keep his wits about him, which made Nikki determined he would and could.

But Deymorin hadn't seen that look, so Deymorin didn't know. Somehow Deymorin never saw that side of Mikhyel; Mikhyel made certain of that, consciously or not.

Somehow, it was a given: whenever Deymorin and Mikhyel met, sparks flew. Nurse said it hadn't always been like that, that as youngsters, they'd been as close as two peas in a pod, which made him wonder if it might not have been different, better even, if he had never been born.

But then, of course everything *would* have been different: Mother and Father wouldn't be dead, and Mikhyel would have gone to Darian Lyceum or maybe Bernoi Judiciary Academy rather than spending his whole young life shunted between tutors and Council offices, courts of law and judgment chambers, and Deymorin might not have spent *all* his time at Darhaven and of course, there'd be no Nikki to argue *about*.

Brothers. . . .

He heaved a sigh, felt Deymorin's arm tighten solicitously, and pressed himself into that extended warmth that was Deymio.

. . . Sometimes, they were very difficult.

The doorway to his apartments loomed before them, a dark mouth in the cream-painted, leylit hallway that swallowed them up, surrounding them with familiar shadow-shapes, one of which was Jerrik, whose presence was reassuring, but Deymorin sent Jerrik to find Diorak, and then he was sitting on his own bed, still in the dark, with Deymorin's stern threat: *"Fall over, fry, and I'll thump you,"* ringing in his ears, while Deymorin propped him up with pillows and pulled off his boots.

And then there was light. And Diorak. And (rings save him) *Nurse.*

And Deymorin was asking Did he want him to stay? after they'd worked the bandage free and stopped the bleeding, and Diorak pronounced the wound a long way from his heart, which made him laugh because that was what the Darhaven farrier told the recalcitrant horses when they leaned on him and jerked their feet away, and laughing made his side hurt, so he objected to them all, wanting only a bath and sleep, but he couldn't sleep: Mikhyel had said he had a duty to Anheliaa, which he hadn't forgotten, he'd just thought he'd get back in time, but he'd lost track . . .

And it *was* his birthday. And he did want his party. So he said to Deymorin, "I'm fine." And he said to Nurse, "I'm fine." And he asked them both to go away and leave him with Jerrik.

Deymorin did, with a final, encouraging grip of his hand. Nurse didn't, and pinched his cheek and called him her last chick, and said she wasn't about to leave him in his moment of need, and then smiled knowingly over his head at Diorak and asked Had he had a good time, which drove the shivers away in a hot flush of embarrassment and suddenly clear thinking.

They'd probably deduced where he'd been. Likely Mikhyel had as well. Knew what had happened, in the way of adults. *They* wouldn't have been caught reading mediocre poetry in a high-priced brothel. They probably knew exactly what went on in such places.

Well, he *knew,* after a fashion. Deymorin would never have let him get this old without a basic understanding. But he didn't *know*.

And after tonight's fiasco, he doubted he'd ever care to go back and find out.

"Arm, boy," Diorak's crusty voice ordered.

He sighed and lifted his arm obediently (never mind the movement sent a jolt clear to his toes), then lowered it again (very carefully) as Anheliaa's hawk-faced physician muttered ominously and began pulling bottles and arcane equipment from his scuffed and scarred leather bag, arranging them on the small bedside table. Among the last was a very ordinary looking, if somewhat small, curved needle.

Stitches? With mixed feelings, he raised his arm again, trying to assess the damage, which act gained him a light head and an abrupt chastisement to *Keep still*.

He cleared his throat, and asked, as steadily as Deymorin himself might have done: "How many?"

Diorak glanced at Nurse, who patted his hand and said gently, "Don't worry, lovie. Two. Maybe three. It's a very small opening, and he'll leave the back open for drainage."

"B–back?"

"The blade went clear through, lovie. But don't worry; you should be feeling quite the thing in a day or two."

"Will it leave a horrible scar?" he asked anxiously.

"Certainly not!" Diorak answered for himself this time, and Nikki slumped with a disappointed, *Oh*.

He'd never had stitches before. Never had a scar. Never broken a bone. Never done so many of the things most young men had accomplished by their seventeenth year. All of which made it very hard to feel like an adult (especially when one's childhood nanny was sitting there patting one's hand, and telling one to Be a brave boy) never mind what the calendar read.

He sighed again, and endured, with no more than a bitten lip, the physician's probe and the dabbing of strong-smelling, stinging substances over his person.

Then Diorak muttered something about *Time* and *numb*

and *your brother* (which made Nikki wonder *which* brother) before he disappeared out the door, taking Nurse with him, leaving that needle soaking in some brown-colored liquid right there on the table . . .

He swallowed hard, and folded his hands in his lap . . . and waited.

If only he had someone to talk to. Not about politics and history, for that he had Mikhyel and tutors, like he had Deymorin to explain about horses and farming and the Facts of Life.

He needed someone who understood the really important things, like brothers, and family. Bertie had brothers, but they were all younger, and besides, Bertie was a bit silly. Phell was far more sensible, but he only had sisters, except for one baby brother, so he wasn't much more use.

Besides, he needed someone who understood that being born into the Rhomandi family meant more than money and social position and private tutors. It meant Responsibility, and responsibility sometimes made people act . . . oddly.

For instance, one couldn't, it seemed to him, blame Deymorin for rebelling against Anheliaa's attempts to cut his youth short—and that's what she'd done, when Mheric died. She'd tried to force Deymorin into assuming the political responsibilities he had inherited as the head of House Rhomandi even before he reached the legal voting age of twenty-four.

According to Mikhyel, Deymorin had claimed at the time that Anheliaa wanted *him* stuck presiding over the Rhomatum Syndicate, the Rhomatum City Council, and the High Court so that *she* wouldn't have to. Which was probably right, but when Deymorin openly defied Anheliaa and took up with his wild set, Mikhyel had felt compelled to fill the void.

Poor Khyel (safe to think of him that way here, beyond pride's reach), *he* had accepted those rejected duties when he was only thirteen, still, by any reckoning, a child. Mikhyel had never told him exactly why he'd stepped in, but as a younger brother whose recalcitrant rear Khyel had covered more times than he cared to count, Nikki could well imagine Mikhyel protecting Deymorin from his own foolhardiness, just because that's what brothers did.

How else to explain the fact that for four long years, while Deymorin caroused the streets of every node city in the Rhomatum Web, Mikhyel had attended those meetings and functions and court sessions, sitting in respectful, *enforced* silence while the Rhomatum leaders discussed City needs and Syndicate representatives argued rights and responsibilities.

When at seventeen, Mikhyel had been allowed at last to voice the opinions he'd been hoarding for those four years, he'd had to fight daily to gain the respect the inherited position—and Anheliaa's aggressive backing—had theoretically granted him. From the transcripts, Nikki knew just how hard a battle that had been against the staunch conservatives, who resented so young a voice, and the more liberal councillors, who resented his views.

That fight had left its mark, both in Mikhyel's black moods and in his appearance.

One of Nikki's earliest clear memories was of Mikhyel's public induction into Council. He could remember sitting alone in the front row of the first balcony—the spot reserved for the family of the inductee—trying not to swing his legs. Alone because Deymorin had been confined in hospital following The Accident no one had ever, in all these years, explained to Nikki, and Anheliaa had been part of the ceremony below.

And that swearing in had been in the spring session following *Mikhyel's* seventeenth birthday.

Hard to identify that somber image and responsibilities with himself, and he wondered, now he'd reached seventeen and knew how little different it felt from sixteen or fifteen, whether he could have done as Mikhyel had done, and stood, alone and on display, the sole inductee that year, before an embarrassingly thin Council, his very presence in that hall the center of a highly controversial vote during the previous session.

Having reached his first majority, Mikhyel had been sworn in ostensibly to fill Deymorin's empty chair: an unprecedented move forced through the Council by Anheliaa, tempered only by the Council's insistence it be a speaking seat only, without voting power. Even so, it was a decision (Nikki knew from Mikhyel's onetime drunken indiscretion) to which Mikhyel had acquiesced out of sheer terror.

But one would never have known from outward appearances as he stood before Anheliaa and the High Council taking the oath, in a voice that neither cracked nor stut-

tered. Slender, of little more than average height, dressed
entirely in black, his now-signature beard and mustache,
grown the moment his body cooperated, making him appear at least slightly older than he was, his sleek black hair
fashionably long but severely contained, he'd been awe-
some—at least to his seven-year-old brother.

In almost ten years, Mikhyel had never changed that
image, never worn anything but black, never made a move
(at least in public) that wasn't carefully contained and elegantly choreographed.

Deymorin resented what he called Mikhyel's attitudes.
Deymorin (on a good day) called him Hell's Barrister.
What Deymorin called him in private, Nikki could only
guess.

But Deymorin just didn't understand how much pressure
their brother operated under day in and day out. Deymorin, who by his own admission refused to assume the
Council seat he'd inherited because of a temper he felt
would prove counterproductive, had never seen Mikhyel
control a temper to match Deymorin's own to manipulate
that stubborn Council, nor chanced to be in the way when
that temper inevitably blew in private.

But Khyel always apologized after and talked the reason
out—confidences which had given an acting princeps'
younger brother a political savvy well beyond his peers—
and the bruises came only rarely these days, and never
without provocation.

Though Mikhyel had never mentioned it, he suspected
Mikhyel felt deserted, perhaps even betrayed, by their
older brother. And perhaps Deymorin *had* been irresponsi-
ble, once, but if so, he'd paid for it when he'd tried to
assume that council seat he'd abandoned to Mikhyel.

Deymorin had never mentioned the circumstances which
had led to his self-imposed exile; when he'd asked two
years ago, Mikhyel had insisted he read the debate tran-
script and draw his own conclusions.

Mikhyel had been nearing his voting majority when he
and Deymorin finally went head to head before Council;
his future had hung in the balance, the compromise which
had prevented him voting coming under fire, splitting the
Council down the middle.

The now-historic debate had centered around Anheliaa's
addition of Khoratum to the Rhomatum Web which had

extended the Tower's power umbrella, absorbing what had been, for generations, prime farm land.

Mikhyel had argued the farmers had been more than adequately compensated, since the price of City property far outstripped that of mere farmland. Deymorin had fought against that expansion, argued that, at the very least, they must make the transition slowly—over as much as a generation—and aid the displaced farmers to relocate to businesses in keeping with their accustomed lifestyles.

Mikhyel had argued Khoratum was an accomplished fact.

Deymorin had argued what had been done, could be undone.

But Deymorin's interest in the family business had come too late. By that time, his reputation had undermined any force his words might have carried. Mikhyel's arguments had carried the day and secured his position in Council.

And alienated him from Deymorin forever.

When the vote went resoundingly against him, Deymorin had officially relinquished his seat on Council to Mikhyel as proxy, privately consigned the lot to the eighteen hells above Rhomatum, and retired permanently to the Rhomandi Outside holdings, where he began expanding the experimental farming and breeding programs their father had dabbled in.

Though few people would ever know, Deymio being Deymio and not inclined to flaunt his deeds, Deymorin had used that newly acquired passion—and no small portion of his personal inheritance—to effect his proposed relocation of dispossessed farmers quietly and on his own.

"And what's bothering the little man now?" A hand pinched his cheek. "Such a melancholy look. Give us a smile?"

Nurse had returned.

He forced the requisite smile, and she laughed and patted his cheek.

"That's my little man. Don't worry, sweet, it'll all be over soon."

As if he needed the reassurance. To Nurse, he was a child, would always be a child.

And not just to Nurse. They all interrupted him whenever he was thinking Important Thoughts, then argued over whose fault it was Nikki was upset.

If his family and the household at large had its way, he'd

spend the rest of his life smiling; his teeth would dry out and bugs would stick to them and the lizards would cling to his nose to lick them off and ...

Diorak returned with one of the Tower Guard in tow. A big, burly man. In case they needed to hold him steady, he suspected, and swallowed—very hard—and determined the man's presence would be superfluous.

More poking and prodding, this time to skin gone numb with Diorak's mysterious medicines. Or perhaps he just no longer cared, since not even Nurse's deft threading of the dreaded needle roused more than passing awareness.

Diorak said not to worry, that the medicine would let him sleep for a short time and he would wake perfectly well enough for dinner so long as he used his head.

Which was all Nikaenor ever did: sleep and use his head. Nikaenor slept and read the histories. Nikaenor slept and listened to the merchants in the streets, Nikaenor slept and studied with the best military strategists and armsmasters the Estate could provide, but all Nikaenor dunMheric had personally accomplished in seventeen years was a stack of bad poetry and a hole under his arm from a singularly inept cutpurse, and a rift between his two elder brothers.

Not a very impressive resumé for a meaningful career as ambassador to Mauritum.

He sighed a third time, and nerved himself against the approaching needle. Diorak's forceps lifted the skin. Diorak's needle pricked, pressed, and *popped* through the skin. He felt it, heard it, and imagined that tiny point piercing his skin, the red blood seeping around it, forming a gleaming drop that slipped slowly along the thread ... then the image faded into inviting black.

"What would you have me say, Khyel? 'I'm so sorry, Papa? I'll never do it again, Papa?' Well, you're not my papa, boy, I'm not sorry, whatever it is you think I should be sorry about, and if it's given you apoplexy, I'd do it again in an instant, believe me."

"Oh, I do, Deymorin. I do believe you."

Mikhyel controlled the urge to steady the bud vase on the sitting room mantle; it was his imagination Deymorin's deep voice rocked, not the crystal. Instead, he cupped the half-furled rose it held and inhaled slowly, deeply, determined not to show his trepidation.

A shame, really, that his older brother avoided his rightful place in the council chamber: with that voice, no one would dare cross him.

No one except someone with a lifetime of carefully fostered immunity. By the time Deymorin's voice had changed, Deymorin's brother had had no doubt Deymorin was a force to beware, and had modified his actions accordingly.

A lifetime had taught Mikhyel how to hold his ground; it could do nothing to dim the internal impact of his brother's presence.

As for the other ... He'd seen what it meant to be a father, and he had no desire to be Deymorin's—or anyone else's for that matter. But for Nikki's sake, to save sweet, gentle Nikki from the fate Deymorin would hand him, wittingly or not ... To save Nikki from that, yes, he'd be Mheric himself, if that was required of him.

The meeting was following what had become an all too familiar pattern over the years. A pattern that led inevitably to shouting and arguments and ultimately to one or the other of them storming from the room before they came to actual blows, and lately with Deymorin leaving the City altogether, deserting the problem. Escaping to Darhaven— the way Mheric had always done rather than face Anheliaa head to head.

At least Deymorin hadn't sons to drag off with him.

It was a pattern he refused to allow this time, regardless how Deymorin provoked him. Too much was at stake.

While Deymorin was bathing their youngest brother's blood off his hands, Mikhyel had received Diorak's preliminary evaluation: Nikki had received a knife wound, annoying but not serious, while walking Beliard Cross-ley, in the vicinity of Gartum Ley. Adding Deymorin's presence, it hadn't required a genius to fill in the details.

Feeling temper and disgust rise, he traced a fingertip through the carving in the mantelpiece, seeking spiritual control within the elaborate stone curves and whorls. He couldn't afford to lose his temper, couldn't let disgust cloud his thinking, and most of all, couldn't let Deymorin win this particular battle: it was Nikki's life at stake.

And he had a promise to keep.

This morning, Nikki's future had been assured. Protected from criminal elements, his income secure for life, of temperament, appearance, and breeding to choose a wife from the best families, Nikki should have been free to pursue his scholarly activities, free to develop into the loving husband and father he was meant to be, to have the life their mother would have wanted for him, the life she'd have provided him had she survived Nikki's birth for more than a few pain-ridden hours.

And now, in one night, Deymorin, with Deymorin's disastrously forceful personality and zest for adventure, had placed that entire vision in jeopardy.

Deymorin, the ever strong, ever wonderful, ever carefree—Deymorin, the ever absent, who by the time their mother died had already defected to Mheric's deadly lifestyle, forcing their mother to settle on second best.

Perhaps Deymorin knew what their mother had asked of him in those final moments, perhaps he didn't, but Mother had had that promise of him—not Deymorin. It had been into his care, not Deymorin's, she had placed Nikki.

Not that it had taken much persuasion. Nothing would have induced him to leave that mewling little curly-topped bundle of not-quite-humanity alone in the Darhaven nursery. Not then. Not for years after, though Mheric had accused him of cowardice and worse for remaining so long in the child's safe world.

Safe. That's what Mheric had called it, and that's what *he* had tried to make it, for Nikki.

Unfortunately, little brothers didn't stay forever in the nursery, and adolescents were in perpetual need of heroes. He had no illusions about himself: he was not the stuff of which heroes were made. Deymorin, also unfortunately, was.

Seventeen today. Hard to forget when piles of presents had been arriving from all over the web for the last week. Particularly difficult when those piles—hidden from Nikki until this morning and now artistically displayed on several tables—dominated the far end of the Blue Salon.

"What I want, Deymorin," he said at last, "I can't possibly have. I *want* you to stay away from Nikaenor. I want you to stop dragging him off to Darhaven and encouraging him to risk his neck on those half-wild ... creatures you favor. I *want* you to stop racing and gambling and whoring. I *want*—"

"Me to stop? Spinning a bit beyond your orbit, aren't you, Barrister?"

"Yes, damn you!" Despite his efforts, his fist clenched, his voice broke as he realized, suddenly and quite painfully, that it wasn't just *Nikki's* soul he was fighting to save. And knowing how *that* presumption would appear to Deymorin, he forced his hand to relax, and likewise controlled his expression and voice before facing his older brother. "I want you to grow up, Deymorin, for Nikki's sake. You're a bad influence on Nikki and all his friends. You legitimize their fantasies. If you can't see that, you're the only one."

Deymorin's dark brows rose. "Because the lad visited a perfectly legal brothel, something his friends undoubtedly do on a regular basis, *I'm* a bad influence?"

"Brothels. Races. Midnight hunts and gambling. Your reputation fascinates him, and he simply can't compete. No sane man would try."

"No sane man? Oh, dear, brother-mine, what *does* that make me?"

"Damn it, Deymorin, don't joke about this. He already flirts outrageously—"

"Meaning he smiles at the young ladies in the opera balcony."

"He fights mock duels with his friends—"

"As long as they're not in earnest—"

"With untipped steel?" That, at least, caused a faint pucker between Deymorin's brows, and he pressed further: "When will it be enough? Would you have him dueling *in earnest* with angry husbands before he's old enough to marry?"

The line deepened, but in contempt, not concern. "Give your outraged morals a rest, boy. The girl was a professional."

"That makes a difference?"

"To your proposed premise, yes. Beyond that premise, Nikki *is* of age, in case you hadn't noticed." Deymorin threw himself into a chair and lifted his leg to a padded stool with a grunt of pain. "Besides, you prudish old woman, nothing happened. Flattery expanded his poetic ego long before it expanded anything else."

"Expanded? . . . Oh." Curves and whorls pressed into his back, holding him firm against equal measures of embarrassment and guilt. At times such as this, he suspected his elder brother of deliberately invoking both emotions, which was damned ... unsportsmanlike, to his way of thinking. Guilt for the leg that pained Deymorin constantly: he'd acknowledged his responsibility for the accident when it happened, and had that apology thrown in his face. The other: if he was a 'prudish old woman,' he had ample reason.

"And the knifeman? Was *he* a professional as well?"

"Khyel, I—" The faint line appeared again. "I'm honestly not certain."

"Not certain." A chill twisted his heart. "Is that meant to be humorous?"

The line vanished. "Come down from your lectern, Barrister. Diorak's pronounced him fit for your damned dinner party—fueled by one of his noxious potions. Nikki got a much needed lesson in real life and acquitted himself quite handily, I might add."

Near Deymorin's hand, a small tray table supported wine and two goblets. Deymorin filled one for himself, offered the other with a grossly over-polite flourish. He refused with a single abrupt jerk of his head, wanting it to steady his hands, needing a clear head worse.

Deymorin shrugged and sat back.

"What did or did not happen is irrelevant," Mikhyel said, doggedly returning to his original premise, "You had no business taking him to that place."

"Pl-l-lace," Deymorin repeated, putting on an exaggeratedly thoughtful face. "Whorehouse, you mean? Cathouse, maybe." His face hardened. "Whatever you call it, taxman, you should love it."

Taxman. Mikhyel thought of Nikki and the need for calm, and raised his chin, refusing to take offense.

"As always, older brother, your assessment of my work is—enlightening. What I think of Tirise romMarinni's establishment in any sense is not the issue. Your taking a child—there's no other way to describe him, regardless of what the law claims—into that section of the City, is."

"I see. And what makes you so certain I took him there?"

"We both know what you consider an ideal coming of age present."

"Unlike some people, I learn from my mistakes."

"Which simply means you made a fool of him at Madame Tirise's rather than in his own bedroom."

Deymorin snorted. "No one *makes* a fool of someone else, brother-mine. The fact *you* had a problem figuring what end to do what to, doesn't mean the rest of the family suffers a similar confusion."

"You, of all people, should know better than to accuse me of that."

It was bitterness speaking, unthinking, immature self-defense, immediately regretted when Deymorin responded with:

"No, I suppose I can't."

Laughter coated the edges of that statement, faint echo of remembered laughter. Laughter from the hallway outside his bedroom door. Laughter that drowned out the soft moans emanating from the woman whose skill drew him to a destiny not even that laughter could forestall.

His hand blindly sought the whorls' solid marble reality, and as soon as he could trust his voice, he said firmly, "All of which is irrelevant. Nikki—"

"—wouldn't have reacted to his natural tendencies like a cloistered virgin."

"Dammit!" He whirled, and struck the mantel, then slowly opened his throbbing fist savoring the incontrovertibilily of pain. "Just once, can't you admit that maybe, just *maybe*, you were wrong?"

"Possibly. When you admit it was nothing but a harmless joke."

"Joke? *Harmless?*" He resisted the temptation to turn and glance at Deymorin's leg; they were both painfully aware they'd left the topic of Nikki far behind them. "Is that what you call it?"

"That's what it *was*, boy, as you'd realize if you'd ever bother to admit you're the only one who even remembers that day."

At times, Deymorin could say the stupidest things. Deymorin remembered with every limping step, every throb of his leg—how not? Certainly Deymorin's ex-cohorts among the Guard, or the devil-may-care toadeaters he'd collected during his years on the town would not agree with that assessment. Some took care to remind him daily he was not fit to fill Deymorin's well-polished boots. Or Mheric's . . .

A man had to wonder, sometimes, just where he fit into the scheme of things. If Nikki provided him a daily reminder of the beauty and the sweetness that was the essence of their mother's memory, perhaps (he considered the idea in a macabre instant of personal evaluation) he'd always wished Deymorin would fill Mheric's void in similar fashion.

If it were possible to miss such a narrow-minded, self-centered void.

But Deymorin, for all he'd inherited Mheric's size, Mheric's temper, and Mheric's politics, wasn't Mheric. Deymorin was wild and daring in his sporting interests, but Deymorin had never, to Mikhyel's knowledge, raised a truly violent hand to anyone. Deymorin argued—gods knew he argued—but never with the irrational rage that had characterized Mheric's anger. He had frequently wondered what it would take to rouse the Mheric he feared was lying in wait within Deymorin.

One undeniable difference: Deymorin sincerely cared about Nikki, which was more than one could say about Mheric, who had died for lack of a wife rather than live for his three young sons.

All of which left him . . . where? As some unfinished sack of human flesh, neither father nor son, child nor adult . . . Certainly he was far more crippled in his chosen life's work than Deymorin had ever been. The one thing he truly, deeply cared about had slipped from his control years ago.

He faced about wearily, vaguely surprised when Deymorin's hard expression wavered.

"Don't you see, Deymio?" he pleaded, hoping to take advantage of that softening. "Nikki idolizes you, and if you don't mend your ways, his attempts to emulate you *could* lead to far worse ends than tonight's. One day, you won't be there. Whether it's Madame Tirise's, or a cutpurse, or a hunt course— Would you have him end up with a broken neck like—"

He broke off, but not soon enough.

"Like Father?" Deymorin finished coldly, the softness vanishing. "Get it through your head, brother-mine, our father *chose* that death above other, less romantic, alternatives. He was out of control of his life. He *wanted* to die. Grant him that dignity, at least."

"You count it dignified to run away from your responsibilities?'' Which heartfelt, double-edged cut gave him the vague satisfaction of seeing Deymorin's eyes narrow and his suntanned brow tighten.

"I count it his choice, brother, for his reasons, and count that enough. He's responsible to whatever gods he believed in at the last, not me. Or you. Or anyone else. He was my father, and I was sorry to lose him. Beyond that, my life continues, and I live it responsible to myself, not Father.''

. . . and not you, was the unspoken end of that statement.

Mikhyel looked away, afraid if Deymorin realized he did not share that regret the discussion was doomed before he'd even broached his point.

A point from which they'd strayed wildly.

"We're not speaking of Mheric, we're speaking of Nikki and his obvious desire to emulate you.''

"That's the second time you've said that. Emulate? Me? Interesting. I don't recall spending hours in the library, but if you say so, it must be true.''

"Don't make a mockery of this, Deymorin, I beg you.''

"Beg? Again, you amaze me, Barrister. Whence this new humility?''

"Dammit, Deymio!" He caught himself, wondering what sort of man allowed such paltry taunts disturb him so. When his blood had cooled: "I'm worried, Rhomandi. I'm worried about Nikki, and I'm worried about the Estate.''

"I'd hardly equate the two.''

"Well, perhaps you should, for once. Nikki spends a small fortune every time he visits a tailor, has no sense where it comes to buying gifts for his friends . . .''

"A tragedy, certainly.''

Mockery continued to fill the air. He refused to look at Deymorin, refused to let that mockery dissuade him from his course.

"More than that, he's begun . . .'' Mikhyel found his voice failing, belatedly realizing he'd missed his mark, that Deymorin was incapable of seeing the matter his way, and seeing no possible means to backtrack. ". . . he's begun incurring . . . debts . . .''

"Gambling? *Nikki?*'' Deymorin's bark of laughter was all he'd feared. "Small worry there, Barrister.''

"Small? Perhaps now, but—''

"All right, brother, all right. I'll take the brat out while I'm here. Introduce him to—''

"Deymorin, *no!*" He turned back in time to see Deymorin's lightly amused look turn dark, and sought desperately to explain. "What about when you're gone? What will happen if he continues your pattern and chooses to follow you into those Outside gambling hells of yours as well? You know the sort who'll surround him there, once you've retreated to the safety of Darhaven and left him alone with the sharps. What about the personal dangers? What about the losses? The Estate can't support two of you."

"The Estate could handle a dozen of us without a hiccup." Deymorin's voice was as cold as his face.

"Because I put limits on your spending."

"You?" Deymorin's foot hit the floor with a thud. An instant later, his hand clamped Mikhyel's arm hard enough to make a larger man wince, but Mikhyel clenched his teeth, refusing his brother the satisfaction. "Get it through your head, boy. *You* don't control any pursestrings—*you* never have. *I* inherited the Estate. I *am* the Princeps. You 'rule' by proxy, *boy,* and never forget it. Any time I *choose,* I'm back on the Council."

"Good gods, Rhomandi, I *know*—"

Deymorin's hold on his arm tightened, Deymorin's voice hissed through clenched teeth. "*I* set those limits on myself, *long* before you even thought to try. I like to have a good time. I like to treat friends to a good time. I gave Rymarik leave to place those 'limits' on the books when you raised the issue, mainly to keep you quiet, but I can break them *any time I please.* I don't please. I've enough for my needs, and no interest in running the Estate into bankruptcy."

"I never said—"

Fingers twisted, biting deep into muscle, and for a moment, it was Mheric's eyes that glittered between narrow slits. "It's not that I don't know the numbers. Not that I don't understand them. It's that I don't give a damn."

"I never doubted it."

Level black brows twitched: a hint of puzzlement, gone in an instant. Deymorin dropped his hold and turned away, deserting him, ignoring the real problem.

The way Deymorin always had.

"As for Council," Deymorin continued lightly, the back of his hand flipping a nonchalance, "you seem to enjoy battling the old fools; overall, you do a good job. Why should I argue? In the arbitration court, your judgment has proven equally sound; I skim the transcripts—when I've nothing better to amuse me. I *know* what you're doing. Like the numbers, the court bores me to distraction. But I'll stretch those purse limits and I'll override those decisions when and where the urge takes me."

"Yours or your parasites'," he said, stupid in his bitter anger, though his blood froze as Deymorin pivoted slowly, and it was more than Mheric's eyes facing him this time.

"My—what?"

"Parasites." He spat the word out, defying his own visceral terror, and dodged Deymorin's backhand.

Too late. He staggered backward, caught himself against the mantle, morbidly certain he'd roused that shadow of Mheric at last. But he didn't care. Couldn't. Or perhaps, he thought, as the once-familiar taste of his own blood seeped across his tongue, he did care, and wanted the truth he'd feared out where he, at least, could face it, once and for all.

Obstinately, past a numbness in his lip, he pursued the point; "Those ... creatures you call friends, who hover around you *waiting* for the next hand—"

He gasped as Deymorin's strong fingers again cut deep into muscle ... twisting ...

"—*out!*"

"I don't give handouts, boy. I give credit where it's due. Call it ... redistributing the wealth, in the only way the system allows. The families I aided were cheated out of the most valuable farmland in the valley by those *friends* of yours on Council. I gave them the dignity of a new life—"

"They were well compensated for the loss. More than sufficient to relocate—"

"To where, Barrister? Bogs and granite? That's what Council never got through their thick skulls. There *is* no replacement for what you stole from them."

"No one *stole* anything."

"Rather well depends on which side the lawmakers are on, doesn't it? You don't compensate for generations of family history and devoted land management with money, Barrister. These were proud people, accustomed to hard work and a unique sense of accomplishment a man gets when the sweat pours down his face at harvest time. A feeling *you'll* never share."

"Thank the gods."

"No doubt. The choice you and your coconspirators gave them was no choice at all: a life of eternal idleness in the City with no legacy for their children, or land so remote and barren it would take years—perhaps generations—before they turned a profit. All I did was give them a dignified option, the only one that same stinking system allowed me to offer—and I'll continue my own brand of economics until someday, someone, dissolves the stinking system."

"You sound as if you'd like that."

A frozen, timeless pause, during which he stared defiantly at the angry face swimming beyond pain-watering eyes. That biting, localized pain surprised him, threw a man off his balance, who'd expected violence. He'd never pushed Deymorin this hard before. Never dared, knowing the man whose temper Deymorin had inherited.

Or so he'd always believed. This control was *not* Mheric, was nothing *like* Mheric.

Then the pressure was gone, the anger was gone, and Deymorin's hand fell away, leaving him strangely anchorless.

"Maybe I would," Deymorin said slowly, not looking at him.

"Your parasites might object," some perverse idiot inside him muttered, while he rubbed his arm against the tingling of renewed circulation. "They'd lose their free ticket." That same idiot continued pushing against this unknown limit, trying to force the Deymorin he *knew* existed into the open.

"Your terms, brother, not mine." Deymorin sounded . . . old. Tired. "They pay their way in this world."

"Now."

"Their *ancestors* were criminals, Khyel, not them."

That wasn't entirely true. Since the Founding, repeat offenders had been exiled to remote city-owned land where they were taught the basics of subsistence, then given a small plot of land, there to subsist as they could, any entitlement to city revenue they might have had reverting to the community share, there to be held in reserve for noncitizens who earned the right to citizenship.

He'd personally consigned no few to that Outside existence. But those were not the folk to whom Deymorin referred. He knew that, and was sincerely shamed to have unconsciously equated them.

"What would you have us do, Deymorin? Reinstate

them? The city property isn't there. The shares aren't. Who would we exile or impoverish for their sakes?"

"Impoverish? We've *personal* holdings in fifteen of the satellite nodes. The previous hard-working owners now work for us. Why? Because they owed the *Estate* taxes that they couldn't pay. Hell of a deal, brother, buying a business to pay the taxes that provide you the money to buy the business."

"Those 'businesses' were barely surviving. Our fore-closure has given them the backing they needed to thrive. Those previous owners are much better off than they were."

"Like the farmers, is it? We rob them of their independence, and they're supposed to smile and say thank you?"

"They're not complaining."

"What *good* would it do? You haven't done anything illegal. What recourse have they?"

"So why don't you take your seat and do something to change the law?"

Deymorin's dark gaze made a deliberate rise and capture of his.

"I tried that once."

"And gave up at the first hint of opposition."

"Is that what you think?"

In the face of that dark-eyed challenge, all he could do was raise a hand, then let it drop helplessly.

"Not really. But, Deymorin, *every* new member has a difficult time being taken seriously. Rings, if you knew what I—"

"Oh, poor, poor Barrister. Shall I call out the mourn-ers? —Difficult? You don't know the meaning of the word. You've had Anheliaa backing you every step of the way since you were twelve. You've had the Council's own ava-rice. Who and what did the farmers and those ill-fated shop-owners have?"

You, he longed to say, but couldn't, he who had led the attack against his own brother, thinking naively that by meeting Deymorin on these grounds and winning he stood some chance of winning his brother's respect at last, of gaining some sign of approval of his efforts, some mote of appreciation for his sacrifices over the years.

He'd realized too late he'd tried so hard for so long that he'd lost sight of what he truly wanted and instead, with that final confrontation, had driven Deymorin permanently into the arms of those people he'd so passionately represented.

"You talk as if the Councillors are ogres, Deymorin," he said quietly. "They're just businessmen, looking for answers to benefit the greatest number of people."

"They're hawks circling for the kill."

"They've achieved their position because they knew *how* to make a profit, and are using that expertise to benefit the Citizens."

"Easy to become rich when you make robbery legal."

"Dammit, Deymorin, there's no reasoning with you!"

"No? I suppose not. But then, that could just be because I have a problem with your basic premise. —Excuse me, *Anheliaa's* premise."

"I resent that."

"Do you? Well, that's a step in the right direction, anyway."

More than a step, Mikhyel suddenly realized, and the bottom fell out of his universe.

Until someone dissolves the system. . . .

For at least five years his brother had been working independently of Rhomatum Council and Rhomatum funds, building a network of loyalties beyond the City's boundaries, in the mysterious darks between the lines. A network with an unknown agenda.

The Council knew *of* his operations, but no one could ever figure what the goals were, never figure whether he posed a threat to the City's interests.

He knew, from his own experience, that Deymorin had powers of persuasion he'd never brought to bear in Council for the causes he ostensibly supported. That very reticence was enough to make a Councillor of Rhomatum nervous and wonder how Deymorin intended to win—and *what* he intended to win.

If his concerns were as benign as this conversation would suggest, perhaps compromise was possible. If not . . . *until someone dissolves the system. . . .*

"What *would* you do, Deymorin?" he asked quietly, "If you were Council?"

"You don't want to know."

"If I didn't, I wouldn't have asked." He crossed the room, sank down in a chair, and leaned forward, elbows on knees, the most earnest, nonthreatening stance he knew short of curling into a ball on the floor. "You said yourself I'm your proxy. How can I represent you if I don't know what you'd fight for?"

For a long, silent moment, Deymorin studied him then: "For starters, turn the rings over to the people."

"The rings already belong to the citizens."

"Not the shares. The rings."

"That's . . . crazed."

"Thought so." A humorless laugh. "Give it up, Barrister. You're not cut out for subversion."

Mikhyel rubbed his face fiercely with both hands, pressed his fingers into his eyes to relieve the building pressure.

"All right, Deymorin. *All right.* We'll play it your way. But we can't just . . . hand them over. For one thing, the people wouldn't know what to do with them, couldn't possibly maintain them, and the economy would collapse along with the power-base. For another, the rings are our personal security. Yours. Mine. Nikki's. And any future Rhomandi generations."

"We'd survive without, I assure you."

"We shouldn't have to. The people wouldn't want it that way."

"The people? Why should they give a damn what happens to us? What have we done for them?"

"We've given them the rings," Mikhyel stated the obvious, increasingly perplexed by this highly circular debate. "We've made Rhomatum's power available to them."

"The Tower has. The ley. Mother nature, not us. The rest is politically convenient bullshit."

"Without the Rhomandi Family, the Tower wouldn't exist. Rhomatum wouldn't. The web wouldn't."

"Our ancestor built the damn building, and for that, we deserve virtual godhood? As I recall, good old Darius went to a lot of trouble to eradicate precisely such antiquated notions as you're set on endorsing."

Deymorin was oversimplifying, trying to start a fight, was as uneasy (Mikhyel, as a veteran of literally hundreds of debates suddenly realized) as he with this change in long-established tactics between them.

"He found the node, Deymorin, and set the rings. For three hundred years, our family has produced the Rhomatum ringmaster—"

"Out of a line that hadn't produced a master in five generations. Darius was the king's bastard, Khyel, or have you forgotten that little fact? He *shouldn't* have been able to make the rings hiccup, let alone establish a whole new web. Proved them all wrong, didn't he?"

"If he was, in fact, Matrindi's son. We've only his word on that."

"We know the Matrindi fell from power after the Exodus. That was politics, not Talent or lack thereof."

"Five generations without so much as a single High Priest of Mauritum Tower would undermine any Family's power base. Maybe Darius had a personal grudge against the Rhomandi Family and saw that final announcement as the ultimate revenge. Perhaps the Matrin-Rhomandi cross was the key. We just don't know, Deymorin. We *do* know, our Family has produced *all* the Rhomatum ringmasters."

"Because we damnwell keep everyone else out of the Tower. Rather increases our chances, doesn't it?"

"When was the last time you stayed around long enough to know *what* we've tried?"

Deymorin drew back, the merest hint of remorse creeping past the assurance. A hint that vanished in an instant. "Well, looks like we've finally broken the string this generation, doesn't it?"

"Have we?"

"Full of oblique answers tonight, aren't you, boy? Tired of bean counting? Into ring-spinning now? Or is Nikki blossoming in other ways than with the ladies?"

"*You* could replace Anheliaa."

"Hell if." Deymorin fell back a step, caught a heel on a flagstone and dropped heavily into a chair.

Mikhyel's tenuous control over his temper wavered. "After all these years, when so much depends on it, do you *still* deny your Talent?"

"What the hell are you talking about?"

"*Dammit, Rhomandi!* You have had since you were nine—maybe before, for all I know. *Why* in all the eighteen chambers of Rhomatum hell do you refuse to act on it? Are you waiting for the moment Anheliaa's gone? Just waiting to destroy what you obviously cannot abide?"

Strangely, Deymorin laughed. "Brother, you're crazy."

"Am I?" And his voice shook with the tremors he could no longer control. Forcing a potential ringmaster into taking action was a risk, the scope of which he had no real inkling, but which life with Anheliaa dunMoren had taught him to fear.

Towers could only be taken from within. Anything else destroyed the very object of the invader's desire. Deymorin had kept his secret for years. Even away from the Tower, he could have been studying how to control the rings, preparing an incontestable takeover, awaiting Anheliaa's inevitable death. Possibly even in collusion with one or more of the satellite nodes.

"I don't know where you got such a crack-brained notion, but—"

"I was all of six, *Rhomandi,* but I remember like it was yesterday. We snuck into the Tower. I touched the rings, and fouled the orbits. Do you *remember,* yet?"

"I don't . . ." Deymorin's head swung slowly from side to side, not seeming to *see* anything. "I . . . recall alarms . . . and thinking we'd be flayed alive for sure. But the alarms quit and we got out before anyone caught us. I always assumed the damned things fixed themselves. I mean, they *do* that, don't they?"

There could be no doubting the innocent ignorance of that statement.

"Never." He stood up. "*You* reset them, Deymorin. All these years . . . have you *never* realized?"

"Realized? Brother, I never even *wondered.*" Deymorin pulled back in the chair as if Mikhyel had physically threatened him. "It wasn't me. *Couldn't* have been. Surely I'd have known—"

Something collapsed inside, some anger that had sustained him for years, and Mikhyel fell weakly into his chair.

"Dear sweet living gods, brother, all these years, and *that's* what's been eating you? *Me* conniving some mythical plot against Anheliaa and your gods-be-damned *rings*?" Deymorin seemed about to say more, but then just shook his head in patent disbelief.

A sphere of nonfeeling surrounded him. Deymorin hadn't refused responsibility, had not left him to deal with an aging, increasingly testy Anheliaa on his own simply for spite. Had not been off preparing a coup. Deymorin hadn't told Anheliaa because Deymorin hadn't known.

And creeping insidiously into the void, another dangerously weakening sense: Hope.

Deymorin, being Deymorin, would do the right thing—if only the brother Deymorin openly despised could convince him of his own Talent. Convince him to help control Anheliaa's increasingly obsessive notions.

"It *was* your doing, Deymorin. And don't you see?" he pleaded, near choking on throat-constricting desperation. "The Rhomandi blood does run true. We need your Talent, your goodwill, here. In the Tower. Not—" *Outside,* he finished silently, but knew better than to say.

"Talent—perhaps, though I've only your say on that," Deymorin said firmly, "The will—never."

"Why not?"

"Rings, boy. I'd be incarcerated with Anheliaa for months, perhaps *years* learning a trade I despise. Isn't that reason enough?"

"And for that, you'd condemn the City to eternal darkness?"

"Melodramatic, aren't we? Frankly, going back to pushing plows and living by candlelight might make a number of citizens I can think of a great deal more palatable. But that's not even a remote possibility. There are plenty of lackeys to keep the Tower going. They don't need me and my mythic Talent."

So much for pleading and reason. Mikhyel rose stiffly and crossed the room to stand looking down at Deymorin, who stared stubbornly forward, calmly sipping his wine.

"You might not have any choice, Rhomandi. The Tower needs a master. There *is* no one else—"

"Bullshit, brother."

"Your tongue becomes increasingly Outside vulgar, Deymorin."

Deymorin just snorted.

He turned to the fireplace.

"And if I tell Anheliaa what I saw?"

"Rings, boy, you *sound* like a six-year-old. She'll ask why you haven't said anything in—what?—twenty years? box your ears for lying, and send you to bed without supper."

"It's not a joke, Deymorin. I've been waiting to say anything. I didn't realize ... And if you really were a threat to the rings, how could I encourage Anheliaa to ... But if you didn't know ... if you still refuse—"

"You do realize you're making no sense whatsoever. But

it hardly matters. *She* can't make me do anything. And neither, little brother, can you."

Mikhyel lifted a hand in tacit defeat. The most important negotiation of his life, and he'd used the diplomacy of a breeding bull. "Just think about it, Deymio, that's all I ask."

"What I think is that it's all in your head."

Mikhyel sighed. "Nikki should be coming down soon. Let's see if we can manage to be civil, at least long enough for his party. We owe him that *much*, poor lad."

Deymorin's sharp bark of laughter held no humor. "You have the gall to say that? After that reception you gave him?"

The memory of Nikki's pale face, of his own fingers pressing into cheeks barely able to produce peach fuzz, filled his soul and once again, his fingertips sought refuge in the patterned stone. "I was worried. I . . . overreacted. I'm . . . sorry for it, Deymio. —Damned sorry."

A rustle of cloth, a creak of wood flooring, and Deymorin was beside him, and Deymorin's hand was on his shoulder. He looked up, met Deymorin's eyes in a way they hadn't managed in years. This time, his brother's touch was almost gentle, his tone a rueful relaxation of tension. "Sometimes, fry, I wonder if I'll *ever*—"

But whatever he was about to say floundered and died in a damnably ill-timed flurry of activity at the salon doors. Tea tray, first. A second wine tray next. And from the midst of a sea of attendants surrounding the large-wheeled mobility chair and its bewigged and painted occupant:

"High time you got here, Rhomandi!"

Anheliaa had arrived.

Chapter Five

Time had been it seemed strange to Nikki that the one night of the year he could be certain the family would dine alone and in the echoing vastness of the formal dining room was on his birthday, but over the years, he'd figured out it was Aunt Anheliaa's way of celebrating while protecting him against well-meaning reminiscences about the parents he'd never known.

Of course, neither had his friends known them, but sometimes Aunt forgot about that.

Besides, Aunt Anheliaa's idea of a party would undoubtedly include *her* friends who *had* known Mother and Father, and who *would* talk about them, and what a shame they'd died so young, and Nikki mustn't feel that he'd caused it, which of *course,* he hadn't....

He shuddered. Maybe family-only parties weren't so bad, after all.

But tonight he'd have preferred the ballroom itself, packed wall to wall and floor to ceiling with people he'd never met and who wouldn't recognize him, so that he could melt into obscurity rather than sit on display at the place of honor at a single oval table with Mikhyel and Deymorin seated to either side and Aunt Anheliaa on the far end watching every bite he choked down.

Even Anheliaa's attendant ... Mirym? ... seemed to be staring at him. But then, she *always* seemed to stare, although perhaps it only felt that way, because she never said anything. Almost two years since she'd arrived, and never a sound out of her, not that he'd heard. Probably that was why Anheliaa, who always demanded absolute silence while she worked, seemed so satisfied with her.

His brothers had argued—he knew that even without anyone telling him, and in spite of the cheerful faces they put on for his party.

Anheliaa seemed very tired tonight, almost fragile. The arthritis, which had confined her to her mobility chair since before he was born, was more painful than usual, if one could judge from the irritation in her tone as she ordered Mirym to cut her meat or hand her the wineglass. And she seemed to drift off in the middle of sentences . . . Of course, Diorak might have given her the same green goo he'd given Nikki against the pain . . .

Effective green goo. He hadn't felt a thing since he'd waked up . . . And on a sudden disturbing thought: could he be drifting similarly? Certainly the pain was gone, but if he was wandering, and could notice *her* wandering, might *she* not notice *him*, and if yes, might she not begin to wonder and ask questions Mikhyel didn't want answered and . . .

Panicked, he made an active effort to join the conversation, and despite the fact the tension in the air was making his already queasy stomach churn, he took small bites of the rich foods and chewed them to liquidity, trying to make it appear he was eating more than he really was. And he smiled and said all the right things, and made all the ordinary, inane responses to meaningless, formalized impersonal comments . . . until the talk turned to the rumblings of discontent out of Mauritum, and the treaty.

"What's Paurini's problem this time?" Deymorin asked, around a mouthful of spiced beef.

Palev Paurini dunTasrek, Nikki's head wasn't *that* fuzzy. Mauritum's Minister of State.

"Not Paurini," Mikhyel clarified, "Garetti."

"Garetti?" Nikki asked. "High Priest Garetti rom-Maurii?"

Mikhyel shot him a faint nodding smile, the way Mikhyel would when he took an interest in politics that didn't come out of a history book, looks that came more frequently these days . . . or, at least, one liked to think so.

"He's complaining about the power differential again. Claims we're leeching Mauritum Node, and trying to charge them for the privilege."

"After the way they took advantage of our worst drought in history and jacked up the price of grain last year?" Deymorin asked, scowling. "Hell, screw the bastard seven ways from yesterday and let him howl."

Mikhyel's thin brows twitched. "Grain? How could the price of Mauritumin grain affect us?"

"Come, come, brother-mine, join the real world, for a change, will you?"

"But the trade restrictions—"

"Trade restrictions?" Deymorin lifted his fork, letting the light glint off its silver-beaded handle. "Gartum work, is it? Maybe Horassidumin? And the bauble in Anheliaa's ear? Obviously Khoratum workmanship. —Or, dare I suggest it, *Mauritumin*?" The fork clattered to the table. "Admit it, Khyel. The black market is alive and well. Has been since Darius closed off the legitimate businessmen three-damn-hundred years ago. What do you expect when half the damn coastline is within spitting distance of Maurislan? Last year, we got grain, seed, *and* the market produce, wherever we could damnwell find it."

Mikhyel flushed, and the hand that raised his wineglass shook, spilling droplets over his manicured fingertips. He drained it in a single gulp. "Who arranged the deal?"

"Who do you think?"

Mikhyel's hand tightened on the fragile-stemmed goblet.

"Khyel, please." Nikki reached across the table and gently disengaged Mikhyel's fingers, setting the glass aside.

"Dammit, Rhomandi!" Mikhyel jerked his hand free, swearing at the dinner table, which Mikhyel *never* did, especially in front of ladies. "I can't believe . . . Have you the slightest notion what your little 'business deals' cost us? The least you could have done is come to me. Asked where the negotiations stood—"

"Come to *you*? Oh, that's funny, Mikhyel. That's *really* outstandingly humorous. What would you have done? Given the farmers an I.O.U. until you could work their little problem into the Council schedule? Maybe made it a part of the overall trade package . . . which *still* hasn't been signed? Council would be damned hungry by now, and blaming the farmers. Shit, Barrister, when have you ever given a *damn* about Outside needs? When it's time to plant, you can't fucking well *wait*—"

Mikhyel hissed. "That's *enough*, Rhomandi!"

Deymorin scowled, drained his glass and snapped his fingers for a refill.

For a moment, the tension was stifling, Mikhyel and Deymorin both militantly avoiding eye contact with anyone. From the far end of the table Anheliaa surveyed them

all from under hooded, painted eyelids. Little Mirym just
gazed studiously into her teacup.

Nikki coughed discreetly.

Deymorin started and glanced at him; Mikhyel did; then
at each other, and Mikhyel said, past a set jaw: "Much as
I might ... appreciate ... the ... depth ... of your feelings,
dear brother, kindly leave that language in the stables
where it belongs. Or have you forgotten altogether how to
act around real ladies?"

Which admonition (even though Nikki would swear the
expression Mirym hid behind her teacup had nothing to do
with maidenly shock and everything to do with humor,
while Anheliaa just looked smug) naturally set the previous
subject aside and his two brothers off on one of the thinly
disguised, tediously polite, contests of wills, which they'd
somehow avoided through the first five courses, and Anheliaa, wide awake now and with a sly grin creasing her face,
joined in, adding fuel to their snipes.

Leaving Nikki to wonder, on his own again, and weary
of the battle, about the treaty and the issues they'd forgotten—or set aside because of his birthday, so as not to upset
him. *What's wrong, Nikki?*

Except he *wasn't* upset. And they were important issues,
especially to someone who hoped one day to be an ambassador to the ancient god-determined city.

God-determined. ...

"It seems to me," he interjected tentatively into the first
pause for collective breath, "that Garetti is behaving quite
reasonably ... for a High Priest of Maurii."

The pause became an extended silence.

Anheliaa's expression soured and she was staring down
the table—at him.

His brothers exchanged a look he couldn't read, and he
considered slipping under the table and crawling its length
to the servant's door the way he had as a child when they
served something he didn't want to eat. But he was too big
now, dammit.

Mikhyel raised a sardonic eyebrow at Deymorin; Deymorin shrugged, then asked:

"Reasonably? Why do you say that, Nikaenor?"

Nikaenor? Deymorin was mad, or Nikki had been a fool.
Either way, he wished now he hadn't interrupted. His brain
wasn't working: too much wine and Diorak's green goo.

However, having been a fool did oblige one to make the attempt to dig one's way out of that pit.

"It–it's been three hundred years since we've had direct trade with Mauritum. It–it seems—to me, at least—only natural that the first few years of renewed relations between our two nodes should be tinged with suspicions." Another exchanged look; he pushed a bit further: "On *both* sides."

Deymorin looked at Mikhyel, and Mikhyel at Deymorin, but when no one challenged him openly, Nikki swallowed hard and warmed to his theme.

"Garetti is in a terribly awkward position, don't you think? I mean, for his entire career, he's had to balance and direct ley-energy like a farmer budgets water in a drought, and now, after years of explaining why his gods favored one company or Family over another, he's got virtually all the power his people need—but he's got to explain the added cost and why and where it came from, or cover the difference out of his own profit—and that means his *god's* profits. And with all that tied up with the religion he supposedly represents—well, it seems to me . . . that . . ."

He'd made himself the center of attention again, exactly what he'd wanted most to avoid. Anheliaa was staring at him. Likely he was making no sense whatsoever. She'd guess about the green goo and Tirise's and the cutpurse and—"Never mind," he mumbled, and took a hasty mouthful of chicken and cream.

"Never mind?" Anheliaa's voice cracked over him like a whip. *"Never mind?* The man's whole life is based on a sham. Of *course* he's in an awkward position. With luck, he'll be out of a job within my lifetime and I'll have the chance to dance on the rubble of his anachronistic church."

"S–sorry." Nikki flicked a glance at her, started to raise another forkfull, found he couldn't hold it steady, and, all too aware of all the eyes following his movements, let it drop again. "Please, forget I said anything."

But, Deymorin said:

"I think we should let Nikaenor speak his piece."

And: "I agree."

That was Mikhyel.

A confused desperation came over him. Deymorin and Mikhyel never agreed on anything, particularly where it

concerned him and *never* in opposition to Anheliaa's
wishes.

"I don't—" He couldn't finish. Not with Anheliaa staring
daggers at him.

Or possibly it was Mikhyel who took that glare, because
Mikhyel's eyes dropped, and Mikhyel's fork stirred his
creamed peas into neat rows.

"It's all right, Nikki," Deymorin said, firmly. "You're
seventeen today, after all. You're allowed to have opinions
of your own."

And thus was the secret to his brothers' uncharacteristic
alliance revealed: they were humoring him.

Because it was his birthday.

Nikki controlled the sudden urge to lose the meal he'd
just forced down, and instead of throwing his half-filled
plate at his patronizing brothers, he lifted his full wineglass
defiantly, and emptied it in two very large gulps, which
settled his stomach in a warm, head-spinning glow.

Deymorin's laughter filled the room. His glass lifted in
response, turning Nikki's defiance into a toast, and forcing
the others to match the gesture and call the issue closed.

More wine followed. Lots of wine, and more laughter.

"Everybody has an agenda, don't you see?" Nikki said
then, in a rush of inspired bravado. "Even if they don't
know they have one. It's only human. Everything we think
we know about Mauritum is based on what Darius *wanted*
us to know, colored by things we can't *officially* know, and
Darius had his own agenda, and probably Garetti is similarly biased, so of course what we think they think will be
colored by what Darius thought so how can we be sure
what Garetti thinks, or what Garetti's religion tells him to
do until we meet him and discuss it face-to-face?"

He paused, breathless. Realized Mikhyel and Deymorin
were staring at each other now, as though they shared
some secret.

"Berul!" they shouted together, and ... laughed. Together.

Deymorin and Mikhyel never laughed together.

Mikhyel spluttered first, being less in practice. Deymorin
eyed him sidewise and placing a hand to his chest intoned dra-
matically: ". . . Maurii *lusts* after additional followers . . ."

And Mikhyel finished breathlessly: ". . . such is the way
of gods. —Oh, gods, Deymio. —Seventeen!"

Laughter burst out again. Berul. That was *Berul* they were quoting. *His* Berul.

They *knew*!

It was as though some dam had burst. When one would sputter to an almost stop, dark eyes crinkling at the corners would meet grey, and laughter would erupt all over again, and Nikki sank into his chair, wanting to disappear, wondering how the market magicians managed the trick.

"Enough!" Anheliaa's voice cracked over the top, and Anheliaa's hand struck the table, spilling her wine and rattling Mirym's teacup.

Obedient as two recalcitrant children, Deymorin and Mikhyel dropped their attention to their plates, mouths pressed tight, shoulders shaking with an occasional spasm. Then Deymorin reached for his wine, took a sip, and in a voice that squeaked only slightly said, "Tolerably good vintage. From Tarlisium Valley, you said?"

Tarlisium wine, hell. They'd been laughing at him. And his ideas. His bookish notions. One might be devastated, but instead, one found oneself delighted at this new side of one's brothers one's bookish comments had revealed.

And if the wine and Diorak's goo weren't making the world seem just absolutely wonderful at the moment.

"Well, Khyel," Deymorin said, "do you suppose the brat's newly-discovered adulthood is too precious to include presents?"

Mikhyel seemed to consider the matter, frowning at him.

At least, he thought Mikhyel must be frowning, as he had to take it on faith that the shadow swimming somewhere down the table was Anheliaa.

"A distinct possibility." That *was* Mikhyel. "Well, Nikaenor?"

Nikki grinned at the room in general, since his brothers were having a tendency to multiply at random, and assured all of them. "Not a chance."

But when faced with the pile in the salon, Nikki was no longer quite so certain. Daunting didn't quite cover it.

He wandered between the two tables checking labels, realizing in something of a daze that fully half were from people he'd never met, many from people he'd never even heard of.

"What did you do? Post a notice in the *Internode*?" he asked, half-joking.

"Naturally," Anheliaa said, sounding quite pleased with herself.

But for him, it was embarrassing, almost like stealing. Suddenly the glow of laughter and wine that had sustained him through the end of dinner seemed to disappear along with the numbing effects of Diorak's green goo. His side hurt, he was tired, and the presents just didn't seem very important, coming from people he didn't know or care about.

"Sit," Deymorin ordered, appearing miraculously at his side just as the world turned sideways, and guided him to a chair. "We've all been through it, brat. Part of the dues. So just open, smile, and resign yourself to thank-you writer's cramp."

And Mikhyel, who had joined them, murmured into his ear: "White as a chicken egg, fry. Hold another bit, and you'll be through the worst."

And, Deymorin again: "Old private joke, Nikki-lad. Not aimed at you. Tomorrow, we'll discuss Garetti and Mauritum—even, Darius save us, Berul."

Mikhyel's choke of swallowed laughter sounded above his head, and Deymorin tossed a grin upward.

"Whatever you want, Nik," Deymorin said. "Promise."

Nikki smiled shakily; Deymio ruffled his hair and Mikhyel pressed his arm; then Deymorin said aloud:

"I'll read the tags, pass the package to you, you open, and Khyel will write." And with a twitching smile meant for Mikhyel alone: "Always had the best handwriting of the lot, Barrister."

Mikhyel's eyes dropped, reasonable enough for someone settling behind a writing table, but *his* mouth twitched as well.

"Got it?" Deymorin asked.

Nikki nodded, basking in this unprecedented united attention, no longer caring if it was just his birthday making it possible. He swallowed a hiccup, then grinned apologetically toward Anheliaa, who was frowning at them: "Th–think I . . . over–ind–(hic)–ulged a bit, aunt. S–sorry."

"Webs, boy, it's your birthday," she said, acerbically, then her lips pressed into a tight smile, and she lifted her own refilled glass. "When better? Just open your presents. Let's see what debts people figure they owe us, eh?"

Such a lovely way to look at it. He accepted the first from Deymorin, more reluctant than ever. Deymorin pressed his shoulder in mute sympathy, then murmured, "Don't let her spoil it, fry. They're sent out of respect for you and the Family, despite what she claims."

"Thanks," he muttered.

Thus began the longest evening of his entire life. He'd never seen so many ... *things* accumulated into one spot. His chair grew deeper and deeper in folds of colorful paper and ribbons—until Mirym slipped into the black comedy.

Sinking to her knees beside his chair, she made bouquets of the bows and dried flowers used to decorate the packages and tied them to everything available: first his wrists, then Deymorin's, then Anheliaa's, Mikhyel's, the lamps ... and finally, at his laughing insistence, into her own curly tendrils, then she folded the wrappings, separating them into color-coordinated piles (rings knew why, except, perhaps, it seemed *something* to do with them) until somehow, by the time they'd narrowed the stack to the Family gifts, the blackness had departed, leaving only the comedy.

More Family gifts than usual, unless his vision and exhaustion had combined to make it seem so, and Anheliaa's taste in clothes for once seemed more in line with his own—or his with hers, and he wondered vaguely if that should alarm him; and there was a translation of Berlio's *History of Greater Agoran,* so new he hadn't even heard it advertised, from Mikhyel; and from Deymorin—

A large, flat envelope. The annual I.O.U.

He met Deymorin's laughter-filled eyes and asked, "Shall I make you a wager?"

The laughter escaped. "Don't count on it, fry."

"Not?" Deymorin wouldn't dare lie, not on his birthday, but if not the I.O.U., what ... ?

Nikki held the envelope by one corner and at arm's length in mock terror, then pressed it to his forehead in mimicry of the leyside charlatans.

"I'm getting an image. By the power of the Lines—"

A hand boxed his ears, cutting his act short. He dropped Deymorin's gift and instinctively covered his head.

"Don't *ever* mock the lines, boy!"

Through a world suddenly spinning, Mikhyel's eyes glared at him, seeming, in that spin, to flicker first at him, then sideways toward their aunt's profoundly disturbed face. Nikki bit his lip, using that localized, personally inflicted pain to settle the outside world's instability long enough to mumble an apology, then retreated into an unfocussed middle-ground, not daring to move, not even to reach for Deymorin's gift, fearing he would leave his supper on the carpet beneath his chair.

Shock. Or the wine. The blow, perhaps, or just the wound, throbbing now past Diorak's medication *and* the alcohol *and* the laughter: any or all were likely culprits—not that the *source* of his sudden desire to die on the spot made very much difference.

A touch of his shoulder; he blinked up, saw remorse on Mikhyel's pale face.

From behind him and through the ringing in his ears, Deymorin's murmur: "Remind me to teach you manners, Khyel," and saw remorse melt into obstinacy.

A flat package arrived into his hands, and he heard, Deymorin again: "Open it, lad," as Deymorin's steadying hand replaced Mikhyel's and Mikhyel retreated silently to the cold fireplace, his back to them all.

Nikki wished, then, that he'd thought to request a fire. He could have, it being his birthday, even though they didn't need it for heat. Perhaps in a fire's warm glow Khyel wouldn't have looked quite so forbidding—or alone.

Clutching the envelope to his chest, he blinked his eyes clear and said shakily, "I truly am sorry, Aunt Liaa. I meant no disrespect."

Deymorin squeezed his shoulder. "She knows that, Nikki. We *all* know that. Mikhyel's just a bit touchy right now."

Beside the fireplace, Mikhyel started.

"My fault, fry, not yours," Deymorin said, but Deymorin was watching Mikhyel, not him, and Mikhyel's shoulders straightened, then, and Mikhyel returned to his chair, his grey eyes blank, if a bit wide.

The hand left his shoulder with a light tap, and Deymorin said, in a much livelier tone: "Now open your damn present and say 'Excuse me, dear brother Deymio, for ever doubting you!' "

Nikki gulped, grinned soggily, and tried surreptitiously

to wipe the blurring tears away, gratefully accepting the handkerchief Deymorin slipped him.

Young Miryem had retreated to her chair and was staring studiously at her lap, Anheliaa was looking distracted again, Mikhyel was scowling at his feet, but Deymorin's hands gripped his shoulders, shaking him gently to attention.

"Hurry up, wretch. I want my dessert!"

"All right, Deymio, all right."

Falling in with Deymorin's attempts to salvage the mood, he ripped the brown paper covering (Deymorin's notion of wrapping) from two thin sheets of stiffened, beautifully tooled, brass-bound leather.

He threw a puzzled glance at Deymorin, who had left his side to lean his shoulders against the fireplace mantle, arms akimbo, comfortable there, as Mikhyel hadn't been. Deymorin raised an eyebrow and lowered his eyes deliberately to the strange object.

Nikki flicked the clasp free with a thumbnail ...

Documents. *Transfer* papers. The names blurring on the lines made no sense until he realized they were registered names, not the Storm and Ashley he knew them by.

"The *greys*?" He gasped, his head suddenly lighter than ever the blood loss and green goo had made it.

This time, his brother laughed outright.

"Deymio, you can't be serious!"

"Of course I am. You handled them better than I on that final leg last month. They like you—far better than they do me. Who am I to argue with true love?"

"What *are* you two gibbering about?" Aunt asked; and Mikhyel interjected acerbically: "Horses."

"Not just *any* horses, Khyel." He felt compelled to explain. "The *greys*."

"As I said."

"But they're the *best*. Last month they won—" He bit his lip, recalling too late his next older brother's feelings on *that* topic.

Mikhyel's face grew very dark.

Nikki looked an apology at Deymorin. But Deymorin, chin raised, a slight mocking smile hovering about his lips, was watching Mikhyel, who was staring at Deymorin.

Suddenly every ache and throb returned in double measure.

The gift was just one more challenge to Mikhyel. All that about handling and love nothing more than pretense.

All the laughter, all the pleasantries at dinner and after . . . all that meant nothing. Nothing was different. Nothing changed.

Nothing ever changed.

"What's all this?" Aunt asked sternly. "Who won what, and why are you looking like a thundercloud, Mikhyel?"

Eyes still glued on Deymorin, Mikhyel answered, "A race through the streets of the City, Aunt Liaa. A race between my brother—"

"Bro*thers*, Mikhyel," Nikki interjected loyally—and fairly. After all, Deymorin had gotten into the race in the first place because of *his* bragging about the greys.

Mikhyel's slender, beringed hand waved the air dismissively. "I refuse to hold you responsible, Nikaenor."

Anheliaa was watching them all, narrow-eyed and calculating.

Nikki bit his tongue, uncertain whether standing up for Deymorin at this point would help or hinder.

"No one was hurt, Khyel," Deymorin said quietly, and with a glance toward Anheliaa, "It was a wager, Aunt, nothing more."

But that wasn't all.

"It was the festival race, Aunt," Nikki tried to explain, "We were reenacting the Transition Day kidnapping."

To which Anheliaa replied calmly, "Well, if that's all . . ."

"It doesn't matter," Mikhyel said, and stood—for emphasis, Nikki knew the routine. But:

"Tell me, boys, which of you played the abducted virgin?" Anheliaa asked, and Deymorin glanced at him, and it was their turn to burst into simultaneous laughter.

"Aunt, *please*." Mikhyel's face took on a faint desperation—and confusion. "Don't encourage them. If we won't allow merchants to bring animals within the City limits to deliver produce, how can we expect them to understand when their so-called leaders—"

"But they loved it!" Nikki cried in protest. "People were lining the stadium roads, cheering."

"Enjoyed making a spectacle of yourself, did you?" Mikhyel asked dryly.

Here it was: Mikhyel's anticipated lecture.

He slumped down, his face hot, his enthusiasm waning, and with it his strength.

And he muttered stupidly, knowing he was courting disaster: "Go to hell."

Which got him (justifiably, he had to admit) the back of Mikhyel's hand.

Not as hard as he deserved, perhaps, though it *felt* heavier than usual, but unfortunately rather more than his already mistreated head could handle. The world began fading at the corners, and the seat cushions slipped from under him.

He heard Deymorin shout something, tried to assure them he was all right, but somehow, the words wouldn't come, and the floor hit him, and then someone was holding him and Mikhyel's voice—more in his head than in his ear—was whispering *Sweet gods, Nikki, I'm sorry,* and he tried to tell him he was all right, but then someone pulled him in another direction and Deymorin's voice was yelling for someone to get Jerrik . . .

"Take your stinking hands off him. You've done more than enough already."

Deymorin's scorn ripped through Mikhyel's already shaken nerves and his fingers went numb.

Nikki's limp arm fell free.

Mikhyel caught it before it flopped, eased it to rest on the boy's knee, and stood up, staggering in mute horror away from the consequence of his temper. A hard edge struck his knee; he grabbed blindly at the chair arm and collapsed numbly into the chair's cushioned seat. Burying his head in shaking hands shielded him from the visible consequence of his outburst, but he couldn't wipe the memory of . . .

(Clear, blue eyes, clouded in shock and pain, tendrils of blond hair, damp with sweat, brushing a bruising cheekbone, soft mouth trailing a thin line of red . . .)

Only—the blood of Darius curse him—this time, it was *his* hand that raised the bruise. *His* hand created that line of blood.

And the face was Nikki's, not his mother's.

He'd *never* struck so hard before, *never* knocked the boy down.

He let his hands fall, stared at them, wishing, for a moment, he could cut them off.

All too often, he'd seen Mheric, in a fit of anger, strike his mother.

All too often, he'd seen that same, gentle understanding he saw now in Nikki override the pain and the shock.

The last time . . .

The door opened. Jerrik, Nikki's valet, come to help Deymorin take Nikki to his room.

The last time, the blow had sent Mama down a staircase.

Jerrik, because Deymorin wouldn't trust him to touch Nikki.

That had been seventeen years ago.

Deymorin wouldn't trust him; more than that, he wouldn't trust himself.

Seventeen years ago. . . .

"Nikki!"

He threw his head up; Nikki's eyes met his, blinking, frightened. He lifted a hand helplessly; the fright vanished in a gentle, familiar smile before the door closed between them.

. . . to the day.

"All right, Jerrik," a voice said over his head. "I can take care of him now. Thanks."

Pillows were at his back and under his elbows, propping him upright. He was in his bedroom, sitting on a freshly-made bed that smelled of rose petals.

Something tugged at his hand, that same voice gently urged him to let go.

He blinked his eyes until they cleared, realized it was Deymorin doing the tugging, that he was trying to take back the horse papers he'd somehow clung to throughout.

Nikki bit his lip, fighting not at all appropriate for an adult tears. He let go of the papers and forced himself to say steadily, "It's all right, Deymio, I . . ." He looked down at his empty hands. "I realize it was just to annoy Mikhyel. I–I won't hold you—"

"Nikki!" Deymorin sounded shocked. "No."

"It's all right—really."

"It's not 'all right.'" Deymorin's hand gripped his chin, not painfully as Mikhyel would, urging rather than demanding his attention. Nikki looked off to one side, concentrating on the grain in the wainscotting, afraid those stupid childish tears would prevail if he met Deymorin's eyes.

"Look at me, brother."

He swallowed hard . . .

"Please?"

. . . and forced himself to obey.

"I meant what I said down there, Nik. Regardless of what passes between Mikhyel and myself, those horses are yours. You were there when they were born—you know damnwell they wouldn't have lived, but for your efforts . . ."

That much was true. He'd been all of ten. His first time to Darhaven; his first real trip Outside; his first attendance at a foaling—

And would have been his last had Gerhard had his way. The foaling-man had been for putting the twins down.

". . . you helped me train them," Deymorin was still arguing.

Deymorin had given in to his pleas to let the foals live.

". . . and last week you proved you could handle them on your own."

And he'd been right. Lucky, more like, as he'd realized since.

"This," Deymorin gestured toward the bound papers lying on the bed table, "was merely a formality."

He wished he believed that. Would, but for the ever-present dissonance between his brothers.

But Deymorin expected him to accept the gesture, and he would, until Deymorin changed his mind—which Deymorin might well, once he'd thought better of it, or the moment someone offered what the greys were worth.

So he smiled and Deymorin smiled and that issue was closed. But swimming in the darkness behind closed eyes as Deymorin pulled his shirt off over his head was Mikhyel's distressed face and he had to wonder what Deymorin would do once he left this room. He'd sensed the anger in Deymorin's supporting arm, sensed it still in the tightness of Deymorin's brow, and the distracted way he dabbed at Nikki's bruised and bloodied face.

"He didn't hurt me, you know."

"Oh?" A sardonic brow lifted at him. "All an act, then, is it?"

"That's not fair, Deymorin. I was light-headed before I ever went down for dinner, and I drank far too much wine. Diorak did warn me about that."

"And this?" Deymorin lifted the rag.

Nikki shrugged. "I fell badly."

"Like hell." Deymorin's hand clenched on the rag, and Nikki expected any moment to see it fly across the room. But Deymorin's hand relaxed, and he folded the rag deliberately and set it on the side table. "He was out of line, Nikaenor, and don't you *dare* make any excuses for him. And don't you *dare* apologize to him, do you hear me?"

"He'd never let me do either of those things."

"How would he stop you? Hit you again?"

That was Deymorin's anger talking, and he didn't bother answering it.

"Deymio," he asked slowly, "why doesn't Khyel ever visit you at Darhaven?"

Deymorin gave him a measured frown. "What difference does that make?"

"Have you . . . Have you ever asked him to visit?"

Deymorin shrugged, turned away, ostensibly to retrieve his nightshirt from the warming rack.

"Have you?" Nikki persisted, standing only to drop his pants to the floor, even that small effort enough to make his head spin, which likely accounted for Deymorin's muffled-sounding answer:

"Not . . . for a long time." And more clearly: "Not that it's any of your business, young snoop."

"Why not?"

Deymorin's head twitched, swung far enough to shoot him a look of incredulity. "You don't give up, do you?"

Nikki chewed his lower lip and shook his head. "Not when it's this important."

Following a frowning, corner-of-one-eye scrutiny, Deymorin dropped onto the side of his bed, resting a hand lightly on Nikki's knee.

"He used to go to Darhaven every fall after the Transition festivals. You did too, when Father was alive. Don't you remember?"

Nikki shook his head, a failure which seemed to sadden Deymorin, so he searched for an image . . . any image . . . of Darhaven prior to the twins' foaling. But he'd been four years old when their father died, and all he remembered of that time was a large, loud, perpetually angry man.

And darkness.

And a whisper admonishing him to be quiet.

But those were elusive images, and likely not Darhaven at all, even were they real, so he asked:

"And after Father died? Why did he stop going? You didn't."

"Man can only take so many rejections, fry. I wanted him to come Outside. Wanted him to know something beyond the City. Khyel just . . . wasn't interested, and I didn't feel it was my place to insist."

"A—and me? Why didn't you ever ask . . . ?" It was an old pain, one he hadn't thought ever to face.

"Mikhyel was terrified of your going, so I didn't . . ." Deymorin's eyes dropped to the papers clutched against Nikki's chest. "You'll never know what it meant to me when you asked to come with me that spring. I thought . . ."

"Thought what?" Nikki asked, eager to have this void filled, to have verbal reassurance of the truths he'd always suspected: that Deymorin truly loved him and wanted to be with him—and Mikhyel, of course—always, and that those forces pushing them apart were superficial, easily discarded once everyone wanted it to be different.

But Deymorin shook his head, grinned tightly, and patted Nikki's hand. "Never mind. Coming out of this thick skull, it couldn't have been very important, could it?"

"It's important to me."

"Nikki!"

"All right. All right." He slumped, shivering, tired, and feeling sorely put upon by self-centered elders unwilling to explain the important details which one had missed out on only by reason of being born late.

"Hands up," Deymorin ordered, and slipped the flannel shirt over his head as if he were a child instead of a newly-acknowledged adult, which he really didn't mind, since moving his arm hurt his side and made his head swim.

He suspected, sometimes, that Deymorin secretly preferred little brothers over adult ones, suspected at times like this that perhaps Khyel's greatest youthful transgression—that which had ultimately driven his brothers apart—had been growing up too fast. He didn't *know* that for certain, of course, but he wasn't about to similarly destroy his own relationship with Deymorin.

Emerging from the warm folds, he looked sideways at Deymorin through his lashes. "So can I ask you something else?"

Deymorin gave a bark of laughter. "You imp. What now?"

"Why don't you like Khyel?"

"Why don't I—" A startled look flashed at him. "I like him well enough." And faded into something approaching wistful. "Hell, you nosy brat, I probably love him, he's my brother, after all. I just . . . I just don't much care for the factions he represents."

"What factions? He represents House Rhomandi."

"He's Anheliaa's front man."

"That's not fair."

"He pushes through any legislation she requests. Supports her every power-hungry move and ignores Outsider petitions."

"Is this about Khoratum again? Deymorin, that's over and done—"

"Khoratum was only the most obvious in an ongoing series of moves. Council has increasingly ignored Outside requests and needs, until now the simplest cross-ley road clearance is nearly impossible to obtain."

"And that's Khyel's fault?"

Deymorin's broad shoulders rose and fell in what might have been a shrug—or a sigh.

"He's the one in a position to stop it. And it's self-destructive. *That's* what I most don't understand, what . . . disturbs me. Khyel is many things, mostly damnably self-serving, but stupid isn't among them. If he's leading Council in this direction, it's for reasons I can't begin to fathom."

"Maybe he doesn't see it as self-destructive."

"He should."

"Why?"

Deymorin studied him, frowning.

"I need to know, Deymorin. I've a right to know, haven't I?"

Deymorin propped elbows on knees, and ran a hand across his face. "You're too young to remember how it was, Inside and Out before—"

"But I read, Deymio. *And* listen."

"Point to the bookworm. After Mother died, Father had to spend more time than ever in Rhomatum—"

"Why did Mother's death affect that?"

"Hah! My point that time, worm. She was Father's shadow proxy for years. She attended meetings and debates and handled all that gods-be-damned paperwork that—" Deymorin's lips pressed into a hard line, and he stared sightlessly, his color deepening beneath his tan.

"That Khyel handles for you?" Nikki finished softly.

Deymorin shrugged. "His choice, Nikki. It was always his choice. After Mother died, what had been unpleasant between Anheliaa and Father before turned into all-out daily warfare. Especially at dinner. I learned more over those dinner table 'debates' as they called them, than any library could possibly cover. They were both stubborn, pig-headed fools, but between them, there was nothing, no possible argument for either side, overlooked."

"And was Khyel at those dinners? Did Khyel hear those . . . debates?"

Deymorin shot him an enigmatic look. "That's the crux of the question, isn't it, worm? No, he wasn't. He ate in the nursery, avoiding the controversy."

"In the nursery. With me? I would have been there, wouldn't I? Maybe he wasn't avoiding anything. Maybe he didn't want to leave me all alone."

Deymorin's enigmatic look deepened. "The *point* is, he never heard those arguments, and when I was trying to make up my mind, when I wanted to discuss an issue with him, he—wasn't interested. If it was Father's arguments I repeated, he wouldn't even listen. After Father died . . . well, by the time Khoratum became an issue between us, Anheliaa had long since instilled her insidiously biased ideas firmly into his head."

"Why? What is it *Anheliaa* wants?"

"That, dear worm, is beyond my meager comprehension, but I strongly suspect she won't be content until she rules the world."

"That's silly, Deymorin."

"Is it?"

"She's too old. What would she *do* with it if she got it?"

Deymorin's grim look broke on a shout of laughter. "Oh, my dear worm, that's youth talking for certain. —It's the ultimate legacy. The greatest mark in history since Darius himself."

"But—" He blushed, thinking about his own, somewhat less ambitious, desires that afternoon in the library. Anheliaa wasn't the only one interested in leaving a . . . mark in history.

"She's obsessed with *something*, Nikki. She's been Rhomatum ringmaster longer than anyone since Darius himself, and in all that time, in her eyes, she has only one significant accomplishment: capping Khoratum. All her other petty little experiments mean nothing to her. They were all to accomplish that one, single goal. —And what did that gain her? Power. More power in a day than Rhomatum uses in a year. More power than the web uses. And from her comments tonight, I begin to suspect that her real goal is toppling Garetti."

"Garetti?"

"Or whoever happens to be in control in Mauritum when she decides to make her move. I think she wants to bring Mauritum to its knees, and she doesn't care who or what she sacrifices to do it."

"But Khyel—"

"Will back her, just like the Syndics back her, because if *she* wins, their coffers grow."

Nikki was silent a moment. It made sense, in a way, but:

"Khyel's four years younger than you, Deymio. Those years you spent listening to Anheliaa and Father around a private dinner table, he spent at Council meetings and public debates. He's grown up surrounded by that Council, Deymorin. He's never *known* anything else. *Won't* unless you explain to him."

"Do you think I haven't tried? He won't talk to me, boy. He listens only to Anheliaa these days."

"That's unfair, Deymorin."

"Is it? —Perhaps. But in Mikhyel's eyes, I'm a mindless wastrel, without the sense the gods granted a newt." And then a strange look crossed Deymorin's face.

"Deymio?"

Deymorin blinked, then, and with a wry laugh: "Sometimes, I think maybe he's right."

He said it like a joke, but drooping shoulders said otherwise.

Nikki reached a hand, hesitantly covered Deymorin's. "Deymio, sometimes . . . sometimes I think you don't understand him at all."

A faint smile, a gentle hand exploring his bruised face and cut lip. "And you do, little man?"

He frowned and pulled away from that exploring hand. "Stop it. I'm not a child anymore. —And I'm *not* talking about this stupid birthday. He *does* talk to me, Deymorin. And Khyel—he respects you, Deymorin, more than *anybody*. He . . ."

But he couldn't say what he wanted to say: that Khyel loved Deymorin as much as he did. He didn't know that was true. Couldn't. He only hoped.

"He what, boy?" Deymorin's voice had gone cold, as if he was intruding where he wasn't wanted.

But he had his own wants, and he was tired of Deymorin and Mikhyel fighting, tired of Mikhyel's temper and Deymorin's absences.

"He wants you to take your place on Council."

"Little chance of that." A distinct flush darkened Deymorin's face. Still, he seemed to relax, as if he'd thought Nikki was going to suggest something quite different. "I'd kill them all in an hour. I don't *do* negotiations. I can't *deal* with people bent on their own convenience above other people's necessity, and immediate capital gains over long-term economic vitality."

Nikki stared at the transfer papers, balanced between desire and pride, and . . . need.

"Here." He held the papers out. "I want a trade."

Deymorin looked hurt and confused, and ignored the papers.

"These—" He set the papers in Deymorin's lap. "For one day: tomorrow."

Confusion grew into a wary frown.

"Promise me you won't run off, that you won't let Khyel *run* you off, until we've had a chance to talk."

"We?"

"You. Me. Mikhyel."

Deymorin's chin lifted.

"Deymorin, I just . . . I love you. I love Khyel. Maybe that means I'm a fool, but I *want* us to . . . at least to *try*, Deymorin. Please?"

Deymorin frowned. Deymorin didn't like being forced into anything. Realizing suddenly he was risking everything—Deymorin's love, what family he *did* have . . . the horses . . . Nikki felt his resolve waver, and cried, before he could change his mind:

"I don't *want* horses, Deymorin. I *want* my *family*."

The frown deepened in the direction of the papers and Deymorin brushed them with nervous fingertips. Then he looked up, and the strain of embattled hurt and anger was almost more than Nikki could bear.

Almost. He lifted his chin, in his best imitation of Deymorin's own obstinate look.

"Deal?"

Deymorin's fingertips moved from the papers to his cheek, a gentle touch that traced his jawline. "Stubble. Dammit, fry, when did you get so old?"

He just bit his lip, afraid to look away. Afraid that if he did, Deymorin would escape.

Finally, Deymorin shook his head slowly. "No deal, Nik."

Nikki's heart sank.

"You keep the greys." A slow grin broke through the thunderclouds. "But somewhere in here, you've a stack of—what, ten, now? Eleven?—I.O.U.s. I'll stick around until . . . until, by the rings, you've got your family, if such a miracle is possible, or until you cry 'yield.' Then we'll call it even." He stuck out his hand. "Deal?"

Suddenly, the world seemed bright again.

"Deal." Nikki grasped the hand briefly, then, as the weight of anxiety lifted and fatigue set in hard, he reached for a not very adult hug and whispered in Deymorin's ear, "Thank you, Deymio. I'll take good care of them, I promise."

"See that you do, fry. And remember—" Deymorin pushed him back, eyeing him sternly. "The next time you run off at the mouth, it'll be *your* job alone to make good."

And somehow he was certain Deymorin wasn't speaking solely of the greys . . .

. . . any more than he was.

Chapter Six

Deymorin took the steps back to the salon one at a slow time. Nikki's deliberately calculated challenge had left him shaken, and he wanted time to gather his wits before facing Anheliaa and, especially, Mikhyel again.

Nikki's attitude toward their middle brother confused and disturbed him. He'd known Mikhyel had raised his hand to Nikki more than once over the years since Nikki had entered the difficult age of pubescence and beyond. (Never before, or Deymorin would have taken Nikki permanently to Darhaven and damn the consequences.) But Nikki had never shown the slightest fear of Mikhyel, indeed, he'd preferred, overall, to live in Rhomatum, and since Nikki had rapidly outsized citified Mikhyel, Deymorin had never really worried, never interfered.

Besides, so had Mheric struck *them*—himself and Mikhyel. They'd survived, and Mheric's hand had been infinitely heavier than Mikhyel's.

But this time . . . The boy had already been dangerously weakened, had been holding up bravely all evening. Mikhyel had had no right to raise so much as his voice; and Nikki had not only accepted the unwarranted chastisement, he begged now for some sort of reconciliation.

He wasn't sure he was ready for that. Wasn't sure the better choice still might not be to haul Nikki off to Darhaven—at least until the boy was independent enough to give Mikhyel back some of his own. But, for the sake of his promise—and for the sake of the glimpses he'd had tonight of the brother Mikhyel had once been—he'd hold his peace.

For now.

His leg having grown to a constant ache again, he stopped at the entry foyer to retrieve his cane. The sheath slipped as he pulled it from the stand, and as he refastened

the safety, he was forcibly reminded of the matter of the
attack on Nikki tonight. The more he thought on it, the
more convinced he was it wasn't a simple cutpurse, that it
had been aimed specifically at Nikki for reasons perhaps
dangerously unknown.

. . . Not from any city I know . . .

Unknown, at least to him. Definitely, Mikhyel needed
to know.

Tomorrow. Now did not seem the optimum moment to
bring the matter up. Better for them all to wait until Nikki
could get Mikhyel more receptive to reason.

He'd been a fool not to mention it earlier, had put his
own pride before Nikki's safety. If anyone could trace those
cutpurses down, Anheliaa could, that near-mythic power of
the rings being one of her true rumored abilities, and Khyel
was the one to convince her to commit the time. If Garetti
of Mauritum was getting nervous, and if strangers from one
of the Mauritum nodes were getting past the wall's gate-
posts and making attempts on Rhomatum citizenry, it could
put a whole new slant on further negotiations.

He'd make it part of this . . . talk . . . he'd promised the
boy. Put Khyel—and through Khyel, Anheliaa—wise to the
real implications of Nikki's evening escapade when Nikki
was there to avert all-out warfare, and maybe, just maybe,
they'd do something about it.

From the look Anheliaa cast him as he limped into the
room, Mikhyel had explained everything—from his own
unique perspective.

"Is what Mikhyel tells me the truth?" Anheliaa barked
before his foot cleared the door.

With his promise to Nikki still fresh in his mind, Deymorin set his teeth and muttered, "Close enough."

Mikhyel flashed an enigmatic look his way, but Deymorin
ignored it, and strangely, after that initial flare, Anheliaa
didn't seem angry. Her silver-haired head swung slowly
back and forth, and her face stretched in a disturbing,
vaguely obscene smile. "Never mind. Boys will be . . ." The
rest of the sentence floated into obscurity; she shook her
head as if to clear it, and continued: ". . . But that's why
I've taken steps . . . His age made me realize . . . It was to
be part of his birthday . . ."

"Anheliaa," he began, keeping a suspicious eye to Mikhyel, lest his civil query inspire yet one more attack on his neglected so-called responsibilities here in the City. "Is everything all right? Are *you* all right?"

"Time to get down to business ..." Having finished whatever line of thought she'd been following, Anheliaa blinked up at him somewhat dazedly. "Of course, Deymorin. Why wouldn't ..." She shook her head, and ordered, in a voice much more typical of the aunt he'd grown up with: "Help me, boys. I must get to the Tower. I've something to say, and it's better said there. —No, girl," she snapped at her mousy little attendant. "The boys are all I need, and Leanna will care for my needs later, as always. Go to bed. Off with you."

Not a thank you, not so much as a kind tone: typical Anheliaa. The mousy little female dipped in a mousy little curtsy, first to Anheliaa, then to Mikhyel, lastly to himself.

As she straightened, her eyes—her one significant feature, large and a gentle, warm brown—flickered over his face and settled rather anxiously on Nikki's empty chair, then travelled up toward the ceiling and back to him in a surprisingly clear question.

"He's fine," he said, smiling down at her, wondering was she mute or simply shy. When his reassurance failed to lift the anxious look from Miss Mouse's face, a wicked spark prompted him to say. "I'm sure he would appreciate a bit of Ceidin brandy to help him sleep. Why don't you take some by his room on your way to bed? Check him out for yourself."

"Deymorin!" Mikhyel's exclamation made the girl's eyes flicker like a startled deer's.

"Don't be silly, Khyel." Deymorin put a reassuring arm around the girl's shoulders, and walked her toward the door. "She's practically one of the family."

Mikhyel stepped in front of them, and pulled the girl free of his hold. "You don't even know her name, Deymorin. Leave her alone."

A wave of remorse hit him as he looked into her doe-soft eyes. Mikhyel was right. He didn't know the girl's name, didn't know a thing about her. He was using her for his humor, as cruel in his way as Anheliaa.

But below those doe-eyes her mouth was moving, a soundless communication directed only to him, and of a sudden he realized:

"Mirym, Khyel."

She smiled faintly, revealing, in that mischievous quirk of the lips, a second noticeable feature.

He grinned back. "Her name is Mirym." And meeting Mikhyel's angry gaze: "And I don't think she minded my suggestion at all."

A second of those faint smiles confirmed that notion, and he winked at her.

"Let her go, boys," Anheliaa said firmly. And to the girl, "Go, go, go. If you want to look in on the boy, do so. Tell him you're checking for me." She chuckled suddenly, a little-used grating sound, and sent a wicked look toward Mikhyel. "Just make certain to knock first."

Mirym bobbed again, and flitted from the room; Mikhyel, the color rising above his dark beard, closed the door silently behind her, the set of his narrow shoulders and his overlong delay at the door betraying the depth of his mortification.

Cruel of Anheliaa, to remind him of that particular night under these particular circumstances. —Almost as cruel as she'd been on the night in question; the night she'd quite deliberately thrown the door wide on Mikhyel and his birthday present.

Without knocking.

"How will she tell him anything?" Deymorin asked, to draw attention from Mikhyel's tense back. "*Can* she speak?"

"She has her ways." Anheliaa's smile widened; and Deymorin's skin crawled, never having had Anheliaa and such pleasant, earthy matters collide in the same thought before.

"And what about Nikaenor?" Mikhyel asked harshly, still with his hand clenched on the doorlatch, then he turned, shooting an accusatory gaze at Anheliaa. "What if Nikki doesn't *want* a strange girl mooning over him in his own bedroom?"

"Then he'd better enter the Harisham priesthood and wear a bag over his head, Mikhyel," Anheliaa hissed, which made him regard his aunt in a whole new light—something of an accomplishment after thirty years. "He's a handsome young man and had best learn to handle such situations. If . . ." her mouth twitched in a not-quite smile, ". . . he hasn't already. That *is* the whole point of tonight's fiasco, isn't it? Now . . ."

She tapped the chair wheels in silent command and Mikhyel obediently fell in behind her. As she rolled through the door and toward the Tower lift, she cackled again and said over her shoulder to Deymorin: "I *still* want to know which of you played the abducted virgin . . ."

Nikki closed his eyes and gritted his teeth and twisted the key another fraction . . .

It would be nice if he could get the guitar in tune. He was wide awake again, despite—or because of—Diorak's goo and wine and brothers, and he didn't want to think about Diorak or his brothers any more tonight, didn't want to read or think or do any of those other things one inevitably ended up doing when one was being ignored because one was supposed to be sick and falling asleep.

So if he could just get Barney in tune . . . just for a song or two. One couldn't think of brothers and stitches when one had to concentrate on one's fingers.

"C'mon, Barney, give me one—more—"

With a singularly appropriate *twang,* the string snapped.

"Shit." The word exploded out of him. Disgusted. Satisfactorily wicked . . .

And safe, here in his own room.

So he tried it again: "Shit. Shit shit shit *shit—*"

The entry bell chimed.

Shit.

Face burning, he set the guitar in its stand beside the bed, winced as the move strained stitches, and pulled the covers straight, praying it was Jerrik, or Deymorin . . . anyone but Mikhyel.

"Come," he said, relieved when his voice didn't break, more so when Jerrik opened the door.

But: "The lady's compliments, sir," Jerrik said, and stepped aside, making way for—

Smiling to mask his utter humiliation, Nikki said, "Hello, Mirym."

His voice squeaked.

Anheliaa's tiny attendant, anxious eyes barely visible over a large tray filled with a wine carafe, a glass and a huge slab of holiday-cake dripping with raspberry liqueur, dipped gingerly into a curtsy.

Keen to help, Nikki threw the covers to the side and swung his feet to the floor, but bare knees and a room that whirled madly reminded him *why* he was in bed at this hour, forcing him to concede and tuck his feet back under before he embarrassed himself further.

But once she'd safely negotiated the distance to the bedside table, Mirym's anxiety disappeared. She sighed in exaggerated relief, the first sound he'd ever heard out of her, as her triumphant grin was the first smile he recalled seeing on her face. Not even the nonsense with the presents had managed to lighten her perpetually somber expression.

An answering smile stretched his own face, and before he thought to stop him, Jerrik (the traitor) had closed the door again, leaving him alone with the strange young woman.

His face went stiff around the smile, and he stammered, "Miss Mirym, I must apologize . . . Why Jerrik let you carry that tray, I cannot imagine, but I'll . . ."

She patted his hand, then turned to the tray, and poured him a careful measure of brandy into the pewter goblet reserved for the evening's finale: the coming-of-age toast.

How appropriate a launch into his singularly empty future: a mute girl mouthing birthday blessings as she handed him the goblet as he lay on his sickbed.

He sighed and took a large gulp before asking: "Did–did you hear . . ."

Her grin widened.

"I—"

She tipped her head in gentle mockery, then cut a generous slice of cake and held out the plate to him, her composure reminding him suddenly of her mild reaction to Deymorin's comments at dinner. Relieved, secretly delighted, he chuckled and dipped his head, accepting the plate, playing her game quite willingly.

Giving the tray a quick survey, he asked, "Where's yours?"

Her head tipped again, this time in confusion.

"I see cake enough here for five, a carafe of wine, which I'm sure is far more than Diorak would want me to have, but only one fork, one plate, and one glass." On a sudden whimsical inspiration, he shouted: "—Jerrik!"

She jumped. Shook her head, mouthing *no,* reaching desperate little hands to stop him.

But he ignored her, except to pat *her* hand, and yelled again for Jerrik, ignoring the bell-pull, which Jerrik refused to answer anyway. This was his birthday, and he wanted a party. His own party with guests of his choosing.

Feeling suddenly quite merry, having sent Jerrik off to fetch glasses and plates for himself and Mirym, he pointed to a small package still resting on the tray. "Is that for me?"

Mirym stared at him for a moment, brown eyes narrowed and calculating. Then her expressive brows raised, her eyes widened innocently, and she shrugged.

Laughing, he held his hand out imperiously. "Well, we've a mystery, then, haven't we?" She handed it to him, and he turned it this way and that, pretending to look for a tag. "It's got flowers on it." He looked up at her, batting his eyelashes exaggeratedly. "Very pretty flowers, too. —Must be for you."

She blushed faintly, and pushed the package back at him, nodding to it and then to him.

"So it *is* for me."

She nodded.

"From whom, I wonder."

Her blush deepened, and all at once he wasn't in quite so teasing a mood.

"From you?" he asked softly; and at her shy nod, "Why thank you, Mistress Mirym. Thank you, very much."

The girl sat down on the edge of the wing chair's deeply-cushioned seat, her hands folded in her lap, her gaze following his every reaction. Suddenly self-conscious, he carefully freed the blossoms from the ribbon, setting them to float in the lemon-scented finger bowl, then peeled the gilt paper back.

"Strings!" He smiled in real delight, and recognizing the packaging: "Fredriri's! Wonderful. His are the best. How'd you know?"

She dipped her head shyly, then, in one fluid movement, brushed her ear, gestured toward himself, and then to the guitar.

"You heard me?"

She nodded.

"Lord, —*playing*? I hate to tell you, but that wretched sound had nothing to do with the age of the strings."

She shook her head, hiding a smile with that small, graceful hand, and glanced toward the ceiling.

"You heard me tell Aunt."

She nodded.

"Well, thank you. Thank you very much."

She shrugged. Then pointed again to the box.

"More?"

Another nod.

"Honestly, Mirym, you shouldn't ..." He lifted out a
layer of tissue and underneath found a guitar strap, hand-
stitched in an exquisite design of red flowers and grey
horses on a deep indigo background. He stared a moment,
open-mouthed, looked up to find those large eyes anxious
again.

And he thought of Anheliaa in the Tower and in the
sitting room, and her silent brown shadow, always with her
needlework, something different at each station about the
house, which he'd never bothered to notice, nor anyone
else to his knowledge, and in which she took an obvious
pride.

"You made this yourself?"

This time, the quick dip of the head was unquestionably shy.

"Mirym, I–I don't know what to say. It's—"

A knock rescued him: Jerrik, with a second tray, and he
found refuge in the wine, the cake and Jerrik's familiar,
cheerful presence.

The earliest Tower lift had been servant-powered: one
stout man whose sole purpose in life had been winding the
wheel that turned the gears. The modern platform operated
on steam from the boilers buried deep within the leythium
mines, and, for access to the ringchamber itself, a lock dependent upon Anheliaa's own mind.

Beyond the lift's bentwood safety-grill, a stairwell of ancient stone, sole remnant of the original Tower, entwined
this modern convenience in stately elegance. It was the
means by which most mortals traversed the Tower floors.

Not so Anheliaa; not even when she was physically able;
in recent years, this lift had become the only real access to
the ringchamber—excepting the Guards' emergency
hatch—a precaution Anheliaa had deemed vital ever since
two small boys snuck up and fouled her precious rings.

For his part, Deymorin was just happy to balance on one leg and the cane and let steam do all the work.

Past Anheliaa's private apartments, past the communication levels where single-ring technicians, each linked to a different node, sat in isolated cells sending and receiving encoded information, and finally past the Tower Guard floor to the ringchamber itself.

As the platform rose into the chamber, flickers of green and gold, bright red and green-blue leapt and pattered over and around each other, scattering from the rising grillwork.

Lizards. The ubiquitous pets of the City.

Mikhyel, with the sure touch of experience, geared the lift to a smooth halt, set the anchor pin, and opened the grill, all without a word. Likewise silent, Deymorin pushed Anheliaa's chair into the glass-enclosed room.

A man in Tower Guard blacks stood at attention outside the lift door, dipped his head at Anheliaa's signal, and took their place inside the lift. Then, with a wheeze of escaping steam, a condensing puff of venting air drifting spiritlike outside the windows, the lift sank slowly back into the floor until its ceiling became an indistinguishable part of the floor's tile pattern.

Presumably, the guard would remain on that lift indefinitely, awaiting Anheliaa's pleasure. And sealing them in here with her. How utterly lovely.

Keeping his back pointedly to the centrally-placed rings on which Mikhyel and Anheliaa set such importance, Deymorin made a slow turn about the chamber. He couldn't remember when he'd last entered this sanctuary for the rings of Rhomatum—possibly not since that time Mikhyel had recalled for him earlier. Whenever it was, he'd been somewhat shorter at the time. And with a child's lack of true appreciation.

This clear-sided marvel was more to be admired than feared, the furnishings of wood, gold, and crystal (all ley-inert materials) were elegant, if somewhat spindly and ornate, in keeping with Anheliaa's aesthetic taste, and a small stone waterfall and pool, a ... lizard-salon, added a welcome natural counterpoint to the otherwise unnatural setting.

He moved closer to the high, arched windows and gold-leafed sill. Directly below, the rose garden fountain sparkled in constantly shifting moonlit patterns that were lovely enough from ground level, but which were obviously designed for viewing from this vantage. Gravel walkways and courtyards glowed about the Tower complex. Beyond the Tower wall, the roofs of the City expanded outward, concentric rings of ice-blue tiles, the silver-lit leys forming eighteen not-quite-even, not-quite-straight spokes.

Lights stopped abruptly at the old wall, resumed to the new, that double demarcation the visible artifact of the damned Khoratum addition—more shops, more housing, and two incredibly expensive private gardens.

The lighted leylines extended beyond the City palisade, cutting through night-dark fields until they disappeared into the forests and foothills. One, the newest and brightest, extended toward distant Khoratum, where yet another storm was in full flower.

Even as he watched, a streak of lightning arced overhead, *over* Rhomatum itself, paralleled that Khoratum line, and struck dangerously near Khoratum peak.

No wonder Anheliaa had been distracted all night.

"Deymorin!"

Mikhyel's voice, demanding his attention. He blinked himself back into the ringchamber, where Khyel was trying to help Anheliaa make the transition between her chair and the adjustable console couch that provided the only substantial piece of furniture in this otherwise spindly-furnished room.

He set the cane down on the sill and crossed to Mikhyel's side, but Anheliaa cursed them equally and waved them away. Edging across in her own manner, she settled herself into the cushions with audible groans of relief, somehow managing at once to assert her independence and make them feel like incompetent boors.

Or at least he did. Mikhyel's blank face lent no clue to his thoughts. Whatever renewed brotherly relations *he* might have sensed below vanished in this, Anheliaa's realm.

Anheliaa leaned back into the cushions, eyes closed, while the sectional couch slowly contorted, configuring to her express needs.

He'd helped his father build that couch, years ago. Even then, Anheliaa had spent most of her waking hours in this room and the chairs she had had 'made her old bones ache,' so her nephew, his father, had spent weeks designing and building a couch that, within the confines of this room, could respond to her every wish.

At the time, he hadn't wondered at the strangeness, hadn't wondered why someone of his father's importance had undertaken such a menial task, or even at the chair's engineering. By his way of thinking at the time, Family did things like that for each other, out of a strange thing called love.

Like the rocking horse he'd made for his new brother the day he'd learned to pound nails. Of course, baby Khyel had taken some exception to the gift when it collapsed underneath him, but Mama had always insisted it was the thought that counted, and his thoughts had been utterly pure.

Well, mostly. Pure thoughts hadn't stopped him from laughing at baby Khyel's indignity.

Now, he wasn't so certain. He knew now that no one came into the Tower who wasn't cleared by Anheliaa first—rarely anyone not directly related or a member of her personal retinue.

Ex-clu-sivity. Control. Anheliaa's hallmarks.

On the other hand, one had to admit, who had instigated that long-ago infiltration of the precious room, perhaps her act had been sheer self-defense against childish pranks.

"Don't hover." Anheliaa waved her hands irritably at the room in general. "You're spoiling my concentration."

He stationed himself gingerly on the only other marginally sturdy piece of furniture in the room: an exceedingly uncomfortable footstool. Mikhyel, more daring (and thirty pounds lighter), settled into one of the spidery chairs, and crossed one elegantly tailored leg over the other.

Flaunting his comfort, damn his grey eyes.

Or damn Nikki's blue ones.

As Nikki had pointed out, the Tower and City politics were their middle brother's life. He couldn't blame Mikhyel for feeling at ease in this place. If the Tower and the rings disturbed *him*, it was a direct result of his willful, lifelong avoidance of the place, and that was his own choice, no one else's doing.

Thanks for the insight, little brother, he thought rather sourly.

In the perfect, geometric center of the room, where memory and knowledge placed the rings themselves, a shimmer filled the space between floor and ceiling. That shimmer was definitely *not* a part of his memory of this place, and he found that difference uncomfortable in its implications.

For two generations, Anheliaa had been free to experiment with the Rhomatum rings without a check rein, so long as the power-flow continued uninterrupted, and experiment she had, without, following Mheric's death, benefit of backup, lacking even an apprentice to attend the rings as she slept. A confidence—or arrogance—only the Rhomatum ringmaster could afford.

As he'd told Nikki, he believed Anheliaa to have had one end only in mind, but this shimmering barrier, a side benefit Anheliaa would undoubtedly consider a parlor trick was, like the mental locks on this room, disturbing to any sane man.

And Khyel spent all day, every day, in Anheliaa's disturbing company.

Of a sudden, the shimmer evaporated, and Deymorin felt a slightly off-target *déjà vu*. The rings he recalled filled his mind's eye, to the periphery and beyond, but while this gently swaying silver structure unquestionably dominated the room, the Cardinal Ring was only slightly taller than he.

Most Cityborn children asked their parents how the lights worked and got Tamshi stories of magic and strange creatures, and underground rivers of light—and the Rhomatum rings. Few ever saw the real thing, only the enormous duplicates in outdoor stadiums erected for festival dances. Or the miniature versions: the clocks that ran the city and every citizen's life, whose cardinal ring (properly aligned, of course) synchronized with the Rhomatum Cardinal, kept everyone in absolute synchronicity.

Rhomandi children, on the other hand, learned about The Rings. For Rhomandi children, there could be no romance, no mystery. He'd been taught the leystream was a source of power, tappable as the power of an Outside water stream was tappable to turn a grinding wheel. At six, he'd been taken on a tour of the original mines, where the natural ley still struggled, the crystals regrowing with painful deliberation that which had been stripped away.

And he'd seen the growth chambers, where humanity provided ideal conditions for leythium seed crystals to mature into the tiny webs used in the bulbs and heaters. Web-filled lights glowed when aligned with that stream; web-filled heaters that likewise tapped that powerstream created the lift for the floaters, the heat for giant boilers that provided steam to kitchens for cooking and heating or to the pipe organ in the ringstadium.

But those were recognizable, understandable phenomena. These solid rings of silver and leythium alloy, each several times the weight of a man, floating freely in that powerstream, defied logic, and made a practical man . . . ill at ease.

Even less logical was their slow change of momentum until the chaotic swings became orbits, taking on a peculiar rhythm, a rhythm you sensed, but could not define . . .

Until only the radical streamer, warping and stretching its mysteriously unpredictable course in and around the other rings, made, in its very irrationality, any sense whatsoever.

Ah, that's better," Anheliaa said, sounding—abruptly— stronger, clear-headed.

Spooky, that's what he called it, this symbiotic relationship between the rings and their master. A relationship he wanted nothing to do with, thank you anyway, brother Mikhyel.

On the other hand, as frail as Anheliaa had appeared at dinner, this disturbing symbiosis might be all that kept her going these days. Despite the disbelief of the Pwerenettis of the City, Khoratum had cost her dearly, the capping itself leaving her in a comatose state for three months. According to Diorak, only the rings had kept her alive during that crisis.

Personally, he would wager it was Anheliaa's own perverse nature.

"Well, hello there," Anheliaa said softly, and leaned over, stretching a hand to the floor.

A small green and gold streak flitted up her sleeve to perch expectantly on the chair arm, its tiny reptilian tongue flickering in and out, tasting the air.

"And where are your friends?" she asked conversationally, and reached again, this time for a container sitting conveniently on a side table. She dipped a finger, stiff and crooked with arthritis, lifted it covered with a red paste that flickering tongue seemed to find delicious.

As if in response to a silent alert, several more tiny heads appeared from the fountain's stony recesses.

He resented her deliberate enticement of the lizards, as he resented this venue. He'd learned the year his voice changed the City's lizards were not for him. His tones were evidently too deep, too resonant for their ... delicate sensibilities.

Anheliaa wanted to keep him quiet and off-balance.

Two other creatures had joined the first, possibly a dozen more roamed the room at will. Leypower attracted bugs, one of its less romantic aspects, in particular, a rather nasty little spider these creatures favored. As a consequence, and since static-generating fur—alive or otherwise—was legally banned from all but the outermost sections of the City, these tiny reptiles had become more common than flies in a barn.

In areas of the City where rats were a problem, they cultivated snakes.

Ten foot long snakes.

Tiny feet skittered over his hand and up his arm, and launched a tiny body from his head over to Anheliaa's chair.

He preferred the snakes.

"Nikki's birthday has forced me to face my own mortality," Anheliaa said, in that same gentle voice she used to the lizards. "I can no longer put off the question of my successor."

"Planning on leaving us soon?" Mikhyel asked, his voice carrying a teasing lightness he had heard Mikhyel use only to Anheliaa. He'd never questioned that difference, had always assumed Mikhyel simply *liked* Anheliaa's acerbic company. Now (*Thanks ever so, Nikki-lad.*) one had to wonder if that lightness hid a very real concern for the future of the City, or even, considering Anheliaa's actions at dinner, a gut-deep fear of upsetting Anheliaa.

"Well, no." Three tongues gathered about Anheliaa's finger, flicking the paste away a granule at a time. She chuckled softly. "But I tire quickly these days. I'd hoped Nikaenor would prove proficient, but ..." She shrugged. And winced. "Even with Talent, a real master requires time to mature, and I've decided I can wait no longer to locate a meaningful apprentice."

Mikhyel's grey eyes turned to him expectantly. Waiting, undoubtedly, for him to leap up and declare himself and his mythical Talent. Well, Mikhyel had a long wait coming;

personally, he did *not* give a damn *who* replaced the woman, as Anheliaa well knew, and Mikhyel, by now, should.

Anheliaa's announcement did, however, make a man wonder if Mikhyel hadn't known about this meeting all along—wonder if he had staged that business before the party precisely *because* this meeting was scheduled.

He returned a senior-brotherly *dare you to say anything,* raised-brow challenge. A challenge the disappointment he sensed in his brother's eyes in one blink made him regret in the next.

But the moment had passed, the look was gone, and Mikhyel was asking Anheliaa soberly, "None of the monitors have shown promise, then?"

"The web won't disintegrate because Anheliaa Rhomandi dunMoren passes from it, if that's what you're worried about," she said dryly.

Mikhyel made a sound of protest, swallowed it at her lifted finger.

"If not, you should be. You take too much for granted, Mikhyel. I've six aides who cover for me at need, and there are eighteen monitors running shifts below us, and three times that number on inter-tower communications below them. Any half-competent controller can keep Rhomatum attuned to the leys now; with Khoratum capped—" She threw an archly triumphant look past Mikhyel to him. "—it practically monitors itself, and storms slide right past the Zone. But I intend to leave a worthier legacy than that. I built Rhomatum Tower into more than a simple leystation, and I *won't* allow it to wither into mediocrity."

Another flickering glance from Mikhyel. "Does this sudden urgency have anything to do with those messages we've been getting out of Mauritum?"

Anheliaa said, showing none of Mikhyel's reticence, "Garetti is an irritant, nothing more. He resents my capping of Khoratum. Likes to claim it undermines his available power—claims that's why he can't give his people all we have. Says we've used it to force them into the trade agreement."

"Why doesn't he simply disconnect the Rhomatum connection, then?" Deymorin asked, keeping his voice low for the damned lizard's sake.

"He's already got one radical line he can't possibly cap—

not unless he learns to breathe saltwater," Mikhyel explained, his voice lacking the contempt it usually conveyed on such occasions. "If he releases Rhomatum, it means releasing Persitum node. He won't affect us to speak of, Persitum node would still be capped and allied only with us, but creating a second uncapped node would cut Mauritum's power in half, since Persitum is the complement of the radical node."

"Don't bother, Mikhyel, dear," Anheliaa sneered. "Your brother is incapable of understanding."

Mikhyel's cool glance drifted from Anheliaa to him, expecting some sort of rebuttal, but Anheliaa could insult him all she wanted. She was, after all, the one who had invoked the lizards, thus setting the parameters. He might even surprise her and abide by those rules, say nothing, and get out of here without argument.

"*Is* it our doing?" Mikhyel asked her, finally. "Has he *any* legal stance whatsoever?"

Anheliaa sniffed. "Mostly, the man lacks Talent. But the fact is, even if he could successfully manipulate that much ley, it would require more power than Mauritum node can supply—power he'd have to get from Rhomatum, and he doesn't want to pay for it."

"And if he decides to come and take what he doesn't want to pay for?" Deymorin asked, regretting anew missing his earlier opportunity to discuss Nikki's attack with Mikhyel in private.

A faint smirk played over Anheliaa's lips.

"That is a concern, of course. It would be difficult, but not impossible, once I'm gone. Too many unsuccessful, but marginally competent and thus purchasable, trainees who could be placed in control here, however disastrously for *our* web. As I said, Rhomatum is virtually monitor free for normal use. I'd like to see stronger ties between Rhomatum and our satellite nodes—something more permanent than economic ones. We've grown far too insular in the past century. . . . But I get ahead of myself. I've been searching for an apprentice."

"Searching?"

A regal tilt of her bewigged head toward the rings. "I've located possibilities. Several of them female and quite personable."

Mikhyel blinked and shook his head confusedly. "Female? Why is that significant?"

"I also want to assure the line before I die," Anheliaa explained, delicately, for her.

"Assure it *how*?" Deymorin, unlike his naive brother, had no doubt as to her meaning and meant to force her to say it outright.

The lizards flitted over Anheliaa's arm and out of sight. She swore softly, then raised a disapproving brow at him, making him feel like a recalcitrant child.

He started mumbling an apology, caught himself and repeated the question instead. But she'd won a round, making him feel that way, and her faint smirk reflected that victory. "After all your practice? Mheric's son, I'm ashamed of you." And in a sudden, all-business turning: "Now, I've been searching, and the rings have conjured any number of likely prospects . . ."

"Pros–pects?" Mikhyel repeated softly.

Deymorin glanced toward his brother, seeking outrage to match his own, but Mikhyel's face displayed only studious interest and puzzled curiosity.

"What she's saying is," he said, ruthlessly clarifying for his biologically backward brother, "we're to set up a stud service."

"Deymorin!"

His backward brother picked the damnedest times to take offense.

"Wake up, Khyel. No verbal dressing will change what she's proposing."

"I'm suggesting—" Anheliaa remained the picture of serenity, not even going through the motions of considering their feelings, or of granting them a choice in the matter. "—you get married and see to your civic responsibility."

"Civic—?" He choked on surprised laughter. "Is that what they're calling it these days?"

"Deymio," Mikhyel broke in softly, his reaction masked behind lowered eyes, "Let her finish."

But his voice was unsteady, a point he was damned Anheliaa would make off *him*.

"Hell, brother, I've done my—responsibility. Long since."

"She means legitimately."

"I've acknowledged them."

"Them?" Anheliaa asked, with some interest—the first she'd expressed in his affairs in years. He responded with bitter lightness:

"A boy and a girl. Their mothers are quite happy, thank you. Married, now, and doing fine."

"Where?"

"I'm taking care of them, thanks all the same," he said coldly, wanting none of her interference in his children's upbringing.

"I don't mean now. I mean where were they conceived?"

"Anheliaa, *really*—" His brother's face had gone bright red and Deymorin, having no real desire to embarrass Mikhyel, prepared to drop the subject.

"Hush, Mikhyel." Anheliaa had no such reservations. "It's important. —Deymorin?"

He laughed harshly. "I really couldn't tell you."

"Frequent meetings, then?"

"Very," he answered dryly, and in a stage whisper to Mikhyel: "Patience, brother, I'm beginning to perceive a warped humor here."

"I had no idea." Anheliaa was paying little attention to them, staring instead at her gods-be-damned rings. "Any possibility they were conceived here?"

"In the City?"

"In the Tower."

"Oh, well. Sorry, Auntie Liaa, dear. None whatsoever."

The intensity vanished. She waved a hand in dismissal and sat back in her chair. "They are of no consequence, then."

"Charming, Aunt. I thought you wanted grandchildren— or whatever our offspring will be to you."

"Not at all. I want an *heir*. Quite a different thing. And it must be conceived within this Tower, on women of Shatum or Giephaetum Nodes."

"What?" This time, he laughed in genuine amusement. "I've a friend you simply *must* meet, Anheliaa. Crazy old loon, and he breeds terrible horses, but you'd *love* comparing breeding theor—"

"Don't mock me, boy. I believe—no, more than that, I'm quite *certain* conception is the key."

Her face took on a passionate glow; behind her, the central ring's spin-rate increased.

"*I* was, you see. Your father, both of you, were conceived

elsewhere. Nikki, at least, started within the City, but Mheric had that wife of his off in the mountains, totally away from ley influence, when *you* happened, and look how you turned out. We were all born within the Tower— excepting Nikki, of course, which could account for *his* inability. According to tradition *that's* the critical factor—yet none of you are even remotely facile with the rings. Not that I would neglect that; it could well be significant, and I do think the proximity of and similarities between Shatum and Giephaetum Nodes can't be ignored, thus the ladies must come from there ... or, of course, Rhomatum, but that would defeat our other purpose."

"In other words," he interrupted abruptly, "we are to take part in a biological experiment in order—possibly—to provide you with a proper ringmaster *and* a comfy political alliance, at once legitimate and functional. How romantic, Aunt. And efficient, too."

The passion dimmed to cold practically; the silver blur of the central ring gained shape and a regular beat. "Romance is hardly a necessary aspect of marriage, certainly not of offspring production, and when it does enter in, it usually interferes with rather than promotes a healthy Family. Just look at what happened to your own parents. They'd have been far better off to be more friends and less lovers."

"Mother died in childbirth, Father in a fit of temper."

"Grief."

"*I* was there, woman. *I* know. *I* took the back of his hand, one last time. *I* heard him berate my dead mother for leaving him with three ungrateful brats, one last time. And then I saw him push a fine horse too hard one time too many—*that's* what killed him, not this mythical pining for Mother."

"Deymorin, please," Mikhyel interrupted, and the unexpected pain in that quiet plea proved more effective at cooling his temper than any blow.

Deymorin bit his lip, shutting off the flow of bitterness.

With a slight nod, Mikhyel asked, "Liaa, are you certain this is the only way?"

"For the love of Darius, Khyel, you're not seriously considering—"

"*Please,* brother, for once *listen* first. —Anheliaa, there's more to this than you're saying. You've run three apprentices out already. Why?"

"You weren't interested."

"I wasn't *what*?"

"Actually, neither of you were. While they were possibly Talented enough, someone with the talent and the desire to replace me isn't enough. I need someone to act as a repository for everything I've learned until the child I've foreseen comes to power."

"Foreseen?" Deymorin repeated slowly, an ominous suspicion growing in his mind.

"Yes, Deymorin," she said, all triumph and eagerness now, "I've conquered time with the rings. I *can* predict the future."

He laughed harshly. Here it was at last. Proof positive. The rings had warped all their minds. "And you sat there while Mikhyel chastised Nikki."

"I'm no charlatan, boy. I know what I'm doing. There *will* be a child, the ninth generation of Darius on a nineley node, and that child *will* be a ringmaster such as the world has never known."

"Really?" he sneered. "Boy? or girl?"

"I—don't know."

"Perhaps Tamshirin?"

"It was human."

"Well, that's a relief. I'd hate to be crossed with something else. —Give over, Aunt. It was a dream. A nightmare, if you want my opinion, which likely you don't, but I'll give it to you anyway. You want grandchildren, tell *him*—" With a jerk of his head toward Mikhyel. "—to get to work on figures that have nothing to do with numbers and leave Nikki alone—*he's* getting along just fine. You have to lay your bets and take your chances like everyone else, Anheliaa. Every good breeder knows, you can breed two champions and get a slug, and two mediocre parents can create singular perfection. You can better your odds with controlled breeding, but nothing—*nothing*—is a sure thing—and certainly not in humans who have the spiritual capacity to expand beyond innate talent."

"Or ignore it," Mikhyel murmured.

"Deymorin, sit down and lower your voice; you're scaring Ohtee."

"*Forget the damn lizard!* I'm talking about my *life*, woman. And Nikki's. If Mikhyel wants to go along with your crazy notions—Rings! let him, I don't give a damn. Give him the whole fucking Estate for a wedding pres—"

Pressure inside his head. Pressure that sent him to his knees with the pain, hands clasped to his ears. A buzz that might be in his head, and might be the rings, whose gentle rotations had accelerated to a silver blur against the night sky.

It was Anheliaa causing that pressure; he knew that as surely as if she'd said it—could almost *hear* her voice ordering capitulation. Anger filled him, and he fought that pressure blindly, saw a break in the silver blur and laughed, hard and bitterly, as if that sound alone could further disrupt the blur.

He felt the pressure waver, saw lightning flash in the distance, or perhaps it was a ring or two as separate edges within the blur, and forced himself to his feet. There were hands on him, pulling—Mikhyel. He tried to thrust his brother away, but Mikhyel held firm: support, that was all, and he clung to it blindly, then, and heard Mikhyel shout: *Dammit, Anheliaa, stop!*

Alliance from Mikhyel. That confused him. His anger wavered. The rings blurred; the pressure increased . . . .

"Anheliaa," Mikhyel again, softly this time and at a distance. And Mikhyel's support had vanished. "Release him, Aunt, or I will." And a moment later: "So help me, I'll do it—and to hell with the consequences."

The pain stopped—so abruptly, he staggered, and would have fallen again had not Mikhyel's arm caught and steadied him.

"You're a fool, Mikhyel," Anheliaa's voice said.

He felt Mikhyel shrug, felt pressure behind his knees and sat, his eyes clearing on Mikhyel, settling again in his spindle-legged chair.

"You'd have lost the arm," Anheliaa said, cold and uncaring.

"I'd have stopped you." Without a tremor.

And then he realized—which realization sent sickness rising in his throat—Mikhyel had threatened the rings. A touch of a hand would have sufficed, but at the speed they'd been spinning . . .

"Rings, Khyel," he said, his voice coming out a thin croak, "I didn't know you cared."

Mikhyel glanced at him, lips tightened into an unreadable

line. Then, he looked away. "She was angry—as you were.
I knew she wouldn't risk the rings. Not for simple pique."
Another undecipherable glance. "Neither would you. Now will
you hear her out?"

"Brother," he said carefully, "Much as I appreciate your
thoughtfulness, nothing—I repeat, *nothing*—will induce me
to accept a wife of that female's choosing."

"Nothing?" Palpable anger again filled the room, the
rings began to swing.

Mikhyel cursed softly, and dropped his head into his
hand.

Ignoring him, he shouted, over the rings' shrieking hum:
"Nothing! I'd rather a common shepherd's daughter."

"Then you shall have your wish!"

And the silver blur expanded, consuming the room, the
stars overhead, and somewhere—a lonely, human sound
within the hum of the rings—he heard his brother call his
name.

Interlude

"Mother?"

Dancer called out before the shimmer of transfer had dissipated. An elbow stung, warning of careless coverage.

"Mother?" Dancer called again and staggered to a leythium pool, haphazardly anointing the elbow before running into the chamber where the inner Sense professed Mother to be. A small antechamber to the world-cavern, a recent budding Dancer had never before entered.

And she was there, calmly watching a pattern forming in the veil; a pattern that was the source of the disturbance that had reached all the way to Dancer's surface bedroom and into Dancer's disturbed, kaleidoscopic dreams; a pull so strong, it forced transfer, unthinking and half-asleep, and inadequately oiled.

A pull so terrifyingly insistent in this pattern's presence it constricted Dancer's throat, making it nearly impossible to ask:

"Mother, what have you done?"

A calm turn. A glow of satisfied purple illuminating the new veil.

{What had to be.}

He was falling.

Father's laughter rang in his ears. "Balance, fool! Expect the unexpected."

Rule number one: Never anticipate. Never lean into a jump ... lead with your chin ... parry a blade not yet committed ... or pressure a woman.

Horse, man or woman: which had outsmarted him this time?

SECTION TWO

SECTION
TWO

Chapter One

"He left last night, Nikki."

"L–left?"

Mikhyel pushed the heavy drape aside and stared out the window and across the sun-gilded rooftops of Rhomatum, needing the bright light, as he needed the hard wood of the window seat pressing into his back and legs to keep him alert and focussed on the difficult conversation that lay ahead.

"Without saying good-bye?" Confusion. Betrayal. Understandable in a sick child awakened too early from fevered dreams.

He answered with a noncommittal shrug. *Coward,* he accused himself, but he could think of no words to explain Deymorin's absence that wouldn't send Nikki off in a blind rage. He needed time. Time to explain, time to think ... to plan.

Time fate wasn't likely to grant him. Fate had given him last night, and he'd wasted it all, staring at Deymorin's empty bed, his mind numb and blank.

The drape fell, shutting out all but a single shaft of the morning sunlight. That single band of brilliance split the room in half, cutting a vision-hazing swath between his windowseat and Nikki's bed.

"Where'd he go?" Nikki pursued. "Darhaven?"

He lifted a hand from his knee. Helplessly.

Coward—perhaps. But he'd never deliberately lied to the boy before. Found it nearly impossible to do so now. But if he told Nikki the truth ...

"Damn him!" Nikki's light voice broke, but not for normal, pubescent reasons.

Disappointment. Betrayal. He'd expected both, but aimed at himself, not Deymorin.

"He *promised* me he wouldn't!" Nikki exclaimed, and a soft *fwoosh* that might be a fist burying itself in a pillow.

"Wouldn't what, Nikki?" he asked over his shoulder.

"*Leave,* may Darius curse his hypocritical tongue."

Mikhyel flinched, safely obscure behind the sunbeam. Unfair, considering. But Nikki couldn't know that consideration. Not today. Perhaps never. Better, perhaps, for him to feel himself deserted. It wouldn't be the first time, and was a safer interpretation than other options.

He drew a resolute breath and at last shifted around on the window seat.

Nikki, hair tumbling wildly about his shoulders, eyes red-rimmed and puffy, was struggling to sit up. Mikhyel crossed the light beam to steady his brother, adjusting pillows to prop him upright.

"All right?" he asked, laying his hand lightly on Nikki's shoulder, unable to resist a momentarily overwhelming need for solid reassurance of this brother's presence.

Nikki nodded, but grasped his wrist when he would have moved away again.

"Please, Khyel, sit here." Nikki released him and patted the bed. "I—" He chuckled ruefully, sweeping his hair back, and giving bloodshot eyes a vigorous rub. "—can't see that far this morning."

He settled where Nikki asked, because Nikki asked, yet not certain he really wanted to be that close, distrusting his own thespian talents.

"Good time last night?" he asked.

Nikki started to nod, apparently thought better of it and settled for: "I—think so."

Mikhyel picked up the decanter, sniffed and raised his brows, but said nothing. Going to tilt the ring, might as well do it on quality. And, casting a marked glance at the tray: "Company?"

"I—" Nikki's eyes closed as if he were pained—or distracted—by the light. "Uh, Jerrik. I invited Jerrik to stay. And ..." His brow puckered with effort. "F–Flowers ..." He blinked in the direction of his guitar, whose top string waved softly in the breeze from the window. "Strings. Aunt's maid ..."

"Mirym?" he supplied, already knowing the answer, and hoping he was wrong. But:

"That's her name, thanks. Nice girl. Gave me a present.

Guitar strings. Nice of her." Nikki's voice faded; his face turned wistful.

So, a present. Strings. Nice girl. A brother could relax on that score.

"He must have said something, Khyel. *Done* something, before he left."

Deymorin again.

Mikhyel clenched his teeth.

"Did you two fight?"

He brushed last night's party crumbs off the sheets and into his hand and wiped them onto the tray, not so much avoiding Nikki's eyes as just not meeting them.

"We always fight, Nikki, nothing new about that."

"But this time it was about me. And Tirise's."

A light touch to his wrist forced him to look up.

"Wasn't it?"

There was a bruise on the rounded cheek. He'd put it there, with a hand made heavier by the very control he'd exercised all night. He'd struck a sick boy out of fear, fear of the flux he felt, the shifting of power that might eliminate him forever.

Or include him. He wasn't altogether certain which was the more terrifying possibility.

"Khyel?"

"Only indirectly."

"My doing, Khyel. Not his. All my fault."

"It *wasn't* the brothel, boy." He only wished it were that simple.

"Then why are you being so evasive? What happened, Khyel? Where'd he go?" And a bit plaintively: "Why?"

(Deymorin's clothing lying in a pile in the middle of the Tower room.

Empty.

"Where is he, Aunt? Where'd you send him?"

"I've no idea . . .")

Anheliaa's look had frightened him, more even than his brother's clothes, suddenly bereft of support, crumpling to the floor. He'd seen men disappear from that room before; he'd never seen that look. Cold. Uncaring. —Triumphant.

Anheliaa had evinced more interest in the criminals she had similarly exiled than for her own nephew—she'd at least been curious where they'd been thrown.

He hadn't challenged Anheliaa further. Hadn't dared,

lest she send him after Deymorin. Now, he felt the coward
for that failure. He should tell Nikki what had happened,
warn him against Anheliaa's encroaching insanity. But he
feared Nikki, in blind love for Deymorin, would pursue the
issue and damn the consequences.

"Khyel?"

"He just—left, Nikki, that's all. Anheliaa made a request
and he . . . needed time to think about it, I suppose."

"What kind of request?"

"Actually, she made it of all of us." He shifted about on
the mattress. The shaft of sunlight burst over his shoulder;
Nikki winced as it struck him full in the face. "Too bright?"
He stood up, eager to restore distance between them.
"Would you like the drapes—"

"It's fine, Khyel." Again Nikki's hand grasped his, a surprisingly strong grasp that belied his seeming infirmity.
"Please, what did Anheliaa want?"

Short of hurting Nikki, he couldn't break that hold. He
sank reluctantly back to the mattress.

"She's feeling her age, Nikki." That, at least, was truth.
"She wants to leave the rings in good hands. She's found
likely candidates, but she thinks it would be best if they
were part of the family, so to speak."

"So to . . . I don't understand."

"You must understand, Nikaenor, she wouldn't ask this
if it weren't important. *Very* important."

"Ask what, Khyel?"

"She's found a number of young ladies—through the
rings, you understand—that would make suitable—even
outstanding—"

"Wives, Khyel? Is that what you're trying to say?"

"Well, uh, yes. I—"

"I'm not nearly so naive as you and Deymorin would
have me," Nikki continued earnestly. "If Aunt Liaa thinks
they're suitable . . . well, I suppose it's as good a reason to
marry as any. Though I had hoped . . ."

Nikki's eyes dropped, his shoulders heaved, and Mikhyel
could well imagine the essence of that wish. Nikki, the romantic, had wanted to marry for Love, the sort of Love
the poets eulogized. And because *his* fondest dream had
always been to see Nikki happily established, he wished he
dared counsel against Anheliaa's tyrannical plan.

But he didn't dare. To counsel against Anheliaa was to

risk exile or worse. Besides, he had no right to counsel anyone. Not any more.

Nikki sighed again, then asked, "What was Deymorin's problem?"

"You need to ask?"

"Not really." Nikki's finger dug through a hole in the crocheted bedspread. "I just wish I'd had a chance to . . ." His eyes slipped around to the bedside table, where the transfer papers Deymorin had given Nikki last night were propped against a lamp. "He's not stupid, just stubborn. He knows how important these things are."

"Of course he does, Nikki." Amazing how easily the lies came once begun. "I'm certain he'll come back as soon as he's had a chance to think about it."

Nikki's forlorn little laugh suggested Nikki believed that about as much as he did, though for vastly differing reasons.

But Nikki's eyes at least were clear when they shifted from the bedtable to meet his.

"So," Nikki said, with forced cheerfulness. "What about the girls Aunt has conjured up? Are they pretty?"

"And then, m'lady, you slide this over and—" The boy's face shone in light golden as the morning sunlight filtering through the windows of Mauritum Tower—and yet emanating from a bulb quite similar to a common silver leylight. "Y' see? Totally misaligned, but it still works."

"Interesting," Kiyrstine romGaretti commented as she circled the table, examining the boy's magic box from a safe distance. It was a plain, green-painted wooden cube, with leather strap-handles on either side. On top was a quite ordinary-looking bulb socket—except it had no swivel-joint, no lever to attune the bulb's positioning within the leyflux, nothing to turn it on, except a tiny sliding switch. "But the color is strange. . . ."

"By yer leave, lady, th' wire inside—th' part what glows—it ain't leythium."

She leaned forward, taking a closer look at the bulb, which was similar in shape to a leybulb, but contained a thin wire rather than a lacy leythium web.

"And you say this works even beyond the node's umbrella?"

"Aye, lady." The boy's long topknot flopped forward

with the energy of his nod, partially obscuring his bright dark eyes. "Even *better* in th' betweens."

Likely that was pride talking. Even so, if just what he had here was real and not some sort of trick ... in all of Mauritum, she'd never heard of such a wonder. Trust Garetti to throw the greatest possibility of his tenure out the door without a first glance, let alone a second.

She turned the entire unit—surprised at its weight and wondering if this undersized youngster had brought it here himself—but the light didn't flicker.

"This is th' little 'un, lady, wot runs on alchemies. I had t' leave th' big 'un wot works on metallurgies Outside 'cuz I couldn't get dis-pen-sa-shun t' bring th' cart 'n' mules into Mauritum, but *it* c'n run a whole cross-ley worth o' lights."

She found, to her annoyance, she was twisting a curl around one finger. It was an old, old habit, long since eradicated—or so she'd believed. Garetti, who despised what she termed childish aberrations, would be incensed if he caught her at it.

In fact, he'd be far more angry at his wife's unseemly reversion, than at her tête-à-tête with the boy he'd just thrown out of the audience hall.

She dropped her hand, inadvertently pulling the curl and painfully endangering her maid's entire elaborate coiffure. Her maid's, not hers. The rings would stop before she'd claim it, regardless of whose head it perched upon.

Her hand crept back toward the curl as if with a mind of its own. She stopped it, then defiantly turned it loose to infiltrate the red strands.

It helped her think.

She'd been in the audience chamber on her regular inspection tour when the youngster had presented his case, and been outraged when Garetti had denied the child so much as a demonstration. She'd felt sorry for the weary child he'd appeared, and intercepted him in this back passageway of the Temple of Maurii, thinking to give him a few coppers for his trouble, perhaps to send him to the kitchens for a cake or two.

On closer inspection, she'd found him perhaps four years older than his size would indicate, and articulate, in a third-level node way. In addition, what had appeared a rather clumsily constructed toy at a distance, was proving far more than merely curious.

"And you are responsible for this—ley-by-artifice?"

A shy duck of the head didn't quite mask the blush that rose over his childishly rounded cheeks. "Not me, m'lady, no. I ain't even an apprentice, properly speakin'. More a fetch 'n' carry, if ya knows wot I means. My master—he's the one wot discovered this 'un. Though I—" His chin lifted ever so slightly, and his voice assumed a note of youthful pride. "I did help with this 'un's makin'. The other scuts, they's scared o' it. Says as how it's evil magic. But I knows better. Anyways, the other one, the one wot uses lode-stones, that was this other feller's, my master's friend's, idea."

"And these two friends' names?"

"They, uh, tol' me not t' say, if it pleases yer ladyship."

"Well, it doesn't please me. Why should I believe you? Perhaps you simply stole the device, and left the poor inventor lying in some ley-side ditch."

"I *ain't* no thief!"

"I've only your word on that. Perhaps I should call the guard."

The round chin jutted forward, all hint of shyness gone. "Go ahead 'n' call 'em."

She laughed at that defiance, honestly delighted. His mouth twitched, and she half-expected him to join her, was disappointed when good sense triumphed, and his eyes dropped.

"All right," she said, sobering, "Say I believe you—for the present. Why did these two clever friends trust their marvels to an apprentice who is not really an apprentice?"

"It were my idea to bring 'em to th' City."

"To solicit funds?"

He nodded. "That, and the Tower's end–endo–" His smooth brow wrinkled, his lips tightened as if determined to remember a word clearly not his own. Then, triumphantly: "—endorsement. And we needs land. A place t' test th' machines."

"So, now we have it: you desire property within Mauritum."

Surprisingly, he shook his head. "Wouldn't be any use, anyway, begging your ladyship's pardon. Like I says, works better between. Just needs a place closer to a metals manufactory."

"Oh?"

"Parts, mistress."

"I see."

Practicality. She hadn't expected that, not of the boy's masters. In her experience, such requisitions generally came from those seeking Mauritum's distractions rather than a node's benefits. One had to wonder if it was the master or the boy's own native wisdom speaking.

"And why did your master wish anonymity? Surely this is a magnificent discovery."

"They says as how I ain't got a chance in hell, that Garetti don't want no competition." His mouth twisted, and the bitter glance he sent down the long hall toward the double-doorway entrance to Garetti's receiving hall, held little of youth. His fresh face darkened further with anger and resentment. " 'Pears they was right. Ignorant old . . ." His voice trailed off to something not quite audible.

Crude, from what little she detected.

"Do you reference, by any chance, my husband?"

Bright eyes shot back to her, wide with terror. "M'lady, forgive—I didn't mean no—"

"Disrespect? He hardly granted you any in there." She gestured toward the double doors. "Now did he?"

"Nor should he, lady." His voice cracked with barely controlled fear. "I'd no right t' say—wot I said. I *am* sorry, lady. Truly."

She shrugged. "We're not speaking of him, now."

The lad needn't have worried; she'd called her husband far worse, though she vented those thoughts in private these days. Personally, she respected honesty, and a spirit not yet cowed, as she'd tell this lad frankly, if she could trust the shadows' apparent emptiness.

"You say you want funding? Support?"

He nodded eagerly.

"I'll see what I can do, boy. Mind you, I promise nothing, but I'll talk with my husband. Failing him, well, I've some money of my own, and I know a few others who might care to—invest in the future. Don't get overly hopeful, but don't despair, yet. Where are you staying?"

"At th' road-camp beyond the Coronum market."

"Outside?"

The boy nodded.

She was appalled. No cabby would have taken such a ragamuffin aboard, whether or not he'd had the fare. It must have taken him hours to walk to the Tower, and carrying that ponderous thing all the way.

"You'll stay here. In my apartments."

"Oh." The lad's voice shook now and his eyes dropped to where his hands twisted his cap into shapelessness. "If 'ee please, lady, thank 'ee. But best I seek help elsewhere."

"Your virtue is perfectly safe with me, boy," she said sharply. "I simply want you where I can reach you easily and quickly."

His face, what she could see of it, turned bright red. "Sorry, m'lady. I meant no—"

"Disrespect." She laughed shortly. "I begin to see you speak your mind first and consider the consequences only when disaster is imminent. Well, I can't fault that. It gives greater credence to your claims."

Another twist and already stressed seams gave, leaving the cap a shredded, useless mass of cloth, his distress making plain he was fully aware of the Tower administration's reputation. He wouldn't be the first homeless child to disappear forever into the Halls of Maurii.

Not that he was a particularly pretty child, having features more to be grown into than admired in adolescence, but he was alone, and with that ingenuous remark, had made it clear no one would note his disappearance. Some within Garetti's circle would claim the boy had come looking, not for patronage, but a keeper.

She felt something tight give in her chest, and she reached a hand to cup his rounded chin until his eyes lifted.

Somehow, she didn't think so.

"Please, child, let me rephrase the invitation. You're tired, and it's a long trip back. Stay the night."

If possible, the flush deepened. "Th–thank 'ee, lady. But, rings' truth, I can't leave th' big 'un alone Outside. Th' man wot I paid t' watch it—I only had coppers enou' fer th' day. My camp ain't hard t' find. I'll go back there 'n' wait. Stay till I hears from 'ee, one way or t'other."

"Fair enough. Perhaps I'll send someone for a demonstration of this ... big 'un. You can find your own way out? —Off with you, then."

She turned abruptly, heading for the west garden, fighting the dangerous softness the boy roused in her. He seemed so determinedly hopeful. Maurii save her, had she ever felt that way? About anything?

Behind her: a scrape. A *thud*. And a horrified gasp.

She turned to find the boy kneeling on the floor, frantically checking his machine.

"Is it all right?" she called from her safe distance.

He jerked upright, tugging his tunic straight, but when his eyes landed on the table he'd used for the demonstration, composure deserted him completely. He reached a trembling hand to smooth the surface, and she thought for a moment that he'd bolt, even if it meant leaving the machine behind. Then his back straightened, and though he shook head to foot, he waited, head bravely upright, as she approached.

There was a long deep scratch on the table. His eyes were filled with tears, but they were not overflowing and they met hers without flinching.

"Why didn't you run?" she asked at last, that curiosity the only important one of several that occurred.

Confusion mingled with surprise and fear, and he rubbed a wrist turning an angry red.

"You were about to run. I couldn't possibly have caught you. Why didn't you?"

"B–Because," he said, his voice a whisper, but steadying with each word, "I done it. It were my fault."

"An honest man in a child's coat. Interesting." She looked pointedly at his wrist. "What happened?"

The wrist disappeared behind his back. "N–Nothing."

"Answer me, honest man."

Teeth closed on a childish pout, then: "I thinks mebbe I did 'er in on th' way here, lady. Honest, I didn't know 'til I tried t'pick 'er up. It's heavy, don't ye see? And when I tries t' lift 'er, 'er slips, and then I tries t' catch 'er, an' that's when—"

"When it scratched the table?"

For a moment he seemed tempted to deny it, then, he shook his head miserably. "I don't make no excuses, m'lady. 'Twere my fault. Shouldn'ta tried if'n I couldn't manage." The last took on the singsong quality of an oft-repeated lesson.

Gesturing toward that hidden wrist she asked: "May I see the damage?" And as she examined the bruise and probed lightly at the rising lump, she murmured: "On the other hand, honest man, if one doesn't press those limits, how does one know where, precisely, they are?"

His mouth tightened into a sulky scowl. "Tha's wot I—"

Bright eyes flickered, and he swallowed the rest, but he watched her with a new calculation, and the rest of that sentence was easy enough to fill in. This was a boy with ambition. The constructive sort. The sort that made an eager boy into a self-motivated, honorable man.

She pressed his injured wrist lightly, then let him go.

The table in question was light, easily carvable wood; terribly delicate, in its own way, undoubtedly expensive—probably overpriced—as were all the innumerable too-ornate creations that littered the rooms of the Temple palace.

"Honest man?" she said quietly, "There are times one can be too honest. Times when people with power can make the wheels of justice run a bit more smoothly for honest men who will accept their help. Will you accept mine, honest man?"

Confusion covered his face, and a hint of fear. But beneath it all, a wicked little glimmer of anticipation.

She grinned conspiratorially, picked the small table up by two legs, and giving a single, practice swing, flung herself around, slamming the thing into a stone pillar with every bit of muscle and weight she could muster behind it.

The shock reverberated up through her elbows to the base of her skull; the table splintered in her hands. She tossed the two remaining intact legs to the floor, and, lifting her massive, still-swaying skirts, she planted her foot through the top twice for good measure—discovering, after two years of suffering their discomfort, a use for her shoe's fashion-dictated platform sole.

It was one of her noisier tantrums. Within moments, a startled palace guard appeared at the antechamber door, pausing uncertainly at the obvious calm within.

"Ah, captain." Her hands still tingling from the highly rewarding impact, Kirystin smiled blithely, and brushed her hands free of splinters. "My young visitor here is returning to his encampment. Help him out with his machine, and see one of the palace cabs conveys him safely to the City gates."

And in a much lower undertone to the open-mouthed boy: "Can you manage from there, honest man?"

The boy nodded wordlessly, his wide eyes taking in the smashed table, her face, and the guard's tacit oblivion toward the table's condition, the bright mind behind those bright eyes obviously at work. He bowed, a deep bend at the waist that never took his eyes from her face. "Thank you, lady."

"You'll be hearing from me." And to the footman who had followed the guard into the room, and was trying not to stare at the ruined table: "Clean that up, will you?" She glided again toward the west garden: "I always did hate that thing. . . ."

The Cardinal Ring sliced its hypnotically regular path through the leylines. The nine inner rings' tranquil, randomized movements gained momentum and purpose; silver flickerings achieved a rhythmic blur.

Following two false starts, the radical streamer, innermost of all at the moment, chose its own dangerous course, becoming one with the silver haze surrounding the central sphere.

Beyond that haze, a glowing sphere . . . an image that shimmered . . . and stabilized.

A face. A woman's face. Pale blonde hair, large blue eyes . . . features some would consider beautiful. But of infinitely more interest than the face (or so Anheliaa claimed) was the aura of power that radiated from the sphere, touching the inner haze with a delicate spring-green, proof (also according to Anheliaa) of her candidate's latent Talent.

"That's her?" Nikki leaned forward in his chair and stared. Finally, eyes wide, he turned to Mikhyel, and as if seeking confirmation of his observation: "She's pretty."

"Did you think otherwise? The rings provided multiple options for each of us; why should Anheliaa choose other than the best?"

"M–Multiple. . . ?"

He laughed as Nikki's rather dazed expression slid past him to Anheliaa.

"You're certain she's the best?" Nikki asked shakily, and Anheliaa laughed merrily, obviously finding his younger brother's complacency to her liking.

"Greedy, aren't you?" she said.

"No, Aunt." Nikki leaned forward earnestly. "At least, I don't think so. I just want to be sure. Mikhyel said we've got to make a good match—for the Tower's sake. I–I'd hope to become . . . fond of the woman I marry. I'd like to be certain I won't have to give her up, that is, if she didn't work out, for another . . . after . . . you know."

"The probabilities are equally compelling for each of the young ladies, Nikaenor. The search parameters I established were for biological viability and compatibility with both you, personally, and the Rhomatum Node. There can be no assurance one is better than another in that sense. Of the four possibilities—for you alone, darling—I chose Lidye dunTarim as the most attractive, both physically and by birth. Her brother is Shatum's third-ranked ringmaster, her father is a fourth term Shatum Syndic—and doesn't look to lose an election any time soon. He also recently purchased controlling interest in the Shatum Tower."

"Shatum Tower?" Nikki turned a puzzled look toward Mikhyel.

"She means—" he began, broke off at Anheliaa's glare.

"I told you to explain all this," she snapped.

"On the contrary, Aunt," he returned, "you said to bring him here."

"Oh, for—" She slumped back on her couch, thrumming her fingers on the chair arm. The image and the sphere wavered and dissipated.

Uncertain what she expected of him, Mikhyel waited for some sign, keeping his face blank, despite his growing inner turmoil.

Finally, Anheliaa cast a hand in the air impatiently:

"Well—tell him. *Tell* him, so we can get on with it."

He dipped his head in silent acknowledgment.

"Diplomatic relations," he said succinctly, to the accompaniment of Anheliaa's thrumming fingers, knowing that Nikki, being no fool, would fill in the blanks, and some bitterness within prompted him to add: "Dynastic linkages."

However, Nikki, being also a student of history, asked:

"With Shatum Tower? Would Darius—"

"There's nothing within Darius' laws prohibiting formal alliances between nodes," Anheliaa said patronizingly. "He was concerned with a priesthood, not the sort of necessary understanding one must achieve with one's neighbors if one is to tell Mauritum to go to hell."

"I . . . suppose."

But Nikki still sounded dubious, and to prevent his dig-

ging himself deeper into Anheliaa's bad graces, Mikhyel
said:

"We have no choice, Nikki. We *need* a ringmaster, therefore we *must* proceed along the course most likely to provide one, and that, according to the rings, is cross-breeding
with Shatum. Three of the four ladies the rings suggested
for you were from that node."

"Oh, I see." Nikki sounded relieved; Nikki hated dis-
agreements, which made him disquietingly susceptible to
Anheliaa's brand of pressure. For Nikki's safety, Mikhyel
argued Anheliaa's side, however, seeing the woman Anheliaa had chosen for his young brother, Mikhyel was less
and less certain he wanted any part of that plan.

Anheliaa said suggestively: "Lidye's cousins threw her a
majority ball here in Rhomatum last year. I thought, perhaps, you might have met?"

"I . . ." Nikki blushed, and stared at his hands.

"Anheliaa," Mikhyel intervened, daring her wrath a second time, "he just turned . . ."

She glared at him. "I *know* that. What do you think I
am, senile? Did you think I'd forgotten?"

Which meant, of course, she *had* forgotten. But:

"Of course not," Mikhyel acquiesced, but he was silently
appalled: Shatum's majority was twenty-two. This Lidye
woman had to be nearer his age than Nikki's.

"Yes, well," Anheliaa continued archly, "The girl is quite
bookish. I *thought* Nikaenor might have met her in the
library, or at a bookseller's. But since that is apparently
not the case, if you'd care to see the others. . . ."

She said, who clearly didn't want one of the others. She
clearly wanted this Lidye.

Damn her.

"N–No. I'm sure she'll be . . . f–fine," Nikki stammered
uncertainly, and what more could the boy do, but agree?
What more, at Anheliaa's dissatisfied scowl, than amend:
"I meant *wonderful,* of course, Aunt Liaa. Thank you."
Nikki's brilliant blue eyes shifted back to him, a desperate
appeal for rescue. "What about Nethaalye? She's from Giephaetum, not Shatum."

He forced a smile. "She . . . passed the compatibility test,
if you will."

"I'm glad. You must be relieved."

He supposed that emotion lay somewhere within him.

But his family's twenty-year understanding with the Giephaetum heiress' family would not have been in total jeopardy in any case: multiple spouses, while not common and certainly not a possibility he'd ever considered for himself, were hardly illegal. However, marriage being something of a theoretical necessity in his mind, he had welcomed the simplicity of Anheliaa's choice for him.

All of which didn't make it any easier to force his forced smile to remain steady. "I'll simply marry her a bit sooner than planned."

Never mind Nethaalye had *planned* the wedding five years ago.

He didn't know why he'd kept putting it off. He liked her well enough; bright, good looking in a quiet way, wellmannered and accomplished—she was all any sane man could want in a wife. Certainly he sought none of the complex emotional ties Nikki craved. He suspected it wasn't the fact of *being* married he avoided, but the bedlam of *getting* married.

"Sooner?" Nikki echoed, "How soon?"

Anheliaa said, "Once you two have formally extended the proposals to the families, we'll have the ladies to the Tower. If all goes as planned ... well, the sooner you're married, the sooner we'll have offspring, won't we?"

"Offsp ..." Nikki swallowed visibly. "Of c–course. But what do you mean, if all goes as planned? All what?"

"If you suit one another, silly goose." Anheliaa was ever so much happier now she was in absolute control. "And naturally at least one of the ladies must prove proficient with the rings."

"I see." Nikki swallowed visibly. "And Deymorin? Where does he fit in?"

"He doesn't," Anheliaa said flatly, and Mikhyel winced, but Nikki said:

"Oh."

And Anheliaa seemed to take that as acceptance of the situation.

Mikhyel reached for his brother's wrist, where it rested on the chair arm, and gripped it comfortably. "Deymio made his choice, Nikki," he said, gently, "No one forced him. He wants nothing to do with the plan. You know he doesn't care about the Tower or the Estate—"

"But he *does*, Khyel. If you'd only listen to him—"

He withdrew his hand and sat back. "I've spent my whole life listening to him, Nikaenor. He doesn't understand the rings—never has understood the dynamics of City economics."

"He just wants people to be happy, Khyel. Is that so wrong?"

"A society doesn't function in order to make people happy," Anheliaa interjected sharply, and Mikhyel said, hoping to stave off the obstinate look brewing in Nikki's eyes:

"Happiness is a by-product of an efficient process, Nikki. Maybe one day, Deymio will figure that out, and when he does, he'll probably take his proper place at the head of Council. But we can't put our lives, and the Principality, on hold waiting for that day."

Despite his efforts, Nikki's jaw set stubbornly, a look Anheliaa rarely saw. Hoping now to stave off open rebellion, and deflect her attention, Mikhyel asked:

"May we see Deymorin's?"

"Deymorin's *what*?" Anheliaa's voice dripped with impatience.

"I'd like to see the woman you found for Deymorin," he persisted, his own temper beginning to seethe.

"I said, it makes no difference."

"It might." Nikki leaned forward, eager eyes flickering in the flash of ring-reflected leylight. "If she's as pretty as Lady Lidye, perhaps Deymorin would come back."

Mikhyel tilted his head arrogantly—a manner he'd learned from her—challenging Anheliaa, knowing she knew she couldn't refuse now without alienating them both. "Call it—curiosity."

Her breath hissed out between clenched teeth, but she faced the rings, which, upon her release of Lidye's image, had resumed their seemingly random swings. According to Anheliaa, those random motions were the rings' response to the chaotic flux of the leys themselves—all except the outermost, whose rotation hadn't wavered since the day his aunt had taken command of the Tower, and the radical, which hardly counted as a ring at all.

Her expression tempered, her eyes glazed as she absorbed that randomness and ciphered the probabilities. Then, without ever moving, she gave the tiniest deflection to the radical, and attuned the rings to her chosen parameters in one economic mental exhalation.

She'd explained the process to him once, when he'd tried to emulate her, hoping to find some iota of Talent within himself, but he'd only managed to frustrate them both. He'd never repeated the trial—and eventually the nightmares of that failed attempt had faded.

On the central sphere, another face swam into view. Not one he recognized; not the individual, not the general district from which such features might reasonably hail, though the set of the mouth held a disturbing familiarity. Red hair, green eyes; hardly what he'd call stunningly beautiful, and as young for Deymorin as that Lidye individual was old for Nikki.

"But that's not . . ." Anheliaa's voice faded into uncertainty.

Not what? Mikhyel wondered. Her puzzled expression gave him neither clue nor reassurance, but he held his peace, her concentration at this stage far too delicate to disturb with superfluous questions.

The image expanded, as if the viewer had stepped back from the young woman. One pace, and a second, back and back—until the sphere pictured a slim, athletic figure, a painted-on costume of silver and black, the metallic gleam of a counter-balance orbiter, and (another positional recession) a stone stadium surrounding a multitiered latticework stage.

A ringdancer? He felt laughter bubble in his throat. "Leave it to Deymorin," he murmured, uncertain whether that bubble was humor, bitterness—or envy.

Nikki raised his chin pugnaciously. "What do you mean by that?"

"Don't get touchy, lad. I think Deymorin himself would appreciate the humor. Appropriate that our egalitarian brother finds his match in a simple entertainer, don't you think?"

"Hardly simple, Mikhyel," Anheliaa said, and her voice quivered with excitement. The image wavered; she mastered her emotional flare and the image stabilized. She was leaning forward in her chair, eagerness and disbelief at war in her age-crabbed features. "Look at the aura."

The Power radiating from the sphere this time was not the innocent spring-green of Lidye's, but an intense, almost blue, green; an aura so strong, so distinct, the rotating rings glimmered a sympathetic, iridescent purple-red.

In one sense, 'simple' was undoubtedly apropos: the inherent (but exceedingly well-compensated) dangers of the ringdance generally appealed only to the most fiscally desperate. But the woman's birth wouldn't matter, not to Anheliaa—that green glow was recommendation enough. Likely she'd even relinquish her dreams of internode alliances, if Deymorin could land this woman.

Of course, first she'd have to bring Deymorin home.

With a grunt that mingled pain and frustration in equal portions, Anheliaa fell back into the confines of her couch, still staring at that image, which shimmered and stabilized. Furtive little Mirym appeared like magic at her side, adjusting the cushion at her back without a word.

Again the image wavered.

"Don't *touch* me!" Anheliaa's temper-flare colored the ringhaze red; Mirym jumped back, then stood there, hands behind her back, chin high, defiantly fearless.

Anheliaa's mouth tightened. Her eyes, still on the image, narrowed to droop-lidded slits.

The red faded; the image stabilized.

Anheliaa murmured a curt *Thank you.* Mirym dipped a slight curtsy and returned to her backless stool, and her endless stitchery. Nikki appeared startled, but Mikhyel had seen it before, this oddly silent little shadow with backbone to rival Deymorin's.

But for all her silent defiance, Anheliaa must approve, since Mirym had been here for nearly two years now, longer than any of the others since Marta, Anheliaa's lifelong personal companion, had died some fifteen years ago—and only Mirym could imply, as she had now, Anheliaa's malpractice—and survive.

An ability that never failed to rouse a tinge of jealous admiration in him.

Silence, then, save for the sound of the rings cutting the air, differential hums that took on a musicality all their own. A seemingly endless silence into which Anheliaa stared with that unfathomable expression.

Suddenly:

"*Damn* the radical and the chaos it represents!"

The image shattered; the rings spun in sudden mad chaos.

Mirym reached Anheliaa first, offering supporting hands.

Anheliaa thrust her staggering backward into Mikhyel's arms; he staggered into Nikki, who held them all upright.

"Out!"

The girl twisted in Mikhyel's arms to look up at him, seeking guidance.

He released her, jerked his head to where the lift was rising from the floor in response to Anheliaa's desire to be rid of them. "Leave. Now."

Still, Mirym hesitated. Nikki reached past him and took her arm, murmuring: "It's all right," and led her to the waiting lift, pausing there, his blue eyes questioning.

Mikhyel nodded, a single dip of the chin, and Nikki complacently accompanied Mirym through the bentwood grill, and released the brake. But his eyes never left Mikhyel's until he disappeared down the shaft and the hatch slid silently between them.

Leaving him alone to deal with Anheliaa.

As they all did. Nikki. Deymorin. Council. —Ever since she brought him here to inform him that she was having him groomed to take Deymorin's place on Council.

"Anheliaa?" He touched her arm, a light touch, but firm.

He'd been all of thirteen.

They all assumed that he, unlike all of them, was not afraid of her. That he, unlike them, could sway her to his thinking.

"Can't trust them," she muttered, still glaring at the wildly spinning inner rings, her upper lip lifting in a one-sided sneer.

They all assumed wrong.

"Can't trust what, Aunt?"

"The rings!" she snarled, then caught herself, buried her wrinkled face in her gnarled hands.

Age. Affliction. The signs had increased of late. Her sanity, never incontestable, had grown terrifyingly uncertain. After last night . . .

He'd covered for her for years, in public and in private, humored her ever-wilder notions, taking them and transforming them into acceptable proposals for Council, praying they'd ultimately prove beneficial to Rhomatum and her people.

There'd been no option. No one else to control the Rhomatum rings. Except, possibly, Deymorin, and he might well have proven a worse tyrant with his anti-city notions.

He'd hoped this newest project would make her happy (and keep her occupied) in her twilight years, while providing the vital master Rhomatum so desperately needed.

Now—

He stood behind her, gently rubbing her knotted shoulders and neck until the fury ebbed and she quit shaking, wondering would this mysterious dancer destroy those dreams and set Anheliaa on some obsessive quest for unattainable, perceived perfection.

"Who was she, Anheliaa?" he asked softly, when at last it seemed safe. "What's wrong?"

Her shoulders lifted wearily under his hands. "I can't trust them anymore, darling. Sometimes, too often, of late, the rings have been inclined to reveal more wishes than fact."

When it became apparent she considered her explanation complete, he prompted: "And that's what you believe that woman to be? A wish? Your wish? Why?"

"The rings refused to give details of the city—I have no idea where she comes from. Maurii's hells, she might not even exist."

"She's a dancer, that much is obvious. We can find her, if it's important."

"A dancer. That tells us nothing. *Nothing!* Every damned node in the web has at least one ringtheater now—barbaric custom that it is. If the woman exists, she's beyond reach." She shrugged his hands away, impatiently. "Just as well. With that chin, she'd undoubtedly prove more hindrance than help."

"Maybe we *should* search her out, then—before she marries elsewhere. Set her to taming my hard-headed brother."

She gave a bark of laughter. "That decides it: she was a figment of an old woman's desperation. We could never be that lucky." She rubbed her forehead and eyes irritably. "Damnable boy. I'd never have imagined he had it in him. I've *still* got a headache."

It was a moment before he realized the *damnable boy* was Deymorin.

He gently pulled her wig free, and ran his fingers through her thinning hair, rubbing gently in the way he'd learned— the way she'd had him taught—fifteen years before. "Transporting that overdeveloped body of his a bit of a strain, was it?"

"Oh-h-h, that's lovely, sweet." Her head drooped backward, her paper-dry hand caught awkwardly at his and carried it shakily to her mouth.

He shivered and conquered the urge to pull free.

She nibbled a fingertip, bit hard enough to draw protest out of him. Sharpened, polished nails dug into his palm, preventing his escape. Only after he ceased to pull did she chuckle and release him, saying, "Wasn't the transport, darling."

Wasn't ... He'd seen the disruption of the rings' orbits. Had that flux been Deymorin's doing? Had she realized the truth at last?

And one had to wonder how she would react when she found out he'd known, for years, and had said . . . nothing?

"Why'd you stop, sweet?" Her voice, in repose, was as thin as her hair.

"Sorry." He resumed the gentle massage with fingers gone suddenly cold. "If not the transfer, what was it?"

"He ... Oh, hell. Doesn't matter. Besides, he's gone."

"Not—" He swallowed and tried again. "Not for good. . . ?"

Silence.

"Surely, he'll be back...." he protested weakly.

And a shrug.

Third Interlude

He was falling.

Father's laughter rang in his ears. "Balance, fool! Expect the unexpected."

Rule number one: Never anticipate: Never lean into a jump . . . lead with your chin . . . parry a blade not yet committed . . . or pressure a woman.

Horse, man or woman: which had outsmarted him this time?

The fall took a lifetime . . .
A brother's voice, echoing his name.
Black hair streaming, veiled stars and moon above.
His answering cry froze in his throat.

Beyond the shimmer of materialization, one could feel the crystalline lace opalesce red and orange: subtle betrayal of latent anger and frustration. Dancer willed those colors—and the emotions—into oblivion before completing bodily transition into the cavern.

Lest Mother add one more human hide to her oft-referenced, never seen collection.

Besides, there was no percentage in frustration: Mother would explain the new pattern in her own time. But she'd woven Dancer into that pattern—nothing else could explain the energy flux Dancer experienced day and night since the pattern began—and that fact made patience exceedingly difficult, particularly when that flux pulled one way, Rhyys' demands another, and the dance itself another still.

Mother (Dancer heaved a sigh of relief) was not lying in wait. Mother was, in point of fact, nowhere in sight.

Or wouldn't have been, had Dancer's eyes been open.

A tentative tendril of thought sent searching through the shifting, spongelike maze of stone and crystal located her, and Dancer followed that perception into the innermost sanctuary, Mother's personal nest, feeling the warmth of the leythium flame before remembering closed eyes and blinking them open.

Mother *was* there, as the Sense had told Dancer, but so much a part of the dense veils, actually finding her took several moments.

She lay motionless on a shelf above the imaging pool, chin propped on cupped palms, gazing fixedly into the flaming liquid. Her couch was composed of shifting leythium, her clothing a filmy drape of interlinking leythium threads; it required a blink of her large, multifaceted eyes to separate her from the shadows and flickering veils.

"Mother?" Dancer began tentatively. "I'm terribly sorry. I heard you call, but Rhyys wanted an audience, and I was the first available victim. It seems Mheric's eldest has disappeared and—"

Those large eyes shifted, and Dancer's voice caught, frozen in that fixed stare.

{I'm supposed to give a storm's hiccup about any of this?}

Dancer smothered comment and thought alike. For Mother, comment was much the same as thought—and vice versa.

{Get over here and tell me what you see, curse these old eyes of mine.}

Those 'old eyes' could spot a mouse in a field from the top of a mountain peak, or the dust on the end of her nose, but Mother liked to think she was dying. Mother had heard somewhere that human elders used their infirmities to manipulate the younger folk around them, a concept she found highly entertaining to emulate, though she'd never admit as much.

Crossing a filmy stream of liquid leythium (evidence that elsewhere someone was drawing heavily on Khoratum resources) Dancer slid onto the couch beside Mother and stared into the flames, seeking pictures in the shadows and colors that danced across the surface.

Anheliaa: appearing older by far than the ten years that had passed since Dancer had seen her. For Dancer, it was a clear, clean image, but Mother might have reason to complain: her own distaste for the Rhomatum ringmaster might well be clouding her visions.

{Smart ass. What else do you see?}

A man ... or what was left of one.

{Deymorin Rhomandi dunMheric. Mheric's eldest brat.}

"Thank you," Dancer acknowledged the information humbly, while mentally noting that soon she *would* be demanding the rumors from Rhyys' dinner table, at least as far as they regarded the man in the pool. "Anheliaa has leythiated him ... like the others."

Mother nodded toward the liquid leythium stream. "Rather more emphatically than the others. Dislikes the lad intensely."

At least in that, Rhyys' rumors held true. Rhyys had said the Rhomandi had argued with his aunt and deserted Rhomatum at last. Evidently, 'deserted' wasn't quite the most accurate description of this Deymorin's departure.

"What else?" Mother hissed, all eagerness. "Where has the creature sent him?"

"He's still in transit, isn't he?"

"I asked you. If I knew the answer, would I have asked?"

Dancer grinned, not the least abashed. "Yes."

{Humph.} Mother's thoughts echoed of amusement. Mother appreciated backbone. *{Well, you're right. Given him quite a send-off. —Curse the vile creature, it's getting better than it deserves.}*

"Mother, Deymorin dunMheric—he's Princeps of Rhomatum. Technically, he outranks Anheliaa in the Rhomatum government, for all he's declared his brother proxy. If she's eliminated him ... there could be a major political coup in motion."

{Meaning the creature will be completely free to do as she wishes? That might be fun.}

"*Fun?* Mother, Anheliaa's an aggressive expansionist. Rhyys has said Mauritum hasn't the power to stand against her. If Anheliaa dares move in that direction, there could be major ramifications."

The veils took on a rosy glow of anticipation. "Oh, good."

He was falling.

Father's laughter rang in his ears. "Balance, fool! Expect the unexpected."

Rule number one: Never anticipate: Never lean into a jump ... lead with your chin ... parry a blade not yet committed ... or pressure a woman.

Horse, man or woman: which had outsmarted him this time?

The fall took a lifetime ...
A brother's voice, echoing his name.
Black hair streaming, veiled stars and moon above.
His answering cry froze in his throat.

... and an instant.
Sunlight, blinding bright, replaced moonlit black hair.
Not Brandy. Not a horse at all. No jump; no father. No duel. No woman.
No brother.

"He's aware, Mother." Dancer felt queasy at the thought. Queasier at the realization of the time Deymorin dunMheric had already spent in that hazy nowhere, the limbo of transition: it had been nearly six months since Mother had last shared her imaging cauldron.

Six months of silence from Mother.

Six months of silence out of Rhomatum.

Six months of growing frustration from Rhyys, whose plans for Khoratum's future revolved in some significant sense around Rhomatum's succession. Six months of eerie quiet, during which one's own plans for the future could grow and blossom into exciting possibilities, shoving the fate of the unknown Princeps of Rhomatum into a forgotten mental recess.

Six months during which the insistent pull of the new pattern had diminished to insignificance, until, of a sudden, it had returned full force and more, so powerful, Dancer had barely had time to escape the practice hall before something or someone forced transfer to Mother's sanctum.

Dancer suspected some*one*, but didn't accuse. Not considering:

"Six months in nowhere. What could he possibly have done to deserve it?"

{Should I care?}

Dancer looked away from the image of utter helplessness, an image that triggered memories of darkness and blood seeping from stone—and memories of loss.

"Perhaps you shouldn't. Perhaps I shouldn't, but I can't help it. Can't I do something?"

{Of course you can. But we won't.}

"Why?" Difficult to contain the anguish. Even more difficult to keep the image clear of the distorting colors of anguish.

{Because Anheliaa did it. Anheliaa set the trajectory. I want to see where it ends.}

"She has no control over it, you know that. *I* know it."

{I should certainly hope you do. And of course Anheliaa doesn't. Anheliaa's not that good. But the rings do. The ley does, and it's all charted according to that creature's subconscious.}

"And you want to know where that subconscious is sending him?"

{How very clever you are.}

"What good is knowing, if the man who arrives has no mind left?"

{Did I say I didn't know? Go away. Your childish loyalties begin to pall.}

"My loyalties are not to Rhomatum. Certainly not to Deymorin dunMheric."

{Where are they, then?}

"To *my* people."

{Harrumph.}

"That means to you, Mother. You know that. Many of us remain loyal to the old ways."

Her pink, double-tipped tongue flickered across supplely-scaled lips. *{That last chicken was ... delightful. When you return, tell them their mother* loves *chicken.}*

Dancer laughed, the bad memories and the helplessness banished for the time being, and hugged her, receiving a staggering shove for the effort. "I will, Mother. —And now, I must return."

{Haven't you something else to tell me?}

Dancer froze, striving for the anonymity of non-thought without overmuch success, knowing better than to prevaricate. "I—didn't want to say anything until ... after. In case I lost."

{You thought I wouldn't know?}

"I hoped you were too occupied."

{Does failure frighten you so much?}

Tears threatened. Childish tears; Dancer knew it, and still they dripped and clouded inferior human vision. "In this. Yes."

Mother's scaled fingers caressed Dancer's body, following muscle contours, tapping at detected weak spots. *(Too much practicing of the same moves.)*

"I dance to win. The moves must be those the judges recognize and understand, those they can compare with the other contestants."

"You allow this single goal too much power over your thoughts and emotions, Dancer," she murmured softly: her human voice, not the sibilant one, not the internal one. "You are what you are, no contest can change or set a value on that—win or lose. You will never dance your best as long as you dance for those whose standards are less than your own."

"Time enough for experimentation once I *am* the Radical Dancer."

"Even if you win this competition, you will only *be* the Radical if you let yourself be."

"You don't understand."

The fingers left abruptly, the voice returned to that internal chill:

(Don't I? You might well win this upcoming competition and replace Betania, but if you win under false pretences, you will continue to dance under them, because you will be too frightened to try anything new, too afraid their standards will not stretch to encompass yours. You will always know the difference between what you are and what you should have been, and one day so will the audience, not in the substance, but in the spirit, and they will know you have cheated them, and you will know you cheated yourself. Then where will you be?)

"Mother, you frighten me."

"Good. You need to be frightened. You're too good, Dancer. You rely too heavily on that ability."

"I practice hard. Harder than anyone."

(You practice conservatism, not art. Tradition, not inspiration; rules, not faith. The radical factor in the ley is rarely conservative: that's where Anheliaa's greatest errors in judgment lie. The radical dances to the most unusual flux and designs its own rules, challenging the universe to join it. Until you gain that courage to laugh in the face of the judges and dance as you were born to dance, you've no right to win.)

"You ask too much of me, Mother."

"I ask nothing of you, except that you leave me alone."

It was clear dismissal. She turned back to the flame, and Dancer, left with no alternative, drifted slowly back to the world-cavern, where transfer to the surface came most easily.

Aimless.

Liquid leythium oozed between bare toes, sending a palpable, revitalizing, iridescent glimmer through Dancer's tired body, and trickling from Dancer's eyes.

Alone.

{Unless, of course . . .} Mother's brushing thought tasted suddenly of excitement: *{You care to stay and see where our favorite Princeps lands.}*

"He's exiting?"

{I believe—yes, he already has.}

Dancer ran back, as anxious for reinstatement into Mother's graces as for the answer to that six-month-long puzzle.

He was falling.

Father's laughter rang in his ears. *"Balance, fool! Expect the unexpected."*

Rule number one: Never anticipate: Never lean into a jump . . . lead with your chin . . . parry a blade not yet committed . . . or pressure a woman.

Horse, man or woman: which had outsmarted him this time?

The fall took a lifetime . . .
A brother's voice, echoing his name.
Black hair streaming, veiled stars and moon above.
His answering cry froze in his throat.

. . . and an instant.
Sunlight, blinding bright, replaced moonlit black hair.
Not Brandy. Not a horse at all. No jump; no father. No duel. No woman.
No brother.

He struck.

Blinding pain. His leg, and not.

His lungs exploded . . . collapsed.

He gasped, inhaled—

—water.

Chapter Two

"Nikki? —Nee–ee–kee. Wait. Oh, please, wait."

Long skirts *whooshed* softly across the salon carpet. Soft-soled slippers pitter-pattered across the foyer's patterned tiles.

Snared.

He should have known his luck would run out.

Stifling a sigh, Nikki paused just short of the Tower's front door, aiming his frustration at the necessary business of working driving gloves on over fingers gone suddenly damp, feeling the complete boor and still wishing he could disappear.

But if he felt this way now . . .

"Oh, Nikki." Lidye's voice was charmingly breathless. "I feared I'd miss you."

. . . what was he going to feel after they were married?

Nikki pushed the final fingertip into place, and forced a smile before facing her.

"Where are you going?" Breathless voice. Exertion-flushed cheeks. She'd dashed all the way across two whole rooms and was still on her feet. Amazing.

Be fair, dunMheric, he chastised himself, and managed more warmth in his expression. "Just leaving to pick up Mikhyel."

He'd had no idea he was such a good actor.

"A whole month already?" Tiny hands fluttered delicately to Lidye's shapely (but all-too-modestly covered) bosom.

Rings save him, he was thinking more like Deymorin every day.

"A month and more; he stayed an extra week this time, you know."

Her long lashes blinked—one, two, three, four . . . then

fluttered, as if the calculation was straining her abilities, then: "Wait. I'll get my bonnet and cloak—"

"No!" The involuntary protest escaped before he could stop it.

"No?" Her lower lip quivered pitifully, and Nikki stifled another sigh, and took her hands in his, rather belatedly attempting to soften his protest.

"Lidye, I'm terribly sorry. I didn't mean that the way it sounded. I'm late already, you see, and Khyel must get back to the City tonight."

"Tonight?" Her head tipped toward one shoulder and she blinked up at him. "Won't you have to travel awfully fast, then?"

He nodded solemnly. "And I'll have to take the open carriage."

"Oh. Dear." She blinked again.

"It might rain, you know. There could be lightning."

"Goodness!" Her hands fluttered free again, this time to land on his elbow.

Sort of like a . . . bug.

"And after last month—I *know* how much you suffered and I couldn't *bear* inflicting such discomfort on you again."

Behind the florid phrases, he berated himself for his lack of sincerity, but after six months of daily contact with the young flower he'd dutifully asked to marry him, the perfume had gone decidedly stale. His only relief had been these drives, and recently she'd begun invading them as well.

Her fingers slid delicately around his arm, her head tipped shyly to his shoulder. . . .

It was all he could do not to pull away.

"But I *so* enjoyed it, Nikki. I shouldn't mind the suffering . . . if I were with you."

Yet another blink, followed by several more.

Made a man wonder (unkind thought) whether she was nearsighted or just had something perpetually lodged in her eye. Made a man wonder as well what god he had offended to make the rings think *this* was his perfect match.

Her attention safely on his driving coat lapel, he was free to frown, an emotional release that made it easier to say neutrally, "But I must return tonight, dearest girl. Khyel has an extremely important Council meeting early tomorrow morning, and I simply can't risk a delay at Armayel."

A lace-covered fingertip tremblingly traced his buttons, and her voice quivered pathetically as she murmured, "And I was *such* a hindrance last time, delaying you for two whole *days*. I—I'm so . . ."

Three, he thought glumly, but who was counting? He shoved such uncharitable, unromantic thoughts from his mind and patted her hand consolingly. It wasn't, after all, her fault she had a delicate constitution.

Thrusting aside the insidious little voice that asked *If not her fault, then whose?* along with the image of her counting the Armayel silver, he said, "I truly would never forgive myself if you took ill. It's cold Outside. Colder than last time—"

"Truly? How strange, that spring should be colder than winter . . ."

Spring. Bless the rings, it was. Three months since the midwinter festival.

And nearly six months since his seventeenth birthday.

Her fingers traced the folds of his cloak, disappearing inside, past his waistcoat to his shirt, stopping just short of his skin, before retreating. "You're certain you can't take the carriage?"

"Not and make the time I must." He pulled away, holding her hands captive—to keep them from creeping over him again—and backed toward the door. "Please, Mistress Lidye, I *must* be going."

Her hands withdrew from his, and clasped beneath her chin. "Then *I* must be generous and forgo my personal pleasure, *dear* Nikki. You *will* hurry back?"

Only if Khyel holds a gun on me, he thought, smiled sweetly and escaped out the door.

A breeze drifted across his skin.

Bare skin. Wet bare skin. Cold, wet bare skin.

Deymorin shivered and tried to force sticky eyes open, decided it required far too much effort, and desisted, wondering, for an instant, whether he'd had a good time achieving this state of mental and physical exhaustion.

He remembered falling . . .

And water. There had been water. *Lots* of water.

But he was dry now—comparatively, at least, since it was air he breathed—dry, and lying facedown in (he inhaled deeply) grass. Outside, to judge from that grass, and from the whisper of wind in the trees and the chill against his skin.

Not such a bad situation, especially since his back burned as if it had been flayed; unless, of course, that flayed feeling was the world's worst sunburn, in which case, he supposed he should move. But moving sounded too much like work. Besides, from the chill, he must be in the shade.

Grass. Flayed back. Sun. Shade. Man had to wonder where he was, and how he'd gotten here.

And who'd done the flaying.

Memory expanded, lazily filling the blanks. He remembered Nikki's party, the argument with Mikhyel, Anheliaa and the Tower ... and her palpable anger, the mesmeric silver blur, the pain pressuring him to concede—and light, blinding light, when he refused.

And falling ...

Khyel's voice surrounding him; Khyel's hair, streaming across a night sky.

... and water. Drowning. Why *hadn't* he drowned?

If only he could see.

He tried to rub his eyes, discovered his hand wouldn't move. Couldn't.

Neither arm could move.

Neither ... foot.

And his eyes were covered—blindfolded.

He muttered a curse and pulled harder.

He was tied down. He was damnwell tied down. Not painfully, not even totally immobilized, but enough to force him to stay right where he was, facedown in the grass and damned uncomfortable, now he thought of it.

Strangely, though his backside was painful as hell, he felt nothing underneath, only the inward pressure of a sharp-edged rock against his ribs, the internal strain on a backward-bent knee. His back was on fire, his other side was ... numb.

"All right," he called experimentally, "I'm awake now. Game's over. What's going on?"

Not so much as heavy breathing answered him.

Immobilization, desertion ... What had the old bat done to him?

Damn her.

"Anheliaa?" he shouted. "Barrister! —Where the hell are you?"

Whispers about Tower justice, rumors about criminals disappearing into the air, never to return. Rumors he'd laughed away as outrageous exaggerations of Anheliaa's power, once upon a foolish time, as once he'd have scoffed at ring-induced headaches from hell.

Somehow, those rumors no longer seemed quite so outrageous.

But there was no need (he thought, to calm his visceral heave) for supernatural intervention. Easy enough, when you were Anheliaa dunMoren, to blind a man with that ring-induced lightning, to strike him senseless with ring-induced pain, then spirit him from the City via the arms of highly substantial Tower Guards, and leave him tied barebuck naked for the wolves to devour the evidence.

After that, rumor would do the rest: magic, if you were Anheliaa. Deceptive, dishonest, and deceitful in anyone else.

A surge of anger ripped through him, robbing him of common sense. He fought his bonds, throwing himself backward, ignoring the pain in his back and wrists, the pounding in his skull simply spurring him on to greater effort.

Thump. One arm flew suddenly free.

He thudded back to the ground, the three remaining restraints twisting his limbs awkwardly, crimping his burning back. A turn of the bound wrist and the unseen rope was in his grip, providing leverage to haul his aching carcass upright.

Thump.

He lay still, both arms free, but with his legs turned uselessly under him. His thinking, already clouded with pain, wasn't helped by the fact his head had struck something exceedingly hard and was humming rather like Anheliaa's rings.

Suddenly:

"Not real bright, are you?" A harsh, but youthful voice floated from the darkness beyond his covered eyes.

Apparently, he was no longer alone.

Even as his buzzing head reached that brilliant conclusion, a hand grasped his elbow and pulled him back onto his stomach.

"Hold still," the strangely accented voice-out-of-the-dark ordered.

A third *thump*.
A leg free.
He waited.
Thump.

Ignoring the objections in every muscle and joint, he heaved up and away from the voice's apparent point of origin, tearing at the blindfold, convinced he'd have the advantage on any youth, if only he could see—

But his body betrayed him. His knees wobbled like a newborn colt's, fire shot down his weak leg and it collapsed under him, and he was falling well before the other's body struck him down.

A fist slammed him between the shoulder blades. "I *said*, hold still, idiot."

Deymorin swore roundly, reared back, and swiped again at the blindfold. The fist struck a second time.

"It's a *bandage*, fly-brain. Touch it again, and so help me I'll knock your fool head in. I didn't haul your ass out of that damned oversized mud puddle to lose you now."

He grumbled and collapsed into the grass, feeling queasily vulnerable, yet oddly relieved. He'd never been blind before, and didn't appreciate the sensation now. Liked less having to lie uncomplaining, without a stitch on, while strong callused fingers kneaded something cold and slimy into his burning flesh.

However, Gravel-voice had implied he was in no immediate danger from that source, and disgusting though it felt going on, as the slime dried, the pain subsided; reflection compared the result to his downward side, and he realized whatever the youth was doing to the back, he'd already done to the front, and decided he was just as glad he *couldn't* observe the damage.

He avoided the question of *why* his eyes required a bandage. Refused to entertain the mere possibility that that final blinding flash might have done something permanent. But if it had . . .

If it had, Anheliaa was going to pay.

Perhaps—anger welled, and he revised the thought coldly—he'd collect regardless.

From somewhere (it sounded overhead, which he sincerely hoped was not the case) came the distinctive bleat of a . . . lamb? Perhaps he *was* hallucinating after all. It was fall, much too late in the year for lambs. But the sound didn't repeat, and he concluded he was mistaken.

"Where am I?" he asked at last, that seeming an innocuous enough request.

"Oops. Missed a spot." The hands left him and more oil dribbled down his sides. Then: "Where do you think you are?"

He cursed softly. "Perhaps that's too hard," he said dryly. "Let's try this one: Who are you?"

The hands' owner laughed. "Does it matter?"

Intellectual debates. Too tired and sore to bother, he gave up, and let his mind drift.

Wherever he was, whenever, and whoever Gravel-voice was, Anheliaa was behind his being here.

Following years of living apart, respectful—or at least tolerant—of each other's idiosyncrasies, Anheliaa had changed the rules of their perpetual conflict without warning. He probably should have expected it: their differences were too legion to coexist forever, but now, the padding, so to speak, had been pulled in an attack he could not, *would* not, leave unchallenged.

First, he had to get Nikki out of Rhomatum—away from Anheliaa's influence. Mikhyel too, if he weren't a willing participant in Anheliaa's schemes.

As for the several hundred thousand citizens of Rhomatum and her satellites, he had no interest in being either their conscience or their martyr. He'd tried dealing with them once before, had determined their priorities and found them—at odds with his own.

Once his brothers were safe, he'd see about arming the citizens with the facts of Tower life. The means existed: flyers, underground newspapers ... perhaps, given his name, the *Internode* itself would take the risk. After that, it was up to them whether they allowed Anheliaa dun-Moren a free rein over their lives or deposed her.

Revenge, however, was another matter—undermining Anheliaa's newest obsession would fill that bill quite nicely. And since liberating her two remaining studs would go a long way toward destroying Anheliaa's little breeding program, even revenge boiled down to getting his brothers out of Rhomatum, and out of range of the Rhomatum rings and Anheliaa's sadistic influence.

She could inflict pain—to that, he could personally attest.

According to official records, she could track known individuals within the City—perhaps anywhere along the nodes.

Which put her about on a par with a good hunting hound.

There were the rumors she could transport people instantaneously out of the City, which might be true, rumor also had her flinging bolts of pure leypower and reading minds.

Any of which, he would concede as possible—now. He just didn't know for certain and until he did, he could hardly plan an effective opposition.

He was willing, under the circumstances, to give Khyel's theory some credence. He *might* have some power over the Rhomatum rings (hard-headed stubbornness, if nothing else; there'd been a moment, he recalled or imagined, when he'd almost broken free of Anheliaa's influence) but a head-to-head contest of wills against a sixty-year veteran of ring manipulation was not his idea of a winning battle-plan. First . . .

In its relentless downward path, Gravel-voice's massage roused a stabbing pain in his bad leg, and he grunted objection; Gravel muttered something totally unintelligible, and Gravel's hands poked and prodded with only slightly more care, asking *Here?* and *Here?* To which he replied in fluent Curse.

Gravel-voice laughed, set both palms flat on either side of his tailbone and shoved.

Hard.

Compressing . . . parts into the ground. Parts that objected highly to such cavalier treatment.

But somewhere in and around or through his curse, something grated inside, and *thunked* . . . into place, there was no other way to describe the sudden release of tension and pressure within.

"What the hell—" Deymorin gasped and twisted away.

"Sorry." Humor touched the gruff voice, but the hand that grabbed his shoulder and held him steady was all business. "How's the back? Better?"

Deymorin settled reluctantly onto his stomach, gingerly flexing his lower back, and found, to his rather grudging amazement, that the subtle tension he lived with almost daily was gone, and with it the sharp bite of pain in his leg, and he forced himself to admit, "I suppose." He shifted, protecting the newest bruise, and said sourly, "Least you could do is warn a fellow."

A throaty chuckle filled the air over his head. "Didn't think. Sorry."

He grunted and settled his head on his forearms as his tormentor dribbled more of the oily substance.

"Used to do it for m' sis, don't you know? After her fifth, her back bothered her like everything ... Sorry about the ropes. Wriggling around, you were, like a landed fish, and you need to stay still while it dries, don't you know? Woke up faster than I thought you would, or I wouldn't have left you that way."

Suddenly Gravel-voice was quite chatty ... A nonchalance a man appreciated when the numbing goo oozed over his hips and buttocks and those businesslike hands started sliming his legs. Whatever Anheliaa's henchmen had done to him, they hadn't missed a hand's-breadth of skin. Made a man wonder what else had been flayed and was already, thankfully, numb.

Someone was going to be sorry they hadn't completed the job.

Another bleat.

It *was* a lamb. Or a different one. And soon, from the sounds, several.

Sincerely disturbed, now, he sniffed the grass—that being the most immediately available clue, sticking into his nose as it was—and rubbed a hand across it, trying to connect the finger picture with a remembered image.

Short. Natural ends. Not clipped—not by scythes, not by sheep teeth. Fresh-smelling.

Spring smelling.

This time, the chill that shuddered through him had nothing to do with the ointment the unseen lad poured across his feet.

Sparing him little more than a passing glance, the Oreno Ley registrar waved Nikki through the express stile. No need for papers when you were one of Mheric dunMoren's multiplicity of heirs, less when you made a habit of visiting the family stable several times a week and were on a first name basis with all the Oreno keepers.

Nikki raised a hand in silent thanks and slipped past, hoping the rest of the walk to the stable would prove as uneventful; the registrar nodded and returned with obvious reluctance to an argumentative traveller.

Threads of that argument reached him as he wove through the growing line of impatient inbounds. Something to do with a gun and City regulations.

Strange argument. Must be an Outsider on his first visit. No sane person would consider travelling near the leylines (let alone within a node city) with a loaded firearm. There'd been some spectacular accidents before their ancestors had discovered the causal linkage between leypower and gunpowder.

Even along the lines themselves, handling explosive weapons was more likely to endanger your foot than your adversary. Anyone accustomed to Cities expected guns of any sort to be confiscated at the gates, and one carried the proper papers and identification for retrieval of said items upon departure.

But in Rhomatum even loose powder could be dangerous, and sometimes, people just didn't understand. . . .

Not that anyone needed such devices. Not in Rhomatum. Within Rhomatum one confined oneself to (the tiny scar beneath his arm twitched) knives. Not even Mikhyel could outlaw those.

Personally, he'd always preferred the power of words. An admirable philosophy which hadn't stopped him, since the events of six months past, from carrying a knife at his belt, and training with the cadets twice a week.

Six months. Had it really been so long since he'd last seen Deymorin?

Nikki worked his way through the crowded streets, past produce carts and street sellers, enjoying his own brand of anonymity, here, where he was just one of many potential customers meandering by to pass the time of day, to comment on the weather or current politics, or to purchase an apple or a freshly-baked meat pie.

Market-grazing, Deymorin called it. And it was a habit he'd picked up from Deymorin, he supposed, although since the market lay between the Tower and the stables, it was natural enough. But Deymorin loved the marketplace, as he loved the stables and farmlands. Deymorin loved the press of people, the friendly shouts, even the jostling that might mean a cutpurse.

Deymorin considered it a personal challenge to outsmart such individuals, and if he couldn't, figured the cutpurse deserved the prize.

He doubted a cutpurse had outsmarted his eldest brother in years.

Dammit, Deymorin, where are you?

He never knew these days how he felt toward Deymorin. Angry, that for certain. Deymorin had made him a promise—the first important promise he'd ever asked of him—and broken it within the hour.

But after six months of *Lidye*—

"Hai-yo, Nikki, lad!"

Nikki forced a smile to his lips and edged past an energetic, four-way argument on the relative merits of various chicken breeds to answer the voice hailing him from a low bench behind a leather-strewn table.

"Where be that brother o' yourn?" the saddler asked the Dreaded Question. "I ha'no seen him for—lord o' my, since afore midwinter. Been holdin' this here—" He held up a bitless bridle. "Bought a' paid, 'tis. Bought a' paid. Just waitin' to set on a head."

Nikki ran a hand over the supple leather and fingered the fine tooling appreciatively. These days, he tended to pass by stalls with little more than a glance at the wares, avoiding the owners because of the inevitable questions Deymorin's Brother attracted. Questions to which he could give only the official response ...

"He rode up to Pretierac last fall, to check out some native ponies and got snowed in for the winter in that early blizzard. We expect him back any day now."

... regardless how unsatisfactory the answer was to both himself and Deymorin's friends. Deymorin didn't get snowed in, and Deymorin especially didn't miss the spring foaling at Darhaven regardless of health or weather.

One thing he knew, Deymorin wasn't at Darhaven. He'd been to the breeding farm twice since Deymorin disappeared: once with Mikhyel, a second time alone, quietly, and unannounced, and he simply couldn't believe Tonio and the other staff could fake their obvious growing concern over their master's continued absence.

It was all very disturbing.

He handed the headstall back, expressed his admiration of the workmanship, said he'd tell Deymorin as soon as he saw him, and sidled out of the stall, mumbling some excuse, uncertain which he used this time.

Mikhyel, being more accustomed to subterfuge, might

have given more complete, more believable answers, had
people ever thought to ask him. But they never thought,
never made the connection with Deymorin on the rare occasions they saw Mikhyel dunMheric walking this same
path, not even when Nikki accompanied him.

Or perhaps it wasn't that they didn't think to ask, not
that they didn't recognize him, but rather that Mikhyel
never stopped, never gave anyone an opportunity to ask.

It was even possible some of the Outsiders dealing their
wares had never seen Mikhyel Rhomandi dunMheric. Prior
to Deymorin's disappearance, Mikhyel hadn't been through
this market since their father had died.

Mikhyel had told him once, years ago and in passing,
that strangers disturbed him, particularly crowds like the
market-grazers. Nikki had thought that quite odd, at the
time, and wondered, perhaps, if he'd heard wrong, but after
accompanying Mikhyel through these streets, after watching his brother's deliberately evasive, forward-staring eyes
as he passed between the stalls, he'd come to realize how
very real that fear must be.

Mikhyel had been going to the Tower Hill offices daily
since he was a child, and by the time he was Nikki's age,
he'd been in charge of them, constantly surrounded by people and buildings and things he knew and had known all
his life. His tailor and barber attended him in the Tower.
He hardly knew other citizens, let alone the farmers and
breeders and merchants Deymorin preferred.

Seemed like a lonely way to live, though not as bad as
Anheliaa, who never got outside the Tower anymore. And
that—one way or the other, Anheliaa's or Mikhyel's—was
how they would have *him* live, if they had their way.

Except, Anheliaa would say, he'd have Lidye to keep
him company.

Day and night.

He shuddered, understanding, after six months of Lidye
dunTarim, exactly why Deymorin had left, and why his
brother had never so much as sent word of where he was
or how he was or when (if ever, Nikki now feared) he was
coming back to Rhomatum, no matter how many promises
or I.O.U.s given.

But understanding did not excuse.

Initially, Deymorin's leaving, his casual disregard of the
promise he'd made had seemed a personal betrayal. They'd

had a deal. Deymorin wouldn't leave until they—he, Mikhyel, and Deymorin—had had a chance to work things out.
Six months ago, that had had ultimate significance. Now . . .

Now, he realized there was more at issue than his own,
admittedly rather childish, desires for an end of strife and
interfamilial power plays. In his selfish disappearance,
Deymorin had deserted, not just him, not just Mikhyel, but
all the Outside as well.

Poor already-overworked Khyel, who hated and feared
the Outside, had been spending at least one week in five
travelling the Betweens, seeing to all the things Deymorin
used to manage. And when he was in the City, he was up
till all hours of the night meeting with councillors, syndics,
and people Nikki suspected, when he saw them passing in
the halls, of being Rhomatum's eyes and ears in other
nodes.

Nikki would have helped, offered to help every time he
took Mikhyel Outside, but Mikhyel insisted on doing the
work himself, insisted it was time he learned about fertiliz-
ers and mulch and foaling and seasons. And Inside the
Tower, Mikhyel said it was his job, and would take longer
to explain than to do it himself. Besides, Mikhyel said, he
depended on Nikki to keep Lidye and Nethaalye occupied
and entertained.

He'd rather be helping Tomas muck stables.

He stopped at Fredriri's booth as he always did whenever
the instrument-maker passed through Rhomatum, partially
because it was *his* interest alone, not one he shared with
Deymorin, or Mikhyel, and partially because he couldn't
resist trying out the new instruments.

He always stopped. He always admired. But somehow,
he never bought—at least, not for his own use. To do so
seemed—disloyal to Barney. And because Fredriri was *his*
friend, he could get the out-of-town news and gossip without Deymorin's fate entering the conversation.

But today, even Fredriri failed him, insistently drawing
his attention to the wares of the seamstress sharing his stall,
Fredi himself obviously more intent on her buxom charms
than in promoting a known nonsale, and unwittingly reminding him of his own impending matrimony and associated obligations.

Nikki was dutifully checking out the embroidery on a
festival blouse of the seamstress' art and wondering list-

lessly if Lidye would like it, when, from the corner of his
eye, he glimpsed a familiar figure.

Mirym.

Anheliaa's servant was weaving her way like a wispy
brown shadow through the crowd, pausing at each stall to
examine the items at length. Strange behavior, if she was
here on Anheliaa's errands: through monetarily generous
to her ladies-in-waiting, his aunt was adamant about loiter-
ing and time-wasting. Stranger still, she hadn't even a footman to carry her packages and protect her from unwanted
attentions.

Finally, before people began to note and comment on
his apparent obsession with a young, unaccompanied female, he approached her, ostensibly to pay his respects.

"And what are you doing here?" he asked conversationally, having determined she was, indeed, on holiday from
Anheliaa's demands.

She raised a basket filled with small packages, and lifted
a gently cynical eyebrow.

He ducked his head and tapped his forehead. "Dim-
witted, eh?"

She shrugged, and, tipping her head toward the stream
of humanity outside the stall, moved into the sunlight and
out of a potential customer's way. Considerate, he thought,
and recalling that long-ago birthday, and his private little
party, wasn't at all surprised at the discovery.

Taking the basket from her hands, he followed her
through the crowd to another stall, not quite certain what
to do, now he'd tacitly fallen in with her.

A surprisingly heavy basket, which upon closer examination of the packages revealed:

"Apples?" he asked, lifting one free of its cloth bag.

She touched index finger to thumb in interlocking circles—her sign for Anheliaa—then brushed an index finger
haughtily past her nose.

"Anheliaa doesn't like them?" he hazarded.

She nodded. Touched her own mouth and closed her
eyes blissfully.

"And you do."

Her tongue peeked out between her lips, tracing a damp-
ening path around the edge.

He laughed, both delighted and worried: she was so ingenuous; she seemed easy prey for the unscrupulous.

"Is anyone here with you?" he asked.

She cast a look about as though checking every potential hiding place, then shook her head sadly, looking like a lost five-year-old.

He gave a shout of laughter that drew attention from passersby, who caught her expression and turned accusatory. One man actually stepped forward, shouldering between them to ask Mirym was this cad annoying her and did she wish to be rid of him.

"I didn't—" Nikki protested, but Mirym laughed silently, dipped a curtsy to her would-be rescuers and pulled him by the arm into the shade between two stalls. When they were safely alone, he said, "Did anyone ever tell you you're a wicked, wicked girl?"

Another innocent blink, a disturbingly familiar fluttering of eyelids. . . .

Rings, another Lidye—or rather, a roguish caricature of the type.

He chuckled. "Still, your champions out there had a point: it's hardly appropriate, your being here all alone, at the mercy of every letch and—"

Another of those eloquent searches of the shadows, mock horror in every line, a search that settled on him. Her eyes widened. A gloved hand crept to her mouth.

Before she could create another scene, he shook her arm. "All right—you win. You win. —Peace?"

She smiled and patted his arm, immediately transforming into a proper young female, and they moved back into the marketplace flow.

Which inspired burlesque, while charming and entertaining and fun, failed to guide him to a proper course of action. While he couldn't just leave her, he had business of his own. Important business. Mikhyel's business, which meant the City's.

He could, he supposed, send her home with one of the grooms, but he found himself increasingly reluctant to leave her company, found himself wondering what she did on her days off, where her family was, where, in fact, she came from.

Though he'd rarely crossed her path since that stolen little party, he'd never forgotten—was reminded of her each time he picked up his guitar and set the embroidered strap over his head, or plucked the sweet-timbred strings.

She deserved better than a lonely day in the market, after which, what would she do? retire to her room and her stitching?

"Have you the whole day off?" he asked finally.

She nodded . . .

"Plans?"

. . . then gave one of her articulate shrugs.

"Would you like to join me for a drive?"

Her dark eyes scanned the horizon, then her head cocked questioningly.

"I'm off to Armayel to pick up Mikhyel. We'll have an early supper and return before dark—well before you're due back. Khyel's been gone twice as long as usual and he'll be anxious to get home." He stopped and maneuvered to face her. "So you see, you must come with me."

She tucked her chin in and gave him a gently skeptical frown.

"To save me from his doldrums." Ignoring the human wave breaking around them, he set her basket on the ground, then held her hand to his chest, urging soulfully: "Please?"

The frown dissolved into a soundless giggle. She shoved him away and reclaimed her hand. Thumb under her chin, she tapped her lips with her index finger while scanning the distant foothills. Tipping her head back toward him, she hugged her pelisse-covered shoulders, giving a mock little shiver.

"I keep a spare cloak at the stable. —Must. Wool, you see. —Not elegant, but *very* warm."

Her lower lip disappeared beneath barely visible teeth, and her clear eyes narrowed. Cautious. Not one to decide on a whim. Possibly even making a mental list of his motives.

He put on as innocent a face as possible, wanting her to accept the invitation for his own sake now. She was pleasant company, delightfully self-sufficient, inspiration to his entertainment ingenuity. She felt . . . comfortable, as no one since Deymorin left had felt comfortable, even his so-called best friends, Phell and Bertie, having deserted him (in disgust, he feared) since Lidye's arrival.

When her face relaxed and she gave a quick nod, it was as if the sun shone a degree brighter.

"Thank you!" he said on a huff of air, brushing a hand

across his brow in only slightly exaggerated relief. "So—to the stables. Walk? Or shall I fetch a cabin?"

Her eyes swept the soft puffs of cloud overhead, glanced toward the human-drawn enclosed cabs working their way a slow step at a time along the crowded cobblestones, then she lifted her heavy skirts to shake a tiny, eloquent foot.

"Your wish is my command, m'lady." He tucked her hand into his arm, picked up the basket, and steered her toward the stables.

He began a cheerful monologue, a totally fictitious commentary regarding the private lives of passing shoppers, a libelous nonsensicality to which she responded with her own comments, revealing an unusual talent for visual mimicry, until by the time they reached the stable, they were both doubling over with irreverent laughter.

Storm and Ashley were vociferous in their welcome of him, accepting Mirym with tempered equine dignity—until she offered them her precious hand-picked apples. After that, she could do no wrong, in their eyes—or his.

Negotiating the carriage through crowded streets required little effort on his part, the market-wise team working their own way quietly past vehicles and pedestrians alike. Once free of the market and past the outer wall-gate, however, their eagerness to be let out vibrated down the lines.

He gave them a notch, but it was not enough: they shook their heads and snorted, eager to have the brisk spring air filling their lungs. While their driver agreed wholeheartedly, Nikki couldn't help remembering Lidye's reactions the last time out, the fear, the fingers clutching his arm—and threatening his control of the lines—at the first sign of open fields.

Equine demands grew more insistent. He hadn't had time to take them out all week. They had energy to burn—and so had he.

A stolen glance: Mirym's eyes were closed, her face lifted to the sun and the breeze, her hands folded calmly in her lap.

Trying to contain his eagerness, not wishing to pressure her into something that *would* frighten her, he asked: "Shall I let them go?"

She met his eyes; a wave of emotion crossed her face too

rapidly to read; then, one hand moving surreptitiously to grip the buggy's side, she dipped her chin.

"You're sure? Don't let me scare you."

Another unreadable look, then she grinned widely, clamped her free hand on her wide-brimmed hat, and nodded vigorously.

He gave the greys the rein they craved, and the buggy surged forward.

Something stank.

Deymorin shifted the arm pillowing his head, and realized:

Curse the rings and their thrice-damned mistress, that stench came from *him*.

This time, he awoke as if from a normal sleep—provided one counted sleeping alone on a grassy slope, clad in nothing but a stained wool blanket, normal. But his eyes opened without obstruction, and his vision cleared (normally, thank the various illegal deities), and his hands and legs were free, if unwilling, as yet, to move. In fact, aside from a pounding headache and smelling like a dungheap, he felt in quite amazingly good health, considering the possibilities memory suggested.

For a moment, he wondered if the whole thing had been a dream: the gravel-voiced youth, the water, the fall ... the fight with Anheliaa, maybe even Nikki's bolt to Tirise's.

Perhaps he'd fallen asleep after making love in this rather idyllic spot, perhaps (his imagination gained momentum) with the shepherd's daughter, and the maiden had left him here while she tended the flock.

Or, perhaps (imagination deferring to cynical practicality, and considering his clothing was nowhere in sight), said gentle maiden had absconded after stealing him quite literally blind.

But the feminine thief had no substance in his memories. His brothers and Anheliaa and her rings did. The residual pain in his back when he twisted around to scan over his shoulder was definitely real. His eyes stung in the sunlight ... possibly the green-stained strip lying in the grass next to him was the bandage that had instigated the row of his last waking moments.

The only thing missing (other than his clothes) was the gravel-voiced youth.

On the other hand, the charred remains of a small fire he didn't remember setting still warmed the nearby air, and if he accepted Nikki's birthday and Anheliaa as truth, he still had to explain the lambs and the abundant, spring-green foliage surrounding him. Nikki's birthday—at least as he remembered it—was in the fall: a good six months ago.

If not, Darius save him, longer.

Assuming his memory was sound, the old woman must have knocked him cold with her mind-invading rings and had him put into winter storage, possibly talked Diorak into keeping him drugged into incoherency.

He rubbed a chin bare of stubble across his supporting forearm, flicked dirt from under a smooth-edged fingernail. If that were the case, his jailers had taken uncommonly good care of him just to flay him and set him out for the wolves.

Which creatures would have been far more appreciative of a free meal in the dead of winter.

He'd put nothing past—or beyond—Anheliaa, not after that painful assault inside his head. He supposed it was even possible she'd used those damned rings to confound his thinking permanently. His recall seemed clear enough up to Nikki's birthday, but all that lay between that and his last blind awakening was a series of disconnected impressions having little to do with coherent reality.

Of course, come tomorrow he might not remember lying here wondering where the sheep belonged and what had happened to the gravel-voiced youth. Perhaps he'd awake to an entirely different scenario. Perhaps he was really in jail, and this lake, the sheep, and everything around him was some fevered dream.

Except, if he were dreaming, there would be, without question, a shapely shepherdess to share his lucid moments with.

At least, bless all the ancient gods and damn the rings, he wasn't blind.

No thanks to Anheliaa.

And he was alive, despite Anheliaa's efforts. If he read Gravel-voice correctly, his previous immobile status had been for his own good, not the wolves' convenience or Anheliaa's pleasure.

Therefore, Gravel-voice might be a potential friendly.

Might.

Gravel-voice had spoken Mauritumin, which was more than the webless so-called barbarians to the north and east did, but with an accent he hadn't recognized, and while he hadn't a guardsman's talent in identifying such things, one was reminded forcibly of cutpurse/assassins with strange accents . . .

And the storms, and the Tower and Nikki's seventeenth birthday, and . . .

Rings save him, the promise he'd made to the boy; that reconciliation which had meant so much to him. Would he ever believe his older brother hadn't simply run away? Considering he felt the promise necessary in the first place, Nikki must share Mikhyel's assessment of his character, at least in that sense. If Mikhyel hadn't told Nikki the truth about what happened in the Tower.

If Mikhyel knew the truth. If, considering Mikhyel's threat to the rings, Anheliaa hadn't scattered him to the winds as well.

But Anheliaa needed Mikhyel—to do the damned paperwork if nothing else.

Of course, she also needed a backup stud for her breeding plan. Nikki, being more complacent, would probably be more to her taste.

Him, she didn't need. Had Mikhyel not risked his hand to stop her, she'd have killed him right there in the Tower. Lacking other physical means of accomplishing that goal, she'd have driven him crazy with the pain until he killed himself.

If it were just himself, he might well tell her where to stick her rings and never return to Rhomatum. His life was Outside, provided she hadn't impounded the Outside estates already.

Even if she had, his people, sharecroppers and employees alike, were a loyal (to him) and self-sufficient lot. She wouldn't absorb them and what was theirs without a fight— and Rhomatum needed their produce, not the other way around, therefore chances were she'd leave them alone.

At least for the moment. Until she discovered he was still alive, despite her undoubtedly fervent wishes to the contrary.

But he had two brothers still living under her Towered roof, and should either of them refuse to accede to her plans, he had no doubt that she'd deal with them as she had with him. Perhaps with more permanent results.

A man had to wonder, who'd weathered that pain and lived, whether Anheliaa had used similar tactics with Mikhyel. That was a disturbing thought. Anheliaa had had her beringed claws in Mikhyel since the tender age of thirteen. Her methods had sent a grown man to his knees; how must they have affected Mikhyel over the years? More importantly, how would they affect his future choices, now he's taken a stand against her?

So much depended on Mikhyel, on his motives and goals and what he had or had not told Nikki. If Nikki didn't know, if he believed himself deserted, he'd join forces with Anheliaa, do whatever Mikhyel suggested to keep what he perceived as his own family intact, because Nikki wanted family, Nikki hated arguments, and *(face it, Rhomandi)* Nikki was inclined toward the road of least resistance.

Mikhyel had power, if he chose to use it, and Mikhyel might well fight.

For several brief instants, before the party, during, and after, Mikhyel had revealed a side of himself Deymorin hadn't seen in years, and Anheliaa . . . hadn't liked it. He realized now, lying here, free of familial distraction, she'd been watching them, inciting fragmentation when peace threatened. She'd *wanted* Mikhyel and himself to fight, which might be sheer perversity of spirit—certainly she had enough of that for any ten individuals—or might be something ominously more pernicious.

For years, for Nikki's sake, he and Mikhyel had avoided letting their differences peak into full-blown battle. The first time they had—that last evening before Anheliaa entered the room—there'd been no fireworks, lightning hadn't struck the Tower—they had, in fact, come close to, if not reconciliation, at least a truce and some seminal understanding.

He wondered now if Anheliaa had known all along that they'd never really hurt one another. If Anheliaa wanted them in opposite camps, she would (following that warped logic) *want* Nikki to constantly smooth their feathers so they'd never reconcile, never compromise, never—band against her.

But they had, when Mikhyel threatened the rings in the Tower. After that, she'd been forced to rid herself of one

of them permanently, and therefore goaded *him* into that
final battle. Gravel-voice wasn't supposed to be here.
Naked, flayed, dumped into that pool below, he'd have had
little chance of survival.

Khyel (if memory was in any sense reliable) had been in
the Tower with them, and obviously knew well the risk of
opposition, even before Anheliaa attacked him. Depending
on his personal motives and his own goals, their middle
brother could as easily encourage Nikki into a similar disastrous protest, or steer him into compliance.

Or he might get himself killed trying to fight Anheliaa
alone, if he had come to the same conclusions Deymorin
was now drawing, and if he was the man Deymorin increasingly believed him to be.

His brothers needed help and he wasn't about to run
away this time. Khyel's accusation to that effect had startled him, wounded him deeply. Perhaps Mikhyel was right
to accuse him of running away when their father died. Certainly from Mikhyel's point of view he'd taken the easy
way out.

But he *hadn't* run away this time, and one way or another, Nikki—and Khyel—were going to know that one
truth. And getting his brothers the truth meant getting to
his brothers.

Which in turn meant figuring *where* he was.

A leyline ran though the deceptively innocent meadow:
the barren strip running through the trees, into the small
lake, and out the other side was far too flat and wide to
be a seasonal stream.

Undeveloped leys did not exist between Rhomatum and
her primary satellites. Even the unsettled tertiaries had
lights erected along them, though the lights barely glimmered, and the land itself had long since been claimed on
speculation toward the time when even those minuscule
intersections would be capped and towered.

The surrounding mountains, and the untapped ley would
argue for the far side of Hanitum, or possibly Persitum
in the Kharatas Range. The latter would account for the
unfamiliar accent—and fit Anheliaa's warped sense of justice. She was perfectly capable of throwing him into Garetti's lap just to watch them both squirm.

Came one of those bleats from above. This time, he was

able to *see* the rock overhang that explained the impression of airborne sheep.

Downslope lay a pool, calm and green-shadowed among budding azaleas.

And in the pool . . .

Perhaps his first—or rather second—supposition was correct. That bare figure rising from the shallows was unquestionably more shepherd's daughter than gravel-voiced youth.

Nikki pulled the horses down to a distance-covering, extended trot, a pace they could hold for hours, hope returning that they might make up at least in part for the time lost in the market. The road they travelled was one the greys knew as well or better than he, and the grain awaiting them at Armayel was sufficient incentive to keep their minds on their business; the air was clear, visibility good, at least until they reached the heavily wooded lands around Armayel . . .

Which left him free to entertain his silent companion; a far from unappealing prospect.

Cheeks flushed with the breeze, hair shaken loose beneath her wind-battered hat, her dark eyes shining with excitement, Mirym looked almost pretty.

He grinned at her, and she smiled back, then threw her arms wide, as if to absorb all the sunshine at once, as if, like a flower, she required that glow to blossom, seemingly at ease in what should have been a thoroughly foreign environment.

Lidye's fears, while frustrating and tedious, had been understandable, and, in a way, expected, since citizens of a node city went Outside only to travel between nodes, and then they rode in sleeper-floaters along the leys, never seeing the open fields and the green forests they passed. Mirym's open, almost childlike enjoyment was the exception, a mystery wanting exploration.

Much as he had of the unknown market-gazers, he found himself making up scenarios to explain Mirym.

. . . She was the unplanned daughter of a Family, her parents banished to the Outside before her birth, forced to raise her in the Barbarous Darkness Between the Lines.

Or perhaps she was a Rhomandi relative, considering she now served Anheliaa, a cousin or even half-sister. But when he tried to track his own, depressingly sparse family web, no possibility suggested itself. The Darius line, after Darius' own multiplicity of wives, had grown thin. Children born, but few surviving to reproduce.

Odd, now he thought of it. And he wondered if this belated observation should concern him, particularly considering Deymorin's mysterious absence. But the deaths of his unknown potential relatives had never been mysterious, only frequent.

There were a few, mostly quite distant, possibilities, offspring acknowledged, but not in the direct Rhomandi line. Deymorin had at least two, but she was too old to be one of his. Or perhaps an old retainer's daughter. Possibly someone Deymorin owed a favor, except Deymorin wouldn't consider placing someone in Anheliaa's control a *favor* . . .

Deymorin. *Dammit, brother* . . .

A tiny cough. He swallowed hard, jerked abruptly back to reality. Mirym, huddled now in the borrowed cloak, was eyeing him strangely, almost suspiciously.

He smiled. "Sorry. Gathering rose petals. —You like it Outside?"

She nodded.

"Do you get out of Rhomatum frequently?"

A puzzled blink. One hand crept out of the cloak's folds and held up one finger.

"First time?" An unaccountable disappointment touched him at her nod, only to quickly fade when she tapped her forehead and flipped her hand like a man doffing a hat.

"Thank you?" he hazarded.

Acknowledgment.

"Well, you're quite welcome, ma'am," he said, and Mirym's head ducked, her fine curls falling forward, hair and bedraggled hat veiling her face.

She pulled her hat free, trying to fingercomb and pat her hair into some form of order, searching her lap for lost pins. Her hair, a pale, colorless brown, was more tightly curled than his, and, free of its severe chignon, it fluffed about her face, catching the sun, making a silvery halo for her face and shoulders, making her unfashionably pointed features look like some fey creature in a child's Tamshi book.

"Please, don't," he objected, and at her startled blink: "It looks wonderful."

Her attempts had tangled one lock behind her ear. Unable to resist, he shifted the reins into one hand and reached to fluff it free.

She dodged his touch, suspicion flooding her face, and pushed into the far corner of the buggy, as far from him as the handrail would allow, scanning the passing ground as if preparing a leap to freedom. Not anxious, not frightened, just eminently determined to avoid what she'd obviously perceived as an advance on his part.

A decidedly unwanted advance.

"Mirym, I'm *sorry*," he said, horrified. "I didn't mean it like that."

A single doubtful blink . . .

"Truly, I didn't."

. . . that became one of her narrow-eyed evaluations.

He chewed his lower lip, trying not to compound the problem. "If you're really worried about your hair, you can fix it when we get to Armayel. Beasley—the housekeeper, you know—will have hairpins. There's even a comb—wide teeth and everything." He patted his own endlessly irritating curls, the short ones sticking out at all angles from under his hat, and flipped the severely braided queue, setting it flopping between his shoulder blades. "You see, I'm sadly familiar with the problem."

Her silent giggle broke the tension, and expanding on the innocuous theme, he proceeded to babble about various ridiculous (and frequently embarrassing) moments resulting from his hair, which nonsense seemed, at least, to amuse her, and before he realized, they were well past the halfway point, and moving into the wooded greenbelt that extended in all directions around Armayel, a vast, natural garden whose upkeep employed several households.

The greys eased their pace, knowing his preferences, and he didn't urge them on. They were making good time, and would arrive soon enough. His monologue died a natural, companionable death, birds and the whisper of the wind through the leaves carrying the conversation.

Watching her, he discovered a new kind of joy, that of sharing something he loved with someone capable of open appreciation of it, and he couldn't help but wonder if this was the special feeling Deymorin had talked about having the first time Deymorin had taken him to Darhaven.

And he wondered if Lidye would have been this pleasant,

had she not been trying constantly to secure his affections. She wanted the position marriage with him could give her, he had no illusions about that and couldn't blame her for that ambition, but the constant need for reassurance, the physical clinging—would Mirym have resorted to such tactics, were their situations reversed?

A light touch on his arm requested his attention: Mirym, who cocked her head and touched her forehead with a fingertip.

Somehow, he didn't think so.

"Just wondering," he said. "Where are you from? What node? What Family?"

Her chin tucked in a gesture he was learning meant a suspicious *Why?*

"Just wondering why Aunt couldn't have chosen you for me instead of Lidye."

The words were uttered before he realized where his thoughts had taken him. Her response was outrage and another scan of the ground racing past their wheels.

The hand he reached to keep her from falling got slapped for its trouble, and he jerked back, palm outward.

"I'm sorry! Honestly, Mirym, I'm not . . . I didn't mean . . . It's just . . . Oh, never mind!"

The horses tossed their heads and broke stride, his tension translating to their sensitive mouths. He threw himself back against the padded seat and distracted himself with sorting the reins. For a time, he was sufficiently occupied settling them back into their easy jog.

A light hand brushed his elbow. He jumped; the horses did; again he steadied them, this time prepared for Mirym's attention-requesting touch, less so for the surprisingly sympathetic expression that greeted him.

"I didn't mean that the way it sounded, Mirym. I'm just . . ."

He stopped, embarrassed that he'd ever brought the topic up with this particular girl. Her position was awkward enough, her duties to Anheliaa forcing her into family politics and what should be private matters. But there was something so calm, so unpretentious and . . . worldly about her. Like Deymorin. And when she pressed his arm encouragingly, as if to say *It's all right,* he relented to that pressing need to say *something . . . to anyone.*

"It's Lidye. I should be thrilled with her, I know. Aunt

claims she's doing exceedingly well with the rings, she's ever so accommodating, and she seems interested in everything I do, but . . ."

He paused, finding no words to describe the vague feeling. Her fingers squeezed his arm, urging him to continue.

In desperation, he blurted out: "She *likes* my poetry!"

An upward palm asked, clear as sunshine on a cloudless day, *So? What's wrong with that?*

"My poetry's *terrible*."

She shook her head until the curls flipped her nose.

"How would you know?"

Her mouth opened, closed, then, with a little shake of the head, she looked away, nose in the air.

"Just know, do you?"

The curls nodded once. Emphatically.

"You'd better watch yourself. I'll make you read them."

She turned back, and before he knew what she was up to, caught his hand and slashed his wrist with a fingertip, then tapped her mouth, committing him to his promise. It was an ancient, childish gesture, one Darius' descendants had inherited from the natives of this valley.

He laughed, feeling like a fly caught in her gentle web. "Just never claim I didn't warn you." He sobered. "Don't you see? She *hates* poetry. Knows nothing about the classics, or even the modern drivel. So either way, it's an insult: either to my intelligence, or my talent."

Her dubious look was back.

"You don't think so?"

She shrugged.

"What if she's just saying it? What if she'll do anything to make this marriage succeed? Her parents were ecstatic when I proposed. They might have pressured her to accept. Anheliaa thinks she's wonderful, whenever Mikhyel mentions her, it's to say how beautiful she is, and what a—" He felt like gagging. "—lovely couple we make, Aunt's friends tell me how lucky I am. So why don't I *feel* lucky?"

The warm sympathy had vanished. Her face remained blank, offering no insight. Tenaciously, he pressed his point:

"Last month, when I went after Mikhyel, Lidye *insisted* on coming along. Before we left, she went on and on and on about how *lovely* the drive must be and how she'd rather spend the time with me than stay in the Tower alone—never mind Nethaalye, is there, and Aunt and *doz-*

ens of other people. But she *hated* the drive—complained of the cold, wanted the carriage to stop swaying, said it was making her sick and covered her eyes the entire way." *Into* his shoulder. "It was *awful*. Until we got there. Then she was all sweetness and delicate sensibilities. She couldn't *possibly* have made the trip back that same day." Or the next. Or the next. "While she was there, she never went outside; she just wandered the house, fingering this and that like ... like an *appraiser*. And when we did return, we had to walk the horses the whole way.... It took us the *entire* day! And despite that, *this* time, she tried to come again. I—" He sought her calm gaze. "Why would she want to, after the first time made her miserable?"

She looked at him, then ahead at the horses and the road, then back to him. Finally, she shrugged, touched first her heart, then his lips, and shrugged again.

"Maybe because she loves me?"

She nodded slowly, deep, emphatic dips of her head.

"Oh, dear."

Chapter Three

. . . Then you shall have her . . .

One had to wonder: was *that* Anheliaa's plan? Grant his 'wish' and wait for him to come crawling home?

Well, Deymorin thought, as that curvaceous figure, hidden now beneath a ragged, gathered skirt and loose peasant shirt, swayed its way up the grassy slope, *you might have a long wait, Auntie-dearest.*

A patched travel bag slung over one shoulder hampered his shepherdess' efforts to contain the shirt's voluminousness with a simple strip cummerbund. Finally, in singularly eloquent silent frustration, she stopped and flung the bag to the ground, took several wraps around her narrow waist and secured the ends with a snap. Then she plucked something long and narrow from between her teeth, and slipped it into that newly-secured waistband with a pat—rather like tucking an old friend into bed.

A knife. A fairly large, serviceable knife. Not that he'd hold that against her: a shepherd's daughter out alone in the hills, particularly one with so tempting a figure, would need to protect herself.

As the unknown female approached, Deymorin tore his eyes from her long, powerful, distractingly sensual strides, and put his head down to give an outward appearance of sleep, while watching her approach through slitted lids.

Perhaps not a shepherd's daughter. Voluptuous, yes, but slim for a country girl, and (she paused to take an irritated tug at the skirt wrapping uncooperatively around her damp legs) singularly inept at the dress. She might well be something quite interestingly different.

Possibly, considering her rather casual—one might even say loving—attitude regarding the knife, some lady outlaw preparing to . . . take advantage of him.

He stifled laughter in the crook of his elbow and the smelly, stained blanket lying half-under, half-over him.

Insane, that's what he was. Anheliaa's games had bent his mind, robbing him of what little sense he'd ever had. Here he was—he, who had been preparing a lecture for Nikki about worldly caution—lying naked as the day he was born, on an unknown hillside, thinking lewd thoughts about an unknown female, while said unknown female carried an undoubtedly very sharp knife in his direction. . . .

The rustle of skirts drew near; a twig snapped beneath an incautious foot.

A toe prodded bruised ribs.

"Lazy bastard, aren't you?" Gravel-voice had returned, too. "C'mon, Rag'n'bones, wakey-wakey."

He cursed roundly and rolled to an elbow, fully expecting third party involvement. Possibly the knife-carrying shepherdess' brother, or (disappointing thought) husband.

But there was only the shepherd's daughter.

Realizing, in some disillusion, that the disagreeable voice must have emanated from her, he squinted up at the backlit figure and found further disappointment in dripping, rough-shorn hair sticking out at odd angles about a freckled face and reddened nose.

"Then you shall have her. . . ."

If this apparition was Anheliaa's notion of his shepherd's daughter, she had a great deal to learn about her oldest nephew's taste in women.

"So, Rag'n'bones," the apparition grated. Then sneezed, sniffed, and ran a dampened cloth under its too-red nose. "Now you've had your eyeful, you going to tell me why I shouldn't dump you back? You're hardly a first-rate catch."

Catch? Dump him back? Fine talk for such a homely shepherdess to the Rhomandi himself—

Another burst of unholy amusement. Rings save him, her attitude had him thinking like lord-and-lofty Mikhyel.

Homely she might be, but she wasn't stupid, neither was she helpless, as the bruise between his shoulder blades reminded him.

Neither was she Anheliaa's, considering the treatment he'd had of her thus far. She might well be impressed with his lordly credentials—certainly with the potential of his lordly purse.

So he opened his mouth to reform her thinking. Unfortunately, all that came out was a rather petulant: "Rag'n'bones?"

(The ground shook with the beat of horse-hooves.

(Hordes galloped down the leyroad toward Rhomatum, their weapons blazing a steady stream of chained lightning.

(Rhomatumin soldiers struggled to intercept, their horses foundering in deep mud that turned to flowing rivers and whirlpools that sucked them down and down into the bowels of the earth herself. . . .)

"M'lord Khyel?"

Not the ground quaking after all, but Gareg, shaking his shoulder ever-so-gently.

"Pardon, m'lord," the overseer said, from the far side of sleep-sticky eyelashes, "but Master Nikaenor has arrived."

Mikhyel yawned widely and leaned his head back in the chair, striving to ignore the aches in his joints and the pounding pain behind his eyes, where that final dreadful dreamscape yet lingered.

Such a lovely spring cocktail: rumors of war out of Mauritum, threats of flood here in Armayel . . . with such a plethora of problems, a man really ought not sleep anyway.

At least Nikki was here—finally. He'd hoped for earlier, hoped to be well on the return trip by now, but he could hardly complain: more than likely, the boy had been forced to adjust his own plans to make the trip at all. Never mind he'd told Nikki to send someone else this time, the third trip in two weeks.

He should never have let Nikki talk him into this carting him one way and the other, but Nikki claimed to enjoy the trips, had objected loudly and at length when Mikhyel had dared suggest he commandeer a driver and coach for these necessary journeys to the Rhomandi holdings.

He had no doubt the boy relished the time with his horses, but most of all, he suspected Nikki needed the time away from the Tower and its perfumed prima donnas. Unfair, to put the entertainment of Anheliaa's two apprentices off on him, but Nikki managed the women so much better than he, and what with one thing and another . . .

If only there weren't so much to do. Always, so much . . .

"Sir?" Gareg, again, keeping him from drifting off.

Good man, Gareg. Mikhyel thanked the overseer, forced himself out of his chair, and headed for the door. Gareg swung his greatcoat over his shoulders while he walked, telling him to take care of himself and get some rest, once he got back to Rhomatum, and that he had every confidence in his lordship's ability to convince Council to do all that was necessary.

A week since, they'd been near blows.

That was when he'd sent Nikki back alone, determined to settle his differences with Gareg once and for all, or replace the overseer with a man of his own choosing.

He didn't blame Gareg, never had. It was simply that Armayel had a major problem; a problem Deymorin had been working to solve before that last disastrous visit to Rhomatum, and he needed *someone* who would explain that problem in terms he could comprehend.

Inexplicable changes in weather patterns of the past few years had brought a confusion of drought and flooding to the valley farmlands, turning small but rapidly expanding portions of Armayel into bogs. Six months ago, confused and resentful at what he could only perceive as Deymorin's desertion, scornful of Deymorin's City-bred brother's patent ignorance, Gareg had tried to carry Deymorin's sketchy plans through on his own. But Gareg's attempts to build those vital drainage channels across public land, without the funds or necessary contacts Inside to gain the legal waivers had gained Council's attention, and at last month's meeting, the Council had given Mikhyel, in lieu of Deymorin, an ultimatum: stop Gareg, or they would.

Not an auspicious addition to an already formidable non-working relationship.

But he hadn't wanted to replace Gareg—hadn't wanted to replace any of Deymorin's loyal employees. He owed that much to his brother, at least, not to turn his staff out. And so he'd pressed Gareg and fought Gareg for information and details until he finally began to understand, past the books and the numbers, what delay of the project meant—not only to Armayel, but to all of Rhomatum.

Gareg's project, had Deymorin gotten the necessary backing last fall, might well have contained the problem before the spring thaws, draining the bogs and shifting waterflows to the areas in dire need. As it was, that bog now extended far beyond Rhomandi land, threatening fully half of Rhomatum's prime produce farms, and left untreated, it would eventually take the City itself.

His own awakening had come too late: the spring thaws had begun, flooding nature-made channels and destroying Gareg's unfinished labors, and Deymorin's original plan was woefully inadequate for the new scope of the disaster.

He and Gareg had worked late every night for the past week—the last two nights, Mikhyel hadn't seen his bed—poring over survey maps, ordering new crews out for updates ... And every proposal they'd come up with would require more money and manpower than he could possibly get out of Council.

"Luck of the rings, sir," Gareg said at the door, and gripped his hand before filling it with the packet containing his books and ledgers, legal papers, notes and the all-vital survey maps of the entire north end of the valley.

He smiled grimly. "If you've any influence with the local gods, you'd best call it in. If you think *I* was hard-headed—"

"Not hardheaded, sir. Ignorant. And so are they. No shame in that. Stupidity, that's something else. And if you show them your maps and present them the facts and they *still* resist, that's stupid, and we all get what we deserve for letting them stay in control."

Deymorin's sentiments in a nutshell. Mikhyel wondered who had learned them from whom until he realized, it didn't matter, that either way those same notions had infected him as well.

"Tell you what, Gareg," he said and returned the old man's grip firmly. "If they prove stupid, I'll have Nikki run me back here, and we'll gather all the 'tweeners together and drive the fools out—chase them over the Kharatas to Mauritum with the other crazies, then build the ditches will they or nil they. Deal?"

Gareg grinned. "Deal. Then get yourself some sleep, hear me?"

He laughed weakly. "Deal."

Outside, Nikki had indeed arrived—in the buggy, he noted with relief, his body ill-prepared for the nonexistent springs of the two-wheeled, single-seat contraption his brother usually drove when he wanted to make speed.

But Nikki was climbing down, telling the groom to unharness and walk the horses out. Nikki was pulling off his driving gloves, and turning back to the carriage ...

Nikki had brought a companion.

Exhaustion washed over him, turning his knees to water. He was not going to be home before dark, perhaps (recalling the last disastrous Visitation) not even tonight. The extended bath and solitary dinner his manservant was to have prepared for him were going to go to waste.

And somehow, regardless of feminine frailty, sleep or no sleep, tomorrow morning, he had to be in Rhomatum, making sense to a hostile and apprehensive group of councillors, talking drainage ditches when those same councillors were fixating on the rumors of impending war with Mauritum. He'd been planning on discussing those problems with Nikki, had planned to rehearse tomorrow's session with his brother on the way home.

Nikki, how could you?

But it wasn't fair to blame Nikki, who even now was handing his fair companion down from the sleek carriage. Nikki didn't know about the drainage ditches any more than he knew about the most recent rumors out of Mauritum. As had become Mikhyel's habit over the years, he'd thought to keep these problems from Nikki until such time as he *had* to know.

And now, perhaps, he'd waited too long.

Mirym's unannounced presence was disturbing in itself. Anheliaa's personal servants simply did not leave the Tower, even on holiday, without a Tower Guard in attendance. One had to wonder if Anheliaa trusted her enough for this private-seeming excursion, and if so, what other duties Anheliaa might expect of her.

Over the months, Mirym had become rather like a piece of furniture: always where she was expected, generally in a quiet corner, stitching, silently going about her duties without question or complaint.

One had to wonder what secrets Tower furniture overheard.

Anheliaa had expressed (frequently) her dissatisfaction with his absences from the City, and his return this time was a week overdue. Without him in Rhomatum to act as a communication buffer between Anheliaa and the Council, it was possible she'd come to suspect the subtle twists he'd put on her proposals over the years and consequently to suspect his motives. If that was so, Anheliaa might well want ears where she couldn't possibly go.

All things considered, he didn't believe Mirym's presence

here today was coincidence, but one had to wonder what Anheliaa had sent the servant to find. Illegal ditches? Subversive drainage canals? Possibly the nonexistent 'tweener coup he'd accused Deymorin of all those months ago.

Perhaps Anheliaa pictured him coming out here once a month just to meet with Mauritumin spies, handing them her precious secrets, arranging a takeover of the City the moment Anheliaa breathed her last. Such a notion would be ludicrous, except . . .

Except for the rumors out of Mauritum, rumors that were, perhaps, no more significant than any in the past; but if ever control of Rhomatum Tower had been contemplated, now would be the time to try. Anheliaa grew more frail each day, and had yet to declare and train a replacement. She herself claimed that capping Khoratum had made the Rhomatum rings' operation virtually automatic, at least for simple power production. For the first time since Darius had tamed the node, outsiders might well be able to supplant the Rhomandis with impunity.

If Anheliaa suspected Mauritum of such a plan, if she mistrusted him to the extent she linked him with such suspicions, she could well be using innocent-seeming young Mirym to follow his movements.

Regardless, he had little choice but to play along, and at least Mirym wouldn't keep them spinning their wheels here for days the way Lidye had on her visit last month. Anheliaa was a serious taskmaster, even, he would imagine, to her spies.

He returned packet and coat to Gareg, received in return a sympathetic press of his arm. There being nothing to say to that, Mikhyel forced a smile to his lips and descended the steps to greet his brother and Anheliaa's spy.

If spy she was . . .

Mirym's face flushed and shining, her hair loose and windblown . . . Nikki handling her as if she were made of glass . . .

Perhaps, he thought, allowing himself the luxury of a momentary lapse of caution, if the boy was fond of her, that in itself explained her presence: a beyond the Tower tryst fraught with Romance—landing his impulsive brother in a great deal of trouble, if Nikki was contemplating giving up Lidye for a servant.

But Nikki's face, that had gone so hollow-cheeked and

somber these last months, was aglow with laughter and a brother whose life had once centered on seeing that look on that face had to welcome the change, regardless the circumstances responsible.

Such a brother might even work to protect the source of that happiness—if Nikki had asked.

Nikki looked up at his approach, and the welcome laughter faded. Nikki's brows, shockingly dark beneath his pale hair, knit in concern.

Mikhyel didn't ask why. Didn't need to. He'd looked in the mirror this morning, he'd seen the dark lines about his own eyes, the thin, pale face he scarcely recognized. Yesterday he'd found grey in his beard.

Late hours. Little sleep when his back did manage to encounter a mattress. Out in weather the like of which he'd never even imagined . . .

Not thirty yet and he looked like an old man.

"Nikki." He grasped his brother's wrist in greeting, then nodded politely to Anheliaa's handmaid. "Mistress Mirym."

"Rings, man, you're freezing," Nikki exclaimed and pulled him unceremoniously toward the door.

"Mind your manners." He resisted that pull, embarrassed, more so when Nikki, refusing to relinquish his hold, sandwiched his hand between two warm ones and rubbed it briskly, a superfluity of gesture out of character for the two of them, and particularly off-putting with Mistress Mirym standing as silent observer.

One didn't want to think what Anheliaa might make of *that* tidbit.

With what dignity he could muster, he gestured with his free hand, inviting Mirym to precede them into the manor house.

But before heading up the broad steps, she exchanged a look with Nikki, a look of mutual understanding that made Mikhyel's blood run cold.

Darius save him, was Nikki party to Anheliaa's schemes as well?

"Let go," he muttered, and shook Nikki's hands off. "Nothing wrong with me about a week's worth of sleep wouldn't cure."

"You could stay here a few days," Nikki said quietly,

that gay abandon dissipating at last. "*Take* the time and . . ."

Mikhyel shook his head, and the sentence died unfinished. Nikki frowned, then hurried to catch up with Mirym.

He longed to ask Nikki what he knew of Anheliaa's plans, longed to ask how Mirym had come to accompany him, but if Anheliaa had made a decision, if Nikki had in fact become her sole choice for the Rhomandi, it was possible Nikki had suddenly acquired political aspirations. Nikki might even want a wrong-thinking, inconveniently older brother out of the picture.

If that were the case, he thought, dragging up the stairs and back into the manor, tomorrow's meeting might well take care of that problem for both Nikki and Anheliaa. By throwing his lot directly behind Gareg, he was bound to alienate Anheliaa, ending his political career more effectively than if he *had* been conspiring with Mauritum.

Because Anheliaa would never believe his assessment of the situation. Anheliaa wouldn't agree on general principle to any plan with which Deymorin had been involved, and in specific with one that would give such importance to Deymorin's constituency.

But before Anheliaa had a chance to remove him from office, he'd have made his case to Council, and as he'd told Gareg—or had Gareg told him?—if Council heard the facts and still voted against the request, Council deserved to float downstream with the rest of the valley.

Inside, the cheerful glow had returned to Nikki's face and, with a great deal of melodramatic handwaving and lordly demands upon a giggling staff, he consigned Mirym into Beasley's hands to, "repair the damage the wind has perpetrated upon her exquisite person."

Mirym, while blushing profusely, played along with his nonsense quite admirably, matching his grandiose gestures with shy posturings and fluttering lashes utterly unlike her normal behavior, sinking into a deep, graceful curtsy when Nikki captured her hand and held it lovingly to his cheek.

Mikhyel wished he knew if it was all preplanned. Perhaps it was an attempt to separate, to place Mirym where she might overhear conversations among the house staff, or to put Nikki alone with him.

Or possibly both. The hypotheticals revolved as chaoti-

cally as Anheliaa's rings. It was enough to make a man
sick, who tried to figure them, so instead, he ordered hot
cider and brandy immediately, dinner for three as quickly
as the kitchen staff could manage, and preceded Nikki into
the study.

"I was hoping you'd be alone, Nikaenor," he said, after
they'd settled beside the fireplace. "I was hoping we'd be
able to talk."

Nikki looked abashed. "I'm sorry, Khyel. I met her on
my way through Oreno Market, and she seemed so alone,
and she had the day off and—"

If Nikki was telling the truth—and (Darius save him) he
wanted to believe Nikki was truthful, and that this was not
simply a rehearsed excuse designed to set him off his
guard—then Nikki didn't understand the implications,
hadn't considered the coincidence of the girl's path crossing
his, today of all days.

Certainly Anheliaa was capable of planning the entire
meeting, planting the girl in the market—everything without the boy's knowledge.

"I'm not criticizing, Nikki. You don't have to explain
yourself to me. You've every right to court any girl you
come across, though I understood you'd settled on Lidye."

"I'm not—"

"Dammit, stop interrupting!" Mikhyel jerked to his feet
and paced the room, rubbing the chill from his arms, regretting his relinquished coat. He sensed Nikki's gaze, hoped
that if he faced it, he'd find the quiet, selfless concern of
old, and know that political aspirations had not yet driven
out innocence.

There was too much happening too fast. He only knew
he *had* to take a stand. Now. On issues based in fact, not
conjecture. But if he fell before Anheliaa's wrath, Nikki
mustn't be taken down with him. Nikki needed options.

Unless Nikki already belonged to Anheliaa. In which
case he, Mikhyel, was in even greater danger. And he
wasn't certain which was true, and that lack of certainty
tore at a temper already in tatters.

It was that flagging control he fought, not Nikki.

He'd learned something about himself all those months
ago, and about his brothers. He'd always assumed Deymorin's
was the temper to beware in the family, the way he'd assumed Nikki was the family peacekeeper.

But he was wrong. Deymorin though tall and physically imposing as Mheric, hadn't erupted into anger when pressured, had contained it, tried for reason. *Deymorin* wouldn't strike in blind anger and damn the consequences.

If anyone in the family resembled their father in that other, darker sense, it was himself.

"Khyel?"

"I'm sorry, Nikki. I'm ... slipping an orbit, as your friends are fond of saying."

Silence. Nikki, as always, just as openly patient, waiting for him to make his point.

Or sitting in judgment.

Mikhyel wondered, with his newly aroused familial insight, whether Mheric had felt the same about their mother, wondered if she'd sat, waiting for him to speak with just that air of ... moral superiority.

Nikki the peacemaker. Nikki, who studied all sides of an issue but never, ever, *committed* to any position.

He stopped beside the fireplace and held out his hands. The warmth spread upward from his fingers, dispelling the chill that reached all the way to his heart. He'd discovered, this past week, that wood fires touched something basic inside him.

The way Nikki did.

Nikki, who might even now, behind that nonjudgmental facade, be plotting his remaining brother's downfall.

He shuddered, wondering, in his deepest self-evaluation, whether these newest suspicions about Nikki indicated a final paranoid breakdown on his part—or the death of his own last vestige of political innocence, that he must suspect everyone around him.

"Sometimes," Mikhyel said slowly and out of that evaluation, "I wonder how Mheric managed. He did it all ... somehow. The City. The holdings. Even the rings, on occasion."

"Father had Anheliaa," Nikki replied smoothly, not seeming to notice—or choosing to ignore—the apparent irrelevancy of his comment. "He had the council, and Gareg, and all the other overseers. He even had Mother to fill out all the paperwork. He just signed the papers and took the credit. You do more. Care more."

"Forgive me, younger brother, but how would *you* know?"

"Don't patronize me, Khyel. I've read the transcripts—all of them. I know what Father did, which decisions he made, and which were made for him. The City survived his tenure on the strengths of his predecessors' past management. Since his death, the City has flourished under your administration; as the web has under Anheliaa; as the Outside has—" Nikki bit his lip and looked away.

"Under Deymorin?" Mikhyel finished for him.

Nikki shrugged, a one-sided, self-conscious twitch.

"It's all right, Nikki. We can be honest with one another. Can't we?"

Nikki's eyes flashed toward him, brows drawn tight above. "What's that supposed to mean?"

He raised a placating hand. "Just that there's no need to avoid the real issues, is there? Anheliaa's will doesn't infiltrate Armayel. —Does it?"

"Khyel, I didn't mean ... I'm not ..."

A discreet tap on the door interrupted him: a footman with a huntbowl filled with steaming cider.

Nikki's mouth tightened, and he jerked to his feet, crossing the room to stare out the window, his back to Mikhyel, while the footman set out the silver and poured the mugs.

Personally, Mikhyel welcomed the interruption, not only for the hot liquid, soothing to both his chill body and a growing rawness in his throat, but also for the footman's presence which gave him the opportunity to gather scattering wits.

I'm not— What, Nikki-lad? A spy? Tempting to believe everything. Nikki's innocence and outrage at having his veracity questioned ... Nikki's assessment of their father's performance ... Of Deymorin's ...

He wasn't even certain why he'd raised the issue, except that he was mortally tired and increasingly uncertain of his own judgment.

Except that he wanted to believe there was *someone* left he could trust.

And he couldn't help but think that, if they could face Anheliaa with a unity of purpose, Anheliaa might be forced to compromise. Such a unity might be possible.

Unless Anheliaa already owned Nikki.

Too much was converging too fast. Mauritum, Deymorin, the flooding ... *He* had to take a stand, but Nikki did not.

Nikki must play the innocent, but Nikki must *be* smart. Aware. Ready to defend himself.

To survive.

While the footman stoked the fire, he rested an elbow on the mantel, closing eyes gritty with lack of sleep, and sipped spiced cider, ignoring the world for a fleeting instant.

But eventually the footsteps retreated and the door closed, and reality, as was inevitable, returned. He opened reluctant eyes to Nikki swinging about to face him, radiating postponed righteous indignation.

"I had to ask, Nikki," he said quietly, before that indignation gave voice. "And if I've accused anyone unjustly, I'm sorry. But I must know where you stand. You're right, I've done Deymorin an injustice all these years. I've learned that much. I don't want to make that same mistake with you. I didn't want to do *anything* to interrupt your courtship of Lidye, or spoil what youth you have left, but I'm afraid I must." He paused for breath, and because he knew that challenging Nikki's sincerity was the best way to lose it. "I need your help, Nikki. Badly."

Indignation gave way to eager anticipation. "You've got it, of course."

Grimly aware he was manipulating his younger brother in ways Anheliaa had never imagined, he warned: "Take care how quickly you promise, brother. You've no idea what I'm about to ask."

Which ought to ensure Nikki's total, blind allegiance.

"Khyel," Nikki said, walking toward him, "if you need me to go muck out the stables, I will, you know that."

"It's not cleaning stables that's at issue, Nikki. I only wish it were that simple."

"Khyel, you're killing yourself, trying to do everything." Nikki closed the gap between them with a hand to touch his arm, as much display of affection as there ever was between them. "It's too much for one person. I want to help. Until Deymio returns—"

"*If* Deymorin returns," he qualified deliberately.

That light touch left him. "I don't understand."

Mikhyel stared up into those blue eyes (Rings, the lad was taller than he, when had that happened?) and found himself caught in a sudden, overwhelming urge to transgress the rules of distance, to throw his arm around his

brother's shoulders, to love as openly as Deymorin always
had.

But he hadn't the ability, had lost it long ago, if it had
ever existed for him, and he'd confused the issue enough
already. Nikki had the right to hear the entire truth and
make his own judgment with a clear head, with those basic
rules of conduct between them intact.

So he moved away from the fire, away from Nikki, and
away from temptation.

"Nikki, I must ask you—rings, don't take offence at
this—*Are* you Anheliaa's? How much has she told you of
her plans?"

Confusion clouded the blue eyes. "Anheliaa's what?
She's told me nothing. Nothing! *What about Deymorin?*"

"Just before he left, Deymorin—in front of witnesses—"

"Witnesses?"

"Myself . . . Anheliaa. Deymorin . . . he renounced any
claim to the Principate."

"I don't believe it!"

"Nevertheless, it's true. Anheliaa says—" Mikhyel
rubbed his eyes, trying to ease what had become a constant,
burning irritation. "She says that as the Rhomatum Tower
ringmaster, it is within her rights to bestow the title as she
sees fit."

"You can't mean that!" Nikki objected. "Deymorin's the
Princeps—he *is*. You *wouldn't* take it from him."

Mikhyel said nothing, there being nothing he could say.
Take? No. But what if Rhomatum needed a real leader,
not the proxy of an absent Princeps. The thaws were well
underway and soon Deymorin's whereabouts could no
longer be explained away.

"Would you?" Nikki persisted.

Even the details, sooner or later, would come out.

"She didn't say that I would replace him," Mikhyel
said quietly.

"You *can't* think I would."

"You might not have any choice. *I* might not. Anheliaa
insists, since we've shown no ability with the rings, whichever wife replaces her in the Tower, that brother will assume the Principate whether he wills it or not." Although
tomorrow's meeting might well swing the balance—away
from Nethaalye.

He wished, now, he'd not avoided Nethaalye these past

months, wished he knew how she really felt about being mistress of Rhomatum Tower. He'd assured her and her parents that her betrothal would stand, regardless, but he'd seen her only a handful of times since she'd come to the Tower. If she truly had Talent, if she truly wished to be ringmaster, he was taking her down with him.

They'd been friends once. Good friends, and he wished he could give her a reasonable say in the decision, but he had no choice.

"But—*why?*" Nikki's protest cut into those thoughts.

"It sets a precedent," Mikhyel said, "So *she* says."

"Precedent? What sort of *precedent?* Council voted the position to the Rhomandi three hundred years ago. The *Rhomandi,* not the Family, and that's Deymorin. She can't change that—only Council can vote it away."

"Anheliaa's not touching the Council's authority—at least ..." And this was hazy in his own mind. "... not legally speaking. She's changing the Rhomandi Family rules of primogeniture. She says that this way the Rhomatum Tower will never again be a part-time consideration. That instead of the Princeps either assuming the position of ringmaster personally, or delegating it to a controllable relative, the primary right to inherit is to be Talent, *not* primogeniture, that *anyone* can learn law and books, but the Tower requires unique, inborn traits which must have precedence."

Which sounded to Mikhyel like one more assumption of power on Anheliaa dunMoren's part. A line of thought he was sure Nikki was perfectly capable of generating on his own, and one which, from the growing chill emanating from Nikki's corner of the room, was well underway.

Mikhyel forced a smile. "Sort of puts my job into perspective, don't you think? Of course, if *I* can learn the dynamics of farming, I suppose her contention has some validity."

"That's not funny, Mikhyel."

Nikki's tone and the chill that filled the room now, while familiar in essence, were painfully new in origin. So: Nikki, gentle Nikki, who had endured all of Anheliaa's decrees without complaint, Nikki, who, with endless diplomacy, had been so agreeable lifelong Deymorin used to joke he couldn't be Mheric's ... sweet Nikki had matured into the family temper at last.

Anheliaa was going to be so pleased.

"And does she?" Nikki asked finally, amazingly—dangerously—controlled.

"Anheliaa? Does she what?"

"Have the right, the *legal* right, to propose and dispose of our family this way?"

Mikhyel shrugged, caught off guard, which he shouldn't have been. He should have been prepared to face Nikki on this at any moment. But Anheliaa and her philosophies had seemed so unreal, had lacked the urgency of flooding and trade agreements, and pending war ... until he realized that his stand on that very topic might well swing the balance of Anheliaa's decision—away from Nethaalye, throwing the decisions precisely onto the young shoulders he'd been protecting.

"As far as I've been able to determine," he said quietly, "there is no precedent. It's never been an issue before: the Princeps and the ringmaster were either the same person, or an unequivocal Rhomandi. But does it really matter? Anheliaa has been setting her own rules for years. Who would seriously consider challenging her?"

"Deymorin," Nikki answered without hesitation. "He didn't really leave, did he? She drove him away because she knew if he were here, she'd lose—she wouldn't dare suggest such a thing to him. She *always* drove him away, from the City, the Councillors, from you ... Damn you, Khyel, if you two had *ever* stopped arguing long enough to talk, you'd have realized you're not so different as you'd like to think. But you never did, *you* always *had* to fight, so *she* always won, didn't she? And she's winning this time as well, because *you* won't oppose her, even though you know damn well she's wrong."

"Nikki, it's not—" Rings, how to answer that cold-blooded logic that only confirmed his own belief? He'd meant to explain long ago, but there'd been no good time, and now, time had run out. "The point is," he said wearily, "Deymorin's not here—*for whatever reason*—and there really *is* no choice. We must do something. Mauritum is pressing us. Our informants suggest they could be raising and outfitting an army."

Nikki choked on a half-laugh. "You're joking."

"I wish I were."

"An *army?*"

"With ley-compatible firearms."

"Ley-compatible. Of course. —And they've found a treasure trove of ancient Tamshi weapons that collect bolts of lightning and fling them at leytowers, blasting the foundations out at the bottom. —And we mustn't forget that Garetti has discovered how to make people and things disappear, just like that—poof!"

"It's possible." Mikhyel said and forced his face to remain impassive, tried to keep Anheliaa's ring-driven powers from his mind, tried to ignore Nikki's open derision.

"Now that's taking the joke too far, Khyel. They're negotiating a trade agreement—"

"They've been *negotiating* for years. They've settled nothing."

Nikki was silent a moment, then:

"An army, you said. —To do *what?*"

"To take Rhomatum, I should imagine. Isn't that the ordinary objective of armies?" Despite his best efforts, sarcasm tinged his own voice at the last, and Nikki's chin raised belligerently.

"Why haven't I been told before?"

"There was no need. We still don't know any of it for certain."

"So why now? If 'we' were keeping Nikki ignorant, why reveal ourselves now?"

"Because ... because it *might* be true."

"And—?"

"And because ... because ..." Nikki's set and thin-lipped mouth wiped all reason from his mind. Nikki wasn't going to listen, Nikki wasn't going to believe anything he said, and Nikki, who loved Outside nearly as much as Deymorin, would never believe he'd come to agree with them. He shook his head wearily. "It doesn't matter."

"You're right, it doesn't. Not to you. It never has made any difference to you. Keep Nikki ignorant, keep Nikki happy. Keep Nikki out of the damned way."

"Damn you, boy, I'm telling you now because I might not be in a position to tell you later—"

"Why not?"

"Because Anheliaa might well have me thrown in jail—"

"Tell me another bogle-tale, barrister."

"Rings, you sound more like Deymorin every day."

"Thank you."

Mockery. Disbelief. Suddenly, he was tired of it all. Tired
of Nikki's accusations, tired of Nikki's determined immatu-
rity, the wide-eyed innocence that disappeared only when
they confronted one another, like now. He was tired of
skirting around Nikki's delicate sensibilities, and most of
all, tired of Nikki's never-ending, nonpartisan evaluations,
first siding with him, then Deymorin ... next he'd be defending Mauritum's right to Rhomatum Tower.

"Impossible as it seems," Mikhyel said past a painfully
tight throat, "war is what rumor suggests."

"I'll grant you—*for the moment*—they might take the
City, possibly even the Tower. . . . What good would it do
them without Anheliaa?"

"We run that risk daily, Nikki. Anheliaa herself has said
the Rhomatum rings will remain aligned and stable with or
without a master. Certainly long enough for a trained outsider to come in and master them. From all indications,
Mauritum is simply awaiting Anheliaa's death and the chaos
surrounding it, but I wouldn't count on that rumor. —The
point I'm trying to make is: if war *is* in the offing, we must
have a meaningful leader ready to take the field. Someone
everyone agrees has the right to command the City forces—
one can scarcely call them an army—we've begun amassing.
It's not a large army. We can't muster one overnight. But
we must give at least the credible appearance of defense.
The Guard's not taken the field in two hundred years."

"Rather more than that. Read your history, brother."
Nikki took a turn about the room. "All the more reason
to get Deymorin back. He already has the respect of the
Guard—he's the only one of us with the experience and
the training to lead them. Neither of us has ever been *in*
the Guard, let alone—"

*"Dammit, Nikki, he's not coming back. Get that through
your head!"*

Nikki froze, turned slowly to stare at him, measuring,
calculating the pain and guilt he'd not been able to with-
hold from that outburst.

Nikki walked slowly back to the settee.

"I want to know what's going on, Mikhyel," he said quietly, firmly, all apparent signs of anger gone. "If Anheliaa
had simply explained the entire situation to him, Deymorin
wouldn't have left. Deymorin's not stupid. He'd not risk all

of Rhomatum for his own pride. And he'd believe the risk. He believed Anheliaa had designs on Mauritum—"

"Mauri*tum?*" Mikhyel could scarcely believe he'd heard right. "How did he think she would take Mauritum?"

"Power. He said she capped Khoratum to give herself the power to force Mauritum to join the Rhomatum Web."

It made a horrific kind of unanswerable logic.

"Where *is* he, Mikhyel? And don't tell me Pretiérac. We both know that's not the case."

"I wish I knew, Nikki," he admitted foolishly.

"Wish you knew *what?* Honestly, Khyel. No more evasions."

Something collapsed inside...

"Where Deymorin is," he said wearily, and Nikki nodded as if he had only confirmed what Nikki had suspected all along.

"What happened that night, Khyel?" Nikki asked.

...that same inside-something that Deymorin had breached six months ago. He could stand firm against his brother's anger; against this soft-voiced reason, he had no defense whatsoever.

"After you'd gone to bed, we joined Anheliaa in the Tower, as I told you. There was an argument—as I told you. Only Deymorin didn't leave, not on his own." He was stumbling, making his case poorly at best. "Anheliaa ... sent him away. They were both angry. Exceedingly. You know how they could get."

"Because he realized she was trying to steal his birthright and he challenged her."

All a man could do was shrug. Too much to explain. Too old and tangled a path ...

"She sent him away ... Where? What's she done with him?"

"Better to ask, how, Nikki. She *sent* him away." And venting his own long-simmering anger toward Anheliaa and fear for his brother's safety. "Damn her—just like some common criminal!"

A long silence, during which a mask of calm settled over Nikki's normally expressive features, a composed detachment Mikhyel didn't trust.

There was a bond between Nikki and Deymorin. Nikki wasn't stupid. Nikki was thinking, weighing the various possibilities, and when the scales had settled, Nikki was going to blame him, as a result of which he'd lose what small influence he had left.

Nikki wasn't stupid, but then, neither had Deymorin been stupid; just passionate and headstrong. And if Nikki was not to suffer the same fate as Deymorin, Nikki must learn what he was up against, learn to play the game according to Anheliaa's rules.

Rules, he, Mikhyel, intended to consciously contest. . .

"Sent him away. You mean, using the rings?" Nikki asked at last, and Mikhyel nodded, being too tired to form words.

. . . Contention that might well send him after Deymorin. Rings, he was a fool. . . .

"Then the rumors are true."

He nodded again, and wearily continued the motion, through:

"And she did . . . *that* to Deymorin?"

And: "Just because they had a fight?"

He stopped in mid-nod, Nikki's interpretation seeping past exhaustion-induced stupidity, and he wrenched his neck in reversing the motion. "No, Nikki. It wasn't quite like that. Deymorin—"

"*Deymorin* made me a promise that night, Mikhyel. Did he tell you that? He promised me a family—" Nikki's calm cracked. "The only thing I've ever *really* wanted. You and Anheliaa, between the two of you, have made me believe for *six months* that that promise meant nothing to him. For *six months* you've made me *hate* the only person who ever *really* loved me!"

"Nikki—"

"Deymorin did nothing that could possibly merit exile. *Nothing!* She had no right. *You* hadn't."

"I didn't—"

"You didn't damn well get him back! You didn't expose her injustice to me—or to the Council. You advised me to play along with her damned high-handed takeover."

"And if you hadn't played along? If I hadn't? What then, Nikaenor?"

"I'd be with Deymorin."

"Are you so certain? You might be dead."

"Dea— Where the hell is he? *Where* did she send him?"

"I don't—"

"*Where?*"

Like the crack of a whip, the shock of such a tone from his younger brother cut through his mesmerized thinking. "Nikaenor, I don't know. Anheliaa doesn't. More than that, she doesn't *care*."

Or so she claimed. It was the fear that she *did* know, that Deymorin was alive and subject to her whim, that she could at any moment make Deymorin suffer again as she had that night and he wouldn't be there to stop her—it was that fear more than any other that had controlled him for six months. That had kept him from telling Nikki the truth, knowing Nikki wasn't going to accept that answer.

Well, neither had he accepted it.

"I've been looking—*discreetly,* dammit—ever since that night, and so far, there's been nothing. Not a clue to where he or any of the others she's exiled landed. It's hard. I don't want to start a panic in the City. I *don't* want to alert Anheliaa, and I don't want to endanger *him!* Can you understand that, *boy?* For all we know, he's in the middle of those same criminals we both agree he shouldn't be correlated with—to—" He threw his hands up in furious, mute surrender. "Whatever."

Nikki scowled.

Upset.

Angry.

But Nikki listened. Nikki ground his teeth and breathed deeply, controlling that justified anger.

"What happened to Ringer?" Nikki asked past that tight jaw, which question made no sense at all. "Deymorin's *horse,* dammit! He was gone from the stable when I went there three days after Deymorin disappeared. He's not at Armayel. Not at Darhaven. *What happened to Ringer?*"

And then he understood. Knew again that other subtle pain in how he'd failed Deymorin. "I . . . I was too late, Nikki," he forced through his tightening throat. "Anheliaa got to him first."

Or more accurately, Brolucci, the captain of Anheliaa's Guard had.

"Destroyed?"

He nodded, that being all he knew. The horse had been gone when he'd been clearheaded enough to ask, and no one knew. Except Anheliaa, who had seen no reason to hide her actions from him. Had piled secret upon secret onto him until he collapsed under their weight, no longer certain who knew what, having to evaluate every thought . . .

Nikki's jaw slowly relaxed, his harsh breaths eased into silence, and Nikki asked calmly:

"That's the real reason you've been driving yourself so hard, isn't it, Khyel? You're worried about him?"

"Exceedingly."

"More than that, you're blaming yourself—feeling guilty."

He shrugged. But the truth of it was, he'd never known whether the constant antipathy between Deymorin and himself had been the primary factor preventing Deymorin from backing down from Anheliaa in front of him, any more than he himself had been able to excuse Nikki's truancy in front of Deymio the night of Nikki's party. Maybe if he hadn't been there, Deymorin would have responded differently to Anheliaa's demands, would have been here to drain Gareg's bog and counsel Nikki more wisely than ever he had done.

"Well, you shouldn't be," Nikki said emphatically. "Neither should I for demanding that promise. Anheliaa's to blame. She sets so much store by the rings, and she's so damned proud of her skill. *She* threw him out. Whatever has happened to him is *her* fault and since *she* lost him, *she* can damnwell find him."

"Don't push her, Nikki." *Please.* He pressed his lips tight over the silent plea, but he knew, with fatalistic certainty, that he would lose Nikki from such a confrontation, leaving him alone to deal with Anheliaa, to present her with her damned heir, to lead the damned campaign against Mauritum, and to get the damned swamp drained.

But if that happened, it was no more than he deserved. He should have confronted Deymorin years ago, should have challenged Anheliaa's high-handed dispersal of criminals, should have told Nikki long before the engagements were settled, should have given him the chance to tell Anheliaa to take her rings and her wives and go to hell.

So many, so very many should-haves . . .

"We've got to go after him, Khyel."

"Don't be foolish. I've good people, trained people working on it."

"*We've* got to go after him. If it were one of us missing—"

"He'd come looking. But it wasn't—" This time, it was a light tap at the door that interrupted him. "We'll talk about this later. I promise you, Deymorin is not forgotten."

A second tapping, louder this time. He knew who it was. Who it must be.

"And if I go to Anheliaa?" Nikki demanded, "If she gives me a different story?"

"Anheliaa has an agenda, Nikki. You know that. You can imagine what it is, if you use your head. Think of that. Think of—think of Berul. And then ask yourself, brother ... and if you lied to me in this ... Who really arranged Mirym's presence here today, and watch what you say."

"Who—?" Nikki regarded him as if he'd gone totally over the edge. Then not. The temper flared. Came under control. "You're out of your mind."

He'd gone too far, challenging Mirym. Mirym had snared his brother's romantic interest at impressionable seventeen and Anheliaa had him, whether or not he realized it yet. No, Nikki wasn't stupid, but he was young, and impressionable, and passionate; and if his cooler, older, supposedly wiser brother had pushed him into defending the very people he advised against, who was the fool? Where the stupidity?

"Disregard what I said." He made a dismissive gesture. "Probably inconsequential. Probably nothing at all. Just ..." He shrugged, somewhat desperate in the face of his brother's stubborn calm. "... trust me."

Nikki raised a single, cynical eyebrow, a gesture so like Deymorin it roused a painful knot in Mikhyel's throat.

Or perhaps that knot was born of the knowledge that Nikaenor was not about to trust him. Or take his warnings.

Not this time.

Perhaps never again.

Chapter Four

"So, Rag'n'bones, have you a name?"

Soap splashed into the pool, scattering reflections of blue sky and shadows, and the carrot-topped apparition appearing unannounced behind him.

"Dammit!" Deymorin made a wild grab after the blanket lying on the bank, overbalanced and followed the soap into the pool. Shaking his eyes free of water, he glared at the apparition through a veil of dripping hair. "After making him smell like a skunk, the least you could do is give a man a bit of privacy while he defumigates."

"Like you gave me, Rag'n'bones?"

Scowling, he ducked his head and swept the trailing hair aside with a bent arm, careful not to crimp tender back flesh. Closer examination of his person had given no clue to the origin of his vast discomfort. It was as if his entire body had been badly sunburned.

According to the apparition—who even now tossed the pack she carried to the ground and settled with her elbows propped on it, obviously planning to stay—this soap would help.

"Nothing I haven't seen already, Rag'n'bones. As to privacy, I hauled your oversized carcass out of this place once, I don't intend to repeat the performance for the sake of misplaced modesty."

Out of the lake was one thing, up the hill to her campsite was something entirely different. Where was her help? If not the gravel-voiced youth, then who?

Easier to believe he'd simply been thrown out the city gates and wandered here on his own. Perhaps he and this female were unwilling companions, or she'd found him sleeping and hit him on the head to rob him. He'd heard of people losing vast chunks of memory through a blow to the head.

Perhaps she knew full well who he was, and was taking advantage of his confused state to place him under some fictitious obligation. He could have mumbled something in his sleep. Something she used against him now.

Now, that *was* paranoid thinking.

On the other hand, that would account both for the lost months and the fact his body seemed as fit as he last recalled, give or taking an aching—

"Get a move on, man. Before you turn blue."

Nothing to argue with in that.

He groped about the rocks where underwater currents had carried both soap and battered washrag and staggered defiantly to his feet, to discover, to his delight, that the stinking ointment she'd spread all over him had turned from irritating-dry to disgusting-slime on contact with water, and itched as if he were one of Anheliaa's lizards shedding outgrown skin.

He scrubbed at the area of greatest irritation.

She hissed, and a barrage of pebbles and dirt struck his back.

"What the—"

"Use it right, or not at all, Rag'n'bones."

Tempted to throw the lot in her face, he followed instead her explicit instructions, given him along with the soap, covering his face, shoulders, and chest with herbal-smelling foam, taking it clear to his fingertips. Bare fingers. The Family ring he'd worn for thirteen years—ever since Mheric's death—gone, like his clothes.

Something else Anheliaa owed him.

Properly foamed, he stood shivering in the breeze, counting.

To his further delight, the throbbing ache had returned to his back and leg, whatever magic she'd performed proving sadly temporary. Having no desire to repeat her 'cure,' he tried to conceal his discomfort, to stand straight and shift his weight smoothly, determined not to show weakness in front of her.

He discovered himself surprisingly conscious of her gaze. He'd never considered himself a particularly bashful individual—had, indeed, spent a delightful summer interlude at a friend's mountain lodge cavorting in what Mikhyel would undoubtedly have considered a shocking state of undress—but he'd always had the *option* of dignity, and the *knowledge* that everyone knew who he was and would treat him accordingly, if he had demanded it.

It was that (he had to admit it) arrogance which had stared openly at this woman as she bathed; she'd caught him at it, recognized that attitude, and challenged it now.

However, his arrogance had been unconscious, while she'd chosen a bathing spot in full view of the campsite—also of her choosing. *He'd* retreated into these prickly poolside bushes to organize his thoughts as well as destench his person in private. If he'd tried to run (ridiculous hypothetical: he could barely walk without staggering) she'd have seen as well from the camp as from her current front row seating.

Besides which, if he chose to leave, wasn't that his right? If she believed that pigsticker of hers would keep him if he decided otherwise—

"Long enough," she said, and he ducked under willingly, relieved when the itch rinsed away with the soap.

"I'd still rather scrub it off," he muttered, when he surfaced, charity not high on his list of emotions at the moment.

Surprisingly, she laughed. "Infinitely more satisfying, I'll admit, but infinitely less effective. Trust me. I know."

"Oh?" He twisted, reaching for that elusive Spot in the middle of his back no human arm could conveniently reach. "Been flogged recently, have you?"

She didn't answer. A backward glance encountered a face gone quite blank, what he'd intended for a joke, albeit a rather low one, gone sadly off-mark.

But the flush disappeared as quickly as it had risen, and she repeated smoothly:

"So, Rag'n'bones, *have* you a name?"

"Dey—" he began easily, anxious (at first) to make amends, then (with an attack of sanity) amended smoothly, "—mio."

"Deymio," she repeated flatly. "That's it? Just ... Deymio?"

"Just Deymio," he maintained firmly, gave up on the infernal Spot (and dignity) and soaped his lower half next.

"No family? No honor affiliates?"

"Honor—?" That *was* an old one. "Can't recall I've heard that anywhere outside a history book."

Another over-the-shoulder glance caught her studying

him with the predatory interest of a hungry cat. Not sexual interest; more the look of a merchant assessing the trade value of an unknown commodity.

"Well?" That predatory gaze lifted.

"None that will acknowledge me," he answered belatedly, and returned rather slowly to his soaping.

Her look said she didn't believe him, but that much was probably true. Anheliaa never had, Mikhyel increasingly didn't, and Nikki . . .

Unless that gap in his memory included some magical reconciliation with his brothers, he'd broken his promise; and considering what that promise had meant to Nikki, Nikki wouldn't want him either.

A convulsive tremor shook him: the mountain breeze, he told himself, and rubbed his arms vigorously.

"Wait." The woman buried herself up to the elbow in the bag, and produced a flask of—he waded over to meet her stretch halfway—*strong* spirits.

Another of her ringing laughs, which, when he could breathe, he echoed.

She gestured at him to try again.

Forewarned, he took a more cautious sip, and found welcome warmth spreading from his throat to his stomach and outward to steady shivering limbs. She squatted on a rock, one elbow comfortably balanced on a bent knee.

"And where are you from, Just Deymio? —Rinse."

The disarming smile he sought came more easily than he expected. Returning the flask, he sank into the water, then settled his backside on a convenient rock, propped his feet on another to soap his legs, and masked the twinge that nonchalance caused with:

"Ah, mistress, 'tis my turn, now. I realize the lady in general retains a prerogative of anonymity, but under the circumstances . . ."

"Under the circumstances," the woman said, "I think I've every right to engage that prerogative." She took a healthy swig, and passed the flask again. "—Ask another."

"Generous of you," he said sourly.

He took a third swallow, while he waited for his legs to cure.

If he asked where she was from, he'd undoubtedly receive a similar rebuff.

And a fourth.

If how she'd found him, or how he came to be here, he'd betray his ignorance, giving her yet another advantage....

"Where are my clothes?"

"You arrived without any."

"I— *What?*"

Her oh-so-ladylike laughter rang out across the grassy meadow.

Deymorin scowled, and, not waiting for her signal, slipped his legs—and much of the rest of him—into the water. Not so chill as before: either he was growing accustomed, or the drink was amazingly effective.

Or, gloomier thought, he was losing all sensation ... dying from the toes up.

A hand clapped his shoulder, squeezed reassuringly: a companionable, unfeminine gesture that made the world go momentarily sideways to a head too full of spirits.

"So, Just Deymio, what brings you to our humble end of the country, naked as the day you were born? Someone rob you? Dump you on your head in the lake?"

"You tell me," he said flatly, and twisted around to stare along that companionably stretched arm, feeling anything but companionable at the moment.

The smile left her face. She started to pull away; he grabbed her wrist, tightening his hold and standing when she jerked to her feet, her free hand flying to her waist and the concealed knife.

But she didn't draw it. Didn't struggle beyond that initial attempt to free herself. Instead, eyes narrowed, mouth tight with anger, she hissed:

"If you don't want to lose something important, *Just Deymio*, I suggest you let go right now."

"Guess I'll have to take my chances, won't I?"

Which priority seemed to confuse her utterly. Tension dropped from her face and wrist alike.

"The last I remember," he said candidly, "I was—well, someplace entirely different. You say you rescued me from the lake. I believe you, and appreciate it. I must assume, however, that you saw me go in, or I'd have drowned, right? Lord and rings, woman, have pity. If you have any idea how I got there—"

"You fell from the sky," she snapped, "like a common cutpurse."

"Fell ...?" His hand went numb. She jerked free. But

he was beyond caring. The world had gone grey and shimmery, the image too close to confirming his worst nightmares. He sank back onto his rock, shivering.

"Relax, friend," she said easily, dropping cross-legged to her chosen perch, almost cheerful, now *she* was in control. "You're not the first; I doubt you'll be the last to arrive thus. —And you put those legs of yours in too soon. Try again."

Grateful for a supplied objective, he resoaped his legs.

Not the first? Falling out of the sky?

Disturbing pieces of a disturbing puzzle. He brushed cold water over his face, clearing the buzz in his head, and threw the least disturbing piece back at her:

"You consider falling out of the sky common?"

"For criminals out of Rhomatum, it is," she said just as matter-of-factly. "Other cities simply toss their overstock out the back gates."

"How pedantic," he said dryly, and lifted a foot. "Now?"

"Yes. Quite." She grinned appreciatively; he took that for the answer to both and rinsed his legs.

She seemed to take this 'dumping' for granted. If there was any truth to it, if other Rhomatum 'overstock' *had* been thrown into this region—if she herself was one—he had no desire to advertise his identity. No sense encouraging them to seek revenge against Anheliaa's justice through him.

"Damn you, Anheliaa dunMoren," he muttered under his breath, and a solid and present hand tightened on his arm. He took the proffered flask and drank deeply, grateful for the warmth and the bite of spirits to wash the bitterness away.

"Not the first to utter that, either, Just Deymio. What did *you* do to incur the lady's wrath?"

"This time?" He laughed ruefully. "Lady, I was born. Anheliaa dunMoren needs no other excuse."

The hand fell from his arm, and she rose to her feet, looking down her nose at him.

"You speak well, Deymio of no house in particular. Too well for streetscut."

He shrugged and settled lower into the water. "I might say the same of you, shepherdess."

"*Shep*—" It was her turn to choke. And gasp. And

sneeze. And blow her nose most inelegantly into a cloth
she then rinsed in the pond.

"Don't you *like* sheep?" he asked innocently, willingly
shifting the conversation onto her.

She just glared at him.

"I suppose that means you're not my shepherd's daughter," he said, with a soulful sigh.

"I'm not *your* anything, my lord nobody. Quite the opposite, in case you hadn't noticed."

He blinked. "I'm *your* shepherd's daughter?"

A cool-eyed scan of his person terminated squarely and
without a hint of maidenly color on his water-covered
lap. "Hardly."

"I'm relieved for that."

Surprisingly, she laughed. "Get your back, Just Deymio.
I'm freezing."

He ducked an increasingly heavy head toward the flask.
"Try a swig of that, shepherdess. Warm y' right up, 't will."

He swayed upright, avoiding a retaliation that never occurred, and stretched once again after that Spot.

His shoulders screamed a protest; the woman's ointment
had taken the sting and fire from the skin, but the bruised
muscles beneath, joints stretched to the limit, still ached
with a fire of their own. Forgetting the woman, he cursed
softly, closed his eyes and stretched again, determined to
reach the Spot.

"Fool." The woman's gruff voice chastised almost gently,
and she plucked the cloth from his hand to give the unreachable spot a scrub.

Eminently satisfying ... until it turned painful. He
grunted a protest, and shied away.

With a laugh (an I-warned-you laugh, if ever he'd been
subjected to one), she grabbed his wet trailing hair and
pulled him back, this time smoothing the lather over the
Spot and down, stopping before getting overly personal.

"Thanks," he muttered, and finished himself, waited silently for the itching to stop, the signal (he inferred from
experience) to rinse, and dipped a final time, staying under
to run his fingers through the hair drifting freely around
his head, working the worst of the tangles free.

Surfacing, he found her standing well back on the stony
shore. Her eyes followed him as he worked his way through
rocks and weeds to dry ground and the stained blanket.

"So," he said, shaking out the blanket, and turning his head away from all the ... things ... that flew free, "you've had *your* eyeful. What's the verdict?"

"I've seen better—and worse. Far worse." She continued that head-tilted consideration, while he gingerly wrapped the filthy thing around his waist, little enough protection against the breeze, which had reclassified itself into a no-argument wind, that whipped around him and threatened to freeze damp skin solid.

"C'mon, Rag'n'bones," she said, grabbing his arm and giving him an uphill shove, "Let's get out of the wind."

He rubbed his bare arms vigorously, and quickened his pace, no longer able to disguise the limp.

"What's wrong?"

"Nothing," he answered shortly.

"Back bothering again?"

"Leg." He hedged.

"Twist it when you fell?"

"Old."

"Break?"

He nodded: a single, abrupt dip of the chin.

She clucked sympathetically. "That explains the scars. Must've been a bad one."

"Doesn't slow me. —Don't suppose you have anything approximating a spare shirt in that bag of yours."

A hesitation, so slight as to be nonexistent—to a less suspicious man. Then:

"A nightshirt. Quite frilly. And you might ..." She took a skipping stride ahead and walked backward, squinting and holding her hands as if taking a tailor's estimate. "You might find it a touch binding through the shoulders."

"Thanks. I'll pass."

"Thought you might." She fell back in beside him, her long strides matching his easily until they reached her camp.

In deference to the gender of his companion, he forced his legs to stay straight, waiting for her to sit before dropping cross-legged to the ground and huddling into as small a package as he could manage, drawing the blanket up around his shoulders.

The woman's seemingly bottomless bag produced an oil-cloth of standard traveller's fare, hard-baked flat-bread and cheese, as well as the flask—or perhaps, from the weight, a second. They shared the largesse in silence, and since she seemed unconcerned about renewing the supply, he ate—and drank—freely.

"Listen, Rag'n'bones," she said at last, and he looked up, surprised to find her face swimming in and out of focus, "we've a while before we have to leave. I suggest you try and get some rest."

"Leave?" he asked, stupid and not caring. "Are we going somewhere?"

"What did you think? Unless you want to stay here and commune with the sheep."

"I—" Think? He wasn't thinking. Hadn't been for a long time. He'd been floating with the moment, hadn't truly looked beyond to realistic options.

Because there weren't any. Reality had taken a holiday the moment he'd fallen from the sky. But he found his head agreeing with her suggestion, found himself unable to formulate any sort of answer . . .

Found himself settling to the ground in absolute, complacent acceptance.

Outside, a groom walked the greys patiently around the circular drive, keeping (so Nikki had explained once and at length) their delicate leg-muscles warm. Inside:

"Khyel, we must be going. The horses—"

"I know, Nikki." Mikhyel turned from the window, letting the drape fall. "I know. But promise me you'll leave the issue—"

"Issue." His younger brother settled his hat and picked his gloves off the table. "You mean, Deymorin?"

"You know exactly what I mean." He looped a silk scarf around his neck, crossed the ends, and fastened his greatcoat over the top, praying it would be enough against the growing chill outside. "It's not just Deymorin. Please, Nikki, it's important. I must be able to trust you to keep your own counsel until I—"

"You've had six months, Khyel." Nikki yanked a glove over his hand. "I'm not promising anything. But don't worry, I won't implicate you without your clearance."

He shook his head wearily. He'd just stay close to Nikki, keep him from taking Anheliaa on alone, for all the help he'd be. Perhaps he could temporize with the Council—at

least until Nikki cooled down ... until his head was clearer
... until—

"Mirym's waiting," Nikki said, and reached for the door.
Mirym.

He'd made a silent supper, listening to their odd, one-
voiced conversation down the table. One-voiced, but not
single-minded. Nikki had seemed able to read Mirym's silent gestures with uncanny accuracy.

And watching, he'd begun to wonder if he was doomed
to read conspiracy into even the most innocent of intrigues.
Except that no romantic tryst could remain innocent where
Anheliaa's nephews—and Anheliaa's servants—were
concerned.

"Nikki?"

"What?" Nikki turned impatiently.

"What about ... her?" He tipped his head toward the
door.

"Mirym?" Nikki's chin lifted. "She's a nice girl. Had the
day off. I gave her an outing. What about her?"

Perhaps he was wrong about everything. Perhaps Mirym
wasn't a spy, perhaps they weren't even a couple; certainly
there was nothing openly romantical in their actions, being
more like the easy companionship his brother seemed able
to establish with anyone.

But this girl was not just anyone.

"Do you love ..." He dropped his eyes to the short-
crowned hat he twisted between his hands, and rephrased
the question. "Do you love Lidye?"

"I'm going to marry her."

"That's not what I asked." This time, he sought out
Nikki's eyes, hoping for clues to his thoughts. "I just ...
can't imagine. You. Her ..."

Nikki's cold stare revealed nothing.

He shook his head, and settled the hat, ready, now, to
leave. But:

"Do *you* love her, Khyel?" Nikki asked, with ill-
concealed eagerness. "Would you rather her than
Nethaalye?"

"Me? Gods, no!" Shock betrayed him into brutal honesty. "I can't stand—" He broke off. "Sorry, I shouldn't
have said that. As you point out, Mirym's waiting."

This time, it was Nikki's hand forcing confrontation.

"Don't you like Lidye?" Nikki asked, staring intently, a look no more readable than the other.

"Nikki, I—" He sighed, and, very briefly, covered Nikki's hand with his own. "I want you to be happy. Nothing more, certainly no less. If Lidye will do that, I'll—" He swallowed hard. "I'll respect her as your wife and try to love her as a sister. More than that, no, I'd not want her as *my* wife."

And with that ultimate betrayal of Anheliaa's plans, he walked out the door.

Angry, more confused than ever, Nikki followed Mikhyel down the steps to the carriage.

Lidye, the paragon—wasn't. Mirym, Anheliaa's spy? And Mikhyel—just where in the eighteen hells above Rhomatum did he stand?

Mirym was standing at the horses' heads, nipping an apple into bits with her teeth, holding the bits out in a gloved hand for appreciative horse-mouths. Gareg was leaning over the carriage half-door, supervising the distribution of furs and blankets in the rear seat, while four men stood at attention beside saddled horses, obviously intending to accompany them.

Brushing past Mikhyel, Nikki joined Mirym, openly demonstrating his opinion of Mikhyel's absurd accusations. She smiled a welcome, but her face clouded with concern as she looked past him to Mikhyel, who was certainly moving more slowly than was his custom, and his feet scuffed the gravel twice as he approached the carriage.

Nikki concentrated on the horses, making minute (and unnecessary) adjustments in the harness. Stubborn pride brought its own reward, as Deymio had told him often enough, when he'd ruined something by insisting he could do it himself. He'd offered to help Mikhyel and had those offers twisted into something . . . ugly; he wasn't inclined to offer again.

Still, he couldn't help but hear when Gareg asked: "Are you certain you don't want to wait until tomorrow, sir?"

He glanced up to see Mikhyel smile wryly. "Not if you want that road by harvest."

"We can have a coach brought 'round—"

A flicker of pale eyes in his direction, then Mikhyel shook his head, said something in an undertone, and took Gareg's hand before climbing into the nest of furs. Their low-voiced conversation continued, shedding occasional references to bogs and manure, while the footman stowed Mikhyel's portmanteau under the forward seat.

Bogs and manure. A mere week ago, Mikhyel had gotten silence and hostility from Gareg, and Mikhyel had shouted at *him* to get the hell back to Rhomatum and tell Anheliaa she was on her own until he'd pounded sense into Gareg's thick skull.

Enough to make a man quit trying to comprehend, and opt instead to ask Mirym whether she preferred Mikhyel's nest in the back, or the simple lap robe of the forward seat.

He was ... not displeased when she compromised, exchanging the lap robe for a larger, warmer blanket from the back, but climbing into the front next to him.

"Think you'll be warm enough, brother?" he asked somewhat sourly.

A touch of color stained Mikhyel's pale face, but it was Gareg who answered harshly:

"You'll be grateful to have blankets along yourself, soon enough, Master Nikaenor. Once that sun sets, you'll freeze that smart ass of yours off without." Gareg pressed something into Mikhyel's hands, then moved forward and said in a stern undertone: "You ease off on your brother, hear me, Master Nikki? He's worked long hours and has no business setting off in this cold. He's liable to fall asleep. If he does, you keep your eye to him and keep him warm. —And *stop teasing him.*"

Somewhat abashed, he glanced back at Mikhyel. "You want a warming brick or something, Khyel?"

Mikhyel shook his head, without looking up, but seeing him huddling into those furs, one was reminded unwillingly of chill hands and weary eyes, and uncharacteristically confused logic.

"Khyel, if you're not up to this, I'll take Mirym back tonight, and come back for you in a day or two."

Which earned him a scowl and an irritable, *Just get going*, for his trouble.

He shrugged, and said to Gareg: "I'll watch him. Nothing more I can do, is there?"

"I suppose not." But Gareg was still angry—or, perhaps, frustrated.

"What about them?" He nodded toward the outriders, mounted now, and quietly adjusting reins and stirrups.

"You'll be glad of them, too, considering the time you're starting. They'll see you to Khorandi Ley, but no further. They've firearms in their saddles . . ." His voice faded into a muttered comment about outlaws and fools and Mauritum spies.

"All right, Gari," Nikki said, laughing and throwing his hands in defeat. "All right. Can we go now?"

"*May* you go, fry." Gareg grinned finally, in the old, friendly way, and waved him away. "And yes, you may." And giving the half-door a tap, as it passed: "Bye, boss. Take care."

Boss. The term Gareg had always reserved for Deymorin.

A good sign, Nikki supposed, though it hurt to hear the familiarity directed elsewhere, particularly considering his new understanding of Deymorin's absence. However, the Rhomandi Family held four different seats in the valley and foothills surrounding Rhomatum, not counting Darhaven, of which Armayel was by far the largest. Mikhyel had faced anger and hostility at each as he'd visited them, trying desperately to cover for Deymorin's absence. If Mikhyel could establish an understanding with Gareg, perhaps the others would come around as well.

But Nikki, if he were honest with himself, did not *want* them to come around. He *wanted* Deymorin back to deal with them in person. The only truly useful result of such a . . . defection . . . would be if it meant Mikhyel could now find room in his schedule for more important things.

Like finding Deymorin and bringing him home.

The reins were quiet, steady, Storm and Ashley, all business now, and pacing the outriders without need of his input.

Mikhyel, when applied to for comment on the deepening sunset, was silent. Sleeping, or, more likely from the occasional smothered cough that escaped him, wanting them to pretend that he was.

Hoping to be left alone—which hope Nikki was perfectly content to oblige.

Mirym, wrapped in her blanket, sat huddled against the side-cushions, her former enthusiasm waning, though not, from her frequent backward glances, due to the cold.

Anheliaa's spy. How dare Mikhyel imply such nonsense? Mikhyel should know better. Mikhyel spent more time around Anheliaa than anyone, and must have seen how competent and honest Mirym was.

He could understand how his incurably serious brother might wonder, seeing Mirym arriving with him. But how those suspicions could survive beyond the initial consideration . . . had to be sheer blind stupidity on Mikhyel's part, as ridiculous as . . . as those rumors of war with Mauritum.

Lidye could be a spy, perhaps, or Nethaalye. They were from political families, they had come to Rhomatum for political reasons—*Anheliaa's* reasons.

Mirym was different. Innocent and fresh. Sensible, as Outsiders were sensible. Sweet and honest, considerate and a multiplicity of other virtues Mikhyel wasn't likely to recognize.

He sighed heavily, jumped as a light hand touched his. Mirym, whose large eyes drifted to Mikhyel's nest and back to him.

"I'm fine. Just—" He shrugged and laughed softly. "We had a bit of a row. Personal, but thanks for asking."

Her hand patted his, then tucked back under the blanket, her gaze wandering to the lengthening purple shadows. She huddled deeper into the seat, pulling the blanket higher, shivering.

"Would you like me to stop so you can move back there?" He pointed to the rear with his chin.

She glanced backward, her face going soft and gentle, and Nikki instantly regretted the suggestion, but:

She shook her head, and tilted her head cheek to palm.

"Khyel's asleep?" Perversely, he argued his own desires. "Don't worry. If he wakes, he wakes. We wouldn't want *you* to take a chill."

Her expression turned puzzled, as if he presented a mystery she couldn't sort. Then she shook her head firmly.

Just as well, he decided. He'd as soon not deal with Mikhyel at the moment. For all his brain found remote reasons for Mikhyel's long silence and for his suspicions regarding Mirym, still he resented being kept ignorant, still resented having his judgment constantly challenged, or worse, ignored altogether.

He wasn't a child. He wasn't naive. But Mikhyel insisted on treating him that way. Mikhyel, who let Anheliaa exile Deymorin without public challenge, who called Mirym a spy, and who thought to scare him into compliance with rumors of war.

Who sang Lidye's praises to him for six months, and now admitted he could scarcely tolerate her and paled at the thought of wedding her.

Mikhyel, who spent a significant portion of every day in Anheliaa's company and upon whose sleeping figure Mirym cast repeated furtive glances.

Jealousy. That strange twist in his gut was common jealousy. Perhaps Mirym, who had rejected his innocently advanced *friendship* on the trip out, wanted Mikhyel so badly she couldn't trust herself even to sit next to him. Obviously, she preferred mysterious and darkly handsome to honesty and . . . and . . . (he raised his chin, in silent defiance) *cherubic* curls.

Another shiver. A tiny cold-sounding sniff and a rustle as Mirym tucked her handkerchief back into her sleeve. He glanced sideways at the girl's bravely steadfast profile.

Perhaps Mikhyel wanted Mirym. Perhaps he raised doubts to convince himself, not Nikki, willing to destroy Nikki's virtuous friendship to silence his own base lust.

Well, Mikhyel was a fool, in more than one way.

"There is another option," he said to Mirym.

She looked a question; he lifted an arm in invitation, the change in direction on the rein rousing a snort of protest from ahead and the tiniest veer in their smooth forward motion.

He apologized solemnly to the horses, and (encouraged by Mirym's silent laughter) went on to assure them they were indeed going to their City stables and warm mash and that he wouldn't *consider* pulling a switch on them.

"I promise to be a perfect gentleman," he said to Mirym, "but Gari was right: I'm a bit chilled myself, now, and two under a blanket is warmer than one."

She grinned and slid easily inside the circle of his arm, tucking the blanket firmly around them both. The outriders exchanged knowing glances and moved in pairs—one ahead, one behind—extending the distance between them and the carriage.

"Wonderful," he said under his breath. And at her inquiring look, nodded toward the riders. "It'll be all over the Tower by morning."

A strike of her palm to her forehead said, plain as words: How could I be so stupid.

He squeezed her shoulders lightly. "Don't worry. Plenty of witnesses to the contrary at Armayel. Hell, my *brother's* in the back seat, and he's the most dedicated prude in Rhomatum. Besides—" He leaned as if to get a better angle on her face. "If Anheliaa tries to make an issue of it, I'll tell her I'll marry you instead of Lidye."

She frowned, a mock scowl, and punched his ribs.

"Guess that's a No." He sighed, a grandiose huff of air. "Can't blame a fellow for trying."

The scowl quivered into a silent giggle, and that into a yawn, and he found himself wishing Anheliaa *would* make an issue of it. Found himself considering giving his priggish chaperone in the back something to talk about.

Unfortunately, he'd made Mirym a promise to the contrary.

"Sleep." He brought the blanket up over her shoulders. "I'll wake you when we get there."

Chapter Five

In sleep, the strong lines softened, giving Just Deymio's face an almost boyish charm.

But there was nothing at all boyish about the thick-muscled forearm tucked, elbow to the fore, beneath the dark head; or to the broad shoulders and lean body attached to that arm.

Kiyrstin dunTareg, you should be ashamed of yourself.

But why, in the name of all the gods, did *this* particular fugitive out of Rhomatum have to fall at her feet—or rather, on her head? The other Rhomatumin outcasts they'd encountered on the road, like those Van had hauled out of Mauritum prisons, had been streetscut: ragged and rough, the sort any City would toss out without pause for second thoughts. That sort one could recruit with a clear conscience; that sort had as much reason as she to keep clear of the authorities.

This one ... sweet Maurii, still shocky from Anheliaa's tender ministrations, dizzy-drunk as a loon, dressed in nothing but a filthy blanket, he'd stood like a noble gentleman until she was seated, never mind her chair was a rock, and there wasn't a soul about to notice was he mannerly or not. Never mind he could hardly *stay* upright.

And that hair. Long, silky despite its twice-over dunking in murky water, short and wavy about the face ... Difficult not to touch it—as a babe's cheek or a cat's fur was irresistible.

She'd heard of the Rhomatumin custom—rumor had it that Darius had picked it up from the valley locals, adopted it as one more calculated departure from the old, Mauritumin customs that considered long hair effeminate.

A bit of whimsy that had survived three hundred years.

The dark, luxurious waves, pulling up and over his shoulders as they dried, were obviously meant to be controlled:

tied back, or possibly, (her lip curled at the thought) forced into the elaborate coifs the ladies of Mauritum were required to contend with.

Somehow, she doubted such a man would endure the latter. A braid, perhaps, long and simple, with those shorter waves loose to soften the strong lines of his face.

Tempting fate, she leaned toward him and brushed a strand back from his stubbled cheek.

He didn't move. Not surprising: he'd inhaled enough of the shepherd's homebrew to put three men under the table—and still hadn't trusted her enough to speak frankly.

A foot twitched, searching the blanket twisted up around the knee. Not a meaningful callus in sight. Evidently the burn and parnicci balm had sloughed any such rough spots away—if they'd ever been there. She'd wager this was a man accustomed to well-fitting footware. Either way, he was going to be sorry for its lack, before the night was out.

The foot twitched again. She unwound the blanket, taking the leisure to admire the exposed limb before tucking the corner securely around the pitiful foot.

Yes, she *must* have seen better sometime.

But damned if she knew who or when.

Good thing for him he'd landed on her and not another member of her party. A man might have let that face scar: one had to get the parnicci balm on fast to stop the burning and remove it gently if one was to avoid that.

Lucky, too, for Just Deymio that she'd not been too delicate to care for certain parts of his body before he wakened. Not that he'd appreciate knowing that—prudish, by his actions lakeside. Too bad for the ladies of Rhomatum.

You are a filthy-minded slut, woman, she told herself firmly. *You haven't the remotest idea who he is or why he's here, but he's damnsure not Just Deymio, and until you know who he is and precisely why Anheliaa shoved such a lovely gem from her little ley-lined nest, he's not for you.*

Not even then, she admitted to herself wryly. Drunk or sober, the man wasn't interested, not a bit of it.

Not that she blamed him; if ever she'd had reason for vanity these past months had eliminated it for good and all. Skin that had once been her maid's pride and joy was rough now, and sunburned, her nose would never recover from the combined effects of sheep and this spring spent

Outside, and her body, never particularly lady-delicate, was, after a winter of living like a bandit, as hard as any man's.

Well . . .

She looked again at those broad shoulders.

. . . most men's.

What to do with him, that was a problem. She couldn't leave him here . . . Well, perhaps she *could*, but she didn't want to. He posed a mystery. One that might have bearing on their mission.

Best to take him back to camp with her. Perhaps Van could get him to talk, find out who he was and whether or not he'd prove useful.

But that leg . . . she frowned, thinking of the scars, wondering if it would, in fact, hold up under pressure. His back was already paining him again, and while she could take another shove at it, if he'd trust her anywhere near it, and while the accidentally discovered cure helped, she really hadn't any idea *what* she was doing, and she did know it was far from permanent—her sister Meliande's back still went bad regularly.

Well, she decided fatalistically, she couldn't afford to let him slow her. Van was going to want to move out, no question. She'd gotten solid information from the shepherd this time: Mauritumin forces had indeed entered Persitum Node, looking for her. The pass was clear of snow at last—

A state that would allow their own small band to get all the way to Rhomandi territory, where, if they were lucky, Garetti's men wouldn't dare follow.

Unless Garetti and Anheliaa had settled their differences. Unless this Just gorgeous Deymio was Anheliaa's spy dropped very specifically on *her* head to lead those men right to herself and Vandoshin romMaurii.

The last of the sunset's ruddiness edged the mountain tops and streaked the sky above; she'd let him sleep as long as she dared. She wrapped her leggings and fastened her sandals, then stood up and nudged him with a toe.

He moaned, muttered, *"Go 'way,"* and rolled his face into his elbow, shading it from outside influence.

"On your feet, Rag'n'bones."

Another moan, a sweep of arm that brushed the hair back from his face, and secured it at his nape with a dexterous twist of the wrist.

And a disarming smile that made her heart flip. " 'Mornin', shepherdess."

"Courting disaster, Rags." She pointed toward the sunset with her chin, and forced her heart to proper behavior. "Time to leave."

"Rags?" His eyebrows arched upward. "First name basis, are we?"

Laughter bubbled. She swallowed it and slung the bag over her shoulder, then nudged his leg again, deliberately dislodging the blanket. If she couldn't get him on his feet one way ...

"Are you well enough to walk? On your own, Rags, I'm not carrying one finger's weight."

"Walk?" He pushed himself upright, flipping the blanket deftly across his lap. "Where to?"

"Away from these ... woolly things. It's getting late and I don't care to explain you to their owner."

"Oh, I see. And yourself?"

"He already knows me. That's *why* I can't explain you."

"I see."

He packed a world of innuendo into those two words; she raised an eyebrow: let him wonder.

Examining a bare sole, he asked, "How far?"

"They'll survive." Not comfortably, but that wasn't her concern.

Another disarming smile.

"Perhaps I'll just wait for the shepherd." He cast a look about the scattered herd. "Careless of him to leave them out so long, don't you think? But perhaps I'm mistaken. Perhaps I don't know anything about sheep. I *am* a bit hazy, you know. One moment, drowning. The next lying in the moonlight—" An upward glance to the moonless, twilight sky. "—well, almost-starlight, with an unknown lady's blanket wrapped about me, and the fair one herself standing over me ... you must admit, this is all a bit overwhelming."

Lady. Fair one. She ran a self-conscious hand through her cropped hair, checked the motion, and dropped the hand. She'd been surrounded by heathens and hooligans far too long. But heathen was better than where he tried to place her.

"Overwhelmin', my sweet arse," she said, scowling hard, and adopting the cant of those same hooligans. "Tryin' t'

turn me up sweet, y'ar. Y' ain't never been o'erwhelmed
in yer life, *Jus' Deymio*. Yer tryin' t' *de*lay me, 'n I don'
like *de*lays. So, on yo' feet, laddybuck."

"Yo'?" He slumped back onto his elbows, a skeptical
half-smile splitting his face. "*Laddybuck?*"

She jerked her head toward the forest . . . "On yo' feet."

He laughed aloud. "You expect me to buy this?"

. . . and tucked her thumbs in her sash, fingers of the
right brushing the knife hilt. "Ee buys what 'ee c'n afford.
One or t'other, makes no nevermind to me, so long as yer
walkin' in that direction, afore I c'n count t' ten. —One."

"You can count?"

"Two."

"*Have* you a name?"

"Three. —Not one I'm inclined to hand you. —Four."

"Charming."

Scornful. Derisive. Good.

"Give me one good reason why I should go with you
rather than wait for the shepherd."

Safer than the teasing and that disastrous smile. "Seven."

"What happened to five and six?"

"Eight. You babbled through them. —Nine. Reasons?
I'll give you two. This . . ." She tapped the sheathed knife.

He shrugged, obviously underwhelmed. "And the
other?"

"Ten." She grinned, feeling deliciously, dangerously
wicked. "That's my blanket, Rag'n'bones."

Lights ahead. Talk of pistols and Khorandi Ley—never
a good combination.

They'd be safe from here: no highwayman ever dared
the leys this close to Rhomatum, so the outriders were leaving them, returning to Armayel and their wives and their
beds.

Their warm beds, lucky souls.

Mikhyel smothered a cough and burrowed deeper into
the furs, seeking the sleep the girl accused him of, trying to
ignore the comfortable coze in progress in the driver's seat.

They made an odd couple, Mikhyel thought, his tall, elegantly handsome younger brother and Anheliaa's mousy
little servant girl. Easy to forget this colorless, silent wraith
might have needs and desires her physical and social limitations denied expression.

But not Nikki. Nikki, in Nikki's own unique way, had managed to find the person within the servant, seeming almost to read her mind at times.

Perhaps Nikki could.

Perhaps Nikki's older brother should mention that observation to Anheliaa, as Deymorin's younger brother should have mentioned his suspicions regarding Deymorin's ring-setting abilities. But somehow, Deymorin's younger and Nikki's older brother opted to hold his peace on both matters—it seeming easier to allow almost-wives, virtual strangers, into Anheliaa's power than to deliver his brothers to her. Somehow, their brother didn't have nightmares of Lidye or Nethaalye—or possibly Mirym—crumpled over on the floor in agony as the rings spun.

Use anybody. Do anything. Anheliaa had no rules, where it involved her control of the Rhomatum Web.

And it appeared, now, he could be as ruthless, where it concerned his brothers.

Lidye and Nethaalye had involved themselves in Anheliaa's plans of their own free will—or their parents'—which made their continued presence in the Tower a matter for their Family honor, not his.

Mirym had the option of leaving at any time; still, he was willing to consider the possibility that Mirym was as much Anheliaa's pawn as Nikki and himself. Last he'd heard, Lidye was all but publicly declared as Anheliaa's chosen successor. He hadn't thought about it at the time. Hadn't cared, but for wondering how to explain to Nikki that Nikki was to be Princeps.

But maybe Lidye wasn't working out. Maybe Anheliaa wanted to force her into calling the engagement off and was using Mirym as a convenient wedge, figuring she could force Nikki to give Mirym up when she found a replacement for Lidye.

If Mirym would make Nikki happy, then, dammit, he should have her. But the transition between engagements would be done with dignity and without ruining Nikki's reputation.

He'd see to that, Anheliaa or no Anheliaa.

At least Nikki had observed some propriety and started back before the sun set. And as Nikki had so succinctly pointed out to his fluffy-headed paramour, they had the web's greatest prude chaperoning from the rear seat. If

Lidye tried to take exception, she'd have nothing but a rapid daytime trip between Rhomatum and Armayel to base it on.

Well—hazy eyes registered starry skies—mostly daylight.

If Anheliaa wanted Lidye gone, if Nikki didn't want her, she'd have no grounds for legal settlement—no breach of promise suit to inflate her Family's coffers—only a civilized buyout.

And if Anheliaa still wanted Lidye, Nikki would have both, somehow, if that was what Nikki wanted.

Another cough, barely concealable.

To avoid another of Nikki's contemptuous backward glances, he fumbled reluctantly after the flask Gareg had pressed on him at the last moment.

Nikki, with his increasingly Deymorin-esque frame and hot blood; Nikki with his warm little paramour tucked beneath his arm.

Mikhyel took a cautious sip.

Nikki, with his unsullied righteousness.

The spirit's bite seared his throat, but it did help the cough. He blinked back tears and hazarded another sip before screwing the cap back in place.

For a time he had tried to follow the one-sided conversation taking place in the front seat, hoping for assurance of Nikki's innocence, fearing clues to Mirym's complicity, but each rut in the road jolted his aching joints despite the buffering furs, each burst of laughter made his pounding head explode, and eventually he simply endured, setting his teeth against those jolts, hiding his ears in his collar, trying fruitlessly to sleep, while the needs of the farmers, and the favors he could call in, the names of the merchants he had to contact for quotes on material and labor first thing tomorrow—some the instant he arrived in the City—raced through his head in ever-increasing columns of figures and faceless names and nameless faces.

And underlying every thought, a disturbing certainty that, faced with the question of Deymorin's whereabouts, and the trouble reportedly brewing in Mauritum, Nikki would pursue those questions all the way to Anheliaa's Tower chamber. There would be no stopping him.

He would do the same, if the figures and farmers weren't demanding attention . . . or if he weren't convinced that there was little or no chance of locating Deymorin without Anheliaa's help, and less chance of securing that fickle aid.

Or would he pursue them? *Was* he truly convinced?

One cough became a convulsive chain. He clamped his jaw, keeping those relentless seizures internal, and pulled the wool blanket up to his chin, knocking his hat to the carriage floorboards.

Or was he too much the coward?

That was the most unsettling thought of all: that, all excuses aside, he might not have the requisite courage; that if he had, Deymorin would never have been sent away.

His threat to the rings all those months ago had been an act of expediency, not bravery: he'd known Anheliaa would never risk her precious mechanism—that *thing* that was more child to her than ever he and his brothers had been.

Except, perhaps, Nikki.

And perhaps Nikki could get out of her what he'd been unable to obtain. Nikki the pet, the always agreeable. Nikki, who hated arguments with a passion. Perhaps Nikki could indeed succeed in locating Deymorin—or Deymorin's pieces.

Unless Anheliaa, assuming she already controlled *him*, was setting out now to destroy *Nikki*. Unless Anheliaa *had* moved Mirym, had gotten her close to Nikki for her own purposes, with or without the young servant's consent, intending to throw Nethaalye into power and *him* into the Principate.

If that was the case, tomorrow's meeting should truly foul her orbits.

By all the gods, he hoped Nikki *could* find Deymio and bring him back to Rhomatum, though it was very hard to imagine his stubborn elder brother alive and well, and not returning on his own for another round with Anheliaa. And if that was the case, he hoped also Deymorin had been living like an ancient king these past months so *he* could send Deymorin to hell for leaving him alone with this godsforsaken nest of snakes.

His throat tightened. Dry. Painful. He took another sip of Gareg's concoction, to straighten a world suddenly canted.

. . . If anyone was going to kill Deymorin dunMheric, he reserved the right to see to it personally. He'd earned it.

Another sip; the dizziness increased.

Rings, all he needed to was to show up drunk on the

Tower doorstep. Fine chaperon he was. Defiantly, he took another sip. And another, and another as the tightness eased to bearable, and the world hazed into uncomplicated.

Activity; inside the carriage and out.

The stables. Rhomatum. Strange, seemed as if they'd just begun the drive.

Or been driving forever.

His objecting leg muscles moved his feet reluctantly to the half-door and beyond. His body slid after in a slow collapse to the ground.

Someone shouted, a sound that echoed in his head and rattled down to his feet, shattering his frozen bones. Hands fumbled over him and gained purchase; he tried to shake them off, tried to tell him he was all right, just tired and cold.

But then he was in a porter-cab, being carried like an old woman through the empty marketplace. Dark marketplace. Their ridiculous, fruitless arguments had made them impossibly late.

And then they were in a floater with ring-blessed warmth filling the air, and Nikki was there. He could hear Nikki, though his eyes had closed and refused to open, yelling at the pedaller to hurry, damn you; and he could feel him— almost. Could at least feel the tug when Nikki yanked his gloves off and the pressure when Nikki began rubbing his hands. Hard. Which hurt, but he didn't say anything because it was Nikki rubbing and he didn't care if Nikki hurt him so long as Nikki was there and safe.

And there was panic in Nikki's voice telling him not to fall asleep; and another voice, gentle, in his head, telling him it was all right, that he *could* sleep—truly sleep—at last.

Darkness imploded about them, the surrounding mountains and forest absorbing what, in the valley, would have been twilight.

Deymorin stumbled over an unseen root, caught one-handed at a nearby tree, and clutched the awkward blanket to his waist with the other. A curse rose, but he swallowed it, his head still ringing from the woman-with-no-name's last wordless chastisement.

Once hidden within the trees, she'd drawn the skirt up between her legs and tucked it into her belt, forming a sort of loose breeches he envied, particularly since the revision allowed her to swing immediately into a long, ground-covering stride, while ignoring the possible limitations of bare feet and a scratchy blanket with a contrary tendency to drift southward, despite the rope belt salvaged from his former bonds.

He paused once and tried a similar wrap, but the blanket was too large the weave too bulky for it to hold, and the following instant, she was at his side hissing, *"Move it!"*

As if she seriously wanted to avoid attention. As if she was anxious to get somewhere in a hurry. Though whose attention, and where remained as much a mystery as the woman herself.

A curious mixture of familiar and bizarre, her body and carriage were designed for action, not a ballroom floor, and yet he'd wager she could dance a *Shilea* with the best professional husband-hunter. She handled the woodland trail with the instincts of the hill-folk, but an occasional muted grunt and reflexive swipe of the hand indicated a less resigned attitude toward minute forest freeloaders than the hill-folk achieved long before puberty. Though she attempted to convince him otherwise, her *natural* accent was that of an educated Citizen, though he couldn't, not having Ben's trained ear, quite place the city of origin.

He would wager she was from Mauritum Web, perhaps Mauritum itself. Perhaps one of those exiles she'd referenced. Perhaps she'd made a political misstep. Perhaps she'd murdered her husband. Perhaps (and somehow more likely, he thought, throwing up both hands to protect his face from a backward-flying branch) her husband had attempted to murder her and she was running away.

Perhaps (as he snatched at the wayward blanket) he'd help that poor sod finish the job.

They followed a trail—of sorts—that was ghostly evident in the waning moon's light; and sometime during that seemingly endless trek, he discovered one good thing about frozen feet: ultimately, they ceased to feel the blisters and bruises and slivers; and another (dour realization), that if they were bleeding, the blood would congeal more rapidly, and he might avoid bleeding to death.

For a time, he managed to busy his mind and warm his fingers imagining the confrontation he was determined to have with Anheliaa. He even briefly considered taking the redheaded apparition-with-no-name back as his bride just to spite his autocratic relative. But stumbling along that blackened trail, he found Anheliaa's thinning grey strands turning thick and red, her large-boned, arthritic body transformed into curvaceous and strong, the wrinkled neck he longed to wring becoming a long and lush neck he longed to wring.

He was hungry. He was thirsty. He was damned cold and his feet hurt, his leg ached and showed a disturbing tendency to collapse at the most awkward moments, and for some reason known only to the gods and the rings, he continued following this woman as if he had no more sense or choice than one of those mindless sheep.

It was possible—perhaps probable—she'd long since forgotten he was there. And who needed her anyway? Given a little sleep to recoup, he was woodsman enough to find food, water, eventually a friendly farmer or goatherd. He'd find out where he was, get word to someone he knew. . . .

And what did she have to stop him? A knife?

Keeping a close eye to the woman's back, he lagged behind . . .

No backward glance, no falter to her stride—if she noticed, she didn't care.

. . . and stopped.

Her ghostly form disappeared into the blackness ahead.

He slipped into the undergrowth, and began counting, using the throb in his leg as a metronome.

One hundred: he slumped wearily against a tree.

Two hundred: he slid down to sit among the dead leaves and needles, elbows propped on his knees, his back propped against the tree.

Three hundred: he let his face drop onto his crossed arms. He was tired—rings, more exhausted than he'd ever been in his life.

She'd get far enough ahead, he'd become too much trouble to pursue. She had no reason to suspect his identity, assuming they'd never met before, and if they had, he'd have remembered that unusual accent. . . . Surely he'd have remembered. Rings, he'd remember that *face*.

Or would he?

(He yawned.)

He tried to imagine That Face as the ladies of his ac-

quaintance did their hair and made their faces up. When
that failed, he tried to imagine her at Tirise's.

He chuckled wryly: that worked much better.

(He yawned again, and buried his nose in his elbow, hoping at least to warm the air going into his lungs: to such
small pleasures had his world shrunk.)

Tomorrow he'd worry about his fate ... about how he'd
gotten here and what he'd do about his brothers ... about
where exactly he was and why this woman had been so
determined to take him with her and who her associates
were....

But at the moment, all he wanted was—

"Move it, Rag'n'bones."

The trees might have whispered that in his ear.

But they hadn't. He sighed, and said, without bothering
to raise his head:

"My name, shepherdess, is Deymio, and I'm bloody
damn hungry, and frozen through. Got any more food in
that bag of yours?" Or at least the flask. Darius save him,
he'd even wear the nightshirt, frills and all.

"I said—"

A point pricked his bare side.

"I'm moving. I'm moving."

He lost all track of time then, beyond caring about right
or wrong or why or even options, worried only about putting one foot in front of the other, and following her whispered directions at each trail juncture.

Eventually, he was catching his balance against every
available support, disregarding the point in his back. But
while that point didn't allow him to stop altogether, it
didn't press him beyond reason, and after a time, he recognized the wisdom in that—if he stopped, he might never
start again. Ever.

And just when he had that figured:

"Hold."

He froze. From behind him, a whistle: excellent imitation
of a moonbird. A signal. From the darkness ahead, an
answer.

A hand pressed his back. "Let's go."

Evidently a satisfactory answer.

"Friends of yours?" he inquired cautiously.

An acknowledging grunt.

"Isn't it rather obvious since the moon's not—"

"I said—" It was the knife-point this time. "—move it!"

"All right, all right . . ." he muttered, and a few steps later: "Can we talk now?"

He took a second, less encouraging, grunt for a yes.

"I haven't thanked you for fixing my back and eyes. Felt as if I was burned all over the first time I woke up. I imagine you kept me from going blind."

"Damn right," she growled. "Don't think to turn me up sweet, Rag'n'bones. Better than you have tried."

"Who are you?"

"Already answered that."

"Who are these friends of yours?"

"You'll know soon enough."

Only the hope of food and warmth ahead kept him from turning and choking her, knife or no knife. He asked through clenched teeth: "How soon, dammit?"

"Open your eyes, Rag'n'bones."

And indeed, the trail ahead took a sudden turn, and beyond it, a welcoming glow limned the trees.

"At last," he gasped and picked up his pace.

"Wait, fool! Take it—"

A sudden sparkling flare, an unpleasant tingling in his legs.

A shout—the shepherd's daughter, he thought.

The next he knew, he was staring up into her moonshadowed face.

"Idiot! I told you to slow up. You all right?"

"What the hell—!"

"I'll explain later." Her hands pulled at him. "On your feet. I *know* it's hard—just *do* it.

With her help—and a stinging blow or three to his face— he staggered to his feet and down the trail toward the light.

On the third step, an unpleasant reminder tingled through his bad leg. He cursed, and stumbled; she cursed back and struck him into action. Together, they stumbled through the trees and into a ring of light.

And a chorus of laughter.

The woman's hands left him to his own uncertain balance, and her distinctive voice joined the chorus. Deymorin shook his head clear; felt a breeze where he'd rather not, and glanced downward, then back toward the shadowed trees where the unpleasant tingling—and his blanket— awaited the next poor unsuspecting wayfarer.

Chapter Six

The floater trip from Oreno Gate to Rhomatum Tower was a nightmare.

Kneeling on the carpeted floorboards, in the ley-lit interior, cradling his semicomatose brother against his chest while Mirym rubbed warmth into Mikhyel's near-frozen fingers, Nikki was forced into the realization that Mikhyel, for whatever reason, had been unable—or unwilling—to complain of his growing discomfort—worse, that *he* hadn't thought to ask was his brother cold, or ill, when he could *see* he was, had heard the coughs from the back and willfully ignored them.

Had the distance between them grown so great that Mikhyel would risk serious illness rather than ask for help? Had anger and jealousy and suspicion so completely undermined his *own* sense of Family that he'd been blind to that distance?

He felt angry, yes, and betrayed. Anheliaa had lied to him for months, and Mikhyel had been party to the lie. But he didn't hate Mikhyel; far from it. Anheliaa controlled the rings. Anheliaa had the vision for the Tower's future.

And Anheliaa alone had exiled Deymorin. Mikhyel's only crime had been to go along with her—as he himself had—trusting her to know best. And Mikhyel had the added curse (one had to be honest with oneself) of *knowing* what Anheliaa had done to Deymorin. *Knowing* that Deymorin's fate could easily be his, had he resisted her plans?

A hand tapped his.

He blinked, his eyes gone hazy with unshed tears.

It was Mirym, gesturing toward Mikhyel's booted feet.

He nodded, then held his brother against mindless, fidgeting objections, while the floater attendant pulled the boots off; clasped a flailing hand and murmured reassur-

ance as Mirym and the nameless attendant began vigorously rubbing Mikhyel's feet.

Mirym. Sweet, generous, unsuspecting Mirym.

She was no spy, but Mikhyel had been living under the
shadow of fear and suspicion for months—perhaps years.
A shadow Mikhyel had done his best to keep from his
younger brother's path. Mikhyel was worried for him, that
was all. And perhaps the fear of losing both brothers accounted for Mikhyel's long silence and wild accusations.

He wasn't certain he could stand to be that alone. Neither, perhaps, could Mikhyel, hence Mikhyel's attempts to
keep himself from taking action against Anheliaa, or from
trusting Mirym too much.

And he'd thrown that concern in Khyel's face—with
Khyel already sick.

What if, his mouth turned dry and sour, what if Mikhyel
had elected to return, to risk his health, *because* of what
he perceived as his stubborn younger brother's unwillingness to take his suspicions of Mirym and Anheliaa
seriously?

He thought of those personal revelations he'd made on
the drive to Armayel and the sourness worsened. What if
Mirym took those comments straight to Anheliaa? And she
to Lidye?

Not-quite-frozen fingers tightened convulsively.

"N-Nikki?" His name was a hoarse whisper past chattering teeth.

"I'm here, Khyel."

"N–not f–feeling so g–good."

"Not?" He strove to make and keep his voice light.
"Could have fooled me. Thought you'd maybe tipped one
too many of Old Nam's cider."

A dry, painful-sounding chuckle disintegrated into a
hacking cough that set Mikhyel to fumbling under the blanket. His hand came up clutching a flask, but another
coughing fit foiled his efforts to unscrew the cap.

He brushed Khyel's hands out of the way, uncapped the
half-empty flask and steadied the opening against Mikhyel's
mouth, trying to get more of the liquid inside than out.
From his damp collar, Mikhyel had had similar problems
on the journey from Armayel. But he got down enough to
ease the cough, and Nikki wiped the excess away with a
handkerchief, which appeared as if by magic from Mirym.

"Try to rest, brother," he murmured, not certain Mikhyel heard him, but trying all the same. "We'll be home soon."

A weary nod acknowledged him, and cold fingers pressed his hand against a fever-hot cheek. He hugged Mikhyel closer, bitterly aware just how much he missed such simple human contact. With Deymorin there'd always been a companionable closeness—a hand tucked in his elbow, an arm about his shoulders, playful punches and quick passes of gentle hands over his arm, or his hair, or his chin.

Displays which had always seemed to embarrass Mikhyel and to increase the distance between them all.

Ever since Deymorin's disappearance, communication from Mikhyel had been confined to terse necessities, requests for conveyance like today's, or to pass the salt at the dinner table. For months, he'd waited for Mikhyel to explain to him—to so much as utter Deymorin's name. He'd waited, but there'd been no mention.

Strangest of all, Mikhyel's sudden bursts of violence had vanished altogether. He'd thought Mikhyel was angry, blaming him for Deymorin's disappearance, avoiding him to avoid losing his temper and doing something he'd regret afterward.

If only he'd known....

Of a sudden, Mikhyel's convulsive shivers stopped, his body grew rigid, and his hand withdrew from Nikki's, his feet pulled up under his blanket, fiercely denying Mirym's attempts to retain them.

Safely concealed, Mikhyel turned to him, determinedly aware and, Nikki realized, utterly mortified. Mikhyel, who always turned away in disgust from Deymorin's open affection and the human contact Nikki craved.

"You can let me go now, Nikaenor."

He grinned, hoping the concern he felt didn't show through. "Rather not, big brother."

"Dammit, boy—" Mikhyel's voice broke along with his hold over his body. His face turned and pressed against Nikki's neck. One hand clenched the blanket, the other groped blindly, gripped painfully when Nikki caught it.

When the fierce spasms eased, a half-sobbed whisper, not to him:

"Dammit, why now ... Of all times ... S–so much to ..."

Nikki laughed softly, and let go Mikhyel's hand to wrap

both arms around Mikhyel's shoulders, rocking gently.
"Told you to let me help shovel the shit."

Laughter, weak but honest. Arms that hugged with what
meager strength was left in them. And as he held Khyel
close, closer than he ever had, he realized in hazed surprise
he was no longer the little brother. Likely he hadn't been
for years. Khyel had always been such a presence, had
cared for him for so long, he'd never noticed that he'd
grown taller.

But more than that, Khyel felt ... frail ... in a way no
one else he'd ever touched felt frail. He could feel the
bones of Khyel's back even through the heavy clothing.
Small bones. He was fragile, in a way stocky Anheliaa, for
all her arthritic age, wasn't. Always lean, he was wraithlike,
now, in his lack of flesh. Always pale, sunken eyes and
hollow cheeks made him positively cadaverous.

Most disturbing of all, the pale grey eyes that stared up
at him, eyes that had always been silvery-keen between
pitch-black lashes, had gone cloudy, the green rim of the
iris faded to near invisibility. Sad eyes—even a bit frightened, until Nikki brushed trailing strands of hair from his
brow and told him to rest, that he was going to be all right.
Then those stranger-eyes drifted shut, and another whisper,
so light he wasn't certain he heard correctly:

"Lord and rings, I love you, Deymio."

Tears welled; he blinked them back, hardly recognizing
his own brother. So it was not embarrassment, not even
disgust that had caused him to turn away over the years.
Jealousy ... perhaps.

He'd always wondered what his birth had done to his
brothers' relationship. Now he feared he knew. He wasn't
fool enough to shoulder blame for his existence, but he was
brother enough to care.

Responding as he knew Deymorin would, he brushed
another dark strand back from a forehead clammy with
sweat, and whispered, "Love you, too, fry." And followed
the touch with his lips. "Sleep now, little brother, you'll
feel better when you wake up."

A child forced too early into adult politics, an adolescent
shoved too early into manhood ... his brothers hadn't
asked for that life. His brothers had been friends once, as
he and Deymorin were friends now. Their parents' death

had changed all that, their individual responses to fate making them enemies.

But it needn't have happened that way. Just as Deymorin's disappearance needn't have happened. There was one and only one person truly responsible. One person whose unwillingness to assume *her* responsibilities had shoved Mikhyel into politics and whose obsessions lay at the root of all Deymorin's antipathy toward the City.

They'd reached the hill that was the Rhomatum Node. The floater track constrained them to a scenic path, orbiting upward, circling the Tower complex, which included, besides the Rhomandi city residence with its private gardens and the Tower itself, the city legislative buildings, the Courthouse, and the Guard barracks.

Most of the buildings were in darkness, the residents gone home for the night or asleep. In Rhomandi House itself, his apartments and Mikhyel's in the North and West wings showed signs of life: Jerrik and Raulind, Mikhyel's man, preparing for their arrival, wondering, no doubt, where they were. Worried, perhaps.

Anheliaa's apartments were also evidencing occupation. With luck, his aunt had assumed they'd changed their plans and retired early.

Mirym was likewise staring at Anheliaa's windows, her highly expressive face devoid of emotion. She'd had the day off; he wondered if that extended to the evening, and just how far from her normal schedule he'd dragged her. He realized, in further guilt, that he'd dragged her off without so much as a word to Anheliaa, or anyone else who might have had occasion to wonder at her whereabouts.

Or who might blame her now for that absence.

But if he'd gotten her into trouble, he'd get her out—later.

Not waiting for the doorman to respond to the floater's arrival, he had a barely cognizant Mikhyel on his feet the moment the anchor engaged. Enlisting the unknown attendant's aid, he got his brother inside, where a servant replaced the attendant, who was out the door before Nikki could gather wit enough to say thank you, reappearing only to set Mikhyel's boots and the flask inside the door, and disappear again.

He made a distracted mental note of the cab company—he'd send a message and a generous tip in the morning, as much for that final bit of tact as for his helpfulness—and asked after Diorak.

The physician had gone home for the night, which indicated Anheliaa had had one of her better days. He sent a footman to fetch Diorak, another to alert Raulind, Mikhyel's valet, a third to tell Anheliaa they were back, and that Mikhyel had taken ill . . . and on a belated thought, as the third man headed up the staircase:

"And if the Lady Nethaalye is not still in attendance to my aunt, you'd best take word to her room as well."

When at last they got Mikhyel up the lift, and to his room, Raulind had the heating vents full open, and was drawing a hot bath.

Nikki hesitated, wondering if they shouldn't just get Mikhyel (who had lost all awareness of his surroundings and was mumbling about war and swamps, resisting all efforts to hold him on his feet) into bed, but Raulind insisted, and in the end, proved justified: the moment the hot water closed around him, Mikhyel relaxed, the fight evaporating with the steam, and their greatest challenge became keeping him from sliding under and drowning.

Raulind persisted, even to washing Mikhyel's matted hair, maintaining Mikhyel would sack him for certain if they put him to bed in his own sweat, and by the time they'd soaped and rinsed and manhandled Mikhyel the two steps up from the bathing pool, they were all three soaked. Nikki helped Raulind to wrap Khyel in a warmed bathing robe of luxurious imported cotton, and to settle him on a grooming lounge in the bedchamber; then shed his own clothing into the pile of towels, and rinsed himself off in the constantly cycling tub before slipping into a spare dressing gown Raulind had foresightedly set out for him.

Raulind was at his brother's back, drying Mikhyel's long straight hair in a narrow stream of ley-warmed and driven air. Nikki silently replaced him, running a comb through the silken strands, gently separating the tangles, giving Raulind a chance to change into dry clothes, and straighten the bath.

"Braid?" he asked Raulind, when the hair was dry, but the valet shook his head, and Mikhyel, whom he'd have sworn was asleep said, quite audibly: "Don't you dare, Raul."

Nikki exchanged a look with Raulind, who shrugged and said succinctly: "Hates it."

Which was a surprising insight into his oh-so-meticulous sibling.

Hell of a way to find out, Nikki thought as they worked Khyel, who was, after that final protest, well and truly beyond critical evaluation, into a nightshirt and bed, where, clean hair a dark stream across the pillow, his eyelashes shockingly black against pale cheeks, Mikhyel appeared quite peaceful.

. . . as a corpse, he thought with a shiver.

All he could do then was sit beside the bed holding his brother's hand, until Diorak, grumbling at the late hour, finally arrived.

The grumbling stopped the instant the old physician got a good look at Mikhyel.

Following a cursory examination, and a curt request for explanation, he chased Nikki from the room with orders for the kitchen and Nurse.

"Nurse?" Nikki chewed his lip in uncertainty. Khyel would kill him. "How serious is it?"

Diorak shoved him forcibly from the room. "He'll live— *if* you do as I say and then keep out of my way. I'll send word— Where will you be? The library, I suppose," he answered his own question before Nikki could open his mouth, "since I doubt you'll do the sensible thing and go to bed. —Now, *go*. Get out of my way!"

He made a final stab at self-assertion: "I'll be in Khyel's study—"

"Go!" Diorak barked. And as he ducked out the door: "Damn fool."

Another log sailed into the firepit from the far side shadows; scattered coals fell in a shower of glittering bits. Flame chased like a living thing along cold, dark surfaces, rousing a hissing, sputtering protest from the damp wood.

Rejuvenated, firelight skipped outward, expanding the shadow's edge, dancing along the strong, handsome lines of the Rhomatum exile's face, and highlighting the clean demarcation of intersecting muscle along bare arms and thighs.

From the shadows of the tarpaulin tent covering their small supply cart, Kiyrstin kept a wary eye to this Just

Deymio, while she exchanged the irritating hill costume for more comfortable leather and smooth linen.

Likely she should have given him the extra shirt she'd carried in her bag; if she'd been kind and sensitive like sister-Meliande she undoubtedly would have—with never a second thought.

But she was neither kind nor sensitive and felt no shame in the admission. On the trail, that precarious blanket had been her only hold on his cooperation: she couldn't have forced him, with no more than a knife and a trail ax at her disposal.

Yes, she told herself, she'd been fully justified on the trail.

Since his arrival in camp, it had become a test of wills, no amount of rationalization could change that fact. She was waiting for him to ask. Beg, if she were honest with herself, and she did *try* to be honest . . . with herself.

But he hadn't begged, nor even asked politely for so much as another blanket.

Standing beside the fire in the suit the gods had given him, he'd been embarrassed (how not?) but his grin had appeared loathsomely natural, he'd bowed rather generally (*not* singling her out in that courtesy) and seated himself (casually) on the nearest fireside rock, finger-combing his long hair into a smooth twist *before* accepting the bowl of stew and mug of water Tarcel placed at his side.

Casual. Tranquil.

The scut didn't *deserve* sensitivity.

Without fireworks to feed it, the laughter had died, and the dozen or so men (the exact number varied day to day) who comprised their small band had quietly resumed their own meal, as if a naked stranger in their midst were nothing unusual. But then, some had joined them with little more to their name—some with less: this Rhomatum exile could at least stay on his feet.

Having finished the meal and complimented the anonymous cook, the Rhomatum simply sat and stared into those flames. Waiting, tired, as she herself was, but too wary to let sleep overtake him, in this camp of unknown elements. Waiting for someone else to instigate, content in his ability to handle whatever situation might arise.

Kiyrstin jerked the final lacing tight. Tough, practical— the fur-lined leather vest provided warmth, protection and a very necessary support that was infinitely more comfortable than corsets ...

And made her look like a rather pudgy, fourteen-year-old boy.

Packing the hated skirt away, she gathered the pile of folded leather and cloth she'd set to the side, and sauntered across to Just Deymio's side.

Dark eyes turned up to her, fire-dazed, tired—and puzzled, for a moment, as if he didn't quite recognize her. But the puzzlement lifted along with an enigmatically raised brow, as that gaze travelled her length.

"Stunning," he said coolly. "You should wear it to the Transition Day Ball. Give the day a whole new meaning."

Transition Day. The holiday reference held no significance for her, but the scorn dripping from his voice, the disinterest from his eyes, did.

"I don't dress to please you or any other person of my acquaintance, Rag'n'bones," she said tightly. "Here."

She wadded the pile and thrust it at his chest.

Hands closed reflexively over the clothing. Fine hands, white lines in the tan where rings once circled, manicured and elegant, as the man himself was, even without a stitch on. Too elegant to ever have the least interest in a woman who preferred breeches to skirts, warm leather to lace ruffles, and whose calloused fingers would snag any fine fabric they touched.

Not that she cared—there was no time, and rarely any desire, for such things these days—but the look in his eyes, when she again intercepted them, showed he'd guessed those thoughts, and mocked her nonexistent interest.

She scowled down at him, lest he dare to presume. His mouth twitched, but (showing uncommon good sense) he kept those thoughts to himself.

He located the broadcloth breeches and slipped them on before standing and sorting the rest of the clothing out on his rock.

She studied that smooth-skinned back with what she convinced herself was clinical detachment, noted the slight blemish (barely visible above the waistband) with a decidedly *un*detached, fiendish satisfaction.

Maybe next time, the man would believe her. Listen to her.

And perhaps sheep would sprout fins and swim.

The parnicci balm, a common enough country burn treatment, made of plants that grew along the ley at the very
edge of the infertile zone, had proven remarkably effective
against these insidious, ley-inflicted burns, but the depth of
the burn varied unpredictably, and one could never be certain until that last bit of dead skin flaked free whether
one had applied the cream quickly enough, or removed it
carefully enough.

"Find yourself another stray dog, Kiyrsti?"

Vandoshin's voice announced his presence before he appeared beside her. A muscle twitched in Deymio's smooth
back. Then, as if determined not to appear unduly startled,
he straightened quite deliberately and faced them, shooting
a triumphant glance at her as he slipped the loose shirt
over his head.

A small triumph she cast into perspective with an indifferent shrug. With that diminutive of her name, he knew
no more about her than she about him.

Less.

She knew his City.

"*Rhomatum* streetscut," she answered Vandoshin, at
once reminding the Rhomatum of, and cautioning Vandoshin with, that fact. "Name of Deymio—so he claims."

Van touched fingertips to brow in formal greeting; the
Rhomatum just nodded warily.

Van gave an easy smile, not likely to take offense, under
the circumstances. "Vandoshin romMaurii, Deymio, at
your—"

"Service, *rom*Maurii?" Deymio finished. "A *Mauritum*
priest? for a Rhomatum citizen? Somehow, I doubt it."

"Which?" Van asked smoothly. "That I'm at your service? Or that I'm a priest of Maurii?"

"Take your pick. You can't be both. —Or was that your
ticket into this elite group? Caught impersonating a priest,
were you?"

"Actually ..." Van paused, his mouth twitching in an
enigmatic smile, "Not. My title is quite legal ... though I,
perhaps, am not."

"Perhaps?"

"Shall we say, I've heard no *official* charges."

"More than that," Kiyrstin interrupted, irritated at the
priest who, obviously finding this duel of innuendo to his

liking, was revealing far too much far too cheaply, "you'll have to wait until we know you better."

The two men exchanged an enigmatic look designed, she was certain, to make a woman suspicious and mean absolutely *nothing* no matter they meant you to think it did, so she ignored the look and continued:

"He's one of Anheliaa's victims, Van. Dumped him right into the old shepherd's lake, crisp fried. Love him, she must."

Vandoshin laughed easily. "What did the Rhomandi bitch get you for, Deymio of Rhomatum?"

Deymio adjusted the laces on the shirt to a precise balance between careless and sloppy, then looked up through a rakish fall of hair. "Apparently, she didn't approve the cut of my clothes."

"Cautious lad." Another laugh. Coming close to overdoing the companionability, Van was: her Just Deymio was the suspicious type. "Not a bad trait. But we're all bandits here, of one ilk or another—hardly the sort to turn you in."

Not that Van was likely to listen to her, any more than the Rhomatum was.

"Bandits?" Deymio's glance scanned the camp this time. "How disappointing." And stopped on her: "Pardon, m'lady." As he unbuttoned the breeches to neatly tuck his shirttail.

Without turning.

She allowed her mouth its own appreciative twitch. "Disappointing?"

"As a boy, I rather thought bandits to live a far more— exotic lifestyle. This is quite . . . meager." Another brief pause to shrug on the loose, calf-length coat: old-fashioned, but the warmest garment she could find that might span his shoulders. "Overall . . ." He stretched his arms forward, nodded surprised approval and adjusted the cuffs. "I'd rather be fishing."

"A fisherman from Rhomatum?" Kiyrstin asked, lightly. "Bit far from the coast, isn't it?"

"Ah, lady," he mocked her, meticulously (so she suspected) avoiding the use of the name she'd not yet granted him permission to use, "I didn't say fisher*man*. I said fishing. There is a difference."

"But not one your average Rhomatum lord would recognize."

"It is, however, your classification, not mine." He lifted a very sad-looking foot. "And does my lady's benevolence perchance extend to boots?"

Vandoshin laughed. "Admit it, Kiyrsti-lass, stalemate." He reached for Deymio's arm. "Come with me, lad, we'll find something suitable for those feet."

My mistress, devastated by your distressing message, has taken to her bed. Please keep her informed of her beloved Mikhyel's progress. She wishes, of course, she could come care for him herself, but her delicate constitution . . . I'm certain you understand . . .

Etc., etc., etc.

Oh, he understood. He understood perfectly.

Nikki crumpled the scented paper into a ball and threw it across Mikhyel's study. It bounced off a bookshelf and disappeared behind a couch.

Good riddance.

But one wouldn't want Mikhyel discovering it by accident on some future date, so one went crawling on one's hands and knees to retrieve the smelly thing, and this time one made certain one got it into the waste box beside Mikhyel's desk.

Such a loving fiancée. No wonder Mikhyel took every opportunity to avoid her.

Still, it was more acknowledgment than he'd received from Anheliaa.

Mikhyel's desk was covered with mail, neat piles his secretary had sorted in his absence, piles of (he pulled the robe's heavy brocade cuff back to flip through a stack or two) letters to be signed, grant requests to be reviewed, various personal and business appointments to be confirmed or rescheduled due to his delayed return.

Even in this small way, Mikhyel refused his help, insisting to bring in a professional, constantly protecting him, to preserve, so Mikhyel had said, his youth.

So Mikhyel had always excused his actions.

Dammitall, he *wasn't* a child, though he was kept ignorant as one. And if Mikhyel had only taught him, let him help, he wouldn't be up there with Diorak right now, having worked himself into exhaustion.

Unless Mikhyel had lied in that reason as he had in Deymorin's fate. Anheliaa might have demanded he be kept ignorant, and if Mikhyel had kept silent at Anheliaa's

bidding, the timing of this revelation might also be her
choosing. If she was about to make her move, having her
disposition of Deymorin suddenly revealed to Deymorin's
youngest brother might have been calculated to catch the
brother unaware and to frighten him into capitulation—

A knock.

He was at the door in two strides.

"Diorak?" he asked before he had it open. "How is—
Oh, hello, Mirym." He stepped back, schooling his face to
hide disappointment. "Please, come in."

She crossed the threshold, a tray-laden footman following
close on her heels. She was carrying a large package which,
once safely within the room, she handed to him.

Mikhyel's packet, the one he'd nursed all the way from
Armayel.

Appalled at its weight, he frowned his disapproval at
the footman.

The footman released the legs on the serving tray and
set it precisely between two wing chairs, then, glancing at
the girl, shrugged.

"Sorry, sir. She wouldn't let go."

"Declaring yourself personally responsible?" he asked
her, and she nodded primly. "Thank you," he said, forcing
his mind to amenities. "I should have seen to it myself."

She cast her eyes ceilingward, then shook her head
firmly, and, oddly, some of the strain and worry seeped
away from his shoulders.

"You're right. He *was* my first responsibility. So I say
for both of us: thank you."

A slight cough, a clearing of the throat, from the doorway: reminder of the footman's presence. He excused the
man and cast himself into the righthand wingchair, reaching
for the decanter.

"Will you join me?" he asked, and tipped the decanter
without waiting for her answer.

Another cough, tiny echo of the footman's attention-
getter.

He paused in mid-pour, surprised when her look, generally so direct, kept shifting uncertainly, sliding from him in
obvious embarrassment.

Aware, suddenly, of drooping lapels exposing his bare
chest, and of the robe's split front exposing most of a bare
thigh, he hurriedly set the decanter down and stood up,

pulling the dressing gown together. He was at once appalled at himself and secretly disappointed that she didn't feel a similar impatience with protocol. Among family—

Except she wasn't family. Odd, that he should forget that. So with a formal gesture toward the other chair: "Please?"

Indicating a tiny measure between her fingers, she relented, easing onto the edge of the other chair, apparently still unable to relax fully in his presence. And somehow, he knew his attire was not entirely at fault. What clouded the air between them now had nothing to do with lust, love, or even friendship, and everything to do with po-si-tion.

He poured a glass to her specifications, another for himself (to his own) and sat back wearily, the energy to initiate conversation beyond him at the moment, knowing that responsibility to be his and resenting that reality, as he resented the socially proscribed customs that kept him from treating her as the friend he suspected she could be.

He had been born into money and power, but a primarily quiet life, divided between the library and stables, with the occasional theater outing or informal dance, had done little to make the class distinction more than theoretical. His friends, such as they were, tended to come from families of his parents' friends, or the stables.

He'd rarely differentiated between the two sources.

The young ladies of his acquaintance tended to be ephemeral—even Lidye. Lidye was a fact of his life, a necessary function to be performed. Even though they were distantly (very) related, and while they came from supposedly similar backgrounds, Lidye still felt like a stranger. Mirym . . .

That afternoon, he'd thought they'd enjoyed an understanding, her manner had been open and friendly. Now, they were back in the Tower, back where she was a servant, never mind she gave honest work for honest pay, and she no longer dared even sit in his company without express invitation.

Their eyes met over the top of the glass she cradled between her fingertips.

Mirym, realizing she had his attention, again glanced upward, concern drawing her brow together.

"Khyel?"

She nodded.

"I don't truly know, yet. Diorak is still with him."

Her concern deepened, all the way over to frightened. And a man had to wonder why his brother's health should matter to this girl, this determined stranger.

Perhaps she feared Anheliaa would blame her for Mikhyel's illness. Perhaps she felt that if she hadn't been along, they'd have stayed the night at Armayel. Perhaps her concern was more basic, a fear of what Lidye would say when she discovered Mirym had spent the day with her intended.

He took a sip, running his tongue around the rim, gathering drops left by his wearily shaking hand, lowered the glass to the chair arm, and let his head fall back against the cushions, eyes closed.

Or perhaps she was frightened of *him*. He could, after all, on the whim of a moment, take away all she had. So simple a concept, yet until this moment, one he'd never considered. Because *he* wouldn't act upon such a whim. That wouldn't be fair, that much Deymorin had taught him.

Mikhyel might. He didn't know for certain, though he preferred to believe otherwise.

Anheliaa would, *had*, without hesitation or regret.

Revulsion shuddered through him.

A touch: hand to hand.

His turned of its own volition, recognizing reassurance given, not requested, accepted that comfort as fingers interwove. For a time, he absorbed Mirym's warmth, her calm, her strength, then, with some reluctance, squeezed gently and released her, heaving a deep sigh.

"He'll live, so Diorak claims." He looked down into the swirling liquid. "It's ... kind ... of you to ask."

A glassy *click* demanded his attention: her barely touched glass stood abandoned on the tray.

An emphatic, one might almost say angry, shake of her head.

Startled, he asked, "I don't—of *course* it's kind. I appreciate—"

A slap on his chair arm stopped him. She tapped his arm, gestured toward Mikhyel's room, then pressed crossed hands to her breast.

"Mirym, settle down. I don't understand what you're saying. I certainly didn't intend to insult you."

Her foot tapped the floor as her eyes scanned the room, settling on him, exuding no small anxiety.

Thinking he understood, he said gently, "Don't worry, Mirym. I won't let Anheliaa blame you. We would have returned today regardless. Your position here is—"

He might have slapped her. She jerked to her feet, hand raised as if to retaliate.

"Go ahead," he said calmly, "If I've said something to offend you, I'm sorry, but I deserve it. I won't tell anyone."

Her jaw dropped. She flounced over to the desk, searched ruthlessly through the private papers for pen and paper, scribbled furiously for a moment, then thrust the result into his hand before dropping defiantly back into the chair and draining her glass.

The note, barely legible past the angrily splattered ink, read:

I asked because I care, you supercilious idiot!

Nikki stared at the note, at her, and inward at himself, not liking the mirror she held for him. He hadn't once considered that possibility, that she could care as a friend would care.

As Khyel's own kin and fiancée did not.

Or perhaps, reluctantly recalling his suspicions on the ride home, not as a friend, and he ... hoped that was not the case. Hoped further his brother had not encouraged any such leaning. He didn't want her hurt. Certainly didn't want her driven from the house following Mikhyel's wedding to Nethaalye.

If she survived here past Lidye's discovery of today's events.

Anger surged within him, unfocussed. All pervasive.

It wasn't right. None of it was *right*.

He thrust himself to his feet, brushing the tray with his trailing hand. The glass tottered and fell, shattering on impact. Red wine spread across the hardwood floor like thin blood, seeking the easy course, working its way insidiously into the grain, like the lies and pretense upon which his very life was based.

A frothy white moth fluttered across the blood: Mirym, on her knees and blotting at that stain with an inadequate lace-edged handkerchief.

"Get up!"

Her head flew back, her eyes wide, surprise throwing her balance, forcing her to catch it with a hand to the floor.

Anger, concern, exhaustion, and bitterness confounded in a dizzying whole, and sought release in the nearest source:

"Dammit, *get up!* You're *not* a servant!"

Her expression shifted; her eyes fell, but not in submission. He followed that blank look to the floor, where real blood joined the metaphoric, oozing through the wine in viscous rivulets.

Mirym stood slowly, holding her cut hand well away from her clothing. She freed the glass shard from her palm with stoic calm, and wrapped her wine-stained handkerchief tightly about the wound.

Nikki watched, spellbound, vaguely appalled at his own lack of initiative, saying nothing when she dipped a curtsy and turned to go.

"Wait!" He reached the door before her, held it shut, though she made no move to elude him.

She didn't seem angry, or accusatory, or any of the gamut of justifiable emotions. In fact, she'd ceased to radiate anything at all.

"Mirym, I—"

A knock interrupted him.

Taking advantage of his momentary confusion, she slipped out the door, leaving him face-to-face with a startled maid.

Nikki, straining to see past the girl, caught a glimpse of embroidered hem disappearing down the hallway toward the east wing and the servants' quarters. He sighed and took the note the maid held, thanking her quietly.

High time you returned. That ridiculous vehicle of yours is to blame. You should have taken the coach.

He's your brother. You see to him.

Attend me first thing tomorrow morning. I've a task for you.

Written in an unfamiliar, rounded hand.

Nikki crumpled the paper in his fist, and demanded of the waiting maid: "Where is she?"

"I—in the Tower, sir."

"At this hour? What's the emergency?"

"None, m'lord, that I've heard."

"Alone?"

"With the Lady Lidye, sir."

Lidye. *She* had written that note for Anheliaa.

"Is there word, yet, of my brother?"

"Your brother, Master Nikaenor," Diorak's voice said,

from beyond the maid, "is out of danger." The old physician waved the maid away and drew Nikki into the privacy of the study, closing the door behind them. "No thanks to you. Whatever possessed you to subject a sick man to that drive?"

"Stupidity, sir," Nikki said abruptly, making no attempt to whitewash his culpability. "I didn't realize how bad he was. I thought him asleep. I should have known better."

"And he, poor stubborn fool, should have said something." Diorak grasped his arm in rough reassurance. "Don't worry, son. He'll have an unpleasant day or two, but he'll survive."

"May I see him?"

"I don't think he'd want you to."

"Why?" Somehow, he couldn't stop his voice from shaking.

But Diorak snorted his disgust. "Drunk! That's why. Damn fool should know better. But he should sleep until morning. Nurse will stay with him tonight. She'll welcome relief in the morning. Best you can do is get some rest yourself."

"I'll try, sir." He grasped the warm, dry hand. "Thank you."

"Doing my job, son. Will you tell Anheliaa, or should I?"

"She's in the Tower."

"Oh. Well, I suppose morning is soon enough."

"No, sir, it's not."

"Boy—"

"Tonight." Nikki said determinedly. "But don't worry. I intend to tell her personally."

"Careful, boy, I don't want to be called out of bed twice in one night."

"If you are, it won't be for me."

"Is that supposed to reassure me? Perhaps I'll just wait here until you return."

"Good night, doctor," Nikki said firmly. "And thank you."

Chapter Seven

Unable to gain access to the ringchamber without Anheliaa's mandate, forced to stand passively as the lift carried him up, Nikki realized the deliberate nature of his arrival would shield his aunt's initial reactions, relegating him to what might well be nothing more revealing than carefully garnered responses.

But for once he had the advantage over Anheliaa. He was no longer the mindless trusting sod he'd been yesterday, or even this morning.

He had to face her tonight, before Mikhyel had recovered enough to interfere. Mikhyel was afraid of Anheliaa, afraid of her anger, afraid of her abilities with the rings, afraid of being sent after Deymorin. Mikhyel *always* intercepted for him, kept him from pushing Anheliaa for answers.

Well, not tonight.

He wasn't afraid of Anheliaa. Well, at least, not particularly. Anheliaa had an agenda, and that agenda included Lidye, and for Lidye, she needed him, and if Anheliaa wanted him, Anheliaa was going to answer a few whys and wherefores.

If she didn't want to answer, well, she could send him after Deymorin.

He slammed the brake with his palm; the lift jerked to a halt.

Anheliaa's chair faced the door, waiting.

At her side: Lidye, who, as he stepped off the platform, beamed and rushed to take his hands, exclaiming over his fortitude—making that horrid drive in *such* weather, and *all* alone—as though their meeting this morning had never taken place, as though never suspecting he'd purposely avoided her company.

"I hate to disillusion you, madam, but I wasn't alone."

"Not?" Some of the fluttering ingenue was missing from that query.

"Mirym was with me."

"Mirym?" She sounded confused, as if the name meant nothing to her. Then: "Anheliaa's Mirym? Is *that* where the little—"

Her blue eyes flickered toward him, and she swallowed the rest of whatever she'd planned to say.

"You didn't even notice she was missing, did you?"

"Oh, we noticed," Anheliaa's dry voice interrupted.

"And did you make any attempt whatsoever to locate her, when she didn't return from the market?"

"Hardly necessary, was it?"

"You didn't know that!"

"Didn't I?" Anheliaa countered, which resurrected, unwanted, the dark suspicions Mikhyel had hinted at earlier.

"You *knew* that sneaking little bitch had insinuated herself into his company and didn't tell me?" Lidye's voice achieved a painful screech. "Anheliaa, how *could*—"

Anheliaa raised one arthritis-contorted hand, and cast Lidye a quelling glance. Lidye frowned and looked away, but she did not finish the accusation.

"Lidye, please leave us," he said curtly.

Lidye raised her softly rounded chin and looked to Anheliaa.

He closed his eyes, and drew a calming breath. "Forgive me, Lady Lidye, I've had a trying day. Aunt, if you please, I must speak with you alone. Now."

That calming breath undermined his store of driving anger. And as if aware of that weakening resolve, Anheliaa smiled, a mere tightening of her mouth, and nodded a gracious dismissal.

As she passed, Lidye placed a light hand on his arm. Forcing his attention from his aunt, he found the woman destined to be his wife blinking up at him pathetically, as if seeking absolution for her unseemly defiance.

Unfair, perhaps, to blame the young woman, who was, after all, simply one more pawn in Anheliaa's grand scheme. And perhaps Mirym was right. Perhaps Lidye's actions were motivated by ... love.

He patted her hand reassuringly.

Perhaps she thought to inspire similar emotions in him. It wasn't her fault that she'd been caught in the middle of a familial power struggle. Naturally here, within Anheliaa's domain, she'd feel compelled to defer to his aunt's desires.

But, dammitall—why now?

Closing the grille behind her, he waited until she disappeared down the shaft and the telescoping hatch fanned out over the opening, a hatch that was guarded with a leylock to which only two, Anheliaa and Brolucci gorAnheliaa, the Captain of Anheliaa's private Tower Guard, held the mental keys. Only Anheliaa knew precisely how that lock worked, but (particularly in lieu of recent developments) he no longer considered its addition five months ago entirely circumstantial.

If he'd done to Deymorin what Mikhyel claimed Anheliaa had done, he'd have taken a few extra precautions himself.

"Well, you unhousebroken brat?" Anheliaa's voice snapped. "What have you to say for yourself?"

"Damn you!" He whirled about, then gritted his teeth against that self-destructive family temper. "What would you say—how would you *feel*—if the answer to that was 'Khyel's dead'?"

"Is he?"

Tempting to answer in the affirmative, tempting to see if *anything* could shake that infuriatingly aloof exterior. But he couldn't. For some reason, he clung with foolish tenacity to the belief that if he persisted in Truth, those around him would someday reciprocate in kind.

He shook his head, dropping his eyes from her cool triumph.

She gave a slight, derisive snort. "I've lived a damned long time, boy, and ceased years ago to panic when one of you boys comes down with a sniffle."

A damned long time. That much was so.

Her cool confidence and austere face had fascinated him as a child, when, constrained to sit for hours in her presence, warned never to make his existence known, he'd watched her, and wondered what her delicate, wrinkled skin felt like from the inside, how the gnarled fingers possibly functioned, knowing from the occasional wince, the care with which she bent them, the curses when she dropped something, how they must pain her, thinking she must be terribly brave and wise, having lived so long in such obvious discomfort, with so many people hanging on her every judgment.

Now, that air of supreme conviction engendered only contempt; contempt for an authoritative old woman's last gasp attempt to control her universe, contempt for her lack of basic humanity and lack of familial loyalty, and contempt for her misuse of her fate-given power.

Propped in a corner like some damned trophy, one of Anheliaa's lizards curled around the handle, was Deymorin's sword-cane.

He wondered why, in all these months, he'd never noticed it. Wondered if Anheliaa had kept it hidden until now, knowing Mikhyel had told him the truth, or whether, not suspecting, he'd simply been that blind.

He picked the cane up, slipped a hand's-breadth of fine steel free of the carved sheath, met Anheliaa's eyes and shot it back home.

"Is what Mikhyel told me the truth?" he asked abruptly.

She raised one painted-on eyebrow. "How should I know? More to the point, why should I care? Such matters are between you two boys."

"Is that intended to put me in my place, Aunt? Or to justify your temerity where it regards my life? I'm not a child, Anheliaa. Neither, for that matter, is Khyel." His exploring fingers discovered the gold band on the tip of the cane was loose. It was a ring. Deymorin's family ring, with its silver-web overlay. He raised his chin. "Certainly Deymorin is not."

Anheliaa's cool expression didn't waver. "And for this sagacious insight you interrupt an important training session?"

"Training session? I saw only one of your apprentices. Hardly sportsmanlike of you."

Her colorless, lashless eyes narrowed. "You sound like your oldest brother. —Bless the *rings* I need no longer suffer *his* audacity. —This is not some sporting contest, *boy*. This is the single most vital decision of my career. *You* should be delighted. Your fiancée shows great promise."

"Delighted?" he asked, deliberately mistaking her meaning. "As a citizen, I am naturally pleased you have a promising student."

"It should. 'Nikaenor Rhomandi dunMheric, Princeps of Rhomatum.' Rather a nice meter, don't you think, poet?"

"Not particularly." He pulled the ring free, held it up between them in two fingers. "Deymorin is, and will be until he dies, Princeps of Rhomatum."

"Dies. Or renounces."

"I'll believe *that* when I hear it from his own mouth."

"Impossible. That person is gone—permanently."

"Dead?"

"I'm sure I don't know."

"*Why* don't you know? You ordered his exile, didn't you? To make certain you would no longer 'suffer his audacity'? Didn't your guard escort him to the perimeter?"

"I prefer to solve my own problems. Personally. Permanently."

"Then Mikhyel was right, you *did* use the rings to send him away."

"Is *that* the grievance behind this vulgar scene? It hardly matters then whether Mikhyel told the truth or not, does it? Since whatever I do with the rings is *my* business, not yours. Or his."

She won't be content until she rules the world. . . . Deymorin's words; among the last he'd heard from his brother, and more prophetic than even Deymorin had realized.

To send Deymorin away in a fit of anger, that was like Mikhyel's backhanded blows: unconsidered before, regretted after. Power, used instinctively and in anger. He'd seen that all his life and could have accepted that excuse from Anheliaa; even if it meant the permanent loss of his brother. Possibly even if it meant Deymorin's death.

But while Khyel struggled to control that misuse of power, berated himself when he could not, Anheliaa had relinquished the struggle before it ever commenced. *Accepted* as her right the ability to destroy life—anyone's life—without accountability. Simply because she had the power to do so.

The cane's carved ridges formed touch-patterns beneath his fingers, the gold and silver inlays radiated a metallic chill.

"What you did to Deymorin . . ." he began, then revised quickly, seeking knowledge and understanding. Anger he had in plenty. "What had he done that was so wrong or illegal as to warrant exile?"

"His was the ultimate crime." She shot him another of those narrow stares. "He refused his destiny."

"The destiny *you* chose for him."

"The destiny the rings chose for him."

"The rings. You yourself told me the rings are affected by personal desire. Your desire."

"The needs of the rings—" Her eyes widened, lids disappearing under the wrinkled brow. "Told *you*? Never!"

He brushed a careless hand through the air. "Of course you did." And ignoring her intense, sudden frown: "The *needs* of the rings cannot preclude the right of my brother, *your* nephew, Princeps and the heir to the Estate!"

"That's where you're wrong, boy. By the rings, I'll choose the bride *and* the groom, if I so choose."

"Don't you think the Council of Citizens might just have something to say about wholesale abandonment of tradition and law? Don't you think the Syndic might?"

"For the power I can give them? They'll agree with anything I demand."

... until she rules the world ...

"You seek enhanced use of the rings. Your 'new' benefits are personal ones. That which the rings give the *citizens*, they do already, and will continue to do with—or without—you."

"Are you so certain? And where do *you* suppose Council will stand if the choice is losing the rings altogether?"

"That's an empty threat."

"Is it?"

Her unwavering confidence shook him, made him think of that new controlled doorway into this room, made him recall her years of private experimentation in this isolated fortress. Brought to mind Lidye's image on the ringsphere, six months gone, and made a man wonder if Anheliaa had conjured other images—perhaps compromising images—with those rings, and which Councillors she had called into this same room during her long tenure.

"Why, Anheliaa?"

"Do I need a reason? Then, perhaps just because I'm an old woman. Perhaps because I'm bored. Perhaps just because I can."

Madness. The room reeked of it.

Breath failed him. All arguments seemed wasted as, suddenly, he realized *why* Mikhyel was frightened of Anheliaa, and why Mikhyel sought to protect him from her.

He took a step backward, felt pressure against his weakening knees, fumbled after an armrest and slid into the chair.

"I won't support you in this, Anheliaa," he whispered.

He thought her eyes flickered at that, but her tone, when she answered, continued indifferent: "Did I ask you to? The citizenry will happily accept Mikhyel. He's already their practical Princeps."

"And if Mikhyel refuses?"

She laughed outright. "He won't." An arch look. And a hissed: "Hasn't."

Hasn't. Fait accompli. Suggestion made and accepted. In spite of what Mikhyel had said at Armayel.

Damn him!

He felt as if all the tension, the worry, the guilt he'd felt for the past hours had just been thrown back in his face. One had to wonder what had prompted Mikhyel's strange confrontation at Armayel that afternoon. If Mikhyel planned all along to usurp Deymorin's title, why go through all that? If Deymorin was officially declared exile, Mikhyel would be the natural heir.

Except that, with Anheliaa's renunciation of primogeniture, that was no longer assured.

Had he fallen headlong into a trap? Had Mikhyel set him up? It was possible Mikhyel hoped to ensure his position. Possibly Mikhyel believed that by throwing suspicion on Anheliaa he would force his sole remaining rival into just the confrontation now taking place, and eliminate that rival permanently, leaving *himself* as Princeps.

Rival. He'd never considered himself anyone's rival—certainly not his brothers'. Without his brothers he had ... nothing. No family. No meaningful avocation. His brothers had actively discouraged him from developing usable skills—*protecting* his childhood, so they'd claimed.

His childhood had been studying history and science—*theories*—his poetry the family joke; his single brush with ambition, the brief dream of Ambassador to Mauritum, had long since vanished, gone to dust in the reality of impending marriage and paternal duties.

A life without accomplishment, without goals, a life full of uncertain worth, and now Anheliaa *used* those multitudinous uncertainties against him to force him to conform.

He freed one hand from its deathgrip on the cane, and ran it distractedly through his hair.

"*Dammit*," he cried, "what gives you the right to be judge and jury as well as executioner?"

"The power of the rings."

"*That's no answer!*" He bit his lip, forcing the anger and the pain, the fear of uncertainty under control. "Duly judged criminals—that's one thing, although I'd argue the Council should be consulted first and with full knowledge of *your* actions. Exiling Deymorin—with no hearing, except by you—"

"And Mikhyel."

He refused to believe it. He took a solid grip on his own careening suspicions.

"Don't put this off on Khyel. He had no realistic choice in the matter."

"Is that what he told you?"

His heart sped. The clammy chill left his hands. "He didn't have to. It was *your* doing. All of it. And it's wrong. Anheliaa dunMoren."

She leaned back, eyes narrowing to heavy lidded slits, hands crossed over her substantial girth. "Your judgment is, of course, all important to me. —I really think you should go now."

It wasn't right. None of it was *right*.

Deymorin always said no one could *take* his pride; that, he had to give away, and *damned* if he would.

"Not until you tell me where Deymorin is."

Her eyes closed completely.

"You don't *know* where he is, do you? Or even whether or not he's dead?"

A faint noise. An almost-snore.

"*Do you?*"

Her shadowed eyelids lifted. A painted brow rose slowly. "Definitely unhousebroken."

He tightened his grip on Deymorin's cane, only a desperate need for information preventing him from proving to her just *how* undisciplined he could be.

"What happens to them?"

"Them? I thought we were speaking of your brother. Them who?"

"Those you . . . *leyapult* away from the Tower."

"Leyapult? Ah, I see: our in-house poet strikes. Leyapult. I rather like that."

"*What happens?*"

She shrugged.

"*Where* did you send him?"

Another shrug.

"You don't know?"

"Don't care."

"Where you sent the others?"

Still another shrug.

"Do you know whether or not they *survive* the transfer?"

And a fourth.

"Damn you!"

"You grow unpleasantly like your father."

"Father?" Of a sudden, the statement's very oddity unified and directed his increasingly scattered thoughts. "Talented of me . . . considering I never really knew him."

"You knew your brother; ergo, you knew him. Beware."

"Beware? Why?"

"I never *liked* your father."

"At least, you admit it. Extrapolated: you never *liked* Deymorin. I suppose that means you don't like me, either."

Her head tipped, slitted, unreadable eyes studying him. "I wouldn't go that far . . . yet."

"And if you decide you don't, will you send me into oblivion as well?"

"If necessary."

For one chilling moment, his mind blanked, until he realized that the rings swung their gentle chaos, same as always. For some reason, she wasn't even considering attacking him.

And then, he remembered that exchange with Lidye when he arrived, remembered Mikhyel's statements and suspicions, and from somewhere, bitter laughter happened.

"No, you won't. You want Lidye. For Lidye, you *require* me. Mikhyel can't abide her. Well, if you want *Lidye*, you'll *find* Deymorin, do you understand me?"

There was no way to tell if she heard or cared. Her face was as blank and lifeless as a bad portrait.

"I mean it, Aunt. I'll go further and wager Khyel will support *me* in this. If you push, Khyel and I will leave. We'll find Deymorin without your help. We may come back and we may not. We won't be here to marry your precious apprentices, or to . . . pollinize your precious future adept. Or do you expect to foist Lidye and Nethaalye onto Council without us? Your apprentices are outsiders. Once one

of them controls the Tower, you effectively relinquish Rhomatum Tower to another node whose loyalties to Rhomatum are shaky at best. Do you honestly believe Council
will allow that to happen?"

Her eyes raked him up and down. Measuring.

"You put a high value on yourself," she said at last.

"You established the market when you insisted on outsiders to . . . crossbreed us with."

"And what is it you expect of me?"

"Cooperation."

"In what?"

"I want to know where Deymorin is."

"I tell you, I don't know."

He nodded toward the rings, whose silver surfaces made
a glittering cloud behind Anheliaa, their excitement an
echo of her growing agitation.

"Find him."

"You *dare* defy me?"

He supposed he should, by all rights, be terrified. But a
cold confidence filled him, leaving no room for terror. "Defiance is not the word I would choose. It's really much
simpler. You want your heir, find Deymorin. You use
those things to locate criminals; you can use them to locate Family. Once I have proof, once I know he's alive
and well—once he's *back*—I'll do whatever you ask, as
long as it's for Rhomatum and not simply your own ego.
Have we a deal?"

"*Deal?*" Her face was an ever darkening thundercloud.
"You arrogant little insect. *No!* You *will* stay. You *will*
marry that girl. Do you understand me?"

The rings became a sudden, silver blur behind her, a blur
he remembered seeing before, a blur that was one with a
confusion of images of Mikhyel and Anheliaa, of Deymorin
collapsed on the floor. He felt dizzy in that memory; dizzy
as well with the knowledge that *he'd* not been witness to
any of it. . . .

Pain gripped his head, a vise pressing in all directions
at once, Anheliaa's voice echoed in his ears, though her
mouth remained a thin, clamped line. The voice demanded:

{*Stay. Wed Lidye. Forget Deymorin.* Behave.}

And when his soul cried: "*Why should I?*"

{*Because I say so. . . .*}

Simple adult-to-child orders.

"And if I refuse?"

Images of terror: Child's fears of darkness and closets and ogres and pain; man's fears of death, dismemberment, impotence and shame.

Child and man, he resisted that pressure, tightening his fists about the cane: Deymorin's proxy, Deymorin's camouflaged protection against camouflaged danger. He concentrated on the bite of fingernails into palm, of contrasting cool wood and flesh-warmed metal.

"Is this what you did to Deymorin?" He thought he shouted the words, but perhaps thoughts lied. Certainly her image, swimming in metallic tones somewhere beyond his touch, didn't respond. "And when he wouldn't yield, was that when you exiled him? Threw him out like an uncooperative servant?" The confusion of sensory input increased, touch, sight, sound—even smell and taste—confounding into one, all radiating insistent need to comply with her wishes. "Dammit, you'll not force me ei—"

The pressure increased. He might have screamed. Certainly some offensive noise echoed about the room and through his head.

The room twisted, the chair disappeared from under him. He grasped blindly, breaking the fall, landing on his knees; very real pain that cut through the unnatural agony of Anheliaa's invocation.

He fought again, pulling himself to his feet, staggering toward where he believed her couch to rest, crashed into what felt like a wall where none should be, grasped for a handhold on a slime-slick surface that wasn't there, and slipped full length to the floor.

This time, he simply curled, grasping his head, no longer concerned with winning, striving only to maintain awareness of reality, somehow certain that if he lost consciousness now, he'd never truly regain it, that he'd be Anheliaa's—and after her, Lidye's—forever.

And as he fought, that internal demand wavered like fresh water entering brine, and a sense of pure anger—Anheliaa's hatred for resistance, any resistance, for failure, of anyone, to bend to *her* logic and *her* needs—ballooned, engulfed the pain.

Images of Mheric, standing in this same spot, defying Anheliaa's will, and after him, Deymorin, whose angry

stubbornness had given her headaches for three months
after his exile. Images of Mikhyel, most bitter of all, standing before the Council, selling them watered-down versions
of her most treasured strategies.

Suddenly:

"Damn you, Mheric, and all *your thick-witted hellspawn!"*
And that pain spread ... through his body and beyond.
He was lying in bed, Nurse at his side ...

He was lying beside a fire, wrapped in a filthy blanket,
next to a redheaded woman, surrounded by strangers ...

And all of him curled and clutched his head, on the floor,
in the bed, beside the fire.

And of a sudden, he was Deymorin, on his knees on this
same floor, filled with Deymorin's strength and Deymorin's
hardheaded stubbornness. And he was Mikhyel standing
beside the rings, terrified, but resolute.

Sight/sound/touch dispersed, segregated, and categorized.
A lizard twitched beneath his cheek; Deymorin's cane
pressed painfully beneath his hip.

And then he was Nikki again, pulling himself up from
the floor of Anheliaa's ringchamber. But not Nikki alone:
his brothers, unspoken, unheard, but unquestionably real,
were standing with him, behind him, before him, around
him, and within: a sphere of protection that siphoned Anheliaa's sanity-threatening-destroying-disrupting pain away.
He could feel Deymorin's arms around him, could *see* the
pain flowing like viscous oil, out of his body and down
through the tiles and stones, and he could hear Mikhyel's
whisper: *No one will ever hurt you.* ...

He wrapped his hand around the wooden hilt and pulled
the cane from under his leg, held it to his face, tracing
each intricate niche with fingertip and eye, absorbing the
surprising heat from the metal bands: deliberate conjura-
tion of his own reality to dispel Anheliaa's.

And as the sensations clarified, he felt strength flowing
into his limbs, *heard* Deymorin whispering *Good, fry. Very
good* ... and: *Get the old witch* ... and Mikhyel, his whisper
frighteningly thin: *the rings, boy, the rings are her strength
... and her weakness.* ...

Staggering to his feet, still gripping his brother's cane, he
advanced against the agonizing pressure.

And as he advanced, another image.

A solution. Mikhyel's solution.

He lunged.

* * *

"Nikki, *no!*" Just Deymio screamed and lunged toward the fire, tangled in his blanket, and fell to his knees, fists clutched to his stomach, cursing in an endless, breathless stream.

"Deymio?" Kiyrstin propped herself on a weary elbow, "Are you all right?"

A shuddering breath. A curse that was half-sob. And a breathless: "I'll kill her."

"Who, Deymio?" She sat up and leaned toward him. "Who do you want to kill?"

Another shuddering, teeth-chattering inhalation.

"Who? ... Oh. Sh-shepherdess."

"Nightmare?"

"I ... suppose."

Suppose, Rhomatum? she thought, as he returned to his nest. If not a dream, what else might it be?

"Don't let it concern you," she whispered. "There have been others. They all have them—particularly the first night or so. Whatever the old woman does evidently wreaks havoc on a sane mind. Want to talk about it?"

"N-n-no. You're probably right. Nothing but a dream. Tired, that's all."

"Let's hope there isn't another. 'Night, Rhomatum."

"G'night, shepherdess."

"Idiot!"

Anheliaa's shout was as potent and as physical as a blow to Nikki's face. His head snapped back, he spun away from rings gone suddenly wild, rings spinning randomly on off-center, canted axes, bouncing and scraping against each other, releasing living wails of protest that echoed through his head.

He struck a wall, rebounded into a stool, and dropped to the floor, scrambling for cover from the storm raging within the room, from deafening light and blinding shrieks. Pure instinct for survival located a small nook, a tiny haven within the maelstrom, and he cowered there, clamping his lips on mindless, babbling horror at the havoc he'd wrought.

Silence, darkness, when they arrived suddenly and without diminution, were equally consuming.

"Idiot, Idiot. Idiot."

Rhythmic chant in the void, invading his silence: Anheliaa's bitter whispered incantation.

Alarm bells—within the Tower and without.

For the first time in living memory, the energy flow out
of Rhomatum Node had ceased.

Idiot, idiot, idiot.

The words were a chant inside Deymorin's head.

Sleep. As if he could. Or would ever again want to, now
he knew the nightmares lying in wait for him.

Idiot, idiot, idiot.

The throb echoed the relentless beat of Anheliaa's
dream-rings.

The shepherdess had said Anheliaa's other victims had
had nightmares. Not surprising. Arriving in the middle of
nowhere, losing months in an instant . . . the human mind
took a while to adjust to such realities.

Six months . . . If not, he suddenly realized, much longer.
Perhaps years. How would he know?

Still, one had to wonder, who had faced Anheliaa's rings
before, if nightmare accounted for the images still so crystal-
clear in his mind. This was not the scene he remembered, not
himself and Mikhyel facing Anheliaa, but Nikki, alone.

And not. *He* had been there. Mikhyel had.

Dream? Reality? Or simply Anheliaa's revenge on him:
torment based on his own deepest fears for his brother?
His own mind set to feed off his own fears?

Anheliaa had been experimenting with the rings for
years. She'd alluded to seeing the future. She'd tried to use
them to force him into compliance, *had* used them—or so
Kiyrstin and the priest claimed—to transport him out of
Rhomatum.

How much did Anheliaa know? Could she read his
mind? Was she in any manner responsible for—whatever
he had experienced, and if so, how was she doing it?

For any ley-related effect to reach beyond the lines went
against all traditional understanding of ley energy; and this
camp was most definitely not on a ley.

So many questions. Questions to which there were no answers.

Here.

*   *   *

"Get up."

Essence of light limning the hand in front of his eyes. Gentle low-pitched hum. Aura of serenity.

"I said, *On your feet!*"

Nikki cringed, seeking the serenity.

"At least manage the *appearance* of a man, damn you!"

Half-hysterical laughter shook him. He let his face slip from his hand and into the crook of his elbow. A *man* knew when to take cover . . . and when to keep his mouth shut. He wasn't such a fool as to let pride risk his life again. His aunt had been out of control. Might well still be.

"Nikaenor! Damn you, get up." Desperation edged her command. Desperation and . . . fear?

He lifted his head.

The room was in shambles. Shards of metal, wood splinters permeated everywhere: remnants of Deymorin's cane. That could have been blood and bone: his arm. He'd have done that, to stop Anheliaa's attack. Had intended to, if it had taken that to stop Anheliaa's attack.

Fortunately, the cane had intercepted the rings first.

Thank you, Deymorin. . . .

"Nikaenor." His name was a breathless whisper. "*Help me!*"

Anheliaa lay in a crumpled heap beside her massive chair, overturned and collapsed in the maelstrom. Beyond her . . .

Only the inner ring still beat the rhythm of the leys: that accounted for the glow within the room. The third and seventh ring hung in suspension, but their movements were erratic and off-axial.

"*Damn you, boy, I must see them. Get me up!*"

His body responded without conscious thought—instincts responding to that commanding voice. He scrambled to his feet and staggered on pain-filled legs around the lizard oasis to his aunt's side. He dropped down, heaved the large-boned frame as best he could—Anheliaa's condition had never affected her appetites—her curses of pain and frustration ringing in his ears the while. Her arthritic fingers clawed at him, seeking purchase, long nails scraping his neck, digging into his arm as he turned her face to the rings.

"Hold me *steady*, damn you," she hissed and he braced himself on his knees, took her weight against his shoulder, forced to watch in unwilling awe as the fallen rings rose and, like sentient creatures, sorted themselves, hanging suspended as Anheliaa tilted and aligned their axes, one at a careful time. Nikki could *feel* the touch she gave each as she released it: a gentle breeze to initiate the swing, holding it on line until the system as a whole resumed its self-possessed, mildly chaotic motion.

The breeze touched the final ring, the radical streamer hissed into motion . . .

Anheliaa collapsed, dragging them both to the floor . . .

. . . and the Tower Guards burst through the hatch and into the room.

Interlude

Mother was positively dancing with wicked glee, leaping and twisting about the cavern terraces, the flickering veils whipping over and around her as much as she around them. Dancer hesitated just within the world-cavern, mesmerized, seeing in this impromptu performance the substance of which the human dance of the radical—that was itself predecessor to the ringdance—was but a pale copy.

Tradition held that the first humans to enter the leythium caves had, upon their return to the world of men, taken a dangerous test of manhood and turned it into a dance to honor the gods of whimsy and chance. Tradition held it was patterned on a dance of the gods themselves.

Seeing Mother now, Dancer could well believe tradition.

{*Got the damnable and gods-be-damned creature, they did!*}

There was an imbalance in the veil. Where the Rhomatum haze should be, the crystal was utter blackness, the linkages battered and rent. Mother's elusive form, at the moment more reptilian than human, slipped, slithered, and leapt through that darkness, arcing up like a fish in water to hover and then settle before Dancer's frozen startlement.

"Creature?" Dancer repeated, feeling dull and stupid, until, of a sudden, the sum of Mother's words, her elation . . . and the blackness that once had been Rhomatum came clear. "Anheliaa's dead?"

The veils echoed Mother's shrug, a fluttering, billowing rise and fall as if the crystal itself sighed.

Which might mean Anheliaa was dead . . . and then again, might not. Either way, one had to wonder who or what had 'gotten' the all-powerful Anheliaa of Rhomatum. But Mother, not being inclined to answer the former, was hardly likely to answer the latter, and since Dancer had little power to affect that surface fact, Dancer could afford to wait for the rumors sure to fill Khoratum court tomorrow.

Besides, the Rhomatum pattern didn't matter any longer. Khoratum's didn't, nor any other of the infinity of crystalline webs and chandeliers save one. Only a single pattern mattered now to Dancer: the pattern born in the waning of the previous year, a pattern that drew Dancer to it as relentlessly as the Towers attracted lightning.

That enigmatic pattern had form now: a central core, strong and stable, hardly lacework at all, a core that sank its roots not into the leylines that ran pulsating and rich between the towered nodes, but in the untouched leythium tributaries that formed a delicate lacework between the internode arteries. Off that trunk, a complexity of branching patterns grew and fluxed, reactive to all the surrounding energies.

And that pattern, having broken free, as new patterns would, of its womblike antechamber—was growing, expanding toward and overlaying the Rhomatum darkness.

But the pattern's radical haze, that cloud of leythium hovering above the web, awaiting direction, fluxed in frightening chaos; colors juxtaposed senselessly, crystalline filaments dissolving before they fully formed.

Dancer reached a cautious hand, touched that shimmering, shifting uncertainty and sensed . . .

Mheric's sons . . . and the source of the Rhomatum dissolution.

Dancer pulled back, startled at the clarity of realization. Turned to find Mother staring.

Expectant.

"You did this. You wove me into this pattern."

An aura of negativity, an accompanying thought: *{Too much trouble./No need.}*

"No *need*? Why not? If not your doing, whose? I don't *want* this, Mother."

"What you *want* is irrelevant. What is, *is*."

"*No!*"

Dancer ran from the chamber, but all exits led back to the Rhomatum dysfunction and the Rhomandi brothers' web, Mother or the ley itself refusing to sever the pattern. Eventually, exhaustion prevailed and Dancer collapsed, shaking with anger and denial onto the chamber's lethium-lattice flooring.

And all that while, Mother only watched. Silent.

The leythium lattice liquefied and ran soothing tendrils up and over Dancer's body, bringing revitalizing nourishment to shaking muscle and whispering soothing reassurance to disturbed and disturbing thoughts.

Done was done, those whispers said, the pattern formed, and Dancer inexorably a part of it. But the pattern was in danger, that disintegrating haze of its radical factor crying out for help.

And Dancer, finding the pattern that was Mheric's sons suddenly and not surprisingly within reach, lifted a hand, and this time did not flinch when realization flowed through that touch.

"You never told me patterns could be individuals, Mother."

{And you should, in a measly twenty-two years of human existence, know all your mother knows?}

But there was an excitement, a thrill of discovery coloring her thought.

"You didn't know either, did you? You haven't *seen* this before."

{The universe always has secrets, human. When we unravel one, it creates others to keep us humble. Such is the beauty of life.}

Mother waxed philosophic and pompous: Mother was bewildered, and strove to hide the fact.

The web was certainly Mheric's sons. The solid core was the eldest, the fluctuating pattern the youngest, the radical haze . . .

That one—Mikhyel was the name memory supplied—was gravely ill, and in tracing the source of that illness, Anheliaa's fate came clear. The new pattern had taken down Rhomatum, but not without penalty, and the backlash of Anheliaa's defensive bolt and . . . Mikhyel's . . . physical weakness accounted for the new web's instability.

Or did it?

Dancer traced the source of the disruption, not to weakness, but to willful destruction. The radical . . . Mikhyel had linked itself to the darkness of Rhomatum, and was destroying itself along with those deteriorating edges.

"He's trying to kill himself, Mother."

"He's trying to kill Anheliaa. Quite different."

"But he'll take himself with her!"

"Yes. Curious, don't you think?"

"Curious? It's horrible."

"Oh, that's a matter of opinion. Tell me, Dancer, is he aware of what he's doing?"

"I don't believe so. It feels deeper, more basic. . . . Protection. Mother, he's protecting his brother from her, and killing himself to do it."

"Why?"

"Love. Family." Dancer closed sense-disrupting eyes, the better to analyze that inner revelation. "Responsibility."

"How useless. Especially since his destruction will destroy an essential part of the brother he's supposedly trying to protect. You humans are so . . . connected. So dependent, . . ."

"Not all humans, Mother."

"Not you?" Mother asked aloud and out of Dancer's thoughts.

"I've no family to die for, Mother."

Dancer felt wetness.

Tears.

Jealous tears.

And Dancer wondered what it must be like, having a family, remembered having had a brother, once, or perhaps it had been a sister, and the warmth of a shared bed and loving arms.

Remembered being sent away to live with Grandmother.

Remembered too clearly the chill and emptiness of being alone.

And sent, on the wave of that remembrance—for that lost sibling, for Grandmother—reinforcement to the veil, strengthening the haze, stabilizing the color, forcing the pattern to fruition.

"You'll release Anheliaa."

"It's the only way to release Mheric's son."

Disgust/acquiescence/endorsement: one of Mother's more confusing signs.

"You should care about that?"

"I don't know if I should, Mother, but I do."

SECTION THREE

Chapter One

"Well, good morning, sunshine," said the blur on the far side of his lashes. " 'Bout time you poked your nose above the horizon."

Gentle voice, a bit ragged with exhaustion about the edges; a voice one part of him had feared never to hear again, and another part wondered whence such paranoia arose, as his eyelids again drifted downward.

Pressure on his hand, the warm one, the one nearest the window felt as if it were encased in ice, and a touch to his face, a thumb that stroked his cheek as if encouraging his eyes to reopen.

Mikhyel blinked slowly, and when that proved efficacious, blinked again, as the blur on the far side of his eyelashes slowly developed solid patches of light and shadow, as sunlight, streaming in through sheer draperies, turned blond hair into a shimmering halo, and as two small patches of clear morning sky appeared in that area where the gods intended eyes to be.

"Nikki?" The whisper that escaped his throat was barely audible even to himself; a second attempt, coming on a startled gasp, produced better results: an affectionate-sounding chuckle.

"Can't fool you, can I, big brother?" asked the vision.

It *was* Nikki.

Relief flooded through him. A dream. It had all been nothing but a bad dream.

With images of Nikki writhing under Anheliaa's mental lash haunting every dream-instant, he'd fought waking with every unconscious breath, *wanting* Nikki safe, *wanting* Anheliaa dead. But he knew now his fears had been unfounded. Nikki, Anheliaa, the rings: it was all fever dream, born of his confrontation with Nikki at Armayel and his conviction the boy would challenge Anheliaa despite any warning and disappear as Deymorin had disappeared.

But Nikki had had more sense than he'd accredited him. Nikki had avoided Anheliaa. Nikki was here. Safe.

"How are you feeling?"

That was easy: terrible. The nightmare that was the drive home, his own collapse, that had to be real, else why was he so tired and sore, and why Nikki's worried presence, here in what was irrefutably his own apartment?

But one couldn't say that to one's younger brother. One had to set a brave example, because one remembered one's own example: an older brother, crippled as a result of one's own stupidity, smiling and saying it didn't really hurt, though the face was pale, and the eyes clouded with unshed tears.

He swallowed hard and managed more voice, though the effort sacrificed what smile he'd conjured. "Better than I deserve."

Another squeeze compressed the warm hand and he wondered if the sound he heard was indeed the bones grating, the way it felt. "That's a matter of opinion," Nikki said gently, which was very kind, if untrue.

His eyes drifted shut again. Tired. Very tired. A light tap to his cheek, another, harder, when he didn't respond.

"Tired, Nikki. Very ..." His voice failed into a yawn, that ended in a squeak of protest as Nikki's other hand contacted his face in a stinging slap.

"Sorry, old fellow, Diorak says to keep you awake this time."

"This? ..." He forced the lids up. "How long ..."

"Three days. Four nights, though."

"Rings. Sicker than ... thought."

"You had a relapse the first night. My fault. I should never ..."

"Don't ... silly."

He hadn't the strength to say what he was thinking, that he was just relieved Nikki was still talking to him, after his deception and the things he'd said at Armayel. Instead, he tightened his fingers, felt Nikki's other hand close over the top, a reassuring warmth that would leave, once he was well. He knew that, as he knew it was only Nikki's generous nature keeping him here now. He tried to be thankful Nikki had waited before leaving him to seek the brother he loved, the only person (so Nikki had said, and surely Nikki knew) who had ever really loved him.

Love had always confused him. He wasn't certain he was capable of it. He *did* understand responsibility and purpose, and he suspected that once Nikki left, the aching void he was sensing in so very large a portion of his person would prove nothing but a momentary lack of responsibility and purpose.

He also knew that, right now, Nikki's hand warming his was the most valuable, most desirable occurrence in the world, and tried not to think how that generosity deepened the pit of debt in which he wallowed. Debt to Deymorin for his leg, debt to Nikki for lying to him, debt to Gareg for his hardheaded blindness, debt to them all for not countering Anheliaa when it mattered. . . .

His eyes tingled. He blinked to spread the moisture over their dry, scratchy surface, turning his head away from Nikki, lest Nikki assign more significance to that wetness than it warranted.

Hair tickled his neck, caught beneath a shoulder when he shifted to avoid it. He tried to raise a hand to pull it free; found even that small effort beyond his ability, and swore softly, at the recalcitrant hair, at his weakness, perhaps at the world in general.

A hand lifted his head from the pillow, another eased the offending strand free, and Nikki was standing over him, settling additional pillows behind him, propping his head up.

"Thank you," he said, before Nikki pressed a cup to his lips and ordered, *"Drink!"*

He obeyed meekly. Fruit juice, he thought. Or soup. Hot, cold, sweet, salt, one would taste much like the other.

Whichever it happened to be, it made keeping his eyes open a bit easier, though everything remained slightly fuzzy. He was beyond caring about that or anything else except the fact Nikki wanted him to stay awake and so he must keep his eyes open—until he spotted the brush reflected in the mirror: a brush that meant relief for a scalp that felt as if Anheliaa's lizards were nesting in it.

And him without the energy to so much as lift his hand.

He sighed. And stared. And sighed again.

Golden laughter bounced off the walls, and the reflected brush disappeared from the reflected bureau top.

"Turn a bit," Nikki said.

Embarrassment came on the heels of sluggish understanding. "Rings, boy, you don't have to—"

"Not the first time, brother." A gentle shove pushed him half over, pillows wedged at his back kept him there as a weight depressed the mattress behind him. "Almost had you yesterday, but you faded on me again."

And then the brush was chasing the lizards out.

He sighed and relaxed nose-first into the pillow, managing to work an arm around to support his body in its ludicrous position, a position no amount of ridicule, regardless how public, could convince him to change at that moment.

He let himself drift with the rhythmic strokes, the meaning of life reduced to such stimulation, and was nearing catatonia when:

"Rings," he muttered to the pillow. "The Council meeting. Gareg's bogs. I promised him, and if we don't get something underway—"

"Relax. The Council knows. The meetings have been postponed. I sent a message to Gari." A hand stroked his temple, smoothing the hair back with a gentle, fingertip massage. Tension abated. "Do me a favor?"

"For this," he answered on a pillowed sigh, "anything."

Another stroke of the brush, another touch of fingertips. "Next time—say something, will you?"

"Next time, I'll have the sense to order the coach, and let you stay home where you belong. I should never have asked you out in such weather."

The strokes stopped.

"That's not—" Nikki's voice caught on what sounded disturbingly like a sob, broke on a heartfelt curse. Something hard bounced off the wainscotting and thudded to the floor.

Pillows meant to support became a trap, a barrier keeping him from seeing Nikki and the origin of that sound. A surge of urgency gave him strength and he thrust himself about, tumbling the obstructing pillows to the floor, and the sight of Nikki's exhaustion, plain now he opened his eyes to see, drove the sunlight from the room.

"Nikki, what's wrong?"

Tense. Stricken. Angry. That tired young face reflected every emotion roused in the young mind's search for explanation.

"I'm sorry I didn't tell you, Nikki," Mikhyel said, trying to help. "I didn't realize myself how weak I was getting—had worked myself stupid the night before and hadn't the sense to realize—"

"Don't you see?" Nikki interrupted. "That's what I—*Why* I—"

Nikki waved a frustrated hand through the air, clenched the hand to a fist and let it fall to his knee. He shook his head wearily and silently replaced the pillows at Mikhyel's back, then retrieved the brush from the floor, and returned to the bed as though the interruption had never taken place.

Mikhyel collapsed into his pillows, but refused to turn away from Nikki's determinedly oblivious face, couldn't find it in him to object when Nikki calmly pulled his hair forward, smoothed the newly acquired tangles, and separated the mass into sections for braiding.

When he'd finished, Nikki tied the plait off, and smoothed it gently. Then he just sat, his hand resting absently on Mikhyel's chest, and stared sightlessly.

It was a look Mikhyel knew from the inside, as he knew the reason for Nikki's distraction. Once and long ago, he, too, had felt guilt weighing him down, crushing his ability to reason; he, too, had felt that overpowering need to do something, *anything* for the brother lying helplessly in bed.

Deymorin had come out of his fevered coma filled with forgiveness, nobly assuming a guilt that wasn't his, laughingly dismissing the *accident* (as Deymorin insisted on calling it) that had crippled him for life as a relatively cheap lesson in stupidity. But Mikhyel had rejected Deymorin's forgiveness, had turned from the comfort offered, too filled with the guilt of that night to foresee what his rejection of the offer would do to them both, himself and Deymorin.

Because Deymorin had never repeated the offer ... which was only right, because the truth was, it *had* been his fault Deymorin was on the Tower ledge in the first place, his fault they'd fought and Deymorin had slipped. If he'd done as he should have done all those years ago, he'd have sent the woman away the instant he found her waiting in his room. Then Deymorin and his cohorts would have gone away and Anheliaa would never have found them crouched in the hallway outside his bedroom, would never have opened that door. . . .

Bile rose; he choked it back.

His fault, as his illness was his fault not Nikki's, and when those grief-stricken, sky-blue eyes filled, and Nikki rose, still with that blind look, to leave, he acted for once on pure instinct. He never asked, never offered in words that which Deymorin had offered, never gave Nikki that chance to think too much. Instead, he caught one shaking hand, and pulled Nikki back, and when Nikki protested, slid his other arm around the boy's neck, drawing his brother close, holding him as he'd wanted to be held all those years ago.

As Deymorin had tried to hold him.

But Deymorin had tried to absolve the unforgivable. Nikki, being innocent and gentle and deserving, could accept the dispensation his older brother offered, never realizing whatever small guilt *might* have been his disappeared the instant his arms closed around Mikhyel's waist and his nose burrowed into Mikhyel's neck.

Spasmodic quivers shook them both and left them gasping slightly for breath, when at last they eased. Nothing so organized or unmanly as tears. Just exhaustion. His and Nikki's.

Four nights, he'd said.

"Nikki?" he murmured.

Nikki's head turned until Mikhyel could feel the warm breath brush his chest. "S–sorry, Khyel." He heaved with a sigh, and burrowed again into Mikhyel's neck. "Just ... tired. Give me ... moment. I'll ..." A wry, breathy chuckle stirred the braid's end-tuft. "... get out of your hair."

"No rush." He tightened his hold. "Want to know what this is all about, anyway."

"Not ... now. Later ... maybe."

"Now, Nikaenor."

"No!"

Nikki tried to pull away; he held on, desperation lending him strength, suddenly certain that if he let go, Nikki would disappear forever. "Is it because I was a fool and let myself chill? That's not your fault, brother. I'll share with you the sin of stupidity, but nothing more."

Nikki quite struggling and collapsed against him, holding him now with similar desperation. "That's ... not all."

The words were barely audible, and in that desperation, he read a fear to match his own, as if Nikki, too, was afraid of rejection. Nikki was no fool, was not one to overreact on a triviality.

"Years ago, Nikki," he said on a slow and painful memory, "I pushed one brother away so hard he's never forgiven me. I may be a fool, but I'm selfish enough not to let that happen twice. I don't know what you've done, but I know *you*, I trust you and your motives, regardless the outcome. But whatever's wrong, maybe I can help. Won't you at least let me try?"

Nikki's stranglehold eased, his chest heaved with a sigh. "I've ruined everything."

"Couldn't if you tried, fry, as I discovered years ago. The world's too large, the variables far too many. What is it you think you've done?"

"The Council. Gareg and the flooding. They were pressing for a report, Mikhyel, demanding to know if you'd stopped Gari. I put them off till yesterday, but I didn't know if you'd—if you were—you were so ill, Khyel, so I ... I tried to handle things. Instead, I ruined any chance you had to bring them around."

Too tired to worry, too filled with relief that Nikki was alive and well, Mikhyel chuckled, and answered lightly: "You faced the Council solo? Brave lad."

"I'd say, rather, stupid. They laughed. Then they told me to leave. They wouldn't listen."

"Did the same to me, at first, Nikki. Did the same to me." He heaved a breath against Nikki's weight. "Humiliating, isn't it?"

"Y-y-yes. But that's not—"

"They aren't laughing at me now, Nikki. And they won't at you, in a year or so. I had no idea you were interested, or I'd have had you sitting in with me before now. I owe you for trying to explain the situation to the old ... well, never mind. Relax. No need to fret. It'll be fine."

"But Anheliaa. The rings ..."

"Later, fry. Anheliaa can wait. Just—don't leave me yet, please?"

Nikki's trembling slowly dissipated, and Nikki's apparent weight increased. His breathing steadied.

Nikki was asleep.

And safe in that lack of consciousness, Mikhyel stroked the curls that brushed his chin, gently separating the strands, welcoming the pressure that made breathing difficult.

He had no illusions about that promise. Nikki would leave, and Nikki would find Deymorin and some pretty shepherdess, and never come back, never sit on Council with him, and Anheliaa would have to settle on him as Princeps and as sire to her precious heir, flooding or no flooding, war or no war. In the meantime and forever after, he'd have this moment, and treasure it—

Without warning, the door opened, and Diorak stepped into the room.

Mikhyel raised a finger to his lips.

"I've been waiting for this to happen," Diorak said, keeping his voice low as he settled in a chair. "Young fool hasn't slept in three days."

Mikhyel winced, wondering at whom the epithet was aimed. "All because of me."

"Because of you, yes. And because of Anheliaa."

"Anheliaa?" he asked, surprised.

He nodded. "He's been driving us all to distraction, fluttering back and forth between your rooms and her apartment door."

A sane man would have been shocked. Instead, a part of him seemed already to know, a part that turned cold and asked: "What happened?"

"Evidently, the rings collapsed—at least power was totally disrupted for several minutes. She reset them, then collapsed herself. She was comatose until early this morning, when she, bless the rings, awoke as if from a proper night's sleep."

"When did it happen?"

"The night you returned to Rhomatum. —You took far too long. I've warned you—"

"Was she alone?" He interrupted, the cold inside a solid ice-lump now.

"Your brother was with her. No one else. You really must do something about the Tower Guard. It took them far too long, following the alarm, to organize and access the ringchamber. They've gotten complaisant."

"Rings, man, it was Nikki in there with her. Why *should* there have been a Guard present? Why should they have worried?"

"What makes you think she was safe with him?"

He resisted an instinctive urge to shield Nikki. Anheliaa's threat was long since past, and such a display would only exacerbate Diorak's already ill will.

"Did he say what happened?"

"Only that they argued. He's been quite closemouthed about the entire incident. Unforgivably so, in some opinions."

"As you just reminded me, I've been gone too much. She's overworked, exhausted. If they argued—even over a supper menu—well, you know how obstinate Anheliaa can be. Nikki must have been terrified when she collapsed and there was no one to turn to. In all probability, he feels altogether *too* responsible for the disaster. I'll talk with him when he wakes. I'm certain there's a perfectly reasonable explanation."

"Don't depend on it. And don't automatically accept what he tells you as truth."

Mikhyel felt his hackles rise: damned if any physician, regardless how old a family retainer, had any right to question a Rhomandi's actions. But, he reminded himself firmly, Diorak was Anheliaa's physician—had been for thirty years. He *deigned* to treat the rest of the Family. Not surprisingly, Diorak had his prejudices.

"As for the Guard," he said soothingly, to halt those prejudices in their tracks, "with that new shielded hatch she installed, they couldn't access the room if the rings were down. Anheliaa's design, Diorak, not mine. Anheliaa's overconfidence in her rings, not mine. Do *you* care to argue with her on that account?"

Diorak grumbled something inaudible.

"And Anheliaa?" he asked. "What does she say about the accident?"

"She's volunteered nothing, and I've not asked. I won't allow anyone, *especially* that brother of yours, into her room at this time. Her condition is much too fragile. In fact, I must return to her now."

Diorak paused at the door.

"You don't know the whole, boy. The City's in an uproar. So are the satellites. There's talk of liability suits everywhere you go. Council's frantic."

Liability. Wonderful. One of those damned contract clauses Anheliaa had insisted Council endorse: the satellites' declared price to divert power from them for tapping

Khoratum. Anheliaa had promised them uncompromised power, and they intended to hold her to it.

"What disrupted the rings? Do we at least know that?"

"*Your brother* hasn't said, but there were bits of wood and steel everywhere, including several impaled lizards. The maids were not amused."

The door slammed behind him; Nikki stirred; Mikhyel quieted him with an absentminded squeeze.

Steel and wood. Deymorin's sword-cane.

The rings.

The nightmare—wasn't.

Mikhyel closed his eyes on a world gone suddenly liquid.

Squeezing in between Vandoshin-the-priest and another large fellow, Deymorin set his shoulder to the supply wagon's tailgate and heaved. With a reluctant, sucking *pop*, the mud released the wheel and the cart surged forward onto the bed of twigs and leaves. The mules leaned willingly into the harness and hauled the cart up the hill to dry ground, and a weary cheer rose from the onlookers.

Deymorin and the other four mud-covered but triumphant men staggered from the bog with the help of several willing pairs of hands. The shepherdess observed her minions from a perch atop a large rock, well beyond range of flying filth.

"Well, it *used* to be a road," the other man muttered sourly—Korrigen, if he remembered correctly—and Deymorin slapped a muddy paw on the one unsullied spot on Korrigen's shoulder.

"Never mind, old fellow. The rains this year ..." He paused, recalling time lost, then revised smoothly: "... last year washed out at least three historically reliable roads in the valley. One entire section of what once was top wheatland in west county had soured by summer's end. A vegetable patch or two have likely followed by now."

"I heard Rhomatum had bumper crops last summer," Kiyrstin commented, propping chin in hand and elbow to knee and squinting into the sunlight. "Rumor has it Anheliaa has figured how to make rain in the Betweens at her whim."

"If she has, she's a fool," Deymorin said without thinking. "Yes, we had rain all summer—in the north end and on the west side. Lousy for hay, but it made for excellent crops—where the land wasn't underwater. Unless the pattern has changed more than this—" He waved a hand at the mudpit that had been a road. "—would indicate, the whole valley will foul, if we don't do something soon. It's a damned mess, and we're still high ground here."

"We?" Using the back of her knife, Kiyrstin flipped mud from her boot heel, her eyes downcast and unreachable. "Isn't that the farmers' problem?"

"It's *anyone's* problem who wants to eat—" he replied, his temper heating at the old argument, cooling immediately when her calculating gaze lifted.

Satisfied. Piecing him together. Culling the salient bits from his conversation as she had been for the last three days. Bits she was increasingly effective at teasing out of him despite his better sense.

"Not the attitude of most dedicated city-folk I know, Rags. Are you Rhomatumin so different, then?"

"I suppose it depends on who you ask. I've a Between farm or two—helps to settle the bar-debts—"

"Or pays for a mistress' jewels?"

He assumed a woeful expression. "Ah, shepherdess, for that, one must have a mistress."

"And you don't? How disappointing. And here I'd had you with at least four or five."

"Five?" He cast a glance down his extremely muddy person. "Shepherdess, I . . . don't know how to tell you this, but . . . the ladies of Rhomatum have somewhat . . . higher standards."

She hissed and flipped mud from her knife tip at his face with deadly, and not altogether friendly, accuracy. He laughed and dodged, taking it on his ear rather than between the eyes, then reached a hand to help her down from her stony perch. She slapped his hand aside and slid lightly to the ground.

"Mistress?" A light, breathy voice arrived on a spattering of pebbles: the mule-boy, slipping and sliding down the forward trail. "Found a place, I did. Good 'n' level. Mostly dry. Got grass fer th' mules. Needs to rest, they do."

"Very well, Zandy," Kiyrstin answered, "We'll stop there—for the night, I think. We're all of us exhausted. Tell the others, will you?"

"Yes'm," the boy said, and was off in a flash of dark eyes, a flop of darker hair, and a light, skipping stride.

"And, Zandy," Kiyrstin called after him, and he bounced to a halt facing them. "If you want supper tonight, remind Van to send someone ahead for Carlonio and Basliisi."

"Yes'm." And he was off again, yet one more strange member of a very strange party. Some twenty-odd, there were, all out of Mauritum in one way or another, some with the casual but alert poise of trained fighters, others with the shifty moves of streetscut and prison bait; and then there was romMaurii, the sleek, deceptively powerful priest, Kiyrstin, the by no means shepherdess, and the boy.

A strange company, indeed, and bound for Rhomatum for reasons as mysterious as they'd been three days ago.

Three days of deadlock, the shepherdess and himself. That first night, she'd taken her priestly cohort off into the shadows, and romMaurii had returned alone, full of pleasantries and little else. Whatever the unspoken and instant dissonance between them that had loosened the priest's tongue at the first, it had been effectively silenced.

The priest, waiting for them as they followed the wagon up the hill, reached out to stop Kiyrstin, who waved Deymorin on.

Hard to believe those two hadn't pieced Just Deymio and Deymorin Rhomandi together. Unless they didn't know. Unless Mauritum was even more ignorant of Rhomatum than Rhomatum of Mauritum. He supposed it was possible that they were as notorious in their own city as he was in Rhomatum. Perhaps they were biding their time, waiting for him to reveal *his* knowledge of *their* doings.

Certainly they were wasting no time crossing the Kharatas and descending into Rhomatum. They'd encountered snow the first day, including a short patch that was as difficult a passage, in its own way, as the bog now lying behind them. They had moved steadily downward ever since, rising well before dawn and travelling well into the night, the two men, Carlonio and Basliisi, always a step ahead, preparing a campsite with firewood and fresh meat.

And *always* avoiding the Persitum Leyroad. Assiduously.

Failing information to the contrary, a man might assume his companions were in a hurry to put Persitum (and by extrapolation, Mauritum) well behind them. Made a man wonder what sort of treasure lay hidden within the tarpaulin-covered wagon—other than the chest containing a strangely varied choice of clothing. Certainly the bedrolls and other supplies carried within could have been packed on the mules' backs, had speed been the only consideration.

Obviously, he thought, a backward glance intercepting frowning suspicion from the priest and uncertainty from the non-shepherdess, speed was not.

By the time Kiyrstin entered the camp with Van, the mules were free of their harness and Zandy, with the help of Damn-his-endlessly-useful-hide Deymio, was rubbing them down.

"If you value this project at all, Kiyrstin, get him away from the boy," Van said, and walked abruptly away before she could object to his attitude.

Unfortunately, he was right. For all she didn't share his absolute distrust of the Rhomatum, it was only prudent to secure Deymio's loyalty *before* he enchanted the boy as he had everyone else.

Easy, helpful, diffident ... with everyone but herself. Somehow whenever their paths crossed they generated sparks as reliably as fur in a Tower.

Still, (she smothered the grin that threatened) that sizzle was not thoroughly unpleasant. Was, she had to admit it, quite stimulating, more often than not.

Three days and never another question, not about who they were, not about where they were bound, or why they moved with such obvious intent or what that intent might be. Each day gaining strength, though he hid the fact.

Or (she revised her thought honestly) he simply didn't announce the fact. When necessity called, as with the stuck cart, he didn't hesitate to lend a (very substantial) shoulder. But she'd seen him each night, after the camp slept, stretching and testing muscle and bone, seen him on the trail, pushing, always pushing. He'd even, wonder of wonders, accepted her offer of another try at his back, though he'd insisted on slightly altering the technique. He'd claimed it helped.

Trying to turn her up sweet, that's what he was doing.

When she reached the mules, he was leaning over, one fore-hoof braced between his knees, flipping mud out of the crevasses as dexterously as any farrier.

"Hah, Rags," she said to the top of his head, "Now we know all your secrets."

His head jerked, flipping his hair back so that he could stare up at her, a frown between his dark brows.

"You're a stablebrat, born and bred."

The frown cleared in a ringing laugh, and he stood free, releasing the hoof and giving the large mule a friendly slap on the shoulder.

"More right than you know, shepherdess," he said, and to Zandy: "He's all right, son. Just go stand him in the stream a while."

"Yezzur," Zandy answered. "Thankee, zur."

"Pleasure, lad. He's a good fellow."

"Thankee, zur."

"Where'd he come from?" Just Deymio asked as they watched the boy lead the beast away. There was a warmth to his voice and a smile on his face; he was a man comfortable with youngsters, even fond of them. Contrary to Van's notions, rather than keeping him from the boy, perhaps this was the real means to securing Deymio's loyalty.

"Hard to tell," she answered. "He doesn't seem to have much of anyone."

"An' don' need nobody neither, mistrus!" A grin flashed back at them, their words evidently carrying on the breeze.

"Quite a character." Deymorin laughed. "I'd like to make his closer acquaintance."

"That . . . might be arranged." A sidewise glance caught a puzzled look. She grinned and said, "Go scrub, Rags, you're a walking mudpit."

Consciousness happened on the sweet scent of warm honeyberry wine and a faint scritching sound. Nikki yawned and stretched, feeling relaxed and rested for the first time in days.

Recalling the circumstances of his last waking moments, he realized, in some embarrassment, that he was still dressed and sprawled across Mikhyel's bed rather than his own.

The sweet smell emanated from a decanter underlit with a warming-candle's glow and setting on Mikhyel's desk situated near the window at the far end of the room. Mikhyel himself, head propped in his right hand, scribbling rapidly with his left, was the source of the scratching noise.

Elbow, ink bottle, and wine goblet acted as paperweights to hold a large scroll open for study. A scroll Nikki recognized well. He'd worked hard enough, in the long nights waiting for Mikhyel's fever to break, preparing it.

Nikki had that desk moved in from Mikhyel's study so he could watch over his brother while he worked exactly as *Mikhyel* now was, with the heavy drapes propped just so to shed light on the desk without disturbing the sleeper. During the endless hours he'd created a meticulous composite of all the contour maps Mikhyel had brought back with him from Armayel, making a single map showing the entire valley and the surrounding foothills. Painstakingly tracking natural water flow patterns, he'd found at least two areas where the vast bulk of the runoff channelled into a relatively confined area. Dams built there, where the rock for construction was plentiful, would stop the majority of the water flowing into the valley and create natural roadways for transport of goods between the leys, and reservoirs of water to tap in times of drought.

He'd been so certain it would work. And yesterday, not knowing when (or if) Mikhyel would awake, he'd presented it to Council—

The scratching stopped.

"Dammit, boy," Mikhyel muttered, "If you were awake . . ."

Nikki gulped, uncertain whether he wanted to draw attention to the fact that he was, a decision made moot when Mikhyel glanced up, his shadowed face darkly frowning.

Worse than he'd feared. Word must have come from Council as he slept.

He turned away from the frown, and sat up, swinging his legs off the mattress. He'd so wanted to explain to Mikhyel first. . . .

"Khyel, I'm sorry. I'm so—"

"Sorry?" Mikhyel interrupted him abruptly, distractedly. "Whatever for? How Gareg and I could have missed it . . . You said you talked to Council. About this? Surely they've begun organizing labor crews. There's no time to lose, what with the spring thaws already well underway."

"I . . ." Nikki blinked, wondering if they were discussing the same topic. "No. It's stupid. They said—"

"It's not stupid, Nikki. It's the obvious answer. Who told you otherwise?"

Everybody, he wanted to say, but he paused, unwilling to point out the plan's obvious flaw, at least for a moment.

Mikhyel's response was gratifying; Council's had been ...
less enthusiastic.

He found his boots propped against the bed steps and
pulled them on. "You really think it would work?"

"You know the answer to that." Mikhyel's eyes scanned
him, a frowning deliberation. "This is what you meant
when you said you'd ruined everything? Council laughed
at—" He broke off with a short, harsh laugh. "But they
would: you're only seventeen, after all. —Well, let them
laugh, Nikki. Just don't let them get to you. Don't let their
blind conservatism undermine your conviction. A leader
can't do that, Nikki. A leader must trust what he knows
and act on it."

A leader. He wasn't a leader. Wasn't any kind of a
leader.

But one remembered Anheliaa's assertions, and Mikhyel's warnings, and most of all that *sense* of Mikhyel up in
Anheliaa's Tower, and one said slowly, testing the waters
of waking reality:

"A *wise* man knows his own limitations and listens to
those who might know more. I didn't expect them to adopt
the plan without debate. I'm *not* the Princeps. Neither have
I Deymorin's—or your—overview of all the economic and
political ramifications of such an undertaking. I just wanted
them to consider it. They ... declined the offer."

"They won't decline it now," Mikhyel said firmly, and
jotted another note on a scrap of paper and stuck it firmly
atop a growing stack on the notepin. "Overview be
damned. We've an emergency situation and if they don't
act quickly, bailout will be a thousand times more expensive. Trust me on this, Nikaenor. There are details to figure—moving that much rock, reinforcing the dam structure
for heavy loads—but that's what engineers are for."

"Feasibility was never in question."

"Then what is?"

"As Councillor Bernard pointed out, the northeastern
reservoir would also cover a good portion of Khoratum
Ley. Khoratum is growing. It's a major importer at the
moment, and will be for years to come. City merchants
expect to be able to load trade goods at one end and have
them transported uninterrupted to the other. They'd never
countenance such an obstacle to traffic flow. Particularly
not a fair-sized lake."

"And did you point out to them that floater-track works below water as well as above, and that, should the tracks fail, goods can be floated across water as well as suspended from balloons? The worst that can happen is two thriving port towns on either end of the lake."

Nikki shrugged. He'd had such arguments prepared, but had never been given the opportunity to voice them. Council didn't want to talk about that. Council didn't *want* to hear that half the vegetable crop wouldn't *be* in the markets this year; that not acting promptly would mean hundreds of 'tweeners thrown onto the City charity lists for which excess yield would not exist. Hundreds who *could* be plowing fields and tending crops and keeping *Council's* household costs down.

Mikhyel turned his frown back to the map. "Those fools will listen if I have to assume Deymorin's authority to force them. Dammit! Why couldn't he be here? *He* has the position—and the personal charisma, when he cares to use it, damn him—to make anyone cooperate."

"Anyone except Anheliaa."

Mikhyel's shoulders drooped. "Except Anheliaa."

Sagging shoulders, sunken eyes, hollow cheeks: fever and worry had his older brother looking twice his age and more. Whatever Anheliaa's 'truth', cooperation—or capitulation—had not come easily for Mikhyel. And a man who had experienced Anheliaa's incentives, a man who looked now on a brother whose eyes mirrored a lifetime of horror, had to wonder how much Mikhyel had endured over the years, and at what cost.

"What happened that night, Mikhyel?" Nikki asked at last, never doubting Mikhyel would know which night. "What *exactly* happened?"

Mikhyel's haunted gaze sought the brandy's warm glow. "I told you. Anheliaa proposed her plan—he'd have none of it. She insisted. He refused. And then ..." His head dropped; he covered his eyes with his fists. And when he continued, his voice was thin, shaking—and not altogether rational. "The rings were spinning—so rapidly, they were this silver ... *cloud* ... in the room. The energy ... was enough to make your hair stand. Then ... he was on the floor—in pain. Awful pain. I ... felt it, too. Almost. And there was nothing I could do ... no enemy. No weapon.

Nothing. And then ... I hardly remember ... I must have been mad. ..."

It was as if Mikhyel had forgotten his presence, as if he talked only to himself.

"You threatened the rings, didn't you?" Nikki said gently, drawing him out of that horror into a present-day haven. "To stop Anheliaa—to save Deymio. You threatened them with your bare hands."

Mikhyel emerged from behind blanketing hands. "How did you know that?" he asked faintly. "Did *she* tell you?"

"I know what you did the same way you know what happened between Anheliaa and me the night you collapsed."

Mikhyel's grey eyes widened, the faint green ring around the iris darkened, growing eerily pronounced, a horrified gaze Nikki returned without flinching, knowing the source of that horror from the inside, though for him, it was far from horrifying.

He'd seen things, *knew* things about his brothers he could only know *through* his brothers. He'd heard Deymorin and Mikhyel, had *felt* them inside, as he'd felt Anheliaa when she used the rings to force herself into his head, only their presence had been anything but painful.

He'd dealt on a personal level with that strange threeway communion while Mikhyel hovered in the balance between life and death. Over and over he'd relived those glorious moments when he and his brothers had been one, until he remembered, as clearly as if he'd been there in Mikhyel's flesh, the lengths Mikhyel had gone to that night to save Deymorin.

In that same way he knew Anheliaa was, at least in part, wrong in her assessment of Mikhyel's loyalties. *Had* been certain ever since he'd confronted Anheliaa and felt his brothers in the Tower with him.

He and his brothers had built their lives around the assumption they had no power over the rings. Even considering this new evidence, he had no reason to suppose the position of ringmaster was a part of any future of his. But together, he and his brothers *had* defied Anheliaa's ring-enhanced domination, and as a result, Anheliaa would never again have quite the same power over him; to pretend otherwise was to willfully be the blind fool Anheliaa called him.

That the threeway communion *had* happened was fact. How it had happened, why, and what its implications might be were simple mysteries, unknowns to which there were knowable—potentially exciting—answers. Answers never even suggested in the histories he'd read, but which lay at the very heart of the Tamshi tales.

Almost, one was tempted to go to Anheliaa for answers. Almost. One was also not stupid.

Whether or not that moment of shared experience ever repeated itself, he, at least, had been profoundly affected. As had Mikhyel, though hardly the same way. He knew, thanks to that moment, he—and his brothers—were ... different.

But he couldn't force that realization on Mikhyel. Of the three of them—himself, Mikhyel, and Deymorin—Mikhyel, the lawyer, was the most insistently pragmatic, his entire life based on rules and absolutes. Mikhyel would deny this wonderful, magical—*thing*—they shared until it withered and died through disuse.

Deymorin, on the other hand and wherever he was with his fire and his redheaded woman, would trust his own senses and wonder how best to use the ability to topple Anheliaa once and for all.

He'd felt *that* in the shared instant, as surely as he felt Mikhyel's resistance now.

Himself—he'd tried for all those long hours sitting beside Mikhyel's sickbed to reestablish that moment, to contact his brothers again. All those efforts had proven futile, and now he wanted more than anything to go into the hills to where those with the old beliefs still practiced, to seek out the old tales about the nodes and their power, to find precedent for what they had experienced and what it all meant, and how best to use it for all mankind.

But that would have to wait. Thanks to that shared moment, he knew for certain now that Deymorin was alive. He had to find Deymorin, save Deymorin from Anheliaa, or bandits, or whoever had held him away from his family for so many months, and then they could decide together what they'd do next.

As for Mikhyel, who had been part of that experience, but feared it: Mikhyel would never join them in that quest. Mikhyel, whose horror continued to manifest in his face, would remain here and fight the Council over the obvious, secure and content—if never quite happy—in the safety of the known.

He slid off the bed. "Get some sleep, Mikhyel. You're going to need it, if you honestly expect to convince Council to implement those plans."

"But you'll be there, too. You'll want to explain—get the credit. I *will* support you, Nikki. It will be different this time."

Nikki shook his head. "I don't care to match wits with them any longer, Khyel. That's your forte. Besides, I've other meetings to attend tomorrow morning."

"What 'other meetings.' "

"The message came just before you woke up." Nikki raised an eyebrow, and grinned without actually feeling much in the way of humor. "Anheliaa has . . . summoned me."

"And then you turn this little knob and . . ."

The small ley-like lamp radiated a non-ley yellow into the forest shadows.

"Intrustin', huh?"

The youngster's eyes glowed in the unnatural light, obviously proud of his master's creation. At the machine's side, the man-mountain, who was the boy's constant companion, turned the crank with methodical regularity in a rhythm as hypnotic as Anheliaa's spinning rings.

And the result was, Deymorin had to admit it, '*in*trustin'.'

Funny how one could misread a situation so thoroughly. He'd seen this Zandy hovering in the shadows, had assumed he was son to one of the men, a cutpurse in training, perhaps. Or perhaps, since he never strayed far from the cart, relegated to mule-grooming by happenstance of being the youngest.

He'd never once suspected the youngster was the heart of the entire operation . . . if, in fact, he was. If, in fact, this wasn't some sort of elaborate illusion, and the boy's guileless delivery designed to set him a false trail.

Kiyrstin had her eye on him, likely expected him to bolt at any moment. Which he might. He knew the measure of his captors now, and knew the lay of the land they travelled better than he knew the streets of Rhomatum.

And he had brothers to save; revenge to wreak.

If, on the other hand, the boy and his contraption were

legitimate, he might just delay his departure—for the sake of that revenge, if nothing else ... as the two watching silently from the cart's far side undoubtedly hoped. A man had to wonder, who was the object of such interest, just who his host/captors believed him to be, and what use they thought to make of him.

He smiled easily and set an arm on the boy's shoulders, waiting for some tension in the boy, some sense of evasion, while he inspected the contraption from all angles, poking and prodding cautiously, looking for some hidden mechanism, a trapdoor or mirrors—all those contrivances the skeptics like Mikhyel claimed magicians used.

Himself, he'd always just enjoyed the show.

The somewhat undersized magician evidenced no objections until his snooping led him to a rather ordinary-looking wire strung around the smaller box.

"I wouldn't, zur," the boy said, wincing.

A downward glance encountered honest brown eyes filled with misgiving; thin shoulders relaxed when he pointed to the wire without touching.

"What's it for?"

"Protection." The boy sounded quite smug. "Figgered this'n m'self, I did."

"Protection?"

" 'Member when y' comed inta camp th' first time? Y' got all tingly, din'cha?"

He nodded cautiously.

"Well, y' see, when the lode-stuff goes through the lines, if y' touches the lines, yer finger gets all tingly. I was 'sperimentin' one night, an' discovers that tinglin' can get'cha a long ways away. So's if we makes this ring-like of thick wire and runs th' stats throughs it, a circle of th' tingly goes 'round the camp and keeps th' wild critturs away. Gots somethin' t' do with th' ley, I thinks, cuz it surely do tingle more the closer we is to the leys. Wasna s'posed t'get *you*, zur. I'm mortal sorry for that."

"Can't argue with its effectiveness in that sense, son. And you say it's all from this—what did you call it?"

"Lodestone Static Encapsulator." The boy enunciated carefully around the rather oversized words. "It's like ley-power, don'cha know, but different. More like lightnin's—"

"Lightning?" He dropped his hold on the boy, took a step back from the box in only partially feigned alarm.

The boy laughed and grabbed his arm, pulling him back, his confidence and ease, in the way of boys, growing with the awareness he controlled something that made adults nervous.

"Perfec'ly safe, 'tis, zur. But lightnin' makes th' bulb glow, too, so m' master says. He says as how they's related, summat, but it's not sudden-like th' way lightnin' does. Keeps on so long as Tomly here keeps turnin' this 'ere handle."

The boy patted Tomly's huge arm, got a half-wit's grin in response. Tomly was a big, good-natured fellow, who kept close to the boy—or vice versa. Deymorin had assumed the two had gravitated to one another in response to such an overwhelmingly adult population. Considering the potential value of the boy's knowledge, however, their relationship took on rather different overtones.

"Best of all," Zandy was saying, "it can happen *anywheres* and *anyone* can make 'er happen. No rings. No ringmasters."

And wouldn't Anheliaa love that. He didn't react, didn't care to betray that fascination to this boy—even less to the others watching his every move from the shadowed woods—but the boy had hit his interest squarely with that comment. If this contraption could put Anheliaa effectively out of business, damned right he was interested.

Kiyrstin had sent him off with the boy, Kiyrstin was going to no small effort to protect this boy's invention, therefore, Kiyrstin was also interested in it for her own reasons, which, as yet, were not the least bit obvious.

"And you say wires contain it? Direct it?"

The boy nodded.

"Master says it stores th' static, don'cha see? Th' lodestone collects it, like it were metal filin's. Squoozes 'em down-like an' then sends th' stat through th' wire. Jus' like leythium an' th' leys."

Not quite. Leypower was everywhere within the energy umbrella. A leythium crystal web, properly aligned within the leyflux, glowed with light and heat. Leypower just *was*, like sunlight. This total, *routeable*, containment ... How could one possibly explain such a phenomenon?

Deymorin scanned the contraption again, still suspecting trick devices sustaining some illusion.

"All this to light that one small lamp?"

"O' course not." The boy sounded personally insulted. Deymorin hid a smile.

"So what *can* it do?"

"Dunno, zur. Not for certain. But Master Harlik, he says a big 'un could do for a whole city. Everything the leys do—maybe *more*."

Deymorin nodded, accepting that prideful exaggeration without a flicker. He'd been fourteen himself, once.

"Master Harlik?"

"M' master. 'Ee were assistant t' Master Alchemist Kormac at Khaythnarum Node. They makes—"

"I had quite a collection of Khaythnarum glasswork, once upon a time. Smuggled in, of course. And an aunt with expensive tastes in Mauritumin jewelry. I'm quite familiar with the manufactory's output, lad."

"Yezzur. Ye'd be 'mazed those what ain't," the boy grumbled, obviously a proud native of the remote island node. "Well, zur, they was havin' lots o' trouble with spon—sponta—nyus arcing in the chem labs, 'specially durin' storms 'n' such, an' they been havin' lots of 'em, storms, that is, wi' lots o' lightnin'. Even—" He grinned with an adolescent's grotesque reverence. "—tornadoes. I meself saw five of 'em touch down in one day only a year since. It were truly wonderful."

Deymorin laughed. "And was your master's task to devise a mechanical solution to these problems?"

The boy nodded vigorously. "How'd 'ee guess, zur?"

"Not an uncommon effort—most minor nodes have tried at one time or another. Generally with less than impressive results. The lightning rods we use in the betweens are apparently far less attractive to the gods of lightning than the ringtowers themselves."

Zandy cast him a suspicious sidelong glance. "Ye don' *really* believes in 'em things, do 'ee, zur?"

"What?" He assumed his most innocent face. "Lightning rods?"

The boy laughed. "Naw. Them lightnin' gods." And in an undertone, with a flicker of bright eyes toward the shadowed witnesses to their little meeting: " 'Ee does, ye know."

"Van?"

Zandy nodded. "Gotta be careful what ye jokes 'round 'im."

In the same low voice, he said: "I will. Thanks."

The boy gave a quick, conspiratorial dip of his head.

"But you don't—believe in the lightning gods."

"Cain't be gods what makes it, or I'd be a god, now woul'n't I? And I acks you, zur, does I looks like a god?"

Deymorin controlled a quivering lip. "Well, I don't know. If I say no and you are, you might take exception and strike me dead. If yes, and you aren't, I look a fool. Since I'd rather be a live fool, I'll say: Absolutely, you are a most *wondrous* god, Alizant the Great of Khaythnarum Node."

Giggles exploded into gales as Deymorin got down on one knee and bent his head in a properly worshipful pose. When the boy grandly bid him rise, Deymorin, feeling all restrictions falling, asked: "And where was your ringmaster? Why couldn't he keep the tower safe?"

"Ain't got a master, zur. Khaythnarum ain't a big node, y'see. Th' ringdirectors—th' ones what are any good—they wants like everythin' t' go t' th' big cities and run th' communication lines or th' 'ospitals. Those we ends up with cain't never seem t' manage both th' storms an' th' kilns. Th' kilns drinks a lotta the ley, don'cha see? And Mauritum, it ain't got extra—not fer us. Th' factory owners, they wants all th' ley fer th' kilns an' lights an' spinnin' tables an' 'platers. They figgered t' takes their chances on th' weather, and then blamed m' master whenever lightnin' zapped th' ringtower."

"And this smaller one, the ... potentiator ... was the result of your master's attempts to divert these storms?"

The boy nodded again. "His 'n his partner's. *Their* masters—they threatened t' toss 'em out, said they was crazy and wastin' time, so they quit 'sperimenting. Tha's when I aksed could I borrow the gens and go to Mauritum, an' they says takes it 'n' go 't 'ell, beggin' yer pardon, zur, an' tha's where I mets Mistress Kiyrstin and Master Van, don'cha see?"

He was certainly beginning to.

"At the Mauritum Tower?"

"Yezzur."

So: Kiyrstin the shepherdess was a lady of Mauritum—no more than he'd already assumed—and of the tower, which he hadn't. Deymorin lifted a brow toward the shadowy observers. "Can't say I think much of your masters—

or theirs. You say a city would require a larger encapsulator. How large? And could you surround a city with that ... tingly?"

"Dunno, fer certain, zur. Master's not fer sure. It's what we wants th' money for."

"Money?"

"Thank you, Zandy." Kiyrstin stepped into the glow. "I'll take it from here. Deymio?" She jerked her head toward the main camp, and Deymorin followed her to the fireside.

They settled there, himself, Kiyrstin, and Vandoshin, well away from the other evening conclaves. Zandy cast him a hopeful look as he passed, moving, with his large shadow in tow, to the far side of the fire, where a round of *Capitulation* was just beginning. Elsewhere, an occasional grunt of despair or satisfied crow marked other games of chance in progress. A few sat solo, one repairing a hole in a shirt, another diligently scrubbing mud-encrusted harness, still another repairing a sandal strap.

A handful were indeed exiles from Rhomatum, he'd learned through bits and pieces of overheard conversation, and those were scoundrels of the first water. Three he knew (by street reputation only) and would himself have opted for their removal—had Anheliaa bothered to consult. Some, like Korrigen, were of that annoying breed of bandit, leywayers, individuals who sabotaged the floater-track between nodes, intercepting freight haulers or some lord's private transport.

The balance were, from their accents, out of Mauritum, and, from the way they looked to the priest for orders, men who'd accompanied Vandoshin from the Tower, possibly, from the way they carried themselves, defectors of the Mauritum Guard itself.

For the most part, they avoided him, on orders, he imagined, from their leaders. One guilt-ridden sod avoided him with almost humorous diligence, ducking into shadows, or dipping his unkempt head each time Deymorin's gaze chanced to cross him. Not someone he remembered meeting, not someone who knew him, or he'd have been betrayed to Kiyrstin long since.

Or perhaps he had and Kiyrstin was waiting the moment to spring her knowledge on him.

All in all, enough to make a Rhomatumin Princeps, even

an exiled out-of-favor Princeps, just a bit cautious with his mouth and his drink, and his currently nonexistent but eminently refillable purse.

"How do you do it, Just Deymio?"

"Do what?"

"Van and I have been trying for months to get his master's name out of the lad."

He chuckled. "Obviously, you both lack younger brothers. For one thing, never call a fourteen-year-old 'Zandy.' Eleven or sixteen, you *may* get away with it. When you're fourteen, you're 'Alizant,' And *very* aware of the fact, and *very* suspicious of adults who don't intuit the difference."

"I'll keep that in mind. And how many brothers have you raised, Deymio?"

"Enough to know when someone's trying to weasel information out of me."

They all three laughed, the polite, civilized laughter of politicians and spies. Laughter designed to express a knowledge of barterable secrets held with prices pending.

"So," Kiyrstin leaned forward eagerly, "What do you think?"

"About that?" He inclined his head toward the shadowed cart.

"Naturally."

" '*Intrustin*' ' ..."

"But ... ?"

"For all I know, Mistress Kiyrstin, it's a clever trick. For all I know, you're travelling entertainers and he's your magician-in-training. Incidentally, he's quite good. Quite ingenuous—a new look to an ancient profes—"

"Oh, shut up." She frowned irritably. "You know damn well it's for real."

"Do I? Tell me, Kiyrstin of Mauritum Tower, why didn't Garetti, starved for power as Mauritum claims to be, leap at the chance to free himself of Rhomatum tyranny and grant the lad all he wished?"

"What do you know of Garetti and Rhomatum?"

"Me? Why nothing at all, lady of Maurii. As for the boy's little toy—what difference does it make what *I* think? *You* obviously intend to back him. He needs money; take him to those who have it."

"And you don't?"

He flourished a hand: "As you see."

A muscle tightened at the side of her mouth. "Actually, money is only part of our goal. We also seek what one might term asylum, and the ability to set up the boy's shop in safety, perhaps an introduction to reliable craftsmen: metalworkers, chemists, that sort of thing. I'm not certain what all he might need."

"The *boy's* shop?"

"From what the boy has let slip, his so-called masters had little concept of how the machines work, and their development appears to have been virtually accidental. Certainly useful applications will require a better understanding of the strengths and limitations of the static. Zandy is a bright lad and I'd like to see him given a chance to explore those unknowns. And I'd like to see him secure for life—away from such leeches as his former master. Zandy pretends otherwise, but I doubt, regardless of his venture's success or failure, that he'll ever get support or interest from them."

"Unless it proves profitable to take credit."

"Precisely. Step in when all the risk to purse and reputation is over. I'm not fond of that attitude, and I rather fancy the notion of foiling at least one perpetrator."

"I see ... purely altruistic."

"Hardly. I intend to profit as well. And I don't mind sharing that profit. As for Rhomatum, that's where we hoped you might help. Our success might depend on a somewhat more intimate knowledge of those we approach than we currently have. Mauritum elite were less than receptive to what we considered the obvious possibilities of the boy's machine. We're hoping Rhomatum might be more broad-minded. *You're* Rhomatum."

"Ergo, I might provide that intimate knowledge."

She nodded.

"So might half a dozen of your fellows here."

"They're not likely to know those we need access to."

"And you believe I am? Would?"

"Come, Just Deymio, the innocent doesn't become you. —Would you back it? Will Rhomatum?"

"Would I support a realistic, universally available power source? Probably, though I'd require more evidence than I've yet seen before committing any resources to it. Anheliaa dunMoren will laugh you right out of the valley, and her tame Council will provide the catapult."

"I wouldn't expect Anheliaa's interest any more than any other ringmaster's. They've too secure an existence with the status quo. I'm talking about the Rhomandi. The Princeps of Rhomatum."

"Oh, my," he said, and a grin spread in spite of his efforts. "That is rather different, isn't it?"

"I've heard he's far more liberal than Anheliaa. Certainly, if our understanding of Rhomatum history is at all accurate, he carries more power within the City than Mauritum's Minister Paurini."

"My, my, my, Mistress Kiyrstin," he said with an airy lightness he in no wise felt. If she was this interested in the Princeps of Rhomatum, she should have drawn some thoroughly obvious conclusions, and one had to wonder *why* she persisted in the farce. "What did happen to your 'tween-ley speechifying?"

"Stuff it, Rag'n'bones. Could *he* be persuaded?"

"Why, how would I know? Me, a common criminal?"

"Criminal you may be, Just Deymio, common, never. And I'll wager you're on more than passing acquaintance with the Rhomandi."

"You're casting blind and hoping I'll snap, woman," he said coldly. "Say I do know Rhomandi. Say I even think he might like very much to discuss this topic with you. Say I think he might kick you out on your shapely derriere. Will either change your decision to proceed to Rhomatum?"

Her mouth thinned. Her booted toe tapped a solidly grounded rock.

"If so," Deymorin continued, "I'd suggest you forget the entire affair and go home to your husband and make babies."

"What we were hoping for," Vandoshin said into a suddenly hostile silence, "was a . . . fellow spirit, if you will. If you did know the Rhomandi, we were hoping you'd help us present the child to him. Perhaps warn us of possible offensive approaches to avoid. We know differences exist between Mauritum and Rhomatum customs, but we don't know what those differences are and only rumors about the Rhomandi himself. We wouldn't know him if we saw him."

"I see. And what, *rom*Maurii, is a priest of Mauritum doing supporting such a heretical machine?"

"Heretical? Unusual term to sit on the tongue of a citizen of Darius' supposedly atheistic descendants."

"Old memories die slowly. Besides, we've very few atheists in the Rhomatum Web, just a number of skeptics where it comes to ringspinners calling themselves priests."

"I see. Well, I've—left the fold, you might say. A descendant of Darius ought to appreciate that."

"I might, if anyone bothered to give me a reason why you left, or why a Mauritum *lady* is running around the woods alone, clothed in rather less than courtly attire, talking like an ignorant transient."

The Mauritum lady in question lurched forward, but Van caught her arm and pulled her back down beside him, a resigned—and one might say slightly bored—expression on his face. "What Kiyrstin tells you is her business, but in my own defense, I might point out she is far from alone."

"Oh? And are you prepared to defend her honor?"

"As to that," an enigmatic smile crossed the hawk-face, "she defends her own quite adequately, and you do her an injustice to mock her thus, Rhomatum."

"Whatever." He was increasingly impatient with them both.

"As for myself, I was present when the boy presented his case to Master Garetti. He received a rejection expressed in such terms as you might suspect. I disagreed with my master, and was informed that a man of my obviously aberrant notions would do well to make himself ... extinct. Discretion suddenly acquiring virtue status, I followed Garetti's suggestion, taking a handful of my support staff who agreed with me. We intercepted the boy and his cart and offered our services, such as they were."

"And Mistress Kiyrstin was one of your staff?"

"Hardly."

"Where did they—" Deymorin nodded toward the Rhomatum exiles. "—enter your plan."

"Suspecting Rhomatum might be the boy's most realistic goal, I—released—the handful of Rhomatumin citizens in Mauritum prisons."

"Using your priestly status to effect the release, of course."

"Of course."

"I still find it difficult to understand why one of your background would forsake it all for what might be no more than a toy."

"I'm not a fool, Rhomatum. If this—" It was Vandoshin's turn to gesture toward the shadows. "—proves out, if there *is* a viable power to compete with the power of the leys, I'd rather be in on the ground floor of its development than near the top of a limited, possibly obsolete within my lifetime, system."

Near the top. Garetti was at the top, and likely to stay there for this man's lifetime. Near the top, for an ambitious man, was frustration, not success. Not a stupid man, this priest, but a definite gambler. Another trait—how had the priest put it?—Darius' descendants should appreciate.

Well, this descendant required just a tad more convincing.

"Correct me if I'm wrong, romMaurii, but economics isn't exactly the only issue at stake here. Won't your Maurii take exception to this defection of yours?"

"I'm convinced the gods of the nodes, if they in fact exist, obtain far too much entertainment value from us humans and our little power games to trouble themselves with one believer more or less."

"I always suspected you priestly types were far more pragmatic than your blind followers."

"And how much contact have you had with us ... priestly types, you of secular Rhomatum?"

"We have our share of priests, believe me. Even without ruling the rings, your ley-gods still wield a powerful argument."

"A philosophical discussion I may one day pursue with you, Rhomatum. In the meantime, will you join us?"

"And if I say no? Will I be free to leave you and your band of cutthroats?"

"Have you reason to believe otherwise?"

"I wasn't exactly invited politely to come *this* far. I've been watched every moment, waking and not. I'd say this does not constitute freedom to come and go as I please."

"You may leave any time you like," Kiyrstin stuck in dryly. "But unless you want to be hanged for a thief—"

"I'd do well to leave the clothes behind?"

Her smile held all the sweetness of a she-wolf.

"Charming. Well, Van? What happens if I say take your contraption and throw it into the nearest lake?"

"I suggest you ask Kiyrstin."

This batting responsibility about like a Pursuit pellet began to pall.

"Shall we test the hypothesis and see?" Deymorin stood up. "You, Kiyrstin of Mauritum, may take your precious encapsulator and toss it into the hereafter, for all I care." He took several steps into the shadows. "Unless, of course, you care to explain *your* part in this whole affair."

Another step.

"Why should I?" Her irritated call followed him. "You've done nothing but evade *my* questions since I hauled your ass out of that lake!"

"Because, my dear, you need me. I didn't ask you to . . . haul my ass out of that lake. I'm appreciative of the fact you did, but damned if I'll let you hold that over my head as some sort of obligation. Perhaps I'd as soon have drowned. Perhaps still, I'd rather die than return to the City—or back some unknown's power play against the woman who tossed me into that lake."

"Would you?" And when he took another step as his answer: "Dammit, Rag'n'bones, *get back here.*"

"If your intent was simple humanity, you'd have let me stay in the forest that first night. You've a use for me— probably have had since you 'hauled my ass out of the lake.' " He took another backward step. "I've little enough reason to trust women, shepherdess. Particularly ones who masquerade as something they most assuredly are not."

"All right. All *right.*" she hissed. "I had my suspicions early on. You're *not* under any damned obligation, but we could damnsure use your help."

"Say please."

A stubborn silence.

Another step—away.

A sullen: "*Please* . . ." And a muttered: "Dammit."

He sauntered back to the fireside, hands sunk deep inside his borrowed coat's pockets. "So, Mistress Kiyrstin, what *did* you do to earn entrance into this elite club of refugees?"

"I killed someone." Her eyes flickered toward him under scowling brows, daring him to laugh. "Or, at least, I tried."

"Oh. Didn't you succeed?"

"No. Dammit."

"Ah. But I'm certain she deserved it."

"He did."

"He? The plot thickens. And who was this hapless victim?"

"She deserves it? He's a hapless victim?"

"Forgive my prejudice, m'lady. Who was this villainous scum?"

Her smile again came from that decidedly wolfish ancestor. "My husband."

From somewhere deep inside, somewhere past the memory of his initial speculations regarding this woman, laughter bubbled. Bubbled higher, and ultimately overflowed.

Chapter Two

Lidye, Nethaalye, even Mirym: Anheliaa wanted witnesses.

"You wanted to see me, Aunt?" Nikki asked from the (open) doorway to Anheliaa's private apartments.

Surprisingly, she'd not tried to force this meeting into the ringtower. Not that she'd get him there without an armed guard and in chains—an option he no longer considered beyond her.

"Come in and shut the door, boy." From her voice, Anheliaa's strength was back.

"But—"

"I said *come in.*"

"Yes'm," Nikki, disconcerted in the presence of the women, mumbled and did as she bade him.

"Well?" Anheliaa demanded, the instant he turned back to her. "Have you come to apologize? If so, get on with it."

"Apolo—" Temper flared. "I've come, madam, because *you* ordered me to come, and for no other reason."

"I might have known. It would be asking too much of the gods for you to have come to your senses on your own and in less than a week."

"I'm far more inclined to thank the gods that I've come to my senses after eighteen *years.*"

"Yessss ..." The single word was more hiss than acknowledgment, "I'm sure you are."

Lidye sat next to Anheliaa's bed, chin lifted in perfect imitation of his aunt's most imperialistic look. A look he'd face the rest of his life if he remained here and danced to Anheliaa's rings.

Nethaalye, she of the absolute horror of sickbeds, who had avoided Mikhyel's, never so much as coming to the door to inquire as to his health, sat on Anheliaa's other side, her face impassive. In all the years of their engagement, Nikki had never seen a single sign of passion pass between his brother and Nethaalye, and yet, in all that time, neither had he ever heard Mikhyel challenge that parental choice.

As he himself hadn't challenged Anheliaa's choice, until three days ago.

From the start, Deymorin had known it was wrong. Of them all, only Deymorin had recognized the trap Anheliaa laid. Only Deymorin had had the sense to tell her to go to hell . . . as he'd purportedly told their father upon the parental attempts at matchmaking *him* with the newborn Nethaalye, defiance which had passed Nethaalye on to five-year-old Mikhyel.

Anheliaa's third witness, Mirym, sat silently in a corner behind her ever-present needlework frame . . . and watched him . . . expectantly.

"Anheliaa," he asked, unable to take his eyes from Mirym's, "may we please speak alone?"

"So that you can attack me again? I think not!"

He tore himself from Mirym's mesmeric stare to face his aunt squarely. "Try another, madam. Too many know differently."

"Your word against mine. They'll know which to believe."

"They? Council? After what you did to Deymorin? And to me?"

"Again: your word and mine."

"And Mikhyel's."

"Mikhyel is mine."

There it was again. That confident claim. And what evidence did he really have to the contrary? A feeling, ghostly after four long days. And as he'd put it to Deymorin, what other example had Mikhyel had? Even when, at five, he'd been convinced to accept Nethaalye as a life partner, he'd been learning to put the Tower and Rhomatum above everything.

Possibly even above his brothers.

He felt the impetus to fight seeping away. What difference did it really make, after all? If Anheliaa was right about Mikhyel, and he was wrong, let Mikhyel be Princeps. He was the only one of them half-prepared for the job, anyway. If he left the City, Anheliaa would take extremely good care of Mikhyel. And if she wanted Lidye as her successor? There was precedent. Let Mikhyel marry both.

It was all politics anyway. Love. Family. Loyalty—those were just words to people like these. Politics and power, that was all they cared for.

"Tell Council whatever you like," he said wearily, "I'm leaving anyway."

"Leaving? And going where?"

"After him."

"Him?"

He didn't bother answering: she knew.

"Not until after you marry."

"Madam, I do not intend to return. What could you or Lidye possibly want with a nonexistent husband?"

"You'll be back."

"Only in chains."

She laughed. "You're already in chains, boy. You've an easy life here. You've no means of your own—no aptitude for any gentlemanly position. If you leave, I'll cut off your funds—we'll see how long you last, then."

"I have considered all that. I'm—provided for. I'll manage."

"I'm certain you think so. We'll see how you fare when I cut off your allowance and freeze your assets at the bank."

She had no right, but he couldn't doubt *she'd* manage.

Besides, he'd thought this out already, during the long nights at Mikhyel's bedside.

"I've not wasted my entire life, madam. I'm quite knowl-edgeable—in many significant realms. History. Politics. E-co-no-mics. I'm sure there are those in Mauritum who will find me ... eminently employable."

Her smile faded. "You wouldn't dare."

"No?" And for once, he knew he had her at a disadvan-tage. *She* didn't dare let him into the hands of their ancient adversary, not without knowing exactly how much he knew or how much he was willing to sell.

Settling into a nearby chair, he leaned back, elbows on the rests, hands casually across his stomach, and awaited Anheliaa's response.

"All this to find that undisciplined brother of yours?"

He nodded.

"And where do you think to travel to? Using what for capital? Travel expenses? *Bribes?*"

"There are plenty who will aid me for the sake of their Princeps."

"You're a fossil, boy. You live on antiquated notions of the world. If you go looking for *that person,* you'll need bribes—and protection. Bodyguards don't come free. You've never had to budget, never even had to balance a bank ledger. How do you *know* what you'll need?"

"I can manage."

"And if I offered to help?"

Hope surged, but it had an uphill battle against suspicion. "In return for?"

Anheliaa's hand crept to Lidye's, clasped it hard enough to make the girl wince.

"You cannot leave her unprotected."

"*Unprotected?* From whom? And what?"

"She came here at your request, has certain expectations. You *must* give her the security of position."

"Your request. But I won't quibble the point. What makes you think I'll marry anyone now—particularly of your choosing?"

"Your word, boy."

"Given under duress and false pretenses."

"Given nonetheless."

"I don't care."

"Then you've no honor left. No pride."

"Possibly they were burned from me four days ago."

"Two can play your little game, boy. I'll press charges—"

He felt a surprising urge to laugh. "Go ahead. *Give* me the chance to voice my story—and my suspicions—in court. Just remember, it will be before the Council as a whole, madam, not you alone."

"Let me *finish,* damn you." Anheliaa surged forward, gasped and fell back into the cushions. Lidye leaned over her solicitously. Nethaalye seemed not to notice. "Thank you, my dear," Anheliaa whispered weakly. "Such a sweet child you are."

"What else, madam?" he asked brusquely. "I'd appreciate some economy of time. I've a meeting I promised to attend this morning."

"You're *at* that meeting. The one your brother is holding with Council is no longer your concern. You've already renounced that interest."

"Then I've travel arrangements to make."

"Travel arrangements. And where do you intend to

travel to? Where will you look for this oh-so-important sibling of yours?"

He thought of that brief glimpse of campfire, the unknown woman, but that vision gave no clue of direction.

"I thought so. All right, boy. Here's the rest of my bargain. You marry this charming woman—far better a bride than such as you deserves—fulfill your part of the bargain, and in addition to not pressing charges and allowing you to retain your draw on the bank, I will endeavor to locate your worthless brother."

A surge of hope. "Via the rings?"

She nodded. A single, curt dip of the chin.

"You'll *have* your wedding—tonight. This afternoon. Right now. Bring the witnesses—"

"Don't be silly. There are arrangements to be made—invitations—"

"Tomorrow at the latest. That gives you time to notify her parents ..."

"And her wishes?"

Lidye twitched, obviously less than delighted with this cavalier deployment of her future. But Lidye had made her choice, as far as he was concerned.

"She wants to marry into this family," he said. "She doesn't care when or under what circumstances. I doubt her family cares. That's between you and them. I'm ... incidental."

"How can you say that?" Lidye cried.

"Easily, madam. Now, Aunt, I want to know where my brother is."

"After the wedding."

"No."

"Don't you trust me?"

"No."

Laughter, harsh and cold.

"Perhaps you're right. After the ceremony, then, no earlier, but before the contract signing. —And *don't* argue, boy. I've no strength to manage the task at the moment. The mere thought of That Person exhausts me. You make your travel arrangements, Lidye and I will handle her family and the wedding details."

"Fine."

"And, Nikaenor."

"What?"

"Don't make plans to leave directly following the ceremony."

"Why not?"

"You've one other duty to perform."

"One other ..." Suddenly, he realized Lidye was not just looking at him. She was *looking* at him. And as suddenly, he felt rather like a spider in Ohtee's sights. "It can *wait.*"

"No, it cannot. Something could happen to you on your ... quest. You've already threatened never to return. You try to limit my scope, boy, and I won't allow it. The Tower, Rhomatum, and the future are more important than any of us. I'll not compromise them on your whim."

"I don't believe in your adept—or *any* of your theories."

"Believe what you want. You won't be allowed to leave until Lidye's condition is assured."

"Then you can forget the entire matter. I'll take my chances finding Deymorin alone."

"Nikaenor dunMheric," Lidye's voice rang out, "you insult me."

"I?" He laughed, that seeming the only alternative left. "You've a strange way of analyzing a conversation, madam."

"Stop it, both of you," Anheliaa snapped. "Behaving like gutterbrats. Nikaenor, I'll compromise. The morning after. Grant me one night."

"You must be joking."

"Do as you're told until the day after the wedding, and I'll find your brother for you. And I'll give you an open account at the bank. Otherwise, I'll call the guard, have you arrested, and take *my* chances with the Council."

Trapped. And no way out without a tangled lawsuit: if he told the truth, lawsuits *would* happen and if he was in the middle of a lawsuit—or in prison—he couldn't rescue anyone.

All politicians lied, when it suited them. Mikhyel had taught him that. If it suited Council to believe Anheliaa, they would.

Avoiding Mirym's eyes, he muttered past the invisible noose tightening about his neck: "All right, madam. I promise. One night."

"So, Rag'n'bones, what's the verdict?"

Deymorin sneezed into the double handful of water he'd

raised to his face, stared down into his hands in some disgust, and let the water dribble free as he swung on the balls of his feet to face his tormentor . . .

. . . and the barrel of what appeared, from his vantage, to be something just short of a hand-held cannon.

Firearms.

Bandits, indeed.

"Verdict?" he asked.

"Willingly or not?"

He blinked. "Excuse me, did I miss something? What happened to my freedom to leave?"

"You're still here. So, are you with us? Or do we consider you merely a good will gift for Anheliaa?"

"Oh, I see. That's the current option, is it?"

Kiyrstin swung the miniature cannon suggestively. "Time to get going."

"Can you really hit anything with that?"

"Try me."

"Think I'll pass, thanks anyway." He swivelled back to the stream, splashed another chilly handful over freshly shaven cheeks, and stood up, flipping the last of the damp from his hands. He pocketed Van's borrowed razor and headed upstream toward the breaking camp.

"Well?" Kiyrstin pattered up beside him, thrusting the gun into the sash at her waist.

"Planning on blowing your foot off?"

She snorted. "Don't worry. We avoid the leys."

"There are other means."

"I'm careful."

He shrugged. "It's your personals."

She stopped. Her hand clamped his arm and forced him to stop and face her.

"You listen to me, *Just Deymio,*" she hissed. "I've had about enough of your 'humor.' Despite what you think of me, the way I dress or the way I speak, I *don't* deserve— no, dammit, I won't *tolerate* your attitudes. I deal daily with two dozen men of highly questionable repute, have done so for the better part of a year now, and none of them would *think* of using the tone and language I've endured from you. I do what I must for a cause I believe in, because I've spent a lifetime watching people like you walk all over people like Zandy and these others. Most 'bandits' simply want a few of the amenities people like you bask in daily.

I see a way for them to have those amenities, and I'm not going to allow someone like you to ruin their chances."

"People like me," he repeated, mildly amused at her vehemence, but also a bit touched. Possibly it was the sun. "What sort of person is that?"

"A pampered, game-playing, self-indulgent son-of-a-whoring-bitch Citizen."

"Oh? Have you met my mother?"

"Damn you!"

He caught the hand flying at his face. "The lady speaks with the intensity of close acquaintance." He tightened his hold when she attempted to evade his touch. With a fingertip still showing its last manicure despite recent close association with mud and grit, he traced calluses and lines of ingrained dirt across her palm, lingered over the partially healed remains of a blister. "Just how old *are* these, shepherdess?"

"Old enough." She jerked free, turned away, and leaned a fisted hand against a tree. "Why, in the name of all the gods, do you keep baiting me?"

"Why?" His answer surprised even himself. "Because it's fun."

"Fun?" She whirled.

This time, it was a fist and remarking the strength required to deflect it, he considered himself fortunate the blow didn't land.

"Yes, woman, fun." He caught and held her wrist with controlled exertion, having no desire to hurt her. "As baiting my brothers is fun. You've wit and a sense of humor, when you care to use it. Intelligence ... Rare enough qualities in a man. Virtually nonexistent in the so-called ladies I've known. You intrigue me."

The glare facing him softened, but the jaw set determinedly. She was attracted to him, he'd seen the look too often to mistake it, but she chose not to act on the feeling. That reluctance in itself intrigued him, but because she so determinedly denied the attraction, he endeavored not to encourage it. He was no green boy to make errors in *that* department.

He was, however, curious. Somehow, he didn't think the fact she was married was the source of the denial; difficult to equate love or loyalty with a man she'd tried to kill. She didn't fit the mold of the woman scorned. She didn't fit any familiar mold well.

"And who, madam," he asked, out of that thought, "is that husband you so sadly failed to send to Maurii's seventh hell?"

Her captured hand tightened to a fist. Her chin lifted in a challenge.

"Garetti."

Garetti. Only one person out of Mauritum would need no further identification: the ringmaster himself, the High Priest of Maurii. A single muttered word that should hold the power to chill any prudent man.

Perhaps he just wasn't prudent. Perhaps he was simply beyond impressionable where it came to corrupt ringmasters. He laughed. Laughter that grew as the implications crystallized.

This time, her off-hand blow caught him full in the face, bringing him partially to his senses. He released her.

Unfortunately, the only thing he could think to say was: "Too bad you missed."

Fortunately, he retained sense enough to duck.

"Nikaenor? Please, Nikki, wait." It was Nethaalye's voice chasing him down the hallway.

He paused, quivering with anger toward her and everyone who had witnessed that humiliating scene in Anheliaa's room, and turned slowly, striving to control that fury.

It wasn't Nethaalye alone, but Mirym as well. Two of the witnesses. How lovely. But their faces as they approached him from the stairwell evidenced only an honest-seeming concern.

"Nikki, how is he?" Nethaalye asked, the moment she was within easy earshot.

"Who? —Khyel?" He clenched his jaw on the answer he most wanted to give her. "Aren't you a little tardy in your concern?"

"Don't take that tone with me, Nikaenor dunMheric. The least *you* might have done was notify me he'd taken ill."

"As I recall, I did. *And* received an answer, the gist of which I'm too well-trained to repeat. —Dammit."

"I repeat, I received no message."

"Well someone sure as hell did. You were 'indisposed' and had 'taken to your bed.' "

"From my maid, then. *Anheliaa's* maid, on loan. Need I say more? I'd gone to bed early, Nikki. I never knew."

"You could have come after—"

"No, I could not. Your brother and I have agreements you are not and never shall be privy to, Nikaenor, and I take no shame in that secrecy. But I do care for him, in my own way, a way you've no right to judge. I ask you again, *how is he*?"

Mirym simply glared at him.

Deprived of anger, he just felt . . . overwhelmed.

"Awake, now," he said. "And working. Why don't you come and see for yourself?"

Anger tightened her brow. "Anheliaa won't let me, she's made that quite clear. For Mikhyel's sake, at the moment, I won't question that. After your wedding—" Her glance this time was full of sympathy. "Nikki, I'm so sorry . . ."

He shook his head, denying that sympathy. "It's necessary. And it will be worth it if it gets Deymorin back where he belongs."

She nodded, and stepped close enough to set a hand on his arm. Then: "I can't go to him, Nikki, but I've convinced Anheliaa to let Mirym help attend him. She's . . . quite wonderfully useful."

He was certainly in no position to argue that. He looked past Nethaalye's arm to Mirym. "Is that what you want?"

She gave a brief, emphatic nod, and set her hand on his.

Death by slow division was possibly too good an end for the bastard.

Kiyrstine romGaretti—she was able to think of herself that way for the first time in months—laughed until her sides ached; dropped cross-legged to the ground and laughed some more; paused to tell Zandy, who stuck his head between two bushes demanding to be let in on the joke, that it was none of his business and to inform Van that they'd be late on the road today, if they broke camp at all; then laughed again.

The Rhomatum was scum of the first order, filled with secrets and falsifications, yet she found herself spilling out details of the failed assassination and not giving a ring-sent damn. Seen through his rather warped sense of humor, the terror-filled, life-threatening night took on a whole new aspect.

They'd had an argument, she and Garetti. All she'd wanted was that he give poor Zandy's machine a second look, consider the encapsulator's potential; a battle (she later learned) he'd been waging all afternoon with Vandoshin romMaurii.

Garetti had thrown her on the bed (his normal method of ending one of their 'discussions') and she'd simply decided: ". . . that this time, he was not going to get the final word—so to speak."

"Meaning the advantages of being romGaretti finally ceased to balance the disadvantages?" Deymio asked, from his seat on the far side of her tree-trunk backrest.

"Something like," she answered dryly.

"And what did you do? Wave the cannon in his face?"

"I . . ." She picked up a twig and began breaking snippets off, throwing them into the underbrush. ". . . caught him with his guard down."

"Is that what they call it in Mauritum? My, my, shepherdess, your antique customs—"

The twig followed the snippets; she twisted around the trunk and shut him up with a punch in the arm, however his conversational sidestep helped her skip lightly over details she'd rather forget. Biding her time until Garetti was thoroughly aroused and struggling with his complex state robes, calculating her strike to the instant of greatest entanglement, she . . .

"Gave him a piece of you he'd never wanted to contact a piece of him?" Deymorin suggested blithely.

She choked.

"Thought so. This is getting good. Then what?"

"He collapsed—"

"With a most satisfying thud and howl, I trust."

"Quite. Into a heap on the floor."

"Groaning and unable to free his arms from the labyrinthine folds—come, girl, do it properly."

"*Girl?*" Again, she almost choked. "You *are* blind, Rag'n'bones."

"How dare you continue to call me that? When *you* provided the wardrobe. Besides, a *woman* would realize that in order to arouse a proper sense of identification and sympathy, you must provide more than the bare bones of—"

"All *right*. Rings. —'Groaning and unable to free his

arms from' —What? Oh, yes. —'labyrinthine folds.' Realizing he was quite at my mercy, I sought a weapon—"

"Are we in your chambers or his?"

"Mine. Why?"

"Well, your choices become somewhat limited, then, don't they?"

"If you only knew. First thing I thought of was a book—"

"How heavy?"

She shrugged.

"What was the title. Perhaps I'm—"

"*I don't damnwell know!*"

He turned an offended shoulder.

"Not heavy enough."

A testing, over-the-shoulder, one-eyed glance. "So?"

"So, I grabbed a manicure knife."

"Manicure knife? What did you do? Cut off his . . ." He waved his hand vaguely. "You know."

She laughed. "No, though I considered it. Seriously. While highly satisfactory, by that time, I want—*needed*—him dead, and that wouldn't do it."

"Dead," he repeated flatly. "And why, dare I ask, was that?"

"Come, come, audience. Think. By then, he was screeching his fool head off, the guards were shouting outside the door—"

"Why outside?"

"He'd locked the door, and I knew by that time he wasn't about to let me get that far and live. Anyway, I settled on that lovely, thick artery that lies in the same—general vicinity, so to speak."

He looked slightly ill. "Remind me never to make you angry."

"You already have."

"I appreciate your forbearance."

"Certainly. Let's see, where was I? Oh, yes. Garetti was screeching, the guards were shouting; I mean—" She fluttered her lashes like a bubble-headed adolescent. "—what *could* I do?"

It was his turn (at last) to choke. "What indeed?"

"I began screeching, too."

"Whatever for?"

"To mask *his* screeching, naturally."

"Oh. Naturally. And then?"

"I hit him on the head."

"With what?"

"The book."

"The same one? I thought it wasn't heavy enough."

"I made do."

"How'd you find his head? I thought it was covered with robes."

"I approximated. I just kept hitting him and screeching until he shut up—and *no,* I don't know which got him, the blood or the book. Then I ran to the window and threw it open, making sure to smear the blood everywhere I touched—although by then, blood covered nearly everything anyway—dropped the knife out the window then stood there as the guards finally smashed the door down, waving my arms toward the window, screaming about assassins in the garden."

His stare was a look of mixed fascination and horror. "I'm—speechless."

Which had to be a first in his life. She dipped her head in humble acknowledgment. "In retrospect, I put on a most impressive hysterical wife act. The guard untying my hands—"

"What?"

"One of Garetti's favorite pastimes."

"That doesn't surprise me, but how did you still—"

She grinned tightly. "Talent. Anyway, the guard was wonderfully solicitous—"

"Not to mention distracted by your artfully displayed charms."

"What?"

"Surely your garments were ripped. Bodice drooping, perhaps a bared ankle rubbing his ... you know."

"No, I don't!" she said primly, retaining what little dignity remained, and honestly uncertain what all she'd done to distract the man. "But he was fully occupied, trust me."

"Oh, I do, dear lady, I do. Remember, I've seen the charms quite ... unmasked."

When she'd caught her breath: "The other guards scattered like bugs out the window and down the stairs ... looking for the assassin, you know, and they never suspected a thing. Meanwhile, my husband was bleeding all over the floor, another guard had finally located the wound through the robes—"

She tipped her head toward him. "Does it occur to you that men are frequently blinded by their own prudishness?"

He leaned back, as if to get out of range. "Dare I ask what you mean by that?"

"Only that it was the last place the guard checked. Very silly. I'd have thought, with your male obsessions, it would be a primary—I'm terribly sorry. Have you swallowed wrong?"

He just waved at her to continue.

"Yes, well, as soon as my hands were free, I rushed to his side—"

"To get—" He paused for breath. "—in the way as much as possible."

Her grin loosened. "Precisely."

"You are evil."

"Why, thank you."

"Unfortunately, dear hubby still survived."

She nodded. "Suffice to say, by the time he regained coherency, I was long gone with a fair bit of capital to my name, a sackful of rather expensive, locally unmarketable jewelry, and nowhere to go."

"No friends or family who would take you in?"

"None willing to risk Garetti's wrath—I knew that without asking. So I left Mauritum."

His deep frown left no doubt of his disapproval. Charmingly chivalrous, but it only emphasized his naiveté. Let this man do the treaty negotiations and Rhomatum would lose its collective shirt.

"I knew where Zandy—*Alizant*—had camped. I knew he was as much at loose ends as I. I thought together we might find a solution. He was willing to hide me in the cart, regardless."

"Generous lad."

"Yes, he is," she said seriously. "And then ... well, you've heard Van's side of the tale: here we are."

"Amazing."

"You don't sound half-sincere."

"Oh, but I am, dear lady. I assure you."

But beneath that polished reassurance, doubt lingered. Or humor. Perhaps that of superior knowledge.

"Rings." She threw a stone into the stream and surged to her feet, calling a tacit end to the coze. "I don't care one way or the other what you think. All I want is your decision. I really don't care to hold you hostage—"

"Oh, was that my choice? You'd have been terribly disappointed, you know. Not much anyone would pay to get me back. Pay you to dispose of me, possibly, but ransom ..." He shook his head.

"I suspect differently, Rhomatum."

"You don't believe me? I'm crushed."

She bit back an unladylike curse, conscious of her language for the first time in months, and despising herself for that returned prissiness. "You're not like these men. You're not like—" She broke off. She'd been about to say, not like any man she'd ever met, but damned if she'd admit to that. The difference she perceived could be—likely was—nothing more than a cultural façade, a *difference* in accent and body language. Beneath, he was no better or worse than Van or Garetti, and she'd been far too free with her mouth already. "Well? Are you with us?"

He rose to his feet and brushed twigs off his backside. "Of course."

Simple and straight, that answer. As though she should already know. As though she was a fool to believe otherwise. Suddenly, all the prodding and pushing, the baiting and veiled insults—*Because it's fun,* for Maurii's sake—all her efforts to contain her gut-level responses, all the sleepless nights wondering whether to trust him ...

... Suddenly all those factors exploded, taking her control with them. "What do you mean?" she hissed. "There is no 'of course' about it."

He shrugged—yet *another* rejection of the *possibility* of threat from her quarter. "I *assumed* you'd realize, when you woke up and I was still here, that I was—"

Deymorin's tailbone hit a rock, his vision blurred and faded. When it cleared, Kiyrstin had gone, leaving in her wake only her dulcet tones ordering the men to pack up.

Evidently, they were leaving.

Evidently, his recruitment was completed.

He dabbed gingerly at his lip, twisted with greater care to splash a final icy handful to ease the throbbing, and headed into the sounds. He'd earned that cut and more. He'd been wondering what it would take to make her blow, and what form that explosion would take.

He grinned behind the back of his dabbing hand.

Now he knew.

"Well, Just Deymio, I see the two of you came to an understanding."

RomMaurii. Come to collect him, he reckoned.

He dropped the hand. "Very handy with her knuckles she is."

"As you're not the first to discover." And giving the bruise an experienced assessment: "Actually, she let you off quite lightly. Must like you."

"Unlike Garetti?" Deymorin suggested, testing those waters.

RomMaurii shot a disapproving glance at the innocent trees still standing between them and the camp. "So she told you."

He shrugged.

"Thought she might."

"And wished otherwise?"

The ex-priest shrugged. "Her affair. But I warn you, since I doubt she bothered, most here have no idea who she is."

"Really? Then why do they follow her orders?"

"Because they respect her."

"Like their sister. Tell me another, priest."

For an instant, he glimpsed the harsh reality behind the priest's smooth façade, then: "Because she's the only one who didn't get sick during the crossing. Hard to ... take advantage ... of someone who's held the bucket while you ..."

"Puked your brains out?"

RomMaurii winced. "Something like."

And that partial explanation was all he was likely to get. "Who does know?"

"Myself. The boy. One or two others." The priest's hawk-face hardened. "No need for you to know who. Just don't speak of it—to anyone. Do, and you're a dead man. Do you understand me?"

"Oh, I understand." As did some dozen or so amoral bandits. RomMaurii exited Mauritum with a handful of professional guards in tow. Kiyrstin gave the orders. RomMaurii's guards backed them.

He decided he preferred the bandits. "I just don't understand, why the caution."

"She takes too many risks."

"Such as?"

"That solo foray into the village for one. Taking you in so thoroughly for another. This is a dangerous game we play. Garetti put a substantial bounty up for her."

"Dead or alive?"

"Alive only. He did not, however, specify condition. Most of these would sell their own mother for that much gold."

"So why are they here?"

"We're paying them."

"Why?"

"Security in numbers ... among other reasons."

"Why *your* special interest in her?"

"You think we're lovers?"

"The thought had occurred to me."

Harsh laughter, which could mean any of a number of things. Bitterness. Unrequited desire. Frustration. Possibly true humor at the very notion. This current ambiguity was one with the priest's ever-shifting posture where Kiyrstin was concerned. Protective one instant, deferential the next. But it would explain the other men's hands-off attitude toward the one woman available.

"We're business partners," romMaurii said flatly. "Any relationship beyond that is ... irrelevant. But I'd advise you to stay away from her. She was married to Garetti for over fifteen years. Cut her bedding teeth with him, and he's not known as a gentle man—in any sense of the word."

"Fifteen *years*—what did her family do? Auction her from the cradle?"

"What would you expect? A love match?"

"Truth?" he asked, though it would explain much.

"Which?"

"All of it."

"I should know?"

"You knew the man, worked with him. Surely you have some idea."

"Correction, Rhomatum. I worked under him. I know he's a man who loves power. Having it; using it ... abusing it. I'm certain you know the type. . . ."

"I've run across my share."

"Figured. There *were* rumors. Garetti is a rich and powerful man. Such attract more rumors than long lost relatives. But Garetti also respects and admires power in others. Kiyrstine romGaretti is a powerful woman, in mind and body as well as politically—or was, until her Family disowned her. I suspect controlling her lent a particular . . . excitement . . . to their intimate life."

"His, perhaps. But no personal confirmation of the rumors?"

"And how am I to take that?"

Deymorin shrugged. "As you please."

The priest's mouth twitched, and his head tipped acknowledgment of a hit. "I was a minor entity within the Mauritum Tower. I was never so . . . privileged."

"And you wouldn't tell me if you had been."

"Do you think to rouse a response, Rhomatum? Sorry to disappoint you."

"I could hope. Easier to help if I know who and what I'm trying to get into Rhomatum."

Laughter, full and easy, from the tree-shadows. "So, Van. *Now* do you understand why JD *had* to join us on our little foray into the future?"

A shadow detached itself from the trees. Deymorin leaned against a trunk, arms akimbo, wondering how long she'd been there, and precisely what she'd overheard.

"Jay Dee?"

Her full mouth twitched. "You started it, Rhomatum. Just Deymio is *so* ungainly. Unless, of course, you care to fill in the blanks . . ."

He felt his mouth twitch in response. "JD, it is, shepherdess."

"But you *are* with us?" the priest asked.

"Say, rather, I've decided you're heading my way and I prefer company other than my own. I'll introduce you to those you want to meet. Beyond that, it's your hand to play."

"You think you can accomplish that?" romMaurii persisted. "We've no travel visas, you realize. I've heard Rhomatum is . . . particular about such minor details."

"I'm quite certain I can get you to Rhomandi."

"You think he'll be receptive?" Kiyrstin asked.

"Think? Woman, I know."

"Why? Personal friend, is he?"

"If I didn't know better, I'd think you were suspicious of me. —Tolerably good friend, I should hope. You might say, he owes me. I got into this little mess standing up for his bloody rights."

With what he considered near inhuman forbearance, she didn't pursue that dropped hint. "But you *will* take us to him? Introduce us favorably?"

"Only if we do it my way, shepherdess."

"Meaning?"

"I'll take the boy, his machine, and one other: you, or romMaurii, makes no difference to me; however, knowing Rhomandi, I'd advise you, shepherdess."

"Because she's a woman?" romMaurii sneered.

"Because she's *not* a ringman, priest. Rhomandi has no use for your sort. Has no patience whatsoever with people who use the power of the rings to control lives. That's *why* I suspect he'll love the lad's toy. That's *why* I think you've a chance. But you and your background will *not* sit well with him, regardless of your claims to more idealistic thinking. Alizant's association with you could possibly make Rhomandi doubt every claim the boy makes."

"I'll go," Kiyrstin said quietly. And to romMaurii's glower: "We'll discuss it later, Van, but I'm going."

"Fair enough," Deymorin said. "But no others. And as for visas, we don't try for Rhomatum."

"Why?"

"We'd never make it. Anheliaa would know the instant one of those men she's exiled crossed a leyline or came into the City. —Hell, she'll know when *I* do. For all I know, she'd recognize *him*—" With a jerk of his head toward the glowering priest. "I want to avoid her and any legal side issues those men's presence might raise."

"Where, then?"

"Rhomandi will likely be one of two places—"

"Not Rhomatum?"

"Highly unlikely. The atmosphere . . . disagrees with him. He's not what you'd term a politically active princeps. Leaves that to his brother, Mikhyel."

"Perhaps we should approach this Mikhyel, then."

"Not if you want my help. Mikhyel . . . doesn't approve of me."

"Speaks well for his judgment. Perhaps I should approach him alone."

He laughed outright. The image of this termagant taking

on Hell's Barrister was almost attractive enough to make him admit to everything.

Almost. He wasn't about to enter Rhomatum until he knew his brothers' current status. "I wish you joy of him."

"I see," she said slowly, contemplatively. "Rhomandi it is, then. But if not Rhomatum, where?"

"One of his Outside holdings. Darhaven is closest and most probable at this season. Or Armayel. If he's not there, the overseer will know how to get a private message to him."

"And he'll dance to your tune?"

"As I say, he owes me."

Another disgruntled mutter from romMaurii, quickly shushed by Kiyrstin.

Easy smiles. Pat explanations . . .

"All right," Kiyrstin said, "When? Where?"

. . . patter agreement: it was all falling into rhythm too easily.

It was possible that *Kiyrstin* and *Van* knew precisely who and what he was and were simply biding their time, that this lot of hooligans was the vanguard of a Mauritumin army. Perhaps this machine was some new anti-ley device they wanted spirited into Rhomatum. And while he and Anheliaa had their differences, none were so great he'd willingly aid and abet a Mauritumin makeover.

But if the boy and his machine were . . . Dammit, no. He didn't need extenuating circumstances. If they were being honest, the machine could wait. He'd fund them all right, put them up anywhere they wanted, if it stood a chance of putting Anheliaa out of business in the long run.

If they were trying to use him . . .

"Not far from here—" he answered after a too-long pause, "two, maybe, considering today's late start, three, days, there's a good place to camp. Protected, easy to find, if you know what to look for. Water. We leave romMaurii and the men and the larger machine there. If Rhomandi wants more proof, *he* can arrange to see the large one. From there, you, me, the boy and his smaller machine will head to Darhaven—"

"Darhaven? What's Darhaven?"

"His primary stud." At her confused look: "Breeding farm. He's . . . fond . . . of horses. A breeder of some repute throughout the Rhomatum Web. He winters his best stock there for foaling and breeding." And had missed out on all of it this year, thanks to Anheliaa.

"Oh." Kiyrstin's confusion disappeared, but she didn't seem quite so thrilled with the prospect of meeting this apolitical horseperson as she'd been to meet the Rhomatum Princeps.

"We'll take one man—maybe two—with us. They can return to the camp with supplies for the others, if Rhomandi isn't there."

"Dammit, *no!*" RomMauri pushed between them. "I will *not* approve this splitting of our forces. We've problems enough as it is. These men have been promised money—"

"That you didn't have? Foolish of you, priest."

"We have it," Kiyrstin said tightly.

"I cannot allow you—" romMaurii began, and she interrupted: "You have no say in the matter. *I* promised the men payment upon delivery. We'll *pay* whether Rhomandi funds us or not."

"Leaving *you* with nothing."

"I'll have sufficient left for my needs."

The priest swept his hand through the air in a frustrated, angry dismissal of them both, and retreated into the trees.

Kiyrstin's worried glance followed him, then turned on Deymorin. "Can't we consider a compromise? Perhaps take the men with us to this ... stud?"

"No," he answered flatly. And when she looked to argue: "I just want to get home. I left rather abruptly, and have several outstanding debts to take care of. After this long, the interest will be—painful."

"And family that must be worried sick."

"Dammit, stop pushing!" he hissed. "I've been away for six exceedingly long months, woman. I've no idea the temper of the City. No idea if *my family* has in some way suffered for my personal idiocy. I'll *not* test that temper, or risk their safety, with a band of bloody-minded hooligans and highwaymen and who-knows-what in tow. I have no idea why your Rhomatum recruits were exiled, and I'll not leave an organized band of them unattended within the confines of a friend's home. Give me trouble on this, woman, and I'll leave. I know this countryside better than a babe knows its mother's womb. You'll not find me. But I'll be honest with you: I'd prefer otherwise."

"Why?"

"I'm not certain I can answer that."

"Try."

He shrugged. "Maybe because of—" He nodded toward the sulking shadow. "—that."

"Spite? To prove him wrong?"

He shrugged again. "Close enough."

Mostly he found he did not want to leave her or the boy alone with the priest. A disturbing reaction he didn't care to pursue more closely. She and the boy were nothing to him.

Couldn't be, even were his brothers' lives not in the balance.

She studied him, frowning, for a long moment, then turned without a word, and followed the priest into the shadows. Voices slowly raised into a never-quite-audible argument. Finally, Kiyrstin appeared—alone—and said curtly:

"Let's go."

And as they headed together for the camp:

"What if Rhomandi's not there? What if we must continue on?"

"We'll have all we need at Darhaven. Better, we'll have transportation."

A suspicious sidewise glance. "Rhomandi's horses?"

"If he won't trust me with them, I'll by-the-rings steal them. My feet have had enough."

Her smile blossomed reluctantly. "Why is it I doubt he'd mind, Rhomatum?"

"Because you can't imagine anyone denying me anything," he answered promptly. He was utterly unprepared for her sudden, and quite sober, agreement.

Chapter Three

Benotti dunTogan shifted his weight in the cushioned seat and checked for the third time whether he'd tracked mud onto the delicately-tinted, undoubtedly priceless carpet.

This overtly elegant room that was the Rhomandi's private library was nothing like the homey, often dusty halls of the City Library he passed twice each day, setting the lamps and turning them off. He'd even been known to go inside the library on occasion—he was an educated man, and enjoyed a good read, now and again. Something other than the currently popular epic poems and the novels that were nothing but thinly-veiled retellings of the latest city-wide scandal.

But this . . .

Everything bound (to order, or he missed his bet) in tooled leather, titles embossed in gilt. Books that must date back to the Founding, yet all looking brand-new. Shelf upon shelf upon hand-carved shelf, floor to ceiling, the highest requiring a fancy, wheeled ladder to reach.

The room smelled of lemon polish and freshly-cleaned leather, and roses (from several large bouquets scattered about the room) and other flowers he didn't recognize, brought in from Outside.

Small wonder the book-loving young lord had chosen an antechamber of this particular room for his newly proclaimed office.

For the better part of two days Ben had sat here—when he wasn't working or sleeping—waiting for a chance to speak with Nikaenor dunMheric. Waiting while a stream of individuals passed through the carved door into that office, first one way, then the other. Every hour or so, the lad himself rushed past, always with a kind word and apology, but always in far too great a hurry and with far too worried a look for such a young man.

He'd heard the household staff talking. The middle brother had been ill, his health was still uncertain, and in general, those swift passages were to visits with this Mikhyel. As if the boy hadn't enough to put those lines in his face. . . .

Rumors chased each other about the Guard. Rumors about the sudden, and hurried, marriage plans, rumors about the young lord's planned departure from the City immediately thereafter.

Rumors within the Guard suggested a reason for Lord Deymorin's long absence. Reasons linked to Lord Nikaenor's planned trip. Rumors that reached the lightwatchmen through a complex, generations-old, communication network.

But Ben the lightwatchman was here because he didn't believe those rumors. He'd seen the brothers together that night—was one of the last to see Lord Deymorin, from what he could piece together—and what he had seen would not support a powerplay from the younger upon the elder's position. Certainly nothing that would suggest—what rumor was suggesting. He'd seen fraternity of a depth that did not turn to jealousy, greed, and murder overnight.

Or even over six months.

Leather, soft and worn, slid under his fingertips. Within the covers of that book rested a slender knife: the stiletto used against the young lord all those months ago. He'd taken a chance, bringing it in here. Had snuck it past the Tower guards, though Jerrik knew he carried it.

Three times, he'd contacted the Guard offices, asking should he bring it in, and three times, he'd been told there was no investigation, that they had no idea what attack he referenced.

So he'd led a little investigation of his own, and one thing he was certain of, no local had forged the steel. It was a product of Mauritum Web.

He just thought the young lord ought to know.

A man entered the room, brushing past the young lord's valet-acting-secretary with a curt: "I'll announce myself." And to Jerrik's objection: "*He* ordered me to attend him—"

"Two hours ago. He's—"

"He'll damnwell see me now or not at all."

The door slammed shut behind him.

Brolucci. Current captain of the Tower Guard. Testy sort. He'd never gotten on well with him ... had, in fact, quit the Guard the day Anheliaa appointed the man captain.

And Lord Nikaenor had requested his presence.

Ben could guess the nature of that meeting. Rumor held the boy needed bodyguards, men to support him in this post-nuptial venture. Individuals had refused, all for various reasons, but underlying them all was one widely known truth: Anheliaa had made it clear that anyone supporting the young lord could kiss their job—and their pension—good-bye.

That was why Ben was here. And if Ben was right in his reckoning, there were others who would join him. Other lightwatchmen, bored with the sameness of their job, trained for more active duty, and not so much as a disorderly drunk to contend with these days. And still active Guards. Men who had trained, and then served under Lord Deymorin. Men loyal to the Princeps, as Ben suspected Nikaenor was loyal. Men who knew the character of the man Anheliaa had elevated to captain and were willing to leave the duty roster that he set, in hopes of a worthier replacement.

The main library door opened again, this time admitting a slight, frothy female. She breezed past Jerrik and swirled into the window seat—*after* checking the sun's angle, as if she were a painter choosing the best angle for her subject.

Mistress Lidye. Ben's heart sank, and he resigned himself to yet another lengthy wait.

He'd had substantial opportunity to observe the young lord's future wife, and somehow, he didn't think the lad was in for the married bliss he'd had with his Tessie.

Dear Tessie. Not one complaint when he'd explained. Just hugged him and said, whatever he thought best. But it sounded to her like the young lord needed help and if he lost his pension, well, he lost it. They'd make do.

Rings, what a woman.

The door to the office cracked open.

"Captain." The young lord's voice, barely audible.

The door stopped.

"Yes, ... sir?" Brolucci. In that voice that made a man want to grind his face into the mud.

"You might bear in mind that my aunt will not live forever."

"With what she's paying me, *sir,* she doesn't need to."

Well, that was unexpected confirmation of every honest Guard's suspicions. Either the captain hadn't noticed an ex-guard sitting in this back corner, or he didn't care.

Brolucci's smug face didn't waver as he turned on his heel, bowed to Mistress Lidye and strode from the room—without so much as a nod toward Ben. Made that ex-guard wonder what the current captain knew that the rest of them didn't.

Particularly considering the expression with which Lord Nikki's future wife watched that captain's departing backside.

Nikki held his breath, counting slowly, trying to force the blinding fury from his head. The wedding was (Darius save him) tomorrow; his plans to leave were at an impasse, foiled at each turn by Anheliaa's wider contacts. There were people available in the City, he knew that from his history books and court records, but those documents never told one *how* to contact such hire-ons. He'd tried contacting Gareg for men and supplies, but the messenger had been ... delayed ... en route, a fact he'd discovered only moments before the captain had (belatedly) answered his request for attendance.

Jerrik rapped the open door once, lightly, then announced: "Visitor, Nik."

Informal, as they had been with each other since they'd played together as children. Jerrik dunDaleri, son of the Darhaven head groom, had been Nikki's best friend from Nikki's first visit to Darhaven—after their third fight ended in a draw just like the first two. They were friends first, man and sevant only on rare occasions.

It was a relationship of which Lidye did not at all approve, so naturally Jerrik felt compelled to stretch that informality to the limits whenever she was about.

And from the look the 'visitor' shot him as she breezed past Jerrik, he was going to hear about this infraction for some time to come.

Nikki resisted the temptation to bury his head in his arms.

Jerrik, equally immune to her airs and his discomfiture, said: "Ben's still waiting, Nikki."

Nikki shut his eyes ever-so-briefly. The old man was Deymorin's friend. Wanted to know about his brother, for certain, and what could he tell him? "Soon, Jerrik."

Jerrik turned away radiating his own brand of disapproval. Lidye, he could ignore without the least qualm. But: "Jerrik?"

The valet glanced back.

"Tell him, I'm sorry. —And, Jerrik? I'll track him down on his rounds tonight, if necessary, but I will see him."

Jerrik grinned and disappeared out the door.

Lidye settled into a chair in a swirl of skirts, waited pointedly until the door closed, isolating them again from the outside world, then:

"I don't like him, Nikaenor," she said, with a speaking little shiver. "After we're married, you must—"

"Don't make me say something we'll both regret, Lidye. I'm not dismissing Jerrik. Not for you. Not for anyone. Now, what is it you really want?"

She shifted ever so slightly in her seat, revealing the barest glimpse of darkness before the sweetly persuasive face she used for him replaced it.

"Please don't be like this, Nikki," she pleaded. "I want the wedding to be perfect. For us both."

"Are we to persist in this charade, even in private?"

Her eyes dropped, long, darkened lashes brushing softly blushed cheeks in a wounded dove imitation that would be quite persuasive—in someone else.

"Nikki, dear, for me, this is no charade." Her quiet, cultivated tones could hold more condescension than another's sneer. "I hope, one day, you'll look back and thank me for making this celebration special for us both."

The wedding. Of course, the wedding. *Always* the wedding.

For three days, she'd insisted on pulling him in on the increasingly elaborate plans. Never mind she hadn't wanted opinions. Never mind she only wanted *oo-oos* and *ah-ahs* and *It sounds wonderfuls*. Fortunately, her parents had arrived last night, giving her the excuse to turn elsewhere for . . . advice.

And not just her parents. Hordes of others from every satellite node were pouring down the leylines and into the

City. More people than ever would have come had the engagement been long-standing, all of them hoping to discover the reason for the sudden decision.

Perhaps one day, if Deymorin turned up dead, he'd tell them all.

"What is it you want now?"

"It's the flowers . . ." she said, determinedly wistful.

"I told you, I don't care. Not about any of it. Order what you want. Anheliaa will cover the cost."

"I did so want the Lavender Nights from Mauritum. But unless we delay another month, and get dispensation . . ."

"You know that's out of the question. Choose something local."

"But they're so *perfect*—"

"How in hell do you know that? You've never seen one."

Delicate, sky-blue eyes narrowed to stormy slits. "Don't you *ever* use such language around me again, Nikaenor dunMheric," she hissed, then collected herself in a breath to say primly: "Of course I have."

"In a painting," he spat, unimpressed. "A florist's advertisement. You've no idea what the color really is."

"I tell you, they'd be—"

"Perfect? Find something less so, in Rhomatum's nurseries." On a sudden inspiration of how to solve both their problems at once: "I've got it. I'll drive out to Armayel today—this moment. Their greenhouses are always overflowing. You could float begonias in the fountain basin, have huge bouquets of lilies and orchids and iris and—"

"How dare you suggest such a thing? It must be roses. *Only* roses."

Because only roses would grow along the leys. Only roses thrived within the city power umbrellas. No self-respecting lady of breeding would have such . . . 'tweener decorations as orchids at her wedding.

Deymio, you'd better *be dying.*

"Choose what you like. Just leave me out of it. In fact, good day, madam. I will attend you tomorrow morning in the garden, not before."

"But the rehearsal—"

"You'll get me to spout that nonsense once—I refuse to repeat the experience. At a rehearsal or at the wedding—take your pick."

She pouted.

"I thought so. Anything else, madam, can wait until after we're married. And now, there's a good and decent man sitting out there who has been waiting patiently to see me for two days. If you will kindly take your leave?"

"That disgusting old lightwatchman? Tell him to go away." She shivered again. "Old people ... bother me."

"Anheliaa, too?"

"Anheliaa is different. Special."

"She's different, all right." He opened the door. "Good-*bye*, Lidye."

She flounced out, crossing the library as far from old Benotti dunTogan as the room would allow. But Ben wasn't watching her. Ben's eyes were fastened on him, anxious and hopeful.

Nikki forced his stiff face into a smile and stretched out his hand. "Ben, how good to see you...."

Interlude

{Well, I hope you're satisfied.} Mother's disgust was bitterness on the palate.

"About what?" Dancer asked, watching that still-weak but steady glow surrounding the new pattern.

{It's alive.}

Only one 'it' held that thought/color/taste.

"So are Mheric's sons."

{Congratulations. —I wonder what the belly-crawling snake is up to?}

Energy flowed from all directions into the rapidly reorganizing Rhomatum Web. Rhomatum's satellites, already weakened from the collapse, were still being sucked dry.

{You send your vital energy to the dying, and that creature gobbles it like a greedy sinkhole, and demands more.}

"Mikhyel survived," Dancer maintained stubbornly, though the experience had undeniably weakened the middle brother. "I don't understand you, Mother. If Mheric's son had died, the pattern would disintegrate. You've woven me into it for a reason, so why—"

{You presume too much. What's happening in Rhomatum? What do your precious gossipmongers bring you?}

She could know, if she truly wanted to know. She could know so much, if, as she put it, it weren't like reading ahead in a book.

One had to wonder when, if ever, Mother had read a book.

But Dancer relayed the gossip. Dancer tried to amuse Mother, because Mother was increasingly hostile and distant these days. Frequently, as now, Mother resided in some remote leythium niche, present in mind only.

"The youngest brother, Nikaenor, is getting married tomorrow."

{Oh? And how does Khoratum's resident dolt feel about that?}

"Rhyys is, to put it mildly, perturbed. Anheliaa was *his* mentor and now she's putting all her efforts into Nikaenor and his bride. But he left yesterday for Rhomatum to attend the wedding, anyway."

{And what of the Trials?}

"Might be back, might not."

One did try to keep the bitterness from creeping through, but it was difficult when Mother read more of heart than word.

{You should care about that?}

"I don't know if I should, but I do, Mother. I keep thinking that if only I could win, maybe he'd accept me. But he doesn't care. He's decided the dance is frivolous."

{The way you dance lately—it is.}

Her derision was a brutal blow to heart, mind, and soul, but Dancer said:

"I have to win, Mother. I have to dance. I have to care: he's all the family left to me."

{And what am I?} And suddenly, Mother was there, arms outstretched and welcoming as they hadn't been for a seeming eternity. "Aphids on a rose petal?"

Dancer reached out to her, and her leythium veils engulfed them both.

Chapter Four

"Nikki, are you certain this is what you want?"

Starched lace tangled in blond curls and caught outside its assigned fold. Mikhyel worked its delicate points free and tugged the lace into alignment, then brushed nonexistent lint from his brother's brocade-clad shoulders, before seeking his brother's mirrored eyes.

Difficult, when those eyes were glued to the notes clenched in unsteady hands. A normal enough condition, so he supposed, in a man about to wed, but less than a week ago, this wedding was still a theoretical possibility. He couldn't, no matter how he tried, convince himself it was entirely voluntary.

So much had happened while he'd slept.

"Nik?"

A blink. Two. A Flicker of blue making brief contact with his mirror-reflected gaze, covering again in an instant.

"Of course I agreed."

He grasped silver and lavender brocade, and pulled Nikki around, forcing his attention off the lines he was striving desperately to memorize.

"That's not what I asked. If Anheliaa has pressed you into this, *tell* me. It's not too late. I'll get you out—somehow."

Nikki just stared through him. He could practically see the words marching between them.

"Dammit!" He gave Nikki a little shake. "You *can't* want to marry that woman."

This time, the blink focussed the blue stare squarely on him.

"As much as you want to marry Nethaalye."

His hands dropped, feeling suddenly leaden.

"It's hardly the same."

"No?"

"Nethaalye and I ... we've had an understanding for years. We get along sufficently well. If she can help Anheliaa in the Tower, so much the better. You—"

"I'm no different, Khyel. There are reasons to marry and reasons not. The pros outweigh the cons—in both our cases."

"I don't love elsewhere. Have never *wanted* love—"

"No? How well you blind yourself, brother. In so many ways."

So cold. So detached. Nikki the poet, the romantic, the only one of them destined for a life-role as loving father and husband—to hear him talk thus was the ... death ... of a singularly precious dream.

And as with everything else of importance in his life, he came into this realization too late. He had convinced Nikki months ago to accept Anheliaa's arrangement. His fault, that the dream was ruined, as it was his fault Deymorin was gone.

"You could still marry her, you know."

"Marry who?" Nikki interrupted his own muttering of lines to ask.

"Mirym."

"*Mirym?* Why would I want do to that?" Bitterness tinged his voice. "She's Anheliaa's spy, isn't she?"

He'd seen the looks that passed between his brother and the little servant girl as they changed guard on him these past days. They seemed to have made some secret pact to keep him under constant surveillance. Not a bad notion, seeing his knees had acquired an annoying tendency to collapse unexpectedly. But Mirym ...

"I should never have said that, Nikki. I was wrong."

"Were you?" Paper crackled, crushed between gloved fingers. "Doesn't matter. I couldn't subject any woman to life under Lidye. Not even if I loved her. *Especially* if I loved her. And I don't love Mirym, Mikhyel."

"No?" It appeared he wasn't the only self-deluder in the family.

"No. —Now, if you don't mind, I'd as soon not make a fool of myself in front of three hundred guests."

"Only three hundred?"

"That's where I stop counting, thanks. —Now, dammit," Nikki's voice broke, he controlled it along with the shaking hand. "Get out of here, will you?"

But as Mikhyel closed the door, a final glance caught a shaking hand seeking the guitar lying on the bed and gloved fingertips caressing the strap.

"Kiyrstin!"

Kiyrstin shoved the trailcake into the pack's side pouch and secured the flap before answering Van's imperative summons to the shadows on the cart's far side.

"You can't seriously intend to go through with this." His whisper greeted her as she stepped over the shaft and into the trees to join him.

There was another man with him, one of numerous float-ins that had joined their group—against her better judg-ment—since they'd crossed the Amaidi channel.

"Who's he?" She pointed at the man with a lift of her chin.

"Someone you'll be glad enough for presently. Karod, here, just gave me some very interesting information con-cerning your pretty-spoken friend out there."

"Deymio?" She scanned the intruder, found nothing to refute her initial impression. "What would scut like this know of someone like him?"

"Who he is, for starters."

"And you believe him. Just like that. A cutpurse."

"A cutpurse out of Rhomatum."

"Ain't—" the man muttered.

"Goodness," she said, "it speaks. 'Ain't' what, sir?"

Van twitched; she raised a warning hand.

"No cutpurse," the creature . . . grunted.

"Not? Then what, might I ask, is your honored profes-sion, sir?"

"You don't have to answer that," Van barked.

"Ain't ashamed. No part of it. I kills people, mistress, and I does it right handily. *He's*—" The man shot a glance toward the camp and Deymio's unsuspecting backside. "That un's th' only one who's escaped me."

"Thus far," she amended dryly. "And when did this . . . abortive attempt take place?"

Rather belatedly, Karod looked to his erstwhile mentor; Van shook his head, cast his hands in the air, and turned away.

Karod cast uncertain eyes toward her.

Kiyrstin smiled encouragingly.

Karod grinned back, revealing one chipped and two absent teeth. "Six month ago it were, mistress. In Rhomatum. Outside a whorehouse. Fancy place—on Beliard Cross. Follered him there. Went in alone, come out with another fancy. But they split up and my partner—my *ex*-partner—he insisted we jump t'other first. Wanted the fancy's purse, he did. That's why this 'un, he got away."

"Fascinating. And the other man, the fancy, did he get away as well?"

The man shook his head. "Got him good, I did."

"I see." Kirystin avoided looking back at the campfire where Deymio was helping young Zandy rig a carrying case for the lesser encapsulator, recalling nightmares and names called in the night, wondering who the fancy this man had killed might have been.

"And who hired you to kill him?"

"The Tower lady."

"Anheliaa?" She laughed. "Dealing with the likes of you? Find yourself another source, Van. You've been taken in by a teller of tales with delusions of importance."

"Warn't th' lady, directly, mistress," the man lifted his chin in determined dignity. "But I reckernized th' one whot gived th' order, and it were one o' th' Tower Guard, don't care whot he were wearin'—has to reckernize 'em at sight, now doesn't I? An' th' lady, she has th' orderin' o' th' guard in Rhomatum, and asides, who else would put a hit on th' Rhomandi hisself?"

"The ..." She shot a look at Van. Not hiding his face now, not in what he obviously considered his moment of triumph. "Leave us, cutpurse."

"I ain't—"

"I said, *leave*! *Now!*"

And when they were alone:

"What's this all about, Van?"

"What he said, Kirystin. Your Just Deymio? He's *Deymorin* Rhomandi dunMheric, Princeps of Rhomatum."

"You're certain of that? On that ... worm's word?"

A lifted brow answered. Of course he did. He'd love to believe it. She only wished believing wouldn't provide so many right-feeling answers.

"According to that worm," Van said with an air of utter confidence, "the Rhomandi has two younger brothers, Mikhyel and Nikaenor. Any of that sound familiar? Rhomandi

was in a bad accident some ten years ago. Broken leg. Bad
limp. That sound familiar, Kiyrstine romGaretti?" His face
hardened, he gripped her arm. "By the rings, woman, wake
up! The man's been leading you a chase, but play our cards
right now, and we've everything we could possibly want at
our fingertips."

"Explain."

"Hostage."

"Thought so." She jerked free of his hold. "Wake up,
priest. If that man of yours is telling the truth, *Deymio's*
the one we're looking for. We should humor him—he's as
much as said he's interested. But, he also said, plain as
plain, he doesn't trust priests. Says he doesn't want to lead
a pack of cutthroats into his home city. Can't say I blame
him. Can say, give him a chance. Only fair, seems to me.
Let me get him where he feels safe, give him that chance,
find out what he wants in return—"

"Don't be a fool. He *can't* help us. Anheliaa threw him
out—after the assassination attempt failed. She wants him
gone. He's got no power, not any longer, if he ever did.
The only way he can help us is as a bargaining piece with
Anheliaa, and I daresay she'll pay well to get him. Or his
hide."

"Get this clear, Van, I *don't* deal with any Tower. Never
again. I came here to deal with Rhomandi or any other
free man with vision and money to invest. I certainly don't
put my body anywhere near someone who can send me
anywhere she damnwell pleases, robbing me of months,
maybe years, and broiling my skin right off my bones. Deymio, Deymorin, or Rhomandi—that man wants to get me
and the boy alone, that much is obvious. I'll find out why.
Then, if that answer's not to my liking, we'll pack up and
go elsewhere."

"And if Garetti's reward is what he wants?"

"What would the head of House Rhomandi want with
Garetti's little pittance?"

"The man was thrown out. Anheliaa controls his
pursestrings. Man like that has cultivated expensive tastes
over the years. Draw your own reasons—there are many
possibilities. Perhaps he plans to use you as far more interesting coin in negotiations with Mauritum."

"As you would use him in dealing with Anheliaa."

"Better him than you!"

"I tell you no! I'll not deal in human lives. Not with him. Not with Anheliaa. I've got a gun; if the man double-deals, he'll not keep me long."

"And if he wants you for himself, Kiyrstin? Is that double-dealing? Or only what you want?"

She had to laugh, painful as it was to admit. "You're definitely thinking inside out today, Van. Man like that doesn't settle for the likes of me."

"Only if you don't want him to. We both know you were high on Garetti's list of bribes—"

Because she was Garetti's wife—no other reason. Sour-tasting thought. Sourer still to realize: "How do you know that? How do you know *anything* about Garetti's dealings?"

"Common knowledge in and out of the Tower, Kiyrstin. Veroucci isn't exactly silent about his exploits."

How nice to know one's boudoir had been a public stage.

Had been, but no longer. And at least Lord Veroucci had been fun, had made life with Garetti bearable the last few years.... Had taught her what married life should be.... Had ultimately, and unknowingly, given her the strength, finally, to break free of Garetti's cage.

So what if he'd scored points telling tales; they were fairly-earned points, over all.

That mental scale balanced, she said, with honest indifference: "Think what you like, I'm going with Deymio. My decision. My reasons. My consequences. I'm leaving virtually all I have with you. You've got the encapsulator. If I don't come back, if the boy doesn't, or if you just don't care to wait, take everything and do as you think best." She turned to leave.

"Damn you, Kiyrstin, no!" His hand gripped her elbow, spun her around. "If you're that desperate—" He pulled her into his arms and pressed his lips against hers, hard. Demanding.

His hips pushed her against the cart, his intentions no longer a mystery.

Strange, she'd had no idea the wind drifted that direction, and for a distracted moment, she played with the unconsidered notion, wondered if perhaps he was right, if perhaps she was—desperate, and whether that desperation might be clouding her judgment where Deymio was concerned.

She opened her mouth to his experimentally, worked her hands up his arms to his neck, twined her fingers through his hair . . .

His movements grew more intense, his hands seeking, prodding, his mouth painful in its insistence.

. . . and decided she wasn't that desperate.

She tried to disengage; he growled and pressed closer, his blind fumbling after her nonexistent skirts less than amusing.

Mud slipped beneath her feet; his hands bit into her clothbound buttocks, lifting her free of the ground, his body thrust against her, holding her clamped to the cart's rough edge.

Shoving splinters into her backside.

Beyond unamused, she tightened her fingers in his hair, and pulled, slowly, then with ever-increasing force until, with a gasp that filled her mouth with breath that smelled of last night's onion stew, his head tilted back.

She freed one hand and sought the knife thrust into her belt, slipped it free and pressed its point to the exposed pulse.

His hips eased their pressure, his hands lowered her slowly, and when her feet touched the ground:

"Better," she said softly. "Try that again, romMaurii, and there will be one fewer priest in the world. Do we understand one another?"

No answer.

She jerked the hair. Hard. The cords stood out in his neck. She ran the blunt side of the point along one ridge, leaving a red line in its wake. "Well?"

"All right," he said on a gasp, and she released him, with a backward shove.

"That's a warning, Van. You don't get a second. *No* one gets a second warning from me. Not any more. We'll pretend this never happened, that we had a . . . disagreement within the ranks and reached a compromise."

He rubbed his neck, stretching his head side to side. "You call this a compromise?"

"You agreed I'm not for you, I agreed not to kill you. Seems like a fair exchange to me."

"And does Rhomandi get the same?"

"No proof he is the Rhomandi."

"Only to you."

"You believe a cutpurse so easily? I'm surprised at you."

"He's not a cutpurse."

"Whatever."

"Not that either, Kiyrstin. He's Mauritum. Garetti's."

"Garetti's ... *what*?"

"Spy. One of his source men." The triumph was back, but tempered this time, with a hint of sullen obstinacy.

"Let me make certain I understand you correctly. Anheliaa hired a Mauritumin spy—correction, Garetti's spy—to assassinate her nephew. A contract he failed to fulfill, and now he's here."

"That's right. And before you ask, I contacted him through old channels. Promised him better than he's getting from Garetti."

"And better than from Anheliaa?"

"He hasn't been in Rhomatum for months. —I *had* to know, Kiyrstin."

"Know what?"

"What we were getting into. Names. Access people within the Rhomatum Tower. We *had* to know. Garetti kept us all too ignorant of affairs in Rhomatum."

"Names. I suppose names like the Rhomandi's. And his brothers. Which, if he's telling the truth—if you are—would have been highly useful to me several days ago. So why hadn't you shared this so-important information with me before?"

"Because I feared you'd react just as you are, dammit. Equating him with Garetti rather than thanking the rings we've got him. Suspicious of all he claimed—particularly where it involved your precious JD."

"He joined us before Deymio," she pointed out, forcing a pause: Van hadn't expected her to notice.

Silly him.

"Yes, well, that was a bonus, wasn't it?"

"Yes, of course." It was almost fun watching the slick-tongued Vandoshin slip around in his own slime. "And how long have you suspected Deymio's true identity? Were you planning on keeping me in the dark about him as well ... until the proper time, of course?"

"Karod wasn't certain. He wouldn't commit until I pressured him."

"Didn't know the man he was hired to exterminate? Careless of him, don't you think?"

"He never got a really good look at him, never thought to equate your find with his target until I filled him in on what I knew. Something I was hesitant to do, until you forced me into it."

"I see. My fault is it?"

"I'm not pointing fingers, Kiyrstin. I'm trying to save your hide—*and* mine, thank you very much. Anheliaa wants her nephew dead. Who am I to argue? I'm sure she has ample reason. We've got him. We need her help. Let's take him to her—as a *group*, dammit—and—"

"No! We don't need Rhomatum, don't need a Tower. Only a safe haven. A few quiet contacts. Deymio thinks he can provide that."

"Anheliaa—"

"Give it up, Van. You know how ringmen feel about the encapsulators."

"I'm a ringman, have you forgotten?"

"Never." She gave him a tight smile and stepped across the wagon tongue. "See you later, Van."

Chapter Five

The wedding ceremony was surprisingly painless.

The weather was (naturally) perfect, give or take a distant rumble and flash in the direction of Khoratum, and fortunately Nikki's rather unimaginative wife-soon-to-be had chosen *The Abduction of Pantrina,* the most common (and implausible) of the Reenactment plays, so that even without yesterday's rehearsal, Nikki only forgot two of his lines, a transgression Lidye happily attributed to his excitement at the upcoming (a delicate blush) consummation.

Rings, Nikki thought, and wondered if his queasy stomach coupled with the desire to put one's fists through walls was the way Tirise's young ladies felt their first night on the job, and decided likely it wasn't, since mostly they seemed to enjoy their life.

Khyel still looked at him as if he were moon-touched, but did justice to both his parts—his own and Deymorin's, as acting head of House Rhomandi. Nikki hadn't explained to Mikhyel his agreement with Anheliaa; and from the way Mikhyel acted, neither had Anheliaa told him. Whatever Anheliaa's reasons were for his own, Mikhyel was both too ill, and too potentially clever to confide in. If Mikhyel tried to help, he might do himself serious harm; and if Mikhyel wanted to stand in the way of his postnuptial plans, he could probably succeed, given sufficient warning.

But soon, within hours even, it would be too late. Thanks to Ben, the expedition to find Deymorin was falling smoothly into place. Horses, equipment, supplies—and men—would be awaiting his orders tomorrow morning.

Tomorrow morning. Only some thirteen hours and a handful of orbits away.

*   *   *

Evening arrived on a sunset-stained lake and the long, sloping pasturelands of a wide, flatland oasis nestled between wooded hills to the north and east.

Darhaven.

About time, Kiyrstin thought as she paused to catch her balance and her breath.

And not a sheep in sight. Plenty of horses, in more sizes, shapes, and colors than seemed really necessary for a creature designed to cart people about between leys, but no sheep, white, black or otherwise.

More importantly, down near that lake, at the far end of the well-worn track they followed, there was a very large stone house, a veritable mansion, surrounded by smaller human dwellings as well as outbuildings, barns, and paddocks populated with still more horses. And in that house—she'd been promised—food, hot water ... and a bed. A real bed with real linens and real pillows.

The man hadn't lied, in one sense: not only had he called the arrival time practically to the instant, he'd never faltered at a turning in the trail, regardless which fork appeared the better travelled.

So, he knew the territory. So might several hundred others in Rhomatum Valley.

"Well, shepherdess?" Just Deymio's voice sounded above her, and his hand settled on her shoulder—for balance, she thought, as he stepped over a tangle of exposed roots, but he paused beside her pressing close to let Zandy squeeze past them. "What do you think?"

"It's very ... green," she answered. "And wet. I should imagine the horses love it."

He laughed easily, and his hand slid naturally behind her until his arm rested across her shoulders. Warmth. Friendship ... nothing more came through that hold. She glanced up at him, at dark eyes oblivious to her, whose depths reflected those sunset colors as he drank in the image spread before them.

"Darius' haven indeed," she murmured, and Just Deymio's haven as well, regardless of who owned it in name. If ever she'd seen pure unadulterated love on a man's face ... which she couldn't honestly say she had, but if she had, she was certain it would match the expression on Deymio's face.

It was a thought that gave her no particular pleasure,

bringing, as it must, weight to Vandoshin's claims, and greater uncertainty to her increasingly uncertain future.

Uncertain, she thought, as Deymio left her and joined the boy downslope, except that her future would *not* include Vandoshin romMaurii. Even should all his warnings and suspicions prove accurate.

It wasn't simply his rather sudden and ineffectual aggression that brought her to that decision: obviously, he'd either had a complete and unfathomable reversal of attitude, or she'd simply been *that* blind to his growing personal interest in her, or that *apparent* interest was just Vandoshin romMaurii's way of getting what he obviously (and erroneously) assumed every other priest and nobleman in Mauritum had had. Whatever the reason, she doubted it would have been enough to sever relations with him altogether.

On the other hand, she *was* certain she wanted nothing to do with any individual who would seriously consider turning any halfway decent human being—let alone a man such as Deymio—over to almost certain death while other options existed. Such cold-bloodedness indicated a cruel streak in the priest she'd never before considered.

But then, she hadn't considered much at all where Vandoshin romMaurii was concerned, had taken for granted relationships any marginally sensible woman would have clarified from the beginning. Six months ago, riding the rather heady optimism of her successful escape from Mauritum Tower, she'd naively accepted Van's appearance and offered assistance as both fortuitous and logical: Zandy's presence in Mauritum had, after all, provided the impetus for Van's departure as well as hers.

Once he'd joined them, once they were on the road and surrounded by *his* men, Van had encouraged her wildest notions, embellished them with diagrams drawn in the dirt, images of non-ley power centers and a web of encapsulator wires radiating out from that center exactly like leylines from a node city, only without a ley's physical limits. He'd sat next to her on a moonlit hillside and pointed to dimly-lit farmhouses and helped her imagine them aglow with Zandy's artificial light.

And she'd accepted that vision as perfectly plausible. Convinced herself that all they needed to do was get to Rhomatum, where the value of an idea was judged, not by

a suspicious, self-serving priesthood, but by the interest of
suspicious, self-serving investors.

She'd honestly believed that once she was in the Rhomandi's presence everything would fall into place. That the
Princeps of Rhomatum, practical and independent thinker
that he was reputed to be, would instantly fathom the possibilities and set Zandy—and incidentally herself—up for life.

Sometimes, she amazed even herself at how simple-
minded she could be.

"Hey, shepherdess!" Deymio's shout filled the air. *"You
going to spend the night up there?"*

She shook herself awake and headed downslope after
Deymorin and the boy, who were once again swinging
along the trail, carrying the encapsulator on a sling between them.

Zandy's future she was less concerned about. Whatever
the truth behind Just Deymio's prevarication, she was certain Zandy would be cared for: youth and innocence had a
way of getting to Just Deymio. When he was with the boy,
his eyes held a hint of the same look he'd given Darhaven.

Obviously you lack younger brothers. . . .

And the Rhomandi, according to Vandoshin's worm,
had two.

Damn.

Of the several barns, Deymio chose the one closest to
the human dwellings—the foaling barn, so he called it—
where (according to him) little would be happening at this
time of day, since (also according to him) mares tended to
be—like all women—contrary, choosing to drop their foals
in the earliest morning hours.

She'd heard more about horses in the past few hours
than she'd ever wanted to know.

As had Barrinni and Thon, the two guardsmen Van had
insisted upon sending with them. Earlier that day, they'd
grown bored and dropped back, remaining shadows in the
woods, rejoining them now as they came up on the barn.

A barn that was indeed quiet. The barn was, in fact, in
darkness, save for the light filtering in through the open
doors between stalls and paddocks. The clean smell of fresh
straw, hay, and grain filled the air, along with the steady
rustle and crunch of horses at their dinner.

Without hesitation, Deymio slipped in with the first occupant. A soft word, a pass of the hand, and the nervous horse settled, nuzzling him with obvious expectation.

Nature of the beast? Or recognition? Difficult to judge when one's exposure to the creatures was limited to Alizant's mules.

He slipped, without word or gesture, into the next stall down, where he received a similar response from its inhabitant.

"We're safe," he said, rejoining them.

"Safe, how?"

"They're a good week or more from dropping. No one will bother coming out to check on them until the final rounds tonight."

"Why not? How can you be so sure?"

He laughed, almost silently. "Trust me. With these two, I'm sure. As to why not, we prefer to leave them undisturbed as much as possible, in these final days. You'll be safe here, until I contact Dal."

We? But she let that pass, marking it for later referral. "Dal? Who's Dal?"

"Th' head groom, m'lady," Zandy's whisper inserted. "Warn't 'ee listenin'?"

"Evidently not well enough."

"You all stay here. I can trust Dal. Anything significant, he'll know. Won't take long." He grinned disarmingly, relaxed and truly happy for the first time since he'd dropped on her head.

In control. Utterly and completely in *his* territory.

"All right," she hissed, "all right. Just hurry, will you?"

"Your wish is—"

"Stuff it. We'll be over there—behind that stack of hay." He nodded and headed for the door.

"And, JD?" An eye glimmered over his shoulder; she patted her pocket. "Don't make me use this."

A fraction more face appeared and his teeth gleamed in the minimal light. "Wouldn't think of it, shepherdess. Might frighten the horses."

He disappeared out the same small side door they'd entered, and Kiyrstin threw herself down in a mound of sweet-smelling hay to wait. With her luck, that sweet smell was likely a cause of sneezing and red, running noses like the damned sheep and so many Outside things, but at this

point, her aching feet and back didn't care in the least
about her nose.

Alizant poked about a bit, then dropped down beside
her, burrowing into the hay, shifting constantly until accepting her invitation to use her lap as a pillow.

She picked a few stray bits of leaf and twigs from his
hair, then left him alone. Such a nice boy. Hard working.
Sincere. And bright. Probably why his masters had encouraged him to leave. Masters, in her experience, preferred to
surround themselves with people less skilled than themselves. Terrible to admit a younger man—or woman—could
do your job better.

Easier to get him—or her—out of the way.

Partners with a twelve-year-old. . . .

She yawned and leaned back against the prickly hay, resting her eyes.

Better than some alternatives she could imagine.

The guardsmen had retreated into a corner to wait.
They'd been friendly enough on the trail, but, like all those
who'd defected with Vandoshin, they said little to anyone
outside their group. Depending on Deymio's findings,
they'd go back—either with supplies and instructions to
wait, or a message for Van and the others to come ahead.

She wished now she'd found a way to leave the
guardsmen behind, along with the gold and the greater encapsulator. But there'd been no chance to discuss the problem with Deymio, and Kiyrstin doubted it would have made
any difference. If Van wanted what Deymio could get here,
he'd have had them followed. Just as well to know, she
supposed, whose eyes were on them.

The boy's head grew heavy in her lap; the last of the
light from the doors faded, and still no Deymio. One more
night on straw and hard ground, when she'd been promised
hot water . . . and a, sweet Maurii, real bed.

Van was right. She should never have agreed to this;
she'd been blinded by the man's charisma and would have
to pay for it in the . . .

The main door burst open; lamplight flooded the stable.

"Kiyrstin? Alizant?"

The lamp swung inside; all pretense of stealth
abandoned.

"Barinni! Thon! Up, you lazy bastards. Dinner's waiting!
Get your butts inside where it's warm!"

"Oh, shut up and give us a lift, JD," Kiyrstin growled, and unwinding herself from the yawning, muttering youth, held out an imperious hand. Deymio's broad paw clamped tight and drew her to her feet with an energetic jerk that snapped her neck. She cursed softly, and he apologized while brushing the hay from her numb backside.

"Took long enough," she grumbled, and shook off his hands, secretly relieved that he'd returned at all. "Zandy? Come, boy, wake up, so you can go inside and fall asleep."

Laughter happened, from beyond Deymio, and a grinning giant carrying a second lantern stepped inside. "Have to watch out for this little lady, eh, Deymio-lad?"

"If only you knew, Dal." Deymio helped Zandy to his feet, steadying him with a far more solicitous touch than the one he'd offered her. When a quiet: *Okay, son?* gained him a sleepy nod, he released the boy with a *Good lad*, and headed down the aisle.

Away from the door.

With the light.

"This the new filly, Dal?" came out of the lampglare, and on a soft whistle. "Thank the gods she didn't lose it —Well done, old girl, well done. —Kiyrstin? Alizant? Come here. You don't want to miss this."

"Don't I?"

But as Zandy was already moving obediently away from the open door and toward that light, Kiyrstin was obliged to follow. Deymio was inside another stall—this one had two occupants, and his grinning face was just visible over the back of the larger beast.

"It's a baby horse," she said, striving for enthusiasm past aching joints and sore feet.

"Brilliant, shepherdess. Isn't she gorgeous?"

"Stunning." She quit striving.

"C'n I come in, zur?" Zandy asked, his voice barely above a whisper.

"Sure, son. And you can speak and move naturally—this little lady needs to become accustomed to it. Just no jerks or jumps, shouts or squeals, regardless of what she does, understand?"

"Yes, zur."

The wide-eyed boy moved cautiously into the stall. The baby jumped back from the new presence in her small world, but Deymio was positioned perfectly to catch her and clamp her quietly against his body in a single deft motion, dexterously averting panic on the side of the baby horse and dismay on the part of the boy.

The boy never realized, and soon he was petting and scratching and cooing as disgustingly as his older benefactor. Deymio backed away slowly, leaving the two together, ready to intercede, should the need arise.

Not the skill of a fair-weather sportsman, and not the first time he'd introduced inexperienced adolescents to the creatures.

Obviously you lack younger brothers. . . .

That he was a master manipulator, she had evidence in plenty before her. Evidence enough to make a woman consider what else Just Deymio might have manipulated in the past few days.

The master manipulator was at the mare's side, now, examining her, first, then at her head, rubbing it tenderly.

"Wish you'd been here when this sweetheart dropped, Deymio-lad," Dal was saying. "Came out runnin', she did. She'll do her mama and papa proud, I guarantee."

"Wish I had, too." Wistful. And as if, maybe, he'd planned to be. As if he had every reason to assume he would have been, should have been, had he not been fighting for his life in a far-off mountain lake. Then, with a disarming, over-the-shoulder grin. "Excuse us, shepherdess. Boring reminiscences."

They moved to the next stall, where noises indicated yet more inhabitants, from where Deymio's deep voice said, defying all attempts to keep it inaudible, "Best take them into summer pasture early. Tomorrow, if possible, those that can manage. Cart the foals, if necessary. I'll take Ringer—"

"Ringer's not here, m'lord."

"Not?"

"Haven't seen him since you left last fall, m'lord." Dal's voice dropped beyond her hearing. Then:

"Damn. Well ... I'll take Skylark, then. You ride Brandy, and keep him separate. Smoker and Koko are safe to pasture breed."

"Make the boys happy, but it'll be hard to predict foaling times next spring."

"Have to make do, Dal."

"Nervous, m'lord?"

"Just not certain what will come of all this, and I want them where I know they're safe."

Reminiscences her pickled petunia's pompoms.

The question was, did he, or did he not intend for her to hear 'm'lord' casually ordering the disposition of Rhomandi's prize breeding stock.

She supposed it was remotely possible Rhomandi's friend—Just Deymio—*could be* a partner in this breeding facility. He certainly was no retainer. JD issued orders, he didn't take them: no great insight on her part there.

Keeping her eyes on Zandy, she asked, loud enough for Deymio to hear: "So, JD, where is he?"

"He?"

Such charming confusion. *Forget who we came to find, did you, JD?*

". . . oh, Rhomandi."

Brush of metal against wood: the far stall door closing; and Deymio stepped back into the double circle of lamplight.

"Unfortunately, no. We'll have to go on to Armayel tomorrow. At least from here we don't have to walk."

"Music to the ears, JD."

He grinned broadly, and assuming a hostlike joviality, he detached Zandy from the baby and waved them all out the barn door and up a gravelled path toward the big house that loomed against the night sky, a single light gleaming in its uppermost tower.

It had been a long day, but every day seemed long since his illness. The doctors called it relapses. Claimed he was working too hard.

Mikhyel called it an excess of in-laws.

Nikki's were bad enough, but Nethaalye's parents had ridden in on the first wave of wedding guests, demanding to know why Nikki and Lidye were getting married before *their* daughter, who, he must realize (as if he weren't involved at all), had been long since promised.

Nethaalye had done her best to intercede with them, but tonight, after an exhaustive morning-long emergency session with city merchants demanding restitution following the power lapse, after Nikki's wedding ceremony and an afternoon dodging questions about both his brothers, for which he had no answers, he'd had Nethaalye's father demanding reassurances, in front of everyone, that his daughter's wedding would be as lavish and well-attended, and complained of his cool treatment of her.

How That Man ever sired Nethaalye . . .

Over the years he'd come to respect the woman he was destined to marry and to heed her opinions, and there were times he'd actually looked forward to the day he'd have her level head to consult of an evening. Having agreed long ago that overt affection was . . . mutually distasteful, they'd settled into a quiet relationship that confused someone like Nethaalye's father . . . or Nikki. He'd explained to Nikki—following Nikki's unfair attack on her—but damned if he'd explain to . . . That Man.

Strangulation. He'd had daydreams of the man and an attitudinal chunk of beef. Perhaps a chicken bone.

Instead, it had been himself who had choked and collapsed at the wedding feast. Embarrassing, but it had gotten him free of the lot, and an early bed.

Free of everyone but Mirym.

But lying facedown on his grooming table, steamed into pleasant nirvana, while Mirym's small, strong fingers rubbed knotted muscles loose with sweet-smelling oil, he couldn't really object to her presence. Certainly Raulind had candidly appreciated the time off, after the strain of the past week.

Nikki had brought Mirym to him, saying she'd offered her services, but Mikhyel knew better. Anheliaa, who had taken to demanding Lidye's constant attendance—which meant Nethaalye, as well, fair being fair—had declared Mirym extraneous and assigned her to fetch and carry for Mikhyel, never considering the embarrassment it might cause them both, or even asking did he want someone fussing over him.

But that embarrassment hadn't lasted. Mirym was well-accustomed to the sickroom, seeming to know before he did when a pillow wanted adjusting or when a glass of room temperature fruit juice was exactly what would make the headache subside. Best of all, when he wanted to rest, the young woman could sit calmly for hours, sipping tea and stitching, or reading, yet always there when a coughing fit overcame him, to support a glass of Diorak's foul-tasting liquid, or to fetch an extra blanket when he suddenly chilled.

Mirym's fingers worked up under his braid, moved it gently aside to infiltrate the tight tendons at the base of his skull. He buried his head in his crossed arms, giving her access, understanding, after years of performing a similar task for Anheliaa, why his old and arthritic aunt was so fond of it, why she'd insisted, following her lifetime companion's death, on his being trained in the art, and he had to wonder, though not for long or very energetically, who had trained Mirym, whose fingers seemed uncannily sentient.

Sweet little thing. He couldn't believe he'd ever harbored doubts about her. Too bad she and Nikki couldn't have . . . but Nikki was well and truly married now—or would be after tonight and the contract signing in the morning—and Nikki insisted he'd have no other wives, no seconds to Lidye's first.

He could understand the reasoning: Lidye was a shrew in a rabbit's pelt; *he'd* have himself a second just to avoid her.

At least Nethaalye was innocuous. And Nethaalye wouldn't mind. Nethaalye was as inclined to stay clear of his bed as he was to keep it clear.

Mirym's clever touch released his hair from its braid and combed it loose, a simple act that was, in itself, a soothing massage. She then worked her fingertips in little circles along his scalp and forward to his temples.

If Nikki wouldn't have her, perhaps he would take the girl as a second . . . if she were interested. But he'd wager otherwise. He'd wager Mirym wanted—

The entry-bell's light chime cut the thought short.

Mirym's fingers stilled and, after giving his shoulders a gentle press, left him.

He let his head sink into the cushions, feigning sleep.

The door opened.

A voice asked: "How is he?"

Nikki's voice.

He abandoned pretense, and shoved himself up on one elbow, answering for himself past the raw pain in his throat: "I'm fine, Nik. Come in—please."

Nikki, edging past Mirym, said from the doorway: "I didn't mean to interrupt you."

"You didn't." He swung his legs down and drew the towel over his lap, accepted the robe Mirym placed around his bare shoulders, with an absent word of thanks.

Nikki smiled at Mirym, greeted her kindly, but the smile was forced, the lines about his eyes painfully pronounced.

"Nikki, what's wrong?" He coughed, stilled it with a sip from the glass Mirym placed in his hand. "Is it the wedding? You can still call it off, you know. The contract's aren't signed. If Anheliaa's forcing you—"

But Nikki was shaking his head. "I can't claim that, Mikhyel, not at all. But . . ." The worried frown deepened. "After the wedding . . ." His eyes flickered toward Mirym.

Darius save them both, had the boy come to *him* for advice about the woman waiting in his own chambers? He asked, as steadily as embarrassment would allow: "Would you like Mirym to leave?"

"Nothing she doesn't already know."

"I *have* been kept out of the information stream, haven't I?" Resentment welled, and he dropped his eyes until he had the unproductive emotion under control.

"I didn't want you bothered," Nikki stated abruptly. "You had enough to worry about, what with your health and the lawsuits and all, and for a while I wasn't certain . . . Nothing was going right, but now Ben and the others—"

"Slow up, boy. Ben, who? What others? And please— *bother* me, will you?"

Nikki's expression hardened with resolve. "That's not why I'm here. I just came to tell you I'm leaving tomorrow. I'm going after Deymorin."

"You've found him?" he asked, and hope surged, only to sink again when Nikki shook his head.

"Anheliaa claims she can pinpoint his location, promised to tell me—tomorrow. Before the contract signing."

But after the bedding. So, Nikki had struck a deal: a wife for a brother—or more correctly, a child for Anheliaa's help. Covered herself, their aunt did. A man had to wonder whether—and if so, how—Anheliaa had likewise insured her plans against the biological game of chance that governed conception.

Assuming Anheliaa had covered that contingency, and assuming she did locate Deymorin, Nikki would be leaving tomorrow, going Out into a world that remained a disturbing mystery to Mikhyel, armed only with aged strangers to protect him against that unknown and to deal as well with whatever, if any, danger Deymorin himself was in.

"Surely you realize I can't let you go, Nikki," he said, out of that worried logic. "Not alone."

"How do you plan to stop me, Khyel? Lock me in a closet and throw the key away?"

Suddenly, it was as if someone had sucked the air from Mikhyel's lungs. And from Nikki's widening eyes, startled at first, then dawning comprehension, he suspected Nikki sensed the effect his seemingly trifling words had had. He was certain Nikki knew when Nikki finished softly:

"Somehow, I don't think so, Khyel. Not you."

Or perhaps it wasn't insight. Perhaps Nikki shared a similar shortness of breath, that same racing heartbeat, the chills that thoughts of the closet and locked doors roused in himself. All these years he'd believed Nikki blissfully ignorant. Nikki had been only four that last time, easily young enough to forget. He'd always hoped Nikki had forgotten it all. The closet. Their father....

That day.

Certainly Nikki had never mentioned it. —Until now.

He was shaking, unable, for some reason, to move except for that palsy. The robe fell and Mirym was beside him, silently urging him to put his arms into the sleeves, then pulling it up and closed in the front, casting accusatory glares at Nikki.

But Nikki remained calm, knowing exactly what monsters he'd conjured, and refusing to back down from them, an adult over whom such monsters should hold no sway.

And he, like Nikki, was an adult now. The monsters as impotent against him as they were against Nikki, except that Nikki was right: because of the monsters they'd shared, his options for controlling his brother's actions—for protecting him from harm—were ... limited: Mikhyel, son of Mheric could never take that particular measure against anyone he cared for—especially Nikki.

"I—" He paused, shamefully aware of his physical weakness, worse of his own character deficiencies. Deymorin was Outside, that much was certain. He hated the Outside. Worse, he feared it, more than ever since this last trip. But for Nikki ... for Deymorin ... He swallowed hard. "I'll go with you."

"Outside?" Nikki's voice hinted of mockery. "And considering the condition you're in? What good would that do?" Nikki smiled then, a mature smile that held only a

suggestion of his former affability, a smile that masked
adult-depth sentiments. "Thanks anyway, Mikhyel, but
you're needed here. Council needs you. The City does, and
Gari, as well. I'm ... superfluous."

A smile, as was that final statement, *designed* to ease the
sting of his words. God, how Nikki had changed in the half-
year since Deymorin ...

God, how they'd *all* changed.

"Superfluous, Nikki?" he protested. "Never!"

Nikki raised a hand. "We both know the truth of that,
Mikhyel. Don't obscure it with false—and unnecessary—
reassurances. I'll legitimize Lidye's claim, then do something useful. For everyone. You needn't worry about me.
Ben—he's a lightwatchman that served in the Guard with
Deymorin—Ben is going with me, and bringing several of
the old Guard with him. I'll be well looked after. And I
will find Deymorin, Mikhyel, I promise."

So, some things *hadn't* changed. Finding a purpose. Being
useful—on his own, not as an adjunct to someone else.
Those were old, old concerns of Nikki's. And maybe Nikki
was right. Maybe this was the time to let him go. To let
him prove himself.

And surely, if Deymorin were in real danger, something
would have come to him, one of his sources would have
found something. More than likely, Deymorin had decided
he'd had enough; more than likely, Deymorin was simply
staying away of his own accord, in which case Nikki was in
no real danger.

"Take care of yourself, Nikki," he said, that being the
only caution he could justify. "If something's happened to
him ... if you're caught up in the same web ..."

"We'd know, wouldn't we, Khyel?"

He stifled a shiver. "Would we?"

"Don't fight knowing too hard, Barrister," Nikki said
shortly, and headed toward the door.

Deymio, don't go ... Mikhyel swallowed the whisper that
never quite happened. The broad-shouldered retreating
figure wasn't Deymorin, regardless of the words and tone.
But a man had to wonder, who had shared with his brothers
those nightmares in Anheliaa's tower, where Deymorin
ended and Nikki began.

Nikki paused at Mirym's side to murmur: "Take care of
him, mistress."

"Don't worry about me," Mikhyel answered for her, drawing Nikki's attention, seeking a final image of Nikki to offset the *sense* of Deymorin. "She plays a wicked game of Rings and Dancers. Or, we talk. . . ."

"Talk?" Nikki glanced back at him granting him that image.

Mikhyel nodded toward a notepad and container of sharpened pencils on the bedside table. "And when we tire of that, she plays the harp for me."

Nikki's jaw tightened, and he turned for the door. "Perhaps one day, she'll do me the honor. Good night, Mikhyel. Mirym."

Alizant fell asleep in the tub.

Deymorin received the news as he climbed the shallow steps from his own bath.

"Damn," he said, filled with sudden guilt, "I shouldn't have left them so long in the barn."

"Wasn't your fault, m'lord," Tonami said, as he tossed a fire-warmed robe over Deymorin's shoulders, and pulled his hair free. "We didn't give you much chance at the first, now did we? And what could you expect, what with you being gone six months and more and without so much as a word?"

Deymorin collapsed onto the grooming couch. "I suppose."

"When Dal came in, I'd have sworn he'd seen a ghost. Thought I had, at first. Worried, we've been." Tonami attacked his hair as he talked, first with the towel, squeezing the moisture from the long strands and rubbing the scalp vigorously, then lifting and spreading the heavy mass to the fire's drying heat.

Felt bloody wonderful, as had the hot bath.

Getting soft in your old age, JD, he thought, and chuckled to himself at the nickname he'd unconsciously adopted from the shepherdess.

Shepherdess . . . rings, he only wished she were.

As for Zandy, he couldn't blame the boy for fading. He'd pushed them all hard, getting here before nightfall.

"Well, we won't wake him."

"Couldn't if you wanted to, from what Jem says."

"Make sure there's something to eat in his room: fruit,

bread, cheese—Koorii knows better than I what will stay edible and still tempt a youngster."

"That, he does, m'lord."

"M'lord? What happened to Deymio?"

"Making sure you remember, m'lord."

"Oh, stuff it. —And have Jem set up a cot in there with him. Don't want him waking up alone and scared, do we?"

"Thoughtful of you, m'lord."

"Oh, stuff it twice, Tonio." He chuckled and sat back in the cushions while his sometime valet/sometime paper-hustler/full-time personal meddler worked the tangles from his hair. He was in no rush.

The Darhaven staff, good-natured and efficient, had had rooms ready before they'd arrived from the barn, though the choice of facilities, on such short notice, had been limited.

His rooms—the master suite, and the associated servant quarters—were always maintained and ready. Beyond those, the housekeeper had informed him, the most recently cleaned and aired was the nursery in which he, Nikki, and Mikhyel had all grown up. He'd assigned the servants' quarters at the back of the house for romMaurii's hounds—and set two men to make certain they didn't wander about; the staff had immediately adopted Zandy; while Kiyrstin—a man had to chuckle at the image—Kiyrstin got the nursery.

The kitchen had set out a buffet in the breakfast parlor, and he'd implored his guests not to stand on ceremony, but to eat when and as they pleased. Personally, he'd been more interested in the bath ... until the water began to cool and his stomach voted otherwise. But he placated the new majority with a glass of wine, wanting to eat his dinner in peaceful solitude, perhaps fall asleep beside the fire in the library.

He was ready for—needed—a night of quiet and normalcy. Rings knew he wasn't likely to get another opportunity in the near future.

Downstairs, Kiyrstin would be waiting for him, because Kiyrstin was increasingly suspicious of him and Kiyrstin wanted answers. He should have confessed who he was before major issues of trust were at risk.

But it wasn't just his honesty at issue. A man had to wonder just how committed Kiyrstine romGaretti was to

Alizant's future. Had to wonder if she, like the priest, was more interested in entry into Rhomatum than in the boy's machine, and if they all weren't in some fashion agents of a Mauritum High Priest who had finally tired of paying Rhomatum taxes.

Prevaricating with the woman would be much easier if only she didn't *feel* so damned comfortable. And perhaps that was his main reason for not telling her: a desire not to disturb the status quo in either direction. Fearful of her discovering his truths—equally reluctant to discover hers.

Tired as he was, he couldn't trust his own judgment—or discretion—any longer, if they met in private; and late though it was getting, she might still be downstairs.

He finished his wine and poured another glass.

According to Tonami, the primary rumor out of Rhomatum was of impending marriages: Mikhyel and Nethaalye (only surprise there was that Anheliaa was willing to approve it, under her newfound qualifications), but Nikki and Lidye dunTarim? That crone masquerading as an ingenue was the gold-digging, fair-haired youngest of a notoriously power-hungry Family. How *could* Anheliaa consider such a match for his unsophisticated brother?

He had to get to Armayel. In addition to the most recent information on Nikki's impending wedding, Gareg might well have sagacious insight into both his brothers' current attitudes. According to Tonami, Mikhyel had been a regular visitor to Armayel since Deymorin's disappearance six months ago.

Poor Khyel. He doubted the Barrister had had an easy time of it with the overseer, particularly since, from Tonami's reports, he also doubted any of last fall's drainage plans had been implemented.

But from Armayel, he'd have easy and discreet access to his brothers. At Armayel, he could meet with Nikki outside the City and Anheliaa's influence. And Khyel as well. He'd promised Nikki a family meeting, after all, once upon what must be a painfully long time ago for Nikki.

A very long time, though it seemed less than a week to him, and depressing as it might be to an older brother, the possibility always existed that the marriage was Nikki's choice. Possible that Anheliaa's ring games and the skip through time had addled his own memories of his brothers, or the months in Anheliaa's clutches had altered his brothers forever.

Before taking action, he needed time alone with them.

Because if it *wasn't* Nikki's choice—or, for that matter, no longer Khyel's—he *would* take action, of some sort, even if that action was no more than hauling both brothers bodily back here to Darhaven. *Let* Anheliaa chase them— see how far she got with the locals.

See how far she got with Council, once they got wind of her high-handedness and realized any one of them could be the next seared and drowned corpse.

See how far she got once Council knew there were options to Anheliaa's autocratic rules. RomMaurii wasn't the only ambitious man fate held captive. There were others who might well desire to be in on the ground floor development of Alizant's machine.

He could be in Armayel tomorrow evening . . . well, perhaps the following morning, since he'd have Kiyrstin and the boy; he couldn't leave them here alone, certainly didn't want to send them back to romMaurii. While it was possible that the priest and Kiyrstin were well-suited, instinct told him otherwise, and barring evidence to the contrary, he'd trust his gut.

Better to harbor a snake than hazard an innocent.

Harbor was one thing. Consort with—that was something else.

He poured another drink.

Chapter Six

"Please tell Lord Nikaenor that my lady awaits." The maid dipped a curtsy, and flitted away in a flurry of petticoats and giggles.

Jerrik closed the door, then approached Nikki with a mincing step and squeaked in a high falsetto: "My lady—"

"I heard, you idiot."

Nikki leaned an elbow on the dressing table and propped his freshly-shaven chin in his hand, staring at himself in the mirror's bevelled edge. The fractured image seemed somehow singularly appropriate at the moment.

"Don't do this, Nik." Jerrik's image appeared above his, and Jerrik's hands rested lightly on his shoulders, friend for the moment, not servant.

"Not exactly the Dream, is it, Jerri?" He grinned tightly, then sat back in his chair and handed Jerrik the comb. "Get to it, will you? Sooner started—"

"Sooner ended? Rings, Nik, it's not worth it."

"For once, old friend, you're wrong. Ouch!" His head jerked with the force Jerrik put behind a tangled curl. "Easy!"

"Sorry," Jerrik mumbled, and worked the snarl loose with his fingers before attacking the rat's nest again. But while the touch gentled, Jerrik's expression stayed angry, frustrated.

Nikki turned and grabbed his wrist. "I'm the one who should apologize, Jerri. It's just ... you don't know the whole, and I can't tell you. If you knew, you'd understand. Marriage for me—for any heir to the Estate—can't be dictated by personal preference. I know that. I always have, despite what I've spouted to you in private. Lidye ... I thought I could love her. I was wrong. wrong." He shrugged. "I've run out of time. Anheliaa has. Anheliaa needs her. The City, so Anheliaa claims, needs Lidye's child. Hers and mine."

Jerrik looked slightly ill, but a squeeze to his shoulder assured him Jerri's judgment did not find *him* wanting.

He released his valet's wrist and faced the mirror again. "It can't be that bad—or that difficult. I mean, animals do it on cue all the time, right?"

"You're not a horse."

"No? Too bad."

"That's it. Tie her up and have someone hold a twitch on her to keep her from kicking."

It took a moment for the image to filter past the blank spot that was his vision of the imminent future, but when it did, he collapsed arms and head onto the table, helpless with half-hysterical laughter. "You're *awful*."

"Got you laughing, didn't I?" A fist shoved between his shoulders and a tug on his hair brought him back upright. "Everything will work out. You know what's expected—or close enough. I *told* you to go back to Beauvina and practice."

He choked again, swallowed the last of the wine in a single gulp, and stood up. "Wish me luck."

"I wish I could say you wouldn't need it."

"You're so helpful."

Jerrik straighted his robe's lapels, tugged his belt tight, and twisted it just so, then paused, and fingered the chain around his neck.

"This better go, Nikki-lad, if you don't want civil war in your wedding bed."

"Thanks," he said and bent his head while Jerrik unfastened the chain and set it and the ring it held—Deymorin's ring—in a box on the dresser.

Anheliaa hadn't seen him slip the ring in his pocket the night the rings crashed, nor had she had the gall to question him about it since. He intended to keep it safe until he could put the ring and the title back where it belonged.

Somehow, he doubted Lidye would see eye to eye with him on that topic.

Jerrik gave his hair a final pass, pulled a curl or two over his shoulder, then pronounced him ready for the kill.

"What romantic imagery."

"Who said anything about romance? Just go break the

lady's heart." Jerrik's voice lost the light-hearted lilt. "Fair's fair, after all."

"My heart's not broken."

"Then it must be mine." Jerrik sighed heavily. "I'll be here when you return, love. —Waiting."

"Oh, stuff it."

"Where?"

"Jerrik!"

He was still chuckling to himself as he left the room.

The route to Lidye's room was eerily vacant, servants and wedding guests alike granting them this one small privacy after a full day of being the center of everyone's attention.

Anheliaa wanted the child conceived as close to the rings as possible, and since Nikki had drawn the line at coupling in the ringchamber itself, Lidye's rooms, in the Tower and adjacent to Anheliaa's, had been the logical compromise.

Consummation in great-aunt's parlor. How appropriate.

In actual fact, he didn't care. He'd ceased to care about that as he'd ceased to care about all else regarding the marriage. At least this way, *his* room, the bed he'd had since he left the nursery, remained his own, in every sense.

Outside Lidye's room, he pulled the silver chain that would ring the little silver bell that would announce his presence to those within. A carefully calculated time later, the door opened on Lidye. Behind her, the room, gently illuminated with vastly expensive flicker-lamps, was empty.

"May I come in?" he asked formally, relieved when his voice didn't break.

Lidye, her eyes demurely lowered, nodded, and stepped back, allowing him access. He stood in the middle of the room while she closed the door—and set the bolt—waiting for some sense of . . . anticipation, he supposed. Or at least remote excitement.

What he felt was nothing.

For all her obvious beauty, despite the feminine curves molding the soft fabric of her modest high-necked nightgown in all the appropriate ways, she left him unmoved, even when she paused in front of him, so close her lace hem touched his bare toes.

Eyes still lowered, she lifted a small hand to his chest.

It was trembling.

His tension melted. He covered her hand with his own, and pressed it against him. Cupping her chin in his other hand, he lifted her face to his and brushed his lips against hers.

Gently, tentatively, she returned the caress, swaying closer, off her balance so that he was forced to let go her chin and hand to put his arms around her.

"Oh, Nikki." She sighed and cuddled against him. "I was so afraid."

"Of me? That's silly. What could I do to you?"

"Reject me. Not want me. That we'd be wed, but ... never ..."

"Breed?" he finished for her. "That would be disastrous, wouldn't it?" He didn't mean the sarcasm, at least, not consciously, but it was out before he could stop it, and regretted instantly, as she broke free, sobbing, and stumbled to the bed, falling into a cloud of soft frills.

"Lidye, I'm sorry!" He sank into the frills beside her, and drew her up to his chest, holding her against violent shivers and wracking sobs. He searched the tumbling blonde hair for her face, found it, and kissed her again, speaking gentle, nonsensical words, soothing her back to coherency.

She was little more than a child herself, for all she was five years his senior. She'd come to Rhomatum at his request, cloistered herself for months with Anheliaa, been thrust into marriage with a virtual stranger....

"It's all right, Lidye," he murmured against her trembling lips. "I won't hurt you. I promise."

Her arms crept up and around his neck, her trembling lips softened, opened, her weight shifted, overbalancing them, and they fell back into the lacy froth and the down-filled mattress.

Just Deymio was sitting by the fireside when Kiyrstin entered the small library.

Curse the luck.

She'd eaten dinner first, knowing he'd opted to bathe, then lingered in her own bath, trusting he'd eat and retire immediately for the night, as eager to be alone with his thoughts as she was to be with hers.

So why, she asked herself, *did you come back down, Kiyrstine romGaretti?*

She told that self it was because she couldn't sleep, that she'd wanted a book ... or perhaps a glass of wine. But a persistent, determinedly honest streak forced her to admit she'd hoped to find exactly what she'd found: Just Deymio alone.

A woman could deny the evidence staring her in the face only so long; she wanted to give him the chance to admit who he was, now he was on his home ground. To explain why he'd kept silent, when to speak for himself, at least to her, would have been so simple.

Perhaps he'd feared for his life, in a camp full of Mauritum ex-guards and Rhomatum criminals, but there was no reason to fear, now. Even if Anheliaa had thrown him out for political differences, even if he *hadn't* the ability to fulfill any of the promises given and implied, they could work things out.

If only he'd admit who he was.

She pulled the maid's borrowed robe more firmly over the housekeeper's borrowed nightgown. "I must admit, JD, you came through," she said, by way of opening.

He started, set his book down, and rose, turning to face her. In his proper setting, dressed casually but as became his station, in creased trousers and quilted dressing gown, he was startlingly imposing. So imposingly different, she momentarily questioned whether he really was her Deymio, or some close relative.

Her Deymio. One did have to laugh at oneself.

"I'd assumed you'd gone to bed, shepherdess."

Doubt vanished.

"Couldn't sleep," she replied abruptly.

"I'm sorry. Are the accommodations—"

"Fine, JD." Though she hadn't bedded down in a nursery since she was seven. "Just not sleepy, yet." She looked pointedly at the other chair.

"Please, sit down. Have you eaten?"

She nodded.

He gestured toward the cut-crystal carafe. "Join me?"

"Please."

He fetched a second glass from another room, a blown goblet with Khaythnarum's distinctive glaze, and they settled side by side, the warmth and crackle of the fire filling the air, its glow the only source of light.

"Bit dim for reading, isn't it?"

He nodded toward a blank lamp. "It ran out. I didn't feel like refilling it, too lazy, I suppose, and the servants have all gone to bed. I wasn't really reading, anyway. Just enjoying the fire. In the City, no one uses them other than for emergencies. Here, they're a singularly pleasant necessity."

"In Mauritum," she said quietly, "the hearth always burns in every home, regardless of weather or need."

"Nice custom. I wish Darius had kept it."

"To many, it's much more than custom. Many still believe if the fire goes out, the family will die."

"You're joking, surely."

She shrugged.

Trivialities. They were discussing folklore and customs when she needed to know—

"Van says I'm a fool to believe you."

"Sorry. Don't mean to come between you two."

"Between . . . ? Nothing like that."

"Oh? Does he know?"

"Damnwell better." Still, the question made a woman wonder what had passed between the two men, what distribution of her favors had been agreed upon without asking her opinion. "Am I?"

He blinked. "Are you what?"

"A fool to trust you?"

"Depends on how you look at it."

"Dammit, JD, don't get abstruse on me."

"I've never yet betrayed anyone who's played straight with me."

"You're a fine one to talk about playing straight, *Just Deymio*."

"I've played as straight with you as I dare. I was rather well outnumbered, wasn't I?"

"You aren't now." She set the goblet aside and twisted around on the chair's soft cushion to face him squarely, tucked one foot up under her, and leaned her crossed arms on the padded armrest. "What's going on, *Just Deymio*? Why should *you* have been around when that horse was born? Who are you?"

"A frequent visitor here. Like Rhomandi, I prefer it to Rhomatum."

"Van says you know too much, that your appearance was too convenient—"

"What's he think, that I'm Anheliaa's spy? Dumped in the middle of a Persitumin pond to ferret out the secrets of Mauritum?"

She shrugged.

"And is that what you think?"

"Personally, I fail to see what difference it makes. I've nothing to hide from Anheliaa."

"And has romMaurii reason to avoid Anheliaa's spies? You told me you were going openly to Rhomatum."

"I thought we were." Obviously, there were no easy revelations immediately forthcoming. She sat back again, and retrieved her wine. "I suppose it's possible he's simply nervous. Anheliaa has rather mythic proportions to some in the Towers."

"Anheliaa has mythic proportions in most directions," he said, lifting a cynical brow. Silence, then, save for the crackle of the fire, as Deymio stared into the goblet he cradled in both hands. Large hands, with prominent knuckles and square, freshly manicured fingertips. They fit the rest of the man, large, powerful, yet elegant and graceful.

"Why are *you* here?" he asked at last. "I mean, other than the boy. What do you, personally, hope to gain in Rhomatum?"

She finished her wine in a gulp.

"Asylum."

He refilled it without asking.

"I tried to kill my husband. He wants his revenge, and is willing to pay handsomely for the chance. Luckily, many of the 'tweener folk have as much reason as I to distrust the man, and have given us some timely refuge."

"And you believe Rhomandi will provide for you free of charge?"

"I'm hoping I know enough to pay my import duty."

"And if I offer you that asylum?" He leaned toward her, within touching distance, but (thank blessed Maurii) not. "Will you go with me now? No questions asked?"

"Go? Where?"

"I said, no questions."

"In return for what?"

"The obvious?"

She laughed. "A man like you? You don't need to settle for the likes of me."

"Selling yourself short, shepherdess. I'm quite serious."

"Rings, man, I'm not a fool. I've no family left. My dowry belongs to Garetti. I've some personal funds—enough for this venture, but nothing to live on. I've a fair head for business, but that will get me nowhere without reliable credentials; I haven't the looks to make a decent whore—"

"I've news for you, whores don't need looks."

"All the same in the dark, are we?" She stood up, turning her back on him, embarrassed at having allowed that bitterness to show.

"I didn't say that." Oddly, he allowed her that privacy ... as he would grant it to a man. Or a friend. "You're not a beauty, I'll not lie to you. But you're not hard to look at. Especially," he was grinning now, she could hear it in his voice, "now your nose has stopped running."

Laughing in spite of herself, she gasped, "Gods, how I hate sheep!"

"Poor sheep. You don't know what you're missing."

She snuck a sidewise glance at him. "Tried them, have you?"

"Unkind." A wounded look crossed his face, which then sobered. "Looks aside, shepherdess, I get more enjoyment out of one battle of wits with you than a night in bed with any other woman I've known—including the best whores in Rhomatum. Damn right, I'm serious. Asylum is yours, if you want it. Safety is. My bed—that's negotiable. Either way, I don't think I'd throw you out."

"I'm disappointed in you, Rag'n'bones. Does this mean I'm not going to be ravished?"

"And here, I thought I was to be the ravishee."

Her laughter was short-lived. "Why?"

"Because I like you, shepherdess. Anheliaa ... the woman is dangerously unbalanced. I'd hate to see you on the receiving end of her wrath, but if you insist on going to Rhomatum, it's she you'll have to face, one way or the other."

"Ah, but you'll be between us, and she already hates you."

"Point to the lady." He raised a toast.

"Besides," she said, "my future is that boy upstairs, and Zandy trusts me. It's not fair to him to build the dreams and then fail to see it through. He's so young. Has such dreams and hopes and faith." She shook her head. "Not even if you were serious, Rag'n'bones. I'll not betray that trust. If *Rhomandi's* not interested, or if he's too cowardly to defy Anheliaa, we'll take the encapsulator elsewhere until we find someone with the vision—and the courage—to help."

He finished his wine and stood up; reached for her hand and pulled her to her feet and facing him. "You're an amazing woman, Kiyrstine romGaretti." His fingertips traced her cheekbone. "The life I could give you . . ."

She could barely hear him past the pounding of her own heartbeat. Stupid, that's what she was, to believe anything he said, worse, to respond to this nuisanceful attraction. But past all the logic or lack thereof, she was convinced that, if he was lying—and he likely was—it was for good and honorable reasons, and that, JD or Rhomandi dun-Mheric, she'd be a greater fool to let this moment slip away.

She turned her hand in his, entwining fingers. "There's tonight. Sweet Maurii, Rags, there's even a bed." She nodded to the fur rugs on the hearth.

The irregular breath he drew surprised her, but when his head slowly bent toward hers, she discovered her own breathing had stopped altogether.

Their lips met.

A touch only, at first: a testing of strange waters.

When he hesitated again, she stretched, wrapping her arms around his neck, pushing up and into him, drawing them into firm contact. His mouth softened, opened in a startled gasp. She pursued the advantage, exploring, tasting.

He broke contact, drew back. "Not exactly the shy sort, are you?"

"If you wanted shy—" She drew a surprisingly shaky breath of her own. "—you shouldn't have requested a shepherdess."

He blinked. "How did you . . ." Then he seemed to think better of the question, eyeing her suspiciously.

"Shouldn't talk in your sleep, Rag'n'bones," she whispered softly, and kissed him again, feeling her knees go weak, or his did, dragging them both down until they were kneeling on the fur.

Deft fingers, his and hers, found their way through laces and buttons, clothing having been tacitly declared super-fluous. One powerful arm left her to sweep cushions from the chairs onto the floor, then Deymio's large body pressed her back into pillows and fur alike, lips following fingers in exploration, finding the pulse at the base of her throat and lower.

She wrapped her hands into his hair—free at last of the confining braid—and buried her face in its clean, smooth strands, filling her lungs with the heady scent of fire-warmed herbs. "Gods, JD," she whispered, delicately tracing the curve of his ear with lips and teeth, "You smell so *damn* good."

The glorious sensations ended abruptly. His hands flattened on her bare flanks, his broad shoulders heaved with deep, controlling breaths whose warmth brushed her sweat-dampened skin.

An infinity later, he lifted his head, drawing gently away.

"What's wrong?" she asked, her voice so hoarse with frustrated lust, she scarcely recognized it.

"I—" His mouth opened and closed as if in a search for words. Finally, he shook his head.

"*Don't* try to tell me you're not interested."

"I—" He repeated rather stupidly, then pulled away entirely, reaching for his dressing gown, drawing it tight.

Hiding the evidence.

"I've just got to go now," he said shakily.

"Is it Garetti?" She jerked upright, achingly aware of the soft fur against excited skin, and rolled to her knees to catch his arm, demanding his attention. "No fault of mine, Deymio. I *tried* to get rid of the bastard. He just refused to cooperate."

He laughed, but that laughter sounded painfully dragged from a thoroughly reluctant well.

"Are *you* married, then?"

"No!" Real laughter now, but with a helpless note. He reached for her borrowed robe, wrapped it about her shoulders when she refused to take it, crossing it deliberately over her nakedness, heaving an audible sigh when her body was out of sight.

The coward.

Afraid he'd break down, make a mistake. Maybe (she recalled her own warning), afraid he'd talk in his sleep.

"Damn you," she whispered and her voice was still shaking.

"Perhaps later. When we're both . . . clearer headed."

"Don't hold your breath, Rag'n'bones."

She jerked to her feet and shoved her hands through the wide sleeves. Standing squarely in front of him, she buttoned the dressing gown into place, daring him to turn his entranced eyes from the entire procedure, then strode from the room.

And slammed the door behind her.

And tried not to hear the curse from the far side of that heavy door, or the crash of glass shattering against the stonework.

*   *   *

Khyel dragged the bright red tunic off over his head and kicked it across the nursery floor and into Nikki's block tower. He *wasn't* going. No one could make him.

But the ogre would try.

He heard the ogre yelling downstairs.

From beyond the ruins of his castle, Nikki's blue eyes appeared.

Scared.

Of *him*.

Nikki had been working on that tower for three days, and now, for no reason little Nikki could understand, Khyel had destroyed it.

Heavy booted *thumps* from the stairs.

No time to explain.

The ogre's curses were just outside.

Faster than thought, he was across the room, and his arm was around Nikki, pulling him to the closet.

To safety.

They'd scarcely time to bury themselves behind toy shelves and suit dummies, before the nursery door slammed open.

Back to the deepest wall in a nearly invisible nook he'd discovered when he was Nikki's age, he huddled around Nikki, pulling the boy's small struggling body to him, pressing the curly head to his chest to keep Nikki quiet.

Within the nursery now, the ogre swore, long and loud.

Khyel shivered. And Nikki, seeming to understand at last that *he* was scared, not mad, stopped struggling and wrapped his small arms around him, murmuring reassurances.

The yelling stopped. In desperation, he clamped a hand over Nikki's mouth.

For a moment, they breathed easier. Of a sudden:
"Nikaenor!"

Nikki collapsed against him with a little whimpering sound. . . .

*   *   *

Mikhyel awoke, choking on a scream.

Slender arms wrapped around him, steadying him against a soft breast.

The pressure in his throat eased, and he relaxed against his silent, compassionate nurse, gripping the arm that wrapped his chest and held him upright.

A soothing hand smoothed his hair away from his face, then left him. Mirym's weight shifted the mattress. A glass pressed his lips and he drank the bitter liquid, forced himself to swallow because it did ease his throat and because, when he did as she asked, Mirym rewarded him with an approving smile and a gentle hug.

"Thank you," he said, when she set the cup aside.

She plumped the pillows behind him, and perched on the edge of the bed, her head tilted in consideration. When she knew she had his attention, she touched her lips and shrugged.

"No, Mirym," he said, guessing her meaning. "I don't want to talk about it. Just a nightmare. An old one. Sorry to have worried you."

The slight dip of her head acknowledged his apology as well as his need for privacy, and absolved guilt as expressively as any words would manage. She pressed his hand, then set about straightening dislodged covers.

He hadn't dreamt about the closet in years. Nikki's comment, combined with his own sense of impending incarceration for his brother and himself, must have resurrected the old, old nightmare.

Covers restored, Mirym picked up the brush and began smoothing the knots from his hair. The girl appeared fascinated by the long, straight strands, taking any excuse to lay brush to it—as did Nikki. He supposed that allure related to their own, tightly curled hair, but for himself, he welcomed the soothing effect of the long, gentle strokes.

He should braid it for bed, like any sane man, but he couldn't, hadn't slept with it that way since his seventeenth birthday.

When she'd finished, he found himself awake enough to dread sleep, and asked her to play. Amenable, as always, she returned to her chair, lifted the harp to her lap, rested her cheek against its sounding box, and began to play.

"I'm sorry, Lidye." Nikki sighed and pushed himself upright, swinging his legs over the bedside. "I just can't. . . ."

He dropped his face into his hands and pressed fingertips against the bridge of his nose.

"Nikki, *darling*." The mattress depressed behind him, rocking him back into her perfumed embrace. "It's all right. This is new for both of us. No need for embarrassment."

"It's not—"

But she wasn't listening. She pulled him backward, slithering and shifting around until her weight pressed him into the bed. Then, she attacked his shirt, opening buttons, pulling at those that resisted till they popped free.

He watched this process in horrified fascination, unable, somehow, to connect it to himself . . . until her teeth closed painfully on the skin she exposed. When he objected:

"Just relax and let me help." Her lips covered his. Her hands brushed the fabric aside, seeking bare skin.

Evidently embarrassment was not a weakness she shared.

To his despair, her touch was painfully unexciting. Painful because he wanted to respond. He wanted to love her. They were, after all, committed to a lifetime together, and loving her would make that life ever so much more pleasant.

Somehow, spiteful of his wishes, his mind kept returning to Anheliaa who wanted Lidye here for Anheliaa's purposes, and Lidye wanting to be here for her own reasons. And all those reasons centered upon a simple biological performance out of him. Nothing more. Certainly no less.

A performance *her* no longer shy hands seemed determined to wring from him. He brushed her hands away, and rolled out from under her.

A curse exploded at his back, a string of words he'd never have believed a well-bred female had even heard, and her hands pursued him relentlessly.

"Lord and rings, Lidye, let be!"

"No! Damn you, you *promised*!"

"I *what*?"

He slid off the bed and out of her reach, stood staring down at her, vaguely, distastefully, aware of the shirt now hanging free, exposing him to the drawstring waistband.

"What's the matter, *Nikki sweet*?" Her voice hissed like Anheliaa at her most malicious. "Afraid?"

"Not interested."

"You're a man, aren't you?"

She slithered off the bed and oozed around him, arms sliding around his neck, body pressing against him. Suddenly, she stopped, stared him in the face, while one hand left his neck to explore him elsewhere, jerking the drawstring loose to insinuate her hand where she damnwell didn't belong.

Speechless with anger and mortification, he froze, afraid if he raised a hand to stop her, he'd do her bodily injury, until, curiosity apparently satisfied, she shoved away, forcefully enough to stagger him, and began pacing the floor, rubbing her hands up and down her arms as if she were chilled.

Taking a deep breath, telling himself this was his wife and that she had every right to do what she'd just done, and every right to be upset, Nikki pulled his waist-string snug and retied it.

"What's *wrong* with you?" She stopped. Whirled. "Rings, boy, Anheliaa warned me you were a bit slow, but *this*." She threw her hands in the air, and began pacing again. "This has to work. Everything's ready *now*."

"Ready? What are you—"

"Anheliaa has taken care of everything. My body is ready *now*. We must—"

The look she threw him was that of a total stranger.

Then suddenly, her ice-blue eyes took on a new intensity, warmed with a greenish tinge. Behind her, the haze of ruffled draperies rippled and flowed as if from an unfelt breeze.

Back.

Forth.

Back. . . .

*   *   *

"One . . ."

Nikki trembled in his arms. Khyel held his breath—it wasn't to Nikki the Ogre counted.

"Two. —You're a fool, boy. You left your coat here as evidence. That's *stupid*. You're stupid as well as a coward."

"Three."

Khyel ducked his head before the door crashed open. Suit-stands, clothing, and standing shelves crashed down around him, and light flooded into the nook.

He curled around Nikki, protecting him from the blows that began before the toys and dummies stopped bouncing around them. Papa was dressed for the hunt; the weighted crop, his staff of punishment. The blows fell hard and fast.

He tucked his face in against Nikki, to absorb the worst with his back. After a while, he ceased to feel the blows. Sensations categorized. His back was numb. Nikki's hair, soft against his face. Dampness dripped down his ribs to his stomach. Breathing grew difficult. Nikki was still.

And then Nikki was gone, yanked from his arms, and Papa's voice was yelling Nikki was dead. . . .

Terrified, he grabbed at a departing small foot.

Papa's metal-capped boot caught his ribs, and for one heart-stopping instant, he thought he was dead—the floor was gone, he was falling free . . . and then, he crashed into the back wall.

The closet door slammed shut.

* * *

Blackness: so thick, he could feel it.

Hands in the darkness, holding him. A voice, kind and gentle in his head, whispering reassurances, drawing the pain from him. . . .

The closet was gone. It was his own bedroom in Rhomatum Tower. . . .

Gentle kindness turned coldly practical. *Leave it braided.* Memory's ear heard Deymorin's birthday present say: *It'll only get in the way.*

And then her hands were on him, expert hands bringing his body to life in a way he hadn't realized possible. . . .

Mikhyel reached after the woman, and pulled her to him, locking his lips on hers as purely instinctive hunger enveloped him.

*   *   *

The door opened without a sound, but Kirystin was
awake.

"Deymio?" she whispered.

The shadow detached itself from the hall shadows, shedding its robe like a lizard shedding outgrown skin, crossing
the polished floor to stand beside her bed, naked and beautiful in the moonlight.

Without another word, she reached out to him. His arms
enfolded her, strong and passionate, his lips, fierce in their
intensity, demanded entrance.

She asked her soul, and didn't argue the answer.

*   *   *

Back, forth, back: the draperies snapped and crackled
now in rhythmic waves. He could hear them, though his
eyes were all for the woman beneath him, who writhed in
ecstasy, her face sweat-shiny in the moonlight. Moon-sil-
vered hair spilled over his forearm, its softness caressed
his fingers.

Vision failed as passion flared and the needs of his body
took possession of his mind. The under-color of the silvered
hair fluxed, red . . . a blink . . . then golden . . . another blink
. . . and pure silver.

The body he devoured with mouth and hands was similarly unstable—sometimes womanly full, sometime slender,
almost boyishly flat.

And when he closed his eyes, the rhythm of the waves
coursed through him, gaining clarity and vigor.

And familiarity.

Not waves. The rings. Anheliaa.

Anger. Frustration.

Betrayal.

The woman beneath him screamed.

It was her doing. That Woman's and Anheliaa's.

He thrust harder, fighting the rings' hum with his own
driving beat. That Woman's screams deafened him to the
hum. Her legs clamped around him, her body moved
against him. Lifting. Insistent.

Forcing him to match the rhythm of Anheliaa's rings.

Interlude

The Rhomatum haze fluxed deep red shading to a bruised-looking purple and blue, enveloping the brothers' pattern with its throbbing insistence.

"Not nice, snake," Mother hissed aloud. And to Dancer: "You see here, child, gross misuse of Talent. It is my feeling we should do something about it. What say you?"

Dancer didn't know what was happening. The flames and the web remained obstinately uncommunicative save to Mother. But the wrongness, the anger, and violence that permeated the region of Rhomatum that emanated from the Rhomandi brothers' web was sufficient to make even the insensitive flinch.

And Dancer was far from insensitive.

"Yes," Dancer hissed back. "Now, Mother. Fix it—please."

Mother's fangs gleamed red in the Rhomatum glow. Her mental touch was a palpable caress to Rhomatum's angry insidious bruise. And where it touched, it left a pure silvery glow in its wake. Not a severance of Anheliaa's influence, but a tempering. And when color returned, it fluxed turquoise and green, with a dusting of glittering gold.

Chapter Seven

"Ease off, you overgrown oaf!"

Kiyrstin's scream echoed in Deymorin's head, bringing him to his senses.

Appalled by his own ferocity, he whispered apology and soothed her with his hands and mouth.

Her mouth reassured him. *Her* hands, free now of his immobilizing grip, stroked across his ribs, around to his back and buttocks. Her legs surrounded him, denying him escape.

As if he would want to.

Her deep chuckle caressed his ears. "Much better, Rags," she whispered, and her fingers buried in his hair, pulled his face to hers.

While the same mindless need that had brought him to her room had not abated, this time he retained wit enough to take them down the short track to oblivion together.

Mirym's slender form stirred beneath him, her silent cries echoed faintly in his head, very real tears salted his lips where they brushed her face.

Mikhyel rolled off, confused and disgusted . . .

. . . and still very much in need.

Blood, black as tar in the moonlight, stained his hands.

Nikki stared at his palms in disbelief, and in greater confusion at the woman lying panting and sweating beside him.

She'd screamed, and scratched: his head echoed with the sound, his shoulders stung where she'd raked him bloody; beyond doubt—he looked again at his damp palms—he'd hurt her, yet she lay there, staring at him.

Hungry.

Wanting more.

She reached for him, raked her bloodied nails down his

bare skin from neck to groin, and unbelievably, his body responded for her.

Unbelievable save for the hum still filling the room.

Anheliaa's rings accounted for that reaction and much else. Anheliaa was in her gods-be-damned Tower, watching and choreographing their every move; he knew, somehow, the bedroom and their naked, sweating bodies were pictured on that central sphere as surely as if he stood in the ringchamber watching it with her.

If he were Deymorin, he'd be on the stairs, storming the Tower the moment he felt Anheliaa's presence, yet instead of hating Anheliaa for that interference, he found he was almost grateful. It changed the unimaginable into the merely distasteful.

However, a part of him rebelled in its own way, a part that ached even now for the love he'd dreamed of, and as the blinding ley-induced heat flared anew, bringing with it those strange, flashing images of Mirym's face and body, he welcomed those images, purposely overlaying Lidye's physical presence with the more exciting, sweet fantasy.

This time, rather than fight the rings' thrumming, he controlled those reactions he couldn't stop. This time, he made love to the Mirym that was not there. If this creature he'd married and Anheliaa had struck an unholy bargain, let it remain between them. If Lidye was to be his wife, let the loving be on his terms, not theirs.

Mirym's tiny hands cradled Mikhyel's head against the ripped bodice of her gown, rocking gently in a tacit absolution he didn't deserve. He'd known he had a cruel streak, justly inherited from his father. He hadn't realized how deep and ugly that river ran until tonight.

Worse, he didn't know from what feral depths that assault had come. He'd sworn himself to abstinence nearly ten years ago, and in all that time, his determination had never wavered, regardless of temptations.

Perhaps that was the problem. Perhaps he had denied his naturally base self so long, he could no longer contain it. Even now, despite post-fever weakness, despite its previous abrupt and violent release, his body strained for relief again.

He shuddered. Mirym made little shushing noises and stroked his hair.

He tried to push her away, tried to deny the response of his body to that innocently sweet touch, wanting only to be free of the memories and disgust.

But Mirym had other ideas. One arm at a time, never quite relinquishing her hold on him, she slipped free of what remained of her dress and undergarments, kicking them over the side of the bed, then brushed his away as well.

As always, her silence was eloquent.

He rolled toward her, taking her in his arms . . .

. . . and felt Nikki look out through his eyes.

And he, gods help him, was with Nikki and the creature Nikki had married, with Nikki's frustrated desire filling him.

And Nikki's words echoed in his head: *"Don't fight knowing too hard, Barrister. . . ."*

He fought fighting, tried to invite Nikki in, and the sensation grew undeniable. He didn't begin to understand, and for the moment, didn't care; he let that sweetness that was Nikki guide his hands and his actions, determinedly passive, ignoring his desire to choke the life from the creature making Nikki so unhappy, fearing it would somehow filter through and destroy Nikki's growing contentment as the compassionate woman beneath him responded to Nikki's gentle loving.

And he, in his turn, absorbed the anger and violence—and sheer lust—Nikki's wife radiated.

Nikki wanted Mirym, not the woman he'd married and even now caressed elsewhere in the Tower. What Nikki wanted, Nikki should have, and following the honor-oath he'd set upon himself seventeen and more years ago, he sheltered Nikki the only way he knew how.

Kiyrstin lay peacefully tucked in Deymorin's elbow, while his arm slowly went numb. As the tingling climbed from fingers to elbow to shoulder, he wondered briefly what would happen if he waked her and tried to explain now.

She'd want to kill him.

And he wouldn't blame her. He'd had no business allowing this to happen, hadn't intended it to happen, hadn't wanted his own objectives between them if and when it had happened. But all those good intentions hadn't lasted past the first real temptation.

He'd lost all good sense, there beside the fire, had forgotten the lies that stood between them. It had taken that stupid *JD* to bring him back, to throw him out of that impossible fantasy and end it before it truly began.

And that noble intention had lasted until, on the edge of sleep, with images of might-have-beens flashing behind his closed lids, he'd found himself beside her, his clothes gone, and her arms welcoming.

Strange, to the point of embarrassing. He'd ceased being ruled by his passions when he was eighteen, or so he'd thought. At the moment, he felt that awkward age all over again.

And caught in the grip of adolescent stupidity, he leaned over and kissed her.

Blood surged anew when, even half-asleep, she responded.

He pursued that response lazily, curious, now the initial urgency was gone, why she was still here beside him. Even in his own assessment, reversion to adolescence was no excuse for his initial actions. While she'd welcomed him into her bed, blind obsession had driven him to seek it, blind obsession that had turned suddenly—brutally—vicious.

She should have been furious, should have given him the same treatment she'd given her husband. But she hadn't. She'd taken her pain in stride long enough for him to regain his control and turn obsession into passion.

"Who do I thank?" he murmured, when he discovered green eyes opened to half-mast, and directed to similarly studying his face.

"For what, Rags?"

"For saving your soul from Garetti."

She chuckled. "Would it disgust you if I said there were several?"

He thought about that. Realized it wasn't disgust he felt, but jealousy, and had to laugh at himself.

"Actually, there was one man in particular," she said, making patterns on his chest with her fingertip. "Perhaps someday I'll introduce you to him. I think you'd like him. You're a great deal alike."

"Dare I ask . . . ?"

"Well, he's bald. In his fifties. Has a lovely paunch—"

"Paunch . . ." he repeated, and she smiled lazily. He grunted. "He was a superb lover, right? Taught you the finer points of passion, paunch notwithstanding."

"Not particularly."

"No . . ." He growled deep in his throat and set about putting her past and present, her paunches and passions, into proper perspective.

She curled into a ball, avoiding his hands. He wrapped himself around her, pursuing her sensitive ribs until they were rolling about the bed giggling and laughing like two idiot children. The covers slipped away; he made a grab over the edge for them and a well-timed shove from behind sent him to the floor in a heap.

"JD?" A face appeared above him, assessed his basic well-being, and began to laugh so exuberantly he was forced to leap up and clamp a hand over her mouth before she awoke the entire household.

When she'd sobered, he removed the hand, propping himself on elbows set to either side of her face.

"So—where's the similarity?"

She lifted a hand to his cheek, followed it with a brief kiss. "He made me laugh, too. Even when all I wanted to do was cry. Or kill. It was the best lesson anyone ever taught me. When the time came, it gave me the strength to laugh in Garetti's face and leave."

"Figuratively speaking."

"Figuratively speaking," she acknowledged.

He caught her hand and pressed his lips to the palm, then traced the blue veins up her arms, across her chest and up her long neck to her mouth. When he paused for breath she said:

"Liable to catch our death, Rags."

"Oh, I doubt it."

"I want my blankets."

He scanned her moonlit body, gloriously rounded, yet lean and well-muscled, so unlike any other woman he'd ever known.

"I like you this way."

"I want you to make love to me like a real lady."

"I've never been a lady before."

"You know what I mean."

"Asking a lot of me, shepherdess."

"You'll survive."

Together, they restored the bedding, and slid demurely under the quilts. They lay there, side by side, on their backs, staring at the moonlit ceiling.

"Well?" she broke the silence at last.

"You said to make love to you like a lady. That's what I'm doing."

He barely freed his hands of the quilt in time to deflect the pillow flying at his face.

Mikhyel tried to explain, when it was over and he lay with his head pillowed on Mirym's heaving breast, but her finger touched his mouth to stop him. Then her hands met in front of his face, fingers forming two interlocking rings.

"You believe Anheliaa was behind this?" he whispered past the horror tightening his throat.

He didn't need her nod. It made sense. Too much sense. Anheliaa used the rings to manipulate minds, why not bodies?

"Mirym, I'm so—"

Again, her finger stopped him. Her arms hugged him close.

"But it *was* Nikki, Mirym. He wanted—"

Her nod brushed his head. She knew. Somehow, she knew. And incredibly, she didn't mind.

He sat up, needing to see her face.

Free of his weight, she lifted the notepad he kept at his bedside for her use, and wrote:

I love Nikki. How could I not love you?

"That doesn't make sense, Mirym."

The three of you are one, don't you feel it? It was Nikki who made love to me through you, but it was you as well. And Lord Deymorin.

"Rather incestuous of us," he said, trying desperately to make light of what she was saying.

She grinned. *A bit crowded, but I don't mind.*

She set the pad aside and held her arms shyly toward him, palms up, inviting him in. An invitation he accepted without hesitation.

A breeze swept over his bare shoulders, chilling sweat and congealing blood.

Nikki shivered, and reached for the covers, only to have them jerked from his hands.

"Get out."

He shivered again and blinked his eyes clear. The bed ropes creaked, and a bare-skinned woman stepped over him, crossed the room casually to the armoire, pulled out a quilted dressing gown, and flung it around her shoulders.

Lidye. It took a long moment to put name to face, and then it seemed ... wrong somehow.

Wordlessly, she sat before the mirror and began brushing her hair in brisk, even strokes.

"Lidye?"

The brush's relentless rhythm didn't falter.

He swung his feet over the mattress' edge, found his robe as well as his uncertain balance, and followed her, staring at her face in the mirror.

For several moments, she didn't seem to notice him, then:

"I said, get out."

"Do you want an annulment?" he asked with a great deal more composure than he felt. An annulment would negate the agreement with Anheliaa as well, but at the moment, it seemed the gesture had to be made.

The brush stopped mid-stroke.

"You must be out of your mind."

"You don't love me. I don't—"

"Love? What's *love* got to do with anything, Rhomandi?"

"Don't call me that!"

"It's your name."

"No! I won't have it."

She twisted about to stare up at him, blue eyes narrowed to dark, unreadable slits. "I'm with child. *Your* child. It will be the Rhomatum ringmaster. *You* will be the Rhomandi. Or should I say—" She turned back to the mirror. *"Are."*

"And if you're not?"

"What? Pregnant? Oh, I am."

"You *can't* know. It's too—"

"Not for Anheliaa. Now, get out of here. Go play your little hounds and hare games, or whatever it is you intend to do with your big brother."

He stared down at the pale blonde, almost white hair falling in soft waves between pink satin covered shoulders. Likely, he should feel a murderous rage.

All he really felt was tired, sore, and numb.

He turned to leave.

"And, Rhomandi?"

He paused. "My name is Nikaenor."

"Whatever you call yourself, never come in here again. Do you understand me?"

"M'lady," he said slowly, distinctly, "if this room were the last refuge in a flood—"

She turned, her expression daring him to finish.

He smiled tightly. "I'd drown first. Farewell, my lady wife."

Kiyrstin's head fell back into the pillows, stretching the skin from her tanned and freckled chin down to the sweating valley between not-at-all tanned breasts.

"Mm-mm-mm." Deymorin hummed into the pounding pulse. "Give me a shepherdess any time."

"S–s–scum," Kiyrstin hissed back on a series gasp. Her elbows slipped and she fell flat to the crumpled linens. "Ringfire, I'm exhausted."

He dropped beside her, pulling the covers up over them both, protecting her from a chill and himself from a scolding. From somewhere, she garnered a last vestige of strength and curled into him, wrapping her arms around him and snugging in close.

"Make yourself comfortable," he said wryly.

"Mm-mm-mm."

"What if I'm not ready to go to sleep?" he asked rather rhetorically, running an adventurous finger over those parts of her he could reach.

Her answer, when it came, was mumbly with sleep. "D'it ... y'sel ... D'mrin ... R'mndi ..."

A wide yawn interrupted her, but Deymorin hardly needed to hear the last.

"D'nMer'c."

Pain.

Shock.

Disappointment.

He was floating. No, he was looking down on his nude body from the doorway to his room. He was asleep. Wrapped in Mirym's equally unconscious, equally bare arms.

Anger. Desire to slam the door, quickly smothered.

The image went dark.

Mikhyel awoke, threw a startled glance at the door.

It was shut.

He shuddered, the faint dream fading, as dreams would upon awakening, and drifted back to peaceful oblivion.

Jerrik was waiting.

Nikki slammed the door to his room, as he'd wanted to slam Lidye's ...

... and Mikhyel's.

The effort only strained already strained muscles.

He sagged against the door, stirring reluctantly when Jerrik's hands urged him out of his robe and into the bathing room where a hot bath awaited him.

Other than a few clucks of disapproval over the marks on his shoulders, Jerrik was blessedly quiet. He did not object when his friend joined him, silently performing the ablution he was too tired to manage for himself. He set his elbows on the tiled edge, rested his cheek on his crossed arms, letting the constantly circulating water buffet his chest while Jerrik soaped and scraped his tender back.

When he was through, they sat side by side on the tile seat, sipping wine, while the hot water bubbled and swirled around them.

"Is everything packed?" Nikki broke the silence at last.

Jerrik emptied his cup and poured another. "Yep."

"Good. Tomorrow. As soon as the signing is complete."

Jerrik leaned back for another look at his shoulders. "Should leave before."

"Can't."

"Too bad."

"Need you to stay here."

Long silent stare then: "Why?"

"Khyel."

"Watch? or protect?"

"Both."

"Hmph. Still wish you'd take me along."

"Can't."

" 'F you say so." Jerrik heaved a sigh, took another look at his shoulders, another sip of wine, then: "Told you to tie her up first."

Interlude

The counterbalance swung, lifting Dancer's body high off the polished wood stage, a silent defiance of gravity that produced a thrill beyond even leythiation.

Feet touched; knees, ankles, even toes flexed and rebounded, dexterously manipulating speed and direction. Random music filled the air from hidden pipes responding to the random motion of the rings.

Random for practice. Next week, in the trials for the new radical, the combatants for the position would contend with rings choreographed to music as yet unwritten, a routine the contestants would see and hear for the first time when theirs was the goal to dance to and among them. At the end of the day, the next radical dancer would be chosen by the population of Khoratum and all those who were loyal to her.

In other words (feet touched, took several, bouncing, delighted steps and pushed off again) taxpayers.

A twisting dive toward a retreating ring. A quick grasp to change direction, and a slow rise to the top.

The only thing that would improve the dance would be to release oneself from the safety line and dance the rings for true. But that was not allowed—until the performance—and then, not required: winding and unwinding the line had become an artform in itself. Most never did release. At least three who had had died.

Normally, releasing in the trials was considered aggrandizing and gauche.

Five steps and leap, and if the gut feeling was correct . . . Dancer reached up, and the fifth ring was in position. Fingers closed, and the spinning ring swept down and through the fourth and sixth, so close, the fourth tugged Dancer's unbound hair.

Dancer laughed and released, sailing across to the descending Cardinal.

The point was to entertain, to dance gracefully among the dance rings. The contestants were expected to keep conservative lines and moves, to give the judges a chance to compare like with like. Any obvious attempt to stand out—though legal—would undoubtedly count against a dancer.

The point was to entertain, but to true believers, the ringdance was a near-religious experience. The ringdance was at least the third incarnation of the traditional dance to Rakdi, the Tamshi god of whimsy and chance.

The previous version had been played out within a web-like structure, a mortal facsimile of the underground leythium caves, constructed on a trick stage with footrests and handholds that would disappear or appear randomly—often with lethal consequences for those who fell through. And modified platforms did still exist . . .

In children's playgrounds.

With the ringtower technology out of Mauritum had come the ringdance. Elsewhere in the Rhomatum Web, they choreographed rings and dance troupes alike.

Here in Khoratum, the troupe was only the warm-up for the real performance, the solo of the radical dancer. Most of those competing would likely end up there, and be happy and content.

For Dancer, there was only the radical. Anything else would be cold. . . . Sterile.

The giant dance rings resembled the Tower rings in shape alone. They were constructed not of silver and leythium, but of tempered steel with a sharpened leading edge, and handholds randomly spaced along the trailing side. The largest was three times the height of a tall man, the smallest, even Dancer's body barely fit through, and they injected a level of unpredictability to the dance that only increased its value and beauty.

The dance was valued secular entertainment throughout the Rhomatum Web, but nowhere did they practice it as they did here in Khoratum. Nowhere was the competition as fierce, nowhere the danger so great.

For Dancer, it was life. If someone else won—

But one didn't think of such possibilities, not when one

danced among potentially lethal circles of sharp-edged steel.

A high reaching arc revealed the land beyond the stadium, and the waiting-court maze itself. At dawn, on the day of the contest, the competitors would be led en masse through that web and into the courtyard to await their turn.

Blindfolded.

Each would have one chance to exit when their number was called, and the rapidity with which they performed their escape would factor into their overall performance rating. Once in the stadium ... then, it was just the dance.

One chance to enter. One chance to exit.

One chance to compete.

At least, if you were Dancer. That had been Rhyys' stipulation, part of the agreement that had let Dancer, an unknown of unregistered parentage, train and compete.

A shudder set the sensitive counterbalance to swinging wildly. Dancer collected scattered wits and corrected with a touch of a toe to a passing ring.

Foolish, to let one's attention wander. But with only a single chance to compete, one waited, until one was *sure* one could win.

But so did others believe.

There were three radical dancers, two had been chosen while Dancer trained. The third was to be replaced next week—the last chance for years to come.

Feet touched, knees absorbed momentum in a smooth, practice ending outside the Cardinal's orbit.

Suddenly, the air shimmered, bringing a familiar-yet-always-unnerving disorientation, a glimmer of protective transfer shielding only Mother could provide as the ring's harness belts disappeared ...

*   *   *

She was waiting in the cave.

"Dammit, Mother!" The leythium webs vibrated purple-red. Dancer had never been so angry—at least, not at Mother. "Have you any idea how hard I fought for practice time? The debts I owe?"

Her webbed fingers floated between them. *[Irrelevant.]*

"Not to me, it's not. And just how do you expect me to explain my disappearance off the rings themselves?"

{The supervisor wasn't looking. Mavis wasn't. They think you finished and left.}

"How do you *know*?"

Mother's shrug billowed the leythium strands.

{Mother knows.}

Which might or might not be the case. Likely it was. It wasn't the first public disappearance Dancer had made at Mother's instigation, but no one ever seemed to notice, any more than they noticed the faint glow that sometimes radiated from Dancer's skin upon Dancer's return.

How Mother knew hardly mattered. Mother knew. Mother did. Perhaps Mother made humans see things Dancer would rather not know about. What mattered was, Dancer was losing precious practice time, and there was still a chance, still time, provided Mavis hadn't already belted.

Dancer stalked to the nook and the oil-pot it contained. Lacking Mother's Talent, one must rely on lesser-mortal precautions against transfer burn. Concealing webs parted before reaching fingertips ... and closed again, but not at Dancer's instigation.

"Don't be stupid, child. I have my reasons." Spoken aloud, not in Dancer's head: concession to human preference.

Dancer turned slowly. Faceted eyes glistened in the leylight.

"Anheliaa's made her move?"

She nodded.

"And Mheric's sons?"

Fangs gleamed.

"It's showtime, child. Want to go watch?"

Curiosity flared and as quickly died.

"No."

Dancer finished smearing the oil and transferred back to the stadium, wondering how to explain this time. As happened, the point was moot. Beyond the fading transfer shimmer, Mavis was already harnessed and in full flight.

Chapter Eight

Light flooded the room along with fresh morning air.

And there was movement. Servants' quiet comings and goings designed to let a man know he'd overslept and they had their own work to do.

Mikhyel yawned and stretched, feeling better than he had in years. When he remembered and glanced guiltily about the room, he discovered, with selfish relief, that all signs of Mirym's attendance were gone.

Even to her little notes; not so much as a scent remained of the previous night's events.

Enough to make a man think those events had never happened. Except that memory also supplied a vision of waking to a final shedding of clothes and a soothing, shared bath, and falling back among fresh linens to sleep cradled, flesh against bare flesh.

In retrospect, embarrassingly primitive and embarrassingly appealing.

Or it would have been, had Mirym taken offense, or had she been here to face this morning before his head had the chance to put the emotions into perspective. He didn't love her—nor she, him—but there had been something very right and . . . necessary . . . something . . .

It was Nikki who made love to me. . . .

. . . uncanny in the girl's instincts.

And she believed—or knew—Anheliaa was behind it all.

She was right. She had to be. He'd *felt* Nikki last night. Felt his undirected desire, his confusion, his anger—and his love.

Suddenly, the warmth and pleasure of the morning was gone. Nikki had committed himself to this farce of a marriage for one purpose, a purpose for which he was likely confronting Anheliaa at this very moment. Alone.

He threw the covers back and swung his legs free; a

squeak and skittering toward the door reminded him he was not alone, and in a highly informal state of dress.

Scrambling back under the covers, he said, with what dignity he could muster: "Send Raulind in right away."

"Yes, m'lord." The maid dipped a curtsy, eyes lowered, but when she straightened, her eyes scanned him quite boldly, and the edge of her mouth twitched.

"*Now,* if you please," Mikhyel said, firmly.

Her mouth fell, her shoulders rose and dropped in an exaggerated, highly improper sigh. "Right away, m'lord."

The instant the door closed behind her, he was out of bed and hunting his own clothes. By the time Raul arrived, all apologies and excuses, he was mostly dressed and ready to leave.

"Nikki?" he asked.

"Your brother was waiting for the lift when I passed him."

"Just straighten up, will you?" he said, and ran down the hall, not waiting for an answer, dabbing a handkerchief at a nick from an unpracticed, too-hasty shave, his hair flapping loose against his back.

"Nikki!" he yelled before he rounded the corner, praying Nikki wasn't already on his way up. Anheliaa would never allow him into the ringchamber, once she had Nikki alone. "Nikki, wait, *please.*"

Nikki's normally expressive face was void of emotion, but he was waiting.

They rode up together in absolute silence.

It was Deymorin and the redheaded woman he'd seen the night he'd attacked the rings; they were in bed and obviously pleasantly occupied. At least Nikki assumed it was the same woman. Her face, buried in Deymorin, was no more visible than it had been the previous time.

Nikki looked away from the spinning rings and the image they surrounded.

"Well? Are you satisfied?" Anheliaa asked coldly.

He nodded, having little choice. Anheliaa had fulfilled her part of the bargain, as he had fulfilled his. The fact Deymorin was obviously in no need of rescue did not change those facts.

Except:

"You're certain this is current, and not some past moment or conjured wish?"

Anheliaa snorted. "Anything else takes effort I'm not willing to spend on that lout's behalf. This was your darling brother's activity as of last night. I've no idea *where* he is. The rings evidently find him equally distasteful. They refused to dwell on him longer or to give further information. An inn somewhere along one of the lines, obviously, or I'd not have found him at all."

Mikhyel shifted, but before he could protest, the image within the rings flared, another overlaying it for an instant, like a darkened room suddenly lit by lightning.

It flared a second time, revealing a boy, in the woods, with a box.

And that box was the source of the lightning-like bursts.

Anheliaa cursed and waved a hand, and the central orb faded to silver. The surrounding haze degenerated to slowly orbiting rings.

"What was that?" he asked, or perhaps Mikhyel did, he was that shaken, he wasn't certain who uttered the words.

"Interference," Anheliaa snapped, and would explain no further.

So he nodded, knowing he'd get no more from her, that she considered her side of the bargain closed.

Besides, the boy was not his problem. Deymio was. There were dozens, perhaps hundreds, of inns along eighteen different leyroads out of Rhomatum. And one had to wonder, if Deymorin had gone away, might he not be in the Mauritum Web? Would Anheliaa's rings find him there?

Somehow, he doubted Anheliaa would answer honestly.

"Now." Anheliaa rubbed her hands together triumphantly. "The signing."

As the lift carried them downward, Mikhyel spoke for the first time.

"I'd like to speak to Nikaenor alone first, Aunt."

His voice was hoarse, but he looked physically better, more relaxed, than he had in months.

Thanks to a tonic called Mirym.

Nikki swallowed bitter jealousy.

"It can wait, Khyel."

"No, it can't." Mikhyel hit the brake and pulled Nikki

from the lift before he, or Anheliaa, could protest, released the lift before they'd quite cleared the threshold.

"We'll meet you there," he called after Anheliaa's disappearing wig, and before Mikhyel pulled him into a small antechamber. "What the hell's this all about? Why didn't you just stay in bed this morning?"

"I wanted to be with you in case . . ."

"In case, what?"

Mikhyel shook his head. "Never mind. Nikki, I didn't want to bring this up in the chamber, but . . ."

"Forget it, Khyel. I've a contract to sign."

"Not if you don't want to."

"This is between Anheliaa and myself."

"Not any longer."

"What do you mean?"

"Do you honestly think you were alone last night?"

"Of course I wasn't alone last night. I was with Lidye."

"Like hell." Mikhyel's eyes were wide, his brows drawn. But it wasn't anger. He was shaking. "I was. *You* were with—"

Mikhyel's face spun away.

The back of his hand stung.

Mikhyel caught himself against the wall and propped there, dabbing at the blood flowing freely from his lip.

"Well, Khyel," Nikki said, his voice echoing the harsh anger welling inside. "The violence has come full circle, hasn't it? Aren't we a fine lot? Only one of us worth anything is Deymorin, and I'm going to drag him down with the rest of us."

"Nikki, Mirym loves—"

"Don't say it. It makes no difference. The dream is gone. There's only one first time. One wedding night. At least for me. I've had mine. I want no others."

"Nikki—"

"I'm going after Deymorin."

"He's safe, Nikki. There's no need. He's *chosen* to stay away."

"Possibly. But he'll have to say that to my face. If I can find him."

"You don't know? Didn't recognize the room?"

"How should I? I've only stayed in one inn in all my life. I'll have to check every damned—"

"He's at Darhaven."

"He can't be. Anheliaa said—"

"I don't *care* what she said. I know that room. You should. Dammit, *you're* the one who reminded *me* of it last night."

"The ... closet? That was ... Darhaven?"

And then he did remember. Remembered the ruined castle and Mikhyel's arms holding him, while their father screamed curses and his brother's body jerked and constricted around him with each blow. And then there was only blackness.

"Thank you for reminding me, Khyel," he said, his voice echoing the freezing cold in his gut. "I'll leave as soon as the contracts are signed."

"Don't expect me to witness such a farce."

"I don't."

"You're not coming back, are you, Nikki?" Khyel's voice was weak, exhausted.

Defeated.

"I don't know, Mikhyel, but I doubt it."

Just outside the antechamber door, Mikhyel said: "Goodbye, Nikaenor. Be well." And without looking back, Mikhyel walked slowly down the hallway toward his own rooms.

She should have been suspicious when Deymio had pointedly requested her to resume her man's clothing, and join them directly in the carriage lane, but somehow, (silly her) Kiyrstin had thought carriage lane meant carriage.

"No," she said flatly.

"What do you mean 'no'?"

"I mean there is absolutely no argument in hell or on earth that will convince me to get up there."

Deymorin—or rather, Just Deymio, as he seemed determined to remain—leaned an arm across the creature's neck and pressed the heels of his hands into his eyeballs. He was pale-faced and irritable this morning, acting as if he'd had a long and uncomfortable night, and, as a result, wasn't excessively long on patience.

Well, neither was she. Never mind she'd slept the sleep of the totally sated, she'd also waked to an inexplicably empty bed, been hailed downstairs by an unknown servant, where she'd had to face that irritable-male countenance across a cursory breakfast table, and was now being ordered to stretch her pleasantly strained muscles and bruised backside across a malicious-looking creature, whose plan for the day obviously included her maximum discomfort.

It did leave a woman to wonder what had occurred while she slept blissfully ignorant. In the hazy early morning, she'd determined to forgive all, to tell him she knew who and what he was and it didn't matter why he'd lied and they'd work everything out.

Now . . .

"Lady romGaretti—" Deymorin began, and she glared at him. He revised quickly: "*Kiyrstin,* please, don't fight me on this. If we take the carriage, we must take the road, and that would take us nearly to Rhomatum before the bridge to Braccitum Ley and the Armayel cutaway. That makes the trip a good two—possibly three—days."

. . . now, by her reckoning, they were back to the bottom of the pond.

"You don't know?" she said. "Goodness, JD, what's happened to your wealth of precision answers?"

"Dammit, don't press me. I haven't made the drive in years. I *always* ride. It's faster—hell, if we get out of here, we'll be at Armayel by this evening."

He was highly agitated. Openly worried. Perhaps he'd received ominous information regarding his brothers. Perhaps . . .

"Deymio," she said in a quiet undertone, and throwing a suggestive glance back toward the house, "can we talk?"

His frown deepened, and he shook his head, a single, hat-dislodging jerk.

So much for clearing the air.

"Well, I hate to be the one to break this to you, JD, but I don't know the first thing about riding. You force me into that saddle, and I guarantee, you'll be a lot more than three days getting to wherever it is you think you're taking us."

"Nonsense. There's nothing to it. It's an easy trail. Beautiful this time of year. You'll love it. Now, get on the goddam horse!"

"Please, mistress?" Zandy's voice pleaded from above their heads. He was already up, clinging precariously, his eyes wide and frightened.

But his fear was not of the tall horse: he was accustomed to riding, or so he said, although the creature was twice the size of the typical Maurislan pony. It was their open animosity bringing that look to his young face.

Kiyrstin gave him a teasing, reassuring glower, then nodded toward the horse.

"He hates me."

"Don't be ridiculous," Deymorin said irritably.

"Of course he does." She kicked his ankle lightly to gain his attention and flickered a glance toward Zandy. "Look at him. He's going to dump me in the rocks the first chance he finds."

"It's a mare," JD said dryly.

"Oh, that explains it. She's jealous."

"Nothing for her to be jealous of." JD's cold, down-the-nose look was a declaration of independence. "Is there?"

So much for a truce for Zandy's sake.

Bereft of viable options, she sighed and reached a foot awkwardly for the stirrup. Without warning, a strong hand grasped her support leg just behind the knee, collapsing it against a broad shoulder, lifting, while another hand thrust rudely against her backside.

She was in the saddle before she was clearheaded enough to object, and by then, objection seemed superfluous: JD's back was turned, Zandy was explaining how to hold the reins, and a groom was adjusting her stirrups.

She tried to pay attention to her instructors, tried to ignore JD's well-tailored shoulders, and the smooth line of his riding pants as he swung easily into his own saddle, the elegant sway of his body as he adjusted to the large beast's antics, tried very hard not to translate those lines and movements to bare skin in the moonlight.

She had to wonder, as she rode behind that well-tailored back, down the lane and into the woods, just precisely what had happened.

The horse circled, forcing his would-be rider into a hopping single-footed dance at the center of the spin, until, thanks to a second uncontrolled beast stopping squarely in front of him, the first paused long enough for the rider to scramble into the antique, patched saddle.

From his seat atop the paddock fence, Ben had a clear vantage on that pitiful ballet as well as countless others, as the motley assortment of horses and riders milled about the holding pen, feeling each other out and adjusting hodge-podge equipment to make the best of a make-shift deal.

It was the old Rhomandi stables they used, appropriated at the young lord's orders. There'd been inquiries when the horses arrived, attempts to have them thrown out, but he'd sent the Oreno representative to the Tower as the young lord had said he was to do, and they'd heard nothing since.

The herd, which had arrived from Armayel late last night, had been assembled from Lord Deymorin's private stock augmented with anything the surrounding sharecroppers and landowners loyal to him could spare. As a result, choices ranged from racing stock to a child's pony, though the latter had been relegated by an increasingly inebriated crew to the position of official mascot.

The oldsters weren't faring badly, overall. They'd all survived arms practice this morning, thanks to the fact the rifles Gareg had sent from Armayel were vastly more accurate than those they'd had in the Guard. Perhaps, if rumor held truth and Mauritum was setting to march, Rhomatum should look into updating its arsenal.

But that was, happily, Brolucci's worry, not his.

His job was getting twenty-three increasingly boisterous, would-be bodyguards in their saddles, and keeping them there.

The Guard received basic horsemanship as part of their traditional training, and most hadn't forgotten; quite all they'd learned, but it would take more than liniment to soothe these backsides tonight.

"Rings, Ben, what's this circus?" Lord Nikaenor's blond head appeared beside him.

"By your leave, m'lord, Brolucci denied the request for use of the City reserve stock."

"To hell with my leave. On what grounds?"

"Declared the mission personal, sir, and therefore 'constituting an unnecessary depletion of City resources in these uncertain times.' I didn't say anything, m'lord, it being your wedding day and all, and Gareg—he was here when Brolucci's edict came down—he said he could manage, from the tenants and neighboring landholders, and, well, sir, here they are, like he said."

The pale curls fairly vibrated with controlled energy.

Lord Nikaenor's gloved hands balled into shaking fists as they rested along the fence rail. But the fists relaxed and:

"To hell with them." The lad's voice was even. Matter-of-fact. "To hell with them all. We don't need them."

"My thoughts exactly, m'lord," he ventured to say.

The smile that flashed at him held little real humor. "Two smart men in agreement—must be right, Ben. Are the horses sound? The men ready? The supplies—"

"Enough for a week, sir. In the wagons."

The smile widened. "Let's get out of here."

"Where to?"

The smile disappeared. "I wish I knew for sure."

"Didn't the Lady know?"

"She didn't. I think I do."

"Need to start somewhere, m'lord. Thinks is better than nothing."

The young lord's eyes flickered toward him, embarrassed, like he didn't think he'd be believed. Then:

"Darhaven." His chin rose pugnaciously.

"Fair enough, m'lord," Ben said easily, "Gareg, he said the last he heard from Darhaven was two months since. Seems to me, a fair bit can happen in a month."

Lord Nikaenor's back relaxed into a natural curve. "Darhaven it is. —And, Ben?"

"M'lord?"

"Have the men pack enough for tonight in their saddle-bags, confiscate a packhorse or two if necessary. If Brolucci complains, he can follow us and make his case in person. I intend to move cross-country. The wagons can catch us up at Darhaven."

"Beggin' yer pardon, m'lord, but there's the pavilion. It's too much for a packhorse, and—"

"Pavilion? What in the name of Darius do we need a pavilion for?"

"Surely yer lordship won't wish to sleep on the ground like a common—"

"My lordship's ass learned to conform to hard ground a long time ago, Ben. My lordship's tyrant of an older brother made sure of that. Just throw my bedroll on a pack-horse along with the others. I'll be fine."

They were prepared in a surprisingly short time, the men, like the lad, eager to be on their way. The young lord's

swinging mount was surprisingly stiff, considering he was
reputed a horseman.

Or perhaps not surprising, considering last night was the
boy's wedding night.

Someone else must have had similar thoughts, from the
good-natured laughter that rippled across the field. But the
young lord did not join that laughter, and the young lord's
face, as he rode stiffly through the gate, held nothing of
regret, and everything of relief.

"JD, either we stop now, or you go on without me."

Kiyrstin drew back on her reins, the approved (according
to Alizant's instructions) method for suspension of forward
motion. The creature beneath her (as usual) ignored her
and continued following Deymorin's mount's black tail into
the swift-flowing stream.

She pulled harder.

The horse tucked its nose in toward its chest and shook
its large head, a performance that set its ears waddling
ridiculously. Its steps grew short and choppy, until they
were plunging about in an exceedingly uncomfortable
manner.

She cursed the fool beast loudly and grasped large handfuls of mane. The plunging increased, the reins jerked
wildly in her fist.

Water splashed everywhere.

"M'lady!" Alizant's horse splashed up beside hers.
"M'lady, please."

He reached for her reins.

The horses collided.

The boy slipped toward her.

She relinquished one hand's death grip on the mane and
grabbed to steady him. The horses shied apart, which re-
sulted in them both sliding inexorably into the stream, only
her frantic grasp on the long mane keeping them heads
uppermost, preventing them from a thorough soaking.

Together, she and Alizant staggered, found purchase on
slippery rocks, and stood there, in the middle of the fast-
flowing stream, clinging to one another, the horses milling
aimlessly around them, as an exceedingly unpleasant sound
filled the air.

JD was laughing. JD had reentered the stream and was
sitting atop his unnaturally quiet mount, arms braced

comfortably on the thick arch of neck—and not a fingertip lifted to help.

She glared up at him, caught the mare's reins and
splashed the short distance to the far bank, climbed a rock
and began pulling her boots off, ignoring Deymorin's highly
vocal objections.

Vocal until Zandy grabbed his stirrup and they exchanged a few words. Then Deymorin crossed to her, took
the mare's reins without a word, and, Zandy in his wake,
moved upstream and to a sandy washout where he jumped
lightly to dry earth, performed some arcane ritual with the
creature's saddle, and placed something on the animal's
front legs. Still without a glance toward her, he treated
their horses similarly, then began to help Zandy unpack
the potentiator.

Obviously, some concern about the machine was reason
enough to halt. Fine. She'd take whatever grace she could
get.

She left them to their toy, and went deeper into the undergrowth and downstream to answer nature's insistence,
wishing she could have packed last night's hot bath in the
saddlebags along with her travel sponge.

Nothing in her life had prepared her for this. The constant sway, the sheer power of the creature, might (under
the right circumstances and though she'd never admit as
much to Deymorin) have been invigorating exercise—for
an hour or two.

All day—that was another matter.

Entirely.

She eased the loose breeches from legs gone bruised and
raw. The rough seams she'd taken in the coarse broadcloth
to accommodate her woman's shape, while perfectly adequate for walking through brush, had rubbed blisters all
the way down the inseams as well as in other, less accessi-
ble, areas.

Deymorin didn't care. Deymorin was in a hurry. Deymorin had spent a lifetime building callus in areas most sane
persons considered sacrosanct. Deymorin had skin-tight
breeches of soft leather with seams to the front and back,
but not between himself and the damned horse.

"Oh, shepherdess," Deymorin's voice came from the
trees. "I'm sorry!"

She growled an angry epithet to the gods in general and

JD in specific, and jerked her rough-spun breeches up, then hobbled her way back to the stream to rinse the travel sponge.

That for his sympathy.

At the far end of the trail was another bath and a hot meal. Nothing else mattered at the moment. Without a word, she brushed past her tormentor and marched back toward Alizant.

"What is it?" A little girl voice asked, from beyond the undergrowth.

Kiyrstin stopped short of the washout, and gingerly pressed a view-obstructing branch of bristle-pine aside.

Alizant was squatting on the bank beside the potentiator, head thrown back, his mouth hanging slightly open, his startled eyes glued to the far bank directly opposite her vantage where a little girl stood watching from the wood-shadows.

Wispy, nondescript brown hair whipped across her face, and her dress, a simple brown shift tied in at her tiny waist with a blue-green sash, fluttered about her knees. Her feet were bare.

"What is it?" she asked again. "Is it broken?"

"I—" Alizant's voice croaked. He coughed, and tried again. "I don't think so, little mistress. It got wet, you see, and—" He glanced downstream, obviously wondering what he should say to this out-of-place little inquisitor.

A twig snapped behind her. Kiyrstin twisted, suspecting Deymorin and ready to stop him.

Bare feet. Bare, dry feet, and a ragged hem.

Across the stream . . . the girl was gone . . . or rather, she was here, passing Kiyrstin as though she didn't exist, squatting down beside Alizant to examine the potentiator.

She stretched out a grubby finger to touch it.

"What's it—" A spark arced to her fingertip. *"Ouch!"* She jerked her finger back, fell to the ground with a thump, giving the potentiator an angry, brown-eyed stare and sucking her finger.

"Are you all right?" Alizant reached to help her, touched her arm . . .

Lightning flared, and the boy literally flew back into Kiyrstin's cover, arms flailing, flattening the brush over her.

"Alizant!" Sacrificing a fair quantity of skin, Kiyrstin wriggled free of clinging bristle-pine and stooped over the boy. He was still breathing, but his eyes were wide open and sightless, and his skin was . . . glowing.

"Zandy?" She reached a trepidatious hand, mistrusting that flare, but fearful if she did nothing, the boy might die. What she *could* do remained highly questionable.

When her first touch encountered nothing worse than an unpleasant tingling, she wrapped an arm around his shoulders, urging him upright. The tingling slowly disappeared, the boy's eyes drifted closed and even more slowly, opened.

"Hello, missy." Rhomandi's voice, obviously not aimed at her. Deymorin squatted beside the small girl. "Did you hurt your finger?"

Finger still stuck in her mouth, the little girl glared across the washout at her, her eyes a clear, bright . . . Kiyrstin blinked and looked again . . . green. She blinked again, and the eyes that softened and turned to Deymio, were the color of the sky above them.

And the finger she took from her mouth and extended pathetically to Deymorin for inspection had a faint green iridescence to it.

Zandy stiffened under her arm, fully cognizant, now, and as puzzled, from the look he turned to her, as she herself was.

Deymio didn't seem to notice anything unusual. He was turning the finger over in his hand, listening to the little girl's shrill diatribe about the Bad Box, and making all sorts of disgusting sympathy-noises until her babbling finally ran down.

"Where are you from, missy?" Deymio asked then.

"On the ley," she said, pointing upstream.

"So far? Are you travelling with your mama and papa?"

"Mother lives there. But it's not far."

"There's no ley near here, sweetheart."

She grinned, seeming to like that endearment, and cuddled up to him, draping her arm around his neck, something not-quite-childlike in that gesture. Then she whispered something in his ear, one heavy-lidded purple eye aimed at Kiyrstin.

"This isn't a ley," Deymorin said, laughter in his voice.

" 'Course 'tis, silly. *All* water's on leys, don't you know? Streams, rivers . . ."

"Like tributaries to the leylines?" Kiyrstin asked, and the little girl glared green-eyed at her. But the green faded to blue and she said lightly:

"Tribootrees, caplarees . . ." And turning blue innocence back to Deymio: "Mammarees. All reeses to the leys." She skipped free of his arm, dancing lightly over the rocks along the stream's edge, singing: "Ley flows like reeses underground, don't you know? Some leads to mamrees, like Khor'tum, and some to dadrees, like Rhom'tum and some to nowhere 'tall. But some . . ." She slipped back to Deymio, pressing up against him, leaning back in the supporting arm he threw around her, and running a small hand over his cheek. "Some leads to brotherees."

Deymio's arm dropped. Slowly, he stood and backed away from her, his face ashen. "What do you know about my brothers?"

"Yours is woorrit 'bout you, Deymio-man." She began skipping about the stones again, the water parting from the rocks as her bare toes approached, closing in again when they were gone. "Nik-ki, Khy-yel, and Dey-mi-o. Stoo-pid. Stoo-pid, brotheree-ohs. One be close, and one be far. When three are one, life 'n' death will spar. Death may win and death may lose. All depends on what they choose. I c'd tell them . . . 'n' I c'd tell you . . ." Her dancing had led her back to the shadows on the river's far side. She grinned, and her teeth flashed . . . like fangs. "But figure it yourself, pretty Dey-mer-oo."

She vanished into the trees, and Deymio, with a swallowed curse, splashed through the water and into the trees after her.

She looked at Zandy, and he at her. As one, they shook their heads in disbelief.

Neither of them was surprised when Deymio returned limping and alone.

They stopped for the night earlier than Nikki would have liked, but a day in the saddle had taken its toll on many of the men. Of course, if they'd had their way, they'd have stayed at Talvanni's Inn, where he'd stopped to inquire discreetly after his brother. It was a favorite stopover for Deymorin, and there'd been just the slightest chance . . .

but, of course, nothing had come of it, except that the men had discovered the inn's homebrew.

It had taken an embarrassing long time to roust them free of the tavern, only to discover they'd bought the tavern out and brought its largesse along.

He'd as soon keep going alone and trust to his own luck, but he wasn't stupid. With Deymorin in unknown circumstance, and his own movements so well announced, he dared not proceed alone.

He'd gained at least that much caution in the past months—along with the stiletto he carried in his boot. Ben had given him that knife along with Ben's suspicions. Hard to believe a Mauritum knife intercepted Rhomandi ribs by accident.

So he set up camp with the others, settling his bedroll off to one side, and sipped a mug of Talvanni's brew, while listening to reminiscences of feats of ever-growing magnitude, feeling very much out of place, youngest of the lot by a generation and more, holding his men's respect by accident of birth alone and uncomfortably aware of the fact.

He felt alone, more alone than he'd ever been, and following that sense, he traced it to a single image: Mikhyel walking slump-shouldered down the hallway.

He supposed he should feel sorry for Mikhyel, whom he'd rejected that morning, perhaps unfairly, but he couldn't help it. He'd *felt* Mikhyel last night. He'd felt Mikhyel's hands loving Mirym and hated him for it, even as he supposed he should thank him for sharing the experience with him in that strange intersection of sensations.

But, dammitall, why Mirym? Why not one of the ever-willing maids? Mirym would be hurt, no way not, because Mikhyel didn't love her. Mikhyel didn't love anyone.

Dammitall—

"M'lor'?" It was a whisper from the shadows.

He jumped, looked around.

A female whisper.

"M'lor' Nikki?"

A whisper that sounded for all the world like . . .

He glanced around. No one else had heard; no one was watching him, so he stood up and followed the whisper. A hand closed around his elbow and pulled him under the broad sweep of a tree limb, then left his elbow to slip around his waist.

"H'lo, m'lor'." A soft voice, rather sweet, in its way. A voice he'd heard before.

Six months ago.

"Beauvillia!" he hissed. "What are *you* doing here?"

Fingers trickled through his hair, pulled a leaf free that went floating out of sight, then laced behind his neck. The voluminous gathers of her skirt pressed against his hips, her soft breasts against his chest. "Sweet m'lor', have 'ee a poem fer me?"

He grabbed her wrists and pulled her hands away. "How did you get here?"

Her eyes, silver-blue in the moonlight, glowed rapturously up at him. "Come to warn you, pretty m'lor'."

"*Warn* me? About what?"

"Sweet, sweet, m'lor'." Soft lips sought his.

"Dammit!" He pushed her away.

"Oh, pooh." She took a little dancing step backward. Trick of the campfire behind him, the sparkle that was her eyes took on a faint, red tinge. One of the men must have brought her along. Which made him wonder who and what else they'd packed.

"Miss Beauvillia," he said patiently, realizing the girl must be simple, and slightly embarrassed that he'd actually been attracted to her once. "Are you alone?"

"Alone? Beau*vina's* never alone." Her hands ran through her own hair, fluffing the iron-curled ends. "Came t' warn ye, but 'ee don' care ... don' wan' ta be nice t' poor Beau*vina*. Thinks I'll go find me a nice, *friendly* gent."

Warn him? He supposed it was possible. Beau*vina* was Tirise's and Madame Tirise was Deymorin's friend.

"Now, Mistress 'Vina ..." He grabbed her as she flitted by. Pulled her into his arms and swayed her back and forth. "Let's not be hasty. I can be nice. What did you want to tell—"

She gripped his lower lip between her teeth, slipped her tongue along the captive flesh, preventing him talking. When she released him: "Mm-mm-mm-much better, Master Nikki." Arms stretched over his shoulders, she swayed her hips rhythmically against him and chanted lightly; "Brohs be left and brohs be right, beware the man who stalks the night."

"Riddles? Really, mistress, I don't have ti—" Her teeth closed again.

"Brohs be not, where you be gone—"

"How do you—*ouch*!"

"But your place be there, so you best take care. And if you do . . ." She paused, frowning. Then in a vastly different, almost sibilant voice: "Shit, there's no rhyme. Just watch your step, fry." She kissed him again, her tongue flickering lightly over his skin. "I will be." With that final crypticity, she slipped free and into the trees.

Just before she disappeared, she turned; an eerie green glow happened where her eyes should be, and he froze. He *felt* that green gaze scan him up and down and back again, and a breeze sighed through the trees. "Too bad you're attached, Mheric's son."

When she was gone, that strange paralysis . . . drained, leaving first his eyes, then his arms and at last his feet free to move.

"Beauvina!" He yelled and ran after her, but she was nowhere in sight. "Dammit, girl, *where are you*?"

"M'lord Nikaenor?" Ben's voice answered, and Ben himself crashed into the clearing.

Nikki whirled angrily. "Who's responsible? Whose idea was it to bring *women* on this expedition? Dammit, Ben, I thought you understood—"

"M'lord Rhomandi," Ben's address and Ben's hand on his arm brought him to his senses. "There are no women with us."

Others had followed the old lightwatchman, others even less familiar to him, and the looks being cast about indicated a conviction that their leader was losing what little credibility he might have begun this day with. Nikki drew a settling breath, raised his head and said firmly, "I just spoke with one of Madame Tirise's ladies. She can't have gotten far. I want her found."

* * *

There were people outside the closet door. He could hear them.

But he hadn't the strength left to call, wasn't sure he would if he did. Nikki was dead, and it was his fault. They'd throw him Outside in the woods and he'd freeze and the wolves would eat him—maybe *before* he froze.

Better to die now.

He didn't remember much after Papa's toe and the closet wall. The door had opened again, and his only thought had been to cover his head.

That had been a lifetime ago. In the darkness and deepest pain of that lifetime, he'd wished Papa dead. Imagined Papa riding across the frozen, broken ground, taking chest-high obstacles as if they were cavaletti, laughing Death in the face....

And Death laughing back at last.

Now, he couldn't breathe, and when he tried to move, things grated inside him like he was a chicken some invisible god was cracking apart for its dinner.

He thought maybe he'd cried for a while.

Cried. Probably that proved he was a coward, like Papa said. And because he was a coward, Nikki was dead. Papa had said so.

Someone opened the door; he caught his lip in his teeth to keep from calling out, causing pain that more than occupied his thoughts until the door closed again. And then, coward that he was, he began to cry in earnest, burying his face in an elbow, never minding the arm bent in the wrong place, that being one small pain in a world of pain.

"Khy?" A soft hand gathered his tumbled hair, gently freeing strands embedded in broken skin, easing torn fabric away from blood-encrusted flesh. "Oh, my poor little Khy."

Only one person in all the world had ever called him that.

The shirt fell away, leaving his flesh bare to that touch. The soft hand brushed across his back, then touched his forehead, and in that instant the pain was gone. He lifted his head from an arm that no longer bent the wrong way, twisted a body that no longer grated to look up at ...

"Mama?" he whispered.

A soft green glow surrounded her.

"Poor Khy."

And him. He raised his hand and saw bone showing black through green-glowing skin.

"Am I dead, Mama?"

And the closet was gone. Green-glowing lace surrounded them, billowing gently as if from some unfelt breeze.

"Do you wish to be dead, little Khy?"

He thought of Mama, who was dead. Thought of Papa, who had killed her. Of the closet, and of Nikki, who was dead now, too, and why, and who had killed him ...

"Yes-s-s." His quivering jaw hissed the answer.

Her hands cupped his face. Her green-haloed face tipped as her blue-green eyes caressed him. "Then probably you're not, my darling."

More cowardly tears squeezed their way out, his efforts to stop them making him shake all over. Her hands left his face, her arms surrounded him and pulled him close.

"My fault, Mama. I killed him."

"Killed who, my little Khy?"

"Nikki. I told you I'd keep him safe and I killed him."

"Oh, I don't think so."

So she didn't know. Even dead, you didn't know everything. He was wickedly glad.

"I do know what you think, child. But Nikki's not dead. Your papa said that to hurt you—to scare you. He's become a cruel man, your father. And that's my fault, really. I should have left him ... oh, long ago."

"But you couldn't, Mama," he said, knowing her deepest fear, having heard this before, in Mama's most private, most terrified, living moments. "You feared for Deymio. Deymio didn't know, would never believe, and if you had left and Deymio hadn't, Papa would have taken it out on him."

"Or so I excused my lack of initiative. Sometimes, I think I just took what seemed the easiest course. My family was long since gone. If I'd left, I'd have had no one. Been on my own."

"I'd have helped, Mama."

"I know, child. I didn't know then how strong and brave you were. But I kept thinking it would get better, Khy. That the man I'd known would come back to me, so long as I didn't change. That all I had to do was love him enough and he would get better. But he didn't. Anheliaa's influence was too strong."

"Anheliaa?" Mama had never mentioned his aunt's part in their own private drama. Not when Mama was alive. "What did she do?"

"Your papa wasn't always like this, Khy. Oh, he was always intense. His life was never simple. But Anheliaa

..." Mama hesitated. The glowing lace pulsed red. Her blue eyes reflected purple. "Anheliaa pushed at him, wanting him to relinquish power to her. She ... got in his head, as she did your brother's. Do you remember, Khy?"

He didn't. Not the child, Khy, but the adult, Mikhyel, did and through Mikhyel, Khy remembered and shivered, there in his closet filled with broken lives. Until now the dream had made sense, in the way of dreams. Now ...

Now, he was the child in the closet, but he was also a man.

"Mama, what's happening?" She didn't answer and panic rose. *"Mama?"*

"Just listen, child, and remember." Mama's voice had changed, grown sibilant and firm. "I didn't know then. I just saw the man I'd loved deteriorating, and I made a fatal mistake, didn't I? I stayed with him when I should have left. I paid for that mistake, and now you are having to pay for me."

Mikhyel, the man, lying in his Tower bed, realized now that Anheliaa had poisoned their father, as she'd tried to poison Deymorin. She'd made him frustrated. Angry. And he'd turned that anger on his own family. As Mikhyel, the man, had turned it on others. First Nikki. Then Deymorin, and then innocent Mirym. And all out of his own guilt.

"But that doesn't excuse him. Doesn't excuse what he did to you ..."

"Or to you. Of course it doesn't, child. He could have run the snake out. He could have run the rings without her. He chose otherwise. Chose not to involve himself in the mysteries. I'm not telling you this to excuse Mheric, but to warn you. It wasn't you who raped Mirym—"

"How did you—"

"Hush, child. That was Anheliaa at work. Anheliaa infiltrates—*rapes*—minds. She makes people do things they then hate themselves for, and in that way, she controls them. You must beware your feelings, be certain they are your own before acting on them. Control is more important in you and your brothers than in other men, because she seeks to act through you. Knowing what she is capable of does not excuse *you* either. Ultimately, regardless of the pressures the world, or Anheliaa, puts on you, *you* determine your own destiny."

"You're frightening me, Mother."

"Good. You should be afraid. Of yourself and others. Remember, what she does to her own, she might do to strangers. You are, perhaps, the most vulnerable because of that connection, but you are also the most prepared. And the snake—particularly this snake—has no scruples, it just slithers and bites."

The light around them faded, taking Mama's touch with it.

"Mama?" he whispered into the darkness in the bend of his elbow, and sobbed as the aches returned in full force.

Dream. It was all a dream. Except that the pain was less than he remembered, and he no longer grated inside.

Voices outside the door, asking Where was he? and another . . . *Nikki's* . . . saying that he'd promised not to tell, crying when they tried to make him.

His own sobs were of relief, now. Mama hadn't lied. Nikki was alive and trying to protect him. He wanted to call out, to tell Nikki it was all right, that even exile into the frozen woods was preferable to believing he'd killed him.

And then Deymorin's voice, so like Papa's, now it had finished changing, was yelling for him, for Mikhyel the Coward.

Light flooded the closet, silhouetted a figure, casting a long shadow over him.

"Papa?" he whispered, and fear set in again. Sent him scrambling over broken toys and fallen shelves for his hideyhole. But Papa's strong arms pursued him, hauled him free of the rubble, shook him to sensibility when he struggled for freedom.

Not Papa. Deymorin. Face thundercloud dark, dirty, and streaked with tears, and in a voice hoarse with grief, Deymorin growled:

"Papa's dead."

*   *   *

Mikhyel awoke, covered in sweat and, thank the gods, alone.

It was a new twist to an old, old dream.

The colors.

The lacy veils.

Mama. Mama had never visited him in the closet before, had never said any of what he'd just heard. The reality was waking to hands pulling him from the closet while his insides grated, reality was a room filled with needles and bandages and pain. It had been months before he'd learned Nikki was not only alive but unharmed, and for years he'd waked from this same dream believing Nikki was dead and that he'd killed him. Had had to go to Nikki's room to prove to himself that Nikki was alive. Had sometimes shaken him awake just to hear him talk.

The first time Deymorin had taken Nikki to Darhaven, he hadn't dared close his eyes until Nikki returned to Rhomatum.

Anheliaa. Mama. Rings, what did it all mean?

He buried his face in shaking hands and for the first time in years, he wept.

Chapter Nine

Almost there.

Deymorin could feel his tension as he rounded a bend in the road and the lights of Armayel glimmered between the trees; he was that uncertain what he'd find waiting. He realized then, that he hadn't been at ease since his meeting with that strange child in the forest.

Kiyrstin and Alizant insisted they'd seen scales, that the child's eyes had changed color, that her skin had glowed green.

He'd never believed in the Tamshi. Wasn't certain he did now, but, if not that . . . Life. Death. Close. Far. *Dammitall.*

"Deymio! Dammit, man, unless you want to kill the boy, slow up!"

He pulled Skylark to a plunging halt—the horse knew exactly where he was and wanted no part of stopping—and (under further equine protest) he circled back to where Kiyrstin and the boy had stopped. The woman was on the ground next to Alizant's stirrup, one hand on the boy's leg, the other holding two sets of reins.

That afternoon's events and a long day in the saddle that would tax an experienced rider's endurance had taken their toll. Alizant was clinging to the saddle out of sheer tenacity, but he'd lost any awareness of his surroundings, didn't, or couldn't, respond when Deymorin shook his arm.

"I'll take him up with me. Help me move him across."

"You must be joking. For the gods' sake, JD, let the boy sleep. We'll get there tomorrow."

"Stay if you like, shepherdess, but by the time you spread your bedroll and build a fire, we'll be sleeping on down mattresses."

"Truth?"

"Truth. Give me a hand with the boy?"

Knowing from experience that there was no convenient

way to carry a semiconscious individual tandem on a horse, he opted for the hold that would leave the fewest bruises on both of them. With the boy cradled crosswise and propped against his chest, he asked: "Can you handle both horses?"

Her weary gaze swung toward her horse and back to him, then she nodded slowly, and hauled herself stiffly into the saddle.

It took rather longer than he'd promised to travel—or rather, stumble—the remaining distance to Armayel, and when they pulled up in front of the darkened manor house, the look Kiyrstin sent him and the long journey settled a senses-deadening weight on his shoulders.

"Alizant?" he murmured, and squeezed the boy to wake him. "We're here, fry. Can you hold on? Just long enough for me to get down."

On the off-chance the whimper was an affirmative, he slid down, dismayed when his own legs collapsed. He grabbed mane and saddle to keep from falling until the tingling in his feet dissipated and he could feel his toes again. He released his death grip just in time to receive a fainting Alizant into his arms.

Kiyrstin, who had neither moved nor spoken, gazed up at the house, shoulders slumped, mindless exhaustion in every line. Balancing the boy's dead weight precariously, he gripped her knee, squeezed lightly to get her attention.

"Don't try to move. I'll get the boy inside, be right back."

A faint dismay crossed her face.

"I promise, shepherdess. Just hang on. All right?"

She swayed, eyes closed, then caught her lower lip in her teeth and nodded.

He staggered up the wide stone steps and leaned his shoulder against the doorframe, arching his back to balance the boy while reaching for the bellchain.

Pain lanced through his hip and down his leg. He cried out and collapsed to his knees, swearing.

"Deymorin!" Kiyrstin's cry joined the bells ringing in his head. Before the ringing ended, she was at his side, taking Alizant's weight into her own lap. "Are you all right?" Her hands were brushing his hair back from his face, urging him to look at her.

Just as if she really cared.

"Deymorin." She'd said, and "Rhomandi." She knew. Yet she persisted in pretending otherwise.

"Why, shepherdess?" he whispered past the pain.

Her hand stroked his cheek. "Why, what, JD?"

He shook his head and lurched to his feet, pain shooting through his knees now as well as his back and leg. He cursed softly and pulled the bellchain, then, glancing down at Kiyrstin, he said, "Much more of this, and I won't be able to move at all."

The door opened behind him. Light flooded out, casting his shadow across Kiyrstin and the boy.

"Who are you, and what do you want at such a godforsa ... ken ... ?"

"I should think that quite obvious." He turned slowly, had the satisfaction of seeing Gareg's face blanch, then flush, before shock gave way to amazement and joy.

"M'lord!" Gareg's hands pulled him into the warmth and the light.

"Rings, man, help the woman and the boy." Deymorin waved him back to the door. "And get someone to the stables, before those three outside tear the barn down trying to get in."

It was a confusion of faces, half explanations and hot baths: a virtual repetition of the previous night at Darhaven, but eventually, the boy was in bed, and Kiyrstin, if she had any sense, considering the bruises and sores, was still soaking her shapely rear in hot mineral salts.

Himself, he was in another library beside another fire ... only the individual sharing a bottle of wine with him was rather less ... physically appealing and the information he gathered was both more precise and infinitely more disturbing.

For the first time since the scent of spring-fresh grass had startled his nostrils there beside the mountain pond, he truly felt the months that had so incomprehensibly passed him by. The men Gareg described—in particular, Mikhyel—bore only superficial resemblance to those brothers he'd eaten dinner with what seemed a mere week ago.

One had been spouting poetry at a brothel and Berul at dinner, the other had been calling Outsiders parasites. Now, the one was ... married, and the other ... hard to judge what Mikhyel had become. A brother wanted to believe the best, wanted to believe that Mikhyel's professed commitment to the drainage project indicated something other than false conciliation.

But if such was the case, why allow this ... *farce* of a wedding?

"Honestly can't say to that, boss," Gareg said, when he put the question to him. "They had a long talk here, when Master Nikki came for him that last time, and ... well, whatever it was regarding, it didn't go well at all. Master Nikki was angry, and Master Mikhyel I fear, not well at all. I tried to stop him from leaving, as late and cold as it was, but he would. I was worried, I don't mind telling you. —When Master Nikki's messenger came through asking for horses and such, he didn't mention Master Khyel, only to say he was to take your part in the wedding play as well as his own, you not being there to do it yourself."

"Rings," Deymorin muttered, and rested his head in his hand, pressing his fingers hard into his temple and brow, trying to put the bits and pieces into a whole that made any sense whatsoever. "What you're saying is that Nikki is already married and even as we speak, travelling in directions unknown with some sort of makeshift army, searching for me?"

"Contracts should have been signed this very morning, sir, and Master Nikki, he planned to leave right after. But I wouldn't exactly call it an army."

"Whatever it is," he realized wearily, "it's obviously headed in the wrong direction, and I'll wager my brother was no more anxious to wed that creature than I'd have been."

"You've met the young lady then, m'lord?"

"Met her? You might say that. Anheliaa tried to pass her off on me when she hit seventeen and *that* was, rings, years ago. —Dammit! I've got to get to the City." If he had the energy, he'd pace the floor. "*Someone* pressured him into this. If it was Khyel, so help me, I'll kill him."

"Not before you hear his side, you don't," Gareg said stoutly, "or you'll answer to me, Lord Deymorin."

Another of those disconcerting moments where understanding seemed to slide sideways on him. The Gareg of old would recognize that statement for the exaggeration it was, but agree with the sentiment. The Mikhyel of this new spring had engendered a loyalty in the Armayel overseer that allowed no such dark humor.

Deymorin nodded. "Not before I hear him out, Gareg, I promise. But I'll get an annulment of that marriage contract if I have to choke it out of Anheliaa. There's no time to waste. If I leave right away—"

"You wouldn't dare," Kiyrstin's unmistakable tones said from the doorway.

He leaned an elbow on the chair arm, and cradled his forehead in his hand. "Who invited you in here?"

"Door was open, JD."

Her footsteps crossed the room; he looked up, saw Gareg's eyes flicker from him to Kiyrstin and back, taking in their decidedly informal dialogue, drawing undoubtedly fascinating conclusions.

"Kiyrstin," he said cautiously, "please leave us. This is personal. Has nothing to do with your—*our*—purpose."

She helped herself to his wineglass, refilled it, and arranged herself on a divan opposite them. "You're talking about leaving immediately. Where's that put me? Where's it put Alizant? Sorry, Rags, but I'm not going to bed until I have certain reassurances regarding our . . . disposition."

"Gari," he said, embarrassed and apologetic, "could you leave us for a while? I'm sorry. I know it's *late*—" That barb aimed solely at the uninvited female, but:

"Don't you mind that, m'lord," Gareg said warmly. "We're grateful to have you home and alive. Rest can come later."

The sad thing was, he meant it.

With the door safely shut behind Gareg, Deymorin said: "You, woman, are a semiroyal pain in the derriere. That poor man gets up before sunrise every day, and this stunt of yours means he'll get no sleep at all. What in all the eighteen *hells* above Rhomatum gives you the right to intrude on a private conversation in that highhanded fashion?"

"If 'that poor man' gets no sleep, it'll be your doing, not mine. Was I wrong to suspect your intentions? Should I be soundly sleeping upstairs? And when I awoke in the morning, what would I have found? Leaving right away, you said? *Tonight?* We had a *deal,* Rhomatum. You were to produce Rhomandi. Rhomandi was *supposed* to be here. So where is he, eh? Where is he, *Jus—*"

"Stop it!" He lurched to his feet, crossed the distance between them in two strides.

She just scowled up at him, her mouth a fine, hard line.

Uncertainty consumed him. Uncertainty over the fate and desires of his brothers, over the goals of this woman, over his own judgment—over reality itself. He was exhausted, angry, and increasingly apprehensive for everyone and everything he cared about.

And he was damned tired of the lies.

He jerked her up to face him.

Which she did without flinching, damn her.

"Enough of this pretence," he said through clenched teeth. "You know *damned* well where Rhomandi is. Have known for days."

Still she said nothing, her whole stance a challenge—a condemnation of *his* behavior.

"Who's the real pretender here, woman? And I might never have known, if I'd managed to control my baser self and had stayed clear of your bed. You want Rhomandi?" He released her elbow with a thrust that set her staggering, and stepped back, throwing his arms wide. "Well, here he is."

A second step set him lurching as the leg twisted wrong, collapsing as it could and did, always at the worst of moments. He caught the mantle to hide the stumble.

"Here he is," he repeated. "As if you didn't know. And at the moment, Rhomandi has concerns other than yours and the boy's—and he damnsure doesn't care what rom-Maurii wants—and he'll be thrown to the bloody wolves before he'll take you into Rhomatum to confuse his thinking any more than it already is. Rhomandi will leave you here. Away from Anheliaa, away from Garetti, away from romMaurii—isolated until he *knows* what's happening and where your loyalties *really* lie."

"Anheliaa? Garet— What *are* you talking about?"

A desperate need surfaced in him, to hear her admit to *something* he could despise her for. To be free of her disastrous appeal once and for all.

"*Whose* are you?" He challenged her. "Anheliaa's? Garetti's? *Did* Anheliaa . . . deliver me to you?"

Her lip lifted in a confused, disgusted curl. "Rings, Rhomandi, that's sick."

Rhomandi. At least she was using his title openly now.

And with that tiny concession, his driving anger seeped away. He collapsed into the chair, aware only of the throb in his leg, and the emptiness in his gut that had nothing to do with the supper he'd been unable to swallow.

He didn't trust his attraction to Kiyrstin, feared mostly what it did to his better sense. For all he knew, she might be a ringmaster herself, and manipulating him from some distant Tower, playing games with his mind. That made as much sense as anything else he'd experienced in recent memory. And if she was Anheliaa's pawn ... or Garetti's ... or her own mistress. Perhaps even the source of the nightmares ...

He met her confused, stubborn gaze.

But if she weren't ...

"If you want my loyalty," he said slowly, "give me yours, now."

She had to be out of her mind.

Kiyrstin shifted her weight, trying to ease the ache in her lower back, only to discover that movement prohibited: velvet and lace were caught in the seat springs—again. Kiyrstin tugged at the skirt, yanked hard when it clung tenaciously.

The seat shifted, bounced, and the green-broke *("Sorry, m'lord, we sent everything else to Master Nikki.")* team shied, narrowly missing a cart filled with crates of chickens.

Deymorin steadied the young horses with a gentle word and a barely perceptible twist of his rein-filled hands; the horses settled back into their prancing, generally forward, motion. To her, he cast a sickeningly sweet and adoring smile that said, clear as clear, *"Do it again, shepherdess, and I'll tie your hands in your lap."*

Clear because he'd said precisely that—or similar threats—several times in the past few hours—before they entered his City.

The Rhomatumin market they travelled was crowded, only his skill with the lines keeping the foolish creatures attached to the carriage from taking out every fifth stall. Skill that drew the attention of everyone they passed—or perhaps it was she that made everyone stare at them like sideshow oddities.

And perhaps, sweet Maurii save her, that's what she'd become: a Mauritumin noblewoman, squeezed (with the help of a tortuous corset) into a dress of highly questionable but very expensive taste, perched atop a splinter-filled training cart next to a Rhomatumin prince (or Rhomatum's nearest equivalent), on her way to bid the most powerful madwoman in the history of the two webs a friendly good morning.

Moon-touched, for certain.

She leaned over, endeavoring to ignore the corset biting into her gut, praying she wouldn't fall out the top and give the onlookers an even greater show, and worked the skirt free, then straightened and stretched her back with a sigh. Deymorin looked to her with a solicitous, *"Tired?"* To which she smiled (so sweetly her teeth ached) and responded, *"No, not a bit."*

Damned liars, the pair of them.

She was exhausted, aching in every bone. The dress she wore had been tailored for a *much* smaller woman, and the corset that enabled them to fasten it in back had accomplished that feat by squeezing her out the ridiculously low-cut bodice.

Velvet and lace. Provided by Deymorin. At Armayel. One had to wonder *why* he had women's clothing there. Particularly clothing he swore was top of the line, fashionably speaking.

Though in *that* he was forsworn, she had only to note the apparel of the women around her—and ignore the stares of the men—to realize that.

Some people, particularly too-charming almost-princes, were just very lucky that other people had long since lost any pretense to vanity, and were morally capable of setting need above humiliation.

Her only consolation was that the too-charming—and elegantly, *quietly* attired—almost-prince was equally tired, and nearly as sore.

Only Zandy, with the resilience of youth and a full night's sleep, had come through yesterday unscathed, and *he* was staying with the old man at Armayel. Zandy, sweet Maurii protect his independent little soul, hadn't said a word when Deymorin told him they were going on without him, had only stood outside the fine manorhouse, his arms filled with squirming Puppy, and wished them farewell.

Another wind-flaring banner, another back-wrenching start that caught her in mid-yawn, jerked her head back and snapped her teeth down on her tongue. She hissed, and yanked the billowing skirt free of another so-called spring, finding a certain satisfaction in the sound of lace ripping.

"I don't know what your problem is, shepherdess," Deymorin said from the corner of a smile, as he nodded greeting to some passerby, waved a cheerful answer to a hail from afar. "You had two whole hours of sleep, after all."

Which was two more than he'd had.

"I just can't imagine, Rags," she muttered. "Female frailty?"

He choked. "Never."

The horses shied again, taking his full attention—while the gentle, dextrous skill of those large, buckskin-covered hands commanded hers. She'd found it difficult enough to sort one set of short reins from one of these creature's backs. For this simple, two-horse team, he seemed to have enormously long strips of leather running between every available pair of talented fingers.

She shivered with remembered passion, and pressed herself as far away from those talented fingers as the carriage's single seat would allow. Carriage. It was a damned training cart, nothing but a seat and four wheels with springs designed for stability and comfort for the creatures between the shafts, not the passengers. But that hadn't slowed JD—oh, no. He'd just said, *"Hold on,"* and let the youngsters fly.

What joints had survived yesterday's torment had rapidly succumbed to this new torture.

And Deymorin Rhomandi dunMheric? He just smiled and waved and exchanged friendly insults with every stall they passed. They all seemed to know him, all tried to get him to stop, asking where he'd been all this time, and he, yelling back his pre-agreed-upon answer: *"Courting myself a new bride!"*

Gods of ley and stone. Bride. Just wait til that tidbit found its way to Rhomatum Tower. Better yet, to Garetti's ears.

Which was, of course, the whole idea, or so Just Deymio had claimed. Which was her reason for being here, in Gartum Market, alone with Deymorin dunMheric, the boy and his machine left behind—Where they'd be safe, or so Deymorin had claimed. Her own plans put on hold while they pursued his more *time critical* needs. They were to arrive openly, *noisily,* to put Anheliaa off her guard and the city in a partying mood.

To make certain *everyone* would notice if the Rhomandi disappeared *again.*

As for Garetti ... last night, Deymorin had simply shrugged that problem away. It wasn't as if they were really married, he'd argued, and if Garetti did hear, if Garetti came (or more likely sent someone) after her, it would simply add more spice to the pot. After all, multiple spouses were not at all unusual, particularly in state marriages. *Family-webs and all, don't you know?*

He seemed to conveniently forget that her 'other spouse' was the spiritual and practical ruler of a web that was barely on speaking terms with Rhomatum, and never mind such arrangements had been outlawed in Mauritum two hundred years ago.

Minor details, she supposed, and caught the side rail as the horses spooked sideways yet one more time.

Somewhere ahead, too far for her peace of mind and bruised backside, lay the outer wall of Rhomatum. It must. She'd seen it from the distance. From this crowded so-called street, all she could see were people, and colorful banners announcing wares for sale, and fringed, *flapping,* awnings, to which the team took continued exception.

But for all the crowds, the streets were orderly and clean, lacking the stink and detritus, the pickpockets and thieves of Mauritum's markets.

Tempting to say something, to compliment Deymorin on his city. Tempting ... she snuck a sidewise glance at his smiling, supremely confident profile ... but resistible.

The profile turned toward her. From somewhere, a sigh happened; his dark eyes met hers, his smile turned gentle and, combining the multitudinous reins deftly into one hand, he squeezed hers briefly as they lay clenched on her velvet-covered lap.

"I appreciate this, shepherdess. I truly do."

Gentle. Understanding. Good-humored—sweet Maurii, why couldn't he have just one solid flaw she could hold against him long enough to clear her head?

She straightened her back, heard a hastily adjusted seam

pop, and forced a tight smile. "Just remember you said that, Rhomandi."

"I'll count on you to remind me."

Another hail from a distant tatter's stall. His hand tightened spasmodically, then withdrew to resort the reins. This time, he actually pulled the horses to a halt, somehow finding a niche that allowed other traffic to pass.

"Here," he said and thrust the reins into her hands.

"JD, what . . . ?"

But she spoke into empty air. He was gone, over the open side in a light-footed hop that left the vehicle's springs bouncing sickeningly. Fortunately for her uncertain skill, some youngster immediately discovered the standing horses and began petting their noses and chattering at her, asking questions without breath or pause for answers.

Also fortunate, since she had no answers to give him.

Rhomandi had disappeared into the crowd. She stood, balancing gingerly against the shifting floorboards, trying to spot him, caught a glimpse of him talking to a rather lumpish man, who was dressed in obviously expensive clothing and waving a lace-edged handkerchief through the air in front of his nose as he spoke.

A large basket of fruit came between them and stopped, while the woman beneath the basket carried on a flirtation with a passing customer.

She was tempted to climb up on the seat, but lacking suicidal tendencies, she settled instead on stretching up onto her toes, reins firmly in one hand, the other hand to the siderail, trying to see over the fruit.

The horses shifted.

She staggered, backed a step onto her too-long hem, jerked it free with the hand that held the reins, and in seemingly slow, inevitable sequence, the horses snorted protest and threw their heads; the child screamed and jumped back; one horse reared, the cart tipped . . .

And Kiyrstin fell to the wooden seat in a billowing cloud of red skirts and lace petticoats.

The horses bolted, people screamed, and fruit flew.

Kiyrstin cursed, loudly and without consideration, fumbled past skirts exhibiting a maddening tendency to blow up in her face, caught the very end of the lines as they flipped over the kickboard, cursed again as the horses simultaneously skittered to a halt and swayed to the side, nearly overturning the cart.

Someone screeched.

Wood cracked and flew, and feathers filled the air.

The horses shied again and were off before she could draw a full breath.

Stretched nearly full-length across the seat, face smothered in her own skirts, the reins wrapped around her wrist, she clung to the siderail, ignoring the chicken screeching in her ear, and the bat of its wings against her head.

When all four wheels felt solidly grounded, she raised her head, batted the feathered beast into the street, and pulled herself upright, staying as close to the center of the seat as possible.

Determinedly blind to the chaos they wrought in their careening passage, she set her teeth, thrust the billowing skirt between her knees with a fist, and sorted the reins into both hands as she'd seen Rhomandi do, slipping them taut one at a time without ever releasing her hold on the rest.

Swaying with the bounce and toss of the cart, she set her feet against the kickboard and pulled relentlessly back against the angry tossing heads, absorbing the jerks in her wrists and elbows, threatening the horses through her teeth, until the tossing eased, and the horses' mad darting scramble straightened to a rapid, but even clipping on the cobbled streets.

As the vehicle came to a bouncing, swaying halt and several knowledgeable-acting men closed in around the horses' heads, the tension left the reins and Kiyrstin's shoulders.

"Are you all right, mistress?"

Noting that her hands were shaking, she folded all four reins—damned if she'd let them go now—into one hand; she raised the other hand to pat her hair into a semblance of order, pulled a feather free, and stared at it, certain she looked far worse than she really was.

"Mistress?"

Her eyes were dry. Painfully so. Perhaps it would help if she blinked.

It did.

She smiled down at the man asking so politely, such kindliness in his voice. You wouldn't think she was other than she seemed: some sort of proper lady who had just narrowly escaped an ugly and painful death.

Of course, that wasn't the case. Couldn't have been.

"*Kiyrstin?* Kiyrstin! Dammit, let me through."

That was Deymorin dunMheric. No mistaking that deep and carrying voice. Besides, one had to laugh at oneself, who else here would call her by name?

She was alone. A Mauritumin outlaw in Rhomatum, a city of legend and mystery . . . and crazed people. Like the man limping and pushing his way through the growing crowd. A crazed man who had played with her emotions until she was dotty with him. Why else was she here, in a strange city, putting her life on the line for two other men she'd never even met?

Surely no sensible woman would do such a thing. No sensible man would leave her in charge of moon-touched horses.

"Shepherdess?" That equally moon-touched man was back.

A soft *thank you* to someone unknown; the cart dipped and jerked, and then he was there, his hands on her arms. "Come, girl, wake up."

One hand left her, popped her cheek gently. She resisted the temptation to strike back. Resisted also sticking her tongue into her cheek like a child defying an errant adult. Neither seemed a proper example to give the children she could hear crying and yelling for their parents.

"Kiyrstin!"

Another blow. Sharper. She gasped, an inhalation that set her to coughing. When she caught her breath: "Damn you, dunMheric! What the hell did you think—"

His mouth on hers cut off the rest.

In the Rhomatum Council chamber, Mikhyel stopped in mid-sentence, his mind no longer tracking the debate as his body took on an aching, aimless desire of its own.

He bit his lip, striving for control, as across the table he saw, not Mhalis Corinelli, but Mirym, or perhaps it wasn't. The hair was red. Or perhaps black.

Or it glowed green.

He shuddered, transferred his gaze to the large window, beyond which the Tower loomed.

"DunMheric?" a voice asked.

He had no idea whose.

He muttered some excuse, and left the room.

They were on the trail to Darhaven much later than Nikki had hoped, but he hadn't pushed this morning, couldn't blame the men, most of them elderly and all of them lacking his motivation for hurry.

Couldn't blame them particularly after losing the benefits of the early stop in the fruitless search for Beauvina.

Beauvina. Gods, who, or what, had the woman been?

The eyes. The strange warning. The disappearance leaving no trace.

All the clues hinted Tamshirin. But Tamshi only appeared to the crazed, drunk, or desperate. He had to wonder into which category he fit.

And this morning, as they travelled toward Darhaven at a comfortable jog-trot, one couldn't help but remember the feel of those soft lips. Couldn't help but flash on one's abortive seventeenth birthday, and the disappointing reality of one's wedding night.

He shifted uncomfortably in the saddle, hoping no one noticed, and silently cursed the entire female species.

The crowd around them was cheering. The seat below them swayed and jerked as the horses plunged, giving their self-proclaimed grooms a handful.

As Deymorin grew slowly aware of these things, he drew, with great reluctance, back from the kiss, scanning Kiyrstin's face anxiously. She was trembling beneath his hands, and strangely pale, the freckles standing out starkly on her cheeks and nose.

But her green eyes had lost that wide, shocked look, blinked, now and again, in the way eyes were meant to.

Lord and rings, it was all he could do not to take her here and now.

He pulled a feather free of her too-short hair, plucked three from her bodice and released them to drift away on the breeze, cupped her face in his hands and brushed her lips lightly with his thumb, then pulled her to him again, telling her to kindly shut up when she protested, wanting just to hold her, to convince himself for good and all that she was safe and unharmed.

Without looking up, he lifted a hand to the crowd to

assure them all was well and flipped it to shoo them away, counterfeiting a lightness of heart he was far from feeling.

Laughter, then, and fading, as the crowd responded to that silent message, or others enforced it for him; he didn't know, or care at the moment, and neither, from her complacency in his arms, did the shepherdess.

He'd been a fool to leave her; the colts were unpredictable and exceedingly strong. He forgot sometimes there were things she couldn't do. Perhaps he'd remember if she would carry on, or faint, or do those other things females were supposed to do at times such as this, instead of—

"Wastin' time, Rags," her lips murmured against his.

"I don't feel you moving, shepherdess."

"Not *my* brothers, Rhomandi. I'm perfectly—"

"Damn," he whispered, and captured her mouth in a final penetrating kiss before prying her fingers from the reins. With the help of their volunteer grooms, he backed the colts free of the detritus of their passage, thanked the men, and worked the cart slowly toward the main road, pausing to tell each devastated merchant to send an itemized accounting to the Tower, receiving in his turn well-wishes for himself and his new bride.

That 'new bride' was sitting quietly beside him, staring straight ahead, hands folded in her lap, the wide slashed sleeves of her short jacket covering a ripped side seam, courtesy of that wild dash through the market maze. Not exactly tiny, this woman. Not what would be termed over-large, either. Just ... healthy. The way a woman could be who spent every waking moment active and alive.

Bride. Damn, he wished she were.

"What say you, shepherdess," he asked, side-stepping his own wayward thoughts, "Shall we make it a grand entrance, or approach the Tower quietly, like wayward children returning home with tails tucked?"

An ironically raised brow, a gaze that took in the wreckage around them, was her silent answer.

"Did make a bit of a stir, didn't you?"

"Don't you dare try to attach this onto me, dunMheric."

"And whose hands were on the—"

Without warning, and with the cart still in motion, she one-handed a swing down to the ground and disappeared into the shadowed chaos between two ruined stalls, leaving him with his hands full of rejuvenated colts who'd received their second dose of red velvet skirts flying behind them.

"Dammit, shepherdess!" He struggled to quiet the horses, searching the market crowd for some youngster brave and skilled enough to trust with them, yelled into the shadow: "Kiyrstin!"

"Hold 'em fer a copper, m'lor'," a voice said from the near side, and he said, without looking, "I'll make it ten, boy. Just don't let them—" A familiar chuckle stopped him cold. A two heartbeat pause later, and without looking down, he hissed, "Get up here."

"Ai, now, that'll cost a bit more, then, won't it?"

"Name your price, woman."

"An apology, for starts."

"You have it. What else?"

"Now, that won't do at all. Try again."

He swung his head around to glower down into her deceptively guileless green gaze. "Forgive me, my dearest, most brave and intelligent lady, for being such a boorish, inconsiderate beast—"

"Try idiot, Rags."

"Idiot, then. I had no business leaving such a frail, dainty lady with such ill-trained beasts—"

"There's that word again. Those poor creatures are just spoiled—like their driver. That'll do, Rags." She moved around the front, giving the colts a pat as she passed, and swung up beside him, ignoring the hand he stretched to help. The instant her feet touched the floorboard, he gave the colts the signal to start.

The cart lurched forward; she settled calmly and without a blink.

"You said the apology was just for a down payment," he said. "What's the balance? Perhaps I'll refuse to meet your price."

"Changed my mind. Paid in full."

"How do I know you won't change it again?"

"I'm up here, aren't I?"

"You might leave me again."

"I don't think so, Rags."

And suddenly, the easy raillery . . . wasn't. Suddenly there was too much of seriousness in her voice and in the green eyes that angled toward his.

"Don't do this to us, shepherdess," he said, and his voice was hoarse.

"Done is done, isn't it?"

He swallowed hard.

Her mouth twitched and she pointed with her chin back toward the central marketplace. "Who was that?"

"Nobody."

"Done is—"

"All right, woman. Barishi ... he's nephew to Pwerenetti, one of the City's most accomplished gossipmongers. I was just filling his ear. Setting the stage ..." He shook his head, helpless in the face of her disbelief. "Shepherdess, he was *nobody*."

Her level gaze never wavered, a balancing of his integrity he'd never before experienced. Finally:

"Looks to me like a gate ahead," she said, "Thought you said we couldn't drive within the limits. What do you plan to do with—" She dipped her head toward the horses. "—them?"

"I suppose you have a point." He drew a deep breath, and forced his thinking back to the immediate task. "What say we put the old witch's nose thoroughly out of plumb and drive right up to the Tower itself?"

She shrugged. "You're the Princeps. Who's to complain?"

"Any number of folk, I assure you." He grinned. "*And* a hefty fine will be forthcoming, count on it. But not before I make my point."

"Well, if that's the case ..."

Chapter Ten

With that impassive understatement only a seasoned butler achieved, the man who opened the massive, gilt and glass doors to Rhomatum Tower said:

"Master Deymorin. You have been missed. Come in, please."

Laughter rumbled, deep and heartfelt, beside Kiyrstin, and Deymorin's hands on her back urged her through the doors ahead of him.

She threw him her most daggerous glance and whispered, as she sashayed past: *"The better to draw fire, JD?"* and he laughed again, entering instead at her side, his arm possessively on her waist.

To a person raised among the sculptured fantastical garden estates of Mauritum, Rhomatum's band upon band of apartment housing had all seemed terribly . . . utilitarian.

Tower Hill itself, however, and the surrounding complex of administration buildings, the oldest structures in all Rhomatum, felt quite familiar, as this House Rhomandi, every bit a palace, felt familiar.

Which made her wonder at the true motives of Deymorin's several-generations removed ancestor. Somehow she doubted all Rhomatumin citizens lived like this. Still . . .

"I could grow to like this," she said, swaying free of his arm to cross the patterned tiles and run a possessive hand along a polished banister.

Deymorin pursued her, reclaiming her waist and hissing into her ear: "Don't bother." And in a louder tone: "Korendi, let me be the first to tell you my good news—"

"Your pardon, m'lord, but your happy news has preceded you. Lady Anheliaa awaits you both."

Deymorin's arm tensed. "Where?"

"In the south sitting room, m'lord."

Deymorin's hold tightened, but his murmur was determinedly easy: "That's as far from her lair as the dragon's been in years."

Korendi, who was apparently, in the universal way of servants, selectively deaf, announced implacably: "M'lord, mistress, if you will follow me ..." and with a graceful sweep of his hand, turned and headed across the mosaic floor.

Kiyrstin would have followed, if not for Deymorin's insistent hold.

"Not yet, shepherdess," Deymorin said, staring after the butler, a dark frown on his face. "I intend to see my brothers first."

"I'm afraid that won't be practical, m'lord," Korendi said from across the foyer and down his nose. "Lord Mikhyel is in Council chambers, and Master Nikaenor is ... inaccessible."

"What do you mean, Nikki's 'inaccessible'?"

"I suggest you address that question to the Lady." The butler turned again for the far corridor.

"Hell of a way for a servant to talk to his master," Kiyrstin murmured, pulling Deymorin's attention away from that arrogant back.

"I'm 'master' to no one in this house, Kiyrstin, in anything other than name. That's something you'd best understand. This is Anheliaa's house, regardless of what any laws proclaim." His hand pressed her back. "Let's go, shepherdess."

Shepherdess. Trust JD to remind her. This time, it was she who resisted, setting her feet firmly. "Not before I clean up, *m'lord*. I'm all over feathers and dirt, I've burst another damned seam—"

He relaxed at last, grinned and pulled one lock of hair in another direction (balancing the dust-caked spikes, no doubt) and pronounced her: "Perfect. Let's go."

"Deymorin," she whispered, while they were still out of the butler's selective hearing, "how did she know? How could she possibly—"

"The rings," he said abruptly. "She'd know the instant we entered the power umbrella. The rest—" He shrugged. "*If* she knows, it's as likely through human eyes and ears as through the rings, though I suspect she might have been watching us since we passed the outer gate."

She shivered, grateful now for the warm arm about her. Garetti raved about Anheliaa's so-called magic, claimed the rumors of her experiments with the rings were Rhomatumin propaganda, disseminated about Mauritum to undermine his influence and force them into the Rhomatum Web.

But since she'd left Garetti's sphere, she'd personally seen people appearing out of nowhere. Fairly solid propaganda, to her way of thinking. However, if Anheliaa had this other power. . . .

"Just how *much* does she know?" she asked, realizing too late how much they should have discussed before now. Realizing, too late, they'd wasted far too many of the past hours in angry, suspicious silence. "What all can she do?"

"I couldn't tell you, shepherdess, something, for the first time in my life, I'm ashamed to admit. But she's not in the Tower now, and without the rings, she's nothing but a vicious-tongued old woman."

However, she sensed fear through Deymorin's arm, not shame, and slipping his grip, she tucked her hand into his elbow and squeezed reassuringly. "Then let's find out, shall we, JD?"

He chuckled and that uncharacteristic feeling dissipated.

The butler led them a long, winding pathway, past art galleries and corridors lined with busts—of family, so Deymorin said—and exquisite tapestries. Art and architecture that were at once familiar and slightly alien, common beginnings taking independent directions, geometries right, yet not, centuries of separation, yet like the language and names, indisputably linked.

They passed a group of people—a guided tour, from the singsong voice of the leader describing this and that anecdote of this or that Rhomandi. The voice faded as they approached, drifted into stunned silence, and the group turned to watch them pass.

Not them. *Her.* They never noticed the man with her was the Rhomandi himself.

She tried not to stare back, tried very hard to ignore them and not insult Deymorin's official visitors. But . . . nature insisted. She lifted her feathered head high, and shoved an extra sway into her hips, and threw the lot a *look* behind Deymorin's broad back.

Deymorin, apparently lost in his own thoughts, patted

her hand and said, "Someday, I'll take you on a guided tour of the whole place. The tapestries are the history of Rhomatum in ..." His voice drifted off, his hand closed painfully tight around hers. "Better yet, I'll have Nikki take you. He's the family historian." His voice drifted off.

Forgetting the tour, she dug her elbow into his side, and smiled placidly into his startled, darkening look.

"I look forward to it, Rhomandi," she said. "Soon."

His expression shifted to bewildered, and he nodded.

Teach him to forget her presence, or worse, to let his mind wander on topics to which she, as his second in this venture, ought to be privy.

They stopped at last before a simple, single door, down a corridor that felt less used than the rest of the house—the south wing, so Deymorin explained in an undertone. The butler pulled a silver bell-chain and slipped inside without waiting for permission from within. He reappeared a moment later and held the door open.

In the center of the room, like some would-be goddess holding court, an old woman sat waiting. Beneath the paint, her features proclaimed an unmistakable linkage to those busts lining the hall, some resemblance even to Deymorin, although that resemblance might simply be a product of sheer size. She was an unusually large woman, but her big-boned frame, meant to support muscle, was covered instead with flaccid flesh; her hunched position, her mechanical chair, and arthritic hands lent her an air—or façade—of fragility.

At her back, her dainty features painted and twisted into a caricature of the old woman's superior expression, was a pale-haired piece of court decoration. Funny: change the clothing styles, the manner, and numerous other minor social variables, and the type was still recognizable—and hardly worth the effort to ignore.

Anheliaa, she'd expected, and the court flower was undoubtedly the leech Deymorin wanted to detach from his younger brother. But in the corner next to a window, her hands busy with a fine silver needle, sat a second young woman whose steady gaze and quietly pretty features, and sheer unexpected presence, made her the most significant unknown element in the room, particularly when the flashing needle paused and she raised soft brown eyes to meet Kiyrstin's gaze steadily.

"Well, dunMheric," Anheliaa's harsh voice matched her features, "your timing is ... predictable. —So, where's the boy?"

Boy? What *boy*? Kiyrstin blinked her gaze free of the young woman's and shifted to Anheliaa, whose beady eyes scanned her, then peered beyond Deymorin to the door.

"Anheliaa," Deymorin said, "I'd like you to meet—"

"Your shepherdess?" The old bat interrupted rudely. "Looks more like a chicken farmer."

Something snapped within her, Something decidedly less than sociable. She shook herself free of Deymorin's hold, and sashayed forward, flounced down onto a divan and dragged it across the floor in scraping jerks, angling herself face to the old crone's chair. She leaned forward, grasped a dry gnarled hand, and pumped it vigorously. "Name's Kiyrsti, Auntie Aneeleeahr. Ain't no cause t' stand on ceremony, now is there, bein' as we're t' be fam'ly an' all. Ain't that so, Deymio-luvvie?"

Deymio-luvvie made his choking noise; she smiled confidingly up at the crone; the crone, with a grunt of pain, jerked her hand free and glared up at Deymorin.

"Bear with 'im, Liaa-dearie, he's been a touch under th' weather-like." She fluffed her skirts, the seam gave another finger's-breadth and feathers drifted free of the folds. "Oh, dearie-me." She two-fingered one and blew it in Deymio's direction with a simpering giggle. "Trust me, dearie, we'll get 'long famous, promise 'ee. This—" Another feather drifted free. "—warn't nothin' but a bit o' misunderstandin' in th' market on th' way t' visit yer sweet sel'. Promise 'ee."

Anheliaa's expression stalled somewhere between shock and outrage; the pouf-piece beside her ... well, who really cared? But over in her corner, the unknown woman's mouth twitched, though she ducked her head to hide the fact.

"DunMheric, I want this ... *creature* ... gone from my sight. Immediately."

"Oh, I don't think so, Anheliaa." Dropping down beside her, Deymorin put his arm around her and buried his head in her chicken-fluffed hair to whisper: *Easy on, shepherdess.* But laughter quivered his breath and her hair. "She's a very clever shepherdess, and," his head came up, his voice hardening, "after all, I have you to thank for throwing us together."

"Me?" Anheliaa's face took on a considering look. "Ah. And how *was* your trip, nephew? Did you find it enlightening?"

"Extremely."

"Good. Pleasantries are over now. Marry whom you will. Nikki has provided me my heir."

Deymorin tensed. That *feeling* returned tenfold. But his voice, when he spoke, radiated calm indifference.

"Has he now? I *have* been gone a while—longer than I thought. Where is the unhappy child?"

"Here." Anheliaa ... caressed, there was no other word for it, the stomach of the woman standing silently beside her chair, and the *feeling* went away.

For the first time in this odd game of unpleasantries, Deymorin deigned to notice the woman. "Lidye, isn't it? Charmed. You couldn't snag me, so you settled on my poor little brother. Not quite up to your weight, was he?"

"He managed, dunMheric." The woman's voice was everything that set Kiyrstin's teeth on edge. Top-lofty, overly controlled, overly sweet, overly everything. And she stroked her own corseted stomach. "As Anheliaa said."

Deymorin pulled himself up, a formidable presence even seated as he was. "Normally, madam, I don't stand on ceremony. In your case ... I suggest you remember who I am and address me accordingly."

An arch smile spread over her perfectly pink mouth. "But I did, dunMheric. *I* am the next Rhomatum ringmaster. The child I bear will be the greatest master of all time. My Nikki is the Rhomandi now ... and Princeps. You'll find the adjustments legally entered in the City ledgers."

"Ledgers, hell. Nikki would never agree to such an arrangement. *Khyel* would never—"

"Why do you *think* Nikki married me?" the blonde confection asked. "Loyalty? Obedience? Or perhaps, dare I suggest, because he coveted the title? And brother Mikhyel filed the papers, *Deymio-luvvie.* As to your personal claim, not to mention your lack of official involvement ... well, I doubt you'll find any opposition to the change in Council. You've been absent so long, after all. ..."

There followed a silence, Deymorin processing that information in ways she couldn't know, could only sense in the slow tightening of his hands into fists. She reached out and insinuated her fingers into one of those fists, which seemed to break the spell.

"So this is how you win, Anheliaa," he muttered.

"I don't win, boy," Anheliaa answered, and from her tone, Kiyrstin could almost believe she meant it. "I accomplish what's necessary and best for the City."

"And what about what's best for my brother?"

"He's content enough."

"Is he? Then why isn't he here with his not-so-blushing bride?"

"Oh, leave him be, dunMheric. He's playing the hero. Gone off with an army to save you."

"Where?"

"Has he gone?" She shrugged. "Who knows? Don't worry. Once he discovers how you've duped him, he'll come running home with his tail tucked. You can exchange adventure tales then, and you can go back to playing in your dirt."

"How *I've* duped him?"

"He thinks you're in dire straits. Has convinced himself I've designs on your life."

"And you hadn't?"

"I wanted you gone, boy. Out of the way. Your life was—*is* . . . irrelevant." Her gnarled hand made another vaguely obscene tour of that stomach at her side. "I've got what I needed."

"So you just let him go? Just like that?"

"He might have been right. And it occurred to me you might be useful, if you'd calmed down. You just might have some supporters to whom your opinions matter."

"So he went with your blessing?"

Anheliaa shrugged.

"Is that why he had to outfit a handful of retired light-watchman with Armayel stock?"

"If he'd shown up with my Guardsmen, he wouldn't have gotten very far with you, now would he?"

Deymorin's brow wrinkled—he really didn't play these games well, his feelings were written much too clearly on his features. He was wondering now if this younger brother had political notions he didn't know about. Wondering were his own goals here any longer worth the risks.

Kiyrstin was tempted, under the circumstances, to step in for him, to play her own cards early and put Anheliaa on the defensive. To ask Anheliaa about the Mauritum spy she'd hired to eliminate Deymorin. A cutpurse whose veracity Kiyrstin no longer doubted: she'd seen murderous hatred before, and that was unquestionably the look Anheliaa turned on her nephew.

But she hadn't properly prepared her forces for this meeting. She'd been too tired to think clearly and had wasted too much time arguing instead of exchanging information, and she really didn't want to spring such knowledge on Deymorin in front of the enemy, so she retained a hold on her tongue—at least for the moment.

"Enough of this," Anheliaa snapped. "Since you've elected to return on your own, the least you can do is make yourself useful. Where's the boy and his cursed machine?"

Zandy. That *boy* was Zandy. How could she know about Zandy? Unless she and Garetti *were* in contact. *Close* contact. Close *friendly* contact. Which would mean, she should know about Garetti's escaped wife as well.

"I haven't the least notion what boy or what machine you're talking about," Deymorin said, though his tell-tale face said otherwise.

"I *saw* him, dunMheric, in that same brothel where you and this *creature* were coupling like animals."

"Brothel?" Deymorin repeated, and this time his face mirrored confusion. "What brothel?"

But that was a mere detail. Anheliaa said she'd *seen* them, and Deymorin said she could have been watching them through the rings. It was possible Anheliaa was just—how had Deymorin had put it?—casting blind and hoping they'd snap, using that expressive face of Deymorin's to gage her distance, but from her face and voice, Kiyrstin didn't think so.

"That brat and his cursed machine must be destroyed, nephew," Anheliaa declared. "Now, where *are* they?"

Kiyrstin controlled an urge to destroy something, or someone, rather more immediate. "You disgusting old pervert. And you call *me* a creature. *Saw us,* did you? And you want to destroy a child and his toy just to amuse yourself? Deymorin was right. I wouldn't allow Zandy anywhere *near* you."

Deymorin cursed softly and she turned to face him.

"Relax, JD. She's playing with you. With me. She *knows* about us all. Zandy, his encapsulator—everything. What's she going to do? Have us killed? Flogged? Incarcerated? I don't think so. Not after that entrance and all those folk you promised to see this afternoon. Not with the city primed for yet another—" She primped her feather-laden coiffure. "—spectacular wedding."

Which declaration silenced them both, aunt and nephew, for an instant. So what if it wasn't quite true? It was close enough to make the old hag think twice. But:

"The boy's not here, then." Anheliaa flung a stiff-necked glance at her blonde-headed incubator. "I *told* you such precautions were unnecessary. I'd have *known* if they'd brought that thing into the City with them."

"Better to be certain, Anheliaa. Better to protect the rings. The ramifications—"

"Enough!"

The blonde woman bit her lip on whatever else she planned to say, but tossed her head defiantly.

"Beware the tone you take with me, girl. It's not too late to replace you."

"I'd still have the child."

"Don't depend on it."

The woman's hands crossed protectively over her stomach, her head dipped in a subtle shift from insolence to respect.

Kiyrstin scanned the fluffy creature deliberately, and said, in a thoroughly audible whisper: "*This* is your next ringmaster, Rhomandi? Perhaps I *should* return home. Another few years and Garetti will own Rhomatum anyway." She let her voice trail off significantly, smiling, closed-mouthed, into the fluffy blonde's indignation and Anheliaa's suddenly undivided attention.

Beside her, Deymorin was a loud silence.

"Who are you, girl?" Anheliaa asked abruptly.

"Deymorin's affianced wife," she returned without hesitation, and the noisy silence choked.

"You're no shepherdess. Nor even farm wench."

"Prostitute," Lidye said through her nose, and flinched as Anheliaa backhanded her bare arm, heavy rings drawing blood from the fair maid's tender white skin.

"At least prostitutes' clients get their money's worth. Can you claim as much?"

"Hush, both of you," Anheliaa hissed. "Where are you from, woman?"

She folded her hands in her lap, and said nothing.

"Well?"

"You told me to hush. I was obeying my—" She scanned Anheliaa with deliberate impudence. "—superior."

"Impertinent."

"But then, you are unspeakably rude, so I suppose that makes us well-matched, if not precisely even."

"You try my patience."

"Good!"

Deymorin's hand clamped on hers. "Enough of this." He stood and pulled her up beside him. "Farewell, Anheliaa."

"Leaving so soon? How sad."

"I'll be back. —Eventually."

"Ah. Bringing me the boy?"

"I'm going to find Nikki."

"And *then* you'll bring me the boy."

"Actually . . . no."

"You must, Deymorin!"

He laughed harshly. "I had something rather different in mind."

"What?"

"If you know about Alizant and his machine, you *know* what. If not . . . you'll find out."

"Deymorin, *no*! You mustn't . . ."

Desperation sat strangely on that brittle voice. Deymorin's head tilted.

"Mustn't . . . what, Anheliaa?"

"That machine. It *must* be destroyed. Where is it?"

Deymorin laughed. "Really, Anheliaa. Do you honestly expect an answer?" All laughter faded from his voice. "I'm not at all surprised you fear it. You're already barred from being a god—Darius saw to that—and this would make you . . . ordinary. One resource among many. Do you really think I'd destroy such a gift from the gods? Find it yourself. Destroy it yourself." He pulled Kiyrstin toward the door. "If you can."

"Rhomandi, stop!"

He paused. His hand fell from her elbow, and he turned ever so slowly.

"You heard correctly," Anheliaa said. "And you can be again, if you take proper responsibility at last."

"What are you talking about?"

"That machine *cannot* coexist with the nodes, Deymorin. If it *is*, as this ... friend of yours claims, from Mauritum, *think* what Garetti might intend. Don't you see? It's the source of these destructive weather patterns your farmers have been so concerned over."

"What do you know about it?"

"Do you honestly think this is the first time anyone has tried to duplicate the power of the rings? We've had two rather spectacular disasters at Gartum and Shatum in just the last thirty years."

Deymorin frowned. "I never heard—"

"Of course you didn't! That machine tames *lightning,* you fool! Do you think I'll spread such information about? Some other simpleton who shares your idiotic fantasies will start distributing them like toys. Rings, boy, the valley would go up in a fireball."

Deymorin's eyes flickered to Kiyrstin, worried, uncertain.

"Deymorin, I don't know," she said in answer to that look, because Anheliaa offered a frighteningly sound argument. "I honestly ..."

His hand found hers and tightened in warning.

"I've felt that monster like a dust mote in the eye for months," Anheliaa hissed, and her eyes narrowed, never wavering from their faces. "*You* know where it is. *You* control its creator. You want everything as it was—"

"No!"

"Shut up, Lidye. —You destroy that thing, dunMheric, bring me its pieces, *and the boy,* and we'll negotiate. Whatever you want—for your brothers, for yourself ... even to this *creature* for wife."

"Not the boy, Anheliaa. He's not the creator. Only a messenger."

"Forget the brat! Just bring the damned machine to me—now!"

Deymorin's breath came and went in harsh gasps. Temptation. Gods, it must be killing him. And if Anheliaa, sweet Maurii save them, was right, perhaps they *should* let the machines go.

She pressed his hand and said, "Anheliaa, let me talk with him."

"Why should I trust you? And why should the Rhomandi listen?"

"I brought Zandy to him. I asked him to help us. Let us talk . . . alone."

Once again, Anheliaa's attention rested firmly on her.

"Have we met?"

"Never."

"Are you quite certain?"

"I've never left my home city."

"And where is that? Who are you *really*?"

"Prostitute." Lidye's prissy voice interrupted.

"Lidye, one more utterance and you'll be stuck in the betweens—permanently. Well, you who are not a shepherdess? What—and—who—are you?"

"Mauritum." She smiled tightly, and played her final card in a very familiar game. "Name's Kiyrstine romGaretti— Garetti's wife, exiled because I attempted to murder him, an attempt which unfortunately failed. You dropped your nephew on my head while I was bathing. While I appreciate the gift, you could have taken a bit better care of the merchandise. He required extensive bodily repair. I thought perhaps I'd give you the chance to make it up. Possibly the chance at inside information of Mauritum Tower. But now that I've met you . . . well, why don't you think about it, Anheliaa dear? Perhaps you'll change your tune to something a bit more . . . friendly. But we are in a bit of a rush, so make that soon, Anheliaa, will you? Very, *very* soon. —JD?" She tucked her arm through his elbow. "Shall we?"

It was a large divan on which he sat, whose cushions seemed wonderfully kind to his old, bruised bones. Deymorin realized that, when he came aware enough to realize anything. The head resting heavily in his lap stirred, a wandering, seemingly absentminded hand brushed his knee, and wandered higher, and he caught it, kept it from climbing too high, having that much sense remaining.

"Shepherdess?" he asked without opening his eyes.

"Mm–mm–mm."

"Where the hell are we?"

"Council Hall."

"Why?"

"You said you wanted to see your brother."

"Oh. Yeah." He yawned, blinked his eyes clear, forcing himself awake. "Rings, she had me scared for a moment."

"When she mentioned Nikki's child?"

"Mmmm-hmmm."

"Thought you'd been gone for years, did you?"

"Something like." He let his hand meander across her cropped hair, picking bits of feather free. "Knew better, of course. Tonio ... Gari ... everything pointed to last fall, still ..."

"Once memories become suspect, it's hard to trust any of them?"

"Quite. Thanks."

"Any time, Rags." She yawned widely and rubbed her nose into his thigh. "Any time ..."

There was a hospitality spread with tea, possibly even wine, on a tray along the far wall. Tempting. But wine would most certainly tip him over into about three days' sleep, and the far wall, at the moment, might as well be in Mauritum.

"Thought I had it figured. Come here, find out where Nikki went, get his marriage annulled. All that's changed, now."

"Funny how a little thing like a title doesn't mean much until it's been snatched away, isn't it?"

"How'd you know?"

"Magic, Rags."

"Female magic, I'd believe. Hypocrite that I am, I was willing to throw the damned inheritance away in a grand hell-with-you-all gesture, but I wasn't prepared—never even seriously considered Anheliaa's legal finagling."

Kiyrstin chuckled and her hand began wandering again. "Always knew you were naive, JD."

He snorted, and grabbed her hand, holding it tight, letting his head fall back against the seat cushions.

"Who was the woman in the corner?"

"Woman? —Oh, Anheliaa's servant. Name's—" Memory took a bit to sort, but he found it: "Mirym. Nice girl. Mute. Not sure where she's from, but she has a healthy sense of the ridiculous. Thought, once upon a time, she and Nikki might be a pair, but ..."

"Hmph," was her noncommittal response. Tired, she was, as he was tired.

Nikki, married and—Princeps? Could Lidye be right?

Had the lad gone ambitious on him? If so, did *he* really want to stand in the boy's way? He had, after all, been ready to give it all up before he'd entered that room.

As for Mikhyel, well, he'd know soon enough. A man had to wonder where his brothers resided in the picture. Man wanted to wait to make his decisions until he knew.

Man who'd been this long with no sleep wanted only to close his eyes and let that absentminded hand wander ... or perhaps not so absentminded.

"Rings, shepherdess, not here."

She chuckled, and the hand retreated, tucked under her chin.

"Deymio, there's something I've been meaning to tell you ..."

But whatever she had been meaning to tell him was lost behind the darkness of his eyelids.

The white-painted fences of Darhaven's pastures spread out below them and Nikki sent a message back through the line that they were almost there, rousing a weary cheer, understandable, considering how early he'd had them up; nonetheless, he was in a hurry, and set them at a canter down the final stretch of road.

But something felt wrong, and slowly he dropped the pace back to a trot, a jog, and finally a slow, deliberate, walk.

"Is everything all right, Master Nikki?" Ben came up beside him to ask, and he nodded to the pastures on either side.

"They're empty. . . . They should be full this time of year. Mares and foals ... they should have the two- and three-year-olds out taking ground work. Something's wrong, Ben. Something's very ..." He stopped altogether. Nerves crawling, though common sense suggested any number of innocuous explanations.

On the other hand, they hadn't heard from Darhaven for months. If Deymorin *was* here night before last as Mikhyel insisted, it was possible ... things ... had changed. Deymorin could be here ...

And he could be in danger.

Brohs be not ... your place be there ...

They'd searched and searched, but found no trace of the woman, and one was forcibly reminded of stories about

... visitations in the forest. Even Darius, in his notes, had mentioned them, and that their cryptic wisdom was often worth heeding. . . .

"Ben," he said in an undertone, "tell the men to keep close and stay alert. I don't like this."

They approached the house in deceptively loose formation, made it all the way to the front approach without sign of any activity, in the barn or the house.

"Ben," Nikki said, and: "—Parli, you two come with me. The rest of you . . . keep those firearms cocked."

He slid down, settled his own pistol in his pocket and walked up to the door, pulled the bellchain, and waited. And waited.

An exchange of uneasy glances later, he pulled again. And waited.

He'd only been here twice without Deymorin—once with Mikhyel, when everything had been uneasy and strange, and once, alone and unannounced, hoping to find Deymorin—and Deymorin, unquestioned owner of Darhaven, simply walked in. He didn't know whether to be alarmed at the delay, or . . .

The door opened.

"Master Nikaenor! What a surprise." It was Tonami who opened the door: another strangeness. "Please, come . . ." And looking past him: "All those men? Are they with you?"

Nikki nodded.

"Oh, dear. Do you plan on staying, then?"

"Depends. Tonio, is Deymio here?"

"Your brother? He hasn't been here in months, you know that."

A lie. That was an outright lie. And Tonio never called him Nikaenor, and Tonio shouldn't be opening doors. . . .

"Deymio?" an unfamiliar voice said from the darkness inside and a hand materialized on Tonio's shoulder, and a pleasant-looking man with a somewhat hawkish face appeared beside the valet. "Did you say Deymio?"

Tonio stiffened, not altogether welcoming of that hand. But Tonio said, steadily enough: "Lord Nikaenor, this is Vandoshin dunGarshin, he's a—"

"Master Merchant out of Mauritum, son." The stranger smiled broadly, and dipped his head, as he'd heard they greeted one another in Mauritum. "Dealer in the strange and wonderful, taking advantage of the new market the treaty has made for us."

Nikki returned the foreign gesture hesitantly, then asked: "Jumping the flag a bit, aren't you?"

DunGarshin smiled easily. "Feeling out my customers, son ... doing a bit of market measuring so when the final signatures are drawn, I'm ready to roll wagons across Persichi Pass."

"I see...."

"But did I hear you mention a man called Deymio?"

"Why?" Nikki asked cautiously.

"Just that it's an unusual name. I chanced to meet a man who called himself that, some time since. Large, well-made fellow, with a limp."

"Where?"

"Out beyond Persitum."

"Beyond the node itself?" Despite himself, dismay crept through. Anheliaa had said the room was along the leys somewhere, and one had to wonder if perhaps Mikhyel was wrong.

And it did *sound* like Deymorin....

A trip through the pass would be tortuous this time of year, considering the mud, and the marginal roadways. Even the leyroad was comparatively underdeveloped, Persitum being the one direct link to Mauritum. And they couldn't take it. Not carrying firearms.

And in the next breath, he chastised his own gullibility. This dunGarshin, who just happened to be here, where Mikhyel insisted Deymio was night before last, just happened to have met Deymio the far side of Persichi Pass? Somehow, he tended to think perhaps this man was being less than completely truthful with him.

"I'd like to hear more of this Deymio you met," he said, forcing a smile, hoping he appeared credulous, "but first I've a lot of hungry, tired horses to see to. —Tonio, I could use some help. Where's Dal? Out in the stables?"

"Dal took the stock to summer pastures."

"So soon? Weren't some of the foals a bit young?"

Tonio shrugged. "He said something about thin pickings here ..."

Another outright lie. They cycled pastures here, and some hadn't been touched yet this spring.

"Well, then, there should be plenty of stable space. We'll just take the horses down to the barns. —Tonio, why don't you come along, while I take care of the horses, I'll tell you all about the wedding."

"I don't—"

Hand again on Tonio's shoulder, Vandoshin interrupted, saying solicitously, "Tonio here is recuperating from a severe influenza, young m'lord. He's probably much too self-effacing to admit as much to a man of your station, but, I'm certain you'll agree, exposing himself to the outside air might be . . . less than salubrious."

"You take the men and horses to the stable, Master Nikaenor," Tonio said, "I'll get the kitchens started on food and—and lodging—"

"Going to let them all sleep in the kitchen?" he teased, gently, trying to rouse some telling response. But Tonio only said absently . . . "I'm not certain where we'll put them . . ."

"Tonio, don't worry!" Vandoshin said jovially. "My men can move their lazy carcasses out to the stables."

"Your men?" Nikki asked, and Vandoshin waved his concerns aside with a flip of his hand. "Not to worry, young sir. Just a handful. I wouldn't dare travel unprotected. I've my samples, after all. Tell you what, while poor Tonio sorts this out, I'll go down with you. Show you the samples I've brought with me . . ." He slipped past Tonio, slid his arm through Nikki's and urged him down the stairs. "Tell me, now, what would you like to know about your brother . . . ?"

"Nikki! Rings curse you, fry, don't be an idiot."

Deymio was muttering in his sleep again.

And wiggling.

Which made him a most uncomfortable pillow. Kiyrstin sighed and hauled herself upright. There was no one else in this sitting room; Deymorin said petitions to this Council were submitted in written form. Civilized, to her way of thinking. She'd seen all too many decisions in Mauritum swayed because of the gender or appearance of the petitioner.

Poor Zandy hadn't had a chance.

Deymorin was still muttering, like he'd started muttering in the middle of her warning about Van's assassin-spy. She doubted he'd taken in a word of it. Typical.

At least he didn't appear inclined to violence. So she tugged on his sleeve, pulling him down into her lap, whispering to him to shut up and rest.

He mumbled something and buried his face in her skirts.

There could be little question the man had met Deymorin. He even mentioned the red-haired woman . . . called her Kiyrstin, said she was a tavern-wench plying her trade at a leyside tavern on the outskirts of Persitum.

". . . a most accommodating young woman," Vandoshin said, with a hint of ribald laughter in his voice. "I'd have been tempted myself, if she hadn't shown such a preference for Deymio. Why, I couldn't say. Possibly some misplaced sense of maternalism."

"Why would she feel that? Deymorin's hardly a child."

"Oh, but he arrived on her doorstep naked as the day he was born, not a copper to his name . . . and such a good-looking man, with so endearing a manner. How could any woman resist?"

Another hint that rang disturbingly true: Mikhyel had said Deymorin's clothing was left behind. He knew the ring had been—that lay secure against his chest, awaiting Deymorin's finger.

Brohs be not . . .

Enough to make a man's skin crawl—and hope the men were keeping pistols at the ready.

He did note that they stabled their horses by pairs, one man always standing at the open door to a stall, casually, but openly prepared. Following their example, he cared for his own and Ben's, chatting with Vandoshin all the while.

Ben sat beside the stall door, making bland conversation.

"Van?" Another stranger appeared in the barn doorway, paused, and said, "Well, well, well. Perks was right, we *have* got company."

"I believe you've got that slightly backward," Nikki said and stepped up out of the stall, pulling his gloves off. "Name's dunMheric. My family owns this place."

"You don't say . . ."

"Bari, that's enough," Vandoshin said, and stepped up behind him, close, as he'd done with Tonio.

Nikki fought off the desire to flinch away, thinking perhaps it was cultural differences, perhaps Mauritumin just tended to stand that close.

"*We* are the guests in this house, and Tonio assures me Nikki, here, is indeed Rhomandi's brother. So watch your manners, or he might kick us out."

Bari stepped through the door ... and others fell in behind him. Several others. Numbers near equalling his small force. And among them—he shot a glance at Ben, received an affirming nod—was a face he'd never forget.

A cutpurse whose blade had been Mauritum-made. . . .

He stepped away from Vandoshin and drew the heavy revolver from his pocket. And of a sudden, at the door to each stall, were two ex-guardsmen, also with pistols in hand.

"What's this, boy?" Vandoshin asked, and Nikki nodded toward the cutpurse. "Strange company you keep, Mauritum."

"Which one, lad? I picked up many companions along the way. I don't tend to ask their politics."

"Perhaps you should."

"And perhaps, from now on, I shall. But please, boy—" Vandoshin took a step toward him, and he backed further, into the edge of the stall door. One foot slipped in, jarring his gun-hand and Vandoshin held up both hands, palms out, face mockingly alarmed.

"Where's my brother?" Nikki demanded, brushing an inquisitive horse-lip away from his ear. "And don't tell me Persitum. He was *here* two nights ago."

"And how could you know that? How should I?" Vandoshin gestured broadly, turning his back on Nikki, as though he considered himself in no danger whatsoever—at least from Nikki. His hands swept the air to include all his men, then fell to his side. "We just arrived yesterday."

"So you claim—"

The horse, impatient with his lack of attention, shoved him between the shoulders. Hard.

Vandoshin stepped forward, a hand rising as if to help. Ben yelled, *M'lord*! and jumped between them.

An explosion happened; Ben flew backward into the stall and dropped to the straw, a surprised expression on his face. In the runway: Vandoshin, an amazingly small, smoking pistol in his hand.

"Damn you!" Nikki cried and leapt for him.

"Councillor Betrissim, it's just not that simple." Mikhyel leaned one hand on the table and pressed the bridge of his nose with the other, trying to assuage the physical headache that had plagued him all morning. Assuaging the human headaches was more difficult. "Once the land has been drained, it will still be years before it's ready to work again, unless—"

"Unless what? We spend yet *more* tax funds on these people?"

"Minimal, I assure you." He dropped his hand and forced his aching body to stand straight. "The land will be soured. It wants—"

"What? Honey poured over it? We might as well *buy* the produce elsewhere."

"No, Councillor. What it needs, we manufacture right here. We just need the roads improved for heavy vehicles, and clearance across the leys for—"

"This is ridiculous. Out with it, man. What is this precious commodity?"

"Manure," Mikhyel said through clenched teeth, and into Betrissim's blank face: "Cattle and horse and pig excrement." And as his head seemed to explode: "*Shit,* you simpleto—"

A heavy blow to his left shoulder spun him around and up against his chair.

He caught himself on the arm, squeezed his eyes closed and fell into the cushions, pressing his palms to his eyes, distantly surprised when his arm worked, the blow had been that powerful.

Betrissim was yelling, Gransiddi was yelling back at Betrissim and someone was bending over him, asking what was wrong.

But he didn't know. He clamped a hand to the throbbing shoulder—it wasn't Betrissim's doing, he was too far down the table, and Farnichi, to his left, wouldn't. He brought his hand away, startled to find it clean, expecting blood, expecting a knife—tempers driven to assassination.

Outside the Chamber doors, someone was yelling: a painfully familiar voice calling for—

Nikki. Curse the radical . . . *Nikki.* And in that instant he realized Nikki was the source of the pain.

And that voice . . .

Mumbling excuses, he forced himself out of the chair, pushed his way past angry voices and solicitous hands alike, escaping out a door a footman opened and (at his hasty signal) closed behind him.

And then he was in the waiting room, where, tanned and healthy and angry, a bedraggled, redheaded female hanging onto his arm, was his older brother.

"Well, Deymio," he said, forcing the words past a pain-tightened throat, "home at last, are you?"

He was prepared for Deymorin's slow rise to his feet, the angry growl in the deep voice as his brother asked: "Where is he, Mikhyel?"

No need to ask who—Deymorin's face said he'd felt the same fear and pain that was hazing his own thinking. But he had no answer. Could only stand there, one hand to a chairback, swaying with the pain bursting in his head like bolts of lightning.

He was prepared for the anger. . . .

"Curse you, Barrister, what have you done with him?"

He wasn't prepared for Deymorin's headlong attack.

"Dammit, Rags, *stop it!*"

A blow to his ear rocked him sideways, but Deymorin held on grimly, rolled back atop his brother and tightened his fingers on the unresisting flesh between his hands, pouring all the pain, all the frustration, and all the uncertainty of the past ten years into that grip.

Mikhyel's face, what of it wasn't flushed red, had turned blue, and drool ran a clear stream through the red on his chin.

He'd long since ceased to struggle.

"You *idiot!*"

Water.

Iced.

And flowing down his neck.

Red hair between him and his brother's face. Pain in his wrist. Sharp enough to break through the fog of fury, pain, and that inner sense that screamed accusations of betrayal at Mikhyel.

He cursed and let go his brother's skinny neck. The next

instant, a velvet-and-lace-covered shoulder slammed his chest, rolling him back and off Mikhyel's feebly-twitching body.

His back struck the floor, his head did, and Kiyrstin dropped onto his stomach, forcing what breath remained out of his lungs. She sat there, one hand flat on his chest, the other poised, ready to strike.

"Well?" she demanded.

"Get the hell off me," he got out on a last gasp, inhaled again and: "Let me finish him."

From somewhere toward his feet, came a shuddering, whimpering gasp after air: Mikhyel. Still alive, then. Dammit.

The nightmare remained. Nonspecific, now he was awake. Only the residue of pain and fear, and, most clearly, the sense of betrayal. Khyel knew where he'd gone—had *advised* him where to go. . . .

No. Not him. Nikki. Advised *Nikki* where to go. And Nikki had been attacked—blamed that attack on Mikhyel . . .

Who denied it with painful intensity, while blaming himself anyway.

Slowly, Deymorin sorted out the kaleidoscopic impressions, realized they were Nikki's mixed with his own and, he reluctantly admitted, Mikhyel's.

"Let me up," he said, and her hand grasped his ice-water-dampened chin, forcing him to face her narrow examination.

"Sane?" she demanded.

He shrugged—or what passed for a shrug when lying flat on one's back.

"You'll not attack him again?" And when he set his jaw to avoid answering: "Don't be a fool, JD. How can he tell you anything if he's dead?"

"Let him up, mistress." Mikhyel's voice said in a hoarse, unsteady whisper. "Please." And Mikhyel's face appeared beyond her shoulder: pale, now, rather than blue, and red about the neck, where Deymorin's hands had gripped, and at the mouth where Mikhyel dabbed with the back of one shaking hand.

Kiyrstin eyed Deymorin rather doubtfully, and asked Mikhyel: "You're sure?"

Mikhyel nodded. And swayed, his eyes closing, a hand

grasping for support where a chair, kicked over during their fight, should have been.

Kiyrstin leaned, never minding the move crushed *his* kidneys, and caught Khyel's frantically searching hand, then with a final, tortuous bounce, she left him to kneel at Mikhyel's side and wrap a supportive arm around his shoulders.

Leaving him to curse and nurse his own injuries.

Damned traitoress.

He rolled gingerly upright—if she hadn't broken a rib in that assault, it hadn't been for want of trying, and turned his wrist to the light. Matching set of teeth marks, top and bottom, oozing red and bruising already.

"You'd better not be rabid," he said sourly.

"Serve you right if I were, you overgrown—"

"Mistress," Mikhyel's hoarse whisper interrupted. "Deymio, I'm sorry, I didn't mean to—"

"For what? *She's* the one who bit me."

"Plenty of cause, JD."

"Fine. So I was a bit . . . out of control. Does that mean you had to dismember me?"

"Just get on your feet, Rags, and give us a hand here."

He groaned and moaned his way to his feet, then reached a hand down to help his brother, figuring Kiyrstin could damnwell fend for herself. But as happened, he had his hands more than full with Mikhyel, who swayed ominously and clutched at his arm.

"Get me out of here, Deymio," he hissed, "Before that argument breaks and someone comes to check what's keeping me."

"Out, where?"

"H–home." Mikhyel doubled over. "Gods, *please,* Deymio."

Mikhyel was weak, and growing more so by the instant, a condition, he realized, now the blinding haze of Nikki was gone, owing very little to their fight. Mikhyel was thin, wasted—not at all the man he'd seen threatening Anheliaa's rings six months ago.

Kiyrstin soaked a napkin from the overturned hospitality tray in tea (having emptied the ice bucket over him), and dabbed the blood from Mikhyel's face, drying it with a second napkin. When she pronounced him fit enough to avoid attracting questions, they made their way to the floater dock and the Rhomandi private cab.

"Deymorin," Mikhyel whispered, clutching his hand to ensure his attention, "he—he went to Darhaven. He'd *be* there now. Oh, *gods*—" he shuddered, clasped his free hand to his shoulder, and strangely, Deymorin felt a twinge in his own shoulder.

"Khyel, what is it? What the hell's happening to us?"

"D–don't know, but it's him, Deymio. Nikki's—*Gods!*"

Mikhyel contracted into a tight, shuddering ball, nearly rolling off the seat, *would* have, if not for Kiyrstin's jumping across to steady him. Between the two of them, they got him unwound and Deymorin clasped him tight, while Kiyrstin brushed his hair back from eyes squeezed tight with pain and leaking tears.

"Khyel, for gods sake," Deymorin whispered, feeling more helpless than when Kiyrstin had had him staked out for the wolves, "tell me what I can do!"

"D–don't know . . . *Ah—Dammit!*"

Shuddering breaths became shuddering sobs, everything he did seeming to make it worse.

"Can you hold him?" he asked Kiyrstin, who nodded, and slid her arm around Khyel.

At the back of the car, through a direct access panel to the pedaller, Deymorin murmured: "Cut the travel time up the hill in half, and I'll triple your week's wages in a tip."

The floater surged forward.

When he returned to Kiyrstin's side, Mikhyel seemed much improved, sitting on his own and somewhat shame-faced.

"I can't imagine what that was all about, Deymio. Sorry to—"

"Rings, boy, it's hardly necessary—"

"He should be apologizing to you, Mikhyel," Kiyrstin said.

But Mikhyel only looked confused. "Forgive me, mistress, I realize I owe you a fair debt—you did after all save me from my loving brother's—"

"Don't let yourself get into that trap, fry. She'll remind you of it—"

"Shut up, JD, and let the man speak."

Mikhyel, seemingly more confused than ever, asked

Kiyrstin hesitantly: "Have we met?" And before she could answer: "Deymorin's *ringdancer*."

Kiyrstin drew back. "I don't know what you're talking about. I've *never* danced the rings. Wouldn't *think* of it."

"But Anheliaa found you . . . it *was* you. Younger, perhaps—much younger—but I'm certain of it. I saw it, too . . . in the rings . . ." Mikhyel's eyes sought his, desperate for reassurance, dropped when Deymorin couldn't give him that explanation he needed, and when next Mikhyel spoke, his habitual detachment had been restored. "I must be mistaken. Deymorin, we must go after Nikki."

"You're that certain he's in danger?"

"Rings, man, aren't you?"

He had no doubt whatsoever. As in the dreams, he could *feel* Nikki's fear and pain. Less clearly now, than before, but it was still there. "How?"

"I wish I knew. I—I *feel* him . . . and you . . ." Mikhyel shook his head. For all his apparent calm, his hands were shaking violently.

"You say he left for Darhaven?" Kiyrstin asked.

Mikhyel nodded. "Anheliaa located you for Nikki using the rings. She thought you were on a leyline, but I recognized the . . . room . . . where . . ." His eyes flickered toward Kiyrstin, and his color rose.

"You're certain?" Deymorin asked.

"Not likely to forget it, am I?"

"I suppose not." He'd hoped, for a time, Anheliaa had been grasping, baiting them to *believe* she'd been able to find them off the ley, as they'd been at Darhaven. But evidently she was more talented than even she believed, had stretched the limits of the web to include the betweens. "Well, then, Darhaven is where I'm bound. We'll get you home—"

"I'm going with you!" Mikhyel said and reached for his arm to emphasize his point. But as he reached . . . or as he touched, he spasmed again in pain, and jerked back, staring wild-eyed at his hand.

"You can't sit a floater bench, brother. You certainly couldn't stay a horse."

"You're not going alone. And I wouldn't trust *any* of Anheliaa's Guard. The rest, the men loyal to you left with Nikki . . ."

"He won't be alone," Kiyrstin said, her voice weary, yet disgusted.

"Pardon, m'lady, but—"

"Don't say it, Mikhyel," Deymorin warned. "You'll regret it, trust me."

Chapter Eleven

Came a time when a body's only real option was to cling with every muscle, ignore the bruises and blisters and pray to survive the ride.

This time yesterday, Kiyrstin would have sworn nothing would get her astride a horse again in her life.

She was wrong.

But she couldn't have let Deymorin head out alone, Mikhyel was right in that. And nothing would stop Deymorin from leaving immediately, which, if they could trust Mikhyel's condition as a barometer for the other brother's physical state, was probably wise.

At least this time, she had clothing—Mikhyel's—that was marginally more appropriate to the activity—and a decidedly better fit, though the back seam was strained to its limit, beneath the pleated back of the outer coat.

At least, so Deymorin had reassured her, she'd supplied the stableboy who'd given her a leg-up his entertainment for the week.

How nice.

"Dey-ey-mo-o-r-r-r-rin," she yelled at his horse's rapidly disappearing rump, as her own beast thumped painfully downhill in its wake. Timing a gasp between thumps, she screamed: "Wait!"

She pulled back on the reins. Unlike her last mount, this creature responded with abrupt willingness, throwing her forward onto its prickly-maned neck. She grabbed frantically for any handhold available, decidedly grateful for the hand that grasped the voluminous folds covering her rear and hauled her back into balance.

"Thanks," she said on a gasp, and rearranged her coat.

"What's the problem?" Deymorin asked, his voice short.

She held up a hand in signal defeat. "I'm trying, Rhomandi. I'm honestly trying. But this creature is . . . how do

I put this? . . . sprung worse than that cart you tricked me into this morning."

"Sprung?" A smile forced its way reluctantly past the grimness. "You're just spoiled, that's all."

"Spoiled?"

The smile quirked. "My horses have, of course, far superior—er—springs."

"Of course. Just give my backside a break, will you? I know you're in a hurry, I understand that and I understand why, but—"

His hand covered hers. "I'll compromise. Downhill, we walk. Flat, we push. Uphill—you call it. Deal?"

"Since I doubt I can talk you down . . . Deal."

"Good." His hand patted hers, and his horse surged forward, taking hers with it, and for a time they travelled abreast, so close, their knees occasionally brushed.

The trail they followed was far worse than the one between Darhaven and Armayel. By midafternoon, they'd been into trees and rugged foothills, following a trail which existed only in Deymorin's vivid imagination. He'd insisted they'd make better time than following any road, ley or otherwise, and she, fool that she was, followed without question.

The sad truth was, she'd fallen disastrously in lust, if not love, with a man with a total aversion to civilization.

The side to side rhythm of the horse's downward motion worked its way into her body, setting her hips, her shoulders, her entire backbone, to swaying. The motion combined with the sound of the birds and the breeze in the branches to create a mesmeric totality. Her eyes drifted slowly shut, her head nodded forward . . .

A thud.

She jerked awake, forced her eyes open.

Deymorin's horse still moved beside hers, but the saddle was empty.

"Rhomandi?" She hauled on the reins, twisted around to scan the trail behind.

Barely visible through the encroaching undergrowth, Deymorin lay flat on his back, motionless.

"Deymio!"

She hauled at her horse's reins, pulling its head around. It objected, scrambling for footing and room on the overgrown trail, bumping Deymorin's mount, who squealed and kicked. She grabbed for its trailing reins, and sorted the two beasts awkwardly until they were both lunging back uphill. Just as she began wondering how she'd avoid stomping Deymorin once they reached him, he swayed upright, holding his head in his hands and moaning, a sight evidently so startling to the horses they stopped dead in their tracks.

Deymorin's hand came away red. His eyes raised blearily to meet hers. "How dare you be short?"

Above and a bit behind, a low branch across the trail explained volumes.

"Forget how to duck?"

"Fell asleep," he said, sourly, and hauled himself slowly to his feet, and took the rein from her hand. "Thanks."

He hauled himself even more slowly into the saddle, declaring himself fit, but for a bruised and bleeding forehead; however, as they worked their way downhill, a dazed look descended over his face, a faraway, unfocussed . . . *pain* that had nothing to do with his fall. Based on this new evidence, she began to suspect the low-lying branch was, in fact, quite innocent.

"Rhomandi," she asked, to keep him awake. "How much of that was for real?"

"How much of what?"

"Your brother's actions. Is he always so . . . theatrical?"

"Mikhyel?" His breath released in a huff. "Mikhyel is normally the coldest fish you'll ever meet. I believe his reactions were quite real. I've—" His eyes flickered toward her, frowning darkly, and he seemed to come to a decision between one blink and the next. "I've had a similar sense. . . ."

"The nightmares?"

He chewed his lip, then nodded. "At least in part. Evidently not as potent as Mikhyel's, certainly not as specific, but enough to know it's more than personal dreams."

A shiver worked its way up her back. No more strange than other stories circulated about rings and ley and adepts, but one never thought to encounter such a story at quite so *personal* a perspective.

"Deymio?"

His eyes were closed. He swayed ominously.

"Maurii! —Deymio, wake up!"

He shook his head and came back. "I—I think we'd better stop. I've pushed you farther than is at all fair."

"Gladly." She hauled on the reins.

"Not here, shepherdess. I'm not that much an ogre. There's an inn just ahead, where this trail intersects a real road."

"Inn. As in bed? Food? Maybe, dare I say, a bath?"

He laughed weakly. "All of the above, shepherdess."

Just ahead proved as misleading as most of Deymorin's estimates, and eventually, finding conversation growing tedious, she broke a twig off a passing branch and used it, when he would drift, as a switch to strike whatever portion of his anatomy was within reach, finally rousing him enough to protest:

"You'll have me black and blue from head to foot. How will you explain *that* to the innkeeper?"

"Obviously, our carriage was set upon by highwaymen. They took you by surprise, tied you up, had their way with me—"

"Poor robbers."

"Hush. But you freed yourself and chased them off—obviously killing one."

"Obviously?"

She gestured to her clothing. "Thank you, by the way, for choosing the one closest to my size and not the hulk."

"You're most welcome, I'm certain. What happened to the carriage?"

"Toppled over a cliff, don't you know? —You *do* have cliffs around here, don't you?"

"I—"

"You must. It *had* to go over a cliff—horses and all. That's why we're stuck with these ... inferior creatures."

"Stole them from the thieves, did we?"

"Naturally."

"I see."

He laughed, but the humor was short-lived. Soon, he was once again staring blankly into the forest ahead.

"What are you seeing, Deymorin?"

He blinked at her.

"When you look out there—what are you seeing?"

His eyes dropped to the reins between his fingers. "Nothing, really. *Feeling,* more like."

"Do you know what's happened to him? I mean, specifically."

He shook his head. "Only that he's hurt. And scared.

Mostly that he feels Mikhyel betrayed him. That's what I sensed first—back on the Hill."

"And why you attacked Mikhyel when you saw him?"

Deymorin nodded.

"How?"

"Does he think Mikhyel betrayed him? *I think* ..." Deymorin's brow wrinkled. "I think he believes that Mikhyel set him up. *Sent* him to meet—whatever has met him."

"And did he?"

"Of course not!"

Gut-level denial. But she had to agree, nothing she saw in Mikhyel would support such a notion.

"Can you tell where Nikki is, through this feeling?"

Another weary shake of the head. "Mikhyel couldn't either. Not for certain. And he seems to ... receive more than I do."

"Particularly when you touched him."

"What?"

"You didn't notice? When you were holding him, he was incoherent. The instant you let go, his head cleared. Perhaps that's the answer. Perhaps we should have brought him along. Tied you two together, used you as a ... Nikki-vane."

"Very funny. Besides, if Nikki's pain didn't kill him, I would."

He sounded serious.

"You're not fair to him, you know."

"Don't get me started, woman. You haven't the perspective."

"Or perhaps you're too close. Tell me, JD, you feel Nikki's pain. What do you feel from Mikhyel?"

The look he flashed at her made her heart stop. Made her wonder if he was going to jump her as he had Mikhyel. Then:

"Flat enough," he said, and his horse plunged forward. After that, she was hard put just to keep up on what seemed to her the steepest downhill stretch yet.

Deymorin, meticulous of propriety, for all the shepherdess was not, stayed in the taproom while Kiyrstin bathed. When the innkeeper's daughter, acting as a personal maid, announced her finished, he ordered dinner to be delivered to the room—her room—before taking his turn in the tub.

Separate rooms, connected by the bath. She'd refused any greater distance between them, citing his attempted desertion at Armayel as her reason ... as if leaving her at a 'tweener inn somewhere between Rhomatum and Darhaven were anything like leaving her safe in the care of his own staff.

He didn't know why the arrangement mattered to him, but he simply couldn't stand the thought of sharing a room with her now, regardless of propriety or what had passed already between them.

Because he still wanted her. So intensely, it was a physical pain. Which in itself was crazed. He was so tired, he couldn't think straight, let alone manage more athletic endeavors, but if they bedded in the same room tonight, he'd get no sleep, of that much he was certain.

And that very desire roused suspicions of what Anheliaa was up to back in that tower of hers.

Putting one thing and another together, he'd become certain Anheliaa and her rings and his brothers' bedroom activities had been a factor that other time, though he couldn't deny personal desire had also played a key role. But Anheliaa had her precious fetus. And Nikki and Khyel were currently physically incapable of acting on such designs.

Which left only his own animal instincts to blame, as he sat soaking his aching joints in the old-fashioned, freestanding tub, and if his instincts had any feeling whatsoever, they'd take a vacation. Go relieve themselves in some randy young stallion with all the springtime energy he'd long since outgrown.

If only Kiyrstin hadn't insisted on coming with him.

Likely he was a fool for pursuing the matter alone, but time was critical, and if Nikki was in trouble, if he'd found it at Darhaven, there was only one likely source.

And Vandoshin was Kiyrstin's partner.

Which fact made him a ten times greater fool to have brought her.

Which he wouldn't have, had Mikhyel not been so damned upset, so inordinately worried—which was in itself odd—and had Mikhyel not decided Kiyrstin was some sort of ally in whatever battle they were engaging and relaxed when she announced her intentions.

Anheliaa and Garetti. Vandoshin and Kiyrstin. Mikhyel and . . . who? . . . Nikki?

A man had to wonder, in his more paranoid wonderings, if they were all in league; and he discovered he didn't much care, if that were the case. If that were the case, it didn't leave much worth caring about.

Crazy. They were all . . .

"Deymorin?" Kiyrstin's voice from the door. Hesitant. As if she, too, were uncertain where matters now stood.

He lifted lead-weighted eyelids.

She was standing in the doorway, wrapped in a service-able robe, its cowl pulled up around her ears, catching drips off her ragged hair. And she was holding two pewter goblets, one lifted in mute question.

He nodded, reached without thinking. She handed it to him, keeping her eyes averted.

"Sorry," he muttered.

"You mind?" She nodded to the grooming chair, and he shrugged.

"Not much room for modesty left, is there?"

She blushed and bypassed the chair, pausing in the door-way to say, "Just wanted to tell you supper was here."

"Kiyrstin, I'm sorry. Don't go. Sit down, please."

She did, and he sank lower into the steamy warmth, un-willing to waste a single energized mote. They sipped the wine in silence. Then both began to speak at once.

He lifted his goblet in a mute toast. "Ladies first."

"I resent the classification, but I just wanted to say, I'm sorry."

"Whatever for?"

"For an excessively ill-timed joke. About you and your brother."

"And I haven't where you and Garetti are concerned?"

"Big difference, Rags. You—care—for your brothers a great deal. I didn't realize, and I am sorry."

He shrugged, there being nothing to say.

"Your turn."

"I've . . . forgotten what I was going to say."

"Well, then, I . . . Deymorin, I'm worried."

"About?"

"Your brother."

"Lord, woman, which one?"

"Nikki."

He stiffened. "What about him?"

"We were being followed—even before you joined us."

"Garetti's men?"

She nodded. "I never said anything to you. Didn't think clearly what their entrance into the Rhomatum Web might mean. Didn't really think they would bother. I assumed they were after me and Van. Now . . ."

"You're not so certain."

"If they did, if they were following us and went all the way to Darhaven . . ."

"They could have him."

And all the Darhaven folk. Damn, damn, and damn.

"A—and, Deymorin?"

"What else?"

"There was a man, Van brought him to me just before we left—I thought he was lying, but now, I'm not sure and—"

"Kiyrstin, slow up. What the hell are you talking about?"

"He said he attacked you in Rhomatum, that he got your brother, Nikki, instead. I tried to tell you earlier, but you fell asleep, and then you attacked Mikhyel, and—"

The man who kept ducking out of sight. He raised his eyes slowly to hers, hardly daring to blink. "And?"

"Deymorin, he said—" She swallowed hard. "He said Anheliaa hired him. And I just couldn't help wondering . . . if Anheliaa decides Mikhyel's the enemy . . ."

"Khyel? Anheliaa adores him—Rhomandi's hells, Anheliaa *needs* him. He's her pet Council manipulator."

"Are you certain? She's got the child, now. Perhaps you've all become irrelevant."

He set the goblet down and lifted handfuls of water to his face, striving to clear his head, a useless endeavor that ended with his face cradled in his elbow, arm propped on the tub's lip, wondering where he'd gone wrong, what he could have done differently. . . .

Hands touched tentatively, brushing his braid to one side, rubbed his neck gently when he didn't stop her. He groaned, and brought his other arm up to join the first, crossing them on the tub's edge, shutting out the world and its problems, shutting out everything but penetrating, relaxing rhythm of those strong, increasingly beloved, fingertips.

*   *   *

"Mother?" Dancer materialized running. The veils billowed. "Mother!"

But she wasn't there, not to vision, and not to that other sight.

Dancer dropped, panting, to the floor beside the Rhomandi brothers' pattern. Dancer's own anxiety and excitement sent shivers through the rapidly increasing veil.

The trials had been advanced by a week. Betania, the departing dancer, had practiced yesterday and decided it had become too dangerous, that her new procreative interests interfered too greatly for her to dance any longer.

Procreation. Children. Crazed, to Dancer's way of thinking. How could anyone choose partnering if it required giving up the dance forever?

Old age. Death. Those were acceptable reasons for quitting.

Of course, if one lost, one would never dance again, either, but Dancer didn't intend to lose tomorrow.

Tomorrow was the day. Tomorrow, all of Dancer's future would be determined.

And Mother was, as usual these days, unavailable.

Tears happened, but Dancer brushed them angrily away, and sought a clue to Mother's whereabouts in the leythium web.

The new pattern that was Mheric's sons was spreading. The solid core that was the eldest brother had gained strength and intensity: purpose and self-confidence, Dancer acknowledged rather grudgingly. The complex branching network, while orderly and actively growing, showed damage: perhaps injury to the youngest sibling, if Dancer were to hazard a guess.

But the haze that was the middle brother had shifted away from the sibling web, moving into a distant blackness, softly pulsating red edged with yellow and orange, its single fibrous link to that network pulsing red, like blood through an artery.

Poor radical. Lonely. Deserted. Self-imposed receptacle for all the pain of a web so much stronger than he alone could possibly be.

Dancer reached out, drawn to that glowing agony, and touched the haze—

*   *   *

Nikki was screaming.

The ogre had him, and there was nothing he could do, no way to stop the torture.

Khyel beat the closet door with his fists, and when his fists grew numb, beat it with his shoulder, finally throwing his whole body against the solid wood, screaming at the ogre to leave Nikki alone. That it was his fault, not Nikki's.

His fault. Whatever the crime.

Finally, he could move no more. He lay on the cold floor, a shapeless pile of broken bones, blood, and tears, and listened to Nikki scream.

Nikki didn't know where he was, couldn't the ogre hear? But the ogre wasn't asking about him. The ogre was asking about Deymorin, and Deymorin's ring. And an army. And why was Nikki here.

And there was lightning outside the door. There was light that wasn't ley and wasn't sun, and Nikki was terrified of it. Pain enveloped his arm and he bent the arm backward trying to avoid that impossible hell-glow.

Mikhyel opened his mouth to scream . . .

. . . And *something* rushed in that wasn't air. Something warm and loving. Something that swept the pain aside, and mended the bones and gave him the strength to stand.

Something that shut out the sound of Nikki's cries and told him Nikki was a man now, and could/should/would handle his own problems, his own pain.

He wanted to object, but the something wrapped around him and said, *{No more, my solemn radical. Save your strength for when your web truly needs you.}*

*   *   *

Mikhyel jolted awake, drenched in sweat.

What in the name of Darius was that? He'd had trouble enough accepting Nikki's intrusions into his rare-enough sleep. This new meddler wasn't Nikki. Wasn't Deymorin. Wasn't even Anheliaa's black shadow.

A hand touched his shoulder.

He jerked away, found Mirym staring at him in silent consternation, her hand raised as if it had been burned.

He wondered for an instant, had that intruder been Mirym, realized in the next that it was not. That the presence in the dream was no one and nothing he'd felt before.

But waking, the confused images made sense: Nikki was being tortured. Someone was asking him questions about Deymorin and Rhomatum. And beyond the door, there'd been ... light. Light that wasn't ley or sun.

Mirym's weight pressed the mattress down beside him. She supported his head, and held a glass to his lips.

He drank deeply, grateful for the fruit juice, and the sleeping draught it undoubtedly contained. Every night he tried to sleep without it. Every night, he failed.

You were in touch with Nikki again, weren't you?

Mirym's message floated in front of him. He nodded, too weak to speak.

And was Deymorin with him?

"Not yet."

You know that for certain?

He nodded.

And was the lightning machine there?

He nodded, caught himself with a jerk. "Lightning machine? What lightning machine?"

She stood up, her face blank.

"And what are you doing here?"

Dipped a curtsy, and left.

He tried to throw the covers back. Tried to follow her. But his arms, his legs wouldn't answer his demands, and before he knew to question, he was asleep.

From beyond the bathroom, a strange sound filtered into Kiyrstin's half-awake thoughts. Deymorin ... crying?

She slipped from her bed and padded her way through the bath chamber, and cracked the door into his room. Definite adult, male sobs, that hoarse, unpracticed choking sound was unmistakable.

As she paused, wondering what she should do, the sound caught on a sharp, suddenly awake breath. A long harsh-breathed pause, then:

"Rings, fry, I'm so sorry ..." The whisper rose from the darkness. "I never knew ..."

There was a thump, then, of a fist pummelling a pillow until the seams were in jeopardy. She opened the door a bit farther; light from her fading fire piercing the darkness.

A pillow flew out of the darkness, and straight at her face.

She caught it reflexively.

"What the *hell* are you doing here?"

"Deymorin, I'm ..." But damned if she was. She raised her chin and finished firmly: "Woke me up, Rags. I came here to shut you up."

She threw the pillow back at him and crossed the room to the bed.

"Get out, shepherdess," and his deep voice caught, "Can't you tell when you're not wanted?"

"So throw me out. I dare you." She sat down, caught his hand when he raised it to strike, knew she'd done right to force the issue when he collapsed back against the headboard, his hand going limp and falling to the quilted bedspread.

"More nightmares?"

Head turned toward the darkness, he nodded.

"Nikki's?"

His head turned slowly side to side.

"Khyel's?"

He bit his lip, an endearingly childish gesture she'd not have credited him.

"It was the room," he said, his voice low, strained.

"The one at Darhaven? The nursery?"

He nodded just as slowly. "I never spent much time there—was out riding with the adults almost before I could walk. With Mikhyel, it was different—at least, after Nikki was born. Before Nikki, we did everything together. After ... it seemed so strange, Mikhyel was always a clever, very serious child, almost an adult himself at nine, but after Nikki was born, he chose to stay in the nursery—refused to join the adults until after Father died. I never understood, at the time. I think, gods forgive me, I resented it, thinking he preferred Nikki's company to mine."

"And the room?"

"The day Father died, he was there. It was Mikhyel's birthday. His thirteenth. Father wanted him to join us on the hunt he'd organized for the celebration. Mikhyel declined the honor. Father got very angry. I didn't know precisely what happened. I was out helping with the horses. All I knew was I heard a lot of yelling, and then Father stormed out, red-faced and furious. Later, we discovered he'd locked Khyel in the storage closet."

"In that room?"

He nodded.

"Poor child."

"I'm ... afraid I didn't see it quite that way. Father always rode rather ruthlessly. That day, he was ... crazed. He pushed his horse at one barrier too many ..."

His voice choked.

"That's how he died, isn't it?"

He nodded. "I fear I blamed Mikhyel for his death. —Poor fry. We had to haul him out of the closet. He was this sort of broken little lump. But I couldn't really see, and no one told me, or let me near him for months. ... Rings, what must he have thought all these years?"

"I don't know, Deymorin. Can't." She slid over beside him, not touching, just to be in range, should he want her. "But I think, just to be fair—"

"I should ask him?"

She nodded.

His breath came and went in deep, shuddering waves. Then, without looking at her, he rolled into her waiting embrace.

"Get up."

Warmth, love, safety. Mikhyel resisted the pull at his shoulder to bask in the unfamiliar sensations.

"I said, wake up!"

A hand struck his face, not so hard as to constitute a blow, but definitely more than was strictly necessary.

He cursed and struggled to consciousness.

Brolucci. Anheliaa's pet captain of the Tower Guards.

"How dare—"

The captain grabbed his shoulder and pulled him out of bed, cutting his protest short.

"Get dressed," the man's voice grated on drug-sleepy eardrums. "The Lady demands your immediate attendance in the Tower."

There were four large guardsmen behind Brolucci, each one capable of forcing his compliance. No way to object. No way to avoid a confrontation which could easily mean imminent exile, if not death.

He staggered to his feet and sought clothing with numb hands.

Mirym. Her presence here last night, and the drug that

still fogged his thinking. He'd been wrong, disastrously wrong, in his judgment of her.

Cold water head to foot helped clear the fog, but worsened the shakes. He fought to steady his limbs, and by the time he was dressed, managed at least a semblance of control, though he made no attempt to braid his hair, recognizing a coordination currently beyond him and refusing to display that deficiency in front of Brolucci.

He made the trip to the lift in a cloud of Tower Guards, like some violent criminal. In the Tower, Anheliaa was waiting, with only Lidye and Mirym. Nethaalye was nowhere to be seen. Anheliaa was declaring her alliances, which included—he felt vaguely ill—Mirym.

He stood just beyond the lift, silent, waiting for Anheliaa's decree.

"Darius curse you, Bro," Anheliaa snapped, "take your hands off the boy, and get out of here."

"But—"

"I said *leave*! And don't come back until I invite you." And when the guards were gone: "Mikhyel, darling, I'm terribly sorry. Brolucci must have completely mistaken my meaning."

"I doubt that."

"Don't be that way, darling. Please, sit down, be comfortable."

"Anheliaa," his voice shook and he fought it steady, "just *do* it, will you?"

"I don't know what you're talking about," she said, irritably. "And if you don't sit down, I'll knock the feet from under you. I *hate* staring up at people."

She'd rather look down at them from her oversized chair. All the same, he sat down—before his knees failed.

"Now, Mikhyel, haven't you something to tell me?"

"The Council has been giving me a great deal of trouble regarding land appropriations for the inter-ley road system. Perhaps you'd be interested in helping me out?"

"Perhaps later, darling. Mirym here, has been telling me some most interesting observations regarding you and your brothers. Most interesting. I did wonder, when Nikki claimed to have heard something I'd told exclusively to you, darling. I very much feared that you'd begun betraying my confidences."

He swallowed hard, every thought muddled and confused, wishing she'd simply *do* whatever she'd planned, and quit playing with him.

"She also tells me that Nikaenor is with that infernal machine, now."

She paused, obviously expecting an answer. He shook his head slightly and whispered, "It was a dream, Anheliaa. Like many other dreams I've had over the years. I don't *know* about any machine!"

"But this is a very important machine, darling. A very dangerous machine, and you're going to help me destroy it, aren't you?"

His dreams knew nothing of machines, only fear and lightning that wasn't. It was *Mirym* who had mentioned a machine ... just after she drugged him. But Anheliaa didn't want to hear that. He hadn't the words Anheliaa wanted to hear. All he could do was stare at her and await the inevitable. He didn't look at the rings. Seeing wasn't necessary. The hum filling the air now told him all he needed to know.

"I'm assuming you're ignorant as to the ramifications of your relationship with your brothers, which accounts for your silence. I thought it time to bring it all out in the open. See how best to use these newfound abilities."

"It's nothing, Anheliaa. Dreams. Nothing more."

"Nothing?"

An ear-filling hum threatened balance. Behind Anheliaa, the rings were a whirring blur, and suddenly, he *was* Deymorin.

"M'lord?"

The voice whispered weakly through the undergrowth.

Deymorin pulled his horse up, scanning the bushes.

"Who's there?"

"M'lord? Please ... help ..."

And then he recognized the voice.

"Ben?" He slid down, threw the reins to Kiyrstin and swept his way through the undergrowth to where the old lightwatchman was resting, propped against a tree, a bloodied strip around his arm. "Rings, man, what happened?"

"They got him, m'lord. Must help ..."

"Easy on, old friend."

He searched the old man for wounds, but besides a few lumps and bruises, found nothing of consequence other than the arm. And when he would have bared that: "Leave it, m'lord. No sense starting it bleeding again."

"What happened? You were with Nikki, weren't you? Where is he?"

A weakly shaking hand rose to hush him.

"Not far ahead now, m'lord. Watch for him, you must. They came at us. Too many. Pistols with more than one shot . . . nothing we could do . . . Nothing. . . ."

"Easy on, Ben." He pressed the uninjured shoulder lightly, turned to find Kiyrstin already with them.

"Who was it?" she asked, and her voice was cold with anger. "Who attacked you?"

"Trader. Out of Mauritum, so he said. Name of dunGarshin. Vandoshin dunGarshin. Had a bunch of men. Waiting for us at Darhaven, they were, m'lord."

"Van." Kiyrstin spat the word out and spun on her heel. Deymorin let her leave, knowing she'd not go beyond earshot.

"What about Nikki, Ben?"

"Got shot, Deymorin. Bad one to the shoulder. Thought I'd taken the bullet, he did, but the bastard's gun had more . . . don't know how. Don't know how many it held. Careful, m'lord. Be careful. Guns don't need reloading."

"We will, Ben. But Nikki, where is he?"

"Ahead, m'lord. DunGarshin's men, they hurt him bad, wanting to know why he was there and looking for you."

"Hurt him how?"

"Knocked him around a bit, but mostly they went after that shoulder, m'lord."

"He's still alive?"

"Very much so, m'lord. They was good—aimed to hurt, not end with a carcass. But he's your very own brother, m'lord, make no doubt. Hurting bad as he was, they had to tie him hand and foot and stuff a rag in his mouth to keep him quiet in the cart, they did."

"Cart?"

"They're making a move on Rhomatum, m'lord. Have him tied up in a cart. Brought Tonio along as nurse."

"Move? With what?"

"The boy's machine, m'lord. DunGarshin, he means to use Master Nikaenor to get past the Tower Guard, where—so dunGarshin claims—the machine will destroy the Rings, unless Anheliaa cooperates."

"Cooperates? How? What does he want?"

"Dunno, m'lord. Money? Revenge, mebbe?"

"Revenge on whom?" he wondered aloud.

"Garetti," Kiyrstin hissed behind him, which made some sense. Money was the more likely goal, but he might also want to destroy all chance of Garetti securing Rhomatumin allies. Possibly set himself up as the primary contact between the two webs.

"What about the others, Ben. What happened to the other men with you?"

"Some dead. Some not. Scattered, they were, to the winds and more."

The pain was getting to Ben, his mind was beginning to wander.

"Ben, I've no one to leave here with you. Only the woman, and—"

Ben's hand fumbled for his. He grasped it and squeezed.

"Be fine, m'lord. Save the boy. Did well, he did. Tried hard. Good instincts, just like you taught him. Just didn't know about the guns."

"We'll be back, Ben. If we're free to be anywhere."

"Can reach old Talvanni's place. Got the strength for that. The boys—they was under orders to head toward Armayel. You get the boy free. Head there. Don't worry 'bout me."

"I'll be back," he said firmly, and Ben patted his hand and said past a hint of a smile, "You're a good man, dunMheric."

He squeezed the hand, and left without another word. But just before the brush closed between them, he glanced back, found Ben staring after him, still with that half-smile, his head tipped back against the tree, and from under heavy lids, his brown eyes glowed ever-so-slightly green.

"Birtram's hells!"

Anheliaa's exclamation brought Mikhyel shuddering back into the Tower.

On the rings' central sphere, a picture of the scene he'd been participant/witness to.

Green glowing eyes. Mother. The dream.

Mikhyel shuddered again.

"Who is that man?"

He shook his head, fighting giving Anheliaa any more information. Surprisingly:

"A nasty old lightwatchman," Lidye hissed. "Name of Ben. Kept pushing at the Rhomandi for an audience, when *I* needed to talk to him."

It was all beyond him—or he beyond it, conversation and Tower alike. He was with Deymorin. *Was* Deymorin riding beside his lady love in search of their brother. The woman had been crying. Angry, he thought, though the thought had no rational basis.

He tried to blink. Tried to break the spell, but Anheliaa hissed at him and he realized he couldn't move at all. Could only watch those rings spin and await the inevitable meeting on the trail. . . .

Intercept romMaurii, determine what he was after and negotiate a deal for his brother's freedom: it all seemed quite straightforward . . .

Until they rounded a bend in the road and sighted the encampment at the Boreton turnout.

RomMaurii and his men—at least three times in number as the band they'd left in the forests west of Darhaven— with wagons and horses, not all of which were Darhaven stock.

"They're Garetti's," Kiyrstin said, in a hushed voice and of the new forces.

"Those chasing you?" he asked, in the same tones, and she nodded.

"Sweet Maurii, what have I gotten you into?"

He reached across and squeezed her hand. "Not your fault, shepherdess."

But as a handful of men, including romMaurii, mounted their horses and rode toward them, romMaurii's possible goals expanded enormously. If he was still Maurii's loyal priest, still Garetti's man, he might well be after the rings themselves, either to destroy them, or to control them, and nothing Deymorin Rhomandi dunMheric could offer would counter that objective.

"Well, well, well." RomMaurii hauled on his reins, bringing the poor creature beneath him to a gagging, head-tossing halt. "Look who's come home. Kiyrstin. Just Deymio. Welcome."

On either side of the priest, large men with pistols drawn,

showed rather better horse sense. RomMaurii alone, they
could easily outrun. These others ... even were Nikki not
involved, he'd not risk his or Kiyrstin's life on any lack of
skill on the Mauritumin guards' part.

"What are you doing here, Van?" Deymorin asked,
keeping his voice casual. "I thought we had an agreement."

"Not being privy to the agreement, the men were a bit
restless when Barinni returned with the report you had
bolted—and with Kiyrstin and the boy. Shame, Just Deymio. So I thought, to keep the boys occupied, you know,
that we'd work a bit closer to Rhomatum. Make ourselves
a little more conveniently to hand."

"Quite a caravan you've amassed." He rose in his stirrups, gazing down the road at the camp. "Where'd all this
come from, priest?"

"Mostly, it's thanks to the generosity of your friend the
Rhomandi. The rest ... well, we picked it up along the
way."

"Picked up a few men as well, did you?"

"A few. But come, JD, join our little feast here. It is,
after all, of your provision—indirectly speaking, of course.
What do you say? A bit of a bite over which to discuss the
status of the agreement?"

"Why not?"

They rode toward the camp, two guards ahead, rom-
Maurii, Kiyrstin and himself abreast, and two more men
behind.

He dismounted lightly, ducked under his horse's neck to
catch Kiyrstin in his arms as she slid off. She propped her
elbows on his shoulders to stop her slide halfway down,
wrapped her arms around his neck, and whispered into his
ear, "What *are* you up to, JD?"

"Two against an army, shepherdess." He brushed his lips
across her cheek and nibbled her ear. "Keeping things
calm. Let's find the lad first."

She stared fixedly over his shoulder.

"Calm? Maybe not." Her hands tangled in his hair and
her lips pressed his, hard, possessively, openly staking her
claim—or perhaps declaring her preference.

Hard to question precise motivation when one's mouth
was the object under attack, and one's lips were taking on a
mind of their own, unmindful of the gravity of the situation.

But a man's somewhat less directly involved brain had to wonder just whom she meant to impress.

"Deymio? Kiyrsti?" RomMaurii's voice, cold and hard, interrupted.

Kiyrstin released her hold, he released his, and she dropped the remaining distance to the ground, avoiding his eyes, meeting romMaurii's glitteringly angry gaze. Enough to make a man worry, until he realized her ploy had shifted Van's scowling attention squarely onto her.

Distractingly on her.

He scanned the camp, searching for any sign of Nikki. Darhaven equipment, much of it, and several times what he'd authorized sent to romMaurii's supposed camp, evidence that sustained the worst of his fears. He only hoped the bulk of the staff had escaped before romMaurii arrived.

One horse nickered recognition at him. He laughed, and said, "Excuse me," and before the priest could object or order him stopped, he had crossed to the horse's head, Kiyrstin at his side, the priest hot on his heels.

He played with the eager nose, scratched the ears, endured a rough boot in the ribs, and said, "I trained this ill-mannered creature years ago. You'd think he'd be better mannered by now."

He slapped the muscular neck, smoothed mane hair carelessly twisted beneath the headstall, and worked his way down the horse's back, ostensibly checking the equipment. But the instant his hand touched the cart, he knew that what had truly drawn him to this particular wagon was not the horse.

"What's in here?" he asked, fingering the tarp stretched over the wagon's bed.

"Supplies." RomMaurii's reply did not invite further investigation.

"From Darhaven?" He snapped the end of a retaining rope loose. "Mind if I—"

"Actually, yes, I do mind. Step away, Rhomandi."

He froze, hand on the next loop. "Ah, who told you?"

"*Now,* dunMheric!"

He shrugged and turned, not particularly surprised to find the priest's pistol in hand and leveled at him. It was an interesting piece. Small, almost elegant. And more than single shot, if Ben had seen true.

He leaned his shoulders against the wagon and said, "I

wondered when you'd confess that particular bit of information. How long have you known?"

"Since you arrived, you self-deluded fool. Just Deymio. Really, Rhomandi, did we truly appear that stupid? —I *said,* step away."

"All right, all right." He rocked free of the wagon, and took a single step forward. "You knew, and you didn't tell Kiyrstin? Not exactly sporting of you, was it? Garetti's man are you?"

The priest shrugged. "After a fashion, only. Garetti and I . . . we did argue at some length about the boy's machine. Garetti couldn't see past the internal problems it would cause. I saw a chance to take Rhomatum." He rubbed the back of his free hand up under his chin and along his jawline in a move he undoubtedly considered tantalizing. "After Kiyrstin's . . . one hesitates to call it an assassination attempt . . . after she escaped, Garetti—saw value in my idea, and sent me after the boy—and incidentally the wife who'd made a fool of him."

"So why, once you caught up with them, didn't you and your men take them back to Garetti?"

"I told you, I had a different—vision. The descendant of Darius should appreciate visions."

"Oh, I do, romMaurii, believe me. —So you want to take Rhomatum? And you're willing to defy Garetti's orders to do so?"

"That's one way of putting it."

"Isn't that rather dangerous to admit in front of Garetti's men, here?"

"They have been . . . brought about to my way of thinking, Rhomandi."

"Turnabouts, are they? How did you manage that?"

"Same way I managed with Kiyrstin."

His heart skipped a beat, and the next pounded loud in his ear.

"How—"

"I convinced them I could do it. I had my doubts about how I was to accomplish this miracle, until Anheliaa herself dropped our letter of introduction right into my lap."

And on the third beat, he knew better than to believe. The man was trying to separate them. He'd seen that kiss. Wanted a rift between them large enough to insinuate himself.

"Me?" Deymorin laughed. "Surely you're joking."

"Not particularly. How about it, Rhomandi? How would *you* like to see Anheliaa thrown out of the Tower?"

"Thrown out? I thought you intended to destroy the rings with that contraption. Now, you're going to replace her?"

"Her power's waning, Rhomandi. Everyone knows it. Everyone also knows she's desperate to find someone to replace her. *I* can. Once in there, given the choice of destruction of the rings or an heir primed and ready, which would any ringmaster choose? Which would you?"

"I think you know the answer to that, romMaurii. I don't *like* ringmen, ringman. I thought I made that clear to you. I don't trust any of you, not Anheliaa, not Garetti, certainly not a man who just stole my horses!"

"But then, there are other things at stake now, aren't there?" The hand reached his lips and he ... kissed the back of a finger, then turned the hand, displaying—

"Where the hell did you get that?" Deymorin hissed.

"What, this?" With a surprised look, he held his hand out, studying—and displaying—the ring on his middle finger.

His ring.

"Why, is it yours? But the man I got it from *did* claim it was his. Would you like it back? I'm sure we can come to an agreement, Rhomandi. Don't you agree, Kiyrsti, darling?"

"How *dare* you—" Kiyrstin hissed, her eyes narrowed to angry glittering slits.

"Still playing the loving turnabout, Kiyrsti?" romMaurii asked. "Don't bother. The man's got too much at stake to trust you any longer. You can see the doubt in his eyes."

For a moment, perhaps, he'd doubted, but only for a moment. RomMaurii was a man who dealt in subterfuge and lies, who derived his own power by undermining the influence of others, who divided opposing forces by twisting perceptions of loyalty.

So when Kiyrstin's haughty challenge met his glance, he gave her a shadow wink. Let the man think he'd divided them. Let her turn to romMaurii ... at least long enough to turn tables on him. Now. Tonight. Tomorrow. As long as Nikki was alive—and at the moment, Nikki was alive and strong. Deymorin could feel that—there was time.

"Shepherdess?" He let a breathy disappointment into the single word.

"JD, *no!* Surely you don't believe . . ." Her voice drifted off uncertainly.

Priestly laughter filled the air. "You've lost him, *shepherdess.*"

"I don't . . ." Kiyrstin backed away, toward romMaurii, turning away as if to hide her face.

Don't overdo, shepherdess, he thought, finding it hard not to applaud her performance, utterly certain it was, indeed, a performance.

And then:

"Mm-mm-ee-oh-oh." Came from under the tarp. And a thud.

A worried older brother hardly had to ask what it was, particularly an older brother who could *feel* the younger past that tarp. Could feel the anger, the pain, and the utter terror that all hope was lost. And suddenly any thought of fooling the man who held his youngest brother captive lost its appeal. Suddenly, any thought of leaving that fear unassuaged until tomorrow or even later was unthinkable.

"Let him go, priest."

"Why, what are you talking about? Him, who?"

"My brother. He's just a boy. *I* can get you into Rhomatum. You can *have* the damn Tower."

More muffled protests from beneath the tarp, protests he ignored, both without and within, concentrating his attention on the priest.

"Let him go. Get him to a doctor—"

"Why, if I had such a person, Just Deymio, what makes you think he'd require a doctor?"

"So, let me see him."

"I have no idea who you're talking about."

"Let me see my brother!"

"Oh, I don't think so. I see you've been playing with me, and that I really cannot trust you, no matter what promises you make. And I really don't need you, Rhomandi. I really don't need you at all. —Subdue him, will you, gentlemen?"

Two guards came around the end of the wagon. Deymorin dodged one, kicked at the other, knowing he had no chance in the world and not really caring, wanting only to do maximum damage to those who'd hurt Nikki.

That blinding anger, and a bullheaded tenacity drove

him. As was the case when he'd attacked Mikhyel, there was no sophisticated science to his technique, no cool awareness of his actions and choice of targets, just release of pent-up fury.

He threw a joint-fisted roundhouse blow, felt it land with a satisfying squish, saw the man fall, took a blow in his side, and kicked at the culprit's kneecap, collapsed with his victim as his bad leg took the double weight.

Strangely, no one interfered.

Avoiding one guard's hands, he rolled and scrambled, fought and clawed his way toward the legs he knew were romMaurii's. If he was going down, that snake went with him.

A foot aimed at his face. He blocked the toe with one hand, grabbed the heel and twisted up and inward with the other.

RomMaurii screamed, and crashed in a sprawling heap that narrowly missed Deymorin's head.

And then he was on top, and once again a face was turning red and purple above his hands. The priest's face, this time.

"Uh, Deymorin ..." Kiyrstin's voice, her touch on his shoulder, slowly edged their way into his anger-hazed brain. He blinked his eyes clear and scanned the semicircle of curious eyes.

Curious. And not a weapon in sight.

"Get away from him, Deymorin."

And then he saw why. Kiyrstin had romMaurii's pistol in hand, and there wasn't a man present ready to question whether or not she knew how to use it. Certainly none who was ready to risk death for the man beneath him.

And more than Kiyrstin held them steady. Spaced around the camp, weapons out and ready, were men he recognized: old members of the guard, men he'd trained with and under. Ben's men.

A slow grin happened from deep within. Rendezvous at Armayel be damned.

"I said, get back, Rhomandi!"

There was a look in Kiyrstin's eyes. A hunger. For this man's blood. And the cannon was aimed unwaveringly at the priest's head.

"In cold blood, shepherdess?"

"I'm not particular, Rhomatum. Chivalry is for fools. Wolf bait should be left for the wolves."

He felt the fear in the man beneath him. But romMaurii didn't concern him. Kiyrstin did. Kiyrstin and tomorrow's conscience.

"Please, Kiyrstin. Garetti was one thing. This—you'll never be the same. We've options."

"Hang him?"

"Tie him up, yes." He jerked his head toward the watching men, both romMaurii's and Ben's. "Tie them all up. We'll leave them here, under guard, take Nikki to Armayel, and send additional men back for them."

The look faltered . . .

"Please, shepherdess."

. . . and died.

"Oh, hell, Rags. You're no fun at all."

A thud happened from the wagon.

He heaved a sigh and released romMaurii's throat, jerked the knife from the man's belt and wavered to his feet. Coming up hard against the wagon, he slashed a rear binding and pulled himself up on a wheel to throw the canvas back.

It was nightmare become reality: blood-matted blond hair, bruised and swelling-distorted features, eyes squeezed tight and a half-naked body curled against further blows.

"Nikki!"

Mikhyel screamed, felt the agony in himself, and an all-consuming anger that launched him from the wheel straight at the hawk-faced man staggering to his feet.

He heard Kiyrstin scream.

He felt romMaurii's throat in his hands, felt the shock run up his arms as the man's head struck the ground.

Vision hazed. All was pain and confusion, anger and betrayal, and overwhelming all else, a need to stop the pain. To protect Nikki from the ogre of death.

"Yes-s-s-s-s."

The word was a satisfied hiss in the hum that was the singing of the rings.

He didn't care. He *had* to be with Nikki. *Had* to know Nikki was alive and well, needed to know the reality behind the image of blood, the wracking pain.

But reality rooted him to the chair in the Tower, where the power of the rings was a palpable vibration in the air.

He fought that reality, straining against the invisible bonds that held him motionless. Sensed a weakness in those bonds and strained harder, demanding freedom.

He *had* to be with Nikki.

"Then go!" Anger. Exhaustion. Frustration in that hiss, and like a released bowstring, the tension was gone.

Lightning happened out of a clear sky.

And thunder.

Kiyrstin knew the cause long before any of the startled men around her. Was prepared, as they couldn't be, for the body that dropped from the sky and into the wagon.

She wasn't prepared for the pistol in her hand flaring white hot. But without so much as a single coherent thought, she sent it flying as far from her as her arm could throw it.

The first shot exploded before it touched the ground.

And then, the fires of hell descended around them as firearms began discharging spontaneously.

The wagon swayed suddenly, the horses taking exception to the fireworks. She yelled at Deymorin, still rolling on the ground, locked in idiotic manly combat, oblivious to all sense of self-preservation, kicked him in the rear when he ignored her, then ran to the plunging horses' heads and slashed their tie rope with her knife.

They tried to bolt. She jerked at their bits, gained their attention long enough to haul herself into the seat and kick the brake free.

Then she just let them run.

Behind her, lightning arced.

And arced again.

Became a steady, blinding stream of destruction that bathed the clearing from out of a clear blue sky.

And Deymorin was in the middle of it.

But she couldn't think about that. Either he came to his senses or he didn't. If he did, he'd want his brother safe, and the boy certainly couldn't save himself, unlike Deymorin.

Damn him. Damn him for a fool.

Kiyrstin gripped the reins in one hand, the siderail with the other, and braced herself against the sway and buck of the wagon, blinking back blinding tears, telling herself

firmly it was just the wind and hair whipping in her eyes
that induced those tears.

What seemed a lifetime later, the cloudless storm faded
to silent daylight, and the horses, lathered and blowing,
slowed of their own accord. When they stopped altogether,
she dropped the reins and slumped, burying her face in
her hands.

Nothing could have survived that lightning bath. Van was
gone. Zandy's encapsulator destroyed. All those men.

Deymorin.

It was over. Six months of her life, her whole future as
she'd begun to imagine it ... gone.

Except for the man—*men*—in the back of the wagon.
Deymorin's youngest brother, whom she'd never seen, who
might be a totally useless human being, but whose undoubtedly bruised and battered and barely alive state he owed,
at least in part, to her. And the other one, whose fall from
the sky had preceded the firestorm. A man whose identity,
she somehow knew beyond any doubt, reasonable or
otherwise.

A thud of approaching hooves, possibly a local, drawn
by the fireworks, brought her to her senses.

Possibly help for the too-silent men in the back.

After all, she still had responsibilities: to Deymorin's
brothers and to little Zandy waiting at Armayel. She
pushed herself upright, sniffed, getting salt water up her
nose, and scrubbed at the tears with an impatient hand.

The hoofbeats stopped beside the wagon and a new
weight taxed the seat's springs to the limit.

And then, there were arms around her and a voice in
her ear whispering, "Don't you dare cry, shepherdess."

Chapter Twelve

Contrary as ever, Kiyrstin wrapped her arms around his neck and burst into tears. Not that Deymorin blamed her; he felt a bit like howling himself, but settled for burying his hand in her hair and his face in her neck.

His body was one enormous bruise and strained muscle, not the least of which was a Kiyrstin-sized footprint on his backside, but he was alive, thanks to that butt-kick, and Kiyrstin was, and—

A muffled protest from the rear, and the pain that wracked his body, pain that was part of him and not, reminded him of other obligations.

"Rings," he said into her hair, "Nikki."

She sniffed, loudly, and pushed free, stared blankly at him. Then her eyes widened, and she whispered, "Mikhyel. Sweet Maurii, Deymorin. *Mikhyel.*"

"Khyel?" And then he realized he should have known. Would have, but for the confusion of emotions already writhing within. His anguish. Nikki's. —And Mikhyel's.

Kiyrstin twisted slowly up onto her knees to look over the seat's high back.

"Oh, my god. . . ."

He didn't ask, didn't *have* to look. He could *feel* Khyel's presence, now that he thought to try, isolate from himself and Nikki. Worse, he could feel the destruction burning into Mikhyel's very bones, the pain to which he himself had been blessedly oblivious the time it happened to him.

He only wished he could say the same for Mikhyel.

Together he and Kiyrstin scrambled out of the forward seat and hastened to the rear of the wagon, to find Mikhyel piled against the backboard, where the wild jolting of the wagon bed must have thrown him, a naked, reddened, shapeless mass on the deflated canvas.

He seemed at first glance to be dead, but an ever-so-slight movement of his ribs, and that other, indefinable sense assured him that Mikhyel was not only alive, but all too conscious.

"He's afraid to move," he said quietly, keeping his own senses uncompromisingly separate. "Nikki's awake, too, and . . ." Somewhere, he found a smile. ". . . smothering, so he thinks."

"We can't just lift him," Kiyrstin said imperturbably. "The skin is already rubbing off in places."

"Wait," Deymorin said, and cut the final lashing. "Khyel, I know you can hear me. Don't try to answer. And, please, brother, don't try to help. Just lie still."

Fortunately for them all, Kiyrstin wasn't a delicate woman like Mirym, or the simpering Lidye. Kiyrstin was strong-armed and steady, and together they lifted the canvas, with Mikhyel lying on it, free of a writhing Nikki and a very unhappy Tonio, both bound and gagged and in a crumpled tangle at the bottom of the wagon.

"Settle down, fry," he snapped at Nikki, whose blue eyes sparked with indignation above the gag, and who seemed amazingly hale for the injured condition Ben's report and his own senses had led him to expect. And to Tonio: "I'm sorry to get you into all this. I'll be right back."

With Kiyrstin's help, he eased the tarp to a grassy spot in the shade and straightened Khyel's limbs as gently as possible, talking all the while, explaining to Mikhyel what he knew about what Mikhyel was suffering, describing, as best he could, what had happened. Speaking for his own sake as well as Mikhyel's sanity.

Nothing seemed broken, but in that seared mess, it was difficult to tell. Tears seeped from under Mikhyel's closed eyelids, the only outward sign he was awake.

"Hang in there, Khyel. Same happened to me. Hurts like hell, I know, but you will live, much as you might not care to at the moment. —Kiyrstin, stay with him, will you?"

Tonio had wormed his way free of Nikki, and was struggling to sit up. Taking the gag from Tonio's mouth, he asked, nodding toward Nikki, "How is he?"

Angling his hands to be cut free, Tonio said dryly, "He'll live, m'lord. Hole in his shoulder, but we fixed that. Rest is messy, but a long way from his heart."

"Good." He handed Tonio the knife. "Cut him loose, will you?"

An indignant squeal sounded from behind Nikki's gag.

"Dammit, boy, I'm not ignoring you. —I've got to go back to the camp."

"You can't—" Tonio exclaimed.

"I must. There's an ointment ..." There was no such protest from Kiyrstin, on the ground beside Khyel, and he turned to ask her: "Any idea where to look, shepherdess?"

She shook her head, her forehead puckered with worry. "Just ... if there's anything left, look for the clothes trunk. It's where we kept all that sort of thing."

He cursed softly as he hauled himself into the saddle.

"JD?"

"What?"

"Be careful."

"Not a firearm left alive back there, Kiyrstin. Anything else attacks me at its own risk."

He forced the horse, much against its greater wisdom, back the way they'd come.

Deymorin was leaving.

Choking on gag-contained screams, Nikki struggled to gain his knees, falling atop Tonio as the world whirled and buzzed around him. He collapsed in a heap, and just lay there for a moment, waiting for his head to clear, kicking Tonio away when he reached for his arms to cut him free.

Settle down? All he'd been through—*for Deymorin*—and all Deymorin could say, all the time Deymorin could spare for him when after months of anguish and separation they were back together, was *settle down*?

Deymorin could spare the time to cut Tonio loose but not his own brother? Well ... *damn* Deymorin Rhomandi dunMheric! Damn him to the eighteen hells of Rhomatum! Who needed him?

He kicked Tonio away again and shoved himself back up to the nest of blankets that had been his bed since last night. Since they'd shot him and stolen Deymorin's ring from around his neck and beaten him, demanding to know why he was there, and why he was looking for Deymorin, and who Deymorin was and why he had been exiled.

Well, he hadn't told them. Hadn't given them anything to go on, not even when they struck that bullet hole. Repeatedly.

It just wasn't fair.

He'd been lying right here in these blankets, under that stifling canvas that "protected him from the sun" ... and from the view of casual passersby; he'd been lying there, victim of Mikhyel's betrayal—Mikhyel, who had told him to go to Darhaven when Anheliaa's rings couldn't *possibly* have found Deymorin there. He'd been lying there, searching for some way to escape before they reached Rhomatum, to deprive these Mauritumin invaders of their hostage and so their bargaining power, when, as if by magic, there had been Deymorin's voice, right outside the wagon.

Unable to hear clearly, afraid Deymorin would leave, he'd tried to call out. There'd been a fight; the canvas had been ripped away; and there was Deymorin.

But only for an instant. Deymorin had leapt away, his face dark with anger, and then the thunder had come—though he'd swear there'd been no sign of storm that morning when they'd stretched the canvas over his head—and lightning had blinded him—and something large and heavy had struck him, just before the horses bolted.

Then had begun a long, deafening stream of thunder, blinding light, and the pummeling of the swaying, bucking cart that left him dazed and terrified.

Silence, after that. And dark. And pain ... blinding, *blistering* pain like that filling him now until all he wanted was to scream. . . .

*   *   *

The monster was grabbing at his ankle. He pressed against the chimney's hot, sooty bricks, tried to squirm higher, but the creature had him, pulled him, ripping the skin from his body. Its roar filled the air around him, drove the soot deeper into his ears and skin.

And above him, Nikki screamed. For Deymorin. Always for Deymorin. But Deymorin wasn't there. Deymorin was never there anymore, would never be there again. Deymorin was gone forever, driven away. By him.

He clawed at the brick and screamed at the ogre to leave Nikki alone and called to Nikki that everything would be all right and to be quiet so the ogre couldn't find him.

But Nikki didn't listen. And Nikki's screams went on and on and on, and he was falling, falling, to where the ogre waited.

* * *

A steady stream of curses and cries of protest and calls
for Deymorin arose from the wagon bed. Evidently Tonio
had removed Nikaenor's gag.

On the canvas-covered ground beside Kiyrstin, Mikhyel
writhed, shedding bits of skin that would be scars, if he
survived, and wasted hard-won breath and precious energy
whispering reassurances to his unseen, but excruciatingly
noisy brother.

Mikhyel was unquestionably conscious and aware. And
not just of his own agony. A reflexive jerk from Mikhyel
and an angry, *"Dammit, Tonio, be careful,"* from the wagon
confirmed her suspicions that Mikhyel was also still cognizant of Nikki's physical state. Much as Deymorin had
sensed both Nikki and Mikhyel on the trail and last night.
One could also assume that Nikki was suffering Mikhyel's
pain now, perhaps without realizing why, or even that it
wasn't his own.

Still:

"Dammit, Tonio," Kiyrstin hissed at the unseen valet.
Concern for Mikhyel's life left her little sympathy for a
man who had the strength to protest so loudly. "Can't you
keep that fool quiet? He's disturbing my patient."

Silence. Blessed silence.

And then a golden cloud appeared above the wagon's
sideboards, and below the cloud, a startlingly handsome,
though somewhat battered and definitely indignant, face.

"What did you say?"

Giving Mikhyel a murmured reassurance, wishing the
more satisfying gift of physical touch were feasible, she
stood up to face this precious Nikaenor directly.

He was balancing on his knees and leaning heavily—and
without obvious discomfort—against the wagon's sideboards, while Tonio sawed the bindings from his wrists.
She saw no indication whatsoever that he shared Mikhyel's
suffering. In fact, he seemed amazingly healthy, for someone whose health had been such cause for Deymorin's recent concern.

She saw now that blood matted the blond cloud in places,
and his shirt was in tatters, but his eyes were bright and
clear—though one was swollen nearly shut—and the shoul-

der wound that had caused Deymorin and Mikhyel such misery, appeared tightly and cleanly dressed.

Certainly his voice was strong enough.

"Let me paraphrase," she stated coldly. "Either you shut your mouth and endure your minor discomforts and complaints quietly, or I'll shove that filthy rag right back down your gullet and with luck, you'll choke."

His eyes raked her up and down, and his expression was one of increasing distaste as he took in her borrowed clothes—Mikhyel's clothes—her shorn hair and the filth.

"I know you," he said then. "You're Deymorin's ringdancer!"

"I'm *not* a dancer. I've never *been* a dancer. I never intend to *be* a dancer. And if anyone accuses me of being Deymorin's *anything* again, I'll—"

"Please don't, shepherdess," Deymorin's voice interrupted, weary but amused, and then Deymorin himself was there, walking his horse up to the far side of the wagon, riding more slowly than she'd ever seen him, and he staggered when he slid from the saddle.

Nikki's face lit like captured sunshine, and he rocked about to face Deymorin, radiating love and adoration and vulnerability. Maurii save them, no wonder his brothers' common sense went southward where this boy was concerned.

Deymorin dropped his horse's reins, leaving the foaming, exhausted creature to its own devices—something he'd lectured her severely against—and reached over the end boards to clasp the boy's hand in both of his own, a quiet, but undeniably heartfelt greeting.

"Do you better when we're not both walking wounded, fry."

"I.O.U.?" Nikki asked softly, with the faintest of quivers in his voice, and giving his older brother a shaky grin.

"Something like," Deymorin said, releasing Nikki's hand to caress Nikki's swollen cheek.

Vaguely disgusted, Kiyrstin reminded Deymorin abruptly: "Did you find the salve?"

Deymorin grinned fleetingly. "Nikki, this is Kiyrstin. Be nice. She saved my life."

"Several times. —Well, *did you find it*?"

"It's a war zone back there, Kiyrstin." Deymorin's voice was hushed. Shaken. Hiding emotions she could only imagine. "I've never ... seen the like. Splinters, blood, bits of this and that—everything burned beyond recognition. The amazing thing is, the fire didn't spread. But not a live body, not an unshattered container anywhere."

No parnicci balm meant no way to stop the searing destruction from moving inward, through muscle, all the way to bone and vital organs. Which meant, quite simply, Mikhyel was going to die.

And Deymorin, from the way he avoided looking at Mikhyel, from the devastation on his face, knew it. After all this, Deymorin was going to lose a brother anyway.

She was shaking. She knew that as she knew, from an inward distance, when Deymorin's arms surrounded her, but little else.

"Nothing else we can do?" he asked gently.

"We . . . we can try immersing him in cold water. I've heard that helps other sorts of burns . . . But, Sweet Maurii, Deymorin, what if I'm wrong?"

"Heard? If? What sort of doctor are you? —Deymorin, what's going on? Who is this patient she's going to drown?"

She stiffened, said into Deymorin's chest. "That's that brother of yours, isn't it?"

"I'm afraid so."

"You tell him, Rhomandi, that if he so much as opens his mouth again, he'll find out what sort of doctor I'm not."

Over her head, Deymorin said, with forced humor in his weary voice, trying, she knew, to disguise his own fear and shelter this younger brother who was, in her humble opinion, damn well old enough to handle the truth. "Nikki, lad, much as I love you, much as I know you've been abducted and tortured and nearly died for my sake, I think I should warn you that Kiyrstin is an escaped convict—an assassin by trade, and you'd do well not to get her angry. At the moment, you are alive and comparatively well."

"You call this—"

"Shut up, Nikki. That weight that squashed you in the wagon was our other brother, as you'd probably realize, if you were a little less sore and bruised yourself. At the moment, he's very close to dying, thanks, to our loving aunt's interference, and if you don't want Kiyrstin to help you precede him into the hereafter, I'd suggest you watch what you say."

"N–not Anheliaa."

The weak whisper rose from the ground behind him.

"Khyel?" At least the brat had the decency to sound remorseful, and when the partially clad, cut, bruised, and flayed brother worked his way gingerly over the wagon's sideboards and dropped to his knees beside the burned one, Kiyrstin found her opinion inclining toward leniency.

"Don't touch him," she warned, and the desperate blue eyes that shifted her way, the reddened hand that sought Nikki's despite the warning, melted the last of her resistance, especially when Nikki, showing some real sense, resisted the natural urge to grab indiscriminately, and instead placed his hand gently in his brother's, letting Mikhyel control the pressure.

Deymorin sank down at Mikhyel's other side. "Khyel, don't answer if it can wait, but what did you mean, it wasn't Anheliaa who sent you through?"

"M–my fault. I . . . did it. Rings just . . . Ni-k-ki hurt. Couldn't *not* . . ." Tears leaked with Mikhyel's effort, and Deymorin, his own eyes damp, brushed hair back from Mikhyel's forehead, then clamped that same shaking hand across his own eyes, squeezing his temples.

"Tonio," Nikki called softly toward the wagon, "is there anything in that medical kit of yours that might help?"

"Medical kit?" Kiyrstin repeated and eagerly pawed through the bag Tonio tossed down to her. But it was nothing useful, as far as she could tell. Standard ointments and herbs, some strips for dressing wounds.

She met Deymorin's anxious gaze and shook her head. His shoulders, his entire body, slumped in weary despair.

"His scalp's not burned . . . under the hair." Nikki commented absently. He was rocking gently, just staring at Mikhyel.

"That's just the way it happens," she answered, only half-listening, worried about the wild look beginning to fill Deymorin's eyes. "The beard, the eyebrows, I've never seen them damaged, but they'll fall out—no way not. May grow back. May not, but it's the skin that's damaged. The scalp—perhaps it's different. Maybe it's just that the hair protects it. I just don't—"

"Forget about eyebrows!" Deymorin snarled. "What can we do?"

"Pull yourself together, Rags. Nothing here, that's for certain. Get him in the wagon, I suppose. Try to keep the sun off him and find water. I know the plant the balm is distilled from, but—dammitall—it's a desert thing, imported from—"

"Oh, Basstisstist's hells, woman. Just let him croak the big one."

They stared at one another in shocked silence. That cackle had most definitely not come from any of them.

"Who's there?" Deymorin demanded of the surrounding woods.

"Thought you'd never ask."

An old woman trundled from out of the shadows, leaning heavily on a cane, carrying a rag-covered basket. Her ragged hem dragged the ground, brushing an eerie path through the roadside dust.

Her head extended outward from her scarf-swathed shoulders . . . rather like a turtle's . . . and turned side to side as if examining Mikhyel with the one eye visible past grey rattails and a headscarf's ragged fall.

"Skinny," she declared flatly, and plucked a drenal leaf from the basket. Her single eye blissfully closed, she flicked the leaf with her tonguetip, and nibbled a corner of the leaf. "Let him die."

Another deft flick of the tongue. Another nibble. This time, Kiyrstin saw the tiny green speck she savored.

An aphid.

More than sufficient to break the strange spell the old crone's arrival had cast on them—at least she and Deymorin were free. Nikki was still staring at the crone, seemingly captivated, his eyes wide and wondering.

"I don't know who you are," Kiyrstin said, "or what right you think you have to interfere—"

"Right?" the cackle screeched. *"You're* the trespassers, Kiyrstine romGaretti, and don't think to oust *me* from my own house."

"How do you know . . ." The crone's eye glimmered green and Kiyrstin's indignant question faded in her throat.

She'd swear fangs glittered in the scarf-shadowed face.

"Yes-s-s. —Now, what are you going to do with this rotting carcass?"

"Sweet Tamshi, don't be angry," Nikki whispered, and stood up, hands outheld in appeal. "Sweet, sweet mother, please help us."

Mystical Tamshi as he claimed, or perfectly human crone, the lad's splendid, though slightly damaged, body quite ob-

viously caught the attention of the single visible eye, which
widened and openly scanned him.

And he, in his turn, was staring almost reverently at her.
"He's not a carcass. He's my brother. And I'm afraid he
means far too much to me to just let him die here. If you've
any advice for us, or if *you* can save him, please, help us
now."

A sly smile stretched the wrinkled face. "M-m-m-much
better, pretty human." The rag-draped, grey-haired head
raised its nose in Kiyrstin's direction. "Much better."

The last time she'd seen that look, it had graced a child's
face. A child whose eyes had a disturbing tendency to
change color, and whose fingers glowed green.

That same color tinged the long ragged fingernails that
stroked Nikki's arm. Seeming oblivious to that oddity,
Nikki took the green-glowing hand in his and turned that
devastating sweetness on the attached crone.

"Please?"

Green-glow spread even to Nikki's curls. Then:

"Oh, hell. Move over, brat."

And in a drifting cloud of filthy rags, loose dust, and
bugs, the crone sank down at Mikhyel's side and placed a
claw-fingered hand on his forehead.

It was an ancient room this court at the core of the building within building within building maze. Traditional in a
way the ring stadium itself was not. Technology changed
the Dance and increased the danger to the radical dancer,
but the tradition which housed the aspirants to the coveted
position would never change, not so long as one true believer remained.

And in Khoratum, there were many more than one.

Seven had been led here, blindfolded, at dawn. Sunlight
slanted, now, across that vast expanse, the only indication
of passing time. Three competitors remained, each waiting
anxiously for their number to be called.

Randomly chosen numbers, so tradition said.

Others, long since gone, had boasted you could rig that
order, get yourself out first while the voters were fresh. If
you had the connections. And the money.

But if you weren't one of those with connections and
money, if you played fairly, according to the old rules, you
never knew when your time would come, so you used this

room to keep muscles loose, the spirit ready, and trusted that the best dancer would win.

A dancer had to believe in the ultimate justice of the system. There was no other option, not when dancing was your life.

Not when you only got one chance.

Two of the remaining three cavorted nervously about the tile floor, challenging each other with increasingly complex tricks performed to hand-clapped rhythms.

In the shadows along the west wall, Dancer completed one more warm-up routine and began again. Always the same routine: a series of bends and stretches that warmed and flexed each muscle group, advancing into long, slow moves of balance, flexibility and strength, and ultimately to five strings of rapid, tumbling moves to hone reflexes.

The others had long since ceased to gawk, absorbed as they were in their own tight competition. They'd watched each other practice, knew each other's strengths and weaknesses, and counted on the weaknesses of the other dancers to make them stand out rather than on the intrinsic quality of their own performance.

Dancer knew this, having heard their strategies, and struggled instead for personal perfection. Struggled to ignore Shasari's flashy moves which might work into the composition and might not, determinedly trusting the voters to look beyond the momentary difficulty of a single move to the synchronicity of the entire dance.

A slow-motion, single-hand walkover. A cardinal point, delayed pirouette. One never quite achieved perfection, and so the practice was never in vain. Still, as nerves grew increasingly frayed, even the flawed executions wavered.

Only one would be chosen. Several might die—the dance had its built-in dangers, and competitions always included those who miscalculated their own skill.

In the midst of a backhand walkover, a tingling engulfed Dancer's body, and the tiles beneath Dancer's fingertips faded to green nothingness.

*　　*　　*

"First priority must be the eyes-s-s."

The old woman's index finger traced long slow circles, a continuous double-loop pattern, around Mikhyel's eyes, just below the arched fingertips of her other hand. And with each completed figure, the angry redness within its borders lightened.

From the moment the old woman's hands touched him, Mikhyel's agony had eased, Nikki's inner connection told him that, when Nikki thought to ask it, and now that finger was healing the deep burns—his eyes told him that.

It was—wonderful.

And Mikhyel would be fine now. This wonderful, magical creature would see to that. Just as the old Tamshi stories promised.

Nikki crouched beside the Tamshi, watching her every move with an eye to the minutest detail. Each inflection of the sibilant voice, each subtle color shift of her fingertip's clawed end suggested a full explicatory stanza—perhaps even a complete ode unto itself.

The creature's single, green-glowing eye flickered toward him. Her wrinkled upper lip stretched lopsidedly, revealing an abnormally sharp canine.

"This interests you, young dunMheric?"

"Very much, Sweet Mother." Mother, as in Mother of the Earth. That was the way the old stories said to address these spirits of the leythium underworld.

"Yes-s-s-s." The smile stretched to the other side of her mouth. "It would."

He didn't ask how she knew. Tamshi just did. Tamshi could read the hearts and souls of ... certain ... special ... individuals, those who could themselves see past the illusion and know what they faced.

And *he* had known her for Tamshi from the moment he saw her exit the woods. Perhaps ... just perhaps—

A crackling glow in the forest's deepening shadows cast flowing streams of pastel color over Mikhyel's pain-creased face. Nikki leapt up, squinting into the radiance, which coalesced into a human-seeming form running toward them, as if from a great distance.

"Dammit, Mother!" Sound reached them before the creature itself did, and the sentiment flowed oddly on the musical voice. And with a sobbing catch: "How *could* you?"

Then the creature was standing before them, glowing, graceful ...

And furious.

The Tamshi looked up slowly, her single eyebrow raised cynically. "Well, Dancer. How do? What brings you here?"

Dancer. Spoken as a name. As Mother had been a name.

"You know damnwell how I do. The trials are today, I've yet to dance and *you* dragged me here without so much as a by-your-leave. You and your damned web—"

"Watch your language, brat. You're in company. Show some respect."

"Respect? Why? This time you've gone too far—"

"*I've* done nothing, human-spawn. I ask again, what brings you here?"

'Human-spawn'? Nikki studied the creature, at least, what he could see of it past the glow. A *human* who called a Tamshi mother, not, as he had, human to goddess, but as child to parent? Who dared argue with and curse at her? who glowed and appeared from nowhere?

"N–not?" The creature Mother called human, and Dancer, knelt on the Tamshi's far side. "Mother, you must have. *I* certainly didn't. The others—Mother, they were there, waiting their turn. They will have seen ... The trials ... my turn ..."

The creature's lips began to quiver, liquid gold spilled from large, long-lashed eyes, dripped from pearlescent skin to land on Mikhyel's cheek, making tiny, glowing puddles in the seared flesh.

Golden tears. Pearlescent skin. Human? Somehow, Nikki didn't think so. Human-*spawn,* the Tamshi had said. Perhaps some magical combination of human and Tamshi? The tales hinted at such.

{Never again ... only one chance ...}

Nikki's heart skipped a beat. Dancer's lips hadn't uttered those words. Nikki had ... *heard* them in his head. *Heard* them as if they were his own, half-formed thoughts. Thoughts which, from her expression, Mother heard perfectly well and in their entirety.

Mother's hands left Mikhyel to cup Dancer's face.

{I'm sorry, child.} Her thoughts were much clearer than Dancer's. *{But it wasn't me. Wasn't my pattern. Was never my pattern.}*

Dancer's eyes scanned Mikhyel, then, and Deymorin, and lastly, himself. Scathing, hate-filled eyes.

{Theirs.}

No hint of question in that. But:

{Possibly. Probably, at least in part. But not willfully, Dancer, and design is everything.}

A scholar had to wonder what it all meant, particularly

a scholar who'd felt his brothers these past days—who felt
them now, when he tried—in a way that defied rational
explanation. Particularly a scholar who had waited all his
life for a moment such as this, an opportunity such as this.
And one remembered childhood dreams of Tamshi in the
closets and adult dreams of taking oneself into the hills to
find a teacher—

"Dammit." Deymorin's verbal hiss to the redheaded
woman seemed painfully loud to someone listening with
that inner voice as well as his ears. "He's hurting again, I
can feel it. Why'd she take her hand away?"

Deymorin didn't hear them talking. One who could hear
had to wonder if Mikhyel heard. One who could had to
wonder if perhaps one didn't share, at least in some small
part, the Talent these two exquisite creatures so obviously
possessed.

"But, Deymorin," the redheaded woman's voice was less
obtrusive, being in his ears alone. "Look—*look* at his face."

Where the tears had fallen, Mikhyel's skin was clear.

{How . . .}

That was Dancer.

{Residual ley, child. —I'll explain later.}

Explain. As a teacher explained to a student. That came
through, underlying the silent words. Mother was Dancer's
teacher. If Mother taught Dancer, might she not teach others? But Mother had also called Dancer, who was obviously
an adult, 'child.' So perhaps Dancer was, in truth, Mother's
child. Which would mean Dancer wasn't human, and so
perhaps Mother might not take a human on as a student.

But then again, she might.

Mikhyel groaned, then, ever-so-softly, or perhaps the
sound was just in Nikki's mind, and Mother without sparing
so much as a glance down, replaced her fingertips absent-
mindedly on Mikhyel's temples. To Dancer, she said aloud:

"Since you're here, make yourself useful. Go back and
bring me the oil."

"For *him*?" Dancer answered, also aloud. "Why should
I?"

"Oil?" Deymorin cut in eagerly. "Parnicci oil?"

"Oh, you humans." Mother waved a talon-fingered hand
carelessly, setting rags to fluttering. "Something like. Parnicci is an . . . adequate substitute."

"And you know where it is?" Deymorin asked Dancer. "Can get it?"

"Know; yes. Can; yes. Will—" Dancer's nose rose. "No."

And Nikki, listening with that internal sense, felt something new. Something strong and vital: Deymorin. And as clearly as if the emotion were his own, Nikki felt Deymorin's anger, felt it growing, feeding on the need for something to replace the personal exhaustion and the fear for Mikhyel's life. Knew, before it happened, that that temper must flare, felt Deymorin's weight shift as if it were his own, felt legs flex and set.

"You—" Deymorin made a flying leap for the kneeling creature.

Dancer swayed, graceful as a willow in a breeze, and brushed Deymorin's attack aside as casually as Mother had brushed Mikhyel's suffering aside. Deymorin crashed into the bushes; his redheaded woman cursed and rushed past them to his side.

Dancer twisted into a supple curve, wide eyes following that rolling tumble, and the woman's pursuit, and Dancer nodded solemn agreement at the redheaded woman's, *"Damn fool, JD,"* then turned back to comment indifferently: "Temper."

"What would you expect of Mheric's son?" Mother answered, while that other 'voice' said *{Nice move.}* "But pay him no mind. Just go fetch."

"No! I must return to the waiting chamber!" The glow still surrounding and obscuring Dancer flared orange and red, colors Nikki just *knew* were a result of the creature's anger, which was a palpable force in the air.

"Must?" Mother hissed. "Hah! You always have a choice."

"But it's possible my number has not yet been called. That the others haven't noticed my absence. There's still a chance—"

"And is your dance more important than this man's life? I can't wave my hand and heal him, you know that. It would take days and would be a blasphemous misuse of the ley."

"The dance is my *life*, Mother!"

Mother just stared at the other in silence—if radiant disappointment could be termed silence.

"Can't *you* go get it?"

Mother's single eye narrowed in a worried frown. —Or perhaps not worried, Nikki corrected himself meticulously. The ancient diaries warned of placing too great a human value on Tamshi feelings. Perhaps it was puzzlement that creased the cronelike skin about that eye. Perhaps Dancer's response was simply a . . . curiosity to Mother.

The Tamshi sat back, removing her hand from Mikhyel's forehead. This time, Mikhyel remained silent, not due to unconsciousness, Nikki knew when he queried that inner sense, as he'd known Deymorin's feelings. Mikhyel was awake enough to fear the fact his eyes would not open. Enough to be embarrassed at his weakness and his nakedness before strangers he could not sense but not see.

Nikki absorbed the feelings, fascinated with their depth and clarity.

"Touch him," Mother hissed.

Nikki dropped again to his knees and reached eagerly for Mikhyel's forehead, wondering what else he might sense, only to have his hand slapped away.

"Not you, idiot."

He flushed, mortified, and clenched a stinging, bleeding hand.

But Mother paid him no mind. Mother's eye was fastened on Dancer.

Dancer's chin lifted obstinately, and Dancer's hands remained folded.

{Touch him, and then *tell me to leave!}*

Dancer jumped, then stretched a reluctant, quivering hand to Mikhyel's forehead. Dancer's large eyes closed. Moments later, golden tears were seeping between the long lashes.

"Dancer?" Mother asked. "Dancer!" And then she swept Dancer's hand away from Mikhyel, replacing it instantly with her own.

Dancer collapsed, clenched hands pressed to his bare middle, slender shoulders shaking under a veil of hair that was dark, nearly black, at the scalp, shading to the color of time-bleached bone on the tips that brushed the ground.

Mother hissed her disgust. "*Now*, human, you may return to your . . . . dance."

Human. Unequivocally.

"You–you know I can't without help." Dancer's musical

voice was barely audible. "We're much too far from a node.
I *still* don't understand how I came to be here."

"No? Haven't listened very hard, have you?"

Eyes of a color as uncertain as the hair blinked across
Mikhyel's body at Mother, closed briefly, then scanned
them all: Mikhyel. Himself. Deymorin, who had propped
against the wagon wheel, his bad leg thrust out before him,
and finally returned to Mother, seeking confirmation.

"The pattern." Dancer murmured, and then more loudly.
"*They* are a node. A *human* node!"

{High time you woke up.}

Dancer's eyes fell. "Nonetheless, I still can't, Mother.
You, or someone, brought me here. Without the oil—"

"So. Because of your inadequacies, I must take life-giving
energy from this innocent young man to send you back to
make a travesty of the dance. Very well." She lifted a hand.

"I didn't say that, Mother."

"Then what *do* you say?"

Dancer's head tipped, those amazing eyes ... absorbing
Mikhyel, and Dancer's translucent, high-tendoned hand
reached again for Mikhyel's brow, drew back before making contact.

{To the cave.}

Mother raised her hand again. There were webs between
the fingers.

"And, Mother." Different tone, this time, teasing, and
mildly disgusted. "You look ridiculous. Put yourself back
together. You're embarrassing me."

{Oh, go screw a knothole . . .}

She waved her hand, and the creature she called
human disappeared.

"Mother?" Nikki asked, when Dancer was gone. "Can
you teach me as you did him?"

"Him?" Mother squawked. "Who him? What him?
Teach? I don't teach hims."

"Dancer, of course."

The redheaded woman, Kiyrstin, laughed. Nikki frowned,
not at all certain he liked this *friend* of Deymorin's.

"What's so funny?" he asked.

"Oh, nothing. Nothing, child. Really," she said, and
added condescendingly, "I'll explain later."

He stared at her, indignant without knowing over what,
then turned to Deymorin for support. But Deymorin wasn't

listening. Deymorin's attention was for Mikhyel. *All* for Mikhyel.

Support came on a quiet hiss and from an unexpected quarter; "You would do well, Kiyrstine romGaretti, to question your own senses before you ridicule those of others."

Nikki, somewhat mollified, smiled at the scowling redhead, then turned back to Mother, placing a hand on her rag-shrouded arm, eager to take advantage of her mood. "Does this mean you'll teach me?"

The Tamshi seemed taller than before. And she leaned back to stare down at him, her second eye a glitter in the darkness beneath the rattails.

"Why should I?"

"Why? I ... Well, because I want to know."

"You ... want to know. Fine. And why should you, above all others, receive this precious knowledge of the ages?"

"I ... Well, I hear you and Dancer 'talk.' That must mean I have at least *some* Talent. And because I respect the old ways. And because I'm ... dedicated to making people understand each other and if I could—"

"Bat's poop, if ever I've heard it. You're dying of vulgar curiosity and jealous of a skill someone else has that would impress all your friends if you had it, and you think that by batting those baby-blues at me you'll get it. Well, go suck an aphid, human."

"But—"

"Tell me, human, whose brother lies so near to death before him. Tell me what you feel when you look on him?"

"I feel ... sorry for him, concerned, of course. I want him to be well. But you're caring for him now, so he'll be all right, won't he?"

"Will he? And how do *you* feel, human who has been so terribly ill-treated?"

"Why ... I'm quite well, thank you. The pain is ..." He realized suddenly and with no small surprise: "Gone."

"And how does this dying brother of yours feel, oh great and Talented one?"

"He's ... well, obviously he's in pain." Nikki probed gingerly with that Talent—touched the searing pain, the fear, and more: a gratifying, soul-warming concern over *his* well-being that assured him Mikhyel loved him and had never betrayed him, no matter what he'd thought. . . .

"Hmph." Mother grunted, then: *{And have you not yet wondered why he feels such pain and you feel none?}*

"I . ." He felt a coldness inside him, sensing a test and having no idea what the right answers might be.

{There are no right answers, human. Only Truth and Character. If you know the answer to the question now, it does not explain why you never thought to ask it.}

"Can I learn?"

{Only if you can teach yourself.}

"I don't understand."

{When you can come to me—on your own, we'll discuss it.}

"Come to you?"

{Maybe.}

"Where?"

{If I'm in the mood.}

"How?"

"If you have to ask, I haven't the time to waste."

And slowly, Mother began to glow all over, the rags fading into billowing, glowing lace draperies, her body, serpentine-lithe beneath them, her skin glowing in faintly scaled iridescence.

Kiyrstin had to assume she'd become immune to miracles. Or perhaps, the satisfaction of having her suspicions regarding Mother's nature validated outweigh the shock of confirmation. Whichever happened to be the case, Mother's transformation mixed with Nikki's pouting frustration simply made her want to laugh.

Nikki's 'baby-blues' flashed outrage at her, and she smiled back, feeling quite charitable with him, now someone who mattered to him had called his innocence-incarnate bluff. It had been an entertaining exchange, if somewhat disjointed toward the end—obviously the lad was hearing things she could not. —But then, Deymorin had been *feeling* things for days, so that didn't particularly surprise her either.

She'd heard enough, however, to know the lad had come up against something he wanted badly and couldn't have, which seemed to her a very good thing. On the other hand, Nikki didn't, as she would have expected him to do, leave

Mikhyel's side in a petulant, ill-used huff. Didn't complain or further press the creature he called Mother. Instead, Nikki sat back on his heels and watched and listened, taking in all he could, taking advantage of current opportunity rather than sinking his trust in some future revelation.

Which said much for his basic nature. She could see value in him—hope for the man he might become—provided Deymorin ceased to encourage that patently assumed naiveté.

Meanwhile the creature who was, Kiyrstin was convinced, also the little girl from the streamside, was rattling on, growing quite talkative, now she'd shed her cronish rags, complaining about upstart humans playing with lightning, and getting themselves burned by thinking they knew more than they did.

"Getting burned," Kiyrstin repeated into that hissing stream of words, testing both her suspicions and the creature's veracity. "You mean like Alizant's potentiator burned *you*?"

Green, pupilless eyes scanned her, narrow and calculating, the hissing stream temporarily dammed.

Into that suspicious pause she asked blithely: "How's your finger, missy?"

"Oh, *that* thing." Slender shoulders lifted bonelessly. "Lightning in a box. That's between you humans and the sky. *I* object to your foolish Rhomatum ringmaster's noxious, so-called experimentation. Certainly, there's much one can do with the ley, much we could teach you silly creatures, but we're not so foolish as to turn such short-sighted morons loose with the secrets of the universe."

"We?" Deymorin asked, and Kiyrstin was relieved to see the conversation had managed to pierce his unhealthy absorption in Mikhyel. "There are more of you?"

"Of course. Aphids and oranges, are all humans so ignorant about reproduction? You certainly practice enough. We don't get along nearly so well, but we certainly know how it all works. My valley counterpart—Rhomatum's 'god,' don't you know?—has burrowed in, waiting for you irritants to leave the surface and quit mistreating his node. I'd think—"

Mikhyel spasmed suddenly, and threw his head back as if trying to remove the clawed hand.

"Stop it, child," the Tamshi said, her voice amazingly

gentle of a sudden. "We're going to save you in spite of yourself."

"What are you talking about?" Deymorin asked harshly.

"Why he's here. Why that," her head swung in the general direction of the destruction, "happened."

"You know?" Kiyrstin asked.

"Well, of course, I know. Anheliaa caused it—well, sort of. The boxed lightning helped. The boys, here, did. Actually, come to think on it, Anheliaa was barely a factor at all. That creature couldn't possibly have managed such a magnificent display alone. —Ley doesn't like it, you know."

"Doesn't like it?" Kiyrstin asked, wallowing in a morass of undefined 'its'. "Doesn't like what?"

"Lodestones, potentiators. Encapsulators. Eatorators, feetorators. They argue. All the time. Like the ley argues with lightning. Like brothers. Doesn't like lodestones, doesn't like kitty-cats and chickens." The creature's mouth stretched, exposing impressive dentition, and a forked tongue flicked. "The ley and I . . . disagree in that sense."

"But what about Mikhyel?" Deymorin asked. "Why is he here? How? He said *he* did it, not Anheliaa."

"Think, Mheric's son. Your dear auntie knew about the boxed lightning. Your dear auntie needed a node to arc the ley-energy from Rhomatum to the machine. Your dear auntie was watching you and your pretty brother, there, through your skinny brother, here, and when you two pulled him through from Rhomatum tower, you became the node your dear auntie required to perform that magic. Anheliaa might have started the argument, but once begun, nothing would stop it until the box—or the rings—had been destroyed." Mother grinned. "And ley doesn't *like* to lose."

"But why . . . how . . ." Deymorin rubbed his forehead confusedly. "What was that about saving Mikhyel in spite of himself?"

"How? A node wants to be whole. Division is against nature. Why? For that, you'll have to ask him, now won't you?"

A glow began directly above Mikhyel's head, moved slightly to one side.

"Ah, *here* we are."

Dancer. But then, who else would arrive in a bubble of light, Kiyrstin asked herself, then immediately regretted the question, not really interested in an alternative answer.

The young woman arrived carrying a bowl of translucent light-veined substance, and the light in those veins ... pulsed, like blood in human veins. Dancer's boyishly flat body glistened now as if covered with oil, and the glow that had surrounded her the last time was dissipating rapidly.

Boyishly flat, but definitely not male. One did have to wonder how *Deymorin's* brother had gotten to his advanced age without knowing the difference.

And one had to wonder why, if Nikki didn't, Nikki was staring at the creature as if entranced—as was Tonio, sitting silent in the wagon bed. Only Deymorin seemed immune: even when Dancer knelt opposite him and handed him the bowl.

But then, Deymorin had eyes only for his brother.

Vaguely disgusted, Kiyrstin pulled a blanket from the wagon bed and draped it across Dancer's bare shoulders. A knowing glance met hers, and at that look, she was no longer certain *what* she touched, except that a sweet smile and musical *Thank you,* assured her the gesture was recognized and, in some sense, appreciated.

The next moment, the look was gone and Dancer had turned away. Fingertips dipped into the phosphorescent oil, and smoothed it almost tenderly over Mikhyel's face, in and around the hairline, around the Tamshi's reptilian fingertips that raised one at a time for coverage beneath, and down over Mikhyel's chin and throat. As she had feared, the short hairs of his beard and mustache came away onto Dancer's fingers, to swirl and disappear in the strange oil when she dipped again.

It was as if the oil absorbed them.

And where the oil touched, the skin cleared—without the sloughing characteristic of the parnicci balm, without the wait, like ... magic. And the dark eyelashes and brows lying within the double loop Mother's finger had earlier traced, showed no sign of sloughing.

Face, ears, and neck covered, Deymorin, at Mother's instructions, dribbled the luminous substance down Mikhyel's body, a small section at a time, warned against wastage. Dancer's long fingers followed the golden trail, spreading the oil into even coverage, not actually touching Mikhyel, Kiyrstin slowly realized, but gliding a hair's-breadth above his seared skin, the oil following the fingers, not preceding fingertip pressure.

With Dancer's spell apparently broken, Nikki—ignored, and effectively shoved to one side—retreated to the wagon. He leaned crossed arms on the sideboard next to Tonio, pouting, but with enough sense, she would judge, to realize he'd been a public—and heartless—fool, and perhaps, just perhaps, he was bright enough—and caring enough—to think about how and why.

She'd known his sort: impossible to live among the wealthy and privileged and not see them. Youngest, beautiful as a child, breathtaking as an adult ... heady stuff for anyone. Add two older brothers vying for the right to love him and it was small wonder he was more than a little self-centered. Instinct urged her to go to him, to reassure him, but her better sense held her back: more admirers, he didn't need. Not if he was ever successfully to grow up.

One side completed, Deymorin and Dancer eased Mikhyel's unresisting body over, revealing the real damage of the fall from the sky and the wild wagon ride.

"He's a bloody mess," Mother commented phlegmatically.

"We can see that," Kiyrstin returned. "Will he live?"

"You worry too much. Of course he'll live, Mother's here, now. But there will be scars." Mother grinned. "Of course, we could send him through again and start fresh."

Mikhyel, obviously awake, shuddered and muttered a protest. Dancer passed a reassuring hand over his hair and hissed: "That's not funny, Mother."

"No need to get huffy, human-spawn." Mother sniffed. "It was just a suggestion. —So what are you waiting for, Mheric's son? Pour away, pour away!"

And indeed, once the oil had done its work, Mikhyel's back looked painful, but not life-threatening, and when the Tamshi withdrew her fingertip anesthetic at last, Mikhyel sighed audibly and cradled his face in crossed arms, appearing almost comfortable.

But he never truly awakened again, and by the time they covered the deepest, still-raw wounds with simple, human dressings from Tonio's kit, and lifted him into the back of the wagon, it was obvious to all of them that he was not going to waken.

"What's wrong with him?" Nikki asked, propped on his elbow in his own makeshift travel-bed next to Mikhyel's.

"Attitude," Mother said, and sniffed indifferently.

"He'll return to you if and when he decides to, and nothing you can do will change it. —Dancer, time to leave, child."

Dancer was sitting cross-legged at Mikhyel's head, fingertips to Mikhyel's temples as before, the glow markedly diminished, though still hazing her delicate features. But when Mother would interfere, Dancer brushed her hands off and hissed in excellent imitation of Mother herself.

Mother frowned, clasped Dancer's thin wrists and pulled them forcibly away.

Dancer's eyes opened, and they were filled to overflowing—with normal, clear, *human* tears.

"I can't, Mother. Not yet."

"Again, I'm hearing *can't*!"

"*You* made me part of this pattern, for all you deny your hand in it. I must stay until that pattern is healthy!"

Mother hissed, her eyes, burning an angry red, reflected off Dancer, who faced her without flinching. Then the Tamshi whirled about and returned to her basket of leaves, whisked it into one hand, cradled the oil bowl in the other and disappeared in a swirl of lacy veils and a red glow that crackled and snapped, then popped out of existence.

Dancer stared after her, eyes wide, lips beginning to quiver.

One began to suspect there was much one missed in a conversation between these two.

"She didn't mean it, Dancer," Nikki said gently. "She couldn't."

A blink and the trance broke. "You heard that?" Dancer whispered.

Nikki nodded. "I hear her very clearly. You . . . only bits and pieces."

"Interesting . . ." But the lilting voice shook past Dancer's obvious attempts at composure. Then Dancer's chin raised. "Makes no difference. I couldn't leave. Not without knowing . . ."

"Without knowing what?" Deymorin demanded harshly. "I've had damnwell enough of half-sentences and allusions. I want to know what's wrong with my brother!"

"He's . . . willing himself comatose, Deymorin Rhomandi dunMheric. Perhaps to death."

"You can't know that."

"I can. You can. You just don't want to hear it."

"Why would he do that?"

Dancer's eyes met Deymorin's as firmly as they had Mother's. "He's running from you, Deymorin dunMheric."

"From me? *Why?*"

"Embarrassed. Frightened. Beyond that, I'm not certain."

"Of what?"

"Your rejection, I think. Your scorn, I'm certain. Mostly, of being alone. I think he wants to die rather than be alone any longer."

"He's not alone, dammit! So, stop him. Make him wake up."

"I can't."

"Who can? Mother? Bring her back!"

"You know the answer, Deymorin dunMheric, or you wouldn't have asked."

Deymorin's head dropped, his hair fell forward, masking his face.

"Deymio?" Nikki said, and put a hand on his brother's, but Deymorin brushed him away, and raised his head, throwing his hair back to scowl at Dancer.

"How?" he asked abruptly.

"You must follow that link—somehow. Touch might help, it does with Mother and me. I don't know with you. Your linkage is ... different than ours."

"Don't know? What sort of teacher are you?"

Dancer winced, as if struck.

"No kind at all, Deymorin dunMheric. I'm part of this pattern, but only as an observer. I ... can't be more. Don't know how to be. But don't let him die, Deymorin dunMheric. Please. He's your radical factor, your delicate link, but he's an important one."

"Links, hell. He's my brother," Deymorin said, and set his fingertips next to Dancer's on Mikhyel's face.

* * *

Images of Mheric: wreaking terror and hatred and pain.

Images of himself, towering like some avenging angel, and of nightmares and tears and a pillow called Deymorin.

The Deymorin-self that walked this shadow-realm absorbed those images and feelings and longed to take the years back. He'd known his father's vicious temper, had felt the back of Mheric's hand often enough. Had intervened and diverted his father's anger when Mikhyel was young, knowing his smaller brother was more fragile than he ever was.

He'd never guessed Mikhyel was aware of his interference, diversions he'd no longer created after Nikki's birth . . . after their mother's death. He had been with the cadets by then, had joined the adults at home and Darhaven.

Mikhyel had opted to stay with Nikki. By preference, so he'd thought.

For honor! Mikhyel's soul screamed. *For need!*

Need *he* hadn't seen. Mheric had, to his eyes, simply ceased to care about his children. *He'd* seen nothing, experienced nothing like the terrors Khyel's mind held.

But a green-tinged voice whispered *Nothing?* and he remembered a thirteenth birthday, and a bleeding, broken bundle of humanity dragged screaming from a mass of shattered toys, and was no longer certain what was real and what imagined.

But Mikhyel believed, and, somehow, because of that belief wanted now to die.

Deymorin felt that in his brother, as Dancer must have sensed it, but the why of Mikhyel's determination still eluded him. Fear of Anheliaa he'd have understood, but Anheliaa wasn't the danger—not to this Khyel-self. Mheric was gone, now. Nikki was grown. There had to be something. . . .

Following that thought, the confusion of shadows and images vaporized. At the far end of this tunnel, Hell's Barrister barred a door: the blockade Dancer had encountered. He sensed that, as he sensed now that Dancer had been guiding him along this shadow path within Mikhyel's soul.

The Barrister had confused Dancer, but Deymorin knew better—or Deymorin hated the Barrister more. He gripped black-shrouded arms to cast the Barrister aside . . . and found he held nothing but empty rags that withered and vanished on an unfelt breeze: a meaningless façade to keep the world away.

To keep *him* away.

Deymorin gripped the doorhandle to Mikhyel's innermost self, and sensed:

Guilt, because he saw Mheric and their mother arguing and did nothing. Because he saw Mheric striking their mother and did nothing. Because he saw Mother falling and did nothing.

Never mind, the Deymorin-self insisted with gentle sarcasm against the Mikhyel-self's guilt, there'd been nothing child-Mikhyel could have done.

Guilt, the Mikhyel-self insisted, *because at their mother's bedside, he'd assumed the duty of Elder Brother—promised to protect the blond-haired baby so like their mother—and, frightened of the horrors Deymorin had endured for him, had wanted, in this innermost self, to deny that duty.*

Never mind Deymorin never had endured any such, at least, not as Mikhyel imagined. Never mind, no sane human would *want* to assume such a horrifying responsibility.

Guilt for his desire that Mheric be dead and never touch him again.

Greater guilt when that wish came true.

Hatred, for the image in the mirror, an image so increasingly like Mheric's it had made Mikhyel avoid mirrors throughout puberty.

Never mind, the Deymorin-self interrupted gently, that Mheric's face had been thicker, warped into massiveness through years of hard laughter and hard anger, of never feeling anything part way and never controlling those feelings. Khyel's face was that of an esthete, almost feminine as a child, fragile now, especially in its current gaunt desolation.

The dark, straight hair, the full curved lips, those were Mheric's, the Mikhyel-self insisted, to which there was no argument . . .

And with that acquiescence, Mikhyel's imagery erupted around him, engulfing him in Mikhyel-reality:

. . . Mikhyel, fighting daily the urge to smash that revelatory mirror, resisting the urge to take the pieces and slash the face and hair to destroy that likeness, fighting those instincts because Nikki would have wondered, and worried, and Deymorin would have demanded explanations he'd never accept . . .

. . . Mikhyel's growing the beard, not, as everyone assumed, to make him look older, but to mask, as did the stoic veneer and somber clothing, that despised similarity . . .

. . . and the greatest, darkest similarity of all, a similarity turned undeniable six months ago, when *his* hand had drawn the blood and *his* hand had so nearly destroyed the very child he'd promised to protect . . .

. . . and for lack of courage: hiding behind fatalistic logic

as Mheric had hidden behind anger, he'd stood by as Anheliaa tortured Deymorin and sent Deymorin away, had
stood by while Anheliaa forced Nikki into marriage, aiding
and abetting her with lies until the truths had built to overwhelming proportions and flooded a vulnerable child with
righteous indignation ...

... and then not having the sense to let Nikki go searching blindly, but instead aiming Nikki right into the face of
the danger ...

And the Mikhyel-self had to wonder—had he wanted,
deep inside, to lose Nikki as he'd lost Deymorin?

He should have gone after Deymorin, the Mikhyel-self
insisted, it should have been he in the stolen wagon when
Deymorin lifted that covering cloth. Instead, Khyel had
seen, through Deymorin's eyes, Nikki sprawled there helpless and battered—terrified—all because he'd been too
cowardly to go with him, hadn't, when it most mattered,
kept the promise to their mother. . . .

"Oh, Khyel, . . ." Deymorin murmured into the flood of
self-incrimination, and opened the door.

Chapter Thirteen

It was a room Deymorin had never seen before: book-lined shelves, fey, graceful statuary that defied gravity and engineering, a fire in the hearth. And a painting above the mantle: their family portrait with a stranger as the father, a stranger whose face was a caricature of his own.

Reality as Mikhyel would have it: a room of safety, warmth and privacy. But it welcomed him now, the fire and the books, and Mikhyel himself, comfortable in dressing gown and loose hair, seated in a deep-cushioned wingchair, the goblet he held a ruby-red jewel in the firelight.

Mikhyel smiled, and gestured to a second chair, identical to Mikhyel's in every respect, even to a wine glass that floated in the air, awaiting his hand to cup it.

And with that thought, he was in the chair, though he hadn't consciously moved; and the wine was warm and soothing on his tongue.

And somehow, in that endless instant between standing and sitting, all the explanations had been made and met, accepted and countered ... images and experiences shared on a level that defied mere words.

Or at least, all that required sharing. There remained a core of reticence Deymorin hadn't touched—a protected realm of personal horror Mikhyel reserved, not for deceit, but out of respect for Deymorin and Deymorin's good memories of their father, for which Deymorin thanked him.

But what he had learned left no room for doubt, not of those fears, or the acts that engendered them, or of the infinite courage of the boy who as a man accused himself of the most shameful cowardice.

Acts of which Mikhyel's thirteenth birthday had been— only perhaps—the worst.

"I never knew, Khyel," he said, because some things *had* to be said, for honor's sake—for love—because saying was harder, and spoken explanations somehow more real. "After Father died, Diorak wouldn't let me see you for days—nearly a month. They just dragged you screaming from the closet and took you away to the healers' Tower at Barsitum. They said you were upset by father's death. That I'd frightened you, and to stay away."

Mikhyel stared into the wineglass, turning it in the firelight, searching, Deymorin knew in the way of this place, for words to describe the indescribable.

"You did," Khyel murmured at last. Which hurt, though he knew it wasn't meant to. "I was alone. Completely, utterly alone except for Anheliaa. All in a day, I'd killed Nikki, killed Mheric, and killed you."

That was too cryptic even for the underneath feelings to sort. Deymorin knew, out of those shared experiences, that Mheric had told Mikhyel Nikki was dead, knew Mikhyel believed he'd smothered, or crushed, their four-year-old brother in his desperate attempt to protect Nikki from Mheric's riding crop. But Mheric? *Himself?*

Khyel sensed his confusion and smiled with infinite sadness, and Deymorin remembered, then, his brother's anger toward their sire, the hatred, the wishing. . . .

"I was afraid you see, that you'd realize those wishes had killed Mheric."

In this shadow-world of truth, Mikhyel could never call Mheric Father.

"I knew you loved him, and I was certain, once you knew, you'd hate me, and that we'd be dead to each other forever."

"And are we, Khyel?" He had to ask, though his heart screamed for it to be otherwise.

And there were tears in Mikhyel's eyes, he knew that, though Mikhyel tried to turn his face away, in this place, where there was nowhere to hide, because there had never been a need.

"I tried, Deymio. I tried . . . so hard to love him. And all I ever wanted was for him to be dead. I was never sorry, after—not even for your sake. I *couldn't* help being glad he was gone, even though it made you hate me more and—"

He left his glass floating in the air and reached for Khyel's thin wrist, felt it relax and twist, entwining impossibly, in this place of impossibilities, with his own.

"Khy," which he'd never called his younger brother before, "had I known, I'd have killed him myself."

Though he meant it with all his heart, Mikhyel chuckled softly, and said, "No, you wouldn't, Deymio. You're no killer. You'd have stood between, taken the blows until he killed you."

"Which is all you ever did, fry."

"Only for lack of viable options, brother."

Which in this land of truth, he knew had to be, for all it hinted at a darkness within Mikhyel that a man hated to admit he saw. That Mikhyel *could* kill. *Would* kill, and without remorse. And he knew, somehow, it was self-awareness of that darkness that made Mikhyel want to die now.

"Please don't die, Mikhyel."

"I must, Deymio, don't you see?"

"No, I *don't* see!"

Mikhyel grasped his wrists, demanding silence, forcing him to feel Mikhyel's deepest fear, drawing it like a dark, malignant growth from that final, untouched citadel at his core, forcing him to understand the true source of Mikhyel's agony and shame and wish to die.

Mikhyel knew and accepted beyond a doubt that he *did* have it within him to kill their father, and that he felt nothing but relief that their father was dead. But it wasn't that soul-deep flaw that drove him now toward suicide.

It was Deymorin himself. Deymorin and Nikki. Mikhyel feared their impossible, but undeniably real unity with a horror so deep it eclipsed all else for the instant Deymorin shared it. Feared that through it he had the capacity to kill his brothers, just by wishing. Feared that soul-deep likeness to Mheric might one day drive him to it. Just by wishing. A casual, infinitely evil, thought.

"I'll take my chances, fry," Deymorin whispered, into that horror. "Better that than to lose you this way."

"What better way?"

"Not at all, dammit!"

"Why not? You and Nikki together and safe—that's all I truly wish for, now."

"What about happy? Do you think we—I could be, knowing this? Khyel, for the gods' sake—for ours—"

"Deymorin, I've done so many things wrong, made so

many mistakes ... I've finally done something right. What better time?"

"I'm older."

"And so should go first?"

Gentle, wry laughter, that drew Deymorin in, but only made him want to weep, because he knew he was losing this battle that he wanted so deeply to win.

"Besides, you'll *be* happier. You and Nikki both." For Khyel there were no tears, only resolve. "You need each other, not me."

"You know better than that."

And Mikhyel did, had to, in this place of absolute Truth, which brought tears to his silver-grey eyes at last.

"Please, Deymorin, don't do this to me," he whispered on a shaking breath. "Don't you understand? I'm tired, Deymio. So ... damned ... tired."

"So ... *sleep!*" His voice cracked and he tightened his grip on Mikhyel's thin wrists. "All day, a week, a month. As long as you want. I'll personally keep everyone from your door. You don't damnwell have to *die*."

Mikhyel buried his face in their still-clasped hands, and his shoulders shook with mingled laughter and tears.

Deymorin knew, then, what Mikhyel would never knowingly say: that it wasn't physical exhaustion that was destroying him, but the constant life and death decisions, a pressure he'd lived with since before their father had died. Of fighting the constant desire to just *be* Deymorin's brother again, to be able to make a mistake and not have to justify it, not have to wonder if that mistake would ruin someone's life.

Deymorin dropped to his knees in front of Mikhyel's chair, trying to see Mikhyel's face, slipped one hand free of Mikhyel's grip and slid it under the satiny fall of loose hair, urging Mikhyel's head up.

And it wasn't the bearded man who looked at him with tear-filled eyes, it was the brother he'd deserted so long ago to Anheliaa's den ... and the brother he'd chased onto a moonlit balcony.

Their combined memory shied from that second image; he drew it back firmly.

"Didn't I risk my fool neck once trying to save your hide?"

"Risked your neck? I don't understand, Deymio."

And he drew Mikhyel with him into the memory of that birthday so long ago, the practical joke gone so sadly awry, and sensed another deep Mikhyel-self guilt: debt to the brother he'd grounded forever. A debt he could never possibly repay.

"Why, Deymio?" Mikhyel whispered. "Why did you have to follow me to the roof?"

"I was horrified, Khyel. I thought ... I'd always sensed that you were unhappy. I just didn't know why. I wanted to break you free of Anheliaa's poisonous influence. To make you laugh again, like you did when we were children. When Anheliaa interrupted you and Tirise, and you bolted, naked as the day you were born, up to the roof ..."

"You felt guilty. Feared I meant to jump...."

"You thought I was angry and very sensibly dodged when I lunged ..."

"It was my fault ... and you almost died."

Mikhyel's image wavered wildly between child and Barrister, Mikhyel's guilt flinging a wall between them, trying to force his hatred. Instead, he held tight to hand and neck, countering with his own images of that night, forcing them at the Barrister, who shriveled, leaving the child unprotected against his assault.

For an instant, they shared the moment, the race to the rooftop, the low stone wall, the fall ... Khyel's anguished cry ... the anguish in Khyel's face when the black of unconscious lifted.

And the child was crying, *wanting* to believe, *wanting* it to have been different, to have accepted the love offered, and the absolution. But it was more than a child within Mikhyel, and the adult had accepted the responsibility and tried to live with it.

"Not your fault, fry, *never* your fault." And with that hand on Khyel's neck, he drew him, child and man, into an embrace that transcended physical limitations, that melded them briefly into one entity. And he whispered/thought/believed, *"There's a word for what happened, brother. It's called an accident. Not fate. Not malice. Just an accident, which, I can tell you now, hurt you far more than ever it hurt me, my poor Khy."*

And there was quiet then, their two minds thinking as one, just for this short time. And he knew they'd never agree on that issue, that Mikhyel would forever shoulder a blame not his. But for his part Khyel would know that, even if the accident had been his fault, Deymorin understood it happened in all innocence, and that Mikhyel's insistence on shouldering the blame only increased his value in Deymorin's eyes and Deymorin's heart.

And then they were apart, two individuals sitting beside the fire, sipping vintage wine.

"Nikki won't be pleased, you know," he said at last to Mikhyel.

"Because he should be here?"

"He thinks he should, at any rate. But he's wrong, isn't he?"

"Perhaps ... another time."

"Another time? Then you will go back with me, won't you, Khyel?"

Hesitation, born of fear. "You don't need me. I'm happy here. Safe."

"Safe, perhaps. Happy—can we truly be happy alone, Khyel? I know I can't. Please, brother, come home."

The pattern was nearing completion, and in it, Dancer found new melodies, new harmonies to experience.

Most unusual of all, was this sense of human caring, of real family, a sense Dancer absorbed vicariously and without shame, suspecting in it Mother's—or the ley's, as Mother insisted—purpose for Dancer's own inclusion in the dunMheric brothers' web.

As Mikhyel rose out of his self-induced otherwhere, and Deymorin wrapped him in his arms, the jealousy, the sense of exemption that had surrounded Mheric's youngest son strangely vanished, and Nikaenor knelt with his brothers, exuding relief and joy uncolored by any negative emotions.

Mikhyel's eyes leaked cleansing tears, one hand sought Deymorin's long before his eyes blinked open, the other reached for Nikaenor, circling the younger man's waist and drawing him close.

But when Mikhyel's eyes did open, it was Dancer's they intercepted, not his brothers', and for a long frozen instant, no one moved or spoke. And within those pale eyes, Dancer saw much that was at once familiar and not. And Dancer remembered the pattern, alone in the dark, trying to absorb the damage: selflessly, foolishly destructive.

But most of all, Dancer saw the courage it had taken

this middle brother to return to the other two when to stay in that inner sanctuary would have been so much easier, a courage greater than simple endurance of pain, and constructed wholly of love.

And with that realization, Dancer sensed a pattern completed: Dancer's own pattern.

Then Nikki said, "Khyel?" and grey eyes flickered to meet blue, and the spell dissolved, flowing into the ground.

Having learned all that was appropriate, Dancer wrapped the blanket tighter, and slipped off the end of the wagon, then edged past the human woman, seeking the solitude of the evening shadows.

"Dancer?" The woman's touch was light, but insistent, her voice a whisper on the wind.

Dancer paused, uncomfortable as always in human social interactions, but less so after having shared souls with the dunMheric brothers.

"Tell your Deymorin thank you," Dancer said without turning to face the woman. "It was a brave thing he did."

"He didn't do it for you."

"I say it for Mikhyel, because Mikhyel might not realize when he truly wakes."

"Why not?"

"Memories can be . . . hazy after what he's been through. And it's best not to force him to remember. Let him know only what he asks to know. At least for now. Let him find his own level of understanding."

"How do you know?"

Dancer shrugged. Personal experience was only half-truth. One knew such things because Mother wanted one to know. Truth shouldn't need justification.

"Can't you tell them yourself?"

Dancer shrugged again, wanting to be free of her and her questions, wanting time alone to think and process new perceptions.

"Are you leaving?"

"I'm going to try. Mother said—" Dancer's voice caught. "She said I'm no longer welcome, but perhaps, if I can reach a node . . ."

"Stay here, Dancer. At least until you're sure. They'll want to thank—"

"No!" And on a gentler tone: "I want no thanks, Lady Kiyrstin. I deserve none. What I've done, I had to do."

"As did Deymorin."

"I . . . wouldn't know about that." The issue was growing hazy. Too much new sensation and imagery coming far too fast. Dancer felt a loss of connection, a latent desire for something outside Mother's world, outside anything Rhyys could offer, and felt in that desire a personal deficiency, a disloyalty to those who were dearest. To those who deserved more.

"Mother took me in, years ago," Dancer said, trying to explain for them both. "She taught me. Gave me love and family, such as she could. I think, maybe, this was her attempt to give me what she thought herself incapable of teaching. And she's left herself alone, cut herself off from me. Perhaps that's as she wanted it. But perhaps it's not."

"How will you know?" the woman asked.

Dancer looked away, the memory of that room and Khyel's loneliness too powerful to ignore. And as Deymorin, had said, such an existence was wrong . . . for anyone.

"I won't, will I? Until she lets me come home."

But the human woman was shaking her head. "No, Dancer. There must be another answer. Wait here. Let me get—"

Dancer smiled, sad but content, and slipped the blanket from his shoulders.

Postlude

"Well, brothers," Deymorin said, closing the sitting room door behind the messenger. "Ben wasn't *at* Talvanni's—or anywhere else between the inn and Darhaven."

He crossed the room and settled on the couch between Kiyrstin and Mikhyel. Kiyrstin tucked her feet up and curled into the curve of arm awaiting her, and decided that Armayel was a very comfortable place, and that Deymorin's was a very comfortable arm.

Alizant, playing in the garden outside with a very amiable litter of pups, couldn't be happier. Three days ago, he'd greeted them at a spot well down the drive, where he'd awaited their return, so Gareg claimed, every day since she and Deymorin had left for Rhomatum.

It was, of course, quite possible that the nearby pond and puppies learning to swim after sticks accounted for both the choice of lookout and his dedication, but Kiyrstin would never suggest such a thing to Alizant.

They'd brought Nikki and Mikhyel here to Armayel to convalesce and to give them all time to regroup. Nikki's wounds had proven more extensive than any of them had supposed, due to his deceptive ease of movement and apparent overall lack of discomfort.

Ultimately, they'd traced that strange dearth to Mikhyel, who somehow, through that strange three-way linkage, had been absorbing Nikki's pain. Protecting Nikki, so he insisted, in his less coherent moments. Since then, they'd also discovered that Nikki could, with conscious effort, stop what was for Mikhyel an agonizing flow of sensation.

Nikki could contain the feeling, but no effort of Mikhyel's could stop it, and the instant Nikki's concentration faltered, the flow resumed, sometimes with the shocking surge of a burst dam.

But two days of rest and Armayel kitchen's excellent

food, and youthful resilience had eased that problem, and today Nikki paced the room like a caged animal wanting action, while Mikhyel sat, tired and pale, and a bit hazy at times, but relatively free of pain—his and Nikki's—at last.

Four days of healing, four days of Nikki's men, survivors from the holocaust, drifting to Armayel's door, and four days of messengers sent out to Darhaven and Talvanni, and all points between, of taking account of the dead, which were too many, and of the missing like Ben. Poor old light-watchman, so loyal to both Deymorin and Nikki. Kiyrstin felt as if she'd personally known him.

Nikki paused in his stalking, tension in every line, and said, with the hint of ill-temper that seemed to color his voice more often than not, "I could have told you that. Ben is dead. He died at Darhaven."

Shocked silence filled the room. Four days since the fire-storm in the forest, and not a word of Ben's fate had passed Nikki's lips. Not a word of concern for Ben or for any of the men he'd led to their deaths.

Only a sullen retreat into glowering silence.

In response to this sudden, coldblooded announcement, Deymorin's arm tightened on her shoulders. On Deymorin's far side, his pale face naked of both hair and control, Mikhyel shuddered and pulled his quilt up, as if he sensed Deymorin's perturbation as a physical chill—which possibility lay well within the scope of probability.

It was likely Mikhyel was aware of the source of Deymorin's distress ... and equally likely he was not. The extent and nature of the brothers' link appeared ... mutable, to say the least, and Mikhyel, drifting in and out of consciousness as he tended to do, might well have missed Nikki's comment.

Mikhyel undoubtedly missed the frown that creased Nikki's brow when Deymorin murmured reassurances to Mikhyel, set his other arm about his shoulders or bent solicitously over his black-haired head.

Ever since Mikhyel had awakened, there in the forest, the two elder brothers had been unwilling—or unable—to be separated for any length of time. Perhaps trying to make up for lost years.

And perhaps not. It was too soon to know, their wounds too fresh to test. Someday soon, Kiyrstin would expect answers. She could afford to wait, but whatever emotions were driving the apparent obsession, the overt expression was taking its toll on Nikki.

She'd watched him, over a handful of days, pass from childishly self-centered, to bitter and confused. And watching Nikki watch his brothers now, seeing the frown lines deepen, Kiyrstin had come to believe that beyond the obvious jealousy lay very real pain.

Nikki had to know by their very silence that his brothers disapproved of him, had to be turning his words over in his head and wondering where he'd gone wrong, that his two most ardent supporters in the past united now against him—cast him, to a younger brother's way of thinking, out of the family unit.

She'd heard a great deal of reminiscing, over the past four days, and it was obvious to even the most biased observer that Nikki had never been anything but the center of both Deymorin's and Mikhyel's attention. Considering that other link which now tied the three together, Kiyrstin could only imagine how his brothers' equally overt ostracism, intentional or otherwise, must feel to Nikki.

With regard to herself and Deymorin, Deymorin's fascination with Mikhyel changed little. Mikhyel was still very ill, fading in and out of reality with disconcerting ease. Right now, he needed Deymorin desperately. She knew that and accepted easily whatever time or interest Deymorin had left for her. Besides, Deymorin was, for her, an added bonus to an already full life.

She was an adult, entering Deymorin's life as an adult and without a lifetime of expectations. She could afford not to worry about Deymorin's obsession until Mikhyel was well—or obviously beyond help. Even then, her concerns would be for the unhealthy obsession, not for some perceived personal slight.

Nikki ... Nikki was on the brink of adulthood. From Mikhyel's comments these last few days, and from those of the men he'd led, Nikki had been in the act of making that difficult transition to manhood when he'd left Rhomatum in search of Deymorin.

Considering the confusion and distress Nikki must be facing now, between the obsession of his brothers for each other and the guilt of knowing his slightest twinge added to Mikhyel's distress, consideration of anything or any*one* beyond that narrow personal sphere might be more grace than was fair to expect of him.

"Ben is dead. Are you sure, Nikki?" Deymorin asked at last and slowly.

"*Yes*, I'm sure." Nikki's clear blue eyes looked defiant. His chin raised, proud, obstinate, very like his oldest brother—then crumbled, in confusion, at Deymorin's dark frown. "Well, maybe not *sure*, but he took a bullet right in the gut, Deymio. He certainly wasn't about to make Talvanni's. What made you think he'd be there?"

Mother, Kiyrstin thought, and from the look Deymorin sent her, he thought the same. But they said nothing, having agreed to avoid all mention of Mother or Dancer or any of those strange events.

But Mikhyel, a worried look on his face, wouldn't have heard them anyway. Mikhyel's eyes were fastened on Nikki, and his voice was at its clear best when he asked, "Don't you care whether he's alive, Nikki?"

And Mikhyel flinched visibly when Nikki said, "Well, of course I *care,* but he *was* my bodyguard, Khyel, and I wasn't in much shape to ask questions, now was I?"

Kiyrstin tensed, but Deymorin's arm kept her silent.

"You've got a lot to learn about leading men," Deymorin said quietly, and Nikki at least had the grace to *look* ashamed.

Four days ago, Kiyrstin wouldn't have trusted that look at all, but now she was less certain. The men he'd led, like Mikhyel but with less bias, spoke well of their young leader. The goal of the look might be to placate older brothers, but the heart behind it at least appeared genuine enough.

Which led her to believe Deymorin when he claimed this attitude his youngest brother had been displaying was temporary, aberrant, that Nikki was truly a good-natured child. "Give him time," Deymorin had said.

The problem was, Nikki wasn't a child, and Nikki was running out of time. All tolerance aside, she called him spoiled.

She'd said as much to Nikki's brothers, when Nikki was out of earshot. Mikhyel had tried to take all the blame, but Deymorin had said, "No more responsible than I," and in that, she figured they were both right. Nikki suffered from a plethora of protection, and sad lack of doing for himself. Unfortunately, the first time he had taken control of his life, things had gone awry, and there had been Big Brother Deymorin to rescue him.

Hard to grow up when your brothers were so competent.

But Nikki was young; there was still hope. Especially if he could be convinced to forget about Mother and all that had happened in the forest.

Which Mikhyel had forgotten, as Dancer had predicted. And, if Dancer's other advice had been equally sound, it was just as well Mikhyel had spent the hours following his awakening fading in and out, as nothing would quell Nikki's rattling account of the Tamshi and her apprentice.

Eventually, Deymorin and Kiyrstin's pointed disinterest coupled with Mikhyel's obviously confused distress had evidently convinced Nikki to keep his fascination to himself.

As for Dancer—Dancer had simply disappeared into the forest shadows, leaving the blanket in a faintly-glowing pile on the ground, and Kiyrstin could only hope Dancer's peace with Mother was by now a fait accompli.

She'd certainly earned it. Or he had. Another point that had somehow become irrelevant in the past days. When one considered glowing bodies arriving out of nowhere and crones shifting into scaled creatures before one's eyes, it was difficult to trust one's senses absolutely. More difficult still to think such trivialities mattered.

"So, brothers, what do we do now?" asked Deymorin finally.

"I must return to Rhomatum," Mikhyel said, his voice ragged and thin. "Regardless of what has happened to us, the City still has needs, and the Outside does as well."

"We've been through this before, Khyel," Deymorin said firmly. "It's too great a risk. Anheliaa might not even recognize you now, since you've obviously defected. And I hardly need a proxy, not being Princeps any longer."

"If Anheliaa wants to challenge us, she'll have to do it in court. And in court, she hasn't a chance. What she's done is too grossly illegal, even for her most partisan supporters."

"And if Anheliaa has you arrested quietly? And leyapults you permanently?"

"I think Kirystin had the answer for that." Mikhyel leaned forward to grin at her across Deymorin's chest. "Chickens, was it?"

"Crates of them," she responded immediately, grinning back at him. "You need to make a *big* impression. Right off. The instant you pass the gates. Helps if you have a big fellow like Deymorin to kiss you, after. Right there in front of everyone."

A soft chuckle rewarded her efforts. "I'll keep that in mind."

"We could all just fade away together, you know," Deymorin said, "Anheliaa used us to attack Alizant's machine. If she has any concept of the havoc she wrought, she might well believe we're all dead."

"You going to run away again, Deymorin?" Mikhyel murmured, and Deymorin tensed, his tightening brow hinting at their previous animosity. "Somehow," Mikhyel continued softly, "I don't think so. I doubt you could leave Darhaven and Armayel to Anheliaa's whims any more than I can leave Rhomatum."

Deymorin's arm relaxed.

"Hell, I suppose not." And he grinned. "But I can dream, can't I?"

"That's wonderful," Nikki snapped. "You've both got your allegiances, your duties, your obligations. What have I got?"

"Oh, grow up," Kiyrstin muttered, discovering clemency's limits.

"Excuse me?"

"You keep complaining no one treats you like an adult. Well, start acting like one! You've a wife—"

"Only in name."

"Funny way to put it when you've a child already on the way."

"That's what it is! That child is Anheliaa's, the way Khyel—" Nikki broke off, staring in dismay at Mikhyel, who shrugged and avoided everyone's eyes.

"Fine," Kiyrstin said, completely unwilling to let Nikki wander off into extraneous recriminations, trusting Khyel to understand Nikki's meaning. "Then rear the child. *Fight* Anheliaa's influence with your own. And if you grow weary of that, you're Princeps now. I should think that would keep anyone occupied."

Nikki's eyes widened in panic, sought Mikhyel's.

"She's right, Nikki," he said. "It's official. The Council has confirmed the change."

"No! Deymorin's the Princeps—"

"Hell, boy, *I* don't want it!"

Which made Mikhyel laugh, a nice sound, a healing sound, and Deymorin grinned back at him.

"But—"

"I think it's a fabulous notion," Deymorin insisted.

"But I don't know—"

"We won't desert you, fry."

{We'll be there as much or as little as you like.}

A startled glance chased about the room, each man wondering who had 'said' that.... As if it really mattered.

Kiyrstin chuckled to herself and burrowed in closer to Deymorin's side, not the least surprised to have 'heard' along with the brothers, no longer finding much of anything surprising.

Deymorin's arm squeezed briefly, then he asked:

"What about you, Kiyrstin? What do you want?"

"Right now? To sleep for about a hundred years. After that ... well, Garetti will be back. He's got a cause, now. Anheliaa drew first blood."

"I want you, shepherdess." His hand brushed her hair back from her forehead. "I want you safe."

She shrugged. "I can take care of myself."

"We could annul your marriage," Mikhyel said. "It would keep the locals, at least, from trying to collect on Garetti's reward."

"Annulment? After fifteen years?"

"Under the circumstances—I think our courts, at least, would uphold me."

"After putting her through hell," Deymorin protested.

"I'm not ashamed of what happened—or of anything I've done."

He leaned away, staring at her with the strangest expression on his face. A mixture of pride, frustration, lust, and ...

Love.

"Neither am I," he said finally, then grinned. "Still, we could just live in disgrace for a while. Maybe have a fry or two of our own. It would drive Anheliaa out of her mind, which might be fun."

"Deymorin, I don't *care*. I ask only two things. One, that I be with you."

"Done." His mouth on hers created a pleasant, momentary diversion. "And the second?" he asked against her lips.

"No sheep."

More Top-Flight Science Fiction and Fantasy from
C.J. CHERRYH

SCIENCE FICTION
☐ FOREIGNER (hardcover)   UE2590—$20.00
☐ FOREIGNER   UE2637—$5.99
☐ INVADER (hardcover)   UE2638—$19.95
☐ INVADER   UE2687—$5.99
☐ INHERITOR (hardcover)   UE2689—$21.95

THE MORGAINE CYCLE
☐ GATE OF IVREL (BOOK 1)   UE2321—$4.50
☐ WELLS OF SHIUAN (BOOK 2)   UE2322—$4.50
☐ FIRES OF AZEROTH (BOOK 3)   UE2323—$4.50
☐ EXILE'S GATE (BOOK 4)   UE2254—$5.50

FANTASY
The Ealdwood Novels
☐ THE DREAMSTONE   UE2013—$2.95
☐ THE TREE OF SWORDS AND JEWELS

     UE1850—$2.95

Buy them at your local bookstore or use this convenient coupon for ordering.

PENGUIN USA   P.O. Box 999—Dep. #17109, Bergenfield, New Jersey 07621

Please send me the DAW BOOKS I have checked above, for which I am enclosing
$_____ (please add $2.00 to cover postage and handling). Send check or money
order (no cash or C.O.D.'s) or charge by Mastercard or VISA (with a $15.00 minimum). Prices and
numbers are subject to change without notice.

Card #_____ Exp. Date _____
Signature_____
Name_____
Address_____
City _____ State _____ Zip Code _____

For faster service when ordering by credit card call **1-800-253-6476**

Allow a minimum of 4-6 weeks for delivery. This offer is subject to change without notice.

C.J. CHERRYH
THE ALLIANCE-UNION UNIVERSE

C.S. Friedman

SEAN RUSSELL

THE INITIATE BROTHER

☐ **THE INITIATE BROTHER (Book 1)** UE2466—$5.99
☐ **GATHERER OF CLOUDS (Book 2)** UE2536—$5.99

MOONTIDE AND MAGIC RISE

☐ **WORLD WITHOUT END (Book 1)** UE2624—$5.99
This is the story of Tristam Flattery, who is sent on a dangerous journey for his king to find the seeds of a plant which bestows immortality. Tristam thus finds himself on a voyage of discovery that has more to do with magic than with science.

☐ **SEA WITHOUT A SHORE (Book 2)** UE2665—$5.99
When the Age of the Mages ended, all the secrets of their magical arts were thought to be lost to the world. But the new era's most talented young naturalist, Tristam Flattery, finds himself in a search for the lost secrets of the Mages.
